BLOOD
OF OUR
FATHERS

BLOOD OF

OUR FATHERS

Sonny Girard

POCKET BOOKS

New York   London   Toronto   Sydney   Tokyo   Singapore

Dedicated

to Mother Superior and Tom Talk,
without either of whom
this book would never have been written

and

to Anthony, Angela, and Danielle,
who gave me something to write for.

POCKET BOOKS, a division of Simon & Schuster Inc.
1230 Avenue of the Americas, New York, NY 10020

Copyright © 1991 by Sonny Girard

Girard, Sonny.
    Blood of our fathers / Sonny Girard.
        p. cm.
    ISBN: 0-671-72740-0 : $19.95
    I. Title.
    PS3557.I69B57   1991   90-27130
    813'.54—dc20   CIP

First Pocket Books hardcover printing June 1991

10 9 8 7 6 5 4 3 2 1

POCKET and colophon are registered trademarks of Simon & Schuster Inc.

Printed in the U.S.A.

Author's Note

During the course of reading this manuscript, you will come across conversations or thoughts of characters written in Italian. Sometimes those words have been spelled correctly and are grammatically correct as well. In other instances words or colloquial expressions have been purposely misspelled to indicate their phonetic sounds, which are more easily recognizable to those who have no background in that written language. For example, the word *compare* is not nearly as familiar to most people as its phonetic, Americanized, slang version of *goombah*, which is how it is spelled in this book.

S. G.

The Five New York City

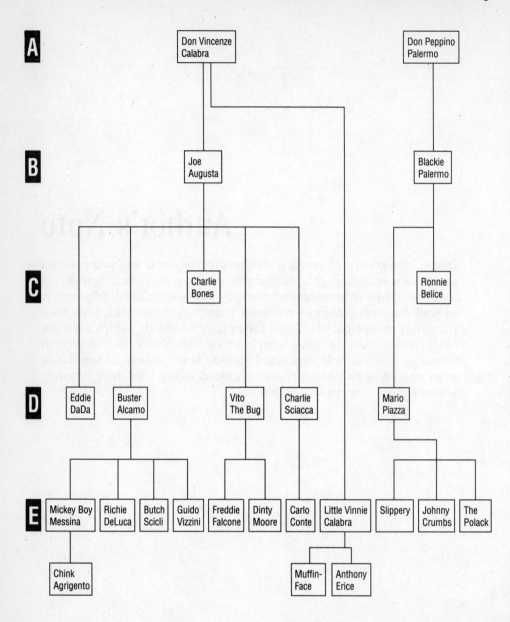

A Don Vincenze Calabra — Don Peppino Palermo

B Joe Augusta — Blackie Palermo

C Charlie Bones — Ronnie Belice

D Eddie DaDa — Buster Alcamo — Vito The Bug — Charlie Sciacca — Mario Piazza

E Mickey Boy Messina — Richie DeLuca — Butch Scicli — Guido Vizzini — Freddie Falcone — Dinty Moore — Carlo Conte — Little Vinnie Calabra — Slippery — Johnny Crumbs — The Polack

Chink Agrigento

Muffin-Face — Anthony Erice

NOTE: There are other unnamed Captains, Soldiers, and Associates too numerous to mention.

Mafia Families

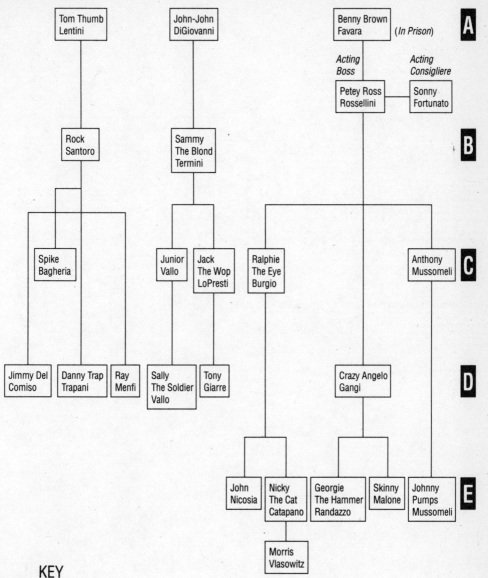

A Tom Thumb Lentini

A John-John DiGiovanni

A Benny Brown Favara (*In Prison*)

Acting Boss
Petey Ross Rossellini

Acting Consigliere
Sonny Fortunato

B Rock Santoro

B Sammy The Blond Termini

C Spike Bagheria

C Junior Vallo

C Jack The Wop LoPresti

C Ralphie The Eye Burgio

C Anthony Mussomeli

D Jimmy Del Comiso

D Danny Trap Trapani

D Ray Menfi

D Sally The Soldier Vallo

D Tony Giarre

D Crazy Angelo Gangi

E John Nicosia

E Nicky The Cat Catapano

E Georgie The Hammer Randazzo

E Skinny Malone

E Johnny Pumps Mussomeli

Morris Vlasowitz

KEY
A. Boss
B. Underboss
C. Captains
D. Soldiers
E. Associates

Prologue

May 22: Brooklyn

The phone was picked up before the first ring had finished. "Yeah."

"It's me," the caller stated. "Is everything taken care of for tonight?"

"All done."

"Are your people where they're supposed to be?"

"Hundred percent."

"Where's Mickey Boy?"

"Out for dinner with some 'young lady' early, then he'll meet his partner, Richie, at Pastel's."

"Who's the girl?" the caller inquired.

"His kid brother's ex-girlfriend. That's why he's leavin' her early to go whorin'."

"What if he changes his mind, will you know where he is?"

"No problem. Somebody'll be on him all night."

"I don't have to remind you how important tonight is . . . that meeting's the beginning of everything, and we must know where everyone is . . . especially him. If you have to, go grab him yourself. I don't want to do it that way, but if we're left no choice . . ."

"Don't worry, you could count on me."

Part
I

May 22: Flatbush, Brooklyn

Michael "Mickey Boy" Messina held the pay phone's receiver to his ear, but his attention was captured by the hazy blue-gray quality of the Brooklyn twilight. All the gold and magenta sunsets he'd seen while upstate in prison couldn't compare to the polluted glow that ushered in the most pleasurable part of his day here at home.

On the other end of the line his partner, Richie DeLuca, argued that Mickey Boy should never have made an appointment with Laurel. ". . . All she could be is a pain in the ass. You shoulda ran the other way when she said she wanted to see you."

"Nah, Rich, I couldn't do that," he said while running a hand through his thick chestnut waves. "What was I gonna tell her, I just called to say hello after six years, but no I won't meet you for a cup of coffee? That's not me."

Mickey Boy glanced at his watch. "Just give me about two hours. I'll waltz 'er in an' outta some joint around here an' have her home before she knows what happened."

When Richie continued to nag, Mickey Boy interrupted him. "Yeah, yeah, I know. I'll meet you at the back of the bar. Lemme go an' get this over with. See ya later."

Time had changed more than just Mickey Boy's personal situation; his only family (a widowed mother, Connie, and a half brother, Alley) had moved to Massachusetts, and his immediate mob superior, Sam LaMonica, had died only days before his release from jail. In the scant three months he'd been home, he'd become acutely aware of an eroded code of honor and a totally dead sense of obligation among his peers; the "me" generation seemed to have overtaken the mob, and it equated respect only with dollars. Richie's attitude about Laurel was just a small example of those differences that irritated him and detracted from the joy of his homecoming.

Had things been that much different before he went away? he wondered lately. Or had he just been too caught up in the life to see its faults? If jail'd had a positive effect, then, it was to make him think, and to make him step back and see things clearly.

But eating himself up inside or complaining to deaf ears wouldn't accomplish anything. The only thing that counted, that would make a difference, was to be at the top. Then people would have to listen, he told himself as he pulled his white Mark VII away from the curb.

As Mickey Boy drove slowly down the tree-lined street, a brown Oldsmobile 98 pulled into the spot by the phone that he'd just abandoned. The Oldsmobile's passenger door opened, and a burly, well-dressed man went to the phone. He picked up the receiver, deposited a coin, and dialed without losing sight of the white Lincoln.

Mickey Boy stopped at the familiar brick house and honked his horn. He flipped open his glove compartment and rummaged through the various Sinatra tapes that filled it. Would the mellow moods of his *Point of No Return* album be too intimate? The upswing beats of *Come Fly with Me* better? Maybe *Ol' Blue Eyes*? He was about to press the horn again, when his jaw dropped and his mouth hung open; *Ol' Blue Eyes Is Back* remained clenched in his fist. Mickey Boy sat mesmerized, watching Laurel on her way to his car—hurrying, smiling, waving.

"Mickey, hi!" Laurel squealed excitedly when she entered the snow-white interior. She bounced off the seat and threw her arms tightly around his neck, engulfing him in her tawny mane and Calvin Klein scent. Her skin felt like cool satin against him; his cheek burned where she kissed it. The sensation of touching her flesh through the flimsy fabric of her dress shot up his arms, leaving him barely enough strength to push her away.

"You're a woman," he muttered, more to himself than to her.

"I certainly hope so," Laurel said. She settled into her seat and tugged at the hem of her dress, which had hiked enough to expose her upper thigh. "I would have been sorely disappointed if I had grown up to be a man."

Mickey Boy's eyes stayed glued to her hemline as she tried to pull it down. "No, that's not what I meant," he replied. "It's just that everybody else—me, my mother, Richie—we all look the same. I guess I expected you to also." Looking up at her, he added, "I don't think I could call you kid anymore."

Laurel's gray-green eyes shone, reflecting her obvious pleasure at his reaction to her. She straightened up and primped her hair, her dress pulling taut over her breasts to display their globular form as thoroughly as if she were nude. "Six years makes a big difference when you start out at sixteen, like I did. Remember, you were what, twenty-five, twenty-six when you went away?"

"Twenty-six."

"That's why you look pretty much the same," she explained, as if to one of her third graders. "Except, maybe a little thinner," she said, studying him as she spoke. "Am I right, you lost weight?"

"Well, you know how it is in jail, having to fight for your life every day, back against the wall. Wanna see my scars?"

"Stop, silly." Laurel giggled, and playfully slapped his arm. Even that nonsexual but feminine gesture electrified him. He turned the air-conditioner vents directly on himself, wishing he could lower the temperature without seeming either ill or foolish.

Mickey Boy kept glancing at Laurel as he drove: manicured crimson nails; silky blue and green print dress; navy high heels. The last time he'd seen her in heels she was wobbling off to Alley's prom looking like a foal saddled in pink chiffon. A kid—his kid brother's girl. Scrawny, stick-people Laurel. Now her effect on him was intoxicating and distracting, rendering him oblivious to the car that followed two lengths behind.

"Instead of eating around here, I figured we'd go uptown for dinner," Mickey Boy said as he entered onto the Belt Parkway toward Manhattan. "My friend Freddie's got a great place up there; you'll love it." He looked at Laurel again. She reminded him of a picture in one of those high-class fashion magazines—why, she even wore pearls. "I can't get over it . . . a woman . . . a twenty-two-year-old woman."

"Please keep your eyes on the road, Mr. Messina," Laurel teased, an impish, sexy, self-satisfied glow in her eye. "I'd like to become a twenty-three-year-old woman someday."

The brown Oldsmobile stayed a short distance behind, and one lane to the right of Mickey Boy and Laurel.

"Where the fuck is he taking us?" the driver snapped. "He's supposed to be stayin' in the neighborhood."

His more patient associate looked at him and smiled. "Maybe she's kidnapping him," he joked.

"She musta done something," the driver growled. "She's definitely not his type . . . not sexy enough."

"Classy though . . . and nice legs. I wouldn't exactly throw her out of bed."

"Or knock myself out to get her there either." The driver cut in front of a red Pinto, ignoring the honking and upturned middle finger directed at him. "My taste is more hot . . . more sexy-looking."

"You mean trashy-looking."

"Call it whatever you want, but I know what I like." The driver cursed again as he followed the Lincoln past the brightly lit Verrazano Bridge.

Because he was seven years older than Alley, and especially because they were both fatherless, Mickey Boy had hovered over him, and, as a result, Laurel. He was her champion when a local teen gang tried to shake her down at school, her chauffeur when Alley was still too young to drive, and her Santa Claus when he delivered her a snowball of a new kitten after Missy had disappeared.

Yesterday, when she had insisted on seeing him, he'd felt that her motive was to take advantage of that past relationship and cry on his shoulder about her split with Alley. He had been uncomfortable at the thought, but felt obligated to accommodate her. Now he found himself surprisingly eager to hear her side, to hear her affirm his disbelief of his half brother's version, and he prodded her into discussing it.

Most of what Laurel told him he already knew: how close she and Alley had been; of the plans they'd made for a future together. What was new to him was how Alley had distanced himself more and more from her during his time at Harvard. Weekend visits home had been eliminated so he could "study" in the dorm, vacations cut shorter and shorter each semester.

She was at the end of her synopsis as they crossed the Brooklyn Bridge. The famed New York skyline, romantically luminous before them against the indigo night, was lost on her as her eyes stared at the felt inside the car's roof. ". . . What he neglected to mention was that the family he was interested in was his roommate's sister, Ellen, who was a sophomore at Wellesley."

"That's it?" Mickey Boy asked, sure there was something more she wanted to say but was holding back.

Laurel stared at him, her lips drawn taut. For a brief moment she appeared ready to blurt out whatever it was. Instead, she turned her head and said in a flat, emotionless voice, "What else is there to say? Brooklyn yuppie goes to Harvard, meets high-class Wasp girl, dumps low-class Brooklyn girl."

"I'm sorry—"

"Don't be," Laurel snapped. Her face burned scarlet. "He did me a big favor . . . made me take a step back and take a good look at myself . . . made me make some changes."

Unconsciously, Mickey Boy reached a hand out to comfort her. Laurel responded by wrapping her long, tapered fingers firmly around his. The strong sexual and emotional impulses he felt in her presence, the

6

urge to reach out for her, were tempered only by his memory of their former link.

"You know how these educated guys are—all book learning and no smarts," he said. "If it was me, I woulda' never let you go for nothing." Feeling awkward with that statement, Mickey Boy tried to lighten his tone. "At least not for some Wasp broad from Boston. Maybe a nice Puerto Rican, but not a Wasp."

"Oh, you," Laurel cooed. She dug her fingernails into Mickey Boy's palm.

The light pain she inflicted felt exquisite, the delicate stab of each nail sending vibrations through the muscle between his neck and collarbone and down to his nipples; he squeezed his thighs together unconsciously as he drove.

Seemingly more relaxed, Laurel continued her tale of her shattered romance. "Up until about four months after he was married I was really screwed up. Then one day I just said, Fuck him!—Oops, cover your ears." She giggled girlishly while turning on her left hip and bringing her free hand to his ear.

Mickey Boy smiled, then frowned as he had to slow to a halt behind stalled traffic. He turned toward Laurel, who slowly drew the backs of her fingers down the length of his jawline. The tingling in his neck resumed, nearly causing him to shudder. He tried to focus beyond her, on the dancing lights reflecting on the East River like thousands of glittery gems, but couldn't. As if by magnets, he was drawn to look directly into her doe-soft eyes. At that instant Mickey Boy knew he was lost.

Neither one spoke for the remainder of the trip.

In the brown Oldsmobile the passenger removed the pistol digging into his waist and slipped it into the glove compartment. He settled back, resigning himself to a long evening.

Arm in arm, Mickey and Laurel left the parking garage. They snuggled close together as they crossed the narrow side street and turned northward onto Second Avenue, the Roosevelt Island tram cables traversing their horizon. Halfway up the block, Mickey said, "There it is," and pointed to a green canopy whose fluorescent white letters announced Ristorante Numero Uno—#1.

When they stepped through the entrance into the restaurant's small but cozy bar area, Freddie Falcone had his pin-striped back to them, inking a new reservation into an open appointment book.

"We'd like a table for ten, right now!" Mickey Boy demanded loudly.

The silver-haired owner began to turn, his mercurial temper on the rise. "Hey, where do you think—sonofabitch!" he cried.

Both men kissed each other on the cheek, parted, then hugged.

"Boy, you look great!" Freddie said. "I think I should check in there for a rest myself, but not for six years like you." Grimacing, he pinched a thumb and forefinger together. "Maybe like a half a calendar or so."

"Six months?! You don't even have to take your shoes off for a skid bid like that. You gotta do at least a year to even rate a shower."

Freddie hugged Mickey Boy again. "Boy, am I glad to see you finished with that shit. You know, things are a hell of a lot different from before you went away."

"Tell me about it," Mickey Boy lamented.

"I'm talking about problems: law, law, and more law," Freddie whispered. "But what am I telling you this for now?" He motioned at Laurel, who stood quietly off to the side. "I see that tonight's strictly R&R."

"Oh, Freddie, this is Laurel."

"A real pleasure," Freddie said, extending a hand to her. "Well, how you kids like the joint?"

Mickey looked around at the stucco and natural brick walls, antique gas-style lamps, and fresh floral arrangements that gave Numero Uno an understated elegance. Between the restaurant's ambience and Freddie's gushy reception, everything was perfect for the impression he wanted to make on Laurel. And one look at her told him he'd succeeded.

"Beautiful," he answered Freddie while still turned toward Laurel, his gaze fixed on her. Catching himself staring, he quickly added, "You must get some pretty high-class clientele here."

"Most of the time we do," Freddie replied. "But then once in a while we get a real *jedrool*, like our illustrious U.S. Attorney, who just left."

"He eats here? That rat! Just let me in the kitchen for about two minutes when he orders his next meal," Mickey Boy joked. "I'll fix him something he'll never forget."

"I wouldn't mind making him a little *pasta alla morte* myself, but business is too lousy." Freddie exaggerated a sigh, then said, "Right now I can't afford to lose any customers . . . not even him. Besides, I couldn't even afford the poison to make the sauce." He hooked an arm in Mickey Boy's, whispered something in his ear, and led him toward the dining room. Laurel was left to follow a few paces behind while the two men engaged in private conversation.

Mickey suddenly turned and looked for Laurel. When he saw her annoyed expression, he reached out a hand to her.

"Listen, Fred, we could go over that anytime. Right now me an' Laurel got a lot of catching up to do. I think you understand." Laurel's returning smile warmed him inside.

Freddie slapped his own face comically. "Sorry, I guess I just got carried away." He raised Laurel's free hand to his lips. "Sorry again," he told her, "but you're probably gonna lose him one more time before you get to sample our fabulous food." Freddie straightened up and explained to Mickey Boy, "Remember my friend Eli, the meat guy that you did that favor for before you went away? Well, he's here, and will probably want to say hello."

Eli Kantor, a kosher provisions distributor from Bridgeport, had contracted Mickey Boy to convince a fortune-seeking beau of his daughter, Eleanor, that it would be wise to find greener, and healthier, pastures elsewhere. One conversation with the stubby barrel of Mickey Boy's .38 Smith & Wesson pressed against his nose convinced the young lothario to abandon not only his design on Eleanor, but his local bartender's job and rented room as well.

"Let's get it over with, so I could spend a little time with my girl," Mickey said, not aware of the possessive term he'd used until Laurel squeezed his hand affectionately. He felt more comfortable and at ease than at any other time since his release, some ninety days before.

Freddie was only partially correct. Not only did Eli Kantor pay his respects, but Laurel lost Mickey Boy twice more—once to Numero Uno's resident bookmaker, a Lou Costello look-alike named Dinty Moore, then to the telephone when Mickey called to cancel his appointment with Richie.

"It's really nice to see how much your friends think of you, but . . ." Laurel said when Mickey Boy finally sat down.

"I know, and I'm really sorry. I should have figured it would be like this on my first night up here." Mickey shrugged, and with a sheepish smile added, "I guess I wanted to impress you, but next time I promise to find us a hideaway . . . that is if you want there to be a next time?"

"Only if I don't have to wear a pin-striped suit to get your attention."

"Nah, I wouldn't change a thing about the way you look . . . no more 'Dungaree Doll.' "

"I told you before, I took a good look at myself," Laurel said with a distinct edge of bitterness. "I worked hard at the changes I made."

Mickey could have kicked himself. He made a mental note not to give her any more openings to bring up her split with Alley. The breakup seemed to have scarred Laurel deeper than he would have expected to a girl her age. He felt sorry for her, and wished he could say something to help. Freddie saved him when he appeared with his tuxedo-clad maître d'.

"Kids, this is Renato. He'll take your order. Renato, these are personal friends of mine, Mickey Boy and Laurel. Make sure that that *strombolata* in the kitchen makes everything *perfètto*, *perfètto* for them, or down the stairs he goes . . . headfirst, like the last chef. *Capisce?*"

"No problem, Mr. Fred." Renato turned a dazzling set of Chiclet-size caps on the seated couple. "*Signor* Mickey, *Principessa* Laurel, would you like a menu, or would you allow Renato to suggest?"

"Could you imagine," Mickey Boy said after the maître d' had left with their order, "having a clown like him for a hack in jail? '*Skinyours* and *Skinyourinis*,'" he mocked. "Not that most of the guards ain't clowns anyway."

"I know prison's no joke, and it's fresh in your mind, but it seems to pop up in every part of your conversation . . . and it comes out very bitter," Laurel said. "Was it a very painful experience? I mean, like physically?"

Mickey Boy laughed. "No, nobody raped me or beat me up, if that's what you want to know."

Laurel blushed.

"Yes, it was bitter . . . and boring," he said while toying with his fork. "I learned when I was growing up, though, that when people ask you how's everything, or how're you feeling, the best way to chase them away is to tell them."

"Try me," Laurel said in a near whisper. She crossed her ankles with his. "Tell me how it was."

Mickey Boy toyed with a soup spoon, studying it to mask his uneasiness. He'd never articulated his emotions to anyone before, especially about jail. Being glib about his prison time was usually part of the macho image he liked to project to girls at discos. With Laurel, however, he didn't feel like he needed a front. He believed she was truly interested, and he wanted to tell her.

Laurel nodded and gave his ankles an encouraging squeeze.

Staring into her eyes for support, Mickey said, "For six years I lived every day by itself. I couldn't think about yesterday 'cause I'd get mad, an' didn't think about tomorrow because it seemed too long to wanna think about."

"I don't know how you did it. I know I couldn't."

"You have to make yourself," he said. "If you can't do that, you just can't do the time. That's why you read sometimes that guys hang up. I seen a few guys try to kill themselves. They couldn't stop feeling, couldn't shake the outside world."

"But don't you need the outside, the support of loved ones?" Laurel asked.

Mickey shifted his gaze to Laurel's mouth as she spoke, wondering what it would have been like to have her waiting for him during his years in prison; how it would have been to kiss those pouting lips good-bye after each visit and go back to a barren cinder-block cell. Deciding that his time would have been even more miserable than it was, he continued. "Jail is the whole world when you're there. It has to be. Other places are just figments of your imagination. As a matter of fact, the hardest time guys have is when they either get a visit or call home. I guess it makes them realize they're away, that there really are people they love . . . but somewhere else." Mickey sipped his drink. "I'm rambling on like a lunatic, right?" he asked with a grin. "Once you wind me up, I don't stop."

"No, no," Laurel said. "Please, I want to know all about how you feel. It's the real human inside the tough guy everyone else sees. I feel privileged."

Mickey wanted to tell her as much as she wanted to know; the catharsis felt good. "Well, bottom line is (a), yes, I feel bitter about going away, especially since I didn't deserve it. Oh, I was a little involved at the end, but I wound up looking like I was the main guy in the whole operation, and carrying the weight for somebody else." The memory of how he'd been set up made his head throb and his skin flush. ". . . But that's another story, for another time. Anyway, (b) is the other end: I feel just like the kid I was before I went away . . . especially with you."

Laurel looked away.

Mickey was puzzled by her sudden change of mood. "I'm really happy you asked for us to meet," he said, hoping his honesty would become contagious. "I probably would have been dumb enough to hang up and never see you."

"Meeting might have been a mistake."

"Mistake is my middle name. Remember, I'm the same guy you used to know," Mickey Boy said. He leaned over the small table and raised her hand to his lips. "Only smarter. No more jails for this guy."

"I certainly hope not," Laurel whispered. She brushed her fingertips over his cheeks, then under his chin, practiced fingers that knew each of his most sensitive spots. "You should have learned your lesson by now . . . and I'd hate to see you leave again."

Mickey Boy smiled. Did Laurel really think he'd sacrificed six years of his life just to become a shoe salesman like her father? His jail time was just another rung on the mob ladder he'd stepped onto in his early teens. Once he'd gotten over his early folly about becoming a lawyer, it had been straight ahead, no detours. "Don't worry, hon," he said. "I ain't going no place but up."

Freddie was back, this time with two waiters. While the waiters served an array of mouthwatering dishes from a rolling silver cart, Freddie presented Laurel with a long white, beribboned gift box. "I'll have you know this hoodlum of yours made me send somebody all the way to Lexington and Fifty-eighth for these," he told her.

Mickey was pleased at how unnerved Laurel became, blushing and fumbling with the pink satin ribbon until she finally exposed the dozen long-stemmed American Beauty roses he'd ordered. Thankfully, whatever was troubling her earlier seemed completely gone. He chuckled to himself, realizing the only other living person he'd ever bought flowers for was his mother.

Laurel became the teenager he remembered again. She jumped from her chair excitedly and, still clutching the roses, kissed him full on the lips. "Oh, Mickey, thank you. They're beautiful!"

Instinctively, Mickey brought his hand to Laurel's hip, then pulled it back as though it had been seared and jammed it back in his pocket.

"I think we just lost another one to the fairer sex," Freddie whispered to his waiter, just loud enough for Mickey to hear.

2

May 22: Bensonhurst, Brooklyn

Just as the Seville rolled into the darkened back lot, the building's steel door swung outward. While one of his underlings inspected the premises, Vincenze Calabra, one of just two of New York City's five Mafia family chieftains to bear the title of don, surveyed the outside to be doubly sure. Five foot eight inches tall, with a swarthy complexion and thinning silver hair, only the facial puffiness usually attributed to good living and a mottled nose that widened each year belied the fact that Don Vincenze had been a handsome man in his younger days.

After receiving an all-clear signal from his man, the husky sixty-seven-year-old don slid from the car's interior and stepped onto the flinty pavement. The only movement on his otherwise stony face came from dark, piercing eyes scanning the area as he limped toward the unlit entranceway. With a wave of his Avanti cigar he dismissed his bodyguards and went in.

"How are you tonight, Joseph?" the don asked after kissing on both cheeks the man who waited in the shadows. "And how's everybody at home, especially my lovely godchild, Christina?"

Joseph Augusta, publicly the owner of the Shore Haven Funeral Home and privately the underboss of the Calabra Family, answered while he rebolted the mortuary's door, "We're all good. As a matter of fact, I just called home to check up on Chrissy and make sure she gets there by curfew. I'll tell you, it's no picnic raising girls, especially when they're sixteen-going-on-thirty, like Chrissy. You know, years ago, when *a buon oumo* my father-in-law used to get mad at my wife, he'd say, 'Instead of having kids, I shoulda raised chickens. At least when they aggravate me I could cook 'em an' eat 'em.' "

Both men laughed.

"But me," Joe Augusta continued, "I wouldn't give up a minute of the pleasure that *sfatcheem*'s brought me. Not that I'm not crazy about my Elizabeth too," he explained. "It's just that with Chrissy being the first, and so much like me, well, you know what I mean."

Don Vincenze smiled knowingly. "You forget, Joseph, that I raised two daughters. Maybe not as spirited as your little flower, Christina, but still girls."

The two mafiosi walked through the funeral home's elaborately decorated lobby toward the front office. Joe Augusta trudged ahead, his broad shoulders hunched forward while the older man paused to admire the splendor of his possessions—gold-flocked foil, red floral carpets, and huge crystal chandeliers surrounded him. He smiled, then puffed out a cloud of anise-scented smoke into the room.

"You look tired, Joseph," Don Vincenze said when he had settled into a leather armchair across the desk from the funeral director–underboss. "So business must be very good."

"You know the old joke, Vincenze, 'People are dying to get in.' But all jokes aside, we are doing very well." Joe Augusta reached under his desk and brought up a black leather attaché case, which he pushed across the top of the desk. "We made a good investment when we bought this place."

"No, we made a good investment when we put you here, Joseph," Don Vincenze responded. He fingered the supple calf appreciatively, his five-carat diamond ring sparkling in spite of the room's dimness, then slowly opened the case. After riffling through the currency for an instant, he closed the case and locked it.

"You've done an excellent job, Joseph. Better than anybody else could've done." Don Vincenze shook his head slowly from side to side. "Who would have thought that the young man who made so much use of a pistol would have turned into such a good businessman?" he said with a chuckle that hinted of some remorse.

"Unfortunately, that's the only future I see for us now," the underboss said. At forty years old, Joe Augusta's face was etched with lines that bespoke a weariness beyond that of physical labor, and which made his prematurely graying temples appear to be taking over the dark brown balance of hair right on schedule. "The old days are gone forever," he said with what had become his permanent funereal expression: lips turned down at the corners, eyes joylessly blank. "That's why I believe John-John's got the right idea about tonight. It's a shame—"

"I know how you feel," Don Vincenze said abruptly, his jowly features tightening into a hard glare. He spat a small piece of cigar tobacco onto the rug, then added, ''Let's not get into that again now. Just remember, what's right is not always important . . . what's best for us *is*.''

Joe Augusta grimaced. He shifted uncomfortably in his seat, then asked, ''All right, what about tonight? Are we gonna take care of the list I got here: Mickey Boy; his partner, Richie; Carlo Conte?''

''No, forget about that for now. I'll take care of them when I'm ready,'' the don said. ''You *did* take care of that other problem tonight though . . . right?''

''Buster's got two guys on him.''

''Good. For now, let's just concentrate on what we gotta do here, okay?''

''Whatever you say,'' Joe agreed. ''I wonder if John-John and Petey will react the way you figured.''

''Don't worry, Joseph,'' Don Vincenze said. ''I know them better than they know themselves . . . *all* of them . . . and especially our young friend, Mr. Petey Ross,'' he added disdainfully. ''Now, have you got everything in order for our guests? Peppino and Blackie should be here soon.''

Joe Augusta smiled. ''Of course. Let me put your briefcase away for now, and I'll show you.''

With Joe Augusta leading the way, the two men descended a stairwell, which led to another, smaller lobby area. After momentarily fumbling with his keys, Joe unlocked and opened one of two ornately carved wooden doors and stepped into the darkness.

A flipped switch instantly revealed a funeral chapel devoid of its traditional trappings, and redone for a very private banquet. In the center of the room, an elegantly appointed rectangular table stood proudly. Ten place settings of bone china and crystal stemware, one for each of New York's five family leaders and their underbosses, glistened on a white damask spread. Off to the right, a longer, narrower piece of furniture strained under the weight of a row of shiny silver chafing dishes, small blue flames warming their innards. There were enough breads, condiments, and desserts for a small wedding. The only reminder of the true location of the scheduled feast was a mocha-colored, brushed-metal casket that sat humbly on a platform at the far end of the room, as peaceful and unnoticed as its occupant.

While Joe Augusta retreated upstairs to greet their fraternal guests, Don Vincenze remained downstairs in the newly created dining room. Limping slowly around the room, he stopped and touched each lavish item he found: a Rosenthal goblet, a Lenox dish, a bottle of Brunello '64. He lifted a white cambric dinner napkin, held it a moment, then brought it to his lips, luxuriating in the way it skimmed over without so much as one fiber catching on his rough skin. *You came a long way from fishnets, Vincenze,* he thought—and smiled.

The appearance of Don Peppino Palermo abruptly awoke Don Vincenze from his reverie.

At seventy-eight years of age, Don Peppino was the senior member of the elite gathering that Don Vincenze was about to host that evening. Hawk-faced and frail, he was a staid, colorless plodder, an immigrant who'd never turned in his old-country ways for American style. His dress was old-fashioned and simple: dark wool suits that might have been new or twenty years old and tieless white-on-white shirts buttoned to the collar—and he ran his Family the same way, his crew being the only one where each member was required to kick in a fifty-dollar "sign of respect" to the boss each week, regardless of how broke any one of them was; all the other Family bosses had given up the practice of a tithe years before, and only took shares of moneys their members earned, which Don Peppino did in addition to the fifties he collected.

To the meeting that night Don Peppino brought his nephew and underboss, Blackie Palermo, a tank-shaped ex-boxer who constantly wore dark glasses to hide the false eye that replaced the one he'd lost in the ring.

Don Vincenze stepped forward to embrace and kiss his old compatriot, saying, *"Peppino, fratello mio, come sta?"*

Don Peppino returned the warmth. *"Bene, grazie. È sta, Vincenze?"*

"Molto bene," Don Vincenze answered. Then, pressing his lips close to Don Peppino's ear, he whispered, *"Stasera sta la notte . . .* tonight's the night . . . *our* night."

During the next hour, at precise twenty-minute intervals, three more late-model automobiles shuttled through the Shore Haven Funeral Home's back lot. Each car discharged a pair of white male passengers, paused until the men entered the building, then continued on its way. Each twosome was welcomed by Joe Augusta. They exchanged fleeting, somber-faced embraces, slight kisses on both cheeks, and whispered words of greeting before they were brought downstairs to meet with the two dons.

The first to arrive was the silver-coiffed, deeply suntanned Giovanni "John-John" DiGiovanni, with his next in command, Salvatore "Sammy The Blond" Termini.

The dapper, polished John-John's appointment to the top spot of his Family had been based more on his reputation for good business management skills than on his street smarts or strength of character. Since becoming boss, he spent half his year in Palm Beach exercising control over a steady flow of runners and messengers from New York, and satisfying his penchant for young, blond would-be actresses.

15

Don Vincenze and Don Peppino, heirs to the two largest Families, and therefore the most powerful bosses in the city, greeted John-John and Sammy The Blond together.

"It looks like life in Florida is pretty good," Don Vincenze told John-John after they had hugged. He eyed everything from John-John's navy crocodile loafers to his blue plaid sport coat to his lapis lazuli cuff links and ring. "I should try to get down there for a while myself."

"Anytime you can make it, Vince, you'll be my guest. I got a beautiful private estate, and the cream of the crop as far as young ladies go," John-John replied.

Gonoude bastard, Don Vincenze thought, but only smiled. He then turned to Don Peppino, who was talking to Sammy The Blond, and joked. "I think our friend John-John wants to kill me. He just offered me a young floozie if I go to Florida."

Don Peppino answered without looking at John-John, "What's worse is that before those *putanas* kill you, they'll destroy your brain. We seen it happen to too many of our friends, eh, Vincenze?"

John-John laughed with the two dons despite the rebuke in Peppino's remark, then excused himself to inspect the colorful variety of foodstuffs. Soon afterward, the next guest filled the doorway.

After a brief pause to survey his surroundings, Tomasso "Tom Thumb" Lentini stepped into the room. Tom Thumb's hulking four-hundred-pound body dwarfed an otherwise normal-size head, which had been poorly endowed with small, dark, beady eyes, one thick, Neanderthal brow, and a nose that nearly hooked into his mouth. As Machiavellian in nature as he was repulsive in appearance, the oversize mafioso allowed no one except his underboss, Rock Santoro, whom he had practically raised, and who escorted him that evening, to become intimate with him.

Tom's underboss, Rocco "Rock" Santoro, was another ex-pug, whose short-cropped hair and stony features brought to mind a model for ancient Roman coins. "The Rock from Ridgewood," as he'd been known when he'd fought in the ring, and Don Peppino's nephew, Blackie Palermo, were inseparable childhood companions who'd boxed in the same clubs, married first cousins, but were recruited and *made* by two different crews. They still remained best of friends, however, and were, in fact, godparents to each other's children.

Unfortunately, Tom Thumb didn't share his underboss's fondness for members of Don Peppino's Family.

"How are you, Don Vincenze?" Tom Thumb asked after a violent fit of coughing.

"I seem to be fine," Don Vincenze replied. "The question is, how are *you*? Between your lust for food and all those cigarettes you smoke, you're pushing yourself to an early grave. Not that we couldn't use the business here, but I'd hate to see you go, my friend. Besides, I don't know if Joseph could find a coffin big enough to fit you."

"That's what Rock always says, right, Rock?" When he received no reply, Tom Thumb turned to see his underboss in a friendly huddle with Don Peppino and Blackie Palermo. Tom's eyes glistened with embarrassment. "Oh, well," he said, his fleshy lips pulled tight, "when do we eat?"

Don Vincenze patted the giant mobster reassuringly on the arm. "As soon as Petey Ross gets here. Be patient, Tomasso, he should be here any minute."

The seven mafiosi were exchanging small talk when Joe Augusta ushered in the final two guests.

At forty-six years of age, Pietro "Petey Ross" Rossellini was the youngest chieftain of any of New York's five crime families. Movie-star handsome, with coal-black hair and ice-blue eyes, he attended the meeting that night as acting boss, subbing for Benedetto "Benny Brown" Favara, who was being held without bail in the Federal House of Detention on an assortment of charges dating back nearly fifteen years.

The only thing to mar Petey's otherwise perfect features was a furrowlike scar on his chin which was the result of a jealous girlfriend who happened to own a .22-caliber automatic.

To offset his youth and relative inexperience in mob political matters, Petey Ross appeared with his grandfatherly *consigliere*, sixty-seven-year-old Antonio "Sonny" Fortunato.

"Well, well, my friends," Don Vincenze began. He spread his arms as he spoke. "I think a little food would be nice before we discuss our business. Unfortunately, I thought it would be wiser if we had no outsiders present, and so we have no waiters."

A round of sniggers filled the room.

"I hope you don't mind if we serve ourselves. *Mi casa su casa. Buon appetito.*"

After brief huddles among the separate duos, the five bosses seated themselves at the dinner table while their companions went to assemble their meals for them.

When he was done serving Don Vincenze, Joe Augusta excused himself to phone home and check up on his sixteen-year-old daughter, Christina.

3

May 22: Bull's Head, Staten Island

"Hello, Mama? Hi, it's me," Christina Marie Augusta said while trying to control her speech through clenched teeth. Her catlike eyes, almond-shaped with huge golden-brown centers, squeezed shut in concentration. "What, Mama?" She hurriedly covered the receiver as a moan escaped her. "Ooh, ooh, stop."

Male lips pulled at Christina's bare, distended nipples, sending rapturous spasms up and down the length of her body. She spoke into the phone again, rushing the words out. "Yes, Mama, I'll be home byonebeforehegetshomegoodbyeIloveyou." She barely hung up in time for her mother to miss her cry as a broad finger drove up between her parted legs.

"Oooh. God, do I love you." Christina clung tightly to her lover's muscled frame while he mounted her. "Oh, Georgie, don't stop. Oh, yes," she whispered as he bucked back and forth, jamming his pelvis into hers.

A while later, spent, he rolled off to her side, still tightly embracing her.

"I wish we could stay like this forever, Georgie."

Christina's lover brushed away the few black ringlets that perspiration had pasted to her forehead, then planted a gentle kiss there. "If I don't get you home before your old man walks in, we *will* be like this forever . . . only in one of his boxes."

"He'd never hurt me, silly."

"Sure, he wouldn't hurt you. But do you know what they'd do to me?" He swung his legs off the bed and reached for a cigarette. "I'd wind up with this thing you like so much stickin' outta my ass—bloody end up!"

"But you're so tough and strong," she teased, hugging him from behind. Her firm young breasts crushed against his back, sending more thrilling sensations through her.

Georgie reacted to her teasing with genuine concern. "Strong, my ass, Chrissy. My own people would do it to me. They'd say I was outta my mind sleepin' with Joey A's sixteen-year-old daughter. An' you know what? They'd be right." He started toward the bathroom, leaving her pouting on the mattress. "Maybe they should put me out of my misery, 'cause I am nuts," he yelled through the open doorway.

Suddenly he dashed toward the motel's bed and leapt onto it, grabbing a surprised Chrissy as he landed. She playfully tried to elude his grasp. "Yeah, I'm crazy . . . crazy about you." He kissed her lips with a loud smacking sound.

"And I'm crazy about you, Mr. Randazzo, even if you are a scaredy-cat," Chrissy giggled. She looked at him sternly. "What kind of daddy are you going to make for all our babies when we get married? We'll have all little scaredy-kittens."

"Only half of them," Georgie answered, kissing her again. "The other half are gonna be little airheads like their mommy . . . that is, if I live long enough to make any. If we don't get our asses outta here fast, your old man is gonna bury me an' put your cute little body in a convent. That means *no* little airheaded kittens." He released her and bounded off the bed.

"I am not an airhead!" Chrissy shouted after him. "And you're still a scaredy-cat!"

Georgie "The Hammer" Randazzo primped himself in the mirror, running a metal comb through his coarse ebony hair. Assuming his best John Travolta pose, he checked his silk shirt to make sure enough buttons were open to expose the three gold chains and eight charms that lay in the hairless valley of his chest. He looked at himself sideways, ignoring the too-big nose that ruined an otherwise perfect profile, flexed a bicep, then reached for the black leather jacket that he had carefully draped over one of the room's chairs earlier that evening.

Georgie had earned his nom de guerre at the tender age of nine, when he'd dented his brother Mario's head with a ball-peen hammer. Now, at twenty-two years of age, he made sure his reputation in the neighborhood kept pace with his nickname by doing collection and other strong-arm work for "Crazy Angelo" Gangi, a soldier with Petey Ross's family.

"C'mon, baby. Seriously, I gotta get you home before I wind up as ground-up meat in a *sopressata*. An' I really gotta meet Skinny soon. We got something important to take care of." He leaned over, ruffled his hand through Chrissy's dark curls, and pecked her on the cheek.

"All right, all right. Here I come," she said, and with an accompanying burst of giggles threw her arms around his neck and pulled him back onto the bed.

4

May 22: East Side, Manhattan

"In the beginning I thought you were really horrible," Laurel said between sips of hot cappuccino. A dish of homemade cream puffs sat half eaten between her and Mickey. "I remember the first day I ever met you. I came to your house for your brother to help me with some math, and you were just getting dressed to leave. You were all in gray: suit, tie, even your shoes."

"Why was I horrible?" Mickey asked while pouring anisette into his espresso. "Was it my gray shoes? Did I insult you?"

"Oh, no, you were very polite, but very cold. It was like I wasn't even there. Then you gave him twenty dollars. I thought, 'Wow!' That was like a fortune at that age. Why, my Christmas Club check that I saved for all year was only fifty."

"Cold, rich, with gray shoes—I had to be a horrible guy. Add not working to the list, and I had to be worse than the Boston Strangler."

"When I asked why you were home during the day, he said you worked nights. What a joke that was."

"I did. I was a cat burglar," Mickey said with a teasing smile. He was amazed at Laurel's memory. As far as he himself remembered, she was just always around, with no specific beginning and no outstanding details—as much a part of Alley as his winter coat or summer Windbreaker.

Laurel reached for a pastry, then continued. "And when I said you had to be rich to give him that much money, he said that he had lent you all his money from the bank, and that you were paying it back at twenty dollars a week." She laughed, but her words were bitter. "I should have learned from that not to trust him."

"I guess he was just trying to impress you." Mickey enjoyed watching Laurel as she spoke. He took pleasure in the way her eyes widened to emphasize a point, how her nose creased to show her disfavor, when her tongue would dart out to moisten dry lips—and he interjected just enough conversation to keep her talking. "So because I ignored you I was horrible."

"Well, some of that, and some because you were always with that beast, Tracey Shea."

"Tracey, a beast? She was gorgeous."

Laurel looked at him with an incredulous expression on her face. "Are you kidding? She looked like a hooker."

The mention of his old flame made Mickey wonder how Laurel compared in bed. Probably not the hot stuff Tracey was, but that was why he couldn't stay with Tracey, or any of the other rubber-holes he dated—they were good for some fast fun but not to get tied up with for any length of time.

Mickey forced himself to dismiss Laurel's sexuality from his mind. "C'mon," he said. "You probably didn't even know what a hooker was at that age."

"I knew more than you think," Laurel said, an impish gleam in her eye. "Like when you started going with my friend Diane Berger's sister, Nancy. We knew everything you two did."

"Everything?"

Laurel nodded mischievously, her golden-brown hair loose and springy.

"Now, you can't say she wasn't pretty," he said, trying to turn her conversation away from the intimate details of his relationship with Nancy, with the Laughing Face.

Laurel drew him directly back. "I don't think you ever got past seeing those enormous boobs of hers that she was always showing off with those low-cut sweaters and no bra." She stuck her own chest out for emphasis.

Mickey stared at the outline of her nipples against the thin crepe fabric of her dress. Not huge like Nancy, but . . .

When she noticed the focus of his attention, Laurel held her pose for a moment and smiled. "Besides, you probably never saw her without the pounds of makeup she wore." She shuddered theatrically. "Ugh!"

"Now, now, let's not be catty," Mickey replied. His hand vibrated imperceptibly as he poured another cup of espresso. "So when did I stop being horrible?" he asked, trying once again to shift their conversation from his sex life.

"Well, it happened a little at a time," Laurel said with a giggle. "The first time I had dinner at your house was the start . . . when you came home with that trained monkey on roller skates."

"Zip? I seen him at my friend's birthday party for his kid, an' couldn't resist bringing him home—cost me three hundred balloons that day."

Laurel began to laugh. "Your mother was livid when he took the hamburger from her plate, but I was hysterical." With a finger pointed in mock anger, she added, "But part of you always aggravated me. I absolutely hated when you used to call me kid. 'Hiya doin', kid?' or

'What's up, kid?' " she imitated. "I wanted to kick you in the shins so bad."

"Why didn't you?"

"I was afraid you'd kick me back." Laurel bit into another chocolate-covered cream puff.

"C'mon, I'd never kick a 'kid,' " he teased.

Laurel stuck her cream-coated tongue out at him.

Mickey wanted so badly to reach out and hold her, kiss her, taste the tongue that was pointed at him. The thought that she probably viewed him as a big brother, and as such that they would never be more than good friends, saddened him. *Why did Alley have to get there first? Anybody else . . .*

"So that was what changed your mind about me?" he said. "Zip the Chimp?"

"That was the first day you really spoke to me like I was alive, and I saw you weren't as bad as I had thought. Before that I was very frightened of you."

"C'mon, me?"

"Really. By that time I knew what you did for a living, and besides, I was at the school yard when you and your friends beat up that guy, Sandy, who used to hang around."

"But he was dealing to kids."

"I know," Laurel said, "but when I saw you hit him with baseball bats I got nauseated and wanted to throw up. Between seeing that and you not talking to me, I thought you were terribly mean. Later on, when I got to know you, I saw you weren't really that bad."

"That's all, just 'not bad'?"

"Well," Laurel teased. "Maybe you rate an 'okay,' but if you stick to your new job and stay out of trouble, you might get a 'great.' "

Job? It took a supreme effort for Mickey Boy to keep a straight face. Laurel was a typical middle-class sucker, he thought—but a sweet one. "Did I ever tell you, in all the time I know you, that I think you rate a terrific? Huh, 'kid'?"

Laurel cast her eyes down at her empty cup. Her tightened lips and fidgeting fingers gave Mickey the same uneasy feeling he'd had earlier: that she was struggling with herself whether or not to tell him something she'd been hiding.

After studying the cup for a moment or two, Laurel brought her watery gray-green eyes up to meet his, forced a smile, then kicked him in the shin.

A burly, well-dressed man stepped up to Numero Uno's bar, ordered a shot of brandy, and paid for it in cash. Drink in hand, he meandered over to the open archway that led to the dining room and looked in.

When he didn't see Mickey Boy or his date, he panicked. Had they left by a back way? he wondered.

Suddenly the man spotted Mickey Boy coming out of the men's room. With a sigh he downed his drink and returned to his partner in the brown Oldsmobile.

5

May 22: Bensonhurst, Brooklyn

The war was over. Ravaged remnants of frutti di mare, veal alla marsala, and shrimp scampi lay scattered across the fifteen-foot linen battlefield. Decapitated broccoli stems waited patiently to be removed from the front lines of Lenox china. The triumphant generals celebrated their victory by reviewing a parade of miniature pastries and downing over-size cups of freshly brewed espresso laced with Sambuca.

Don Peppino, frail-looking but flushed with the contented glow of having eaten more of the rich food than either his heart specialist or wife of fifty-two years, Sylvana, would ever allow, tapped his glass with a spoon.

"Well, now," he said, looking around to make sure he had every-one's attention. "I think it's about time we took care of business, so we could all go home and dream of Don Vincenze's generosity in hosting our little get-together. Don Vincenze, since you called this meet, would you be kind enough to start."

Don Vincenze rose slowly, surveying each of the hardened faces as he did: the foppish, deeply suntanned John-John, probably eager to be back on his way to some twenty-year-old bimbo in Miami; the unsightly giant, Tom Thumb, seemingly more interested in gobbling another chocolate *pasticciote* than in discussing business, but still the most for-midable of all; Petey Ross, the youngest of the bosses, a fine-looking grape pulled off the vine too early to be the award-winning wine it might have been. Not the same quality as when he'd sat among their forerunners, the Don thought. Not one of them could shine the shoes of the old-timers, guys like Lucky Luciano, Trigger Mike Coppola, and Three-Fingers Brown. What would Lucky do today? Probably the same thing he was about to.

"You know," he began quietly, standing slightly hunched over the table, both thick hands planted firmly on its edge. "For years an' years, as a matter of fact for as far back as I could remember . . . from when we took over from the Moustache Petes . . . our whole idea was to keep a low profile. Those guys who didn't all wound up dead. No matter what happened, though, the rest of us tried our best to do the right thing an' stay out of the limelight.

"Like when this rat city made OTB an' took away most of our horse business. We had guys, an' I know that in your Families you had some of the same kind of fellas, that wanted to shut 'em right down . . . an' we could've, like that!" he said with a loud snap of his fingers.

All heads reflexively nodded agreement as they listened.

"Then when the feds started using this fuckin' RICO, an' Hobbs Act, an' *tutta marrone*, we sat by an' didn't make a goddamn peep. Even *a buon oumo* Funzouale, who was closer to me than anybody, refused to make any big issues. To the end, how did he fight back? By bringing bundles of cash up to his big-shot Madison Avenue lawyers. It's a shame he had to beat 'em by croaking, but at least he didn't die in the can like too many of our friends are doing."

Everyone nodded and mumbled a few words in memory of Don Vincenze's predecessor, Frank "Funzouale" Tieri, who remained free by dropping his pants in front of a federal judge at a post-conviction bail hearing. The startled justice was mortified by the network of post-operative scars that made the septuagenarian's lower torso resemble a fleshy roadmap, and released him on bail pending appeal. Consistent with the Court's appraisal, the illness-ravaged Funzi didn't live long enough to surrender for his imprisonment.

Don Vincenze continued. "Everybody figured, an' that goes for me, too, that if we stayed cool an' let them eat up a few of our people, maybe get a few headlines along the way, sooner or later they'd slow down an' get off our backs. A few guys might suffer, but then we'd go back to business as usual. But they didn't go away, they got worse." Don Vincenze waved his beefy hand to encompass the entire group. "*We're* going away . . . all of us. Each one of our Families is getting eaten up a little more every single day!"

Again they nodded.

His dark eyes bristling, Don Vincenze kept his audience mesmerized with emotionally charged claims that U.S. attorneys were using them as stepping-stones to political careers or huge fees as mob lawyers when they left the office, and that the FBI was using them to garner support for tough measures that were ultimately aimed at suppressing political dissent.

"When there's another war, an' they lock up the protesters with no bail, the suckers'll be screaming like stuck pigs. 'Too bad,' the government'll tell 'em, 'but this has been the law for years.' And it *will* be the law . . . made off our backs. Too bad that by that time it won't only be too late for the suckers, but it'll be way too late for us—we'll be forgot about; scapegoats rotting away in Leavenworth or Lewisburg."

The other mob bosses remained as silent and still as the casket's lifeless occupant while Don Vincenze turned his accusations on federal judges who sentenced fellow mafiosi with disproportionate harshness.

"A nigger or spic gets caught with six kilos of *babania*, tells 'em he's shooting it in his arm, an' he gets six years. We're spotted having a cup of demitasse together on Mulberry Street, an' we get hit with RICO—twenty years for each piece of pastry we got on the table."

His bitter joke brought a round of assenting snickers.

"Look what they did to the guys on Big Paul's case: one of 'em got 165 years for stolen cars! What the hell did that judge think he was sentencing, an oak tree?"

Don Vincenze lowered his tone as he prepared to sit. "Now we come to the big question: What are we gonna do about it? That, my friends and brothers, is why we're here tonight. Not that we don't enjoy getting together, but we put our balls on the line meeting like this, because that's the one question that I or any of you can't answer alone. This is when the blood of our fathers, an' their fathers, an' our sacred oath to each other, and our honor . . ." Wagging a finger for emphasis, he added, "Don't forget our honor—pulls us together to move like one person.

"Probably we won't be able to come to no real decision tonight of which way we're gonna move. At least we'll hear what each of our brothers thinks, kick it around, an' set a definite time limit for us to make that decision. We gotta decide soon, 'cause La Cosa Nostra depends on it . . . our future depends on it . . . our lives depend on it.

"When all of you finish, I'll talk again an' tell you how my Family feels. Who wants to start?"

Don Vincenze had done his job. He'd laid the foundation and posed the question for what could have the most profound effect on the mob since Lucky Luciano's sanguinary takeover from the old-line Sicilians in 1931. The don sat down, confident that his speech would trigger a specific response from each of his guests—a response he was counting on.

6

May 22: East Side, Manhattan

Most of the customers, including the provision salesman Eli Kantor and the obese bookmaker Dinty Moore, had already left by the time Freddie Falcone pulled a chair up to join Mickey Boy and Laurel. At Mickey Boy's urging, Freddie began to tell one of the underworld anecdotes he always seemed to have an endless store of. That particular tale concerned a friend of his and Mickey Boy's named Slippery, who had recently attempted to swindle an out-of-towner and another mutual friend nicknamed "The Polack" by convincing them that a building custodian he'd introduced them to was really a powerful mob boss.

"Well," Freddie continued, eyebrows raised high and hands waving in front of him, "Slippery buys this old janitor—who looks just like George Raft—a black polyester suit from one of those joints where you get a suit, two pairs of pants, a toaster oven, an' a trip to Hawaii all for $39.95. Then he throws a three-dollar pinky ring an' a pair of shades on the bum an' gives him orders not to say a word, but just to grunt a lot, an', when he gives him the high sign, to kiss the sucker on both cheeks like he's a real wiseguy."

"Is this a joke?" Laurel asked. "I feel like there's going to be a punch line and I'm going to be the only one who doesn't get it."

Freddie raised a hand in mock oath. "May God strike me dead if I'm lying," he said. "Every word I tell you is the Gospel."

Turning his attention back to Mickey Boy, Freddie went on. "So Slippery and his partner, Johnny Crumbs, bring the janitor to meet The Polack and the sucker in the Grand Hyatt Hotel. They play the part like the janitor's a real Don Corleone. They're tasting his drinks before they give 'em to him and standing by the bathroom door when he takes a leak—the whole works. They do everything but kiss his fugazy ring."

As far as Mickey Boy was concerned, no one told a story like the silver-haired Freddie, who made even dull ones seem funny. As always, the contrast of his usually debonair friend's comical expressions—nose twisting or eyes squinting as he spoke—tickled him inside; he struggled to fight back the laughter welling in him.

"No, don't laugh yet. You ain't heard the best part," Freddie cried out through his own laughter. "The story they tell is that the janitor, who they call Don Cheech di Catania, is the biggest godfather in the country, an' is looking for a replacement for Meyer Lansky. For fifty large, the sucker could buy all of Florida as his territory."

Mickey Boy finally exploded. Oblivious to the few remaining customers, he and Freddie rollicked in their chairs, slapping the table and each other.

"Who's Meyer Lansky?" Laurel asked.

"Well, not only does the sucker fall for it hook, line, and sinker, but so does The Polack," Freddie continued, gasping as he spoke. "This moron's been in the streets all his life an' still don't know who's who."

"Whattaya think they call him The Polack for, nothing?" Mickey Boy replied.

"I know, but even dumb has a limit," Freddie said.

"Not with this guy. If dumb had an organization, he'd be its poster kid."

Freddie drew in a deep breath, trying to regain his composure. "Now, get this: The Polack says he always heard of Don Cheech but never thought he'd get to meet him, and actually helps convince his pal that the whole scam is true."

Mickey Boy and Freddie wiped their eyes with Numero Uno's red linen napkins.

"Who's Don Cheech?" Laurel asked, a baffled expression on her face.

Freddie ignored her again. "To make a long story short, the new Meyer goes back to Miami, tries to make a Lansky move, an' gets the shit kicked out of him in a bar."

"You're kidding?!" Mickey Boy was astounded by the stupidity of the victim. It was no secret among knock-around guys that there were always legitimate suckers who wanted to become involved with racketeers, and who they could invariably fleece. This one, however, was the most gullible of any he'd seen or heard about before.

The punch line to Freddie's story, that when the would-be gangster from Florida finally realized he'd been taken he sent his battle-ax of a wife up to try to collect from Slippery for him, drove Mickey Boy to more laughter.

"I don't think it's very funny to swindle people out of their money," Laurel said. "That's what your friends did, isn't it?"

"You feel that way, pretty lady, because you don't know who Meyer Lansky is," Freddie teased.

Laurel blushed with embarrassment, then replied defensively, "Well, I'm sure you two geniuses don't know who everyone is. For example, who was Horace Mann?"

While Mickey Boy remained quiet, having no idea at all whom she was talking about, Freddie didn't hesitate a second. "Of course we know, don't we, Mick?" he asked with a sidelong wink. "Well, Miss

Smarty Pants, he's the guy they named the law after, about bringing a young girl across a state line to do the job on her—Horace Mann was a famous pervert!"

It was Laurel's turn to laugh, the first time that evening, Mickey noted, that she seemed completely at ease.

After toasts to themselves, the slick con man, Horace Mann, and to themselves again, Freddie shifted his seat closer to Mickey Boy's. "Eli, Dinty, an' me put a little something together as a welcome-home present for you. It's not much, but it'll help you buy a new suit."

Mickey Boy accepted the folded bills, dropped them into his jacket pocket without looking at them, then kissed Freddie's cheek. "Thanks, pal. You know I love ya!"

"Anything I could ever do for you, kid, don't hesitate or be ashamed to ask," a misty-eyed Freddie replied. He turned to Laurel. "All kidding aside, sweetheart . . . you don't mind if I call you sweetheart, do you?" Without waiting for a reply, he went on. "This guy you got here is a piece of bread—they don't come no better. Make sure you treat him right."

The same troubled look that had come and gone all evening crossed Laurel's face again, quickly followed by a weak smile.

"I apologize, but I gotta run; I got an appointment downtown that can't wait," Freddie said. "Meanwhile, everything here's taken care of . . . tips an' all. No, no, don't say a word," he said, stopping his guests' attempts at appreciative gestures. "Your enjoyment is my thanks." He then added, "I also made arrangements for you two to catch the last show at the Café Carlyle. Ask for Ambrose an' tell him you're the people I called about—that's all taken care of too."

"No, Freddie, please," Mickey Boy said. "You did more than enough already."

"Friends could never do more than enough for friends. Are you my friend?"

"You know I am," Mickey Boy said, truly warmed by Freddie's generosity. For a street guy, he felt he was lucky to have two real friends like Richie and Freddie. Most so-called "friends" were backstabbers, just waiting for a clear enough target—and in his life, backstabbing often proved fatal.

"Then it's settled," Freddie said. "Go enjoy yourselves, an' don't insult me with no more thanks or by not going." They kissed again— this time Laurel was included.

Mickey Boy waited until Freddie had left, then counted the money he had been given: one thousand dollars.

Night chill forced Mickey and Laurel close together as they left the restaurant, she, clutching the roses tightly in her arms.

Using a handful of his jacket front, Laurel pulled him into the silent doorway of an optical shop. Reflected bits of streetlight made her eyes appear watery and pleading. "Can we not go to that Café . . . ?"

". . . Carlyle," he said while holding her waist. The taste of her breath excited him; his heart beat faster in his ears. *No, not yet.* "You heard Freddie . . . we don't wanna insult him."

"I'd rather go back to Brooklyn."

The evening couldn't end that quickly; he couldn't let it. Who knew when there would be another one? "But it's still early, and—"

"To your apartment."

"But, Laurel honey, I've been trying so hard not to—"

Her mouth smothered his.

One block up, on Second Avenue, the driver of the brown Oldsmobile turned on the ignition and pulled out of his parking spot.

7

May 22: Lower West Side, Manhattan

Visions of Chrissy—pouting, smiling, nude—flashed repeatedly before Georgie The Hammer's eyes as he made a right turn onto West Street from the Brooklyn Battery Tunnel; the exhilarating scent of her lingered seductively in his nostrils. He continued pushing his black 'Vette northward through the light traffic, totally oblivious to the new towers of Battery Park City on his left, or the World Trade Center to his right.

A few blocks up, at the corner of Debrosses Street, he stopped for his partner, Skinny Malone, to run into Ponte's restaurant to get cigarettes. Georgie wanted to go in himself and dial Chrissy's private number, but was afraid Joe Augusta might have gotten home already. Chrissy's mother was a doll, and would overlook anything the two youngsters did—her romantic instincts overcoming her strict Italian upbringing—but if by some chance the old man was home, he'd raise holy hell. Then, once he'd found out who the culprit was . . . *Why take stupid chances?* Georgie thought.

"You okay?" Skinny asked when he returned his bony frame to the passenger seat. His trademark newsboy cap, this one light blue sailcloth, was settled low on his forehead, just allowing his pug nose, ever-smiling lips, and a few straggly tufts of black hair to show underneath. "You look sick."

"I was just thinking about something."

"I knew I smelled something burning! I thought it was a bag lady torchin' some firewood."

Georgie remained stony-faced. "Funny," he said, and eased them back into the traffic lanes. They passed the westernmost part of Greenwich Village, where rough-trade gay bars dot a couple of blocks of shoddy old uninhabited buildings facing the Hudson River. Despite the late hour, crowds of homosexuals lined the street, dressed in everything from hooker-style drag to studded leather motorcycle outfits.

"Look at them," Skinny said. With exaggerated motions he made sure his window was tightly shut. "I'll bet we could get AIDS just by opening the window down here."

Georgie nodded blankly. It was hard enough trying to picture Chrissy's face without Skinny's bad jokes; every image seemed to have her father somewhere close by.

"What the hell is it with you?" Skinny bellowed. "You're always in a fog lately."

"I'm okay . . . just a little down."

"When are you ever up?" Skinny said. "Ever think maybe you got manic depression, or maybe hypoglycemia? You really should go see a doctor, get a glucose tolerance test."

"Will you stop with your fuckin' diseases! I just got some problems, that's all."

"Ain't we all?" Skinny countered. "C'mon, pal, wanna talk about 'em? I can't stand you always lookin' like the world's comin' to an end."

"Nah, nothing you ain't heard before."

Skinny pursed his lips as though in deep thought. "Let me see . . . I'll bet the first problem is my little darling Chrissy. Solution: Give her to me an' you'll never have to worry about her again," he teased. "I'll marry her an' take her as far away from her old man as I could—maybe even Belfast. I wanna see that dago bastard give the Irish kid a problem over there."

Georgie began to laugh. One thing he had always been able to count on, from the days they were both kids together in grade school, was Skinny perking him up. "You know, one of these days somebody's gonna hear you pull that dago or wop shit, an' you're gonna wind up in the middle of a fuckin' Irish stew."

"See, I told you we all got problems!"

Georgie groaned. "Boy, do I wish I had your head."

"An' do I wish I had your girl!"

"No, really, I wish I didn't let things bother me, like you do. Like even that beef we got with Little Vinnie's got me twisted up in fuckin' knots, an' you don't even give a shit."

"Of course I give a shit. I wish I owed that dirty guinea bastard more money," Skinny said. "See, all your problems—outside of Chrissy, that is—boil down to three things: money, money, an' more money. Now, if you'd listen to the skinny Irish kid an' let us move a little coke or speed, you'd only have to worry about Chrissy's old man castrating you. That sounds simple enough to me."

"Let's just do like we're doing!" Georgie ordered. "If I listen to you, I'll really wind up in the trunk of a car."

"Listen to me an' the only car you'll wind up in is an armored one," Skinny replied. "When you make your deposits!"

They passed the new convention center and the World War II aircraft carrier, *Intrepid*, then turned right and proceeded eastward. Two more rights and they were headed back toward the water on a narrow one-way street.

Georgie pointed through the windshield at something on their right. "All right, there it is." The metal-faced Parthenon Diner, reflecting the light of the streetlamps, shone out from between dark warehouses. The area was totally devoid of life.

They drove around the block one more time, carefully checking everything in sight as they approached the diner. A vagrant pissing in a doorway that night could be their undoing sometime in the future. If, however, a problem did arise at a later date, it certainly wouldn't be due to their neglect.

All memories of Chrissy instantly evaporated from Georgie's mind as adrenaline pumping through his body fine-tuned his senses. At that moment nothing existed but his and Skinny's being locked in a particular point of time and space together, trying to accomplish a mission.

Georgie parked beyond the diner, on the opposite side of the street. He and Skinny sat silently for a while, checking the environment, making certain it was safe. Georgie dried his palms, which had become icier and wetter than their normal clammy condition, by rubbing them along his pants legs. Skinny jumped as a sheet of newsprint blew past the rear window of the Corvette.

When Georgie was sure that the riverside traffic was moving, he said, "Let's go," and swung his door open. No lights went on in the car's interior.

Skinny Malone tossed his blue cap on the seat, then hurried after his partner, skipping once to catch up. Cool night air brushed the two men's faces as they moved nimbly and noiselessly along the building line toward the diner.

Using a key Skinny held in his gloved hand, they entered the counter section of the eatery. Georgie peeked out the window, straining to see as far down either side of the block as he could. All clear.

When Skinny disappeared through the swinging doors that led to the kitchen, Georgie hurried to the refrigerated pastry case. The last meal he'd eaten had been coffee, toast, and a cold pork chop for breakfast. Most of the day the strain of recent problems had kept him too knotted up to consume anything but Pepsi-Colas and Snickers bars, then, in the evening, Chrissy had kept him too occupied to care about food. Tomorrow would be back to high protein and pumping iron, he vowed, but for now lemon meringue would do. As two of his fingers greedily shoveled a blob of cold yellow pudding into his mouth, some dropped to the wooden floorboards, narrowly missing his shoes. *Shit!* he cursed silently while licking his fingers clean, then reached for a chocolate doughnut.

"C'mon, let's get moving," Skinny said, rushing out of the kitchen. His normally clowning manner was gone; in its place a serious, efficient technician. He shot a glance back at the swinging doors, then quickly looked to the front, his mess of hair flapping as his head jerked.

With the doughnut set between his teeth, Georgie drew a candle from the pocket of his leather jacket. Using an ordinary disposable lighter, he melted the bottom of the candle, stuck the hot wax firmly on the counter, then lit the wick.

Within seconds the two men had locked the diner and were rounding the corner into 12th Avenue's northbound traffic. They remained in the vicinity, driving up and down adjacent streets, waiting for the candle to ignite the gas from jets Skinny had opened. No trace would remain of the candle, and they would collect the balance of their fee from the owner.

"Payday!" they yelled in unison when angry orange flames finally exploded through the diner's windows. "God bless the Greeks!"

8

May 22: Bensonhurst, Brooklyn

Don Vincenze remained expressionless, his dark Sicilian eyes scanning each of his fellow mafiosi's faces. He'd just sat through a long, heated confrontation between the debonair John-John, who'd implored them to practice extreme patience until such time as the government relented in its current drive against organized crime, and Petey Ross, the youngest of the bosses, who'd demanded quick, decisive action.

"We gotta make a stand, an' we gotta start now!" Petey had yelled. "Otherwise we're gonna be like the old dinosaurs, an' die out. I say we gotta start using real bullets if we're gonna survive," he'd gone on.

"Kill a couple of gung-ho prosecutors an' hatchetman judges, an' you'll see a whole different ball game."

Now Don Vincenze was tired. He'd had enough, and focused on the current speaker, Don Peppino, hoping he'd finish quickly.

Don Peppino, the most venerable of the bosses, firmly supported John-John's call for *paziènza!* Still seated, the old mafioso spoke between puffs on a dark, twisted DeNobili cigar. "We lived through Dewey. We lived through Kefauver and the heat from Valachi. We'll live through this." He looked directly at Petey Ross. "Violent solutions are not new. I remember when the Dutchman wanted to kill Dewey. We didn't go for it then, and I don't think we should go for it now."

Petey Ross winced at the reference to Dutch Schultz. Though he hadn't even been born at the time, Petey knew all about how Schultz had died in a bullet-riddled phone booth after insisting that he would murder the popular New York prosecutor, Thomas Dewey, in spite of Lucky Luciano and the rest of the ruling council's deciding against it.

"*Fratèllo mio*, believe me," Don Peppino went on, "we carry a lot of the blame for our problems, and before we look outside for solutions, we should look to ourselves. Our good friend Carlo knew this was going to happen, many years ago. Why do you think that for twenty years, except for a couple of special deals, he wouldn't let us bring in no new members? The books stayed closed for twenty years and, take my word for it, if he was alive today, they'd still be closed."

Don Vincenze smiled inwardly. If it were up to Peppino, he thought, the youngest made man would be in his seventies.

"Unfortunately," Don Peppino said, "a lot of our problems came from bringing in new people who really don't belong, and by associating with outsiders who don't have the same upbringing or sense of honor that we do. Maybe what we should do is a little housecleaning on our own, then go hibernate like a bear until this *tempèsta* . . . this storm, passes."

"Don Peppino," Petey Ross called out. "I hate to interrupt you, an' believe me, I don't mean no disrespect by it, but you know some of us, like me an' Thumb," he said, pointing at the ugly giant whose Family had been war-torn for years, "we ain't got very big houses to start with. If we clean ours any more, there'll be nothing left. We'll be sleeping in open lots, if you know what I mean."

A burst of laughter followed Petey's assessment. Even the generally humorless Peppino allowed himself a chuckle.

"Seriously," Petey said. "What we need is more men comin' in to replace what strength we already lost. I got good standup guys waiting for us to make them." He formed a thumb and index finger into a pistol's shape. "Guys who already done work for us and proved what kind of men they are. They deserve to be in our thing, to wear our shoes, as much as anybody. An' we need them to build our houses up so we could survive." Petey turned his attention to John-John. "Maybe then we could hang out in Hollywood or Florida with young star-babies too."

John-John slammed his browned fist on the table. China, silver, and glass seemed to rattle all around the room. "Listen, you!" he shouted. "I'm telling you right now, keep your fuckin' remarks to yourself!"

Sammy The Blond clung to John-John's sleeve, whispering, trying to calm him.

"If the shoe fits, wear it!" Petey answered. "An' you picked the wrong guy to warn about anything. I'll—"

"Petey, that's enough!"

All eyes turned to Don Vincenze, his own eyes boring into Petey Ross like black lasers. Aware of the bitterness toward each other that the two men had brought to the meeting, the don had let them battle all night. He couldn't, however, allow them to continue any longer without it reflecting on him—and his leadership.

"Remember where you are and who you are among," Don Vincenze said. His voice was flat, his face expressionless. "I realize the emotions involved in what we're discussing, but we can't take out our frustrations on each other. We are together. We are one person. You know there was some doubt as to whether you were ready for the position we *allowed* you to fill . . . temporarily, whether you were too young and immature. Don't prove those of us who backed you wrong." He glared at Petey Ross's *consigliere*, Sonny Fortunato, sending an unmistakable message with his eyes: *This is your fault.*

Sonny looked away.

"I hope there will be no more childish outbursts," Don Vincenze warned. "And I hope there's nothing more behind this anger than just what this discussion caused."

Petey Ross's embarrassment at being admonished like a schoolboy was apparent. He paused to look directly at each one, but quickly skipped by John-John. "Don Vincenze, Don Peppino, my brothers, I offer you my deepest apologies, and, of course, there's nothing more than what this discussion causes in me." He paused. "I know that being wound up in the problems we got is no excuse. I hold all of you in the highest regard, and would rather kill myself than dishonor you."

"There is no need to kill yourself . . . controlling yourself will be enough," Don Vincenze said. "Your apology is accepted. Don Peppino, please continue."

Don Peppino began again, softly, as if he were never interrupted. "Sometimes I think I'll never get used to the new ways, and most of the time I'm happy for it. We got a history. We got ways of doing things that stayed the same under Democrats and Republicans, through

World War Two, Korea, and peacetime. Ours is a way of life that never changes . . . it can't change." He pointed a finger as gnarled as his cigar at his fellow mafiosi. "I warn you, if we try to go against our own ways, we'll destroy this thing of ours. *La Cosa Nostra moriro . . .* our thing will die.

"The only hope we have is to go back to the old ways. We're old-country people being poisoned by a new, contaminated world. I say let's turn the clock back and try to be more like those who wore our shoes in the past. Maybe we should take a tip from our brothers from the other side. You don't see them in big, flashy cars, with jewels all over themselves like Christmas trees, or throwing around big money on *putanas* in nightclubs."

No, Don Vincenze thought, *they're too busy selling drugs and burying the money.* Despite the fact that he, like the older Don Peppino, had been born in Sicily, he was totally Americanized and, like most American wiseguys, had nothing but contempt for their European counterparts.

Don Peppino paused to relight his DeNobili, then added, "If we can't come to an agreement among ourselves, maybe we should put it before the whole commission. After all, whatever we do affects them too."

Don Vincenze laughed inside. He knew it would be nearly impossible to get all the ruling mob bosses in the country together during those dangerous times—and knew that Peppino knew it also. Besides, as ruling chieftain of the largest of all the Families, the only one with recognized branches nationwide, Don Vincenze himself would have to be the one to instigate that type of meeting—something he wouldn't do under any circumstances. *Ah, Peppino,* he thought. *How you love to needle these fools.*

"You know how my Family stands," Don Peppino said, putting an end to the buzzing he'd begun with his suggestion of a full commission meeting. "Unless someone comes up with a better idea, one that makes sense, that's the way it will stay." He nodded toward Don Vincenze to indicate he was finished.

Now all eyes fell on the only Family boss who hadn't spoken: Tom Thumb. Like Don Peppino, he chose to remain seated while he spoke. "Youse all know that I don' talk a lot, so don' worry, 'cause I ain't gonna start tonight."

A rash of laughter eased the anxiety in the room.

As promised, Tom Thumb's speech was short and sweet. Between phlegmy coughs and spitting into his handkerchief, the beetle-browed giant argued for more time to make a decision and against consulting the entire commission. In closing, he said that if forced to commit himself to one side or another at that time, he would have to side with young Petey Ross and vote for retaliation against their government enemies.

Don Vincenze took the floor again, thinking that Tom Thumb bore more watching than he'd first estimated. He said, "Well, fellas, as you could all see, we got ourselves a hell of a problem. We *all* agree with that. The only difference we got is how to solve it." With a nod of his head he motioned toward Petey Ross. "When I heard our hotheaded young friend talk, I must admit, I was ready to accept his violent way. On the other hand, Don Peppino and John-John make a lot of sense too."

The seeds were planted; now all they had to do was grow, Don Vincenze thought. He looked around the table, satisfied that everything had gone well, and continued. "The probable truth is that our answer is somewhere in the middle.

"Like Don Peppino, I grew up in the old days, an' with our old ways—but these are not the good old days. Much as I'd like to close my eyes an' find this mess is gone when I open them, I know it won't happen. These are new times and new problems, an' they need new solutions.

"Maybe what we gotta do is set up a big fund to start reaching judges, politicians, an' reporters that could help us. Everybody's got a price—and for those who don't, well, maybe we let Petey get his wish and set up a small hit squad that can't be tied to us. At the same time, we might wanna hire one of those big lobby guys in Washington, like the ones that work for Cuba and China. If they could help them, they could sure enough do a job for us. Big money talks everyplace—from the Fifth Precinct to the White House.

"Like I said, those are only some ideas for us to kick around. What we gotta come up with is exact plans, though, not ideas."

The late hour was having its effect on the sixty-seven-year-old host as well as the senior member, Don Peppino, who listened with his eyes shut.

"My brothers," Don Vincenze said. "Nothing is going to be decided tonight. We're a little lucky because summer'll be here soon, an' it should be pretty quiet, what with judges, prosecutors, and FBI agents going on vacation. I say we give ourselves three or four months where we go over things with each other, and be prepared to have a final vote by the end of the summer. Is that agreed?"

Each member signaled his assent with a nod.

"Okay. How about Labor Day . . . or, better yet, how about we get together in September, at the Festa San Gennaro? There should be enough confusion at the feast for us to make arrangements to meet with no problem. Agreed?"

Again they nodded.

Tom Thumb began to speak, was interrupted by a violent coughing seizure, then said, "Two things: Three votes is law, an' no commission."

"As far as the vote, I'm sure there's no problem with everybody going along with the majority as usual," Don Vincenze replied. "And I also think that we could shelve bringing it to the commission till after San Gennaro. That okay with you, Peppino?"

"S'awright."

"Good. Now let's go home an' get some sleep—we earned it."

The Mafia generals and their aides, mind weary and eager to go about their personal business, exchanged hugs, kisses, and hints at further appointments.

Petey Ross and John-John shared every formality through an undisguised veil of iciness.

Don Vincenze noted the friction.

9

May 22: Sheepshead Bay, Brooklyn

Mickey's attempt to mount Laurel ended unsuccessfully with her coaxing him onto his back so that she could take charge. Her mouth was all over his in an instant—biting, sucking, probing; the almond-sweet taste of Amaretto mingled with her breath, hot with passion, to overwhelm him and drive his tongue deeper toward her throat, almost as though he wished she could swallow him up. When he tried to push his erection into her from his position underneath, she firmly resisted again, shifting her lower body off his.

"My hero," Laurel moaned in Mickey's ear just before darting her tongue in. "My strong, strong hero," she continued throatily as her lips slithered down his neck and across his collarbone. If Mickey was already hot, Laurel's mouth set him ablaze. Every nerve ending in his body seemed raw and vibrated. It troubled him, though, that she knew exactly where each of his most sensitive spots was. How much practice had it taken to make her this perfect? How many . . . ?

When Laurel's lips approached his navel, her tongue dancing in and out like a snake's, Mickey Boy reached down to pull her away.

Laurel lifted his hands off, kissing each palm before she set them at his sides. "Relax," she whispered, a lewd sparkle in her gray-green eyes.

Putana, his mentors' voices rang in his head. *Only a goddamned whore does that.* He wanted to stop her, scream no! and yet . . .

Mickey groaned with pleasure at the sight of Laurel's hair splayed over his midsection. When she engulfed his hardness in the warmth of her mouth, he knew he should pull her off, but instead he pressed his hands on the blue satin sheet and arched his hips upward. He came instantly, excited yet repulsed by the sight of her face draining him.

I must be going crazy, he thought—and shuddered.

Directly across the street from where Mickey Boy's Lincoln sat, the passenger of the brown Oldsmobile spoke into the pay phone. "Yeah, he's tucked in for the night."

"You sure?"

"We been here for almost an hour. He's up there with *a goomarra*."

"That *sfatcheem*! If he ain't just like his old man."

"You knew his old man?" the caller asked.

"Probably better than anybody else." He quickly changed the subject. "Okay, you done good. If youse're sure he ain't comin' out no more, get home yourself . . . and be careful."

"*Ciao*."

Laurel lay in the fetal position, her legs tightly shut. "No, Mickey, I told you before . . . not without protection. Wait till tomorrow."

Mickey's body was plastered to hers, his manhood trying to burrow underneath her from behind. He slid a hand under her arm and fondled her breast, rolling the hardened nipple between his fingers. "C'mon baby," he whispered while kissing her neck and ears. He felt a tremor shoot through her body. "I want to be inside you, hold you . . . just a little bit. I swear to you I'll pull out." He pressed his almost painfully swollen erection harder against her—but to no avail.

"Mickey, I can't," Laurel insisted. She gasped when he squeezed her other breast.

Mickey continued to manipulate her flesh, enjoying the subtle change in skin texture on the underside of her bust, at the hollow of her back, along the insides of her thighs. "I want to be inside you so bad," he pleaded, then kissed her on the neck once more.

When Laurel turned to face Mickey, her legs remained locked. She encircled his neck with her arms and kissed him, hungrily sucking on his tongue, then pulled away and whispered, "My poor, horny baby. Do you have Vaseline?" With a lascivious smile she added, "I'll make you happy."

Mickey Boy couldn't believe his ears, but was in no condition to argue. He ran to the bathroom, grabbed a jar of cocoa butter cream, and within seconds was impaled deep between her buttocks, his hands clutching her hanging breasts.

Soon afterward Mickey lay awake, staring at the ceiling. Laurel slept nestled in the crook of his arm. One of her arms was slung over his chest and her long, waxy leg curled on top of his groin. She felt so right lying there, he thought: not like an intruder who was cramping his movement and numbing his arm, but like a part of him that belonged there, that made him complete, a part he didn't want to lose.

Laurel, however, was an enigma to Mickey Boy—and a potential problem. Something was definitely on her mind, something that had to be connected in some way to what he considered her perverse sexual habits. There was no way he would ever have allowed any girl who did the things Laurel did get close to him, to possibly be an important part of his life. Yet there he was, after she'd forced him to use her like a common whore, a *putana*, wondering why she was so troubled, and why he was feeling sorry for her. He didn't want to think of where, or with who, she'd learned to use her mouth and ass so well. *Putana!* the old men's voices haunted him. No, it was all wrong—she was all wrong. Alley had probably told the truth after all.

The last thing Mickey Boy needed or wanted was an emotional attachment—whore or not. *Especially now*, he thought.

Since the time in his early teens when he'd seen that creep *avvocato*, Nicolo Fonte, for what he really was, and had decided that it would be on the underside of the law that he made his living rather than as a phony attorney, Mickey Boy had more than paid his dues—knocking heads together, robbing to bring money to his bosses, going to jail— and was now ready to accept the rewards.

While some of the aspiring mafiosi he'd grown up with had bought their positions as button-men, without ever having proven themselves, he'd earned the respect of his peers the hard way, but still wasn't made. An attachment to any female now could only divert a portion of the energy he would expend toward his singular goal: getting that prized membership in the Calabra Family.

But visions of Laurel pushed their way to the front of his mind: her on all fours, her thighs opened and her ass pushed back toward him, guiding his hardness into her rectum—he could almost feel her sphincter muscle pop open for him again; feel the tightness as he drew back; hear her squeal with ecstasy and pain.

If he was aware of his own vulnerability, having been denied sex and affection for so long, how could he still be vulnerable? he wondered. How could the simple joy of touching, the warmth of flesh on flesh, override years of experience and common sense?

Don't be a sucker flashed through Mickey Boy's head over and over. Run the other way, that's what he should do—and fast!

Mickey looked down at Laurel's face, infant-peaceful in her slumber, her golden-brown hair tossed loosely over his pillow. He kissed her gently on the top of her head, smiled, and went to sleep.

10

May 23: Bensonhurst, Brooklyn

They departed as unobtrusively as they had arrived. At precisely arranged intervals, the dark-colored late-model cars rolled into the funeral home's parking lot, paused to receive their charges, and speedily moved on. John-John and Sammy The Blond were the last of Don Vincenze's guests to leave.

When John-John's driver steered his Cadillac onto the Van Wyck Expressway a half hour later, John-John was still fuming at Petey Ross's insolence. He pounded the door's leather armrest with his fist. "Somebody'd better cut that punk bastard down to size!" he yelled. "Who the fuck does he think he's playing with, the kids in the park?!"

The driver and John-John's other bodyguard remained mute in the front seat while Sammy The Blond sat alongside their raging leader in the rear.

"He wants to talk about Hollywood?" John-John continued. "I'll send him to Hollywood—in a fuckin' box, that piece of shit!"

Not tonight I hope, the driver thought, finding grim amusement in his boss's ire. If he had to be pulled out of Irene's warm bed and open legs in the middle of the night, then it was only fitting that John-John suffer too. As far as he was concerned, the sooner his easy-living boss took off back to Florida, the better.

While John-John glared out the window, his pampered brown cheeks rippling in anger, Sammy The Blond argued that he shouldn't let himself be aggravated by someone who really wasn't in their league to begin with. It was beneath him to even acknowledge someone with Petey's youth and inexperience, let alone do battle with him.

"Leave him alone and he's bound to step on his own prick anyway," Sammy went on. "How long do you think Vincenze and Peppino are gonna put up with his bullshit? He's like one of them things that makes a big show in the sky, then fizzles out . . . whattaya call them, uh . . . meters? Yeah, he's like a meter that's gonna burn out before he knows it."

The driver peeked into his rearview mirror, hoping John-John would be mollified by Sammy The Blond's assessment. Who the hell wanted to sit in an all-night diner or after-hours club while his boss carried on like a lunatic over something he didn't have the balls to take care of anyway?

"You're right as usual," John-John replied to Sammy. "Where would I be without you?"

I know where the fuck I'd be without the two of you, the driver joked inwardly.

Sammy patted John-John on the arm. "Don't even think about that, pal, 'cause you always got me. Whatever you do, wherever you go, you know The Blond is with you one hundred percent—friends to the end."

3:07. Just enough time to throw Irene one more hump before going home to his wife, the driver thought. He exited the highway at Queens Boulevard and drove past Union Turnpike before veering into the service lane.

"I'll tell you one thing," John-John kept on. "If that cocksucker fucks with me again, I'm gonna give him the lesson he deserves—his last one."

It seemed like forever to the driver until Sammy The Blond tapped him on the shoulder and said, "Over there, see my car?"

The driver carefully pulled up parallel to the gray Jaguar XJS, leaving an alley just wide enough for his superiors to step into. He and the other bodyguard drew their pistols as they waited for their bosses to enter Sammy's car; they would be relieved of duty as soon as it began to roll.

Still holding his .38 in his right hand, the driver backed up to let Sammy The Blond pull out in front of him.

Sammy pressed the automatic door locks, then gave a short wave to his men. John-John was sunk back in the seat, his eyes closed, while Sammy bent slightly forward to start the ignition.

Just as the driver began to breathe a sigh of relief, his mind already charting the quickest route to Irene's, a blazing fireball erupted with a thunderous roar. It drove Sammy's Jaguar nearly a yard off the ground and rocked the driver's Cadillac, whose windows imploded with shards of the other car's safety glass mixed with his bosses' blood. The Jaguar's mutilated silver hood rocketed skyward, savagely deflected off an overhead streetlamp, then shot down onto the Cadillac's roof, jolting the driver for a second time.

As suddenly as the deafening explosion had ignited, it disappeared. Pain seared from the driver's shut right eye back through his eardrum and up to his scalp, which felt as though it was being ripped from the bone. His right arm shredded, he used his left sleeve to wipe at the blood that blurred his vision.

Seen through his one good eye, the grisly scene alongside him was more reminiscent of war-torn Beirut than tranquil Forest Hills: the Jaguar no more than a charred metal frame; his own interior scorched and full of glass; his partner slumped in a crimson heap. The acrid odor of

41

burnt rubber, leather, and flesh added a bitter taste to his blood-coated tongue. Was the wetness in his pants piss? He hoped so.

Dazed, but driven by instinct to escape, he slammed his foot to the Cadillac's accelerator; the auto careened along the avenue on its two good wheels, smashing and mangling parked vehicles as it went.

The driver stumbled out, then, using one hand, tried to drag his semiconscious partner behind him. When he realized the other man was too badly injured to escape, he stopped, stared for a moment at the Jaguar countersunk into the asphalt, then took off on his own. The consequences of being identified by his license plates could be dealt with at a later time. The most important thing at that moment was to report what had happened—but to whom? He spotted a subway entrance on the other side of Queens Boulevard and began to drag himself toward it, stumbling over the concrete islands that divided the ten-lane street.

As the only survivor of the explosion vanished into the bowels of New York's transit system, mumbling "That fuckin' Petey Ross" over and over, the first wails of sirens reached his throbbing ears.

11

May 23: Sheepshead Bay, Brooklyn

From now on the condoms hidden away in her lingerie drawer would be like an American Express card—she'd never leave home without them again, Laurel thought with a painful chuckle while pushing a cold compress into her rectum. It was only the second time she'd experimented with ass-fucking, and definitely the last. Mickey Boy was no thin-dicked stockbroker too timid to hurt her. She'd had no trouble controlling the broker, making him push in gently, then pull back fast to give her the greatest sensation and least pain. Last night, however, it was as if she were being ripped open as Mickey Boy'd rammed into her like an animal off a leash.

Sure, he'd been in prison for six years, she understood that, but he must've been laid since coming home—he certainly hadn't been sitting alone in his apartment with his thing in his hand waiting for Laurel Bianco to come along.

Speaking of coming, she thought, thank God he'd come so quickly, or he might have ruptured all her muscles inside. Pressing a freshly soaked wad of toilet tissue inside her sphincter, she laughingly pictured herself needing an adult-size diaper like eighty-six-year-old Nanny Rose.

Served her right for breaking her own cardinal rule: No sex on the first date! She'd purposely left the condoms home as an alarm system in case she weakened and considered laying him. *What a pain in the ass that decision turned out to be*, Laurel thought, amused by the unintended pun.

Her "sex in stages" rule was based on men wanting most that which is most difficult to obtain; she didn't need any sex manual to teach her that. It was usually easy putting the average guy off for three to four dates (one actually went as far as six), giving up a few hot kisses and a little tit to keep him coming back until she was ready to dazzle him with the repertoire of delights she'd picked up from Alex Comfort, Shere Hite, et al.

But Mickey Boy was different. Though she'd meant to play him like the others—no, better than the others—things had unexpectedly changed. She'd changed. It was the first time in ages that she'd been excited herself, wanted to be satisfied. No excuse. Even when she'd been aroused before, especially at the heavy petting stage, like with Larry, the blond tennis pro she'd met at East Hampton, she'd managed to control herself and pull the string one date further. What had mattered more last night, she admitted inwardly, was that if she hadn't accommodated Mickey Boy, he would have left her to rush to the Brown Derby or Pastel's and pick up some slut who'd fuck his brains out all night. Out of the question. Too much of a chance his one-night whore could turn permanent enough to keep him from coming back, like the others. That would have ruined everything. No, better he woke up where she could see him.

Laurel peeked from the bathroom to make sure Mickey Boy was still asleep, then returned to the sink to wash the rest of her; the sound of a shower might wake him. Yes, she thought, she'd positively done the right thing. Locked into their past as he was, if she hadn't made the move, he would probably be sleeping with some overly made up bitch like Nancy Berger right now.

She smiled, remembering him trapped in the optical store's doorway, practically whining, ". . . But, *Laurel honey, I've been trying so hard not to . . ."* So cute. A strong, untamed animal, recently let out of its cage, who she could control with a flick of her tongue and a spreading of her legs. But how much control? How many feels of her tits would get him to give up his monochromatic gangster dress, like last night's outfit? *Tan shoes, ugh!* How many times would she have to give head to get him to read Michener? Or lay him till he'd listen to Mozart? Probably more than her body could stand.

8:10. Still too early to call Shari. "Shit!" Laurel cursed under her breath, hoping Mickey Boy would remain asleep a couple of hours more. Animal that he was, he'd probably wake up with a raging hard-on, she thought, one he'd never allow to be satisfied with another blow job. And her ass was out—forever!

Having already scrubbed her face and let it dry, Laurel turned to the task of applying fresh makeup. Couldn't let Mickey Boy see her looking like this. Not that she was ugly, far from it, but hers was a beauty that needed help. A little black mascara and eyeliner hid what she called her "pop-eyed" look, dabs of umber shadow snipped the roundness off her slightly bulbous nose, and carefully brushed-on lipstick deemphasized the puffiness of her lips; pale pink that morning would give her face a nude, sexy look. Thank God for Revlon, Maybelline, and Charles of the Ritz—lessons at the latter had been costly, but were worth every cent.

What needed no help, however, was Laurel's body. She'd been blessed with a good percentage of her mother's full, round bust but not that side of the family's thick thighs and wide pelvises. Instead, she'd inherited the Biancos' long legs, narrow hips, and tight, bubble-like ass. The ass and tits might sag in time, but with a little nip here and a tuck there . . .

Naked, Laurel tiptoed to the side of the bed and picked Mickey Boy's white-on-white shirt off the carpet. She couldn't very well prepare breakfast in last night's dress. Besides, nothing looked sexier to a waking male than a girl clad in his shirt and nothing else. She'd read that in some sex book but couldn't remember which one. After all the material she'd consumed, titles couldn't help but become confused. As long as the substance remained clear in her mind, though, all was well. She slipped into the shirt, then lifted his necktie and used it to gather her hair up in a ponytail. A peek of neck at the top and ass at the bottom. Perfect! Now to the refrigerator to see what was available. Guaranteed he had none of the sexy fixings, like caviar or croissants, that Gael Greene recommended in *Delicious Sex*. Bacon and eggs would be the best she could hope for.

Before walking the few steps from the living/bedroom area to the open kitchenette, Laurel stopped and looked down at Mickey Boy. She shook her head at how everything about him looked rough: tousled hair that would never appear refined; square jaw that had begun to look charcoal halfway through their meal at Numero Uno; a serious, tight-lipped expression even while he slept—definitely not the type she'd envisioned Prince Charming to be. Her eyes wandered down through the thick mat of chest hairs to the nearly flat stomach to where the blanket covered legs she knew from experience were hard and muscled. No, he'd never fit in with the Hamptons crowd or look right in a Brooks Brothers suit, she thought while touching the wetness that had begun to form between her legs—but he got her so goddamned hot.

Cursing Mickey Boy under her breath, Laurel went to the kitchen area. Would postponing her plans make them better or worse? Easier to deal with or more difficult to accomplish? The best thing was not to think and just enjoy the pleasure she'd unexpectedly found, she concluded, and dialed Shari's number.

Morning arrived at slightly past 10:30 for Mickey Boy, announced by the aroma of freshly brewed coffee. One of the pleasures of having a studio apartment's main area done up as a bedroom, aside from sending a clear message of his priorities to female visitors, was, when one of the latter stayed over and decided to fix breakfast, to have cooking scents from the small kitchenette envelop him while he lay snuggled between two layers of satin. For too many years he'd awakened to the smell of farts from the bunk below, and covered himself with coarse, hairy blankets that shed all over the cell—he hated to think what his lungs looked like, probably padded an inch thick with green wool. Yes, that was all over, and the memories were bitter, but he clung to them because they served to heighten the sensuousness of even ordinary experiences. Like now.

Laurel stood at the stove with her back to him, her hair bound by his necktie and her body covered by his white shirt. Nice. Real nice.

"Hey, sexy!" he called.

Slowly, Laurel turned, placing her hands on her hips as she did. One pearlized button held the front of her makeshift gown together, promising lusty views with the slightest move; two rosy dots lifted the fabric to feminine peaks at the chest. "I was sent by the management," she purred. "What would you like: coffee, tea . . . or me?"

Mickey's blood raced through his temples and groin. "Not much of a contest," he answered in an equally throaty voice. "Coffee, black with sugar."

"Oh, yeah?" she said, pretending to take offense, her head cocked high. "Well then, I'm leaving."

"You'll be some sight walking out like that," he called when she'd reached the door.

With her back still to him, Laurel lifted the shirttail in mock defiance.

The view was breathtaking. "Besides, who told you you could wear my shirt?" he asked, his hardness lifting the top sheet to form a small tent. "Take it off this minute."

Laurel turned, and with the deliberate motions of a stripper, removed the wrinkled garment, held it straight out in front of her for a moment, then dropped it onto the blue shag rug. "There, for your smelly old shirt," she said.

Wearing nothing but a licentious smile, she began moving slowly toward the bed, her hips swaying seductively with each measured step.

Mickey thought he'd come before she reached him.

"Now, what was it you wanted?"

Focusing his gaze on the bikini-trimmed crescent of dark curls between her legs, he answered, "What you wouldn't give up last night."

"Close your eyes," she whispered, standing just out of his reach. "I've got a surprise for you."

What a fuckin' time to play games, Mickey thought, but complied, the vision of Laurel's nakedness remaining before him. He listened closely for the sound of her moving nearer, readying himself to pounce.

After a few seconds that seemed interminably longer to him, Laurel said, "You can open them now." She held out two boxes of Trojans in her hand. *"Voilà!"*

"Where the hell . . . ?"

"I called my friend, Shari, at King's Pharmacy, and she had them delivered while you were sleeping, darling," she answered with a giggle. Laurel's tone became serious as she added, "Now, put two of them on . . . just to be safe."

It was an hour later when Laurel snaked her hand between Mickey's perspiration-soaked legs; her teeth tugged softly at one of his nipples. She looked up and smiled, capturing him with her youthful glow, then buried her face again on his chest.

Mickey appreciated that youth; he wallowed in it. Life had always been too serious for him, and had made him feeler older than his years. Until now.

A bite from Laurel sent a trill up his neck. "You wanna kill me?" he moaned.

"Mmmm."

His manhood stirred again under her skillful touch. "Did one of my enemies send you to love me to death?"

"Mmmm." She began to suck at his other nipple.

"Laurel, it's late. I gotta get up," he said, not really wanting to.

"You *are* up." The pun was muffled by her lips trailing down his underbelly; she gripped his erection tightly in her fist.

"Oh, God, don't do that," Mickey Boy groaned as she took him into her mouth. Would he ever break her out of that habit? he wondered. Did he really want to?

When Laurel brought her head back on an upstroke, he quickly rolled to his side and off the bed, leaving her wide-eyed and empty-handed.

"Hon, really, I got a very important appointment downtown at two, an' I gotta shave an' shower, an'—"

"Great, I'll shower with you," Laurel said, already on her way after him.

The bathroom door slammed shut before she reached it.

While absorbing the energy of Frank Sinatra's "New York, New York" from the Lincoln's tape player, Mickey Boy caught the light at the base of the Manhattan Bridge and swiftly eased into the plodding Canal Street traffic. Laurel snuggled next to him, his arm draped across her shoulders, her hand resting on his thigh.

Bisecting Lower Manhattan from the Bowery to the Holland Tunnel, Canal Street also divides two major areas that border on either side: Chinatown and Little Italy.

On Mickey Boy's left, as he crawled westward along that thoroughfare, the reds and golds of pagoda-topped buildings and phone booths glinted in the afternoon sun. Bustling crowds scurried back and forth from open-air stand to open-air stand, picking at eels, bok choy, and other Oriental delicacies that a multitude of nearby tenement apartments and touristy restaurants prepared inside.

On his right, jewelry display windows, gaudy as gangsters' dress, stood shoulder to shoulder to shoulder, supporting colorless brick buildings, three and four stories high, that seemed to stand guard for the famous, oftentimes infamous, Italian enclave behind. Ronald Reagan dined at Angelo's Restaurant; Lucky Luciano's headquarters was at the Cefalu. Robert De Niro was born and raised there; "Crazy Joe" Gallo was shot to death there.

When Mickey Boy reached Little Italy's main artery, Mulberry Street, he removed his arm from Laurel's shoulders to concentrate on turning into the narrow block. Wary eyes followed his Lincoln's progress as it crept along, only inches between each fender and an insurance claim.

Laurel pointed at the green marble front of CaSaBella Restaurant. "Didn't we go there once, for your mom's birthday?"

"Yup. How could you forget that place?" he replied. "After all, it's not every day you get to bathe in marinara sauce."

"Don't you ever forget anything?"

Mickey pecked at her pouting lips, then replied, "Only things I want to."

"You know, I love coming to the city, but almost never get to," Laurel said, scanning the neighborhood like a tourist. "Everyone I dated stayed in Brooklyn . . . although I did get out to the Hamptons twice."

Irritated and jealous over Laurel's talk of being with other men, Mickey Boy's first instinct was to look away from her. He tried to think of other things, scores he'd done with guys from the blocks he was viewing, but flashes of crime led to flashes of sex . . . Laurel having sex. Desire for those images began to suffocate him. He turned back to her, hoping the reality of her would replace the disgusting pictures in his mind.

It did.

Laurel motioned toward small groups of men loitering on both sides of the street. "It's so hard to picture you ever being like them."

Wiseguys, hustlers, gamblers—these were Mickey Boy's people. The European-style cafés that lined both sides of the street were his favorite haunts.

"What makes you think I'm any different?"

"I don't know, you just are . . . at least, I hope you are." Laurel hugged his arm affectionately. "Believe it or not, I can sense that there's something better in you, something you never gave a chance to come out."

"Don't get romantic movie ideas. What you see is what you get— nothing more."

"Didn't you ever want to be something more?"

Laurel's question triggered a vision in Mickey Boy's head: Nicolo Fonte, the *avvocato*. Phony bastard.

To Laurel, Mickey Boy answered, "No."

"Regardless," Laurel said. "I'm glad you don't bother with those kinds of people anymore. Much as I like the area, I wish you didn't have to come down here to service your account; the less you're around them, the better." She kissed his cheek.

Mickey Boy smiled—everything would be all right. "There's Angelo's," he said, deliberately changing the subject. "That's where President Reagan ate when he came to New York."

"They must have great food there."

"Good, not great," Mickey Boy lectured. It felt good to be able to teach a teacher. "Most people know the difference between good and bad food, but when it comes to telling good from great, forget it. They don't know if they're eating Sidgie, Napolitan, or Genoese cooking— everything's Italian." He squeezed her thigh. "Stick with me, kid, and I'll make you an expert before you know it."

"As long as I don't have to cook it, I'll eat anything."

Don't remind me, Mickey Boy thought, remembering Laurel's proclivity for oral sex.

Just before he reached Broome Street, Mickey Boy parked by a fire hydrant that had been striped red, white, and green to resemble an Italian flag. "That's it," he said, pointing to a sign that matched the fire plug, and read Focacceria Villarosa.

"Please hurry," she said. "I don't like sitting here alone."

Mickey Boy kissed Laurel again. He promised to return quickly, and assured her she would be unbothered where she was parked. "If you wanna change the tape, pick what you like from the glove compartment."

"Mickey!" she called as he was getting out of the car. "These are all Sinatra tapes. What kind of choice is that?"

"Of course there's a choice," he answered, incredulous. "You got his early years with Dorsey, the Latin stuff with that guy Jobim, his new stuff—take your pick."

Laurel groaned. "Never mind, darling," she said. "Just try to hurry."

Humming the bars to "My Way," Mickey Boy scanned the block, checking doorways and parked cars, then crossed the street and entered the Villarosa.

As per instructions, he stopped the first waiter he spotted. In a low voice he said, "I'm here for Buster."

The waiter motioned with his head toward a back hallway flanked by rest rooms and other doors.

Mickey Boy darted beyond a steel fire exit at the rear of the hall, turned sharply to the left, and passed through a three-foot break in the rusty chain-link fence that separated the eatery's yard from that of the social club next door. He entered the club's antiquated kitchen, where drinks were scattered atop the brown vinyl covering. A nattily dressed bruiser, who Mickey Boy vaguely remembered seeing around before he'd gone to prison, kept the game's score at a portable blackboard.

"Buster here?" Mickey Boy asked.

With a jerk of his chalky thumb, the scorekeeper pointed to a curtain-covered doorway.

The main room of the club was even shabbier than the kitchen Mickey Boy had just left. Dark oak paneling was dingy with years of accumulated grime, and formerly white ceiling tiles had absorbed so much nicotine that they ran from pale amber at their lighter parts to deep umber at others. Outsiders would have been skeptical that the dilapidated surroundings serviced expensively dressed, oftentimes extremely wealthy members—but then again, outsiders were not admitted.

Sebastiano "Buster" Alcamo sat with three other men at a felt-topped card table. At fifty-nine years of age, the bulky Sicilian had already been a captain in his Family under the old bosses, but, in a surprise move, was demoted to common soldier by Vincenze Calabra in a recent shakeup.

A perpetual scowl etched deeply into Buster's jowly face gave him the appearance of a bulldog with a thick bush of steel wool glued on his head. He winked when he saw Mickey Boy, lifted one fat finger to signal that he'd be a short while, and continued his game.

Mickey Boy had never been particularly fond of Buster. He considered the former skipper too domineering and greedy to suit his taste, and was more than a little disappointed when he found that he'd claimed him after Sam LaMonica's death.

Despite his misgivings, however, Mickey Boy had resigned himself to the fact that Family members, like relatives, could not be chosen by him—at least not at that stage of his career. Also, things could have been a lot worse. He could have been scooped up by a wiseguy that he liked even less, like Charlie Sciacca, who regularly abused his underlings when he drank too much, or Willie The Bug, who had a habit of dragging his men together in the middle of the night to impress some waitress or barmaid with his power.

"Wanna cup o' coffee?" asked the craggy-faced old man who saw to the needs of the club's members.

"Yeah, please." While he waited for Buster, Mickey Boy leaned on the small service bar, watching a soap opera on the brand-new color television—bookmakers and gamblers who regularly inhabited the club couldn't afford to get shut out of a heavily wagered sporting event because an old TV broke down.

He was running a lemon rind around the lip of his glass when the front door opened, and three young men entered the room. One glance at them caused his head to pound mercilessly; he turned his back to them, hoping he hadn't been noticed.

"Mickey Boy, is that you?" the all-too-familiar voice asked from only inches behind him. "Hey, hiya doin', pal? How does it feel to be out?"

Mickey Boy turned to stare into the dark, smiling eyes of "Little Vinnie" Calabra, Don Vincenze's twenty-eight-year-old son. His first impulse was to smash the black-haired young mobster in the face, wipe away the thick-lipped grin that always reminded him of a sneer. Instead, he said, "Excuse me, I gotta take a leak," and walked away, leaving a red-faced Vinnie with his hand still outstretched.

As soon as he shut the cubbyhole bathroom's door, Mickey Boy knew he'd made a mistake. He would have been better off staying in the large room, in full view of everyone—especially Buster.

When the door swung open, he was needlessly drying his face with a paper towel, the cold water having practically sizzled off his skin on contact. His eyes, however, watched Vinnie and one of his followers, a lanky youth with badly pockmarked skin, who had also managed to squeeze into the tiny room.

Though another forced smile stretched Little Vinnie's features, his eyes remained hard and angry. "I see jail taught you some bad habits," he said.

While Mickey Boy continued to play at inspecting his face in the mirror, his gaze remained fixed on the two men behind him. "I'm sure

50

you've seen worse," he replied. "A lot of guys could be real scumbags to guys who are supposed to be their friends."

"What're you trying to say, Mick?"

"Nothing you don't understand." Mickey Boy leaned closer to the mirror, resting his hands on the sink to keep them from quivering.

When Little Vinnie reached out to touch his shoulder, Mickey Boy spun underneath Little Vinnie's arm, grabbed it, and forced him into a hammerlock. "Move even an eyelash an' I'll break his fuckin' arm!" Mickey Boy snarled at the other hood.

The man stood still, a look of indecision on his acne-scarred face.

"You got two choices, Vinnie. Either tell the punk with the English-muffin face to get out, or learn to jerk off with your left hand . . . or you could scream, so we could tell Buster what's on our minds." Mickey Boy put more pressure on the twisted arm.

"What are you waitin' for, you fuckin' asshole?" Little Vinnie yelled at his man. "Get out!"

Mickey Boy waited until the bodyguard had left before releasing Little Vinnie, then locked the door.

"Jesus, Mick," Little Vinnie whined while rubbing his arm. "What're you, crazy?"

"Listen, you little prick," Mickey Boy said through clenched teeth. "I lost six years of my fuckin' life 'cause you set me up. Six years of fuckin' retards telling me when to eat, sleep, an' take a shit, while you were out having the time of your life, an' playing Mr. Stand-up Guy to people that didn't know better."

"Mickey, no, I swear—"

"Don't swear nothing to me, you dirty scumbag."

"Mickey, you got it all wrong. I—"

"No, I got it right!" Mickey Boy shouted. "One of your old brown-noses told me what the real deal was." He mimicked Vinnie theatrically. " 'Mickey Boy, please . . . I gotta sell this load of medical shit I'm stuck with . . . please, pal, just go look at it an' see what it's worth'—that's what you said, isn't it?"

Little Vinnie's mouth hung open, but no words came out.

"Well, isn't it?"

"Yeah, but, uh—"

"I had nightmares about those fuckin' words every night for six years—what a sucker I was."

"But, Mick," Little Vinnie pleaded, "I didn't know the feds would be there. By the time I reached the drop, you were already pinched."

"By the time you reached it? I sat there for a fuckin' hour waiting for you, then the minute I went to leave, the feds were all over me like white on rice. I went to look at one load of scalpels an' shit, and they had me down for running a hijack ring for three years. How much did you fuckin' make? A million? Two?"

"It wasn't like that, Mick. You know how they exaggerate everything."

Mickey Boy went on. "It didn't dawn on me till later on why you needed me, of all people, so bad. We're almost the same size, coloring— I was the perfect patsy for you."

"That ain't true!" Little Vinnie's soft baby-fat face glistened with perspiration.

Placing his hands together as if in prayer and wagging them back and forth, Mickey Boy bemoaned, "Of all the fuckin' guys in the world to resemble, it hadda be you? God couldn't bless me an' make me look like a nigger?"

"C'mon, Mick, I—"

"Every guy who got his truck hijacked said I looked like the guy who sat in the car when it happened. Even the owner of the warehouse where the swag was kept said he once saw me give money to the guy who rented it from him." Mickey Boy glared at Little Vinnie, then added, "These fuckin' people never saw me in their fuckin' lives—they saw you, pricko!"

"No, I swear on my father . . ."

Mickey Boy stepped forward, his fists clenched. "Mention your old man again, an' I'll drag you in front of him, see what he says."

When he saw Little Vinnie cower against the wall, he backed away. "Instead of swearing to lies on him, you should go kiss his feet every day that you're still alive. It's only outta respect for him that I don't shut your lights for good. Who'd know but me an' your loyal friend who told me what you did? An' you know what? He'd be deep-sixed right after you. No witnesses."

"Mickey, listen," Little Vinnie stammered. "Even though you're wrong, I understand how you must feel, an' anything I could ever do for you—"

"The only thing you could do for me, you little prick, is to stay the fuck away from me, 'cause if you don't, my respect for your old man might not be enough to save you."

When Mickey Boy left, both of Little Vinnie's followers rushed into the bathroom. Ignoring them, he went back to the club's service bar; he needed a cup of coffee to help him regain his composure.

"What the fuck!" Buster suddenly bellowed, heaving his cards up in the air. They descended on the others like confetti. "How the fuck could you not play trump?!" he roared, his lips turned down at the ends matching the sag of his jowls. "You'll play a hundred years an' still never learn this fuckin' game!"

The man Buster was screaming at glanced around the table for moral support. He received nothing from the others but silence and averted eyes.

Standing, Buster peeled three hundred-dollar bills from a thick bankroll and flung them onto the green baize. He was still cursing when he reached Mickey Boy. A cup of freshly poured espresso, prepared to his liking, was rushed to the bar to meet him.

Buster shook Mickey Boy's hand and kissed him on both cheeks. "Good to see you back with us," he said, speaking so calmly that it was as if someone else had been ranting over the card game a minute before. "How're ya feelin'?"

Trying to shut out the incident with Little Vinnie and concentrate on handling himself well with his new boss, Mickey Boy answered blandly, "Well rested, that's for sure."

"That's not the kinda rests we want though," Buster said with a hearty laugh. "I hope you don't go makin' a habit of it."

He put a heavy arm around Mickey Boy's shoulders and led him toward a table near the front window, where a shield of obsolete wooden blinds shut out the rest of the world. Two men who had been peering out between the slats quickly moved away as Buster and Mickey Boy approached.

"Listen," Buster began, "I guess you know why I sent for you."

Mickey Boy nodded, his face expressionless.

Buster spoke in a fatherly tone, explaining that he'd asked to have Mickey Boy assigned to him after Sam LaMonica had died. "That should make you proud, 'cause I don't have no assholes around me," he said. "If I thought you was an asshole, I woulda let one of our other guys pick you up."

Mickey Boy acted as surprised as he believed the moment required.

"Don't look so shocked," Buster said. "We got our share of assholes too."

Don't I know it, Mickey Boy thought, remembering Little Vinnie again. He also knew that Buster's talking badly about other members of their Family was just a game meant to make an underling feel like he was on the inside with his boss.

His face remained blank while Buster enumerated the advantages of their association and gave him a list of unpardonable sins, the last of which being involvement of any kind in the drug business.

"Remember, no second chances," Buster told him while forming his monstrous fingers into the shape of a pistol—a reminder of how violators wound up.

"Oh, and everything goes on record," he added. "I don't cheat on my boss, an' I don't expect you to cheat on me. Besides, that's the only way we'll go to bat for you if you have a beef with another crew . . . remember, those who eat alone die alone. Any questions?"

Mickey Boy shook his head.

"My guys usually report here on Monday nights, but bein' as you're on parole, I'd excuse you."

Hallelujah, Mickey Boy thought—too soon.

"Except that with this new shit goin' on—you seen what happened this morning, right?"

Mickey Boy's response was a look of bewilderment.

Buster eyed him in disbelief. "Where the fuck you been? John-John an' Sammy The Blond got blowed away in Queens."

"I didn't have the radio on," Mickey Boy explained. His insides fluttered with excitement—it wasn't every day that mafiosi of that stature got killed.

Shaking his head, Buster said, "Bad, bad thing. Whoever whacked them used a bomb."

Someone had broken a cardinal rule: no bombs.

For years, underworld leaders had prohibited the use of explosives, arguing that they couldn't chance killing innocent victims. Their motives weren't based on humanism, but survival: the mob needed support, or at least indifference, from the general public in order to operate. The outcry for vengeance over the accidental killing of an innocent bystander could bankrupt them.

To hundreds of Busters around the city, agitation over someone's divergence from their rules would be mixed with a dread of future chaos. Executions were okay—as long as they were carried out by the book.

". . . So I still want you to see me every week, maybe more now," Buster continued. "Just instead of comin' on a Monday night, like everybody else, sneak in during the day, like you just did. I'm here all the time, so any day's good. Okay?"

Of course it was okay. What could Mickey Boy do, say no? Not a chance.

"Oh, one more thing," Buster added with a snap of his fingers. "You know Little Vinnie, Vincent's son?" he asked. To law enforcement personnel, knock-around guys, and those in the media, just plain "Vincent" or "Mr. Vincent" mentioned in connection with New York's underworld meant one person: Don Vincenze Calabra.

With a wave of his hand, and to Mickey Boy's chagrin, Buster summoned Little Vinnie to their table.

Once Vinnie was seated, Buster asked Mickey Boy, "You know Crazy Angelo? He's a good fella with Petey Ross's crew."

Mickey Boy knew of Crazy Angelo rather than knew him. "He's got the club on the west side of Avenue U, right?" he asked, still burning that he had to sit at the same table with Little Vinnie.

Buster nodded. "That's him. He's got two kids around him, one they call The Hammer, an' some Irish punk, I don't remember his name, that owes Little Vinnie here some money."

"I know Georgie," Mickey Boy said. "The other guy, I don't know who he is."

"It don't matter; neither one of them count anyway; they ain't good fellas. We already settled the beef an' made arrangements to get paid with Crazy Angelo; his is the only one whose word counts for anything. The other two you just respect like you do a dog for its master, otherwise they'd be in a lime pit someplace."

Buster continued. "The only thing is that Vinnie's father don't want him going over there to collect the payments. He told me to send somebody else, and you're it."

Mickey Boy was elated and sick at the same time. Anyone in their crew would give their right testicle for an opportunity to carry out an assignment directly for Don Vincenze. The fact that it was Little Vinnie's money, and especially since he'd personally have to hand it to him, made him want to puke. There was no way he would see Little Vinnie regularly, Don Vincenze or no Don Vincenze. His problem was to get out of it gracefully.

Buster saved him. "Drop whatever you get off this Hammer kid with me," he said. "I'll see that Vinnie gets it."

When their meeting was over and Mickey Boy was ready to leave, he embraced Buster, then started for the door.

"What is it," Buster suddenly bellowed, "you two with different Families? I thought we was all together here."

Laugh now, you little prick, Mickey Boy thought when he saw Little Vinnie enjoying the fact that he was fuming. When he kissed the don's son on the cheek, he envisioned biting him on the throat.

His dead mentor's favorite saying repeated in his mind, *Chiana, chiana, met in ghoule . . . wait, wait, then stick it in their ass*. Sam LaMonica had told him many times, "If you never learn another word in Italian, Mick, when you got a problem with somebody always hold your temper, and remember, *Chiana, chiana, met in ghoule!*"

Relieved that his baptism by Buster was over, but still bristling over his confrontation with Little Vinnie, Mickey Boy hurried out the way he'd come in. Following Buster's instructions, he stopped at the restaurant's counter and left a business card naming him as sales representative for an Italian provisions company. An order would be called in the following day to cover him in case his parole officer found out he was in Little Italy.

Before leaving, he also bought some hot sugary zeppoles, rice balls, and loaves of Sicilian bread. Mickey Boy looked at his watch to see if he had time for a *vastede* sandwich, the strips of beef lungs in spicy gravy he hadn't eaten in years.

"Oh shit!" Mickey Boy mumbled when he realized how long he'd kept Laurel waiting in the car. On his way out he groaned, "Who the hell wants to hear her now."

The pockmarked young hoodlum dropped the slat of the blind he'd been looking through, then returned to the table where Little Vinnie sat. "Yeah, the white Mark VII with the broad in it is his," he said.

Little Vinnie spoke in a low voice. "Make sure you find out everything there is to know about him: where he eats, who he sees, when he shits—everything! The cunt too. I wanna know if she's even got a pimple on her ass or lays a fart. *Capisce?* We're gonna teach Mr. Mickey Boy Messina a little respect . . . and soon!"

12

May 23: Little Italy, Manhattan

Arnold Selkower peered out through the tiny opening in the body of a blue step-in van. While the scope of his vision encompassed the entire intersection of Mulberry and Broome streets, he concentrated on the shuttered storefront bearing the message PRIVATE . . . MEMBERS ONLY on its painted glass door, and displaying a copy of a New York State charter in the lower corner of its blind-covered window which read Lower Manhattan Fishing Association.

Just as Selkower and his employers, the Federal Bureau of Investigation, were not duped into believing that seafaring sportsmen congregated at the fishing association, the sign on his truck which read C.T.C. EXTERMINATORS fooled none of the club's regulars. During the course of his using up numerous rolls of 35mm film, he was intermittently waved at, posed for, and vulgarly given either the finger or the more demonstrative Italian salute. One of the younger showoffs even mooned him.

None of these actions, though, impeded the fulfilling of the agent's assignment, which was to record anyone who entered or left the building where Calabra Family Soldier Buster Alcamo and his underlings hung out. That day especially, after the early morning bombing of John-John DiGiovanni and his underboss, Sammy The Blond, any Mafia meeting could be significant. All around the city, Arnold's brother and sister agents were busy gathering every bit of minutiae they could on the mob.

At 3:51 P.M. Arnold photographed a well-dressed young man, his arms filled with brown paper sacks, leaving the Focacceria Villarosa next door to the club. What had attracted the agent's attention was the fact that the roughhouse-looking fellow had spent nearly two hours inside the restaurant, while his female companion idled that time away alone in his illegally parked white Lincoln.

Arnold noted the car's description and plate number for future investigation.

13

May 24: Glen Cove, Long Island

The Cadillac showroom's garage door rolled up just seconds before the navy-blue limo started into its driveway. Petey Ross waited until the door was shut before he, Sonny Fortunato, and two of his armed button-men got out. The taller of the two bodyguards placed himself on the side of the closed entranceway, his right hand in his outside jacket pocket, while his companion followed Petey and Sonny past a dozen or so mechanics to the rear.

When Petey and his men reached the manager's small office, Don Peppino was already seated behind the desk. From his ill-fitted suit to his humorless expression, the hawk-faced old man looked as gray as his surroundings, a promise to Petey of a difficult, unfriendly meeting.

Blackie Palermo, dressed to suit the atmosphere in a black knit shirt, matching slacks, and the customary dark glasses to cover his missing eye, stood by the door with his thick fighter's arms folded across his chest.

Purposely using a tone as bleak as Don Peppino's appearance, Petey Ross said, "It's a terrible thing that happened to J.J.—I was sick when I heard."

"Were you?" the withered mafioso asked, one silver eyebrow raised questioningly. "I was hoping you would feel that way. Anytime one of ours is eliminated without permission, it's a terrible thing. It makes me very sad."

"I hope you know that we had nothing to do with it."

Don Peppino stared directly into Petey Ross's eyes, the oldest of New York's mob bosses testing the youngest. "I'm glad to hear that from your lips, Pietro. You do understand how it looks, especially after the way you acted the other night."

"An' like I told you the other night, I ain't no Johnny-come-lately. I'd never hit one of our own kind without an okay from you an' Vince." He added, "An' to be honest, I'm a little disappointed that you two would think I would do anything like that . . . especially the way it was done."

"Instead of taking offense because we question your involvement in this terrible situation, I think you should be happy that we're taking the time to let you defend yourself."

"Defend myself?!" Petey Ross shouted. "What did I ever do to have to defend myself?"

Sonny quickly interrupted. "I hope you understand there's no disrespect meant to you or Don Vincenze. We really do appreciate this chance to speak for ourselves."

Fuck this greaseball and his flowery greaseball bullshit! Petey bristled inwardly while pacing in front of the door where Blackie Palermo stood. He looked to the bull-like Blackie for some sign of support, but received only a noncommittal shrug.

"It's only natural that Petey should be upset," Sonny continued. "After all, he values your respect and is as confused by this whole thing as all of us. We want whoever's taking over for John-John to know that too . . . by the way, who is taking over?"

"Alphonse Vallo."

"Junior?" Sonny said, his voice unable to mask his surprise. "Like I said before, we'd really appreciate it if you talk to him an' Don Vincenze for us, an' explain everything."

Don Peppino gave Sonny his well-known Mona Lisa smile. "Of course," he proclaimed, then embraced Sonny to signal the end of their discussion. "I'll explain everything to Don Vincenze, and then together we'll go talk with Alphonse Vallo; he's a reasonable man."

Petey Ross struggled to contain his simmering temper. He followed Don Peppino to the door. "I think it would be a good idea if we sat down with Junior face-to-face an' ironed this thing out."

"Of course," Don Peppino agreed. "I'll arrange something and let you know through my nephew."

Then, in a manner that could have been considered either familial or patronizing, the old don reached up and pinched Petey Ross's cheek before he kissed it. "When you get to be my age, and I hope that you will, you'll understand that people always think better when their brain is not clouded with anger—try and control it."

It was a blistering Petey Ross that waited for Don Peppino and his nephew to leave the building before he spoke. "That fuckin' zip's got some pair of balls!" he yelled. "Pinch my cheek like I was a fuckin' two-year-old? I wanted to beat his fuckin' greaseball head in, that cocksucker!" With a wide sweep of his arm, he sent papers, stapler, and a white plastic cup flying off the top of the desk. Stale coffee splashed over the wall and floor.

"Calm down, pal," Sonny urged. Bubbles noisily plopped in the water cooler's overturned bottle as he drew a cup for Petey. "Getting crazy ain't gonna solve nothing."

Petey gulped the icy liquid, then crumpled the cup in his fist and tossed it into a metal pail. "Yeah. I guess he's right," he said with a sigh. "It does look like we done it. I just get pissed at his fuckin' attitude."

He nervously straightened his tie knot and brushed back his thick black hair with his palms. "Thanks, bud," he said, grabbing Sonny around the shoulders and leading him toward the door. "If I had another hothead like me around, I'd be up shit's creek without a paddle."

"An' a hole in the boat."

"An' a hole in the boat," Petey laughingly agreed.

Before walking out to join their bodyguards, Sonny paused. In a serious tone he cautioned, "Remember, when I say be calm, that don't mean go to sleep. *A buon oumo* your father never trusted Peppino, and between you an' me, I don't either."

"Nah, he's okay. He just wants everybody kissin' his greaseball ass. If him an' Vince really thought we had anything to do with whackin' out J.J. they never woulda made a meet. Don't worry, bud, we're cool."

"Okay, you're the boss," Sonny replied with a shrug. "Just be careful."

Petey smiled. "Careful's my middle name."

14

June 2: Canarsie, Brooklyn

Mickey Boy sat in the rear of the Arch Diner, positioned with his back to the window for a view of the entire room. He waited for his partner, Richie DeLuca, whose loyalty and business acumen during the past six years now kept him from feeling the financial pressures that plagued most ex-convicts. What would he have done for a car, clothes, or a place to sleep without Richie, he often wondered these last months.

Most of the money he'd accumulated before his incarceration had gone for lawyers; the rest had been piddled away over the jail time at a hundred dollars a month for commissary, and flowers sent to his mother on five occasions each year.

Richie, however, had scrupulously saved from the small bookmaking business they'd started together, and annual earning events—selling football-pool tickets each season, Christmas trees in December, fireworks for the Fourth of July, and grilled sausages at the Feast of San Gennaro each September—to present him with the key to a vault that held $34,000 in cash.

When Richie entered, George, the diner's host, ushered him to where Mickey Boy was devouring a rare tenderloin steak topped with poached eggs. Though the all-American–looking Richie was the same age as Mickey Boy, he appeared years younger. His naturally blushing complexion looked as though it wasn't yet ready for a razor, and his straight blondish hair was worn side-parted and sprayed enough to make it seem as though he'd been prepared by his parents for school photographs.

"If I knew you were going to be dressed, I would've put a jacket on," Richie apologized. His yellow V-neck sweater over designer jeans contrasted sharply with the double-breasted gray suit that Mickey Boy wore, and made him look even more collegiate.

"Naa, don't be silly. I gotta pick Laurel up later and take her to dinner. This way I don't have to go home an' change," Mickey Boy explained. "What do you want to eat?"

Richie ordered a spinach salad and iced grapefruit juice from a shapely brunette whose hips and bust looked ready to burst through her black rayon uniform. She gave Mickey Boy a broad smile before leaving.

"Jesus, is she hot!" Richie said.

"Yeah, she's a firecracker all right, an' she's been giving me the eye since I got here."

"Did you pull your usual routine and give her your number on a twenty-dollar bill?"

"Nah," Mickey Boy replied. "Not for me." He quickly changed the subject. "Well, how'd we do this week?"

Richie took a packet of neatly folded papers from his jeans. "We were really doing great until Sunday, but the Yankees killed us. We blow four dimes on them," he added, referring to a four-thousand-dollar loss. "All in all, though, it was okay." He handed Mickey Boy a pink NCR duplicate of a slip he read from. "We wind up sixty-three sixty to the good. If you deduct the twenty-one thirty-five we were in the red, that makes a total win of forty-two an' a quarter for the week."

They followed their tally sheets as Richie continued. "So, forgetting the quarter, we've got to give the office their twenty-one hundred for their half of the win, making forty-two hundred for them and twenty-one sixty for us." Richie lowered his voice, as though one of their bosses were sitting at the next table. "If I bring them the cash tonight, before we collect, I can get away with giving them an even four dimes. That'll be another deuce in our kick to whack up."

Business had certainly picked up since he'd come home, Mickey Boy thought with satisfaction; sometimes it was even too good to be true, like a present from the gods. Between the one or two new customers he'd been able to bring in and the recommendation of strong customers Richie'd been suddenly given by friends of theirs, the business Richie had been hanging on to by mere threads while Mickey Boy was away had now become a viable source of income.

Calculating his and Richie's profit to be about a thousand dollars each, he said, "Take a nickel off the top an' bring it to Buster. You could give it to him after we collect."

"Five hundred?! Can't we skip it this week? I've got a couple of maneuvers I wanna do and I'm a little tight." Like Mickey Boy, Richie had been claimed by Buster after Sam LaMonica had died, but was less inclined to share profits with him. In addition to being greedy, he claimed, Buster was a throwback to the stone age of gangsterism; he called him Fred Flintstone with a .45.

"First of all, anything we do with that office is on record; Buster knows the figures before you do," Mickey Boy lectured. "If we take care of him on what he knows about, he ain't gonna bother trying to find out what else we got going. An' second, like it or not, he is our man, an' we gotta do the right thing with him. If you're short cash, I'll lay it out for you." He scanned a second paper. "What about your guys, no problems? My customers didn't get hit too hard this week, but yours took a beatin'."

"The only one of my guys who isn't paying is Ex-lax," Richie said, using his customer's betting code name. "He's the one I promised the fifteen hundred dollars to at three points. He owes eleven sixty-five, so we only gotta give him three forty-five in cash."

Richie's skill with numbers never ceased to amaze Mickey Boy. "You shoulda been a fuckin' accountant instead of a crook," he mumbled while marking Ex-lax's name on a third sheet of paper for a fifteen-hundred-dollar loan at three percent interest a week. "Okay, Ex-lax is down—what a shitty name, Ex-lax. Could he shit out forty-five dollars a week with no problem?"

"A lot more; his drugstore does real good. He wanted three thousand, but I'm keeping his figure down so we could shy him his own money when he blows it on other ball games. Even if we lay out half of what he loses for the office, we're doubling the juice on our actual cash."

"How many other guys does he owe?"

Richie laughed. "This guy? Forget about it. He was scared to death to even do business with me . . . says he can't have guys who look like hoods hanging around the store."

"And you look like Joe College, so he ain't afraid of his customers knowing he gambles?"

"Customers, my ass," Richie replied with a chuckle. "It's his wife he's afraid of . . . this guy's totally pussy-whipped."

Mickey Boy shook his head. He couldn't understand how any man let a woman determine the way he conducted his life.

"Check around anyway; see if any of our friends know him," he said. "Unless you taught him how to bet, he had to be doin' business with other bookmakers. The last thing we need is a guy who's in hock to half of Brooklyn."

A few minutes later, after their dishes had been cleared away by the still-flirting waitress, Mickey Boy asked, "Your guy a stringbean who looks like he's wearing one of them phony noses and glasses?"

Richie turned to look toward the entrance. "That's him." He whispered, "Don't forget, I told him that I had to stand good for the money, and that I'll pick up his payments every week," then rushed off to guide the newcomer to their table.

"How are you?" Mickey Boy said while crushing Ex-lax's bones in a viselike handshake. He was pleased to see its intimidating effect.

Ex-lax spoke in a thin, nervous voice, "Fine, fine. I'm Irwin, and you're . . . ?" He rubbed his knuckles as he sat across from Mickey Boy in the chair Richie had previously used.

"Right now I'm the Bank of America, but you could call me Bruno." Mickey Boy knew from experience that the average workingman didn't want to owe money to loan sharks named Bruno, especially when they pulverized fingers on first encounters. He searched Irwin's eyes for the slightest hint of the beat artist that he knew lurked in the meekest of clients. Finding nothing obvious, he said in an even, businesslike tone, "Listen to me, an' listen good: the way we give you our money is the way we want it back." The suggestion of others behind the loan was another subtle intimidator he liked to use.

Mickey Boy spent the next few minutes running down his rules and expectations that went along with the loan: three percent a week interest; any payments above the agreed-upon interest would reduce the base amount that it was figured upon; payments to be made on time.

"Don't think we don't know that if you were a good credit risk, you wouldn't be here at all," he continued. "You'd be at a bank, signing over your house, car, an' kids."

"Absolutely not," Irwin said. He pushed his glasses up on his bony nose and with convincing sincerity assured Mickey Boy that his problems were not with overextended credit, but with a government lien for taxes from a previous business. "Because of that, my declared earnings are below what a bank wants to see when they extend a loan." He smiled. "Banks only like to give you money when you don't need it."

"And you like to gamble," Mickey Boy added.

"And I like to gamble—but I know my limit."

"I hope so," Mickey Boy said, staring at the druggist until he looked away.

"Do you require any collateral?" Irwin asked while studying his clasped hands.

"You got blood in your veins?"

"Excuse me?"

Mickey Boy gave him a sinister smile. "Your body is the only collateral we need."

Irwin's hands fidgeted nervously, and his lip sucked in where he was chewing it.

Fearing that he'd softened his new customer up too much, Mickey Boy changed his approach. He assured Irwin that there would be no problems as long as he made every attempt to pay, and if a legitimate problem did arise, was honest enough to admit it rather than avoiding him. "We're no animals," he said. "I brought plenty of groceries to customers who lost their jobs. We just don't like people who try to make jerks out of us."

"Absolutely not, not from me," Irwin said. He appeared greatly relieved; at least the gnawing at his lip stopped.

"Great, then we'll be friends . . . and we're good friends to have," Mickey Boy said. "Any problems you ever have with anything—unions, other street guys, anything—you just call Richie an' he'll get to me right away."

Irwin hesitated, then said, "Thank you, I appreciate that."

Mickey Boy turned to Richie. "Remember, you're responsible for this money—no excuses. If he don't pay, you pay."

"No problem."

"I'll drop off the fifteen hundred to you tonight," Mickey Boy told Richie. "That means that every Tuesday I get what I'm supposed to . . . not Wednesday, Thursday, or Friday, but Tuesday. Understood?"

Richie and Irwin both shook their heads.

"Good, then we're finished."

Irwin bid his adieus and left quickly—without shaking Mickey Boy's hand.

"No problem with this guy," Mickey Boy said after Irwin had left. "He'll be okay. Now, before we go to the lawyer for Chink, I gotta stop by Crazy Angelo's club."

"Jesus," Richie replied. "That's one of Petey Ross's guys. After what happened to John-John, word is out don't walk on the same side of the street with any of them. I'd sure hate for us to be there if it turns into a shooting gallery."

Mickey Boy laughed, then said, "Hey, pal, it's an order from the top . . . an' orders are orders."

He signaled the sexy waitress for his and Richie's check. While holding her hand, he pressed two folded twenty-dollar bills and a third one that he'd obviously written on into her palm. "My name's Mickey Boy, an' this is Richie. What's yours?"

"Lorraine."

"Sweet Lorraine. I like that." He sang, *"I just found joy, I'm as happy as a baby boy . . ."* then winked at her and gently squeezed her hand over the money. "Keep the change." He left the diner humming the Sinatra version of "Sweet Lorraine."

"I thought you weren't interested?" Richie teased.

Mickey Boy smiled. He threw his arm over Richie's shoulders, drew him close, and said, "I'm not; I gave her your number. When she calls, tell her I died . . . or got married," he added with a laugh.

Richie's expression was serious when he replied, "Same thing."

Twenty minutes later Mickey Boy parked his car on West Sixth Street off Avenue U. He sent Richie to Crazy Angelo's club with instructions for Georgie The Hammer to meet him on the avenue, at the Café Mazzoli. While Angelo's club was surely under police surveillance, the legitimate retail store three blocks away was probably not. At least if word of his meeting with Georgie did reach his P.O., he could argue that he wasn't responsible for who shopped in the same places he did.

The white marble counter of the Café Mazzoli was piled high with boxes of Italian cookies, candies, and nuts that Mickey Boy had picked out as gifts for his mother, Laurel, Richie's aunt, and Buster, and the proprietor was grinding six pounds of fresh espresso beans for him when Richie arrived with Georgie in tow. Mickey Boy leaned toward the grinder and took one last sniff of the rich coffee aroma before the two reached him.

"Hey, Mickey Boy, hiya doin'?" Georgie cried out.

When they hugged, Mickey Boy could feel a pistol in Georgie's waistband; when he shook his hand it was as if he'd grabbed hold of a dead fish. "Fine, I'm great. How are you, kid?" he said, thinking what a bad combination wet, nervous palms and a pistol was.

"Not so good since John-John got hit," Georgie replied. "For some reason, everybody's pointing at us. Word from Angelo is stay alert, even though he swears we had nothin' to do with it—but who knows if these guys ever tell us the truth?"

"Let's hope the old men straighten it out," Mickey Boy said. "That way we could all do what we're supposed to do in this life—make money."

Georgie hooked his arm in Mickey Boy's and led him from the rear of the store, with its huge burlap bags of coffee beans piled high, toward the front, where they would find privacy among the chrome and glass of espresso-brewing appliances and serving sets. Richie took over the shopping chores, fingering boxes of panettone and jars of wine-soaked cherries.

"Boy, you've grown up," Mickey Boy said. "When I went away you were just a kid hanging out by Spumoni Gardens." He laughed. "I remember you always wanted to hang around with the big guys; we couldn't get rid of you."

"Yeah," Georgie said, laughing along. "An' just when I thought I made it, I found out there were bigger guys. When does it stop, Mick?"

"When they make you Don Giorgio," Mickey Boy said. "An' I ain't even sure that you don't find out that there's some secret guy we never even heard of who tells you what to do." His humor left when he realized how true his words were. "I was surprised, though, that you didn't come with our crew. What happened?"

"Tell you the truth, Mick, I really had a tough time deciding where to go, especially knowin' that once I hopped on board with somebody, there was no changin' my mind. I was a nervous wreck for weeks," Georgie said, appearing as though he were reliving those anxiety-ridden days. He claimed there would have been too much pressure if he had joined Don Vincenze's Family; their enforcement of mob rules was too strict, and they were too solid in their upper ranks for advancement. "Angelo's a great guy to be with. He really lets us do whatever we want, and over here, in this crew, everybody's got a chance to be a star—young guys they just made are captains already."

Mickey Boy was disappointed in Georgie's judgment. His instincts told him that the underworld had an order—needed an order to survive. As far as he was concerned, the smaller, less-disciplined Families and their promising young men like Georgie were not only distorting what the wiseguy life was supposed to be all about, but were doomed. They made mistakes, taking their bestowed criminal freedom for a license to make enemies by robbery and abuse, and they brought the heat, their struggles for power drawing the public's attention and ire. Unfortunately, everyone, in every Family, would pay the price.

Suddenly, Mickey Boy had an overwhelming desire to get his task over with, and get the hell out.

"Listen, about that money you owe Little Vinnie, I really don't know what it's all about, but I'm here 'cause Buster sent me to collect," Mickey Boy said, trying to distance himself from any association with the don's son. "But for him an' Vincent not to wanna let Little Vinnie or one of his asshole buddies come an' get their money themselves, it's gotta be bad. I'm just telling you so you know to be careful from them too, not only John-John's guys."

"I know," Georgie said while nervously trying to open a package of imported vanilla creme wafers. When it didn't open easily, he flung it across the store. "Sure it's fuckin' bad."

"Sorry," Mickey Boy said, waving apologetically at the proprietor. "Put that on my tab too."

Georgie continued as if nothing had happened. "Crazy Angelo had to get Petey an' Sonny themselves to straighten it out with the old man. I hear Petey had to leave a big-time marker with him to get me off the hit parade." Georgie looked to make sure Richie, who had wandered closer to examine a set of porcelain demitasse cups, was out of earshot. "You know, between you an' me, I really had nothing to do with this fuckin' beef; that's the kind of luck I got. It was all Skinny's shit."

"Who's Skinny?"

"My partner, Skinny Malone. Between bein' Irish an' growin' up in Coney Island, he's a little wild. He don't understand our rules too good, but he's a good earner, an' he's a hundred percent stand-up guy."

"If he don't learn to play by the rules, he may wind up a hundred percent dead guy," Mickey Boy warned. "And you along with him."

A momentary spark of fear glimmered in Georgie's eyes, then disappeared. "Naw, he's okay. Anyway, by the time I found out he beat Little Vinnie for a cigarette load, it was too late." He pulled Mickey Boy close and whispered, "Not only that, but off the record, what makes it fucked up is that he gave me and Angelo a square end—but I swear, he didn't tell us how he got it."

"It wouldn't have been too hard to ask," Mickey Boy said. "That is, if you or Angelo really wanted to find out."

Georgie shrugged. "Anyway, on the q.t., that's why Angelo fought like a bastard to save him. He knows Skinny does the right thing."

"Please, I never heard that," Mickey Boy snapped. He wanted no part of information he was supposed to be duty-bound to report to his superiors.

"Sorry," Georgie continued. "Anyway, how I got involved was when Little Vinnie an' his guys decide to roll on Skinny."

He excitedly recounted driving up to the bar where he hung out, and finding his partner cornered by Little Vinnie's goons. "So I pull around the corner an' walk to where they are with the *pistola* in my pocket. Just as I come around the corner, whap, the bigger guy hits Skinny with a slapjack."

"That was a break for you," Mickey Boy said. According to mob procedure, had Little Vinnie called a *sit-down*, Skinny would have been a hundred percent wrong and forced to pay in full immediately. Instead, he told Georgie, they had screwed up. "You should've thanked these jerks for makin' you fifty percent right."

"I thanked them all right," Georgie said, a smirk on his face. "I grab this guy by the collar an' crack him on the head with the forty-five. The other tough guy takes off, so I take everything out on the guy I got—busted him up pretty good."

He threw his hands up and shrugged. "How am I supposed to know they're with Vincent's scummy kid? I don't know nothin' till I see Little Vinnie pullin' away from the curb—I recognized him right away, but he just turned his head an' took off like a bat outta hell. What a fuckin' dog."

That's Little Vinnie, all right, Mickey Boy thought while shaking his head, *leaving his men and running*.

He placed a hand on Georgie's shoulder. "Listen, pal, I'm not here to tell you whether you're right or wrong. All I can tell you is to watch your step with them. You know, you're still the kid at Spumoni Gardens to me, an' I don't wanna see you get hurt."

"Why, you think they'd look to cop a sneak on me?"

"God forbid!" Mickey Boy said. A sneak, an off-the-record murder, was exactly what concerned him, but he felt Georgie should have been smart enough to get the message without putting him on the spot again by asking—there was no way he'd talk badly about his Family to an associate or member of another, even if it was Little Vinnie who was involved.

"Please, Georgie, don't put words in my mouth. Just use your head, an' remember that Mickey Boy's always your friend."

"I know that, Mick."

"Good, I'm glad that's settled. I don't wanna have you hitting me on the head with a forty-five," he teased. "Now, did the Irishman leave something for Little Vinnie?"

"Yeah, here." Georgie counted out two hundred dollars in fives and tens.

"Is that what he's supposed to leave? I don't even know."

"That's what he's getting. The way we left off is that Skinny would do whatever he could each week, an' that's it. I tried to talk to Skinny, but . . ." He shrugged helplessly.

Mickey Boy knew the figure in dispute was between fifteen and twenty thousand dollars, and that Buster would go through the roof when he received the paltry sum.

To him, both sides of this argument stank. Sooner or later there would be a bad end, and Mickey Boy wanted out before it came. *Fuck the glory*, he thought. *Let somebody else earn brownie points with the old man.*

The chance of his parole officer violating him for consorting with Petey Ross's men would be his excuse to bow out. Even if he had to lie, and say he'd been warned by his P.O., it would be worth it. Dying for the truth didn't make much sense.

While grasping Georgie's clammy hand once more, Mickey Boy kissed him farewell on both cheeks. "I don't know if it'll be me next time, or if they'll send somebody else," he said. "But just try to be careful, okay?"

"Sure," Georgie replied. He started to push the door open to leave, then turned and said, "An' Mickey Boy, try to make sure they send somebody else. Not that I don't wanna see you, but I hate to have you in the middle of our beef."

Mickey Boy smiled sadly.

15

June 2: Bensonhurst, Brooklyn

Little Vinnie Calabra sat impatiently in a booth at the Richelieu Restaurant, just minutes from where Mickey Boy and Georgie were meeting. He and one of his henchmen waited for the one he'd begun calling "Muffin," after Mickey Boy had pointed out that his pockmarked skin resembled the inside of a toasted English, to show up.

Vinnie cursed inwardly while staring at the entrance. *Idiots! I'm surrounded by fuckin' idiots!* Too bad about Mickey Boy, he thought. That was the kind of guy an up-and-coming boss needed—not the shit he had around him. But Mickey Boy wasn't a friend anymore, and if he wasn't a friend, he was an enemy—and enemies had to go. In fact, Mickey Boy was more than an enemy: He was a threat to his future. God forbid the old man found out what had happened more than six years before, that he'd set up Mickey Boy because the feds were hot and heavy on his own ass. One goddamn bad move to get himself out of a jam, and it could ruin everything he'd ever hoped for—the "great don" would have him cleaning piss in his joints' bathrooms for the rest of his life. *Boy, would I ever like to know if he fucked up when he was young.*

Little Vinnie's entertaining thoughts of confronting his father with some damaging secret from his past were interrupted by the arrival of his tardy associate.

"Sorry, Vinnie," Muffin said when he reached the table. "I got stuck in traffic."

"Forget about it; just keep doin' like you're doin'. If you showed up on time, the shock might kill me," Little Vinnie said. He slammed a hand on the table. "C'mon, c'mon, I ain't got all fuckin' day! What'd you find out?"

The trembling would-be mobster smiled weakly as he withdrew a slip of paper from his pocket. "Mickey Boy lives on Emmons Avenue, in a building called The Gardens," he read. "He's in apartment—"

"I don't care about his fuckin' apartment number," Vinnie whined sarcastically. "I ain't goin' up for fuckin' dinner. What time does he leave an' come home? Where does he hang out? Where's a good spot to catch him and spill his fuckin' guts all over the sidewalk?"

"He goes out every morning sometime between ten an' noon, an' don't come back till the middle of the night. Twice a week, on Tuesdays an' Fridays, he goes straight to Jasper's Barber Shop on Avenue U an' Twenty-first Street, for a mud pack, manicure—the whole works. A little guy named Alex works on him in the second chair, but Richie DeLuca's usually there with him, in case you was gonna try an—"

"Don't think, just talk."

Little Vinnie's hood continued his report, listing Mickey Boy's visits to his parole officer, daily meetings with Richie, and infrequent trips to see his family in Boston. "The only time he don't meet Richie is when he's with his new girl . . . he's goin' hot an' heavy with her." He flashed a salacious smile and moved his bony fist back and forth to indicate sexual intercourse.

"What about the cunt?" Little Vinnie snapped. Couldn't these idiots get it through their thick fuckin' skulls that his interest had nothing to do with Mickey Boy and the slut's sex lives. "Who is she? Where does she live? Work? C'mon, stop all the bullshit!"

"Her name's Laurel Bianco, an' she lives with her parents on East Fifty-third Street off Avenue N. Her father's a—"

"Aaii!!" Little Vinnie yelled. When he noticed other patrons staring at him, he lowered his voice to a near whisper. "What the fuck do I care if her old man jerks off elephants for a living? I ain't hiring him! Where is she all day when she ain't ballin' Mickey Boy? That's what I wanna know. Does she work, go to school, hook off a fuckin' corner . . . what?"

"She's a third-grade teacher at P.S. 131, on Fort Hamilton Parkway an' Forty-third Street, in Borough Park. She drives a red Volkswagen Rabbit—I got the plate number—an' if she don't meet Mickey Boy, she goes straight home from work. She don't look like she's got no close girlfriends or nothin'," he said. After hesitating for a minute, he added, "Vinnie, I don't think we should bother with the broad. It'll only make Mickey Boy more mad."

Little Vinnie grabbed his man by the lapel. "Listen, you fuckin' imbecile, if you gotta be afraid of anybody, you gotta be afraid of me.

I'll pull your fuckin' lung out an' feed it to the first stray dog I see."

"I ain't afraid of him, Vinnie, I just think—"

"That's another thing," Little Vinnie growled. "I said, don't fuckin' think! If you could think, you wouldn't need me. Just do what I tell you, an' don't try to be no fuckin' Einstein. *Capisce?*"

"Okay, Vinnie, you're the boss."

When he released his hold on his lapel, Little Vinnie turned to his other associate, who was sitting quietly. "You understand too, fucko? Who's the boss?"

"Yeah, Vinnie, you know you're always the boss."

"Make sure you two idiots don't forget it!" Little Vinnie felt pleased: The Boss. That was what he was destined for if he didn't fuck up along the way—and if Mickey Boy didn't rat him out. Eventually, he would be called Don Vincenze, and have everyone suck his ass the way they did to his father. Everyone, including Mickey Boy Messina—if he lived that long.

Leaning over the table, Little Vinnie pulled his men toward him. "Okay, here's what we're gonna do. . . ."

16

June 2: Downtown Brooklyn

"Shit!" Mickey Boy shouted while slamming a hand on his dashboard. "There's no way I'll get back in time to pick Laurel up. She'll be like a raving lunatic tonight." Though his irritability was caused more by a desire to be with Laurel than what her temperament would be like that evening, he'd used her for a vocal excuse to avoid being ribbed by Richie—he was in no mood for that. The situations between Little Vinnie and Georgie, and Little Vinnie and himself, troubled him deeply, and he had looked forward to relaxing with Laurel later that night; she had become the only ray of sunshine in his life. He reached over and flicked off Frank Sinatra's crooning in the middle of "You're Nobody Till Somebody Loves You."

"If you wanna see this bum lawyer some other day, it's no problem," Richie said as he steered Mickey Boy's Lincoln off the expressway at Atlantic Avenue. "Maybe if you go pick Laurel up you'll come back to life; you ain't said a word since we left Avenue U." He laughed. "You sure you ain't in love?"

"No, this is more important," Mickey Boy said, ignoring Richie's teasing remark. "She'll just have to understand." *Some goddamned joke,* he thought. *How could she understand anything when she still thinks I'm out selling mozzarellas?*

Restless, he rummaged through the glove compartment, found one of the *Trilogy* cassettes, then replaced the album he'd just switched off in the tape player.

Turning to Richie, he said, "Go on, fill me in on the whole story."

Chink Agrigento was a longtime friend of Mickey Boy's and Richie's, who worked as an electrician most of the time, but dabbled in small-time hustles like selling football pools on the job or chauffeuring gamblers to and from a local crap game at night. When someone he introduced to his boss swindled the man, Chink was arrested and charged with conspiracy in the scheme.

"Chink swears he didn't know what was going on," Richie said.

Mickey Boy sat with his head back and his eyes closed. As always, the emotional tug of his favorite song, "My Way," seemed to fortify him. Laurel would just have to wait while he took care of business.

"Anyway," Richie went on, "Chink hires this shyster named Kepler—Phillip Kepler."

For a twenty-thousand-dollar fee, Phillip Kepler brought Chink a deal. He told him that even if he was innocent, it didn't make sense to take a chance on a jury believing it; a fluke conviction would get him at least five years in jail. Instead, he said, the prearranged one-and-a-half-year sentence the D.A.'s office was offering would put him back on the streets within six months, in time to see his first child born.

"I never heard of a one-and-a-half-year sentence with the state," Mickey Boy said. "It's either one and a half to four and a half for a first offender, or one and a half to three for a guy who's got a record."

Richie laughed. "Too bad you didn't tell Chink that before he copped the plea. Afterward, he finds out he's got a one and a half to four and a half, and that he'll probably have to do three years of it in the can."

"That cocksucker," Mickey Boy growled. And to think that he'd wanted to be a lawyer at one time, crossed his mind. Now, with centuries of experience, if he counted all the horror stories of the guys he'd met in jail, to say advocates of the law were not his favorite people would be putting it mildly. Maybe that hump, Nicolo Fonte, had done him a big favor after all when he'd chased him as a kid, he thought.

And though Mickey Boy was none too fond of lawyers in general, he harbored a special hate for the Keplers of the world—vultures who preyed on those who were in trouble.

A memory that would always stay with Mickey Boy, and which defined his opinion of members of the legal profession, was of a discussion he had had with an attorney who used to represent his old boss, Sam LaMonica. "You know how all you guys have dreams of how you'd like to make big scores?" the lawyer had said. "Well, you know what mine is? It's that one of you guys makes that score—a really big one—gets away, stashes the money . . . then gets pinched and hires me to represent him." *Cocksuckers!*

As they pulled into the parking lot near Kepler's office, Richie continued. "Now Chink's up in Dannemora and he gets a new lawyer who says if he could get a statement from Kepler of what went down, how Chink really didn't understand what he was pleading out to, he could pull back the plea and at least get Chink out on bail for a while . . . at least a year."

"And Kepler don't wanna give him the statement."

"Worse. Every time Linda calls Kepler, he makes a play for her, tells her that Chink's gonna be away for a few years, and that, pregnant and all, a young girl's got needs that have to be taken care of. All the bullshit: dinner, dance, and drop your pants. Linda finally got disgusted and called me. All the poor kid does is cry." Richie's fair complexion was blood red by the time he had finished the story.

"Just calm down," Mickey Boy said. "We'll take care of this with no problem."

When they entered the elevator at 26 Court Street, Mickey Boy checked his watch again, hoping the time had miraculously gone backward so he could get to Laurel somewhere close to the hour he had promised. *Shit!* he cursed inwardly when he saw reality, then whispered to Richie, "Listen, we're going up here for three things: a letter that he fucked up, the money that Chink paid him, and the understanding that he quits hittin' on Linda. He's a lawyer, and should be easy to deal with."

Richie's jaw muscles rippled in anger, but he remained silent.

As soon as they got off on the eleventh floor, Mickey Boy grabbed his partner by the arm. "I know how you get with your temper sometimes, but you gotta control it. Let's act like businessmen instead of hoodlums. Remember," he added, "class works every time."

"But—"

"Just let me do the talking," Mickey Boy said. "You just take out your thirty-eight and play with it, classy like, while I talk nice an' quiet; I won't even need mine." He winked. "Just wait till you see his face when he spots the gun."

"I don't want to play with it. I want to shoot the bastard!"

"If you can't hold your temper an' act right, I'll come back tomorrow with somebody else," Mickey Boy said. "Just stare at him so that he sees how pissed you are, but don't say a word. Like I told you, class works every time."

Richie was muttering to himself as they entered the single door with an inscription in gold that read Phillip A. Kepler, Attorney at Law. An overweight and overly made up bleached-blond receptionist announced them to Kepler on an intercom phone, then hung up, saying they would have a short wait until he would see them.

Mickey Boy remembered Laurel again, and cursed silently. He tried to put her out of his mind by studying Kepler's secretary—her purple low-cut dress said "Catch me, I'm coming, boys"; her perfume was overpowering but expensive.

I'll bet that piece of shit inside is humping her too, he thought. *Probably the only decent thing he ever did in his life.*

"You can go in now," the secretary sang flirtatiously, straightening up in a vain effort to appear sexy.

Mickey Boy answered with a smile; Richie ignored her.

Inside the plushly carpeted office, Mickey Boy saw the personification of the type of lawyer he despised. *Fuckin' shyster*, he thought, shutting the door behind him.

Kepler sat behind a large walnut desk, shuffling some papers. He looked up over gold-framed bifocals as though the two men had caught him unawares. A nutmeg tan covered his smooth bald head and framed the shiny, capped ivories that he flashed easily. His cologne was every bit as powerful as his secretary's perfume.

The attorney rose, straightened his light glen-plaid suit, and walked toward them with a hand extended. "You must be Messers Russo and Smith." A large diamond lit up his browned pinky.

I'll bet Chink paid for that, Mickey Boy guessed to himself. "I'm Russo," he said. *Dirty cocksucker!* raced through his mind when Kepler dropped a baby-soft hand in his. That simple touch of pampered flesh ignited all the animosity he had tried to suppress since hearing of Chink's mistreatment.

Mickey Boy closed his hand on Kepler's much the same as he had earlier that afternoon on Ex-lax's. The only difference was that he simultaneously brought his right knee up into Kepler's crotch with all the force he could muster.

Kepler was taken entirely by surprise. His eyes bulged and the scream he tried to unleash lodged in his throat as two of Mickey Boy's powerful fingers dug into either side of his windpipe.

Already folding into the fetal position from the blow to his groin, Kepler was lifted and thrown back onto his desk. Papers and other deskly objects made no sound as they fell to the thick, money-colored pile.

Mickey Boy pulled his snub-nosed revolver from his waistband and forced the barrel in between Kepler's expensive dental work.

Richie stood frozen at the door, his mouth wide open.

"Listen, you dirty cocksucker," Mickey Boy hissed from between clenched teeth. "You robbed some money from Chink Agrigento an' sent him to the can—right, cocksucker?"

73

Though Kepler's teeth chattered frantically on the pistol's blue-gray steel, he did his best to nod.

Mickey Boy's face felt as if it were on fire as he demanded Kepler send a letter to Linda Agrigento, detailing how he'd misinformed her husband about the plea. He jammed the pistol farther into Kepler's mouth while he continued. "And you're gonna put twenty grand in hundred-dollar bills in the fuckin' envelope—understand that too, cocksucker?"

More clicking sounds.

"Good. Now, before I take this thing out of your cunt-lapping mouth, remember this: If you make a sound, even to say good-bye, I'm gonna kill you an' that fat bimbo cunt outside. *Capisce?*"

Mickey Boy completed his instructions. "If you fuck up an' call Chink's wife, or don't send the letter and the money . . . or even send twenties instead of hundreds, I'm gonna come out to your house an' pull pieces of skin off you till you die." He began to remove the pistol, then stopped. "Oh, and if you think that going to the law could stop me, cocksucker, just remember we got a fuckin' army out there just to squash slimy cocksuckers like you."

He gave Kepler exactly twenty-four hours to take care of everything: ". . . And not a fuckin' minute more." It took all his self-control not to squeeze the trigger—one squeeze to exorcise the visions of Chink, Laurel, Little Vinnie, and six lost years out of his life.

His anger subsiding, Mickey Boy pocketed the gun and walked to the door. Kepler remained doubled up on his desk.

Mickey Boy and Richie waved and smiled to the receptionist on their way out.

Once they had finally boarded the crowded elevator, Richie spoke his first words since entering Kepler's office. "You're right as usual," he conceded dryly, "class works every time."

17

June 5: Bay Ridge, Brooklyn

Driving along Eighty-sixth Street, Buster Alcamo checked his rear and sideview mirrors again for any sign of an unwelcome escort. A beige Buick followed close behind. Buster turned on Fourth Avenue and proceeded in the direction of the Belt Parkway. The Buick stayed with him.

"Ready?" Buster inquired of his passenger when they were about thirty yards from the roadway's entrance.

"Go 'head."

"Here we go," Buster said as he gunned the engine and shot into the winding approach to eastbound lanes. The Buick peeled out after him, leaving a sizable gap between itself and any cars behind, then, without warning, spun sideways and blocked the only access route to the highway.

Buster hurried forward at no more than two or three miles over the posted speed. Seconds later he pulled into a shorefront parking area that abuts the Belt. At night it is a lovers' lane, offering an enchanting view of the twinkling Verrazano Bridge, but in the early afternoon, when the two mobsters drove in, its rocky edge was filled with sunbathers, fishermen, and general meanderers, none of whom paid any attention to them as they hastily changed places with two occupants of another car, which had been waiting.

When Buster and his passenger, Don Vincenze, exited at Bay Parkway in the new car, two decoys were headed toward Long Island in theirs.

Of all the made members of their Family, Buster was closest to the powerful don. Vincenze had noticed Buster more than thirty years earlier, when he was beginning to form a power base for his eventual rise to the top. He quickly learned that Buster was dependable, loyal, and above all closemouthed; not once had even his most insignificant confidence been violated. Over the years, Bastiano handled everything with equal dispatch for the don, from picking up his laundry to brutally eliminating those who had earned his disfavor.

Because of that relationship, all of mobdom had been shocked when Vincenze demoted his most loyal ally from a captain to an ordinary soldier. Social clubs around the city buzzed about the prospects of an intra-Family rift. But there was no rift, there was a problem. And Buster's demotion offered the most expedient and palatable solution for the don.

For his part, Buster was all too ready to serve his boss in any capacity. The only thing he asked for this extraordinary favor that had been requested of him was that he report to no one but the don himself. Rewards were never mentioned by either man. Nor were explanations given to others as to why Buster had been demoted yet continued to function as Vincenze's bodyguard and chauffeur. Eyebrows might have been raised, but voices remained silent—or low enough so that they didn't reach the ears of Don Vincenze.

The two men passed through Bensonhurst and into the Hasidic Jewish community of Borough Park, where they parked on a side street in front of a small brick house turned yeshiva. Buster had to slow his pace to accommodate his slightly hobbled boss as they walked around the corner to a kosher delicatessen. When they entered, two associates of theirs were already seated at a table in the rear.

Alphonse "Junior" Vallo, the older and more rugged-looking of the pair, and new boss of the murdered John-John's Family, rose first. He moved to embrace the don, but was held firmly at arm's length.

"Not here, Alphonse," the don said. "We don't want to attract attention, do we?"

Junior Vallo appeared disturbed by the rebuff, but did not mention it. "Don Vincenze, a pleasure to see you again," he said. "You know my kid brother, Sally."

After all four men shook hands, Buster and Sally "The Soldier" Vallo went to a table near the entrance of the deli, leaving the two bosses to talk privately.

"How's everything going?" Don Vincenze asked.

"Okay, except my guys wanna go whack out Petey Ross's whole crew overnight. They are pissed."

"When Peppino and I picked you for the job, we figured you had enough respect and influence with your people to control them—I hope we weren't wrong."

Junior Vallo replied quickly, "You don't gotta worry, I could handle it. The only thing is, I gotta give my guys some satisfaction. There's a lot of bad blood between Petey's Family and ours for a lot of different things besides John-John."

"Out of the question for the time being," Don Vincenze said. "There will be plenty of time for them to get it out of their systems, but not right now; you gotta control the situation for a little while longer. In a few weeks they could start with a couple of Petey's guys that ain't made. If something happens, and you do have to take out a good fella, make sure that he disappears. I don't care what you do with the ones that ain't straightened out yet, but our kind of people can't turn up dead—no matter what."

"That's no problem, we got the lime pits upstate; all they could find is dust an' worms. It's just gonna be tough holdin' my men back that long."

"It's something you must do."

"I'll try my best."

"Unfortunately, that's not good enough—Peppino and I must have your guarantee."

Junior Vallo smiled, a snaggled top canine giving him a sinister look. "If that's the way it's *gotta* be, then that's the way it's *gonna* be."

"Good," Don Vincenze replied. "I knew we could count on you. Take your time and figure out who Petey's key men are. . . ." He formed the image of a pistol with his fingers and added, "The people he depends on for this. Those guys gotta go close together when we tell you."

"It'll be our pleasure."

Don Vincenze frowned. He couldn't believe that he had to sit and discuss business with an idiot who hadn't come any further than when he was a punk kid on some street corner, fighting other punks for fun.

"Don't be so cocky," he said. "Our Mr. Ross has a lot of heavy hitters with him. You'll have to whack as many as you could in a short time, then go underground."

"Then what? We gotta stay hidden like bums when we could be out finishing them off?"

"Let us handle the rest," Don Vincenze said, shaking his head to show his irritation. Maybe Peppino was right, that these younger ones weren't worth two cents. If so, it only made his task more necessary. He continued. "When our big-shot friend is out of control—see, control, that's the most important thing—when he loses it, he's done, *finito* . . . and we'll be waiting to pick up the pieces. Then we'll do like I told you an' split his crew up. You get half their men and first pick, like you were promised. Just one thing: You gotta be extra careful that our little secret never comes out."

"Are you kidding . . . never!" Junior said. "I'd die first."

Don Vincenze stared into his eyes, and with no expression on his face, whispered, "Yes."

At that moment a pudgy, cherubic waiter arrived at their table, pad in hand. "And what can I do for you young gentlemans?" he asked in a heavy Yiddish accent.

Junior respectfully deferred to Don Vincenze to order first.

"Why don't you make me a lean pastrami on rye," the don said.

"Poof," the waiter replied while emulating a magician's wave of his wand, "you're a lean pastrami on rye."

"Don't be a fuckin' smart guy," Junior growled, his tight-lipped glare diffusing the waiter's humor instantly.

Don Vincenze soothingly patted one of Junior's tensed hands. "Relax," he said, then turned to the startled waiter. "That'll be fine: two pastramis on rye, with mustard, and two Cel-Ray sodas. Oh, and please bring us some extra pickles." He smiled reassuringly at the frightened man.

"You have to try to calm down, my friend," Don Vincenze said after the waiter had disappeared. "I know you're under a lot of pressure now, but that will all end sooner than you think. Remember, I'm in your corner, and so is Peppino. He'll keep Petey Ross from fighting back as long as he can, while you pick away at his men. Do you think you are able to do that?" he asked, making no attempt to hide his annoyance.

"I'm fine," Junior countered. "Everything'll be just like you an' Don Peppino say."

"Good. I gotta tell you, though, we were a little disturbed about how John-John was handled. You do know our rules about bombs?"

Junior Vallo shifted restlessly. "You don't know how terrible I felt that I had to break that rule," he began. "But it was the only way. Number one, I was pressed for time—you told me that it had to be that night. Number two, I couldn't trust nobody. I'm sure you could understand that."

Don Vincenze remained expressionless.

"My kid brother Sally was the only one I could work with. Knowin' how good Sally was with demolitions in 'Nam, I hadda make a quick decision. There was no other way to get close to them an' make sure they went . . . I didn't wanna disappoint you."

Don Vincenze smiled, trying hard to hide his disgust. "I'm never disappointed in you, Alphonse," he said. "But this time you were lucky that no innocent parties were hurt. Please, see that no other rules are broken. *Tu capisce?*"

Junior Vallo acknowledged the implied threat with a nod.

18

June 8: Flatbush, Brooklyn

It was a dank, drizzly evening when Mickey pulled up to Laurel's house. She was already waiting in the doorway, and was in his car before he knew it.

"Well, what do you think?" he asked cheerfully. "Only fifteen minutes late."

Laurel shook the dampness off, then snapped open the vanity mirror. "Please," she said while checking her makeup and patting back wisps of hair that clung to her forehead. "I'm so used to you being at least an hour late that I feel like you're forty-five minutes early—talk about conditioned reflexes."

Finished with the mirror, she leaned over and kissed Mickey. "Ooh, what miserable weather," she complained as she moved back in her seat. "It's the kind of night I'd rather be a couch potato."

Mickey smiled. He had quickly settled into a relationship with Laurel that was as comfortable as an old shoe. It seemed to him that as soon as he was in her presence, the tensions of his life faded and he was instantly rejuvenated. And, while they still had some rough spots to clear away between them—some sexual, some communication over his life-style, and some overcoming her past with Alley—he was confident they would work themselves out in time.

In spite of the weather that evening, Mickey felt great. He ejected *The Best of Sinatra* from his tape player. "Look in the glove compartment for the *Ring-A-Ding-Ding* album," he told Laurel. "Did you ever hear Sinatra sing 'A Foggy Day in London Town'?"

Laurel covered her eyes and groaned, "Not more Sinatra, please."

Mickey Boy sang the lyrics about seeing his love and the sun suddenly shining through the fog.

"How sweet—and romantic," Laurel cooed. She stretched to kiss him again. "But he's still a bum," she said. "You really should read Kitty Kelley's book."

"Forget about it! I'm not interested in anything that bitch has to say. If she needed cash that bad, she should've asked him for a loan instead of peddling that bullshit!"

"I should have learned by now that instead of not arguing about politics or religion, like with most normal people, with you I can't talk about Frank Sinatra or what you do for a living," Laurel teased. "So, we will no longer discuss Mr. Sinatra." She settled back, buckled her seat belt, and folded her arms. "By the way, do you know what that louse did to poor Natalie Wood?"

The rain had become heavier by the time they passed Bush Terminal and entered onto the stretch of the Brooklyn-Queens Expressway that runs a hundred feet or so above Hamilton Avenue.

"Where to?" Mickey asked when the entrance to the Brooklyn Battery Tunnel came into view. "To the left an' a nice lobster fra diavolo at Freddie's, or to the right an' a bloody porterhouse at Peter Luger's."

"Please, nothing that reminds me of water; it's wet enough out here," Laurel said. With an imperial wave of her hand, she ordered, "To the right, James—directly to Peter Luger's and a nice juicy steak."

Halfway across the overpass, and at its peak, Mickey noticed a pair of headlights coming up fast behind him. *An accident looking for a place to happen*, he thought.

Alternating his eyes between his rear and sideview mirrors, he tracked the fast-approaching auto while he veered to his extreme right, allowing it a wide berth; when it was a couple of car lengths behind, he lifted his foot from the accelerator.

Assholes, he cursed inwardly, and turned to look at whoever it was as they passed him.

Fear shot through Mickey Boy when he looked in the passing car's window and saw a rubber face mask, grotesquely distorted by the rain. He jammed on his brakes—but it was too late. The other auto smashed him broadside, driving his two passenger-side wheels up onto the concrete embankment. For a split second he envisioned himself and Laurel bursting through the guardrail and plummeting to fiery deaths below.

Reacting quickly, Mickey Boy held the steering wheel tightly while he tried to pull it to the left. Sounds of crunching metal, Laurel's shrill screams, and the explosion of his two right tires chilled his bones and shriveled his testicles as he careened along the railing for what seemed like an eternity. Each scrape and tear of his car's body felt like it was tearing his own; a burning pain ran up Mickey Boy's left arm.

When the mangled Lincoln spun out into the middle lanes, the other car was already driving off toward the exit ramp. Mickey Boy looked around frantically, praying he and Laurel wouldn't get hit by any other speeding vehicles. Perspiration poured off his forehead and into his eyes.

Horns blared as cars and trucks pulled to screeching, skidding halts, thankfully not hitting one another and building up a cushion against the rest of the oncoming traffic. Mickey Boy saw some headlights swing sharply by him, and people running toward his car in spite of the steadily falling rain; pinpoints of iridescent light flickered off the wet metal and pavement around him; he smelled burnt rubber.

Mickey's eyes darted back and forth between Laurel, who'd continued shrieking through the entire incident, and the scene outside. "Laurel baby, you okay?" he yelled.

"I'm all right, I'm all right," Laurel gasped. "At least I think I am." She trembled uncontrollably.

Mickey reached out to comfort her with his right hand. The sharp pain persisted in his left arm, leaving him barely able to remove it from the steering wheel. He pulled the injured limb close to his body as if in an invisible sling.

Two men knocked on his side window. Mickey had to turn completely around to try to bring it down with his right hand, but the electric power didn't work. He tugged at the door handle, but the door was jammed, too, forcing him to kick it till it opened, and then only a few creaky inches.

"You two okay?" one of the men asked, yanking the door open a little wider.

"Yeah, we're fine," Mickey Boy answered; he heard the wailing of sirens in the distance; the burnt-rubber smell was more pungent mixed with the humidity outside.

Laurel cried, "What happened?"

Mickey was sure she hadn't seen the mask. If she had, she would still be hysterical. *Thank God!* he thought.

"That guy must've been drunk as a skunk," one of the men said.

"When I saw him running up on you like a maniac, I knew he was gonna hit you—it was almost like he was aiming for your car. Boy, are you guys lucky you didn't go through that rail." He rambled on, rain dripping off the peak of his Mets cap. "You were lucky you hit it full side instead of front first. Boy, these drunk drivers oughta be shot!"

Mickey pulled the door closer to keep the rain out. "Yeah, drunk driver," he agreed for Laurel's benefit—but he knew better.

19

June 9: Bensonhurst, Brooklyn

It was an ordinary sunny day, with any sunny day's steady flow of wandering pedestrians and golfers to and from Dyker Beach Park. Mothers with carriages who lolled outside the playground, elderly retirees who sat on sidewalk benches as a daily routine, and out-of-school teenagers who hung around by the corner gate all watched Little Vinnie pound the edge of his fist on the side wall of the 19th Hole cocktail lounge.

"What the fuck is wrong with you two?!" he screamed. Veins bulged in his crimson temples like a 3-D roadmap. "Whatta youse think God put guns on this fuckin' earth for, to shoot metal ducks in Coney Island? Youse might as well carry fuckin' water pistols!"

Little Vinnie's pockmarked underling, the one he now called Muffin-Face, held his arms outstretched. "But, Vinnie," he pleaded, "we thought we could run him off the expressway. We had him good over Hamilton Avenue, but instead of goin' through the railing, he bounced off."

"Fuck what you thought!" Little Vinnie howled, oblivious to his audience on the other side of the street. "I told youse before about tryin' to think—*don't!!!* I should kill the both of youse an' put us all out of our misery."

"But Vinnie . . ."

Just then Little Vinnie spotted a shapely female figure in pink shorts and a white halter top crossing 14th Avenue toward the park. He'd recognize those black ringlets and that pert, wiggly bottom anywhere. "Hey, cuz!" he yelled.

Chrissy Augusta turned, waved, and continued on her way without stopping.

"Hey, cuz, wait up!" Little Vinnie shouted, then started in her direction. "I'll finish with you fuckin' idiots later," he called to his relieved associates.

Much as he'd tried to get next to Chrissy, who in spite of his calling her "cousin" was only his father's godchild, he'd received no confidence from her at all. If anything, the spunky teenager acted as though she couldn't stand him. Little Vinnie figured it was the years of teasing and pinching that she'd endured from him in her childhood. Would he ever love to pinch that cute little ass now.

The twelve years that separated him from Chrissy meant nothing to Little Vinnie; going out with girls many years their junior was commonplace among knock-around guys. Besides, marrying Chrissy would probably thrill his father, and virtually ensure him at least a position as captain, maybe even underboss, if, God forbid, the old man died too soon and Joe Augusta became boss. With a father and father-in-law occupying the top two spots in his Family, he'd be a shoo-in for eventual leadership. All he needed for his climb up the Mafia ladder were two things: to be made, and to marry Christina Marie Augusta.

"Where you off to, cuz? Maybe I could give you a lift?" Little Vinnie said, flashing his brightest smile.

"Thanks, but no thanks," Chrissy snapped. "And I'm not your cuz—'Winnie.' "

Little Vinnie grinned and extended a hand to her. "Deal, no cuzzes for no Winnies."

Chrissy ignored his hand. With a sneering smile she said, "Goodbye, Vinnie," and walked off.

"Where you off to in such a hurry?" Little Vinnie asked, keeping pace with her as she marched past the park's main entrance. "Got yourself a new boyfriend?" he teased. He was absolutely sure she didn't—not his sweet Chrissy—but he was desperate for her to stay and talk, and added, "You know your old man wouldn't like that."

"I'm only going over to Fourth Avenue to buy some clothes," she said. "I'm really okay."

"C'mon, lemme drive you over," Little Vinnie insisted. "You know it's not safe for pretty young girls to walk by themselves. You have no idea what kind of slime is out there."

Chrissy looked at him and smiled.

Little Vinnie took her gently by the arm. "I'd never forgive myself if something happened to my favorite girl. That is, unless you really have got a hot date an' I'm crampin' your style?"

"Okay, Vinnie," Chrissy said. "Otherwise you'll have the whole world believing I'm balling half of Bensonhurst in the afternoons."

"Goddammit, don't even talk like that! I hate when you talk like these other bimbos around here. Besides, would I ever do something like that to you?"

Chrissy smiled again.

Little Vinnie led her to his car, played the complete gentleman by holding the door for her while she got in, then drove as slowly as possible toward the shopping area, stopping at the first hint of yellow to make sure he got caught for lights. At the intersection of Fourth Avenue he made a three-corner U-turn and stopped in front of the high-fashion boutique, Something Else.

"Want me to wait for you?"

"No, Vinnie," Chrissy said. "The next thing you'll want to do is help me in the dressing room. Besides, I really want to take my time shopping, and to be by myself for a while. Thanks anyway." Lifting two fingers to her lips, she blew him a kiss, then darted from his car.

Little Vinnie was ecstatic when he pulled away from the curb, imagining where on his face Chrissy's kiss might have landed. *Maybe there's hope yet*, he thought.

Chrissy Augusta peeked out of Something Else's doorway. When she saw Little Vinnie's gold Eldorado cross Fifth Avenue, she dashed toward the cab stand nearby.

"Please take me to the Nathan's, and wait with me there. I'll give you a good tip," she told the cabbie.

When Chrissy's taxi reached the fast-food drive-in, only two blocks from where Little Vinnie had accosted her, Georgie The Hammer was already waiting in his Corvette.

20

June 24: Fort Lee, New Jersey

John "Johnny Pumps" Mussomeli dressed himself in the bedroom of his sixteenth-floor apartment. He strolled out into the early summer humidity that surrounded his balcony garden while inserting onyx and diamond studs into his tuxedo shirt. The breathtaking view of Manhattan never lost its effect on John, who, when he was growing up in Brooklyn's East New York section, saw nothing more lively than the Spanish-Italian shopping area along Liberty Avenue.

As a child, John regularly replaced the rubble-strewn lot across from his bedroom window with conjured-up images of the skylines he had seen in magazine photos. The older he got, the more he replaced his daydreams with the real thing. Mothlike, he gravitated to the bright lights of Las Vegas, Atlantic City, and, most of all, "The City"—Manhattan.

His move to Jersey came as the result of being sent to collect money by his Uncle Anthony, who was a cousin of Petey Ross's. That particular collection, a monthly payment from an Atlantic City casino, was one of many assignments that Johnny Pumps was given because of his indirect relationship to Petey, and was set for the King Cole Room of the St. Regis Hotel.

After the money had changed hands and the casino's bagman had left, an expensively dressed redhead approached Johnny's table. Displaying the chutzpah that had earned her the editorship of a major publishing house, she told him that she had caught the payoff, knew it was a shady deal, and was sure he was a mafioso—all of which she found fascinating and exciting.

Two and a half hours later, Johnny Pumps had her bent on the rail of her Fort Lee penthouse, staring over her naked back at the galaxy of twinkling lights across the Hudson.

John leased a place in the area within two weeks, and since then had engaged in outdoor sex with various playmates that he'd picked up during his regular late-night rounds of Nell's, Au Bar, and the China Club.

More important, the apartment-length terrace, with its professionally designed evergreen forest, had become the most important place in the world to him. In the course of any activity at home, as for example when he dressed that evening for a cocktail party at Regine's, he would amble out through the sliding glass doors dozens of times, reveling in the beauty before him.

Johnny Pumps looked at himself in the mirror: He checked his hair, dark as his tuxedo, to make sure no grays were creeping in; stretched an exaggerated smile ten times to tighten up the flesh under his chin; adjusted his bow tie.

Satisfied, he opened the drawer of a small table below his reflection and withdrew a nickel-plated .25 automatic. Earlier that week, two of Petey Ross's button-men had disappeared and three of his associates were gunned down. Even though John was far removed from the Rossellini Family's activities, securing cash and future promotions by that very indirectness, he wanted to be sure he wouldn't be caught with his proverbial pants down. He also found it exhilarating to carry a weapon; the power of life and death secretly at his manicured fingertips.

With his pistol secured beneath his satin cummerbund, he opened the door and walked out into the narrow hallway.

Johnny Pumps saw the blur charging at him from the stairwell at the same time a crushing blow to his solar plexus doubled him up.

Strong hands gripped him firmly under each arm. Though speechless and filled with agonizing pain, he was aware of his heels dragging first through the deep gold shag carpet of his living room, then onto the green artificial turf of his beloved terrace. His skin dampened when they crossed from the air-conditioned coolness of the interior to the stifling summer moisture of the outdoors. He tried to reach his gun, but couldn't even come close.

Bitter-tasting bile forced its way up from his middle, pushing an earlier meal of take-out Chinese food in front of it; he retched over the phony grass and his black peau-de-soie loafers.

The four powerful hands that had been carrying him lifted John's folded body effortlessly onto the balcony railing. When he felt the wrought iron press against his haunches, he tried to push forward, but two of his aggressors' hands had moved underneath his shoes like stirrups, and were forcibly launching him in the other direction. The glittering skyline of Manhattan that had so captivated him was upside down as he began to tumble earthward, end over end.

The final bit of good fortune Johnny Pumps had was to lose consciousness seconds before he exploded over the concrete sidewalk.

21

June 26: Borough Park, Brooklyn

12:08. Laurel shifted impatiently from one burning foot to the other while waiting in front of the deserted school. She had repeatedly told Mickey Boy that the children were being dismissed at 11:30 sharp, and had pleaded with him to be on time. Now, more than a half hour later, she was wilting from the heat and he still hadn't shown up. "Damn him!"

The weeks since they had become lovers had seen Laurel waiting for him all too often. If she wasn't sitting in the car while he spoke to some unsavory-looking friend of his, she was pacing back and forth either at home or at the school where she worked, counting the minutes, and sometimes hours, that he'd be behind schedule for a date. What would his excuse be this time, she wondered; undoubtedly that miserable after-hours club that he and Richie were building in Bensonhurst.

Laurel had tried. She had begged Mickey Boy not to get involved in anything illegal, anything that could send him back to jail, but he had only laughed. A little gambling or drinking business was nothing to worry about, he'd claimed, especially since he wouldn't be able to stay at the club anyway due to his parole. Richie would run everything, and he would receive a share of the profits.

Listen to Mickey Boy and everything was easy, Laurel thought; everything was ". . . *a piece of cake.*"

Unfortunately, an image dating back to her teens was too vividly etched in her mind: Mickey Boy being led from one of his *nothing* social clubs in handcuffs, his head bowed low to avoid a photographer's flashbulb. She tried not to think about it, but was not very successful. Some piece of cake.

What irritated her most was that she sensed there was something better in him, a potential for intelligence and goodness that, for some reason or other, had never been developed. Instead, he was bent on committing himself, body and soul, to the underside of society. More and more, it seemed to her that gangsterism was in his blood.

In spite of her anger, Laurel let out a small laugh. *How did I ever get hooked like this?* she wondered. She hadn't intended for a relationship to blossom as it had when she'd first insisted on seeing him, and still felt guilty about her original motives—but then again, she hadn't counted on falling in love. Philosophy 1: Ends justified the means. Or did they? She could never remember how that discussion had ended.

Laurel looked at her watch again. "Damn him!"

It wasn't until 12:28 that she heard his tires squealing a block away.

Mickey Boy could see he had a petulant, fuming time-bomb on his hands the minute Laurel got into his rented car. Dropping into the passenger seat, she slammed the door and turned wordlessly toward its window. She continued to stare out while he spoke.

"Gee, babe, I told you I'm sorry," he apologized again to the back of her head. "I really got hung up at the new after-hours an' had no idea what time it was. I left my watch home 'cause I don't want my P.O. to see it when we go there, and I was afraid dust from the construction might get into it. Here, look at my shoes; did you ever see them so dirty?" He stretched to touch her shoulder.

Laurel shook him off.

"All right, be mad at me," he said, reversing his tactics. "This way I don't have to give you the surprise I brought for you."

"Don't try to bribe me."

"Would I do something that low? Me?" Mickey Boy teased. "Especially to a teacher? Why, a future attorney general could be in your class; then someday, if I make you mad, you'll sic him on me."

"The only thing I want to do to you right now is give you a good hard punch in the nose—one that really hurts and makes it bleed."

"First of all, you can't hit me 'cause I'm just healing from the accident. Look, I could even drive a little bit with my left arm again," he said.

No response.

"Second of all, if you hurt this beautiful nose, you're gonna have a lot of people mad at you."

"I'm not afraid of your tough-guy friends."

"Forget about my friends, it's all the girls at Pastel's I'm talking about. They'll rip all that pretty hair right outta your head by the roots."

Laurel turned to face Mickey Boy. She threateningly waved an insignificant fist in his direction. "If only you weren't driving."

Mickey Boy smiled—he had won again.

"If you do that, you'll only have to kiss the parts that you damage," he said. "So since I'm driving and you can't hit me now, why don't you make nicey-nice an' kiss the spots first? Then you could always bang me around when we're alone." He lowered his head, trying to make direct eye contact with her. "C'mon, babe, how about it?"

"Why can't I stay mad at you?"

" 'Cause you're crazy about me."

Her anger gone, Laurel slid over to Mickey Boy's side. She snuggled close enough for him to drape his right arm over her shoulders.

Though his eyes remained on the road, scanning all around carefully, he playfully slipped his hand into the neckline of her blouse and began to fondle her breast; his rolling of its nipple made her shudder.

Protesting, Laurel grabbed his hand, but it only increased the pressure on her sensitive area. "Oh, don't do that," she moaned without making the slightest attempt to move away. "Stop, you bastard, you're getting me hot."

Mickey Boy pinched her distended nipple, forcing a squeal through her parted lips. While the sound gave him some satisfaction, a feeling of control over Laurel that he liked, it scared him. Driving had become a time when he had to be especially alert, had to check for cars with masked occupants trying to kill him. He pulled his hand from her blouse and his arm from her shoulder.

"No," he said when Laurel snaked her hand to his crotch and began to fondle him in return. "Laurel, not now. . . ."

She persisted.

Passing beneath the green and white entrance sign of the Prospect Expressway, he tried to push her hand away, but she ducked her head underneath his arm and down between his legs; he felt her tug at his zipper.

"Laurel, don't do that . . ." he whispered, eyeing the mirrors nervously. His heartbeat quickened as he felt himself sliding into her mouth. What would he do if Rubber Mask showed up then? He could picture himself and Laurel being found dead, him with no penis, and her with it jammed down her throat. "Laurel, stop, you're gonna make me crash!"

Through the lust-induced pounding in his ears, Mickey was barely able to hear Laurel's garbled words: "You started it."

While waiting in the large outdoor lot on Court Street for an attendant to take their car, Mickey slid a dainty peridot ring with guardian diamond chips onto Laurel's finger.

Seemingly ecstatic, Laurel hugged and kissed him, then pointed out that it was yet another milestone in their relationship: her first gift—outside of the roses he'd given her on their first date, of course.

Thank God the credit card pushers had made a decent choice, Mickey Boy thought. He had bought it sight unseen, supplying them with her birthdate and one third of the retail price. Two days later they delivered the ring.

Holding hands and still admiring his gift, they walked around the block to the parole department at 75 Clinton Street and took the elevator to the fourth floor.

They found Mickey Boy's surly case worker, Anthony Spositoro, behind his desk, studying some papers. As always, his short, wiry gray hair and bushy moustache reminded Mickey Boy of a recently clipped schnauzer. Between that and the blotchy red skin that always looked like it had been scrubbed raw, he thought it no wonder the P.O. was so miserable—who the hell would want to see that in the mirror all the time?

"How're ya doin', Mr. S.?" Mickey Boy asked, employing his most radiant charm. "I want you to meet my girl, Laurel. She's a schoolteacher and a helluva great influence on me. Laurel, Mr. Spositoro."

Anthony Spositoro looked up over half glasses from the paperwork he was studying. He managed a weak smile for Laurel, then in a curt, dry voice said, "While it's a pleasure meeting you, I think it would be better if I spoke to Michael alone. There's a chair directly outside my office."

Mickey Boy led her to the seat Spositoro had suggested, then cursed inwardly when he realized she'd hear every word from that spot.

When he returned to the room, Mickey Boy handed Spositoro the weekly report he was required to fill out; on it, questions about changes in living quarters or employment, a financial disclosure, and a statement that he hadn't had any encounters with law enforcement personnel, even for something as minor as a traffic ticket.

As he studied the sheet, Spositoro asked, "How's the job going, Michael?"

"Fine, no problems. It's a lot of hard work, but I'm working for some great people."

"I'm sure you are," Spositoro replied with the faintest hint of sarcasm. "Let me ask you something, how many accounts do you figure you see in the course of a day?"

Mickey Boy's answer was purposely ambiguous, and long. He spoke rapidly, claiming that although most stops were just social visits to keep his company's name on customers' minds for reorders, that distance between stops, traffic conditions, and individual accounts' problems really determined how many visits he made on any given day. As an example, he told the parole officer a fabricated story about a pizzeria account in Washington Heights whose delivery had mistakenly gone to a competitor. He said that the store owner was furious, and wanted nothing more to do with the company. Only his efforts, he claimed, in tracking down the lost merchandise and correcting the error saved the pizzeria's business for his boss.

"It took me hours," he said. "I even went myself and brought the stuff over from the guy who got it by mistake."

Spositoro let Mickey Boy finish his entire story, then slumped back in his chair. He stared directly into Mickey Boy's eyes. "Is that what happened at the Focacceria Villarosa on Mulberry Street?" He tossed across the desktop a photo he'd been holding—a photo of Mickey Boy leaving the restaurant, a time marked across the bottom of it.

Despite rapid thumps reverberating in his ears, Mickey Boy held his composure. Aware that most of Little Italy's social clubs like Buster's were under police surveillance, he had prepared for some flak in the event a lawman had spotted him entering or leaving the nearby restaurant. But as time had passed without any mention of it, he'd figured he was safe, and had become relaxed, sloppy. Now he struggled to retrieve lines he had rehearsed weeks earlier, excuses about how difficult it had been to open the Focacceria as an account.

Spositoro fell forward on his desk. "Cut the bullshit!" he yelled. "I don't know who you met in there, but you wouldn't let your girl—or whatever girl you were with—sit alone in a car for two hours because of a nickel-and-dime pepperoni account. Give me some credit for knowing what's going on."

That dirty puke, Mickey Boy thought, having caught Spositoro looking toward the doorway as he shouted. If there had been a different girl with him that day at the Villarosa, Spositoro would certainly make sure Laurel heard about it. *Fuckin' rat stool pigeon!*

"Don't think you're playing with fools on this end; we know very well what the deal is. You just got lucky that—"

"I'm not trying to—"

"No, you let me finish!" Spositoro yelled. "Then you can run your bullshit excuses by me again. You got lucky that the agent who took the pictures didn't recognize any of your pals going in before or after you—but I know better," he said with a smirk of superiority.

Spositoro's voice turned to a growl. "I'm warning you. Let me catch you with one of your mafioso friends and I'll have you shoveling ass-high snow at Ray Brook for the next four years. Do we understand each other?"

Mickey Boy glared at Spositoro's forehead, envisioning two neatly placed bullet holes. It took all his restraint not to blurt out what was on his mind while answering, "I'm sorry you feel that way, Mr. S., but I'm trying very hard to keep that job." His words were slow and deliberate as he insisted he'd spend as much time at a location as he deemed necessary to secure or service the account. What was he supposed to do, he asked, tell people to buy fast because his parole officer didn't want him to spend too much time in one place?

"No disrespect meant, but if anybody in the parole department or the FBI thinks they could do a better job than me, they're welcome to try—I'll even do the driving and buy them lunch," he offered with a sarcasm equal to anything Spositoro might have dished out. "But as far as violating me because you don't like the way I sell, I think I'll have to talk to my lawyer about that."

"You can talk to whomever you please," Spositoro replied. "All I'm doing is putting you on notice that I see through your little charade. Now, do yourself a favor and try to toe the line out there, because I'm just waiting to drag your ass in." He motioned toward the doorway with his head. "That's a very nice girl you've got . . . maybe too nice. It would be a shame to only see her on visits for the next few years."

"Am I finished?"

"That depends on you, Michael . . . that depends on you." Spositoro stood and walked to his filing cabinet. He spoke with his back to Mickey Boy. "I'm putting you on weekly visits instead of monthlies, but I won't be here next week, so just sign in. I'll see you in two weeks."

Since Laurel insisted she wouldn't ride with him until he calmed down, and since they were both famished, they opted to eat before taking the car from the lot. Mickey Boy guided her along Court Street to the Queen Italian Restaurant, cursing loudly all the way. She looked away each time someone ogled them because of his raging behavior, and stood by petrified when he challenged one man for staring. Fortunately, the man had the good sense to turn and hurry off.

It wasn't until he had guzzled two Johnnie Walkers on the rocks that Mickey Boy finally relaxed somewhat. "I'm sorry, babe. It's just that I can't stand when a little shit like that flexes his muscles with me—every fuckin' week now I gotta report. If he didn't have that badge, I'd bash his goddamn skull in."

"All right, the reports aren't that bad, just a nuisance," Laurel said. "He does worry me, though, when he says he can send you back to prison. Can he?"

"If he could, that dirty puke, believe me, I'd be eating nuked ham hocks in MCC right now."

When their own food arrived—creamy spaghetti carbonara and chicken rollatines with mushrooms in wine sauce—Mickey Boy attacked it as though it were Spositoro's flesh.

Laurel waited for him to calm down some more before continuing. "I'm just afraid he'll keep piling up little things until he can send you back. Can't you stay away from your friends until this is all over?" she asked, as she had on numerous occasions. "It'll only be until your parole is over. I'm sure they'll understand."

Mickey Boy shook his head at how little Laurel understood him. "Honey, I gotta be on the string with this dirty bastard for another four years. Could I possibly go that long without earning?"

"You have a—"

"I'm already behind six years of makin' money. If I only made seventy-five to a hundred thousand a year, you're talkin' about over half a mil. What should I do now, see if I could make it a whole million?"

The wide-eyed expression on Laurel's face made Mickey Boy laugh. Coming from a family where her father was a retail shoe salesman and her mother worked as a file clerk in a hospital, the idea of clearing a couple of thousand dollars a week had to be startling. In spite of all the turmoil that lingered inside him, Mickey Boy felt proud.

"Besides, the last six years I had free room an' board," he said in a light, joking manner. "Who's gonna pay my rent now, Spositoro? You? Do I look like a pimp who sits home an' lives off his women?"

Laurel answered innocently, wondering why he couldn't make do with what he earned on his job.

"Laurel, wake up an' smell the coffee. You don't really believe I'm working for these people, do you? I'm always with you; how could I be working?"

"But you said . . ." she began, then seemed to realize his meaning. "Well, when I'm in school I figured you're busy seeing accounts. I believed you."

"Honey, when I picked you up today, where did I tell you I was?"

"At the new after-hours club."

"And yesterday, where did I tell you I was?"

"With your friend Buster."

"Laurel, you're a smart girl. How could I be doing these things an' seeing customers at the same time?"

"I'm not dumb because I don't know how gangsters act," Laurel snapped. "My mother doesn't wonder where my father is or what he's doing each day, but she knows he's at work. I mean, I'm not used to having to question those things. I trusted you."

Aware of Laurel's displeasure about his continued mob involvement, Mickey Boy had avoided the subject as much as possible. He kept most of his activities secret, and when she did question him, he changed the subject. Sooner or later the air would have to be cleared, however, and to him, in the mood he was in, that moment was as good as any.

He explained gently, but without apology, that on their first date he had misled her into thinking he was working because he had no idea how close they would become—it had been none of her business then. Later, once they'd become involved, he found no reason to upset her by telling her the truth. Sure, mob life had its bad points, he said, but there were peaks that were unattainable for the average workingman: freedom and respect of others the prime benefits, financial gain third behind them.

"There's just no goddamned way I'm gonna kill myself working sixteen hours a day like Alley's old man, or stick shoes on people's smelly feet like yours does, an' then have to worry about the price of broccoli. It just ain't gonna happen."

Mickey Boy shrugged. "I'm sorry, I didn't mean to put down your old man, but he's him an' I'm me."

Smiling weakly, Laurel admitted feeling foolish over not having read the signs before. "I guess I wanted to believe you so much that I ignored what was right in front of my face. Besides, I did see a check you had from your boss."

"Honey, that's all I get—checks, no money." It always amazed him how the educated people he knew never had the shrewdness or common sense that he did. Alley was one example: He could design a city from its pilings to its TV antennas, but had trouble understanding the word loyalty—he hadn't even come up to visit once in six years. Before him sat the other side of the coin: too loyal to see the truth.

Mickey Boy chuckled, more at Laurel than with her, then explained how he bought those checks each week. The arrangement, as he described it, was good for him because he got to show his parole officer a job; the benefit to his supposed boss was to hide cash that would otherwise be heavily taxed.

"Between the Lincoln he leases for me and my salary or commissions, he hides almost three thousand a month. That's more than a ten-thousand-dollar score for him at the end of the year, just from the taxes he'd have had to pay on that thirty . . . and it makes us owe him a favor."

"But if you get caught, you'll go back to prison. I know that much."

Mickey Boy grinned reassuringly at her. "I'm not getting caught. No one knows what I'm doing except me, the owner of the joint, an' now you. Him an' me won't tell—how about the girl I'm nuts about?"

"I don't know, did I ever meet her?" Laurel teased, her effort at humor strained.

Mickey reached across the table and took her hand. "You remember what I told you the other night? Well, let me tell you, it's the God's honest truth. In my whole life I never told a girl I loved her—you're the first, an' if it's up to me, the last. That's all within a few weeks," he added with a smile. "Imagine how crazy I'm gonna be about you after a hundred years!"

Liberated from the need to deceive her, Mickey Boy made an effort to convince her that their future would be a good one if only she would learn to understand his life and stick with him when the going got rough. "Do that for me, an' I'll lay down my life for you. I know it's not easy sometimes, but it'll be worth it—I promise."

Laurel looked down at her hands with the same troubled expression he'd noticed on several occasions. He wished she'd open up to him and clear her mind. Whatever her problems, he was strong and would gladly shoulder them along with his own.

"Laurel baby, is there something on your mind? I just feel like—"

"No," Laurel answered too quickly. Her uneasy expression remained. "I'm just very confused. I've got more feelings in my body and things going through my mind than I've ever had before—and not all of them good either," she admitted softly. "I'm going to try to overcome them because I love you too, more than I ever thought I would. I just hope I can."

"Don't worry, baby," he replied. "Just remember how much I care for you—and what I'd do to anybody who even thought about hurting you." He tucked his hand under her chin and lifted it until their eyes met. "An' take out of your head that I'm going anyplace but wherever you are. After all, who would want to go out with you if I wasn't around?"

"Spositoro."

Mickey Boy threw his rumpled napkin at her while jokingly threatening to kill both her and the parole officer. Taking advantage of their lightened mood, he said, "Now for something more important: Are you gonna take the ride to Boston with me?"

For the last week Mickey had been prodding Laurel to accompany him to see his family in Massachusetts. What puzzled him was how she had suggested it on their first date, almost challenging him to show his face with her in front of his mother and Alley, then later on, once he'd agreed, backed off.

"Didn't you want to go? Remember at Freddie's?"

"That was then!" Laurel snapped. She shifted nervously in her chair. "Right now I feel very funny about seeing your mom," she said. "You know how Connie is—not that she scares me, or that I'm ashamed of us being together, but she's so proper and all."

Proper was exactly the way to describe his mother, Connie, Mickey thought. She was so classy and straight that being around her too much made him feel like a slob. But he loved her dearly, and hadn't seen her in much too long a time. He'd made it a practice, since coming home, to visit her in Massachusetts every other week, but had missed the last two visits, waiting for Laurel to agree to go too.

Laurel continued. "I just feel like she'll look down on me like I'm the neighborhood tramp or something."

"Don't be ridiculous; Mom always loved you."

"That was before," Laurel said. "Things change."

Mickey tried to convince Laurel that his mother had to know Alley was a jerk for giving her up, and that no one, including himself, would have had a chance with her if Alley hadn't been one. He also insisted that his mother would be happy to learn that he wouldn't be alone, that Laurel would be around to care for him.

"Do me a favor an' don't say no just yet," he asked. "We got another week till I told her I was coming, an' I might not even have to—Mom's thinking of takin' a bus down an' spending the weekend here in New York. If she does, then you could come with me to pick her up, an' the three of us could go for dinner. Believe me, she'll be thrilled to see you."

"Sure," Laurel said. "Connie'll just think I'm a sort of family hand-me-down. Laurel Bianco, the Messina receptacle that the boys pass around when they're horny. Good thing there aren't more brothers."

"I don't ever want to hear that again!" Mickey shouted.

Patrons at neighboring tables turned to stare.

Ignoring the onlookers, Mickey continued in a gentler voice. "You're my girl, an' everybody'd better respect you the way I do—the way I want you to respect yourself."

He signaled with a raised hand for their check, then turned to Laurel again. "I won't press you, but I really do want you to come with me to meet Mom. There's nothing to be afraid of with her," he said, wishing that Connie Messina, who was a caring, devoted mother, were less intimidating to others with her rigid moral standards and lofty ideals.

"C'mon," Mickey insisted. "Promise you'll think it over."

Laurel hesitated, then smiled—a troubled smile. "I promise."

22

1956: Brooklyn

It was the year of *Peyton Place*, and as if she were a protagonist in Grace Metalious's steamy novel, Connie Partinico was having an affair with a married man—she was also six weeks pregnant.

Connie had met her lover, who at thirty-five was her senior by nearly a decade and a half, while trudging home from the train station one muggy Friday evening after work. She'd looked especially chic that day in a yellow plissé shirtwaist she had bought with her employee's discount from Bergdorf Goodman, where she worked in the lingerie department. More than a few heads turned along 18th Avenue's store-lined pavement to appreciate the *Vogue*-model image her enviable figure, upswept blue-black hair, and dark almond-shaped eyes presented.

Work-weary and sticky from the humidity, Connie was waiting patiently on the corner for the traffic light to turn green, when a powder-blue Cadillac whizzed by, kicking up sludge that had settled into a small pool nearby. The lower portion of her sunny outfit was instantly converted to a muddy Jackson Pollock–like print.

Like most male drivers, the speeding motorist had looked at Connie as he'd passed, and, as a result, had seen her being showered with mud from his wheels. He quickly double-parked and hurried toward her.

Despite numerous apologies and conciliatory offers that ranged from providing dry cleaning for her soiled dress to replacing it entirely, Connie stubbornly refused to acknowledge him. She walked on toward home, eyes straight ahead, controlled anger fighting its way out through her pores as perspiration.

He, meanwhile, pursued her for the better part of two blocks, babbling incessantly about how sorry he was. He left only after Connie exasperatedly assured him that she was not angry, wanted no settlement, and would appreciate being left alone. She suggested he use his money to pay for the parking ticket she'd seen a policeman placing on the windshield of his car.

For the next ten days Connie received elaborate yellow floral arrangements from various shops in the neighborhood. All bore brief expressions of regret and were facetiously signed "Mudslinger."

The first two offerings were immediately dumped into the Partinico trash can, Connie infuriated by the thought that some stranger had intruded upon her privacy. Indignation was supplanted by amusement on the third day, and curiosity about the persistent "Mudslinger" by the end of the week.

Conversely, Connie's mother became more and more frightened as her living room began to resemble a funeral chapel—God only knew what kind of maniac was lurking out there for her only child.

From the moment she stepped off the RR train each evening until she bolted the front door behind her, Connie was constantly on the lookout for "Mudslinger." When he did eventually contact her, however, it was not in Brooklyn at all, but directly in front of Bergdorf's employee exit, on East 58th Street, in Manhattan. The shock of seeing him there, where she worked, perched atop the lustrous fender of his Coupe de Ville with a bouquet of yellow roses in his hand, totally disarmed her.

Connie consented to his offer of a lift home and was agreeable when he suggested a detour to Cafiero's on President Street for dinner.

Everyone seemed to know him at the family-style eatery, and accorded him openly deferential treatment. Veal al forno was the traditional Tuesday night special, he said, and the two of them heartily devoured platesful of the tender potted calf, washing it down with several glasses of homemade burgundy blended with Coca-Cola and fresh-squeezed lemon. They chatted throughout the meal, becoming a great deal better acquainted by the time the last sweet morsel of citron-spiked cheesecake was gone.

After dinner he gave her a delightful tour of the nearby outdoor market section of Union Street. Freshly baked breads, fresh fish on ice, and copiously stacked fruits and vegetables flowed over from small turn-of-the-century stores to wooden stalls and pushcarts. All this was absorbed by Connie through the rosy-cheeked glow of fermented grape.

In the following weeks she dated him a half dozen more times and thought of him continuously. When Connie mentioned having read rave reviews of the new Rex Harrison show, *My Fair Lady*, he managed to acquire a pair of third row center aisle seats. He was apologetically unsure as to whether they were the best in the house because, as he sheepishly confessed, he had never been to a Broadway production—nothing but movies and nightclubs to that point.

He, on the other hand, introduced her to baseball from an Ebbets Field box seat halfway between Roy Campanella and Gil Hodges. Carl Furillo was her favorite; "The Duke" was his.

Their only major difference in taste was in music. She was crazy about Elvis the Pelvis's "Don't Be Cruel"; he called it garbage next to Vic Damone's "On the Street Where You Live." They settled on "Que Sera, Sera" as their song.

They became lovers on the fourth date, after seeing Carroll Baker in

Baby Doll at a downtown cinema and stopping for a few drinks at the Turf Club on Flatbush and DeKalb. It was in his car, just before registering at the St. George Hotel that first time, that he disclosed his unhappy marital status to her. His loveless marriage to a *paisano*'s daughter from his home village in Sicily had been arranged by his uncle, a man of respect. Connie was too drunk and too sexually aroused to care, and within a half hour had lost her preciously guarded virginity.

Now Connie was carrying Mudslinger's child, and she was sure he'd be thrilled when he learned of it. Of course he'd be shocked at first, she thought, but then the boyish enthusiasm that she alone seemed to find beneath his serious, sometimes brutish exterior would burst through and prompt him to replace his unwanted spouse with the girl of his dreams: her.

My little tough guy, Connie reflected, watching him cross from the bathroom to the bed, where she lounged naked. While she found the aura of ferocity that surrounded her lover strangely exciting, she loved him for the normally shrouded gentleness he uncovered for her.

"Hon," she said, affecting a little-girl coyness as he reached her. "If you could choose one thing that would make you really happy, what would it be?"

He entwined his arms with hers and pecked lightly at her eyes, nose, mouth. "Just to be like we are right now."

Connie freed herself from his grasp and sat up, her supple legs crossed in a lotus, her womanness gaping open at him. She ran a single finger along the puckered scars he had picked up at Anzio when he was closer to her age.

"C'mon, really, babe," she kept on. "Tell me what would make you happy. Make believe I'm like the genie in Aladdin's lamp and could grant your every wish." She bowed at the waist, arms wide, breasts dangling; her ebony hair cascaded over his hip. "Your wish is my command."

A bearlike arm reached beneath Connie's chin, lifting it so he could behold her graceful features. While staring adoringly at her, he said, "Listen, sweetheart, you know I'm not much for fancy words, but you also know how nuts I am about you. Just be you, just the way you are now, an' my wishes are all taken care of."

"I'm pregnant," she blurted out, then wistfully bowed her head again. She waited for his reaction with bated breath, hoping for a joyful embrace and a promise of marriage.

"You sure?"

She nodded vigorously, then lifted her head to stare expectantly into his eyes.

"Don't worry," he assured her, "I know a good doctor who'll take care of it for you."

Connie screamed, suddenly realizing what he meant. "For *me?!*" It was as if her sensibilities had been jolted with electric current. "For me? Take care of it? What happened to *us?*" Her voice bordered on hysteria as she added, "You want to kill our baby?!"

He looked pained by her distress, and sat up to wrap her in his arms. "Baby, I'm sorry. I told you I don't talk that good. When I said you, of course I meant us." He stroked her hair lovingly. "Don't be upset; Daddy'll take care of everything, an' we'll be just fine."

"Then you want our baby?"

"Sweetheart, there's nothing I'd love more in this whole goddamn world than having a kid with you," he replied with heartrending sincerity. "You gotta know that—but it's just not right. I love you too much to make you raise a kid without a husband. An' as for the kid, believe me, I know what it's like to grow up without an old man. It's no picnic."

Connie pulled back to face him directly. "But our baby doesn't have to be without a father." She paused, then added, "And I don't have to be without a husband."

Wretchedness distorted all Mudslinger's features; his eyes softened and his face turned red. Glumly, he clasped both her trembling hands in his and raised them to his lips, as if seeking absolution. Then, in a barely audible voice, he muttered, "I can't—I wish to God I could. I love you so much."

Connie broke his hold. She got off the bed and stepped away from him. "You don't love me," she stated in a sad but even tone. "And I can see now that you never did."

"That's not true!"

"What a fool I've been." Her self-pity rapidly changed to indignation. "You invested in a few lousy flowers and got yourself a steady lay!" she shouted. "I actually bought all that crap you shoveled at me!"

"Connie baby, you don't understand."

"No, don't hand me any more goddamned lines! This is the first time since I met you that I understand anything at all." Angry tears began to flow as she struggled into her panties and bra.

"Honey," he pleaded, "just give me a chance to explain."

"Explain?! What can you possibly explain? That all these stories you've been handing me about how miserable your marriage is were all lies? That you want to have your cake and eat it too? Well, I'm sorry, Mister, you'll just have to find another goddamned bakery—this one's closed to you!"

Mudslinger sprang from the bed. With one sweep of his muscular arm he sent the table lamp flying across the room. "For Christ's sake!" he bellowed. "You don't wanna give me a fuckin' chance to get a fuckin' word in edgeways!"

His tantrum quickly dissipated Connie's, partly from shock and partly from fear of him clubbing her with those fat fists of his. "All right, say what you have to and get it over with."

"I ain't gonna fuckin' talk if you ain't gonna listen!" he yelled.

All dressed, except for her shoes, which she held in her hands, a teary-eyed Connie sat on the edge of a chair across from her lover. "I'm listening," she said. Her lips quivered and tiny rivulets ran down her cheeks.

Mudslinger tried. He told her how much he loved her and how she'd brought him alive, awakened feelings that he had been unaware he'd even possessed. Connie sobbed quietly while he explained that although she saw only the good side of his life—money, good times, the respect he got from others—the laws he lived by were more strict than those of the average man, and the penalties much worse.

"I could go like that!" he said with a snap of his fingers. "All I gotta do is break one of our rules." He sank back on the rumpled mattress, his eyes questioning, looking to her for some response.

"I understand and sympathize," Connie whispered. "But you chose that life yourself, and I really don't see what that has to do with me or our baby." She blew her nose.

"Remember when I told you how my marriage was arranged by my mother's brother? Well, it was, an' as far as my uncle an' the rest of our people are concerned, it's final. They don't give a shit whether I love her, or even like her—it's our law: You don't ever leave your wife and kids. Final. If you do, you're finished; you might as well go to work. I'd become a big fat zero overnight."

Connie stared at Mudslinger's sagging features, the tears welling in his eyes. Her heart broke as much for him as for herself. It was them that was hurting because some old gangsters wouldn't mind their own goddamned business. She went to him and lowered herself onto the rug at his feet; she placed her head on his knees.

"Nobody, not your uncle or his miserable friends, can ever love you as much as I do—or as much as our little baby will." She looked up beseechingly at him. "Leave them; we can go away. You're a smart man, you'll make money anywhere. I'll work—anything as long as we're together."

"Baby, try to understand," he implored. "All my life, from when I was a little boy, all I wanted was to be in the streets like my uncle Nino. When other kids played ball, I stayed at the club with the wiseguys. I shined their shoes an' washed their cars so they'd like me. When I got older, I robbed an' brought 'em a piece of the money so they'd think I was worth keepin' around—I ate, slept, an' drank this life. Now, finally, I'm on the way up, an' I'm goin' right to the top."

Mudslinger smiled, but it was a joyless smile. "Could you picture me waitin' on the bus stop with a brown paper lunchbag with oil stains? Honey, please, ask me to cut my arm off for you an' I'll do it in a second—I swear, right now; go get a knife—but I can't turn my back on my people or my obligations."

"What about your obligations to us? Don't we count?"

"Of course you do, baby. I'll tell you what," he said with renewed enthusiasm. "If you want, have the kid. I'll make sure you get the best of everything: best doctor, best hospital, prettiest maternity clothes you ever seen. We'll even buy a house somewhere, maybe on the Island, so we could spend a lot of time together with the kid. How's that?" He lit up like a Christmas tree, his grin wide and toothy, his eyes sparkling with vitality.

Connie began to cry again. "Are you so blind? Can't you see that I don't want any fancy maternities? I love you; not part-time, but for always." She bawled uncontrollably.

"Please, I beg you, if you love me like you say, then leave them. Marry me and be a father to our child. Please, oh, please . . ." She clung to him desperately, her head tilted up on his tear-soaked lap, searching his face for the slightest hint of the answer she wanted; the answer she and her baby had to have.

Mudslinger turned his head from Connie. With tears beginning to run from his eyes, too, he said through clenched teeth, "I can't."

Connie rose to her feet and stared at the pathetic-looking figure that she had cherished with all her heart. "I love you very very much—you have no idea—and I feel terribly sorry for you," she whispered, "but I never want to see you again. As far as me and my baby are concerned, you died tonight."

She was already moving away from him when he reached out for her. "Connie, please, don't do this."

Connie ignored Mudslinger's tearful plea. She gathered herself together, then coldly stated, "If you ever cared for me at all, even a little bit, please respect my wishes and never bother either one of us again."

The door slammed shut.

Part
II

23

July 2: West Side, Manhattan

Despite the radio's claim that it was ninety-three degrees, Mickey knew better. The temperature along Eighth Avenue's concrete corridor had to be at least a hundred. While driving northward toward the Port Authority Bus Terminal, ribbons of heat undulated upward from the pavement, distorting his vision of the cars in front.

Thank God for air-conditioning, he thought. With any luck, his mother wouldn't have too much luggage for him to put in the trunk, and he'd be back in the coolness of his new Lincoln Town Car before he had a chance to work up a sweat.

Next to him, Laurel chewed on her cuticles as she had all morning. While looking out the window, she repeated, "I still can't believe you got another white car."

"Well, if I was a cowboy I'd have a white horse, wouldn't I?" Mickey joked. "Besides, black looks too much like a gangster's car."

"I'm sure the company had a few colors in between. You know, the whole world is not black or white."

"Of course it is," he said. "You're either a good guy or a bad guy, an' I'm letting everybody know which one I am. Why, I ain't a good guy?"

"You've certainly decided to show it in a big way. Any bigger and you'd need a bus license to drive it."

Why tell her that since their so-called accident he wanted as much protective bulk in a car as possible, and that in fact he'd already inquired about bulletproof glass? No need. He felt sorry enough for her, and didn't want to give her any additional worries.

Facing his mother again seemed like all Laurel could handle for the

103

moment. No doubt she was exaggerating in her mind what his mother's reaction to her would be, but she believed it and was nonetheless braving it for him. For his part, he would do his best to put her at ease—though he'd had little success thus far.

Continuing in a light vein, he answered, "You never know when things'll get bad and I might need a few fares."

Laurel nodded blankly at his attempted joke, her mind obviously elsewhere.

Mickey took her hand, not surprised to find its palm cold and clammy. "Relax," he said, trying to reassure her with a smile. "Believe me, she's gonna be thrilled to see you."

"Sure, like Jack the Ripper was to see another prostitute."

"What's this bullshit about Jack the Ripper an' goddamn hookers?! I don't wanna hear you mention either one in the same breath with you or my mother again—understand?"

Mickey squeezed her hand affectionately. "Remember what I said about respecting you?" He waited for a response from Laurel, but none came. "I told you everything's gonna be okay with her, and it is. Now, c'mon, give me one of those big smiles I fell in love with."

Laurel forced a wan smile.

They double-parked across from Port Authority's two-block-long brick terminal, where they would have an unobstructed view of the main doors beyond a lineup of yellow cabs.

Devoid of those workers from the adjacent garment center who had left for extended holiday vacations, the area was now dominated by a few scantily clad prostitutes, some tough-looking street hustlers from the Times Square porno district, and huddles of raggedy homeless, who on other weekdays were somewhat camouflaged. In the gated doorway of a closed luncheonette a woman sat on a filthy blanket, primping her unwashed face and hair in a hand-held mirror. Another woman, elegant in a black dress and high heels, and carrying a leather cello case, walked by on the way toward the bus terminal; she didn't give the woman on the floor as much as a second glance. A one-legged black man, clad totally in white, from wide-brimmed hat to patent leather shoe, boogied in his wheelchair.

Mickey couldn't wait to get the hell away from there, and turned his head away.

Laurel, oblivious to the outside, wiped her palms on her white linen slacks, fidgeted with her navy-blue sailor blouse to make sure no buttons had come undone, and checked her hair and makeup again in the car's vanity mirror.

"Wanna soda?" Mickey asked, willing to brave the heat for her. He pointed at an open-front Korean vegetable store. "I'll go see if that joint has a Perrier if you want. Or I could go get you something at the Burger King."

"No, I'm fine, thank you," Laurel snapped.

"You sure? You look like springs an' bolts are gonna start popping out of your ears any minute. Maybe a cold drink'll relax you. I want you in good shape when I knock off all those fireworks in the school yard on the Fourth."

Laurel shook her head, and grumbled, "Peter Pan." After a moment she asked, "You're really going to do that again?"

"Hey, this is my first Fourth of July home. I got six years' worth of fireworks to make up for."

"I remember when I was younger," Laurel said, a nostalgic spark seeming to brighten her mood. "All us kids used to run to the school yard to see you and your friends put on a show. I loved the fancy one that used to burst into multicolored showers—it was like getting lost in a fantasy."

"Well, wait'll you see this year's stuff. I got one that's gonna spell Mickey Boy loves Laurel, all the way from Canarsie to Red Hook—you'll be a shtar, shweetheart," he said in a poor Bogart imitation.

By one o'clock Mickey had teased, joked, and cajoled Laurel into appearing almost normal. She seemed a bit more at ease, which made him feel better about pushing her into the confrontation with his mother. Both women were major pieces in the jigsaw puzzle that would make Mickey Boy Messina a whole person. If he could force them together, he'd be able to concentrate on the last two missing pieces: becoming a made member of the Calabra Family, and having children of his own—kids on whom he could bestow the solid, two-parent family unit he'd yearned for himself but could never have.

Mickey was watching the Port Authority's entrance when, through his peripheral vision, he spotted two familiar figures walking out of the West 40th Street exit onto the avenue: his mother, Connie, accompanied by his brother, Alley.

Laurel spotted them at the same time. "Oh, my God!" she cried.

Before Mickey could tell her that everything would be all right, that he was one hundred percent behind her and it was better that she see Alley and get it over with, Laurel had darted out of the car and was hurrying down Eighth Avenue. When, looking over her shoulder, she spotted Mickey take off after her, she broke into a run.

Mickey ran along the gutter, searching for a spot to cut between the closely parked vehicles that lined the curb; horns blared as cars driving in the lane closest the curb nearly hit him. Finding a space between a taxi and a brown compact, he sped through without losing a step.

He gained on Laurel when, moving frantically, she began to cross

39th Street, saw she couldn't get through the bumper-to-bumper traffic, and instead turned into the block. She smashed into a huge black man covered in layer upon layer of brownish rags, reeled off him, and was headed facefirst toward the pavement when Mickey caught her by the waist and pulled her to him. Their motion flung them against a parked van; Mickey's face scraped the van's sideview mirror; his teeth clamped shut on a piece of his cheek, making him scream out; the vehicle's layer of filth blackened his tan safari suit. Sweat covered his body and ran down his face, the saltiness burning his eyes and the spot where the mirror had broken his skin. As he clung to Laurel, he could feel her heart beating as rapidly as his own.

The man in rags stood a few feet away, shouting obscenities and waving his arms wildly.

"It's all right, baby," Mickey gasped. "It's all right." His face throbbed inside and out.

Laurel struggled against him. "No, no," she cried. "Please let me go."

Mickey shook her. "Laurel, stop! Everything's okay—I'm here with you now."

"Mickey, you don't know," Laurel sobbed. "You just don't know." Energy spent, she seemed to wilt, and melted against him.

"I don't care what he says," Mickey assured her, remembering why Alley had told him he'd dissolved their relationship. "What's done is done. You're my girl now, an' he's gonna treat you like a queen, or else he's gonna deal with me." He lowered his tone, whispering gently, "C'mon, just calm down . . . everything's gonna be okay."

Laurel continued to whimper. "Mickey, no. You just don't know what—"

Suddenly they looked away from each other and at two people in the crowd that had stopped to watch them.

"You!" Alley said accusingly. His features were distorted and the briar pipe he pointed shook; his mother clung to his arm, trying to control him.

Though much younger than Mickey, the moustachioed Alley appeared to be the same age; thick plastic-framed glasses magnified his eyes as angry slits. "I see I was right all along," he continued.

"Please, Alley," Connie begged.

Alley's face was a fiery red. "No," he insisted. "I was right all along about that little tramp."

"Hey, just calm down!" Mickey barked. "You treat her like she was me—an' watch your goddamn mouth!" Laurel tried to pull away from him, but he grabbed her wrist and held it tightly, while adding, "And that's not a request."

The implied threat went right by Alley. "How long have you played with both of us?" he asked. "Since you were fifteen? Fourteen? Or is this just a recent maneuver to exact your revenge against me?"

Connie stepped in front of Alley. While using her body as a buffer between the brothers, she tried to push him back in the direction she and he had come from.

"Is that it?" Alley yelled over his mother's shoulder and pleading voice. "Or was my brother just next in line? Did you already fuck the rest of the neighborhood?"

"Shut up!!" Laurel screamed while struggling to get out of Mickey's grip. "Shut up!!" she repeated hysterically. "You bastard, you have no right to talk—you killed my baby!"

24

July 3: Canarsie, Brooklyn

Used ten- and twenty-dollar bills stood in five-hundred-dollar stacks atop the cast-off wooden desk of Morris Vlasowitz, executive officer of V & V Fruiterers, Ltd.

1:43 P.M. Morris was confident that sometime within the next seventeen minutes Nicky "The Cat" Catapano would march through the doors of the already deserted warehouse to collect his monthly share of V & V's cash profits.

The fact that Nicky The Cat represented the interests of Petey Ross's crime Family didn't disturb Morris one bit; the gang war he'd read they were involved in had nothing to do with him. Besides, if not for the backing the Rossellini mobsters had given him, he would still be supplementing his salary as a Key Food department manager by squeezing petty gratuities from their suppliers. Morris would take his help where he could get it. Who else but racketeers could have provided enough money, open credit lines, and commercial accounts—like catering halls, restaurants, and supermarket chains—to drive a V & V from relative obscurity two years earlier to the third largest purveyor of fresh fruits and vegetables in the Brooklyn Terminal Market.

Morris estimated that by 2:45 he'd be one step ahead of the predicted heavy traffic, and on his way to his new home in Glen Cove for a long, relaxing Fourth of July weekend.

Using the intercom that ran from his mezzanine office to the floor of the distribution area, Morris inquired if the only remaining employee, his son David, was through making sure the walk-in refrigerators' temperatures were properly set for the days to follow.

The eldest of five offspring, David, who at twenty-eight was V & V's accountant and corporate secretary, was the only one allowed to remain with Morris when he met his underworld associates. David answered in the affirmative, that temperatures would keep their products from breaking down without freezing, then climbed the concrete stairs to where his father sat like a modern-day Midas.

Less than five minutes before their appointed meeting, Nicky The Cat pushed through the red swinging doors of the warehouse. He was accompanied by a dark, bony-faced man who Morris knew only as John. Before they had walked ten feet into the building, however, four well-dressed men, holding drawn guns and opened wallets, rushed in behind them.

Morris, looking down on the scene through his office window, pressed the intercom button to hear the conversation. A static-dulled "FBI, nobody move!" filled the room.

"What the fuck is this?" Nicky The Cat shouted in surprise. "Are youse crazy?"

"Nicholas Catapano, John Nicosia, we have warrants for your arrests, and the arrests of Morris and David Valsitz," the officer said, mispronouncing Vlasowitz miserably.

Morris's first thought was of David; he was mortified that his son would be involved in the forthcoming mess. His second concern was for his money. While his visitors were being led at gunpoint upstairs to where he was, he frantically collected the exposed cash and stuffed it into desk drawers.

David ran back and forth like a trapped mouse. "What are we going to do, Pop?" he cried while wringing his hands. "What are we going to do?"

"Calm down," Morris replied. He continued to hide the money. "I'll see if I can talk them into just letting you go—maybe I can pay them."

"Morris and David Vlasowitz?" the lead officer asked when he entered the office. "FBI. You are both under arrest."

"B-but, I, uh, I don't understand," Morris stammered. "What's this all about?"

"You'll find out soon enough." He waved his pistol at the frightened father and son, then, having seen the last part of Morris's attempt to conceal his money, went directly to the drawers and pulled them open.

"What have we got here?" he asked, a sly smirk on his face. "Evidence for the court?"

One of his associates emptied the office trash can onto the carpet and began stuffing the liner with cash.

"Can't we work something out?" Morris begged. "Just for my boy. I swear, I'll never mention the money. You can keep it all."

"You trying to bribe a federal officer?"

"Morris, shut the fuck up!" Nicky The Cat yelled. "Whattaya wanna do, get us another fuckin' charge? Just keep quiet till you see the fuckin' lawyer."

David stood trembling in the corner of the room.

"All right, gentlemen, assume the position against that wall. Let's get this over with and get you downtown."

The two seasoned hoodlums leaned against the indicated wall, faces forward, legs back and apart to facilitate a body search. A .38 revolver was removed from John Nicosia's waistband.

"Is this necessary?" Morris continued to plead while being roughly forced into place with the others. "We have nothing illegal on us."

The response he got was clipped and gruff. "We'll decide what's legal or illegal. You just do what you're told."

When all four men were lined up in a row, the intruders removed silencer-equipped .9mm Browning automatics from their jackets and began to fire. A sound similar to muffled applause accompanied the hollow-tipped shells as they erupted and spread through the four hunched bodies, tearing out huge chunks of flesh as they exited. Screaming, the victims clawed their way down the blood-and-gore-splattered wall that the bullets' impact had forced them against.

The assassins didn't stop firing until their pistols were totally emptied, leaving the lifeless bodies of Morris and David Vlasowitz, Nicky The Cat, and John Nicosia slumped together in thick crimson pools.

Before they slipped out into the brilliant July sunshine, Junior Vallo's gunmen carefully removed all traces of their fingerprints, spilled kerosene around the office, and from the top of the stairway tossed in a lit book of matches.

25

July 4: Sheepshead Bay, Brooklyn

Mickey Boy slammed the receiver down in its cradle. For nearly two days Laurel had refused to come to the phone or see him when he'd gone to her door. The last he'd seen of her was when she'd jumped into a cab on 39th Street. He could have kicked himself later for letting her get away, but he had been so shocked by her charges at Alley that he'd loosened his grip on her wrist enough for her to bolt.

Still clad in his underwear, Mickey Boy poured himself a cup of yesterday's coffee, then climbed up onto one of his barstools that served as kitchen chairs. For two days he'd been miserable, caught between what he knew from years in the streets that he should do and what he considered his irrational caring for a girl he was better off without. Sinatra was probably right on the money when he sang, *Let her go, let her go, let her go.*

Mickey was haunted by Alley's angry countercharges when he'd gone after him: *She's a little tramp . . . she went to bed with all my friends and then told me the baby was mine. . . . Instead of blaming me for her goddamned abortion, she should have thanked me. . . . You let her make a fool of you.* It was a good thing their mother had been between them.

Depressed, and not wanting to be alone, Mickey Boy decided to stop by Buster's club. After three weeks of disobeying the order to make an appearance once a week, he figured he'd be sent for sooner or later anyway, and felt it better that he show up without being summoned.

The possibility of making the trip all the way to Manhattan only to find an empty club didn't enter Mickey Boy's mind—holidays were no different from other days for the membership of the Lower Manhattan Fishing Association, who for the most part were gainfully unemployed. The only exception the regulars made for weekends and holidays was to break up their card games and bullshit sessions and leave before sunset for the benefit of their wives and girlfriends. He estimated his arrival at about two P.M.—plenty of time.

The trip to Manhattan annoyed him. Despite the upbeat sounds of Sinatra's "Come Fly with Me" resounding throughout his car, Mickey Boy's mind kept wandering back to the disastrous meeting two days before. He was angry at everyone: at Laurel for letting herself be used so sickeningly—and for using him; at Alley for acting like such a spoiled brat in spite of all Mickey'd done for him since Albert, Sr., had passed away; at his mother for coddling Alley and returning to Boston with him, while leaving Mickey alone on a street corner—he was her son and needed someone too. Most of all, however, Mickey Boy was angry at himself—for being weak. When "The Lady Is a Tramp" came on, he shut the tape player.

After parking in Beansy's lot on Baxter Street, Mickey Boy walked around the corner and up Mulberry Street toward the club. Despite the fact that the Fourth of July was a holiday that normally sent people away from the city in droves, Little Italy was bustling with tourists and neighborhood people. Acquaintances of his from Don Peppino's clan were seated in the shade of Cinzano umbrellas outside the European-style Cafe Napoli; he waved to them but didn't stop.

When he reached Buster's club, Mickey Boy hesitated for a moment, tempted to forgo his convoluted method of entering, but resisted. Instead, he followed the procedure Buster had given him and went through the Sicilian restaurant next door, into the connected backyards, and finally in through the rear of the Lower Manhattan Fishing Association.

Buster sat in the same spot as always, surrounded by his pinochle cronies, a fistful of cards clutched in a tight fan before him. If not for the fact that the burly wiseguy wore different clothing from their last meeting, Mickey Boy thought with amusement, it would have appeared as though he had never left his chair.

Unlike other times he had visited, Mickey Boy was not kept waiting. Almost immediately, Buster gave his cards to a bystander and removed himself from the game.

"Where the fuck you been?!" Buster shouted on his way over. "I was ready to send the troops out after ya. You know, the way bodies are droppin', if I don't see one of my men for a couple of days, I start to worry . . . an' you stay away for three fuckin' weeks!"

"I'm alive."

"Well, if Richie didn't tell me, how the fuck would I know? An' then he tells me you was in an accident." He led Mickey Boy toward an empty table near the front, signaling for coffee as they walked.

"The accident was nothing, just some jerkoff speeding on a wet road," Mickey Boy lied. He was still bothered by the mask, but couldn't think of why anyone would want to kill him. Could it have been Laurel they were after? An old boyfriend? Maybe it was just a psycho who had a thing for rubber faces and whose path just happened to cross theirs—not likely.

He also didn't believe his accident had anything to do with the war between the murdered John-John's Family and Petey Ross's, and told Buster so. "Even that guy Johnny Pumps that got thrown off the balcony in Jersey an' the guys I saw on the news this morning that got blown away in Canarsie were with Petey Ross. Besides, nobody we know could do such a bum job. If anybody wanted to croak me, I'd'a been laid out in Torregrossa's that night."

"Listen to Buster, an' you'll live to be an old man: There's nothing in the streets that's between just two crews," the mob veteran lectured. "You never know when it could spill over an' affect us." He poked a hard finger into Mickey Boy's chest. "Don't you become the first sign that it happened. Besides, anytime something like that's goin' on, it's open season for guys to settle old beefs an' drop bodies around." He laughed. "Drives the law crazy, tryin' to figure out who's with who."

After repeating his warning once more, Buster brought up the subject of the collections from Georgie The Hammer and Skinny Malone for Little Vinnie.

Mickey Boy's insides twisted at the mention of the don's son. He did his best not to grimace as he asked, "Ain't you been getting it? I sent the last couple of weeks with Richie."

Buster had received the money all right, but to Mickey Boy's surprise, relieved him from picking it up anymore. Petey Ross's men were just too hot, he claimed, especially for someone on parole to be around. "I ain't like most good fellas—I look out for my men," he boasted.

"That I know," Mickey Boy agreed. As far as he was concerned, one of Buster's few good characteristics was his caring and strong defense of his men—even in situations where they were wrong. Buster was reputed to have never lost a man to a mob execution, though he'd had a few "on the carpet."

"And as for not showing up, you know the beef I had with my P.O.," Mickey Boy added. "The only reason I took a chance today is because I figured with the holiday and all there'd be no law around—even the feds gotta rest sometimes."

"Don't believe it. They're like fuckin' cockaroaches, all over the place. But as long as you listen to me an' come in through the Focacceria, they could go an' fuck themselves!"

Buster leaned back in his seat and stared at Mickey Boy; the look in his eye was strange, not the look of anger over an underling not reporting, but one bordering on amusement.

Mickey Boy felt the same disquieting sensation as he had just before his parole officer had tried to trap him. Was there anything he'd done on his own that Buster might have discovered? Some deal he'd started and not put on record?

"I know all about your problems with the P.O.," Buster finally said. "But you're gonna hafta start spendin' a lot more time with me anyway."

Here comes the move to find out what I've got going, Mickey Boy thought. *Why the hell did I have to come here today?*

Just then, Little Vinnie Calabra came out of the back room with Muffin-Face and his other stooge in tow. Leaving the two men behind, he walked to the table where Mickey Boy and Buster sat. "Is it okay if I sit down, or is it private?" he asked.

To Mickey Boy's irritation, Buster invited Little Vinnie to join them. He then turned back to Mickey Boy. "I don't know if you heard it yet, but we're openin' the books again soon, an' I'm proposin' you to be made."

This was one time that street gossip had failed. Word on the street was that Don Vincenze and Don Peppino had closed the Mafia rolls to new members for the next few years, and because of that Mickey Boy was caught totally off guard by Buster's announcement. His head began to spin. Had Buster actually said those words—words he'd waited what seemed like a lifetime to hear?

Outside of a slight detour in his youth, it had been a straight, single-minded run for Mickey Boy up the mob ladder. The detour was Nicolo Fonte.

Short and wide—not fat, but just wide, looking as though he'd been pressed, front and back, in a giant vise—with a warm, fatherly moustache, balding head, and sympathetic brown eyes; an *avvocato*, one of those storefront attorneys who gained their only riches from being the singular hope for the poor in their immigrant Italian communities to get justice; not a lawyer, but a self-described "man of the people." That was Nicolo Fonte.

Mickey Boy could still see the weary faces of Nicolo's clients: Mrs. Cangiano in her uniform of black mourning, trying to collect some back money for a husband killed in a pier accident in 1941; Mr. Scarputti, gentle old shoemaker, being evicted so his new landlord could double the rent; husbandless Anna Gela, a black-haired beauty, arrested for assaulting the manager of a carpet store, who had taken scrimped welfare dollars for her baby Anthony's linoleum floor, then refused to replace it when the linoleum proved inferior and cracked.

Mickey Boy had admired Nicolo Fonte, almost loved him like a father; swept his floors and cleaned the cigar slime from his ashtray; wanted to be an *avvocato* too; wanted to be a "man of the people."

But then, suddenly, Nicolo had turned on him. One day, for no apparent reason, the *avvocato* had lost the patience and nurturing that had made the twelve-year-old boy nearly love him. The visions he'd planted in Mickey Boy's head of going to college, then law school, became a nightmare as Nicolo ranted and raved, cursed and insulted— laughed at him, saying how did a dumb guinea kid, one who was lucky he could tie his shoelaces, ever really believe he could become a lawyer—and finally, threw him out.

Mickey Boy then turned back to the streets. And from the first time he'd understood the hierarchy of those streets, he'd worked toward one goal, and one goal only: to participate in the blood and fire ceremony that would initiate him as a made member of the largest non-uniformed army in the world.

To him, as to all the other aspiring mafiosi around the country, becoming a good fella, or wiseguy, was more than just formal entry into a criminal organization. It meant they had reached the epitome of honor and respect, and would be considered equals to those more infamous members whom they'd only heard of or read about: Lucky Luciano, Frank Costello, Vito Genovese. Now Mickey Boy would be one of them—a man who was no longer a dog tolerated or respected for his master, a man whose word counted in mob sitdowns, a man who could someday be boss, a don.

When Buster shook his hand and kissed him to seal their new relationship, Mickey Boy threw his arm around the older man's neck and gave him a sincere, bruising hug.

Little Vinnie sat quietly, his thick lips pursed, his cheek muscles rippling.

Seeing the anger the don's son was trying to hide gave Mickey Boy an added measure of satisfaction. *I hope they don't make that little shit too*, he thought.

Feeling better than he had in days, he hugged Buster again. "What can I say but thanks?"

"You don't have to thank me," his boss answered. "I told ya from the first day ya came here that you was a good man. I had that thing in my head when I took you on, but to be honest, I didn't think the books would open up this soon myself. When Vincenze asked me if I wanted to get anybody straightened out, the first thing I did was propose you an' Richie."

"Richie too? That's great! I'm so shocked, I don't know what to say."

"Don't say nothin'," Buster answered. "You ain't in yet." He turned to Little Vinnie, stared at him for a moment, then snapped, "Well, ain't you gonna congratulate him?"

"Sure," Little Vinnie said. His eyes were fiery pin dots as he shook Mickey Boy's hand and kissed him on both cheeks; Mickey Boy squeezed Vinnie's hand until those eyes became watery.

Buster seemed not to notice the enmity between the two young men, and continued speaking. Because of the war between the Rossellini and Vallo factions, he said, no one would actually be given official membership immediately. The two dons were using the promised inductions as a bargaining chip to end the hostilities; only then would the weaker *borgatas*, or Families, be permitted to grow.

When disappointment shrouded Mickey Boy's face, the burly mafioso offered some encouragement. "Don't worry, it'll happen," he said. "Anyway, you're in a different class now than you was before. When I introduce you around to other good fellas as a proposed guy, they'll give you all the respect like you was already made. Once it cleared with the old man, it was like you already had it." With a snap of his fingers he added, "He okayed you an' Richie like that!"

"Don Vincenze went on your say-so?"

Buster laughed. "Well, not exactly, now. Sure, he trusts what I say, but believe me, he knows more about every guy connected with this crew than their own mothers. If you got a boil on your ass, Vincenze knows about it, and what to do about it."

Little Vinnie, unable to control himself any longer, blurted out, "What about me?"

"You know that's up to your old man," Buster replied with an accompanying shake of his head. "An' before you aks," he said, mispronouncing the word *ask* in Brooklynese, "he ain't told me nothin' yet."

"Excuse me," Little Vinnie said, and left the table.

Buster made a sour face as he watched the don's son walk away, then continued. He explained that they had to wait for word back from all the Families that no present members objected to either his or Richie's induction, and that they would additionally have to check both their natural families all the way back to Italy. "You ain't a half-breed or nothin', are ya?" he teased.

"No way," Mickey Boy answered seriously. "One hundred percent guinea blood in this kid."

Buster smiled. He told Mickey Boy a story about an associate of theirs who they had almost inducted, then discovered was half Greek. Had they already brought him in, Buster said, they would have been honor bound to kill him in order to reverse the error. Some Families, he added, wanted to allow membership if only the father was Italian— but not Don Vincenze's. "My God," he said with a huff. "I remember when you had to be Sicilian to get in. Next they'll wanna bring Jews in . . . or *tootsoones*, if they're light-skinned an' the nigger blood's on their mother's side."

When Buster had exhausted his lesson on mob induction policies, he turned to the subject of him and Mickey Boy spending more time together. "You know, you really got lucky," he said with a laugh. "Between havin' to be careful of your P.O. an' the war goin' on, I can't break your balls too much."

Having fun at the expense of a proposed new member was a mob tradition, Buster said. "My guy used to call me out in my pajamas, four o'clock in the morning, just to teach me that our loyalty to each other comes before our own family or anything else."

His reminiscence made him laugh out loud. "One time he calls me on Christmas Eve, just when I'm sittin' down to eat . . . all the fish— calamari, scungilli, shrimp—was on the table, nice an' hot an' callin' me. But I hadda go, so I get dressed an' run over his house. When I get there, he gives me a paper an' tells me I gotta go pick up somethin' for him. I aks him do I need a *pistola* with me, an' he tells me yeah."

Mickey Boy couldn't fathom the humor in being called away from the most important holiday dinner of the year.

"Well, here I am, with the loaded piece in my pocket," Buster continued. "I get to the place, an' another good fella that I know hands me a pint of spumoni an' tells me to make sure I get it back to my man before it melts." He became hysterical with laughter. "Boy, was my wife mad as a sonomabitch. We was just newlyweds, an' she didn't talk to me for a week."

When he had stopped laughing, Buster cautioned Mickey Boy that there were, however, downsides to formal button-man status, one of which was their superiors' intolerance of errors. "Once you're in, there's no second chances," he said. "Fuck up, an' you wind up with your head air-conditioned like that!" He snapped his fingers again.

Nothing Buster could possibly have said would have diminished Mickey Boy's enthusiasm. He'd eaten, drunk, and slept being a wiseguy from the first moment he'd learned that they were the men hanging around the local social clubs who wore monogrammed shirts and alligator shoes. When his adoptive father, Al Messina, was driving a cab day and night to give him twenty-five cents at a time spending money, they were handing out five-dollar bills to kids who cleaned their brand-new cars or brought them sandwiches from the nearby deli. He'd made up his mind then that he'd never be a crumb, a sucker like Al—or a phony hard-on like Nicolo Fonte.

And now, after twenty years of dedication, six of them in prison, neither threat of death nor physical torture would change his mind.

"I don't care if I gotta carry a *ton* of spumoni on my back *every* Christmas Eve, or walk a tightrope over fire for the rest of my life," he said. "I want in!"

Buster smiled. "That's what I figured you'd say. You never met Don Vincenze, did ya?"

Mickey Boy hated to admit he'd never met their Family's boss, though that was the old man's style, to insulate himself from underlings. "No, but I seen him around," he said. "Don't worry, though, I won't embarrass you an' not recognize him."

"Thank God for little favors," Buster teased. "Vincenze is a great guy; you'll see, you're gonna love him. An' now that you're gonna be one of us, he'll probably wanna see you soon."

"Just say the word, an' I'll be there . . . I'll drop everything," Mickey Boy vowed.

"Any questions?"

There was little information about mob life or procedures that Mickey Boy lacked. As he had with sex, the future button-man had learned the ins and outs of their subculture from war stories—gossip—exchanged among his peers; he never forgot anything about either subject.

There was one thing that bothered him, however. "What's gonna happen between you an' me?" he asked. If Mickey Boy was going to be Buster's equal, he would have to be assigned to a captain, or skipper, to whom he would answer directly. It was bad enough getting used to one guy. Now, after finding out that Buster wasn't as bad as he'd previously thought, that despite his undisguised avarice could be gotten around easily, he'd have to start fresh with some unknown quantity. It was exactly like what he hated most about jail: No matter how adverse the conditions, after a while he, like every other inmate, would get used to where they were, would learn to get around the worse aspects of the location, when, wham, they'd be packed up and shipped to another joint, where they'd have to adjust to new administrative quirks and rules.

Buster grinned in response to Mickey Boy's concern about them parting company. "Don't worry, you an' me's a team. The day you get in is the day I go back to bein' a skipper. I get my regime back," he said, referring to the group of soldiers assigned to each captain, "an' youse two are in it. We're goin' up the ladder together: you, me, an' Richie."

Mickey Boy was as happy for Buster as he was for himself and Richie. Along with just about everyone he knew, he couldn't figure out why someone with a reputation like Buster's had been brought down in rank in the first place.

At that moment any problems that Mickey Boy might have had before he entered the club—Laurel, rubber-masked assassins, Spositoro—were the furthest things from his mind.

"You play pinochle?" Buster asked when they got up from the table.

"Does a bear shit in the woods?"

"Good, sit down an' play a few hands so's I could win some of that money you an' Richie been hidin' from me," Buster said with a wink.

It was nearly three hours later when Mickey Boy was on his way out of the club by the back route. Little Vinnie stood in the kitchen with his two GITs—gangsters in training.

"Drive carefully," Little Vinnie called, his smile forced and taut. "I heard you almost got run off the highway."

Mickey Boy spun around. No one, not even Richie, knew he was pushed into the rail. All he'd said was that the car was hit. The challenging glare in Little Vinnie's eyes confirmed his suspicion.

Not now, Mickey Boy told himself. Between the good in his life, like being proposed for his button, and the bad, like the problem with Laurel that was tearing his mind apart, it was not the time to make a rash move. He'd take care of Little Vinnie another time; do what he should have done as soon as he'd been released from prison. *Chiana, chiana, met en ghoule!*

Slamming the door loudly behind him, Mickey Boy left.

26

July 4: Little Italy, Manhattan

Dressed like a tourist from Lake Woebegon, in denim shorts, a red baseball cap, dark glasses, and an I Love New York T-shirt, Arnold Selkower felt as though he'd covered every centimeter of blistering concrete within sight of the Lower Manhattan Fishing Association. His feet burned and his body was sticky with hours of accumulated perspiration.

Arnold cursed those mobsters whose latest round of warfare kept him from spending this holiday in the above-ground pool of his Douglaston home. With each new Mafia-connected body discovered in the metropolitan area came an increase in forced overtime for him and his fellow agents: weekends, nights, holidays—nothing was sacred. As far as Arnold was concerned, the Justice Department would better serve the public's interest by allowing the racketeers to eliminate each other without interference.

Arnold checked his watch. He'd wait until 2:05 before leaving to join his wife, Sylvia; that way the Bureau would get all it had coming from his half-day assignment.

At 2:08 P.M. Arnold started down Mulberry Street toward the Chinatown side, where his car was parked. He hadn't moved ten feet when he found himself face-to-face with someone who set off alarms in his memory bank. An instinctual curiosity about the well-dressed young man who'd entered the restaurant next door to the Lower Manhattan Fishing Association a few weeks earlier and stayed for over two hours prompted Arnold to change his direction and follow.

Arnold lifted the Canon AE-1 that hung from his neck and snapped three profiles of the young man as once again he approached and entered the Focacceria Villarosa. Even though the restaurant was not the focus of Arnold's surveillance, something about its latest customer bothered him, and he decided to investigate further—with a Mafia war in progress, any small lead could prove significant.

After waiting five minutes so as not to attract the suspected mobster's attention, Special Agent Selkower stepped into the Italian eatery; the appetizing aroma of garlic-filled specialties that greeted him when he was barely through the door made his mouth water.

A quick scan of the dining room told Arnold that his subject wasn't there. Chances were he was in the men's room, which Arnold considered a lucky break. While the young hood might cautiously watch the front door for lawmen or rival hit men, he would be oblivious to an already seated tourist who was dressed like a nerd.

Parched and hungry, he took a seat where he could observe the entire area, possibly sneak a couple of photos of his subject and whoever else he would be meeting, and grab a bite to eat. Though Arnold was sometimes an epicurean adventurer, like being the first in his crowd to try sushi, when he learned that the Focacceria's daily specials included half a sheep's head, cow's intestines in red sauce, and sliced-up lungs on a bun, he opted for nothing more exotic than pepperoni pizza and a Coke.

After another half hour had elapsed with no sign of his man, and the waiter had made it clear that his welcome was worn thin, Arnold decided to unobtrusively examine the premises. The first place he looked was the rest room. He prepared himself for an encounter with a mini Mafia convention in progress along the urinals, or to find the young man he was looking for murdered in one of the toilet stalls. All he found, however, was an empty lavatory.

From there Arnold explored the narrow passageway that led to a rear exit. Without making the slightest sound, he opened the metal door and poked his head through—directly into the chest of one of two monstrous goons who were about to enter the restaurant.

"Aaii!! What the fuck you lookin' for?" the hood demanded; his unshaven jaw was pushed forward and his fists were readied for action.

The last thing Arnold wanted was to have to flash a badge to save himself from being battered into the ground. "Oh, excuse me," he whined. "I thought I could go out this way and get to the next block."

The two giants eyed him suspiciously.

Why didn't I go home to Sylvia at two o'clock? Arnold demanded of himself. His fingers moved tentatively to his shorts pocket to feel for his wallet.

"Be a nice fella an' get the fuck outta here the way you come in," the larger of the two growled. "Don't be no fuckin' Daniel Boone."

"Yes sir!" Arnold yelled over his shoulder while hurrying toward the front. Not only was he grateful to be leaving with his body and investigation intact, he was exploding with joy at having solved the mystery of the disappearing hoodlum.

Even the threat of Sylvia's ire couldn't dissuade him from rushing off to his office to develop the pictures of the two monsters that had confronted him in the backyard—when they had entered the Lower Manhattan Fishing Association earlier that day.

Arnold saw no need to wait for the other young man to leave.

27

July 4: Flatbush, Brooklyn

The acrid scent of burnt gunpowder filled Mickey Boy's nostrils, but after being deprived of it for six years in prison it smelled pleasingly sweet. It was just like the first time he'd gotten hold of real garlic in jail, after being there for about two years. For twenty-four hours after using it to cook a sauce in the unit coffee urn, he'd refused to wash his hands, touching his fingertips to his nostrils constantly to savor the odor as if it were the finest perfume.

Mickey Boy lit another rocket and sent it whistling skyward, invisible against the black night until it burst open into an umbrellalike shower of hot pink sparkles. The deafening cacophony of exploding firecrackers nearby helped him escape into a special mindlessness of his own, a relief from thoughts of Laurel. Off on other blocks ashcans and cherry bombs thundered mercilessly.

As he had intermittently, Mickey Boy scanned the crowd of mostly teenage faces for Laurel's. It wasn't there. Why couldn't she be there to share the joy he'd felt at Buster's news? Why did he have to be tied up with someone who'd gone with his brother? There were thousands, no, goddamned millions of broads out there that would half die to have a guy like him nuts about them: girls without ties to his family, girls who wouldn't care what he did for a living, or break his balls. Who the hell needed this shit anyway?

Before launching another projectile heavenward, Mickey Boy checked the street again—no Laurel.

"Mickey, are they crazy, or what?" a female voice shouted only inches from his ear. Mickey Boy turned to Linda Agrigento, whose husband, Chink, had finally been released on bail after the visit Richie and Mickey Boy had paid to his attorney. She pointed at Richie and Chink, who were filling a large silver garbage pail with fireworks they intended to detonate all at once.

"Nah, they're just big kids," Mickey Boy replied. Looking at Linda's heavily swollen abdomen, he laughingly added, "Little Chink's gonna have some competition for his toys."

At least Chink would be home when Linda gave birth to their first child, Mickey Boy thought. Hopefully, the baby's arrival would be what Chink needed to get him out of dabbling in the street life, a life he didn't have the cunning to survive in.

While he was happy for the couple, Mickey'd felt a pang of jealousy when he had greeted Linda with a kiss, and had felt her baby-filled body press against his. He thought again of Laurel's last words as she was running away, felt the pain in her voice. How long, he wondered, till they could straighten out their lives—or, was he really getting a break? He'd probably be better off without her anyway.

Whore . . . putana . . . tramp! Why did the only girl he'd ever really cared about have to turn out like that?

He lit another rocket.

Hours later, the night almost over, Mickey Boy checked his inventory and saw that there were only a few more assorted fireworks left. Chink and Linda had gone home, leaving him and Richie to entertain the few stragglers that remained. Feeling the same type of melancholia that usually overcame him when he heard Sinatra sing *A quarter to three . . . there's no one in the place, except you an' me . . .* Mickey Boy grabbed a twinkling star out of the box.

Then he saw her.

Laurel stood alone at the outside of the yard's chain-link fence, her fingers entwined in the rusted metal wire. An unnecessary white cotton blazer rested on her shoulders above navy slacks and a red halter top.

"Here, finish these off," Mickey Boy told Richie, and started toward her.

Laurel didn't move.

As Mickey reached her, pastel pinks, yellows, and blues shone on her face, reflections of a rocket burst Richie had sent up. Far from enhancing her features, the colors accented weary circles under her eyes and shadowed tense muscles around her lipstickless mouth.

"I couldn't miss the first good fireworks show here in six years," Laurel said. She spoke softly while staring beyond him. "They're beautiful."

"I'm glad you like 'em . . . you okay?"

"I'll live." Laurel turned and walked slowly toward the far corner of the block; Mickey fell in alongside her. They continued, not talking or touching, until Laurel grabbed on to a lamppost with a slew of names painted over it. Mickey leaned against a parked car.

"Oh, Mickey." Laurel sighed. "There's so much to tell you, and I don't even know where to start . . . much less what I really want to say."

Mickey said nothing. He watched Laurel's tortured face, the reflected pain that, he thought, was no less than he himself felt inside.

"I remember when I'd want to get away from the whole gang at the school yard, and wander down here by myself," Laurel said, looking upward as though she were talking to either the heavens or herself.

"Alley would always find me hanging around this lamppost, and accuse me of sneaking off to meet someone." She laughed. "How stupid he was . . . and how smart."

Turning to Mickey, she said, "You know he accused me then of having an affair with you . . . or at least wanting to . . . like he did the other day. I guess he knew me better than I knew myself."

"Laurel, listen—"

"No, please. Let me get what I can out, or I may never be able to again." Laurel smiled sadly. "This is two days' courage." She continued, rambling on first about how her mortification at hearing that she was pregnant had turned to joy, then about the sacrifices she'd been prepared to make for the baby and her future with Alley.

While Laurel spoke, Alley's bitter accusations rang in Mickey Boy's ears. *I didn't know whose it was . . . She went to bed with all my friends . . . Who knew how many guys she was sleeping with?* He wanted to ask her about them, confront her once and for all, but couldn't bring himself to.

Laurel went on to explain how adamantly against her having the child Alley had been, how he'd argued that he couldn't finish school knowing she would be in Brooklyn with their baby while he was up in Cambridge. He'd sworn, begged, reasoned: There would be other babies for them; he loved her and would marry her as soon as he graduated. "He promised me castles in the sky . . . but I had to get rid of the baby. That was his one condition."

Mickey saw the shimmer of tears running down Laurel's face as she spoke. *Who else did you go to bed with?* was in the front of his mind and on the tip of his tongue. *He called you a whore . . . a fuckin' tramp. . . .*

"That day I was like a zombie," Laurel said, lowering her voice even more. "All I remember was when they laid me on the table and put my legs in the stirrups that I was crying, and the nurse asked me if I was sure that was what I wanted to do. I wanted to scream no! but didn't. Instead, I shook my head yes and cried like an idiot while they killed my child. I was brought up Catholic, but I kept telling myself I was doing it for Alley . . . for us . . . and that was more important, and that we'd have dozens more." She stared directly into Mickey's eyes. "It didn't work . . . not in my mind or my conscience. I made Communion and Confirmation, went to church every week . . . until then. I can't bear taking the Host in my mouth; I can't defile it."

Mickey felt helpless and clumsy. He wanted to touch her, but was afraid to. Instead, he just stared, waiting to hear the rest.

Laurel stared back at him for a moment, then said, "I'm so sorry for what I did to you."

"Honey, please, you got nothing to apologize to me for." In his mind Mickey added, *If you hurt anybody, it's you, not me.*

"No, no," Laurel insisted. "I've been so guilty." She paused, then blurted out, "Alley was right, I used you to hurt him."

It was as if a knife had pierced Mickey's heart. How could she? All her words of love . . . of passion . . . nights in bed . . . her mouth all over him. All lies! The old-timers in the street were right. *Putana sì . . . whore that you are!* he screamed inwardly. His temples pounded and his throat was so dry it felt as though he might suffocate.

Laurel threw her hands up in despair and added, "I didn't know I'd fall in love with you though."

Mickey slumped back on the car, thoroughly confused by her changes and his own vacillating emotions.

"That first night, when I asked you to meet me, it was to use you, to eventually get you to bring me to where Alley was so I could humiliate him and make him eat his heart out . . . make him sorry he'd treated me the way he did." Laurel shrugged helplessly, tears streaming down her cheeks. "But then I realized he'd been right all along, that it really was always you—when I had a crush on you as a girl; when I tingled if you even touched me innocently; and when I used to fantasize that it was you in bed with me instead of Alley. I made all the excuses to myself, Mickey, but it was always you. I'm so sorry I tried to use you."

Mickey couldn't remember either of them moving, yet there she was, wrapped tightly in his arms; kissing, crying, and rambling on. "I traveled all the way to Cambridge by bus and tried to find him at Winthrop Hall, where he was living. Someone mentioned a bar called the Boathouse in Harvard Square, so I went over there. That's when I saw him with *her*." Laurel bit her lower lip, then continued. Alley had laughed at her, called her vile names and said she'd slept with all his friends back home. He'd claimed it was Mickey Boy she'd always wanted anyway, that she'd probably had sex with him too.

Laurel pushed herself back at arm's length to stare into Mickey's eyes. "Mickey, I swear," she said. "I had never even kissed anyone but him . . . and if he hadn't pushed me, threatened to go elsewhere if I didn't give it to him, I wouldn't have gone to bed with him either."

Clutching Mickey again, she began to cry. "I felt like I wanted to die. Everything he had told me was a lie . . . just to kill my baby so he could marry her."

Mickey wanted to cry himself—for joy. He squeezed Laurel so hard he felt her gasp.

"That's enough, baby," he said. "Forget anybody you knew after him. Both our lives started when we started loving each other." He kissed her again. "Like they say in jail: Everything else is history."

"That's another thing," Laurel sobbed. "Mickey, I can't . . . jail is always . . ."

"I don't want to hear it. Not tonight," Mickey said. "Tonight I just wanna go home . . . an' from now on I want it to be our home. I want you there with me all the time."

28

July 14: Todt Hill, Staten Island

An early morning breeze, thick with a preview of the day's stifling humidity, carried the scent of grassy dew through the open window of the Eldorado and into Little Vinnie's nostrils. After a night of partying, which began at Jimmy Weston's early in the evening, moved to Club A as heavy doses of Stolichnaya and tonic took effect, and wound up in a drunken ménage in the Rego Park apartment of two Air France stewardesses, Vinnie needed outdoor sounds and smells to keep him awake. As it was, he had dozed at a red light on Lefferts Boulevard and was snapped out of it only by the screams of angry horns behind him.

Little Vinnie was surprised to find his father had visitors at that early hour. Before his mother had died, he remembered, there were always well-dressed men waiting in the kitchen for the don to make his entrance, wrapped in the old maroon terry robe that he'd refused to part with despite the constant urging of his wife; she'd bought him three others that hung unworn in his closet. Since that time, however, any meeting before noon meant something extraordinarily important was up. Squeezing past Buster's Buick and Joe Augusta's funeral limousine, Vinnie made his way toward the front door.

Even though wiseguys expected their daughters' husbands to drink and discreetly fool around with other women, Little Vinnie wanted to make a good impression on Joe Augusta, and tried to straighten himself out before he entered the house. He wasn't doing at all well with Chrissy on his own, and could certainly use some help from her father. If anyone would understand the value of a marriage between a don's son and an underboss's daughter, it would be Joe.

At that moment Little Vinnie decided to spend the afternoon at Manhattan Beach, where he was sure Chrissy would be. As he fumbled with the door's lock, he pictured Chrissy as he'd seen her three days before. He'd gone to the beach to collect a gambling debt from a new customer who worked at the seaside's food concession. A hardness began to form between his legs as he remembered a barefoot Chrissy prancing up to the food stand for a hot dog and a Coke. Nothing had stood between his hungry stare and her nude body but a few skimpy centimeters of bright yellow fabric and a network of matching strings. He envisioned the droplets of moisture that had dotted her cleavage. Even his wildest daydreams of her were no match for how magnificent she really looked without her clothes. What he wouldn't give to see the rest of her, he thought.

The kitchen was empty when Little Vinnie got there, still thinking about the raven-haired teenager. He looked out into the rambling back-yard, with its orange and white terrazzo patio, matching gazebo, and Olympic-size pool, but no one was there either.

A flash of alarm shot through Little Vinnie's tired body. Maybe his father had taken ill, while he himself was out whoring, and was in his bedroom with his two top lieutenants; maybe he had already died. *Daddy!* Little Vinnie screamed inwardly as he hurried to the basement door to check their little-used den before climbing the stairs to his father's bedroom.

Sure enough, the door to the opulent Spanish-style basement was ajar; male voices floated up the staircase. Relieved, Little Vinnie sank back against the doorjamb.

Despite his original intention of making a grand entrance, a silent voice told him to remain where he was and eavesdrop on the mafiosi's conversation instead.

It wasn't long until Little Vinnie was able to piece together a picture of Machiavellian scheming and manipulation as the don and his un-derlings reviewed and charted the course of the Rossellini–Vallo war. For nearly half an hour the future mafioso listened to the brilliantly diabolical revelations of how his father had engineered John-John's car being bombed by his own people, how he'd set up Petey Ross to be falsely blamed for the murder, and how, with Don Peppino's aid, he'd restrained Petey Ross so that Junior Vallo's killers could gain an advantage.

Little Vinnie smiled as his father's voice, strong and commanding over those of Buster and Joe Augusta, who seemed to be the only one who hadn't supported what was going on, detailed plans for how the war should proceed and eventually end. That was how he himself would have to think if he were ever to fill the old man's shoes and become the next generation's Don Vincenze. It had been the ultimate stroke of good fortune to have happened upon the meeting, he thought. *Destiny!*

"Now for our final task," Don Vincenze continued. "About my son . . . this is what we must do. . . ."

Little Vinnie eagerly pressed his ear to the opening; his heart beat so strongly, he was afraid they would hear it downstairs. This was it: the beginning.

Suddenly Little Vinnie's face turned ashen. "No . . . oh, no," he muttered, trying not to believe his own ears. Head spinning, he reeled through the front door toward his car. Everything he'd hoped and prayed for since he was old enough to realize that his father was different from those of his friends—that he was special—all of it was going down the drain. In one brief moment the don's son had learned that his world was about to be shattered, that his very existence was being threatened with destruction.

While racing along the Staten Island Expressway toward the Verrazano Bridge, Little Vinnie Calabra made up his mind that he wouldn't go down without a fight. He would battle to the end, using every bit of the guile and ruthlessness he'd inherited in his blood—and he'd have to begin immediately.

Foot to the floor, he sped toward the familiar streets of Bensonhurst, where he would gather his thoughts—and troops. He'd teach them all . . . even his fuckin' old man!

29

July 23: Sheepshead Bay, Brooklyn

Laurel rolled the second Trojan over Mickey's hardened penis.

"For Christ's sake," he muttered, his eyes rolling up at the ceiling. "There's gotta be a better way . . . I hate these goddamn things, an' you got me wearing them in sets. I don't like this."

"Relax, you will," Laurel smilingly ordered from between his open legs. "You know if I could take the pill, I would. Then we wouldn't have to worry about accidents."

"Whattaya mean we?" he muttered.

Ignoring Mickey's grumblings, Laurel completed her task of jacketing him. Once done, she straddled his hips, then slowly lowered herself, engulfing his erection as she moved. "Now," she moaned while tightening her vaginal muscles around him. "Isn't this good?"

With her eyes closed and her pelvis undulating rhythmically over his, Laurel whispered throatily, "In *The Joy of Sex* they call this Riding St. George. From now on that's what I'm going to call him," she said, emitting a soft groan. "St. George . . . or, maybe, St. Michael."

The Joy of Sex . . . More Joy of Sex . . . Great Sex . . . Fantasex. All Mickey had heard from Laurel in the two weeks they had been living together were quotes from erotic manuals she claimed to have devoured after Alley'd left, in order to make herself a more desirable female. "I swore to myself," she sobbed that first night, "that no guy was ever going to dump me again. I was going to be the dump*er*, not the dump*ee* . . . and I wouldn't allow myself to get pregnant again until I got married."

Mickey had winced as she'd gone on to describe how she had practiced her newly acquired techniques on men she dated, driving them wild in bed, then refusing to see them again. He felt like vomiting when he pictured faceless men fucking her, her legs splayed wide or her ass raised high in the air to accept them.

It was a toss-up, he thought, who needed to have their head examined more: her for letting one shattered affair dominate her life, or him for staying with her? If only he didn't love her so goddamned much.

When Mickey was about to come, Laurel dismounted him and skillfully squeezed the base of his erection, staying his ejaculation and prolonging their sexual play. "Saxonus," she whispered as she moved forward to lower her breast into his waiting mouth. "That's what they call that little squeeze. I may keep you going all day like that." However, her expert ministrations quickly lost out. When he saw her eyes roll upward and her teeth suck in her bottom lip, he pumped hard into the spasms overtaking her, and exploded in an accompanying orgasm so strong it threatened to turn him inside out.

Two hours later Laurel and a thoroughly sated Mickey were on their way to Manhattan to spend a day away from his mob associates, alone, with no other obligation than to have a good time—that's what she'd asked for.

Mickey relaxed as he drove, crooning along with Sinatra's "Young at Heart," until Laurel interrupted with a subject she'd been harping on for weeks: his after-hours club. "Can't you get out of it?" she nagged. "I'm so afraid you'll get arrested."

"I told you before, nothing's gonna happen," Mickey Boy answered impatiently. "It's just a club; it's nothing."

Once again she reminded him that she'd witnessed his arrest at another of his "nothing" clubs.

"Honey, please, let's have a nice day," Mickey Boy implored her. "Besides, I only got pinched that time because I had a one-armed bandit in the club . . . that's a slot machine."

"I know what they are. I lost almost forty dollars to them when I went to Atlantic City," Laurel answered more pleasantly.

"Gee, that's terrible . . . one bet, right?"

"No, all day, Mr. Smartass."

"Well, if you want to try to win back your fortune one night, we could fly down."

"Are you crazy? That's got to be terribly expensive."

Mickey Boy laughed, proud of how easy it was to impress her. "I should tell you it does cost a lot," he said, "but it's really a freebie. I got a hook at Resorts that puts me on their plane for nothing . . . well, whattaya say?"

With eyes squinted seriously and a teacher's admonishing finger pointed at him, Laurel replied, "Only if you promise to get out of that miserable after-hours club."

Ten-thirty that same morning, Chrissy Augusta slid down the banister of her Bensonhurst home just as she had thousands of times since she was six years old. She bounded into the recently modernized kitchen, where her father and eight-year-old sister, Elizabeth, were halfway through a Marx Brothers–type breakfast preparation. Soiled bowls and utensils and open food containers were everywhere; albumen ran from half an eggshell that had fallen onto the terra-cotta ceramic floor.

"Boy, Mommy's gonna kill you guys when she sees this mess," Chrissy exclaimed while stretching to kiss the unshaven cheek of her father, who was clad only in brown silk pajama bottoms. "Where is she anyway?"

"Across the street by Aunt Marie," Elizabeth answered. "She'll be back soon." When Elizabeth bent over to receive her own peck from her older sister and idol, she inadvertently spilled milk on the chair she stood on.

Whereas Chrissy had been known as "Joe's clone" when she was growing up, Lizzie was a miniature copy of their mother: straight brown hair, almond-shaped green-brown eyes, lean and lanky build. The only trait she lacked was her mother's dexterity. Elizabeth was as clumsy as her mother was graceful; Chrissy had inherited that particular attribute the child had been deprived of.

"Don't worry, I'll clean it up." Elizabeth giggled. She immediately reached for a sponge and knocked a small potted plant into the sink.

Joe Augusta groaned.

"I'd better keep a radio with me today so I can hear if a woman in Brooklyn killed two clums-o's who ruined her brand-new kitchen," Chrissy chided.

"Where are you off to so early?" Joe questioned over his shoulder. "I hardly ever see you anymore."

"One, it's not early; most people are probably getting ready for lunch. Two, I'm on my way to the City with my friend Camille; they're having

128

a big sale at Bloomie's. And three, you never see me because you're always out. I almost have to lay in one of your coffins if I want to see you."

Joe Augusta bellowed, "God forbid!" while turning toward the snappy-mouthed daughter that was his pride and joy. If only she'd been a boy, he often thought, she would have made perfect wiseguy material.

When Joe caught sight of her, Chrissy was already at the kitchen doorway. "Whoa! Wait just a minute there, miss," he hollered. "Where do you think you're going dressed like that?"

The full-figured sixteen-year-old seemed to have been molded into pink-floral-print shorts that left the bottom of her bottom peeking out, and a scanty halter top of the same fabric.

Chrissy stopped in midflight and turned, hands petulantly on hips. "Daddy!" she screeched. "It's summer. What do you want me to wear, my red fox jacket?"

"Lower your goddamned voice or I'll smother you with that fox. Just go put some clothes on so you don't drive all the guys in the City nuts. I don't wanna have to go looking to kill some pervert who tries to attack you." Turning back to his cooking, he continued. "Go put on something decent or you ain't leaving this goddamn house." With a shake of his head he added, "I'm surprised your mother even lets you buy stuff like that."

Feigning more anger than she actually felt, Chrissy stamped up the stairs. She didn't want to keep Georgie waiting too long. Recently he had become very nervous about being in one location for any period of time, and might leave if she didn't hurry.

"Make sure you show me how you look before you go," Joe's voice boomed from downstairs.

Chrissy quickly slipped a pair of baggy painter-style jeans and an oversize button-down blouse over the outfit she wore, then darted down to the kitchen for approval.

"How's this? Are you happy now that I look like a boy?" Chrissy asked while smiling brightly. There was a limit to the patience her father showed with her, and she had no intention of reaching for it. If the ebullient, fun-loving Chrissy could help it, *"I spent the day at home"* would not be her diary entry that evening.

Lizzie was the only one enjoying the scene, laughing and clapping her hands.

"Don't laugh, you little witch," Chrissy admonished her jokingly. "Just wait till you're my age and he drives you crazy too."

"Aah, now you look fine," Joe said. "By the way, how are you getting there, and what time are you gonna be home?"

"Command Bus, and sometime this evening. We're going to eat dinner uptown . . . either Yellowfinger's or Friday's."

"Just make sure you check in with your mother by phone, get home before curfew, and be careful. You know not to bother with strangers, don't you?"

God! He still thinks I'm a baby, Chrissy thought. She bowed mockingly from the waist, saying, "Yes, sahib," then turned and ran for the door.

"Oh, Chrissy!" Joe Augusta shouted before she was out. "Come here for a minute."

"Shit," she muttered, then yelled, "What now?"

"You need money?"

Christina Augusta sighed with relief. "Did you ever meet a girl who didn't?" she cheerfully called back.

"Go in my blue plaid jacket that's hanging in the closet down here and take a hundred . . . only one."

Within seconds Chrissy had taken the money, kissed her father again, and was out in the July sunlight.

Georgie's 'Vette was nowhere in sight when Chrissy reached their rendezvous spot at the entrance to Dyker Beach Park. She walked along the perimeter of the golf course, cursing her luck, until the familiar opening bars of *The Godfather* sounded on a car's horn behind her. Georgie The Hammer pulled to the curb on the opposite side of 86th Street, waving frenetically for her to cross. "God, I'm not even ten minutes late," she complained under her breath.

Chrissy had barely settled into the passenger seat when an overwrought Georgie slammed the gas pedal to the floor and peeled out, stunning pedestrians and other motorists to a halt and leaving a lengthy streak of his Michelins on the pavement.

"Shit, Chrissy, didn't you ever hear of being a few minutes early?" Georgie jumped the light on 8th Avenue and sped onto the expressway toward Manhattan.

"My God, I'm not even ten minutes late," Chrissy said, echoing her earlier sentiments. "You're getting to be as bad as my father with his curfews."

While scolding Georgie for giving her a bad time, she struggled out of the baggy layer of clothing her father had forced her to wear, then bent forward and pulled her halter away from her breasts to let the air-conditioner's breeze circulate between them. The coolness made her nipples bulge through the cloth.

"Whattaya live in the fuckin' twilight zone?" Georgie yelled. "Don't you know there's a fuckin' war goin' on?"

Chrissy sat upright, unbothered by her boyfriend's distraught manner. "Oh, you silly boys, playing at war with captains and generals

130

and things. Forget them today. Let's just spend a beautiful day together. Like my new outfit? I bought it specially for you."

Georgie began to lecture about the realities of men dying, when he turned and noticed Chrissy's nipples bulging through her blouse.

"Chrissy, are you on fuckin' drugs?!" he screamed. "You can't walk in the street like that. I'll wind up havin' to kill somebody." He slapped a hand to his forehead. "Some choice I got in life: Either I get killed by Junior Vallo's guys or I go to the can for murder 'cause some jerkoff pinched my girl's tit!"

Anger flushed Chrissy's face. "If you're going to keep sounding like my father, *and* cursing, Mr. Randazzo, then this girl is not going anywhere with you. Either we're going to spend a fun day together, or I want to go home."

"Chrissy, can't you understand . . ." Georgie began, but when he saw the teenager's pouting face, said, "Forget it, you won't understand anyway."

Chrissy smiled.

Georgie's voice took on a patronizing tone. "Chrissy darling, I think you're gorgeous . . . your outfit's gorgeous . . . everything's gorgeous. In fact, the day is gorgeous . . . the highway is gorgeous. But honey, you can't walk around Manhattan with your gorgeous tits hangin' out."

Suddenly he banged a fist on the dashboard, and screamed, "Your gorgeous fuckin' nipples look like they're gonna tear the fuckin' gorgeous material in half . . . *darling!*"

"I thought you liked my little titties," Chrissy teased. "And my nippies are going down already. They were only cold from the air-conditioning. Here, look."

When Georgie turned, Chrissy was facing him, holding her bare breasts over the top of her halter.

Both lovers burst out laughing.

"I give up," Georgie said. He expelled a gush of air like a deflating balloon. "All right, where to today? How about we stop at that big toy store an' get you that teddy bear you said you wanted?"

"Oh, thankyouthankyouthankyou," the still-bare-bosomed Chrissy squealed while throwing her arms around Georgie's neck. "It's F.A.O. Schwarz, and it's a Molly Bear, not just a teddy."

Georgie The Hammer reached for her exposed bust. "Please, baby, put these things away before we get killed or pinched. Now, where is this toy store?"

Chrissy pressed his hand harder onto her flesh. "Don't be such a fraidy cat," she continued playfully. "And the store's on Fifty-eighth and Fifth."

* * *

The two couples met at the stuffed animal section of F.A.O. Schwarz.

While Laurel was inspecting a paunchy Mr. Jeremy Fisher to bring to her class in the fall, Mickey had wandered a few feet away toward a ten-foot-tall giraffe. On the other side of an étagère packed with furry things he heard a youngish female explaining the merits of a Steiff bear that sold for over two hundred dollars. She dramatically asserted that she'd positively die if she couldn't have it. When a male voice, seemingly unimpressed, argued that if she would be patient, he would send Skinny with a forged credit card later in the week to make the purchase, Mickey Boy recognized it and parted the menagerie on one shelf to push his face through. "No domestic squabbles here, please," he reprimanded.

Georgie spun toward him. "Who the fu—Mickey Boy!" he shouted, then hurried around the display. "What the hell are you doing here?"

"We were on our way to Central Park and stopped for a Frisbee," Mickey Boy said as he hugged Georgie. He pointed toward Laurel, who was paying for a Squirrel Nutkin she'd decided upon. "Then she got involved."

"Serious?"

"Sort of." Mickey Boy paused, reminded of his and Laurel's differences: her sexuality; his life-style. "We're like everybody else, I guess; we got a couple of rough spots."

"I know just what you mean, pal," Georgie said with a conspiratorial snicker. "But when you're talkin' problems, I got trailers full." He jerked a thumb toward Chrissy, who'd wandered into view. "See that cute little fox over there with the cute little ass? Well, she wants that cute little bear she's holding, that costs a not-so-cute two hundred mahoskas."

Mickey Boy admired Chrissy's briefly clad figure. "She certainly looks like she's worth it."

"That, an' a lot more," Georgie quickly agreed. "The problem is that I'm always broke. This fuckin' beef we're havin' with Junior Vallo's crew is destroying me."

"Tell me about it," Mickey Boy replied with a knowing nod of his head. He'd had some tough times too lately. After a few winning weeks his sports business had gone thirty-two thousand dollars behind, making it a good probability that he wouldn't see any relief until football season began in September. "It's the old story," he said. "Eat like a bird, shit like an elephant. Why do you think me and Richie opened the after-hours on Cropsey Avenue?"

"At least you could open a joint. Me, I can't stay in one place long enough to earn," Georgie said. "What's worse, before the war started I could borrow between scores. Now, with so many of our guys getting whacked out, even the shys say we're bad risks."

Mickey Boy understood—helping men on one side of the conflict could cost much more than money if the other side happened to find out. Could he depend on Georgie to keep it quiet if he lent him some cash? Not likely.

"This shit'll be over before you know it," Mickey Boy said, dismissing the idea of a loan. "Then you'll be okay . . . hey, by the way, congratulations! I heard you got proposed."

"Yeah, you too," Georgie said, then with a sigh, added, "Boy, do I need that badge too." He pulled Mickey Boy by the arm, leading him a bit farther away from the girls. "Between us, an' I know I could trust you, see that little sonofabitch over there," he said while motioning affectionately toward Chrissy with his eyes. "She's a great kid, an' she robbed my heart, but if I tell you whose daughter she is, you'll shit."

"Please, Georgie, if it's a wiseguy, I don't wanna know."

"Mick, this is just between us. You know I would never say you knew."

Thank God he hadn't opened his big mouth and promised Georgie a loan, Mickey Boy thought. "Somehow I know I'm making a mistake in askin', but I have the feeling you'd tell me anyway," he said. "So go on, who does she belong to?"

Georgie whispered, "Joe August."

"Are you sick?! Do you really wanna get fuckin' killed?"

"That's why I need that button," Georgie said. "Once I'm in, I'll tell him that I wanna marry her. As long as I'm doin' the right thing, an' especially if I'm a good fella too, what could he say?"

"Say? He don't have to say nothing, just deep-six you when nobody's looking . . . how old is she?"

Georgie hesitated, then said, "She'll be seventeen."

"She'll also be forty, but not soon!" Mickey Boy made sure his back was to the girls, then motioned wildly with his face. "Sixteen! Lord have mercy if her old man ever finds out."

"Honest, she'll be seventeen in less than three months. I figure we could get engaged after I'm made, an' married when she's nineteen."

Mickey Boy shook his head. "I sure hope whatever you got ain't catching."

Mickey Boy and Georgie called the girls over and introduced them. Chrissy still clung to the stuffed bear. "Well, Georgie, can I have Molly?" she pleaded. "I've got money from my father too."

"I don't want your old man's money. When I give it to you, it'll be from me alone."

"But she looks so sad. Look at her poor button eyes," Chrissy said in a little-girl voice. She cuddled the expensive animal under her chin. "And look, honey, see how she loves me?"

"Chrissy, don't start!"

"Okay, you brute," she said, then turned and winked at Laurel. "C'mon, Molly, he's a mean man. You don't want to be in his company today anyway." Chrissy left to return the animal to its shelf.

"She's adorable," Laurel said.

"Yeah, she's a good kid," Georgie replied. "A little air-headed, but all in all she's okay."

"Don't be fooled," Laurel said. "She's a lot smarter than you give her credit for. She just did a pretty good job of teasing you."

The three of them were laughing when Chrissy came back with a small stuffed monkey. "Don't worry," she told Georgie. "I'm buying a present for my sister." When she noticed their grins, she asked, "Am I missing something?"

"Absolutely nothing," Laurel answered. "We were just laughing about how you maneuver this hunk of yours."

Chrissy giggled. "Oh, Georgie's a piece of cake."

"Why don't you two spend the day with us?" Laurel asked. "Mickey and I were just going to the Sheep Meadow to play a little Frisbee."

Mickey Boy pinched Laurel's rear. "Leave them alone," he said. "They probably have their own plans." The last thing he wanted was to be with his underboss's daughter and her secret lover.

Chrissy clapped her hands together. "Oh, yes, Georgie, can we go with them? Pleasepleaseplease?"

"Come on, darling," Laurel said. "Be a sport and I'll be one too . . . nothing more about your after-hours club—for today." She reached up and gave Mickey a smacking kiss on the lips.

Defeated, Mickey Boy and Georgie shrugged their shoulders helplessly.

On their way through F.A.O. Schwarz's side exit, Georgie pressed something soft against the back of Chrissy's exposed legs—her precious Molly Bear, which he had lifted.

"Oh, Georgie," Chrissy cooed. "I love you."

After gorging themselves on pushcart frankfurters and doughy pretzels smeared with mustard, the foursome spent the next couple of hours chasing their spinning red Frisbee across Central Park's lush grass, then, at the request of the girls, set off in search of the carousel.

Laurel and Chrissy walked ahead, arms entwined, chattering like long-lost friends. The two men brought up the rear, discussing underworld gossip and the instant attraction that their dates seemed to have toward each other. Mickey Boy's stomach churned over the last observation. Though he liked Georgie and thought his girlfriend was a doll, he knew their situation would inevitably lead to catastrophe, and wanted no part of it. If he had to dirty himself with problems, he could create plenty of his own.

They found the merry-go-round by following the irresistible whistle of its calliope, and used up six tickets each before their growling stomachs pulled them away.

Mickey Boy drove to Campagnola, where they dined at the front table, looking out on to First Avenue. Chrissy found the atmosphere of warm woods, stucco walls, and garlicky aroma what she imagined an authentic trattoria in Italy would be like and swooned over the veal topped with artichoke hearts. Mickey Boy paid the entire bill and also treated to frozen hot chocolates and fudge sundaes at Serendipity, where he loaded both girls up with novelty items from the front counter, all the while humming Sinatra's version of "New York, New York."

Molly Bear accompanied them to both places.

Before the two couples parted, Laurel and Chrissy exchanged phone numbers, promising to keep in touch with each other.

"You'd do us both a big favor if you'd take Chrissy's number and throw it out the window," Mickey Boy said while driving home. He explained the precarious situation Georgie and Chrissy were in and why he didn't want to make a habit of seeing them.

"I don't think their problem with her father has anything to do with us," Laurel replied. "They're sweet kids and really love each other, and are pleasant to be with. Considering the fact that we don't socialize with any of my friends because you feel uncomfortable around them, I would think you would welcome the opportunity to go out with one of yours."

After first correcting her that Georgie was an "outside sort of a friend," rather than a close one, he admitted having had a good time in Georgie and Chrissy's company, but remained adamant in his rejection of any future outings. "First of all, what they do *does* affect me," he said. "It's a matter of respect. If I keep seeing them, it's like I'm slapping her old man in the face. It just ain't right."

"I didn't know you were that friendly with her father."

"I'm not," Mickey Boy replied. "But he's a very respected man with my friends, not Georgie's. And besides, if they ever found out that I knew and didn't say nothing, I'd be in as much hot water as him—an' I ain't been humping her."

"Don't be disgusting," Laurel replied.

After a brief silence, all too brief for Mickey Boy, Laurel began again, this time questioning the relationship between him and Joe Augusta, and asking him to clarify his statement about his friends and Georgie's friends.

Mickey Boy did his best to avoid direct answers, teasing and kidding with her instead.

"Besides, they're an accident looking for a place to happen," he said. "And I just don't want to be involved, period!"

"Don't worry, you won't," Laurel said. "I promise." She was, however, more optimistic than he about the young lovers' future, romantically portraying them as a modern-day Romeo and Juliet, who, unlike Shakespeare's characters, would eventually overcome their obstacles and live happily ever after. And, although she'd promised not to involve Mickey Boy in any more social engagements with the troubled pair, she insisted there was no harm in her maintaining her own personal friendship with Chrissy.

Mickey Boy reluctantly agreed.

30

July 23: East Side, Manhattan

Early on the same day that Mickey Boy, Georgie, and the two girls met, a black Fleetwood Brougham made its way south in Lexington Avenue's right-hand lane.

Sonny Fortunato sat in the front passenger seat, with Petey Ross right behind him. When they stopped for a light by Citicorp Center, Sonny looked into a visor-mounted vanity mirror. "They're still there," he muttered to their driver. "Four cars back and one lane to the left."

As he neared Fiftieth Street, the driver signaled left and slowed up to merge into the steady flow of late morning traffic. He had barely completed the switchover to the adjoining lane when the light changed; the vehicle that followed him also moved to the left. Before the cross-traffic movement could begin, however, Petey's man gunned the Fleetwood across the intersection, swung sharply to the right, and pulled to a screeching halt in front of the Waldorf-Astoria.

Petey and Sonny leapt from the car and darted toward the entrance. Sonny lost no time, slipping in through the lustrous brass and glass revolving doors. Petey Ross, though, hit the swinging door to the right, found it locked, then bounced off and followed Sonny through the revolving center doors.

Taking the up escalator stairs two at a time, Petey quickly bypassed Sonny, but, to accommodate the sixty-seven-year-old, had to hold himself to a semi-trot through the lavishly appointed lobby. They moved quickly over the maroon and gold carpet—past the exclusive boutiques that lined either side, in front of the main desk, and by those patrons imbibing at Peacock Alley's open café. People just shook their heads as the two men rushed by.

Petey Ross looked over his shoulder and saw one gray-suited figure following them through the crowd. "Sorry, bud, we gotta speed it up," he called to his *consigliere*, then broke into a run toward the overhead Cocktail Terrace, with its white piano bar and potted palms. Their hands skimmed over the brass center railing as they ran down the marble staircase leading to the exit. Those who were quick enough moved out of their way before being roughly pushed aside; muffled complaints echoed off the glossy beige walls.

When the two winded mafiosi burst from the hotel onto Park Avenue, a burly soldier of theirs swung open the rear door of a brown stretch limousine, its motor running.

"One in gray," Petey Ross panted to his underling while he pushed Sonny into the auto ahead of him.

An ex–high school fullback, the bodyguard started immediately toward the building to throw the most important block of his career.

By the time Petey and Sonny pulled up at a stately white building on Central Park South, they had fully recovered from their police surveillance escape; the cognacs they had poured from the limo's bar had helped considerably.

"Twenty-one-oh-two," Sonny announced to the desk clerk of the residential hotel. He and Petey waited in the deco-style lobby while the clerk phoned the apartment for clearance to send them up.

Seconds later the two leaders of the Rossellini Family stood patiently outside the door to Apartment 2102 while being eyed through a peephole.

Both men stiffened when the door finally swung open.

"You can't be too careful," Rock Santoro said, his hand still on the doorknob, his rough fighter's face attempting a smile. Responding to their astonished looks, he added, "I know you guys were a little shaky about me being here, but I want you to understand something: My loyalty is one hundred percent with my Family. No matter how close I am with Don Peppino's guys, that stops dead when my crew's interests are at stake."

Though Petey and Sonny had specifically requested that Rock not be invited to their meeting because of that very relationship he'd just mentioned, at that point they were left with little choice but to trust Tom Thumb's judgment.

I hope that fat fuck knows what he's doing, Petey thought as he bent forward and kissed Rock on both cheeks. "I hope you don't misunderstand how we felt," he said. "You know, these are bad times; any little mistake . . ."

"I would've felt the same way," Rock agreed. "C'mon, Tom's outside."

Rock guided them through the living room and out its sliding glass doors to a penthouse garden, where Tom Thumb leaned against the rail, a pair of binoculars pressed into his fleshy face.

Petey Ross looked around, taking in the lush jungle of ficus trees and flowering plants, yellow and white striped patio furniture, and a seven-foot statue of a nude man and woman embracing and spouting water from their touching lips. He let out an appreciative whistle. "Boy, this is some setup you got here, bud," he said. "Broads' drawers must drop to their ankles as soon as they step outside."

"Naah, you're the guy with all the girls," Tom Thumb replied. He patted his sizable middle. "My vice is pasta. An' this here joint belongs to my diet doctor. He makes me use it once in a while, like when I got a special meet set up." With a laugh he added, "I probably bought it anyway, with all the cash I give him these last few years . . . an' all for nothin'."

"You never lost nothing?"

"Lose, gain, lose, gain," Tom Thumb said. "Between losin' an' gainin', I musta went through more weight than you got left in your whole crew."

Petey masked the sting he felt at Tom Thumb's barb with a smile. "Thumb, you're the greatest."

"C'mere, Pete, take a look through these," Tom Thumb said, pointing out over Central Park. "You could see all the way to Harlem. An' you might catch some hot little numbers runnin' around the Sheep Meadow."

"Only if you bring them to me here, bud. I get dizzy from heights, so I can't go near the railing."

Tom Thumb roared with laughter, which precipitated one of his coughing seizures. "I don't blame you, Pete," he said between wheezes. "After what happened to your guy Johnny Pumps over in Jersey, I wouldn't go near a railin' either. C'mon, let's go inside an' talk."

The living room–dining room area was meticulously done in a style that Petey had seen before only in magazines: mauve upholstery and Oriental rugs, likewise-colored furniture that looked like it was made from granite, paintings that might've been upside down as easily as not.

Once they had settled into soft modular couches that faced each other across a concrete couple fornicating on a chrome and glass table, and Rock had poured them all chilled Orvieto, Tom Thumb, sitting on the same side as Rock, said, "I figure Rock here already told youse how he feels, but I wanna make it clear that I'm behind him all the way. His word is like my word, an' youse know I back that up with my life."

"Enough said," Petey interrupted. "Sonny told you when you two set this meeting up that whatever you decided would be okay with us."

Tom Thumb replied with zest, "Good!" He downed his wine in one gulp and held the glass out for Rock to refill. "Now that that's outta the way, let's get down to business. You know, from the very beginning somethin' about this whole situation stunk. Like take John-John gettin' himself blowed up. I told Rock the same day that there was no way you guys was involved with that. Right, Rock?"

Rock nodded.

"You, I wasn't too sure about, my hotheaded friend," Tom Thumb said while pointing at Petey Ross. "But I knew Sonny would never let that happen."

"Thanks for the vote of confidence, bud," the youngest of New York City's mob bosses retorted, his handsome face tightening at the insult.

"Listen, pal, we're all friends here, an' we gotta call things the way we see 'em. Remember, we're here to help you."

After a few phlegmy convulsions, Tom Thumb continued. "Another thing that don't make no sense was the old men makin' Junior Vallo take John-John's spot. Between us, Junior's an asshole. He couldn't run a fuckin' cake sale, let alone a whole crew."

"Yeah, but you know how those two old zips are," Petey argued, referring to Don Vincenze and Don Peppino. "They wanna be able to control whoever they let in there. By makin' Junior boss, they get a lobby boy who'll go along with anything they say."

"Right . . . an' that's what's wrong," Tom Thumb retorted. According to him, a *paisano*—someone who came from the same town in Sicily— of Don Peppino's, Jack The Wop, should have been given the top spot. "Nobody would have been more loyal to them than The Wop," he said. "An' he's not even makin' a peep about losin' out to Junior. I tell ya, it just ain't right."

Petey Ross fidgeted when he heard Tom Thumb echoing his own *consigliere*'s warnings. "Sonny keeps telling me not to trust the old bastards too," he said. "But I talked to Vince and Peppino, an' they told me if Junior won't listen to them an' stop this shit, they'll put their troops behind me."

Tom Thumb let out another thunderous laugh. "A thousand to one you'll never see that day—you name the figure. What they're givin' you is one big fuckin' stroke job."

Because Petey Ross had been saddled with his incarcerated boss's son as underboss, it was his older, wiser *consigliere*, Sonny Fortunato, that he had accompany him to important meetings, discussed his innermost plans and fears with, and depended upon for guidance and advice. Aware of that relationship, Tom Thumb turned to the old *consigliere*, and said, "Go on, Sonny, tell him if I ain't right."

Ever the statesman, Sonny agreed with Tom Thumb's assessment while still defending Petey Ross's wisdom in being cautious. Petey was only an acting boss, he argued, and didn't have enough support to buck the two powerful dons. What bothered him most, however, he said, was that when Don Peppino had met them in his son's Cadillac dealership, he had practically ordered them not to retaliate against Junior Vallo, thereby causing them to lose five button-men before they fired a single shot. And, he added, he never got to sit down with Junior like he'd been promised.

"That alone should tell you somethin'," Tom Thumb said. He reasoned that if either of the two dons had ordered Junior Vallo to a meeting, it would have been held immediately. "I think they just want your crews to destroy each other so's they could break youse up without too much of a beef from the commission, or whatever's left of you guys. You know, Vincenze hinted at that when we was together a couple of weeks ago."

"What'd he say?" Petey demanded.

"He just made it like you guys was bringin' a lot of heat, an' that youse had no control over the situation. Then he tells me that maybe the old-timers like Charlie Lucky an' Costello would've been better off makin' us into three Families instead of five."

"That's all bullshit!" Petey insisted. "I been hearing that shit since the sixties. If they really wanted to do it, either one of them could put together a bigger army than you, me, and Junior combined."

"An' go through an expensive war, face the whole commission to explain, an' maybe start an uprisin' with their own people? No fuckin' way! They'd rather let your two crews eat each other up, then only have to come after me. Smarten up, pal," Tom Thumb said, his irritation at the young acting boss's naïveté obvious. "Tryin' to keep up with what those two greaseballs are thinkin' could keep us here till we die. All I do know is that your beef is no good for nobody . . . me included."

"So we got to end it fast," Petey said. "We could do it."

"Stop dreaming!" Tom Thumb snapped. "The way it stands now, neither one of youse could beat the other. All youse could do is chip away at each other till there's nothing left."

Though in reality Petey Ross's Family was getting the worst of the fracas, having lost nine men within the previous six weeks, he argued that he would still win before the year ended.

"Petey, please," Tom Thumb interrupted after a spell of hacking. "The way I see it, right now youse got a standoff, maybe with you takin' a little more of a beatin' than Junior. An' the only way you stand a chance of comin' out on top is if you get some help. I'm offerin' you that help. Youse wanna take it, or no?"

Tom Thumb's earlier message offering to act as a mediator in the dispute had left Petey prepared for many possibilities, including the chance that Junior Vallo would appear at the meeting with them that afternoon. He was not prepared, however, for the gift that had just been dropped on his doorstep.

"I gotta admit, you . . . . well, you took me by surprise, bud," he stammered. "But there's nobody I'd rather have in my corner."

The four mafiosi stood, embraced, and kissed to seal their pact. When they returned to their seats, Tom Thumb took charge of the conversation again, saying, "Now, before we came here, me an' Rock decided that if we pumped cash an' guns into youse, that would do the trick. But since we been sittin' here talkin', an' I been smellin' how shitty this whole thing really is, I decided we gotta help youse more than that." Motioning toward Rock, he said, "I know he ain't too happy right now, but . . ." then shrugged.

Rock was obviously perturbed. Every muscle in his face seemed to tense as he leaned forward and mashed out his cigarette. "My gut feeling is that committing our guys to a war that's got nothing to do with us is just like when this country got mixed up in Vietnam, and you see what happened there. Thumb knows how I feel about us getting involved, but like I said before, I'm with him all the way, no matter which way he goes . . . even if I gotta die doing it."

"I could only respect your feelings, an' hope that we all get out of this mess as soon as possible," Petey said, feeling his original uneasiness about having Rock attend. "You know, we didn't want this problem either."

Petey raised his glass in a toast, and said, "Thumb, my friend, may you live to be a hundred."

"*Cent'anni*" reverberated around the room.

Young Petey Ross, overjoyed at the boost Tom Thumb's promised reinforcements would provide, momentarily cast aside his misgivings about Rock Santoro, and eagerly asked how soon they could get their new alliance working.

"First we gotta decide whether it's a smart move to let everybody know we're in it too," Tom Thumb replied. "Whatta youse think?"

It was generally agreed that their efforts would be better served if the opposition remained unaware, at least initially, that the Rossellinis had assistance from Tom Thumb's crew. More important, they all felt that if either Don Vincenze or Don Peppino found out about their pact, the two old men might become angry enough to give open support to the Vallos.

The mobsters' resolution of secrecy seemed to placate Rock Santoro a bit, but not enough—not nearly enough to make Petey Ross feel comfortable.

Once again Tom Thumb took command. He sent Rock to find a pen and paper, then designated Sonny to list as many of Junior Vallo's men as they could collectively recall. The names were then categorized into heavy hitters, like Tony Giarre, who were actually murdering Petey's men; those who were important because they were wealthy or politically connected rather than killers; and those button-men and associates who ran day-to-day Vallo operations like bookmaking to keep their Family economically alive.

To take advantage of the fact that no one knew his Family had entered the war, Tom Thumb suggested he send his men to pick off the Vallo killers one by one while Petey concentrated on those workers who were more exposed.

Petey, Sonny, and Rock nodded in agreement.

"If we get lucky," Tom Thumb said, "we might even get to Junior and his brother." He added that it was more important to kill Jack The Wop, who he felt was a danger to them because of his close ties to Don Peppino, and who he felt was more of a formidable enemy than Junior if he should gain leadership after the Vallos were gone.

Rock Santoro grimaced. "If we do that," he said, "and Peppino or Vince finds out—"

"Nobody's findin' nothin' out!" Tom Thumb snapped. "Anybody we whack out disappears, an' Petey gets the credit; war is war. An' that's that!"

"You're the boss," Rock said.

Tom Thumb smiled. "Good. Now, all this talk about whackin' guys out makes me hungry," he said with an accompanying chuckle and a pat on his huge stomach. "Rock, go see what the good doctor's got layin' around the fridge."

When a stony-faced Rock Santoro had left the room, Tom Thumb leaned across the glass coffee table toward Petey and Sonny, and whispered, "Don't worry, he'll be okay."

31

July 26: Sheepshead Bay, Brooklyn

Laurel had the kitchen phone tucked under her chin when Mickey Boy entered their apartment at 10:30 A.M.

"Yes . . . yes . . . he's just walking in now," she said, then held the receiver out to him. "It's your mother." When he took the phone she stomped off to the bathroom in a huff, slamming the door behind her.

"Hi, Mom," Mickey Boy answered. "No, everything's okay." He glared at the bathroom door. "What'd she do, call you right away to complain that I wasn't home?"

About a week after their disastrous encounter at Port Authority, Connie had called Laurel to let her know that she, unlike Alley, welcomed her relationship with Mickey Boy, and would be thrilled if one day their affair resulted in a wedding and grandchildren. Since that time the two females in Mickey Boy's life spoke practically every day; a good part of that time spent fueling each other's distaste for his street life.

That day, Connie said, she had been the one who called to ask Laurel if she and Mickey would like to spend a couple of days with her in Boston while Alley and Ellen took their young daughter, Kimberly, to Disney World for a week.

Mickey Boy declined, saying that if his brother didn't want him and his girlfriend in his home when he was around, then it wasn't right to go there when he was away. He and Laurel were no thieves in the night who had to sneak around behind anyone's back—especially Alley's.

"I told her we wouldn't go," Mickey Boy said when he entered the bedroom.

Laurel stood at the terrace door, back to him, arms crossed defensively over her chest, looking out over the sunlit blue-green water of Sheepshead Bay. She didn't answer.

Moving cautiously, Mickey Boy stepped behind her and began to knead her bare shoulders. They felt like warmed silk, and immediately caused a stirring between his legs. He lifted her hair gently back on one side, then bent and kissed her ear.

"Mickey, please," Laurel snapped. "You think getting laid solves every problem."

Mickey Boy nuzzled the juncture of her neck and collarbone while he slid the spaghetti straps of her peach nightgown down over her arms, baring her to the waist. "It doesn't solve them," he whispered while reaching around her to cup both breasts in his hands; it pleased him that her nipples instantly responded to his touch. "But it sure makes them a hell of a lot more fun to deal with."

To Mickey Boy's surprise, Laurel pulled away and moved into the center of the room, adjusting her straps as she went. *She's really pissed this time*, he thought.

"Mickey, for God's sake, stop thinking I'm an empty-headed female whose life is run from between her legs!" Laurel yelled. "I mean, you spend the whole night out without so much as a goddamned phone call, and expect me to fall all over you because you've got a hard-on and squeeze my tits a little. It just doesn't work that way!" she screamed. "Do us both a favor and go stick that thing of yours in whoever you spent the night with!"

Mickey Boy laughed. "I don't think Richie would appreciate that too much. Besides, I never was much for hairy asses."

He went to Laurel's side and put his arm around her shoulders. This time she didn't resist, but remained wooden. He kissed her forehead.

"C'mon, hon," he whispered. "I got stuck at the club. The blackjack table wasn't doing too good, so I figured I'd sit in at the anchor spot until the table filled up and I could go . . . except, it never filled up." As he explained it, they always had a couple of heavy players, but never enough for him to leave until the game broke up in the morning. "You think I liked being a shill all night when I could've been doing dirty things in bed with you?"

While Mickey Boy spoke, he worked Laurel's nightgown down until she stood totally nude. "You know there's no other girl for me," he said, and bent to suck at her distended nipple. When he rolled his tongue around the hard pink tip, Laurel gasped and moved her body closer to his; her fingers entwined themselves in his hair.

Gotcha! Mickey Boy thought, and lifted her in his arms.

When he placed her on the bed, Laurel was still complaining, "It's no good, Mickey . . . this life is not for me . . ." but with much less resolve.

32

July 27: Coney Island, Brooklyn

"I want you to know, I really appreciate your comin' with me." It was the fifth time that Georgie The Hammer had thanked Skinny Malone since they'd begun their trip in the stolen Cutlass Skinny had supplied.

There was practically no traffic on the Belt Parkway at that late hour, enabling them to drive exactly at the fifty-mile-an-hour speed limit. They passed Cropsey Avenue at 2:13 A.M. Off to their right, Coney Island's Ferris wheel loomed like a huge charcoal shadow against the black sky.

"We gotta talk though, pal . . . about you," Georgie continued.

Skinny groaned. "I figured this was coming," he said, then pulled his denim poorboy cap down over his eyes and pretended to snore.

"C'mon, Skinny, cut the crap . . . this is serious."

"So's a heart attack, but that don't mean I wanna be involved in one. Let's talk about something that's fun instead. Get any new stuff lately? I mean besides my darling Chrissy?"

"Skinny! Stop fuckin' around and listen."

"Okay, Dad, time to give me my evening lecture. Where do you wanna start: Skinny, you been a bad boy an' offended the Don Cheeches, or Skinny, you know you ain't supposed to sell dope?"

"Let's start with the simplest one: why do you wanna fuck around an' not send no money to Don Vincenze's kid, when you're probably makin' more than you ever did in your whole life?"

Skinny pushed his blue cap back on his head; his lips stretched in a taut smile. "Why?" he asked through gritted teeth. "I'll tell you why. Remember when your pal, Mickey Boy, came an' picked up the money the last time, about five or six weeks ago?"

"Sure, I gave him the money for you."

"What happened after that? No, I'll tell you," Skinny rushed his words. "Buster the bugfucker from Mulberry Street calls up Crazy Angelo at the club, and when Angelo ain't there, he asks for me. An' what does that fuckin' slimebucket tell me? Thanks? Nooo. He tells me he's insulted that I left such a small amount. So you know how the Irish kid from Brooklyn answers him? I say, 'Buster, old pal, old buddy, you have my word that it'll never happen again.' And you know what? It won't! I ain't givin' that dago bastard another fuckin' cent!"

Georgie ignored Skinny's ethnic slurs. They had been close friends since childhood, and had always spoken about each other's heritage that way. The only difference was that usually when they insulted each other they didn't mean it.

"Didn't Angelo tell you just to make a few payments for a while, an' then he'd stretch it out until they forgot about it?"

"Yeah, you know what everybody'll forget? Your end and Crazy Angelo's end. The Irish shmuck who did the score'll wind up paying back everything he made, while the boys whose last names end in *o* will spend theirs on every bimbo who's willing to spread her legs for them."

Georgie made a feeble attempt at convincing Skinny he was mistaken, that Angelo had really done his best for them.

"Georgie, please, I wasn't made with a finger. You're just blind to what those guys do 'cause you're drooling all over yourself to be one of them. I don't have to put up with their bullshit 'cause I can't become a zipper or button or whatever the fuck you call it. Even this shit tonight; if not for you, I wouldn't give them the sweat off my balls."

"I told you before how much I appreciate you comin'," Georgie repeated. "But that don't change the fact that you're in the middle of a big problem." What he was afraid of, Georgie said, was that Little Vinnie's people would cop a sneak and kill Skinny, while making it appear as though he was just another casualty of the Rossellini–Vallo war.

"Fuck them and the mountain goats they came in on. Those dumb guineas gotta wake up early in the morning to outsmart this kid. An' if you wanna know the truth, they ain't as pissed over the money as they are 'cause I showed 'em up for the fuckin' idiots they are." After all, Skinny asked, hadn't Little Vinnie and his friends tried to beat him for the stolen load but wound up being screwed instead? "That doesn't exactly make 'em look like Einsteins."

"That has nothing to do with it anymore," Georgie said. "What's important now is that Angelo got involved for us and gave his word. We can't make him look bad now."

"If Angelo's so worried about what those hard-ons think, why don't he reach into his own fuckin' pocket—you know, the one with the padlocks on it—an' send them a thou?" Skinny asked. He added that he didn't expect Georgie to pay anything because he knew he was broke, but insisted Angelo could. "Just some of the cash he drops at the barber every day to make his three fuckin' hairs look like cement would do it."

"Angelo ain't that bad," Georgie said, trying to pacify his friend. In his heart he knew Skinny was right, but was concerned that he would be in mortal danger if he continued to flout mob edicts. "There's a lot of good fellas who are worse, an' you know it."

"There's a lot worse diseases than TB, but that don't mean I wanna start coughin' blood."

"Will you stop with those fuckin' diseases!" Georgie yelled. "Every time I leave you, I feel like I'm infected with something."

Skinny laughed. "I got diseases up my sleeve you ain't never heard of, pal."

"Just make sure one of them ain't lead poisoning . . . at least until I could get made myself, an' can put you under my wing."

"Wing, my ass!" Skinny shouted while throwing his arms up in disgust. "I wish you'd give up all that wiseguy bullshit an' realize that money is what makes you, not their Mickey Mouse ceremony. Remember the old saying Money talks an' bullshit walks—even with your precious goombahs."

Skinny continued to argue that despite the mafiosi's claims that they didn't want anything to do with the drug business, if he brought them money every time he made a sale, they'd grab it. He also begged Georgie to sever his ties with wiseguys altogether. "Don't be a sucker," he said. "Kiss those assholes good-bye and be my partner one hundred percent . . . we'll be rich in no time."

"That's another thing, Skin," Georgie replied, ignoring Skinny's arguments. "Right now nobody knows what you're doing but me. But if word ever gets out you're dealin', man, will you be up the creek."

"I'm shakin'."

"For God's sake, stop bein' a fuckin' jerkoff!" Georgie screamed. He felt like shaking Skinny by the neck until he understood the danger in what he was doing. "If the blanket Angelo's got over you is yanked, you'll be out there alone for Little Vinnie's goons to pick off—that's if Angelo don't have you whacked out himself; he fuckin' hates drugs."

Skinny sat up and pushed his denim cap all the way back on his head so he could stare at Georgie. "Man, did they ever do a fuckin' number on you. Those dago bastards could piss in your face an' you'd swear it was rainin' out." He argued that in spite of all the mob bosses' threats of death to those under their power who dealt in narcotics, every time a big bust came down it involved either their relatives or closest friends. "Do you know any of their sons or brothers that ever got killed for dealing shit? Even one?"

Georgie remained silent.

"That's why they got mansions on Todt Hill an' Georgie's gotta borrow from shylocks just to eat pizza," Skinny said with a smirk. "Smarten up, pal, this is the real world."

"Just wait till I get my button," Georgie said. "Everything'll be different then."

"Nothing's gonna change, Georgie. Once they give you that fuckin' thing, you're gonna be just like them. If they tell you to whack out your own mother, you'll ask 'em how fast, an' is it okay if you use a bomb." Skinny shook his head. "No, pal, the only chance you got not to be a guinea robot is to break away from them now."

"You know I can't do that."

"No. What you mean is you *won't* do that," Skinny replied. Even the darkness of the car's interior couldn't hide the angry red glow that flushed his hollow cheeks. "That's the fuckin' ginzo blood in you . . . an' they say polacks are thick!"

Skinny pulled his cap back down over his eyes and lay back against the seat. "Just do me one favor," he said. "When you get tired of starving, think over what I said."

It was nearly three o'clock when the Cutlass passed the abandoned remnants of the Southern State Parkway toll booths. Georgie veered toward the right and drove off at the first exit. At the top of the ramp he made another right, then continued at a slower speed through an area rich in wide streets, hi-ranches, and plush lawns.

"That's Hendrickson by the school," Georgie said. "I gotta turn there."

After circling the targeted block twice, he swung into a narrow side street and parked.

As they left the car, its doors purposely unlocked, Skinny dropped his cap onto the front seat. He followed Georgie across the street and into the side walkway of a large, marble-fronted colonial home. Moving quickly, they squeezed in between neatly clipped hedges and the coarse stone base of the building; each clutched at a damp towel beneath his dark zipper jacket.

With nervous, jerky movements, Georgie checked his watch. "He should be here any minute," he whispered. "I'm sure we had a fifteen-to-twenty-minute head start. Do you think we missed him? What if—"

"Don't worry. Just put your mask on."

Both men slipped navy wool ski masks over their heads.

Skinny glanced toward the backyard. Even in darkness he could catch the glimmer of white terrazzo, the outline of neatly clipped trees and hedges, and the vivid colors of stained glass torches; a huge scrolled *M* in the middle of an iron gate stood out against a fog-covered moon.

"Boy, he must have a fortune to own a house like this," Skinny said.

"Are you kidding? This guy's got money he ain't even counted yet. We could probably retire just on his grocery bills." Georgie put one hand, damp and shaking, on Skinny's arm. "Thanks again. You know if I didn't need this so bad, I wouldn't ask you."

"Fuck you!"

After a couple of false alarms, the two sweaty hoodlums heard a car turn into the block. The faint glistening of headlights on the side panels of parked cars became more vivid as it approached. Georgie's pulse quickened; remote-triggered metal gears straining to lift the garage door vibrated through his body and made his heart feel like it would stop; his lungs fought for air.

By the time the ornately carved door began its slide into an overhead track, the bright lights of a white Mercedes 500 SL flooded the entranceway. The door was on its way back down before the car was inside the garage.

With Georgie hanging on to Skinny's jacket sleeve, the two men slipped under the wood door when it was only a few feet from the ground. Georgie rushed to the driver's side while Skinny, still crouching low, scurried to the opposite point.

Though his heart pounded unmercifully in his ears, Georgie lost himself in the numbness of extraordinary fear; he felt as though he were moving while dead and suspended in time. Each of his movements seemed to be a dreamlike struggle against invisible forces; the limb that raised a towel-wrapped pistol and fired at a shocked Vallo numbers banker had to belong to someone else. Its sound muffled by the wet towel, the gun spat bursts of fire through the shattered window and into the victim, even as he vainly attempted to lunge away from the attack. Blood and gore splattered over the seat and dashboard.

The pungent odor of scorched terry filled Georgie's nose as he returned to reality. Struggling to keep from vomiting, he looked across at Skinny, who coolly stood back and out of the line of fire and who was, in fact, emptying his own gun through the back of the seat where their target had moved.

The two gunmen, who had both just killed for the first time in their lives, were back in the stolen vehicle and on their way out of Valley Stream within two minutes of entering the garage.

Georgie tugged the perspiration-soaked ski mask from his head. As he drove toward Brooklyn to report he'd scored one for the Rossellini Family, he wished he had something to stop his body from quivering.

Skinny Malone refused to speak to him all the way home.

33

August 2: East Side, Manhattan

He spotted them on First Avenue, while passing the glass-faced U.N. Plaza Hotel, and only then because he'd made an error and been too far out in the center of the street. When the gray Chevy van jumped across two lanes the same as he did, it stuck out in his rearview mirror as if it were a moving neon sign.

Even though he had nothing to hide, doing nothing more unlawful than taking Laurel for a birthday dinner at Numero Uno and maybe a few late drinks at Nell's, Mickey Boy decided to lose whoever it was behind him. As far as he was concerned, lawmen—or guys in Halloween masks—certainly didn't follow people to make sure they arrived at their destinations safely, or to make their evenings more comfortable.

Adrenaline pumping, Mickey Boy signaled left at the corner of 47th Street, but held up traffic till the light changed to red before making his move. A cacophony of blaring horns accompanied his turn—the Chevy van, stuck five lengths behind, didn't. Luckily, he caught the light again at Second Avenue, turned south, then hastily doubled back on 46th Street toward where he'd begun.

"Mickey, what's the matter?" Laurel asked. "Why are you driving like a nut?" She turned and stretched one arm over the back of the seat, lifting herself enough to look through the rear window.

Thankful his was the only vehicle moving on the narrow side street, and not wanting to alarm her, Mickey Boy replied, "I just remembered I wanted to look at something farther uptown before we go to Freddie's."

"That's why we're driving in circles?"

"No, I just forgot where it was for the minute . . . lost my bearings."

"What, another club?" Laurel asked, her mouth twisting with annoyance. "Can't you save it for when you're with your friends? God knows you're with them more than you are with me. I thought tonight was—"

"Whoa, slow down," Mickey Boy interrupted, trying his best to smile. "I know you'll wanna see this."

Lately Laurel had been nagging him more and more, constantly bitching about either his involvement with the after-hours club or things like how he preferred they leave or enter his apartment building in the weeks since their auto accident.

150

When going out after dark, they'd slip through the rear door, then walk along the water's edge to the narrow, hidden lanes of small bungalows, where he paid an old fisherman to hide his car. When leaving or returning alone, day or night, he always followed those same procedures.

And saying he was only trying to avoid his parole officer's watchful eye didn't placate Laurel one bit. "If you weren't doing anything wrong, you wouldn't have to worry," she'd reply each time he offered up the excuse. Bitch, bitch, bitch.

To make matters worse, Laurel had discovered a strong ally in Mickey Boy's mother. Emboldened by Connie's support during their triweekly phone conversations, she gave him little respite from her requests that he give up his mob life for a legitimate one.

In a good mood, Mickey Boy's usual response was to sing Sinatra's "Swingin' on a Star" to her, with final lyrics changed to "Or would you rather be a *nag?!*" On bad days he'd threaten to walk out if she didn't shut up.

"Isn't Freddie holding a table for us at a certain time?" Laurel asked as Mickey Boy raced across the First Avenue underpass. "It's really not fair to him."

"We'll just be a few minutes," he answered cheerfully, struggling to hide his anxiety. "I got a building I wanted to look at, maybe for a restaurant. I figure a legit business should make you happy, an' showing it to you on your birthday might bring it some luck."

Still uneasy, Laurel looked through the rear window again, once again saw nothing suspicious, then visibly relaxed.

Now that he'd ducked whoever it was that had been following him, Mickey Boy drove aimlessly, scanning the sidewalks for an empty store to fit his story. He found a suitable one on glitzy East 86th Street, and spent nearly a half hour checking it out with her—gauging foot traffic, assessing nearby competition, getting rent and measurement figures from the owner of the card shop next door.

Laurel excitedly poured out ideas for the mythological restaurant's decor on the way to their original destination: Numero Uno.

Shit! Mickey Boy cursed silently when he noticed the gray Chevy van parked diagonally across from Freddie's place. It had to be the fuckin' law, maybe even Spositoro himself—who else would know to find him there?

Though outwardly suppressing the anguish he felt—the tension of being hunted—inside, Mickey Boy's stomach knotted and his mouth dried. How long had he been under heavy surveillance? How much did they know? Visions of being returned to jail pounded in his head.

Once inside the restaurant, however, the evening progressed beautifully. Freddie's chef outdid himself in preparing a birthday feast:

shrimp, clams, and crabmeat sautéed with tomatoes and tossed through fine strands of angel hair pasta; imported filets of pure white Dover sole covered in a butter and garlic sauce and served over a bed of arugula; delicate pastry puffs filled with herb-seasoned asparagus and three kinds of cheese. And wine: two bottles of Château Lafite—a gift from Freddie.

Mickey Boy ate and drank with the gusto of someone having his final meal.

The birthday cake made the biggest hit with Laurel, especially when she found the gold bracelet with her name spelled in diamonds that Mickey had ordered stuffed into the middle layer of lemon mousse. She cried and laughed at the same time, while pulling it from its clear plastic sheath.

The evening's comical entertainment hit its peak when, after relating a couple of his humorous mob anecdotes, Freddie attempted a Neapolitan love song accompanied by two violinists he'd shanghaied from a nearby Hungarian café—neither of whom knew anything but Gypsy melodies.

After relaxing early on, Mickey Boy's irritation over being followed intensified in direct proportion to the quantity of bordeaux he consumed. To rate that kind of attention from the authorities, he reasoned, he had to be in deep shit again. A parole violation began to look more and more real.

With a little more wine his pessimism turned to resignation, then to amusement as he came up with his own little getback on the lawmen outside. Just before his and Laurel's private party drew to a close, he went to the front window, peeked between the café curtains to check outside, then dropped a quarter into the wall phone and dialed.

"Hello, Eighteenth Precinct?" Mickey Boy asked. "I'm calling from Numero Uno restaurant on Second Avenue . . . yeah, Numero Uno. There's a gray Chevy van with two guys in it that's been parked across the street for a couple of hours, and with all the robberies in the neighborhood lately . . ."

"Oh, oh," Muffin-Face groaned to his partner when two police cars, lights flashing, pulled up alongside their gray Chevrolet van. "We got fuckin' problems."

34

August 3: Elizabeth, New Jersey

The man who plays alone never loses! Time and time again Little Vinnie had heard his father voice those words in Sicilian—enough times to have learned to do things for himself. But once again he'd depended on those idiots who surrounded him, and once again they'd let him down.

"Idiots!" he screamed suddenly, stomping away from the window he'd been staring out. "Fuckin' moron idiots!"

The brunette in the motel's bed looked up with fright from her pillow. She pulled the blue coverlet over her nakedness and up to her chin, as though it could protect her from the madman she'd let pick her up in Hedge's the night before.

"Get the fuck out!" Little Vinnie screamed at her. He grabbed his pants from the chair they were draped over and pulled some money from the pocket. "There," he shouted while throwing a few bills in her direction. "Here's fifty . . . no, take a hundred. Just get a fuckin' cab an' disappear! Don't be here when I get out of the shower."

The stunned girl finally found the courage to respond. "Hey, buster, I ain't no fuckin' hooker!" she yelled back at him.

"Listen, bitch," Little Vinnie growled. "Either take the fuckin' money or don't . . . I don't care. Just get the fuck outta here before I throw you out the fuckin' window!" He hurled another fistful of bills at her.

Suddenly terror-stricken, the naked girl scooped up her clothes and rushed to dress. Little Vinnie was already in the shower when she slammed the door on her way out.

The previous night had turned into a fiasco, with him having to get a bondsman to bail out both men he'd sent to kill Mickey Boy. Good thing they'd only been caught with a ten-gauge shotgun and not a pistol. At least a few dollars spread around through his lawyer could get the charges dismissed or reduced so low that a fine would satisfy them. *Imagine the nerve of some fuckin' jerkoff calling the cops*, he thought, smashing his fist on the dresser. *What fuckin' luck!*

Still naked, Little Vinnie threw himself on the bed. The sheet where the brunette's body had been felt distractingly rumpled and warm, and the lingering sweet scent of her perfume annoyed him. He shifted angrily to the other side of the mattress and flung the pillow she'd used across the room. *Dirty whore bastard!*

No, stop, Little Vinnie told himself. He had to think, and think clearly. Since the day he'd accidentally overheard his father in the basement meeting, his mind had been befuddled. He'd love to be able to take care of Mickey Boy himself—no fuckin' idiots in between. But how? How to get rid of that no-good bastard without causing even more problems?

All at once Little Vinnie realized he had no choice. The distasteful idea that had been festering in his head for weeks now became his only viable solution—temporary to be sure, but quick and an easy alternative. If Mr. Mickey Boy Bastard thought he was good at carrying grudges, he'd see to it he had enough to be mad about to last a lifetime . . . hopefully, a short one, at that.

Excitedly, he reached for the phone, and after a few calls was finally able to track down the party he wanted. The receiver on the other end was picked up on the first ring: "Spositoro here."

35

August 8: Tarrytown, New York

The restaurant-bar of the Tarrytown Holiday Inn was moderately crowded that night. At a table in one of the darker corners, one of Junior Vallo's button-men, Tony Giarre, sat with his blond girlfriend, Marsha Caltanese. They were in the middle of a discussion as to whether they would go straight to their room to satisfy Tony's libido or make Marsha happy by bouncing around to a few of the area's night spots first, when a visitor approached.

"Hey, pal. What the hell are you doing here?" the newcomer asked.

Tony looked up to see his old friend, Jimmy DelComiso, or as he was more popularly known, Jimmy Del, standing over him, drink in hand. The two men had grown up together on 115th Street in Harlem, been altar boys at St. Ann's Church, and been partners on their first half dozen or so armed robberies. Even after they were made by two different Families, the two boyhood friends continued to bring each other business deals, and only that past winter had completed a mutually profitable sale of stolen securities in Toronto.

"Aaii, Jimmy," Tony Giarre said, flinging his arms wide. He stood and kissed his friend on both cheeks. "Jimmy, this is Marsha. Marsha, Jimmy Del. C'mon, sit down an' lemme buy ya a drink."

After ordering another round of Dewars and water, Tony explained his presence in Tarrytown: "With all the fireworks in the city, an' I don't mean the Fourth of July kind, the only way I could relax a little is to get someplace where nobody knows me—where it's safe, if ya know what I mean."

When the Westchester Premiere Theater was open and showcasing top-name entertainment, Tony had spent many a day visiting with friends of his who ran it, he claimed, and as a result had become fond of the surrounding area.

"So now, with the trouble we got in the city," he said, referring to the war his people were engaged in with the Rossellinis, "every time I get a shot I grab Marsha an' make it up here as fast as my wheels'll take us."

Tony didn't have to explain how he managed to convince his wife, Nettie, that he'd have to be away from home over nights and weekends. He knew his friend Jimmy had used every excuse he himself could think of, and more, on his own wife, Doreen.

"An' what brings you up here?" he asked Jimmy. "I'm lammin' it from Petey Ross's crew, but you guys are safe."

"Me, I got this Brazilian girl I picked up last month at SOB's; she lives up here. This is the fourth trip I made up here since then. I think it's true love this time," Jimmy Del said with a wink.

"You guys are hot shit," Marsha interjected. Forthright under the best conditions, and cuttingly sarcastic when peeved, with a few drinks she was considered by many to be a blatant big-mouth. "You're probably another one with a wife home cooking lasagna in the oven and nursing a bambino on her tit while you're up here fucking around."

Jimmy Del looked to Tony for help.

"Don't worry," Tony assured him. "Marsha knows the score . . . an' she's closemouthed when she's gotta be. Right, hon?"

"Are you kidding?" the platinum blonde replied. She sat up straight and tugged at the bodice of her red Danskin till her breasts swelled over its scooped neckline. "You wish all your tough-guy friends were as stand-up as I am. I've never said a word about anybody or anything I know . . . and believe me, I know plenty. My old man was a knock-around guy in the old days with Tony Bender, and he taught his daughter right."

Jimmy Del smiled. If there was one thing he hated, it was a female who thought that hanging out with a gangster gave her the right to act like one. In his time he'd seen too many "wiseguy humps," girls who wouldn't give a legit guy the time of day, to appreciate their brash mouths and ballsy attitudes, and to him, Marsha was one of the most nauseating examples he'd ever come across. Unfortunately, that night he had no choice but to be in her company.

In his most charming voice Jimmy asked, "How could we stay with one girl when there are so many hot numbers like you around, drivin' us nuts? I mean, we're only humans."

"Boy, I like him," Marsha cooed while elbowing her boyfriend's ribs. "Where is your lucky lady anyway?"

"I was just gonna be on my way to pick her up when I spotted you two. She told me she knows some great joints around here to go dancing. Why don't you an' Tony come along?"

"Oh, I love to dance," Marsha replied. "But Tony won't. He'll only do slow dances where he can mush it up with me." She elbowed her boyfriend again. "Horny little bastard."

"Same here," Jimmy Del said, chuckling. "You know the old saying: Tough guys don't dance. But if you take the ride, you could dance with Sandy while me an' Tony get just bombed enough to still be able to do the right thing later on." He winked at Marsha, then turned to Tony. "Well, how about it, pal?"

"I don't know. It's getting late an' . . ."

Marsha snuggled close to her boyfriend. With one hand rubbing the inside of his thigh and her lips pressed against his ear, she whispered, "Come on, honeybunch. Do this for me now, baby, and later I'll make sure you have the best time you ever had—you know how hot I get when I dance." She began to massage his crotch gently. "Huh, daddy?"

"Okay," Tony groaned. "You know I'm a sucker for a hard-luck story—or a hard-on from a horny blonde."

They all laughed, then stood to go, Tony signaling for the check.

"We could all go in my car," Jimmy Del said. "That way I could drop you guys back here before I head back to the city. Truth is, I really can't hang around that late tonight."

Smirking, Tony patted Marsha's backside. "Sounds good to me. The earlier the better."

Marsha slipped her arm through Jimmy Del's and started toward the door while Tony waited to pay their bill. "Poor Sandy," she said, looking up lewdly under drink-heavy lids. "How can you be so mean to send her home to a cold shower after she gets all hot and bothered on the dance floor? If it was me, I'd cut your balls off."

"If it was you," Jimmy Del said, smiling back at her, "they'd probably be worn out by now anyway." He looked at his watch. "Lemme go call Sandy an' tell her we're on our way."

Daniel "Danny Trap" Trapani shifted uncomfortably from one foot to the other beneath an elm on a deserted Tarrytown block. Humidity made his crotch sticky inside the nylon pantyhose he wore, and his brassiere cut into the skin under his arms.

"Fuck these guys," Danny muttered. He tugged angrily at the bra through his purple crepe dress, lifted the falsies back into place, then adjusted his dark auburn wig. "I know I'm gonna fall off these fuckin' high heels," he complained to the tree. "How these bitches do it, I'll never know."

Danny checked his watch again. *The beeper rang ten fuckin' minutes ago*, he thought, his patience worn thin. *Why don't they fuckin' hurry up?*

Spotting a pair of headlights coming from the wrong direction, he stumbled across to the hidden side of the elm. That's all he needed, some asshole trying to pick him up, or a cop—a fuckin' cop! Visions of being hauled into some suburban police station and being ridiculed by its local yokels went through his head.

Maybe that's what this whole thing was about, he began to wonder as more time passed. Maybe the whole thing was an elaborate practical joke engineered by his friends to make him look ridiculous. "I'll kill 'em," he grumbled. "I'll really fuckin' kill 'em if they did that to me."

When another auto swung around the corner, he recognized it immediately and stepped off the curb to be picked up. *Thank God*, he thought. *Will I be glad when this is over.*

Danny yanked the car's door open almost before it stopped and, pulling a .38 revolver from his purse as he went, quickly ducked inside. Steadying the gun on the back of the seat, he fired four times into the chest of Tony Giarre before the Vallo button-man could reach his own pistol. Without pausing, he shot once into the screaming flash of yellow that was Marsha's head, then spent his last bullet in Tony's face. Both bodies huddled together on the backseat, Marsha's on top, blood from her temple running down over her boyfriend's corpse.

The entire operation, from the moment Jimmy Del had stopped the car until he calmly pulled away from the curb, had taken less than four seconds. Jimmy followed a route they had previously plotted, driving carefully to avoid being stopped. "Are you sure they're dead?" he asked.

"Are you fuckin' kiddin'?" Danny snapped. He pulled the wig off, then, realizing what he'd look like if someone saw him before he changed, immediately set it back in place. "I caught him so off guard," he said, "it was just like he was sittin' with his insides drawn all over his shirt . . . you know, like one of those pictures in a doctor's office, where it shows all the guts. The first four caught his heart and lungs. I'll tell you, it was worth wearin' a dress to catch him like that," he added with a laugh. "Even though I thought you was crazy at first, I gotta admit, it was a great idea."

"You'd better believe it," Jimmy answered. "If this guy woulda smelled anything at all, we'd be lookin' like Swiss cheese now instead of them. This guy had some balls." He shrugged, remembering all the work Tony had done, then asked, "What about the bitch? Better make sure she's gone."

"Forget about her," Danny answered. "I got her straight through the brain. Too bad, she looked like a great hump."

Jimmy Del leered at Danny. "So do you, cutie. If Thumb ever sees you like that, he might just buy you a house in the country and a whole lot more of them pretty dresses."

Danny smiled. "A piece of that union he's got'll do fine."

When they found a spot where the woods sloped away from the main road they tossed the two bodies down, then headed for a Bronx junkyard of Tom Thumb's, where they'd feed their bloodstained car into a diesel-powered hydraulic press. By daybreak, the only evidence against them would be molded into a neat, unidentifiable package.

It was that same sunrise that greeted a badly injured Marsha Caltanese. Pain from three broken ribs made it hard to breathe and her head throbbed from the flesh wound Danny Trap had inflicted earlier that night.

"Jimmy Del!" the stand-up Marsha immediately told the state troopers who found her crawling along the blacktop. "Jimmy Del and his girlfriend Sandy killed my Tony!"

36

August 20: Theater District, Manhattan

The sweet pineapple-coconut flavor of the piña colada brought Laurel no pleasure at all. Her fingers drummed nervously on the tabletop as she sat in the dimly lit Polynesian atmosphere of the Hawaii Kai. It would take more than a thatched hut or some hula girls wiggling their bottoms to make her enjoy herself.

Unlike Laurel, her parents were having a wonderful time. They delighted over every morsel of the juicy Oriental appetizers that decorated the pockets of a huge wooden pu-pu platter. Her mother shoveled dripping tablespoonsful of shellfish drowned in a sauce thick with cherries and pineapple into her father's eager mouth, while he held a natural coconut goblet for them both to drink from.

"Damn that bastard," Laurel swore under her breath. The meal was practically over and Mickey Boy still hadn't arrived.

She should never have agreed to their meeting in Manhattan, she thought. Not that he would purposely avoid showing up because he had wanted to dine at a less touristy place, but she had enough trouble trying to keep track of him when they were both in Brooklyn, let alone separated by a river.

Lately Mickey Boy's obligations to his friends took up a steadily increasing portion of his time, while Laurel was continually relegated to second-place status. Those claims on him by his mob associates had bothered her in the first days of their relationship—now they were absolutely infuriating.

Laurel checked her watch again. Still an hour and a half until the curtain would rise at the Winter Garden for another performance of *Cats*. She had wanted to see that particular production for years but had never gotten around to it. Her opportunity arose, however, when she'd mentioned to Mickey that she would like to take her parents out for their anniversary and he suggested a Broadway show. Since he had never been to the theater, he left the choice of shows to her. Luckily, she'd accompanied him when he purchased the tickets from a scalper friend of his, or she would have wound up spending an uncomfortable evening acquiring a stiff neck in the first row. All the nightclub-oriented Mickey Boy understood was "ringside."

Laurel tried to calm herself by giving him the benefit of the doubt. She pictured him probably stuck in traffic somewhere, and as anxious as she was. *He's really a doll, even though he acts like a bad kid sometimes*, she told herself, comparing him to some of her more mischievous students. *Don't exaggerate, he'll be here before you know it. He just won't do this to you.*

It was a bit past four-thirty when Richie drove his red Nissan ZX into a parking lot on Pearl Street, two blocks from the South Street Seaport. Sitting in the passenger seat, Mickey calculated that if they spent no more than an hour with Buster, he'd still be able to be dropped off at the Hawaii Kai in time to have dinner with Laurel and her parents. That estimate included an allowance for getting stuck in some rush hour traffic.

Mickey was out of the car and moving as soon as it stopped. Outside the lot's entrance, he slipped into his navy-blue suitjacket and straightened his tie while Richie, clad in a white silk blazer over faded jeans, laid an advance tip on the attendant to keep the Nissan up front and away from other cars.

By the time Richie approached, Mickey had already stepped into the street. "C'mon, let's go," he said, and set off to bob and weave his way through six lanes of moving vehicles.

With Mickey setting a hurried pace, they walked along Water Street to Fulton, turned, then a block later turned again, this time into a narrow side street crowded by old warehouse-type buildings. Richie rang the lower bell alongside a black steel door that led to three floors above a store that serviced frankfurter pushcarts. Empty Sabrett boxes and number-ten sauerkraut cans littered an adjoining delivery platform.

When the buzzer sounded, the two men entered to face a narrow wooden stairway. The beige plaster walls that seemed to close in on them looked as though they hadn't been painted, or even washed, in decades, and the rubber-treaded linoleum covering the steps was faded and torn. A single gray camera stared down from the ceiling above the top of the stairs.

After carefully shutting the street door behind them, Mickey Boy and Richie proceeded up. On the first landing another steel door swung open just as they reached it. Dinty Moore, the obese bookmaker who hung out at Numero Uno, greeted them inside.

"Hiya doin', Mick, Rich? How's your lovely lady?" the fat man asked Mickey Boy.

"Great, Dint," Mickey Boy replied. "As a matter of fact, I gotta meet her uptown as soon as I finish with Buster. Is he here yet?"

"Here? He's been here all goddamned afternoon. An' between you, me, an' the lamppost, I wish he wasn't. He's been knockin' our socks off all day at the crap table. Musta beat us for twenty to twenty-five large so far."

"Don't he have a piece of this joint?" Mickey Boy asked.

"A piece?!" Dinty cried. "Him an' Vincenze practically own the whole goddamn thing. They got twenty points each an' then they got a dozen jerks like me, who put up five grand each an' either bring in business or play big ourselves, for five points apiece. It ain't too bad for me 'cause I grab an extra buck a day for handling the door," he added, referring to the hundred dollars he was paid daily to screen the illicit casino's guests.

"Old Buster's got it pretty good," Richie said. "If he wins twenty grand, sixteen of it comes out of his partners' pockets, but if he loses the same twenty, he gets back four of his own money plus four on the twenty grand he didn't take away from the house. Sonofabitch gets a lot of action for his money—it only costs him twelve thousand to lose twenty."

"Who gives a fuck!" Mickey snapped. "I asked a simple question an' got a whole life story. All I wanna do is get outta here fast."

Dinty directed the pair through an aisle flanked by eighteen blackjack tables, only a third of which were in operation, to an enormous back room with a regulation-size dice table set up at its far end.

When Mickey Boy spotted him, Buster was bent over stacks of multicolored chips and surrounded by all males, many of whom Mickey

Boy recognized as wiseguys and associates from either his own, Don Peppino's, or Tom Thumb's Family—no one from the two warring factions was present. The rest of the players gathered hungrily around the table were employees of the Fulton Fish Market, *New York Post*, or other businesses that inhabited Manhattan's southern waterfront district. Toward evening the clientele would gradually change to one of predominantly couples: men who worked during the day, with their wives or girlfriends. At that time the blackjack tables would run at full gear.

Neither Mickey Boy nor Richie wanted to disturb Buster while he was gambling, and consequently nearly ten minutes passed before he even noticed them.

"Go over to the bar an' get something to eat," he shouted above the buzz of other gamblers' conversations. "I'll be with youse in a few minutes." He then picked up the dice to take his turn at rolling.

Richie took Mickey Boy by the arm. "C'mon, let's get something; I'm starved. Besides, it gotta taste better knowing Tubby's paying— even if it is only costing him twenty percent."

"Naah, I'll just have a soda. I'm gonna be eating soon." Mickey Boy checked his watch, annoyed at how rapidly time was moving along.

Back near where they'd entered the loft-casino from was a ten-foot-long wood-paneled bar which enclosed a small kitchenette. An older man Mickey Boy remembered having seen at Buster's club was serving sandwiches, pastries, and nonalcoholic beverages from behind the Formica-covered counter. An enormous blood-rare roast beef sat in a pan of its own juices on the back ledge.

Richie ordered a dish of the meat with hot gravy and a bowl of sour pickles. He refused the offer of a hard seeded Italian roll, he jokingly claimed, to protect his "girlish figure." Mickey settled for a cold Manhattan Special coffee soda.

Before taking their meat and drinks to a table, Richie gave the counterman a ten-dollar tip—for his free food.

It wasn't until almost six o'clock that Buster finally came out to speak to his underlings.

Mickey, whose tie hung open and jacket was draped over the back of his chair, avoided looking directly at Buster to keep his anger from showing. All he could think about was how hurt and pissed-off Laurel would be by the time he showed up.

As far as Mickey was concerned, the entire evening was already ruined. Once Laurel got into one of her bitchy moods, that was it. He'd spend the better part of the night trying to put her in a better frame of mind so they could enjoy themselves—at least until he got disgusted and gave up till they were home in bed. Thank God that still worked.

So far, no matter what their dispositions had been earlier in the evenings, they'd always found a soother between the sheets and had never once fallen asleep angry with each other.

"Gee, fellas, sorry I kept youse waiting," Buster said, a smile crossing his bulldog face. "But it's tough to walk away from a winning streak. Always remember this, an' you'll never be a loser," he lectured while counting a fistful of cash. "Gambling is luck, an' luck is streaks. Press when you're ahead an' quit when you start to lose. Only suckers chase money when they're runnin' bad."

Mickey's jaws clenched as he lifted his eyes. What did he give a shit about kindergarten gambling lessons, he thought. All he wanted was to get the hell out of Buster's sight as soon as possible.

Richie smiled, and kicked Mickey underneath the table—a warning not to say something he'd be sorry for later.

"Anyway," Buster continued, "I'm glad youse are here now. I gotta pay a little visit to somebody, an' I want youse along. Just give me a couple of minutes to clean up an' take a piss, an' we'll be on our way."

As soon as Buster had turned his back to walk away, Mickey's face lit up like a stoplight. "Is this fuckin' guy kiddin', or what?" he growled at Richie through gritted teeth, controlling his tone enough, however, so no one else would hear. "He didn't even ask us if we had something else to do . . . nothing! Just, 'I want.' Whatta we look like, two fuckin' suitcases you carry around whenever you feel like it?"

"You wanna be Gucci or Louis Vuitton?"

"Very fuckin' funny!"

"Listen, pal, you know the score the same as me," Richie said. "Fatso didn't ask if we wanted to go with him, he told us. It's the same way if his skipper calls him; he's gotta go. Now, if you want all the good stuff of being made, then you gotta put up with the other shit too—get used to it."

"Fuck him and you!"

"Fuck me? Why fuck me?" Richie replied. When he saw Mickey smile, he continued. "I know you gotta meet Laurel, but just be cool an' let's play it by ear," he said. "Listen, if it's one-two-six an' out, then you'll only be a little late an' can kiss her ear to make everything okay. If it's the other way around, and it looks like we're gonna get stuck for a long time, then I'll remind you you got an important appointment, an' offer to stay with him myself—maybe he'll drag me to another crap game an' his luck'll rub off on me."

"No good," Mickey said, waving a hand in disgust. The sleeve of his white shirt was folded halfway to his elbow. "Then he'll wanna know what's so fuckin' important, who's involved, is it on record—you know, the whole shit. What do I tell him, I'm goin' to the Hawaii Kai to rob a picture of Don Ho?"

Richie began to laugh, but stopped abruptly when Mickey shot him a hard glare. He appeared pensive for a moment, then asked, "How about we tell him a jeweler's supposed to be comin' in from outta town with a package an' you gotta check it out?"

Mickey shook his head. "He knows I ain't stealing. And besides, I hate to start makin' up lies—especially for something stupid."

"Everybody steals," Richie said. "And when Laurel kicks you in the balls, it ain't gonna feel stupid." He leaned forward on the table, smiling impishly. "You could say that the tipster who's setting up the heist is waiting for you on Broadway an' Fiftieth. This way we'd have to drop you off near where you gotta go."

Mickey glanced at his watch. The idea was tempting, but . . . "Naah, then he'll really start pestering me to know how much, and—"

"We'll just tell him if it goes off he's got an end," Richie interrupted, leaning closer. He snapped his fingers. "No, better yet, we'll tell him you're gonna bring him the stuff to move. That should make him come in his pants—a shot to score and beat us on the figures at the same time. He'll be too busy scheming how to fuck us to ask anything."

"Oh, then who wants to hear him haunt me tomorrow," Mickey groaned.

"No sweat. Tomorrow we'll tell him the score was no good, that the mark carried in all paste 'cause he was afraid of getting robbed."

The idea was certainly tempting, Mickey thought, watching Richie eagerly awaiting a chance to put one over on their boss. He was just about to agree to do it when Buster returned. "Come with me," he ordered, and began walking toward the back of the building.

Mickey threw up his hands, then petulantly snatched his jacket and followed to an office in the rear, where Buster undid the padlocks fastening two large steel plates together on the wall. The burly mafioso removed a reinforcement bar, swung the metal boards open, and stepped through a window onto a fire escape. Once Mickey Boy and Richie had climbed outside too, one of the remaining workers from the club slammed the plates shut and relocked them.

With Buster leading and Richie behind him, Mickey Boy hurried down the fire-escape stairs, then dropped the last few feet from a corroded hanging ladder into a weed-filled backyard which was separated by only five rusty fencepoles from the adjoining yard of a building that faced the opposite street. Pieces of old wood, broken bottles, and dead vermin littered the uneven dirt yards the three trudged across; Mickey Boy and Richie both pulled their pants legs up above their ankles. Mickey Boy stumbled over something soft, but was afraid to see what it was, and kept on moving.

The trio entered the other building's back door into the steamy, sweet-smelling kitchen of a famous seafood restaurant. A half dozen chefs looked up briefly at the intruders, then, as if through traffic were a common occurrence, continued their work: dropping scallops into a deep-fryer, dredging shrimps in flour, shucking clams and oysters. Buster didn't turn around once as he marched through the kitchen. Mickey Boy looked at Richie, who appeared as baffled as he himself felt.

They followed Buster up a staircase to the restaurant's busy auxiliary dining room, then scaled another flight, at the top of which he knocked on the highly polished door of what appeared to be an apartment. Mickey Boy and Richie exchanged more confused looks behind his back.

When Buster pushed the door open and they stepped inside, Mickey Boy caught his breath. Seated at a large round table with place settings for five were Don Vincenze Calabra and his underboss, Joe Augusta.

"Ah, just in time for dinner," Don Vincenze called. With a wave of his cigar he beckoned the newcomers to the table. "C'mon, sit down," he said. "The linguine an' crab sauce is on the way up."

Anthony Spositoro shifted uncomfortably on the front seat of his dirt-covered 1981 Horizon. He had to urinate badly but was afraid it would be his misfortune that Michael "Mickey Boy" Messina would leave the old brick building, after hours of painstaking surveillance, just at the moment he chose to relieve himself. He had been there too long to lose out because of a bladder full of piss.

Not trusting the word of the anonymous informant who'd been jerking him around for more than two weeks about setting up Messina, Spositoro had begun his surveillance of the parolee at 7:55 A.M. in Brooklyn—eight hours or so before the late afternoon meeting in Manhattan the slimy bastard had claimed would take place. No way Mr. Mickey Boy Messina was going to slip him a red herring and get him keyed into a time or place, then never show up.

To Anthony Spositoro's chagrin, however, he'd spent an entire day running himself ragged only to wind up where the tipster had said anyway. Hell of a long day, but it would be worth it if he could score.

At 7:55 he'd dialed Messina's number, hung up when he'd heard his groggy voice, and logged the call in his book.

At 9:03 he'd repeated the procedure, and noted that his target sounded wide awake, and therefore would probably be going out soon.

At 10:21, still not having seen Messina come out, he'd called again. This time it was a girl's voice that answered.

"Michael there?" he'd asked. "This is his parole officer, Mr. Spositoro."

"Sorry, he's out," the girl had replied.

"Dirty lying bitch!" Spositoro had yelled after slamming down the receiver. By the time he'd reached his car again, however, he'd managed to calm himself. If nothing else, the logged calls would help him build a case for the punk not working, he'd thought.

By 11:40 the parole officer had been a hairbreadth from charging up to the apartment and ringing the bell, when Messina's white Lincoln pulled up to the front of the building. "What the fuck?" he'd blurted out to himself, unable to comprehend what was going on. He'd even used his binoculars to make sure it wasn't someone else behind the wheel. It wasn't.

A couple of seconds later Messina's girlfriend had wiggled out of the front door and deposited her classy ass in the Lincoln.

From there, Spositoro had followed the couple to a private home on Brooklyn's East 53rd Street, where Messina had stayed for about fifteen minutes before leaving with another male who picked him up in a red sports car. All the information the agent had garnered was entered into his black book.

He'd also snapped pictures of the house, which he guessed belonged to either family or friends of the girl, and the flashy auto that had picked Messina up—though both car and driver, who the tipster claimed was the parolee's partner, looked as unmoblike as he could imagine, being tied to a punk like Messina made them worth checking out.

During the rest of the afternoon the two unsuspecting racketeers had stopped at a drugstore in Flatbush, two pizzerias in South Brooklyn, and an office tower at 20 Broad Street, before finally leaving their car in a parking garage on Pearl Street and continuing on foot to where he'd been tipped off their meeting with Buster Alcamo would be.

Spositoro's Plymouth had crawled along like a crippled snail in order to remain undetected while following the two men. Luckily, he'd found an open parking spot on Fulton Street that afforded a direct view of the premises they had entered.

By early evening the parole officer had already filled a roll of film with photos of Messina, his companion, and an assortment of unsavory-looking types that had entered or left the shabby red-brick structure.

Despite the discomfort of having to sit in an inferno of a car for so long, Spositoro was thrilled. Active field assignments were the closest he could come, for the time being, to the type of work he would eventually do as an FBI man. Years of night study at John Jay College of Criminal Justice would be worth it if he could only help rid the streets of scum like Michael Messina, whom he especially detested for being a part of an organization that stigmatized all decent Italians like himself.

He'd grown up among trash like Messina, would-be Mafia scum, and knew them only too well. Punks. Lowlifes who'd thrived on abusing weaker, gentler, or less attractive kids. He could still see, almost feel, their hurtful taunts and jibes.

But Anthony Steven Spositoro, Jr., had finally won, becoming part of the fabric of mainstream America, while the small punks had become large vermin that had to be eradicated by society. Now the power of their government was about to bring them to their knees—every confidential report he'd read said the mob was crumbling—make them taste the abuse they'd earned, and he was proud of any part he could play in meting out that justice.

Though romanticism generally wasn't part of his makeup, Anthony Spositoro saw himself as a modern-day Sir Lancelot, his office a shield, the power to send criminals back to prison his jousting pole, and, for the moment, Michael "Mickey Boy" Messina his Black Knight. And he couldn't wait until the day he could wield the power of the FBI to strengthen his game.

At the point where his full bladder was causing him considerable pain, all Spositoro wanted was one shot of Messina leaving with a known felon. Because he was personally unfamiliar with the young, blond, athletic-looking man that the informant claimed was the parolee's partner, he had no knowledge if he had a record, and had to keep working. Just one former convict in Messina's company could lock up a violation hearing, and he, Anthony Spositoro, would make sure that if it happened, he'd be there to record it on film. *Just let him come out with an ex-con*, he prayed. *That's not too much to ask for sitting for hours in this oven.*

At 8:37 P.M. Spositoro abandoned his surveillance in search of the nearest available urinal that wasn't in a bar and grill—he'd taken the oath, and, by God, would stick to it. Then, immediately after relieving himself, he would call his local police contacts and find out for sure what was going on above the frankfurter store. If his new informant was telling the truth, he thought with satisfaction, Michael Messina was as good as in jail already.

Laurel paid for their meal with her American Express card, all the while cursing Mickey Boy under her breath. Amid apologies and excuses for her errant boyfriend, she and her parents then walked a few steps up Broadway to the theater.

How could he do this when he knows how important this is to me? kept flashing in her mind. All the rationalizing she'd done was worthless compared to the fact that he just wasn't there. *I guess that shows how important I am to him.*

Her mood brightened as they approached the lobby packed with theatergoers. By that time she'd convinced herself that Mickey would be there waiting, probably with flowers or some other surprise gift.

I really should have eaten where he wanted to, Laurel regretted inwardly. *Then I wouldn't have this problem. That bastard!*

Twenty minutes later, when the curtain rose to reveal a stageful of mewing felines, the aisle seat on Laurel's left was still empty.

37

September 1: Bensonhurst, Brooklyn

"Where do you want to start?" Laurel asked Chrissy, who was counting her money in the front seat of Laurel's Volkswagen Rabbit.

"I think we should start at Bay Parkway and work our way down," Chrissy replied without looking up. "I hope I have enough left over to buy Georgie a present." She began to laugh impishly, then said, in singsong, "But I doon't think sooo. Especially with the way he's been acting lately."

Laurel had met Chrissy to shop or just have lunch on several occasions since the day they'd spent together with their boyfriends in Manhattan, and spoke to her on the phone almost daily. She found her teenage friend always cheerful, and a great help in presenting a different point of view about the more troubling aspects of Mickey Boy's life-style.

Having grown up in a home with a Mafia tradition—both grandfathers and her father were executive officers in the mob's hierarchy—Chrissy knew the life of a female in that society well, and was always eager to relate that knowledge. The gaminlike adolescent loved being a knock-around guy's daughter, girlfriend, and hopefully someday, wife.

What amazed Laurel most was that Chrissy was totally aware of all the pitfalls in marrying a wiseguy, but found them an acceptable part of life.

"Sure, I know they all cheat," Chrissy'd said during one of their many conversations. "Even my father. I caught him one night coming out of Ponte Vecchio with some bimbo—and not even his girlfriend." She'd giggled, then added, "But I couldn't let him see me 'cause I was with Georgie."

Chrissy's philosophy, which Laurel assumed was handed down like a family heirloom, was that men were men, and as such would always have needs greater than one woman could, or would want to, provide.

"As long as Georgie comes back to me," she'd said, "who cares what he does? Just let him bring home the money—and no diseases."

Overriding everything else was a particular enjoyment Chrissy derived from the power she was able to exert over the men in her life.

"It's like being a lion tamer at the circus," she'd told Laurel. "I know how tough and mean Georgie can be, but not with me. If I pout, he gets like a cuddly teddy bear, and doesn't know what else he wants to do to make me smile. My father's the same way. Sometimes I'll get mad at them, or cry, just to watch them try so hard to make me happy again. I just have to know when to stop," she'd explained. "Even though I don't think they would ever hurt me, well, you never know what could happen if they lose their tempers. But I guess that's the excitement. I don't think I could be happy with someone that I wasn't a little bit afraid of."

While Laurel couldn't agree with all of Chrissy's views, she did admit to herself that she found Mickey Boy's underlying ferocity exciting. She remembered her reaction one night in a bar they had gone to, when he had beat a drunk senseless who'd touched her on the ass. Though she'd screamed at him to stop, that closeness to the physical violence he was capable of had gotten her so sexually aroused that she'd practically raped him when they reached home. Each touch of his knuckle-scraped hand had driven her mad, as she'd pictured it leaving a trail of blood on her pale flesh.

But there was more to life than excitement, and time after time, when confronted by Chrissy with what a joy it would be to be married to a successful gangster, Laurel found herself repeating, "But there are so many bad things that go along with that life."

However, each time, after venting her anger at incidents like Mickey Boy's not showing up for her parents' anniversary or his staying out all night, Laurel's arguments dissolved in reality as she became more emotionally involved with him.

The two girls parked on 85th Street and walked one block up to where a mile's worth of retail shops stand side by side in the shadow of the BMT el. Chrissy wanted to purchase some new fall clothes before they were sold out of her size, and another pair of shoes that would look decent with her Catholic school uniform; Laurel, anything that struck her fancy.

Over the course of the afternoon, Chrissy picked up three pairs of Guess jeans and five sweaters, one of them cashmere, from the various specialty boutiques in the area. She also left a deposit on a white leather jacket. Laurel bought a green Linda Allard blouse to freshen up one of last year's skirt sets, and a taupe knit dress that was an inexpensive but well-made copy of a Liz Claiborne. All they needed to make their day a complete success were the shoes Chrissy wanted for school, and a sexy piece of nightwear that Laurel felt might give her a lift.

"Why don't I try that little store while you look for your shoes," Laurel suggested, pointing to a small lingerie store off the main drag; fluorescent yellow signs announcing a new discount policy covered its entire window space. "This way we'll have time to grab a cup of coffee before I have to meet Mickey . . . not that he'll be on time."

When Chrissy agreed, Laurel crossed over toward the side street. A gold Eldorado held up traffic to let her pass, its driver flirtatiously punching the horn a couple of times as she walked in front of its grille. She smiled politely at both the compliment and courtesy, while continuing on her way.

The only one inside the store when Laurel entered was a tall young man who sat behind the counter reading a sports magazine.

"Help you?" he asked with no enthusiasm.

"Do you have any babydolls?"

"Regular or super-sexy?"

Laurel raised a questioning eyebrow.

"You know, the Frederick's of Hollywood kind of stuff, with openings and parts missing," he said without leering or grinning as she'd expected he might have. "It's just that we keep that stuff in boxes and the regular stuff displayed."

He wasn't bad looking, she thought, kind of cute and sexy in an awkward sort of way. Before Mickey, he might have been just her cup of tea. At that time she would have probably made him show her each transparent or crotchless piece, toying with and teasing him with innocently suggestive remarks and motions till he either suffered in silence or made a move.

But now, even though she wanted something totally shocking and overtly sexual, the thought of him showing them to her made her uncomfortable. "If the regulars aren't for senior citizens, I'll see them," she said.

The salesman smiled. "No, they're really nice. Got some pretty ones on sale over there," he said, pointing to a circular rack at the rear of the store. "If you don't find what you like, just let me know and I'll look in the storeroom for you." He went back to reading his magazine.

If these weren't the sexy ones, Laurel thought while inspecting a black teddy whose front was almost completely sheer lace, then the others had to be strictly for whorehouses or porno movies.

She had pushed the teddy aside and had removed a gauzy white babydoll with white satin tulips that would barely cover her nipples, when she felt someone gently stroke her hair.

Alarmed, Laurel spun around to find herself hemmed in between the racks by a young man who was approximately the same size and coloring as Mickey Boy. Two other youths, one badly pockmarked, blocked any possible avenues of escape. She became more frightened when she saw the salesman was gone and that she was totally alone with the three strangers.

"He went for coffee, an' won't be back for a while," the leering man in front of her said. He reached again to touch her hair. Laurel jerked her head back, banging it against the mirror.

"You'd better leave me alone if you know what's good for you," she managed weakly. It felt like her heart would stop. Fighting to catch her breath, she said, "My boyfriend—"

"Your boyfriend's shit!" the man who was now touching her cheek said with a sneer. "Mickey Boy knows who he could fool with and who he can't."

Laurel pressed her neck flush against the wall. Her eyes darted quickly to both sides, but there was nowhere else for her to move. She stood paralyzed with fear as the chunky young man ran two fingers down from her cheek, over her neck, and onto her breast.

"What you need is a real man," he said while snaking one hand around her waist to pull her close and cupping her breast firmly in the other, "one who's gonna be around for a while," he added, then kissed her full on the mouth. His hand slid down to her ass and held her so tightly that she felt his erection digging into her belly. He tried to force his tongue into her mouth, but licked her cheek instead when she turned away from him.

Laurel thrashed her head from side to side, trying to avoid more kisses; her hands pushed helplessly against his shoulders; a scream stuck in her throat. *Oh, God, help me!* she prayed as urine trickled from her body.

"What the hell are you doing?" she heard a female voice demand. In an instant her attacker backed off, revealing an angry Chrissy Augusta behind him, her hands on her hips as if ready for battle, her packages at her feet.

"Hey, cuz," Little Vinnie said, a nervous twinge in his voice. "Me an' Laurie here was just havin' a little talk, that's all."

"Listen, you shit. If she tells her boyfriend what you tried to pull, he'll hang your shriveled little balls on the nearest lamppost. And if I tell my father . . . and he tells your father . . ."

"Listen, cuz," Little Vinnie pleaded. "There's no need to blow this whole thing out of proportion. We was just havin' a little fun, an'—"

"Get out, Winnie," Chrissy said. Her voice was controlled but her face neared the shocking pink of her tank top. "Now. Or else I'm going right to the phone and calling home like E.T. Or do you and your asshole friends want to try and stop me?"

"No, no, cuz. We was just leavin' anyhow," he said, pushing his henchmen toward the door.

"And don't call me cuz!" Chrissy shouted after Little Vinnie as the front door slammed shut. She turned to Laurel. "You okay?"

Laurel's body vibrated uncontrollably. "I—I guess s-so," she stammered, then suddenly burst into tears.

A few minutes later, relieved but still sobbing, Laurel let Chrissy lead her out of the store and down the street to the Richelieu Restaurant.

"Feeling better?" Chrissy asked after Laurel had finished a cup of black coffee.

"A little." Laurel's hand still trembled. "Thanks," she said. "I really don't know what would've happened if you hadn't walked in when you did. Is that creep really your cousin?"

"Heaven forbid!" Chrissy exclaimed, rolling her large dark eyes upward. "Vinnie's father, who is the most powerful man in the city, is my godfather—he baptized me. He also happens to be your boyfriend's big boss. Didn't Mickey ever mention the name Vincenze . . . or Mr. Vincent to you?"

Laurel shook her head, a blank expression on her face. "Mickey tells me absolutely nothing about what he does or who he's involved with. Sometimes I think it's better for me that way, because I really don't want to know . . . I only get upset . . . but then other times, like now, it just makes me feel left out, like I don't belong."

Laurel sipped at her second cup of coffee. "I met some of his friends, like Richie, and Freddie from the restaurant, and Dinty Moore, but that's all I know . . . oh, and I know he goes to meet someone named Buster in Manhattan."

Chrissy laughed out loud. "Laurel, he's got you just like the old Sidgies keep their wives . . . in the dark. The only difference is that you're not barefoot and pregnant." She laughed again. "At least, not yet."

Laurel frowned. "I'm afraid that given a choice, I prefer it that way . . . on all accounts," she replied sadly. "I don't think I'd like what I saw if the lights went on."

"Oh, not me," Chrissy said. "I make believe I don't understand so I can hear everything that goes on. Not knowing what's happening is missing half the excitement of—"

"You mean like today?" Laurel snapped. "No, I'd rather pass. I don't understand what's going on . . . why something like today happened . . . and I don't know what to do about it, or how much more of the garbage that goes along with Mickey's life I can put up with."

Her enthusiasm undiminished, Chrissy leaned forward, put her hand on Laurel's, and with the seriousness of someone twice her age, said, "All I can tell you is that I don't think it would be a really good idea to tell Mickey Boy what happened. He'll only get crazy, and do something that could backfire and hurt him in the long run. After all, Vinnie's still his father's son."

Chrissy sat back, giving her advice time to sink in. "Why don't you just not say anything and let me see if I can do a little undercover work to find out what the beef is between Mickey Boy and Vinnie," she said, obviously excited by the prospect of becoming involved in a men's matter.

"Worse to worst, I'll be a little nice to that slob to try and find out something. He's absolutely crazy about me, and'll tell me anything I want to know if I work him right. Just don't be stupid and say anything to your boyfriend . . . for his sake."

"Oh, please, Chrissy," Laurel said anxiously, "don't become involved with that dirtbag on my account. I'd never forgive myself if anything happened."

"Don't worry." Chrissy giggled. "Winnie's a piece of cake."

38

September 7: Canarsie, Brooklyn

Ex-lax was already seated in the Arch's side dining room when Mickey Boy and Richie arrived. The gaunt pharmacist stood and shook their hands. To Mickey Boy he appeared older and thinner than at their last meeting. Dark circles under his eyes made him look like a movie version of a concentration camp victim—not as deathly emaciated as Mickey Boy had seen in actual World War II footage, but broken down enough to feel sorry for.

"Well, Irwin," Mickey Boy began while shaking his head slowly, "Richie tells me you got yourself jammed up pretty good with a couple of guys, and need some help."

Irwin nodded without looking up.

"Before I say anything else, I want you to know that the only reason I agreed to help you is because Richie put himself on the line for you. He thinks you been a hundred percent up front with him. I'm not so sure, but I hope for both your sakes he's right."

Mickey Boy paused, searching Irwin's face for a reaction, some indication of the gambler's lies he suspected were behind it.

Unable to detect anything through the man's anguished look, he continued. "There's nothing else you might've forgot to tell him, is there? Anybody else involved that you might owe money to?"

Irwin shook his head.

"If so, now's the time to say it, 'cause, Irwin, I promise you, if I find out you hid something later on, you'll wish I let the other guys get you."

Still unaware of Mickey Boy's real name, Irwin/Ex-lax whined, "No, Bruno, I swear. I told him everything. That's every penny I owe." He covered his face with his long, bony fingers and began to weep. "I don't know how I let this happen. If I lose my business . . . if my wife ever finds out . . ."

The sight of him crying touched Mickey Boy. Sure, he cried sometimes himself—at a sad part in a movie, when Sinatra sang "My Way," or at the sight of a seriously ill child—but never in self-pity, fear, or pain. It crossed his mind that instant that any suffering he'd done, in jail or otherwise, was worth it if the alternative was to be an Irwin.

"All right, calm down," he said soothingly. "Everything's not as bad as you think. It'll all be okay. Now, come on, just take a drink an' listen to me. Crying ain't gonna straighten your problems out—I will."

"Thanks, Bruno, Richie. If you guys help me this time, I swear I'll never go this far again. I was really stupid, betting sports and then running to Atlantic City every weekend. Those crap tables really killed me."

Richie sat silently, allowing Mickey Boy to carry the discussion forward.

"Now," Mickey Boy said, "Richie tells me you wanna do an insurance job on your store. I'm glad you came here for help, 'cause I'll show you how to get more money out of it than you could've ever done by yourself, and . . . I'll keep everybody you owe off your back. Just listen carefully, an' make sure you do everything exactly the way I tell you, an' you'll be just fine."

First, he instructed Irwin that if any of the people who were owed money showed up before Mickey Boy/Bruno and his people had time to reach them, he shouldn't argue with them or, worse, make any commitments for payments because he was scared.

"From now on," Mickey Boy said, "you don't talk to no street guys without me or Richie around. You belong with us now—officially on record. What you tell anybody who approaches you is this, 'I'm sorry, but I was told by my partners that it's out of my hands, an' that they'll get in touch with you.' Got that?"

"Okay," Irwin responded a bit hesitantly. Still appearing nervous and not the least reassured, he asked, "But what if they ask who my partners are?"

Mickey Boy was all too well acquainted with mob protocol where claims of business interests were involved. More than once he had been beaten out of deals by what he knew to be false claims of previous involvement by other mob-connected guys, guys who "came out of the woodwork," as the saying went. Now, as a result, he had no reservation about doing the same thing himself.

"You tell them that your partners, an' make sure you use that word—partners—are friends of theirs, an' will be in touch with them within a couple of days," Mickey Boy instructed.

"We know all but two of the guys on the list you gave us, and none of them are bad guys. Even the two we don't know will be respectful an' go away once you tell them what I said. If it happens that one of them tries to give you a hard time, just call Richie's beeper number. As soon as he sees it's you calling, he'll drop whatever else he's doing and get right back to you. In the meantime, we'll be reaching out for all of them. Is that clear?"

Once satisfied that the pharmacist understood how to conduct himself, Mickey Boy said, "Now, as far as the insurance, what've you got that we could leave traces of for an adjuster?"

"I don't understand?"

"Well, I'll give you a for-instance. Once I knew a guy in the clothing business. He had three different fires in his stores. What he used to do before he torched a joint was take out all the pants an' replace them with cheap metal zippers that he sewed to small pieces of material. When the adjuster came, he counted each burned zipper as an expensive pair of pants. My friend murdered the insurance company. Guys who burn restaurants do the same thing with empty whiskey bottles."

"No kidding?" Irwin said. He seemed astounded at the deviousness of other, supposedly legitimate shop owners. "I really can't think of anything offhand. Maybe—"

Mickey Boy cut him off. "Don't worry about that now, we got plenty of time for that. As long as you agree, we'll start by seeing that your joint gets burglarized in a couple of weeks."

Irwin readily agreed.

What he wanted, Mickey Boy told Ex-lax, was for him to begin stocking up on merchandise from his distributors. "I got a friend of mine's son who owns his own drugstore in Queens. We'll give him all the medicines an' stuff."

"You know," Irwin said, "some of the drugs can go for a lot more money privately."

Mickey Boy had a sudden urge to smack the pharmacist across the face. He sighed heavily and dropped back in his seat. "Listen, 'cause I'm only gonna tell you this once," he said. "Richie an' me don't fuck with drugs, an' I don't ever wanna hear you mention nothing that even sounds like we do. Understood?"

Irwin nodded.

"Now, if you're gonna get greedy on us an' look to peddle that shit, tell us now, so we could step out of the picture before you have a real problem."

"No, no," Irwin said. "I just thought—"

"Please, Irwin," Mickey Boy said, holding a hand up. "I don't wanna insult you, but do us both a favor an' don't think. If I need a prescription, I'll let you handle it. Meanwhile, this is my line, let me do the thinking."

He went on to tell Irwin the nonprescription items he thought it best to stock up on for the proposed burglary: cigarettes, perfume and cologne, radios, watches. Razor blades were good if he could acquire a substantial amount. He cautioned him to build his inventory without drawing attention from his sources of supply. If Irwin's store normally stocked twenty radios, for example, Mickey Boy advised him to boost that figure to thirty or thirty-five, not a hundred.

After the break-in, Irwin would replace the missing inventory plus order larger quantities for pre-Christmas delivery in early November. Mickey Boy also promised to have a friend provide a layout for ads and a contract for a large advertising campaign, to be used to explain to distributors why such large quantities of goods were being ordered.

"Oh, an' don't forget to load up on plenty of toys an' Christmas lights too," Mickey Boy said. "As you get closer to the holidays, we'll keep selling off your extra stuff to our people, an' you'll keep filling in. Then in January, before your biggest bills come due . . ." He snapped his fingers. "*Whap!* Jew's lightning." Smiling, he added, "No offense, Irwin."

"What do you fellas get for all this?"

"Half of what we sell the stuff for, ten percent of what the insurance company gives you, and the contract to rebuild your store after the fire."

When he saw Irwin's eyes open wide in response to his demands, Mickey Boy said, "But what you get is out of trouble, an' wind up with a brand-new showplace instead of the shithouse drugstore you got now. Good enough?"

"I guess."

"Also, all expenses, like the guys who haul the shit from your joint, the burglar who makes it look like it was a real job after you're empty, and the torch, they all come off the top. But don't worry. They're all cheap. Fair enough?"

"Not exactly. I thought you two would take care of everything yourselves."

"Irwin," Mickey Boy said with an impatient huff. "I don't know what you think of me an' Richie, but we ain't common hoods. We ain't burglars, an' we ain't firebugs, understand? We're businessmen, like you, only with a little muscle. Now, do you have a problem with any of that?''

Irwin appeared none too happy, but nonetheless replied, ''I guess it will have to do.''

The obvious displeasure the pharmacist had about how he had to split profits annoyed Mickey Boy. *Greedy prick*, went through his mind. He brightened, however, at the realization that Irwin had no other viable alternatives. *Too bad, Irwin*, he thought. *You'll just have to skip one of those weekends in Atlantic City that you were counting on.*

After shaking hands to seal their arrangement, and leaving Irwin to pick up their check, Mickey Boy rushed off to pick Laurel up after her first day at school—late, as usual.

Though he loved watching any movie starring Goldie Hawn, Mickey Boy focused on Laurel instead of the TV screen. From where he lay, propped up in bed by two pillows, his eyes followed her as she pranced naked from the bathroom, where she'd just showered, to the dresser, where she pulled the diaphragm she'd recently been fitted for from the top drawer, then back to the bathroom to powder, perfume, and otherwise ready herself for lovemaking. This was no unrealistically directed film star who pulled a sheet over her tits every time she moved. This was a girl who let it all hang out, who enjoyed seeing him enjoy every private inch of her flesh.

By rights, Laurel's immodesty should bother him. That's what the old men would say. Even though she was the perfect lady in public, dressing in a classy, conservatively feminine style, they'd say her willingness to flaunt her body like she did with him was one sign of her being a *putana* at heart; that given the chance, she'd probably think nothing of being naked at the beach, in front of all strange men, or dancing naked at a party if she got drunk.

On the first count, at least, they were right. Once, while thumbing through a travel magazine, he'd seen a photograph of nude bathers on the Riviera, and had asked her if she would ever do that.

''Why not?'' Laurel had responded. ''When in Rome . . .'' What about when she used to go to Rockaway, he'd asked. Had she gone to the nude bays then? Even though she'd smilingly denied it, and he'd threatened to kill her if she ever did, he suspected she'd been a regular there at one time—as long as it was before.

Through the open doorway to the bathroom he watched her squat slightly in front of the sink, her fingers buried in her crotch, readjusting the diaphragm she still wasn't comfortable with; his own fingers unconsciously touched the hardness between his legs.

And what would the old bastards say if they knew how his girlfriend behaved in bed? he wondered with amusement. Forget about it. They'd accuse her of fucking the butcher, the baker, and everyone else in her vicinity, including the blind and crippled.

Oddly enough, all those things which would have driven him crazy for most of his life meant nothing now. In fact, he enjoyed, no, loved the unreserved sexuality she bestowed upon him. Didn't they always say to treat a lady like a whore and a whore like a lady? How did they know which was the real person? In his new thinking, the bottom line was that the past was dead, and what she did now was only for him.

Mickey Boy had explained to Laurel, meaning every word of it, what he'd be forced to do if he ever found out she'd cheated on him. He'd done too much in his life for respect to have some slut cuckold him. Painful as it would be, he'd said, he'd be forced to "plant you like a petunia," and, fortunately, he believed she believed him.

He watched her throw a towel over her shoulder and rinse a washcloth to clean him with when their sex was done. Just like a geisha girl, he thought—and that did bother him. Laurel seemed more than happy to go along just as they were. As close as he got to her, he never really felt like he possessed all of her, never felt he had a full commitment. She never talked of kids or marriage, and even kept a bunch of clothes at her parents' house.

Just an hour earlier, in fact, Laurel had made him furious inside when she'd related a conversation she'd had with his mother.

Connie had called earlier that evening to confirm plans for her visit to New York in two weeks for the Feast of San Gennaro. In spite of Mickey and Laurel having repeatedly offered to have her stay with them, she'd refused.

"I think she figures we'll screw more if she's not around," Laurel had said. "She's dying for grandchildren, you know." She had laughed then, and added, "Wrong girl, wrong time—no kids for me till after church, and I don't see that for a long, long time."

Fuck her! Mickey Boy'd thought, but had held his tongue. He'd be damned if he'd let Laurel, or any girl, for that matter, know how he felt or what he really wanted. No way he'd supply a weapon to hold over him.

Laurel slid into bed and snuggled under Mickey's arm. "Mmmm. Just like Ma and Pa Kettle," she said. "Wouldn't it be nice if you were home like this every night?"

Eager to avoid a repetition of dozens of discussions they'd been through, he said, "Are you making another 'old' joke about me?"

"All of you is definitely not old," Laurel purred while stroking his erection.

"Yeah, but most of me is," he replied. "Do you realize that when I was sixteen and out stealing—"

"And getting laid." She squeezed his testicles.

"And getting laid," he said, then cried out when she squeezed harder. "Do you realize that at that time you were only like in kindergarten or the first grade? Could you imagine somebody at that time saying, 'Hey, Mick, see this little girl? One day you're gonna be crazy about her, an' do all kinds of dirty things to her body'? If they did, I'da clocked 'em one for being a pervert."

Laurel plucked a foil packet from the top drawer of the nightstand, removed a condom, and began to roll it down over his engorged penis—she insisted that since diaphragms weren't a hundred percent effective at any time, until she got used to installing one properly she was in special danger and would take double precautions.

Shifting onto her back, Laurel pulled Mickey on top of her. "You pervert," she whispered throatily while guiding his erection into her body. "Do it to me again."

39

September 10: Mill Basin, Brooklyn

Blackie Palermo drove his gray Fleetwood across Avenue U into the small residential peninsula of Mill Basin. Suddenly houses became richer—Georgians, ranches, marble, stone. Thick, leafy trees shaded flagstone walkways and bay windows, while lawns and shrubs spread wider and greener than just a few blocks before, reminding Blackie more of a suburban township than a New York City neighborhood. He turned left into National Drive, the section's waterfront and thereby most exclusive street, then slowed to check address numbers.

"Here it is," he said, stopping in front of an oversize brick colonial guarded by two cement lions and a wrought iron fence.

"Nice place he got here," Don Peppino said, staring out the passenger-side window. "Looks like our good friend makes a little more money than what he reports," he added. "Doesn't my *paisano* Giacomo live around here too? Looks familiar."

Don Peppino gazed around once more, taking in every inch of professionally cared for property within view. It was habit for the old crime boss, who rarely strayed far from his Gravesend home, to inspect everything around him whenever he did venture out. "C'mon," he finally said, "let's go say hello."

The intricately carved door opened just as the two mafiosi reached it. Ronnie Belice, a gaunt, hook-nosed captain in Don Peppino's Family, stood waiting. He looked up and down the block to see if the two men had been followed, then locked the door and kissed them in greeting.

"Everything ready?" Blackie asked.

The captain nodded, then led his bosses through an overpoweringly red living room furnished in white provincial, and into the backyard which rested on the Brooklyn side of Jamaica Bay facing the Rockaway shore.

Don Peppino and Blackie hurriedly kissed their man good-bye, then, with Blackie staying only a couple of rungs below the old man to box him in with his body, they climbed down a ladder from the dock and into a white Donzi Classic powerboat.

Within minutes they had docked at a nearby marina and were on their way out of its parking lot in a sand-colored Cadillac Seville that had been left there for them.

Once confident no one was following, Blackie settled back and relaxed. He switched the air-conditioner on high. "We'll be there within the hour," he assured his uncle.

The two mafiosi proceeded along Rockaway Parkway, through the decimated area of Brownsville that in the early part of the century had been the hub of a thriving immigrant community.

To Don Peppino, the once-cramped but well-kept tenements now resembled bombed-out sections of Europe after World War II. For blocks and blocks on end all he saw were empty lots strewn with debris, burned-out shells of buildings, and unintelligible graffiti on every standing surface. He cursed the ruin of the neighborhood that had spawned doctors, teachers, politicians—and Murder Incorporated.

"Right down that block, on Livonia and Saratoga, I used to go to Midnight Rose's candy store," the old don reminisced to his nephew. "I used to meet the whole bunch there: Blue Jaw, The Dasher, Pittsburgh Phil—the whole bunch. They all used to answer to Albert," he said proudly, referring to his mentor, Albert Anastasia. "In those days I was like an ambassador for him. I used to come out here, then go see Happy Maione and Louis Capone up on the Hill, maybe every two, three weeks. I'll tell you, they had some good crews here till that no-good Jew bastard Reles turned rat. That sonomabitch! Too bad we didn't throw him out the window before!"

Irritated by bitter remembrances of Murder Incorporated's demise, Don Peppino turned his attention back to the neighborhood's appearance.

"Yes sir, it was a hell of a place then," he said. "Now look what these *dizgraziata tootsoones* did to it. They oughtta ship the whole bunch of 'em back to the jungle . . . they destroy everything else." He began

179

to laugh, then said, "Except, if we did that, what would happen to our number banks in Harlem and Bedford-Stuyvesant?"

Blackie smiled at what he knew struck his uncle as a huge joke. He made a left on Bushwick Avenue, followed it for a short while, then turned twice more, the second time onto Knickerbocker Avenue. Spanish bodegas, their windows covered with signs promoting Goya products, and clothing stores with merchandise hanging off gaily striped awnings lined both sides of the street. Various shades of brown faces hovered over open racks of *zapatas*—the same racks that used to carry the latest in Italian-style shoes—while plantain and mango ruled the fresh produce stands that zucchini and broccoli rabe once owned.

"I ain't been around here in years . . . since Ciro's Restaurant closed. *Marrone*, but this changed a lot too," the old man observed sadly. "Remember the Ridgewood Gardens?"

"Remember?!" Blackie exclaimed. "You know how many times I fought there before the accident?" The accident. For over twenty years now he still felt a twinge of pain in his missing eye every time the word was mentioned, every time he thought of that dirty spic Coco Rivera jabbing that thumb into his face, trying to blind him. But at least the pain in his heart was gone, dissolved with Coco in fifteen pounds of quicklime.

Blackie shook off the memories to peer affectionately at his uncle, who'd been his favorite since he was a small boy. He wondered how many years the withered old man had left.

"You know, Unc, you really should get out a little more," Blackie said. "Why don't you let me take you out to dinner, even once a week. This way you'd get to see the old neighborhoods—and you know the guys would love to see you."

"Ah, my little Fava. Remember when I used to call you that? For me to get out an' see what the niggers an' spics have done to the old places only makes me sick. If it wasn't so important that I keep this appointment you made, I wouldn't come here at all. I'd rather stay home, where it's safe . . . no cops, no stool pigeons, no nothing . . . an' just remember things the way they used to be."

"Aaii, but at least you'd get out."

"I'm an old man. Why should I put myself with people I don't like? Why take a chance that some *stroonze* goes bad an' says I said this or that, where I wind up in jail till I die, like Fat Tony or Ducks, when I could sit in a beautiful house, surrounded by beautiful things and a beautiful family? I open my mouth and, ah, I get anything I want to eat, from sweet cakes to lobsters. I press a button and Jimmy Rosselli sings to me. Please, Fava, leave an old man alone to die the way he wishes."

The sullen expression on his nephew's face warmed the old man.

What does he think, my Fava, he mused, *that I'm never going to die?* In an attempt to cheer the younger man, however, he added, "Except for Thursdays, when we still go to the strip to find a *putana* to suck my prick, eh?"

A few minutes later Blackie parked in front of a four-story beige-brick tenement on Starr Street. Lushly filled window boxes, their green paint chipped and faded, hung off the lower sills. The front stoop was chalked over with Spanish writings.

A buzzer admitted them past a glass-paned wooden door with a yellowed lace curtain behind it. As they slowly mounted three flights of creaky stairs, Don Peppino thought of treachery, and how there was no defense against it—no matter who you were. He counted the single naked bulbs that barely lit each landing, not only to mark the end of a wearying climb, but with sadness for the fate of one of his own. The stuffy odor of decades of mingled lives filled his nostrils.

Blackie knocked on the only metal door in the building. It was secured by three expensive, heavy-duty locks that echoed loudly as they were released.

Don Peppino stared at his half-blind nephew, dumb by his own standards, but that's what had made his only brother's son a good safe choice for underboss. At least he could count on his nephew being loyal, not like the *dizgraziata* inside. No, the same thing would never happen to this old man, the don thought with a grim satisfaction. No, he would make sure that when his time to die came, it would find him sleeping in bed.

A bent old woman clad entirely in black opened the door the four inches that were all the sturdy chain would allow, and eyed them suspiciously. When she was able to focus on their faces and recognize them, she began to close the door to unhook the linked barrier. "*Aspetto* . . . wait," she called as she maneuvered the chain.

"Frankie Boy, Frankie Boy, it's been so long," the enfeebled old crone gushed at Blackie in her Sicilian dialect. "Every day you and my Rocco used to play here." She turned her attention to the older men. "Don Peppino, I'm honored for you to come to my humble home." She grabbed and kissed his hand.

"Please, *Signora*, the honor is mine," Don Peppino answered warmly in the same language.

Beaming, the old lady led them through an immaculate but antique-looking parlor filled with crucifixes, pictures of saints, and other icons into a small kitchen, where the man Petey Ross and Sonny Fortunato had not trusted to attend their penthouse meeting, Tom Thumb's underboss, Rock Santoro, sat morosely waiting with a cup of coffee in his hand.

40

September 14: Little Italy, Manhattan

The first thing that Mickey, his mother, and Laurel saw of the Festa San Gennaro was the yellow aura of some thirty thousand electric-light bulbs that turn the night sky from black to brown for a period of ten days each September.

Since 1926, New York City has cordoned off an area as tribute to St. Gennaro, the patron saint of Naples, who is credited with having prevented Mount Vesuvius from erupting during his lifetime. This saint's dried blood is kept in a vial in Italy, where it is said to liquefy on certain occasions. But in New York, the only red liquids of any consequence at feast time are the thousands of gallons of rich burgundy wines that are drunk throughout the neighborhood in restaurants, cafés, and outdoor stands.

In spite of the original one block of Mulberry Street having expanded to include six running and at least three other cross streets, the increase has done nothing to lessen the crush of visitors who pour through the narrow passageways with the intensity of herded cattle.

Food is the main attraction of the gaudy homage to the third-century saint. Homemade retail stands with strings of bare bulbs snaking across the tops of their wooden frames offer a mouth-watering selection of Italian delicacies, including grilled sweet or hot sausages topped with a mixture of zesty fried peppers and onions, deep-fried shrimp and *calamari*—squid—in hot red sauce, fresh raw clams, pizzas, calzones, sugar-coated zeppoles.

And fun. The grandest of all the city's street fairs provides plenty of entertainment for all age groups. Flat-store hustlers challenge young men to impress their girlfriends by throwing baseballs, hoisting sledge-hammers, shooting guns. "Try your luck! Win a stuffed toy! Win a goldfish!" they bark, lending a carnival atmosphere to the festivities. Ferris wheels, carousels, and other children's rides occupy whatever parking lots poker, blackjack, and craps tents ignore. "Buy a T-shirt! Buy a flag! Buy a souvenir of Little Italy!"

Though still in the bordering SoHo district, Mickey Boy's Lincoln was already slowed to a near crawl by San Gennaro traffic.

"Now for one of the better parts of our life," he said, "making money. All legit, but if you're not hooked up with the right people, you can't even get the time of day, let alone a spot to earn off. Maybe now you two'll stop nagging me for a while, when you see it ain't all bad."

Connie, sitting alongside him in front, grimaced. "I know all about the good side of what you do," she said testily. "And I am also familiar with too many of the bad parts—and believe me, those far outweigh the little glamour that attracts you so."

Despite Connie's claim of being familiar with his life-style, he wondered what the hell she or Laurel knew about what it was really like. Outside of what they saw on TV, he was the closest they'd come to knowing anybody from the streets. How could either one of them understand what being a "wiseguy" meant to him?

Mother Teresa, Goody Two-Shoes, an' Al Capone, he thought. *What a sideshow this is!*

"Well, I certainly hope Laurel can do something to change you," Connie went on. "I know my breath has been wasted all these years."

"You're right, Ma. I should change," he said. "First thing tomorrow I'm gonna apply for a job as a brain surgeon . . . or, better yet, as an architect, like Alley."

"Oh, he's not bad," Laurel quickly interjected, reaching from the backseat to pat Mickey Boy on the head like she would one of her students. "He'll be okay."

At least Laurel had the good sense to know when enough was enough, Mickey Boy thought. The last thing he wanted was bickering to ruin his mother's first visit to the feast since moving to Boston.

Having never learned to drive, for six years Connie had been totally dependent for her transportation on Alley, who refused to subject himself to what he termed "the crush of the slobbering hordes." Mickey Boy had changed all that, giving his mother the opportunity to visit, by going to Massachusetts, chauffering her back down, and, after she'd refused again to stay at his apartment, setting her up a few blocks away in the Golden Gate Motor Inn.

It took Mickey Boy four changes of traffic lights to go another block and a half. "Whattaya say we park here an' walk the rest of the way?" he asked, his skin crawling from the stall. "Okay with you, Mom?"

"What do you think, I'm an old lady who can't walk a few blocks? You're the one who has to worry, with that pot belly you're getting," Connie teased. "Laurel's cooking seems to be too much to your liking."

"Don't blame me," Laurel replied. "He's not home enough to get fat on anything I cook."

Here we go again, he thought, and made a quick, jarring left into the nearest parking lot.

The trio walked the few blocks and entered the cordoned-off area at Grand Street, one of those cross streets that gives the Neapolitan fête the grid shape news-helicopters sometimes record for TV. They turned right on Mulberry and walked south toward the festival's nucleus a block away at Hester. Overhead, red, white, and green garlands glittering with tiny bulbs stretched from one side of the street to the other. Mandolins blared a static-filled version of a tarantella over loudspeakers. The sweet smell of hot meats filled their nostrils.

Because his mother seemed mesmerized, staring all around her like a child at Disneyland, Mickey Boy had to put an arm through hers and guide her along. Smiling at her obvious pleasure, he asked, "Good to be home?"

"Wonderful!" Connie replied, and kissed his cheek.

Laurel wanted to stop and have her fortune told by two Gypsy women who had set up a small bridge table in the gutter between a pastry stand and a gambling wheel.

"You must be nuts," Mickey Boy said. "They're all phonies. Besides, I wouldn't want to know what's gonna happen anyway," he added. "That is, if by some slight chance they were for real."

"I don't believe you!" Laurel exclaimed. "What are you afraid of? I'm not."

"If you wanna go, please, do it when I'm not around," he said. "And, whatever you do, don't tell me about it!"

Both his mother and Laurel laughed at him, but bypassed the fortune-tellers anyway.

At the corner of Hester Street they stopped at the Shrine of St. Gennaro, which spends the balance of the year at the nearby Church of Most Sacred Blood. Each of them made a donation to a church representative, who climbed a ladder and pinned their currency to long streamers hanging off a two-story-high board that had been constructed behind the saint. In return, they received small mass cards with color portraits of St. Gennaro. Their duty done, they rushed to the nearest sausage and pepper stand, where they bought sandwiches dripping with oil to eat as they walked.

The flow of human traffic was so thick it almost dragged them along against their will. Mickey Boy suggested they walk behind the stalls, on whatever strip of sidewalk remained clear. Connie and Laurel voted him down. They agreed that the shoves, bumps, and elbow jabs were a small price to pay for remaining at the center of the excitement.

"Where are your stands?" Laurel asked.

"On the next block."

"Why didn't you try to get them close to here?" his mother questioned. "Look how busy. And right near the saint."

"Fat chance," Mickey Boy replied. "These guys got these spots for years." He went on to explain how choice locations were handed down from generation to generation like family heirlooms. The only way they became available was if someone had wanted out for one reason or another, or if they'd done something so terrible that they had it taken away from them. That year, he said, the first spot on that top block had become available since three years before.

"How did that happen?" Laurel asked.

"I hear the guy who had it left New York altogether," he answered, purposely omitting that the previous owner was also purported to have left in a drum of acid. "I could've got that spot because I know the guy who's got it."

"I don't understand," Laurel said. "You just said the person who had the spot left town."

Mickey Boy laughed. "No, not the spot; that guy's gone," he said. "I'm talking about the block. This whole block belongs to someone I know." Each block in the feast, he told them, was designated to street-guys from different areas. Careful to keep substituting "streetguys" for "wiseguys," he went on to explain that they in turn sold, which really meant rented, individual locations for thousands of dollars to people close to them, or as returnable favors to other streetguys.

"I could've probably got a spot anywhere if I wanted to ask, just being home from jail an' all, but I'd rather deal with my own personal friends, if you know what I mean."

He wondered what their reaction would have been if he'd substituted "Family" for "personal friends," then, with a laugh threatening to break through, he continued. "Not only that, but this block had only one spot open. On the next block, which is weaker, but belongs to my friend Buster, for fifteen hundred apiece I got three spots close together. For that kind of money they had to be near each other or me an' Richie woulda got robbed blind. Like tonight, see the crowds? Richie could never keep up with booths on two different blocks."

"Don't you have to stay here too?" Connie asked.

"For this weekend Richie's watching over everything so I could be free to show you a good time."

He stooped to kiss his mother on the cheek, then put an arm around both her and Laurel's shoulders.

"What a lucky guy," he said, and kissed Laurel too. "I get to spend every night with my two favorite girls . . . an' beautiful ones at that!"

"What about next week?" Laurel asked. "I guess I should expect not to see you at all."

"Don't jump the gun," Mickey Boy replied. "The more I think about it, it ain't worth taking the chance with Spositoro breathing down my neck."

Connie looked at him accusingly. "I thought you said it was legitimate?"

"It is, but if he catches me here, he'll question me to death: who, what, where, taxes—the whole nine yards. If Richie says he could handle it, maybe I'll just pop down for a couple of hours at a time just to give him a break." He was happy to see Laurel smile, but knew it would be short-lived once she realized he'd have to cover for Richie at their after-hours club.

When they finally caught sight of Richie, he was standing in front of a booth that sold cups of chunked fruit drowned in cold red wine. In back of him a bubble-topped juice dispenser churned the wine in a fountain. Smiling and waving his hands, he was engaged in conversation with two young females bedecked in traditional red, white, and green. Both girls wore big buttons offering "Kiss me, I'm Italian."

Richie spotted Mickey Boy, waved, then quickly wrote what had to be the girls' phone numbers in his book before excusing himself.

"Well, I'm still young, single, and healthy," he justified to a sneering Laurel. He kissed Connie on the cheek. "How are you, Mrs. M.? It's been a long time."

"It certainly has, Richie. Although time seems to have made you more handsome, like my Mickey Boy."

When Richie bent to kiss Laurel, she warned him jokingly, "You'd better not let any of your alley-cat ways rub off on Mickey—or you're dead!"

"I always knew you had a lot of moll in you," Richie teased. He ordered fruit and wine for them from a teenage boy behind the counter. "An' use the bottle of Chianti I got stashed." To his guests, he explained, "My private stock."

"Don't worry, the sangria is good enough," Laurel said, pointing to the burgundy liquid whirling around in the machine.

"Sangria?" Richie exclaimed in a hushed tone. He pulled her and Connie closer. "More like Kool-Aid-gria. In that machine, ladies, you see a lovely, mouth-watering formula that was mixed by a mad but brilliant chemist—yours truly. That particular batch is about ten percent guinea red that's one step above stain remover but much cheaper. The other ninety percent is a mixture of every red-colored Kool-Aid known to man, plus grape, of course, to make it real Italian."

"Richie, that's terrible!" Connie exclaimed.

"Not really, Mrs. M.," he answered defensively. "First of all, everybody loves it. Those two little chickadees you saw me talking to swore it was the best sangria in the feast. An' more important, it makes money. The way I broke it down, the plastic cup is the most expensive thing we give up. Remember, half this money goes to your baby boy."

"Just because my son is involved does not make it excusable."

"Then think of it this way," he responded. "Nobody will ever get into an accident because they were drunk from what we sold them. They could chugalug the whole machine an' not even get tipsy."

They all found Richie's rationale humorous, laughed with him, and drank their own uncut wine.

Mickey Boy looked behind the counter for empty bottles or other sales indications, but saw nothing to judge by. "How are we doing?" he finally asked.

Richie frowned. "I'll tell ya, between you and me, with friends like we got, we don't need enemies." He pulled Mickey Boy aside, leaving the two women to talk to the counter boy.

"First," Richie began, "Buster demands all his money up front. 'Friendship is one thing,' he says, 'but business is business.' Could you imagine that? If this guy calls me when I'm takin' a bath, I gotta come runnin' with a towel around my waist and a .357 in my hand, but when it comes to us payin' him forty-five hundred for chalk lines on a sidewalk, what does he say?—'Business is business.' "

"Fifteen hundred ain't too bad."

"Don't go 'way, there's more. Since he ain't got enough money in the vault, he sends his electric guy around, who tells me I can't hook into the city's electric lines unless he does it for two hundred an' fifty mahoskas a joint . . . up front. I felt like hitting him on the head with a hatchet."

"Don't get mad," Mickey Boy said. "One day we may be selling the same spots to young guys who'll wanna hit us on the head."

"Well, I got even anyway," Richie said, a sardonic smile on his face. "I sold the electric guy three sangrias."

Mickey Boy only shook his head. "Don't worry," he said, steering Richie back to where Connie and Laurel stood. "We'll make out okay."

"Wait, we still had to go for more money," Richie complained. "Next came the garbage man, who hadda get paid up front too. I tell him we got no garbage. He tells me, 'Buster says everybody pays for garbage even if they got none.' Then comes his iceman, an' his soda guy who overcharges. Remember, the electric an' garbage is all times three."

Richie went on to point out that if it rained for the remaining days of the festival, between having the booths built, buying equipment, and money he'd already laid out for incidentals, they would lose more than ten thousand dollars.

"We really gotta have our heads examined," Richie exclaimed. "Here we are, at the start of football season, which is the biggest action of the year, an' we're laying out ten big ones so we could work in a carnival. Tell me we don't need to be packed in ice?"

At Laurel's request, Richie showed them to another of the concessions he and Mickey Boy operated. It was a game where a trained rodent would disappear into a hole in one of the colored sections of a huge spinning horizontal wheel. A large crowd of bettors were shouting encouragement to the rat, prodding him to slither into the color they'd put their money on, while the teenage boy who worked for the house waited to scoop up their cash.

"This is where we'll clean up," Richie predicted. "Besides, when we're done we could always eat the rat."

"How gross!" Laurel and Connie shrieked in unison.

Laurel insisted on betting green, and lost ten dollars in quarters before Mickey Boy pulled her away, saying, "Don't you know green's bad luck—it's the color of jail clothes."

Since Richie had to return to the wine and fruit stand, Mickey Boy showed Laurel and his mother to the last of his ventures, another game, this one challenging a player, at the rate of two chances for a dollar, to knock a bowling pin over with a four-inch metal ball suspended from a ceiling chain.

"Oh, that looks easy," Laurel said. Mickey Boy didn't have the heart to tell her that the way it was set up it was fixed against her. He let her play until she got disgusted with missing the pin.

"C'mon, let's—" Laurel began excitedly, then stopped. Her eyes opened wide. Stony-faced, she just stared past Mickey Boy.

Alarmed by her expression, Mickey Boy turned sharply to face Little Vinnie Calabra, who stood some fifteen to twenty feet away, flanked by his two goons.

Fists balled and cheeks rippling, Mickey Boy glared at Little Vinnie's upturned sneer. For the previous weeks he'd been too preoccupied to give Little Vinnie much thought. Now, faced with him, the fact that he couldn't have known about the auto accident unless he was involved came rushing back. Had it been anyone else but the don's son, he would have settled any question in his mind immediately. In this situation, however, when a wrong move could cost him his future, if not his life, he had to be one hundred percent certain, no hunches—and then his solution would have to be final and quiet.

To make matters worse, now the slimy bastard seemed to know Laurel. Had he fucked her too? Mickey Boy wondered. Was he one of those she'd practiced sex-manual instructions on? What exotic tricks had she performed on him? His mind raced, pictures of naked bodies pumping his blood faster past his temples. If that was the case, he swore to himself, Little Vinnie was dead—father or no father.

Mickey Boy turned to Laurel, who nervously turned away toward the concession stand. He watched her hand tremble as she fished for change in her purse. Shocked, his mind struggled to push out the lewd images; to know what to say; know what to do. He turned back to Little Vinnie, who flashed a final sleazy smile before moving off into the crowd.

When the numbness eased, Mickey Boy grabbed Laurel by the arm and swung her around.

"Where the hell do you know him from?" he demanded. His fingers tightened into her flesh.

"I—I don't," Laurel stammered while trying to pull her arm from his grasp. "Mickey, please, you're hurting me."

"Tell me where you know that piece of shit from!" he yelled. "Tell me!"

"Mickey," Connie said, placing a hand on the arm that held Laurel's. "If Laurel says she doesn't know him, then she doesn't. Please let her go."

Though he released his grip on Laurel's arm, Mickey Boy's anger remained; visions of Little Vinnie fucking the girl he loved wouldn't leave. "I'm only going to ask you one more time," he said. "Where do you know him from?"

Laurel was still rubbing her upper arm. "Mickey, I swear, I don't know him. I don't even know his name or who he is. He—he just looked so evil, and, well, if you must know, he reminded me of someone else, someone who almost hit me with a car when I was out shopping with Chrissy."

Car! Mickey Boy thought. *Not again? Now he's dead, that fuck, for sure.*

But as Mickey Boy calmed down, doubts crept into his mind. Was Laurel's whole story true, or was she just covering up for past sins? Why did he seem to recognize her? After what had happened on the parkway a couple of months back, it certainly was possible, he reasoned. But then, if she was telling the truth, it couldn't have been Little Vinnie—not with Chrissy there.

Chrissy! That was his answer. That would be how Mickey Boy would find out if there was more than Laurel was telling.

"When did it happen?" he asked dryly.

"A week or so ago, when I went shopping for clothes. I didn't want to say anything because I didn't want you to worry."

Mickey Boy pointed a threatening finger at her. "If I find out—"

"Mickey, please," Laurel cut him off a bit too anxiously. She put two fingers to his lips. "It wasn't him that day, I only thought he resembled the driver, and I really don't know him from anywhere else. Now, please," she begged. Wearing a weak smile, she hooked her arm in his. "Are we going to have a good time tonight, or what?"

Connie sighed with relief, then, shaking her head, said to Mickey Boy, "You'll be the death of me yet."

They stopped back for another glass of wine with Richie, then walked back toward the center of the feast. While Mickey Boy treated his women royally, spending a small fortune playing games and loading them down with souvenirs, he brooded inside and had to force what little conversation he couldn't avoid.

When Laurel and Connie had had their fill of food and sight-seeing, and their feet and legs ached enough to complain, Mickey Boy again suggested the less crowded path they'd refused earlier.

This time they agreed.

Mickey Boy led them between the backs of the wooden stalls and the facades of the turn-of-the-century tenements that make up Little Italy. Residents sat in front of their buildings on wooden folding chairs, and well-dressed hoods scurried in and out of social clubs and cafés, some of them acknowledging Mickey Boy with a wave or a nod. Garbage piled between the stands fouled the air.

As Mickey Boy, Connie, and Laurel passed in front of the Lower Manhattan Fishing Association, the door opened and a burly figure stepped out.

"Hey, Mickey Boy!" Buster called.

Shit! Mickey Boy thought, eager to get away from the feast. He exchanged greeting kisses with Buster, then introduced him to Laurel and a suddenly ill-at-ease Connie.

"A pleasure to meet you, Mrs. Messina," Buster said, taking her reluctant hand in both of his. "I feel like I know you for ages—I mean from hearing your son talk about you, of course."

41

1961: Brooklyn

It was the year of JFK's inauguration, and akin to the rest of the country, Connie was beginning her days of Camelot. Full of hope and promise, she was getting married. Years of suffering the piercing wounds of personal loss coupled with agonizing loneliness were finally at an end. Any tears she would shed now would be joyous ones.

Back in 1956, Antoinette Partinico had originally been aghast at the gravid situation her only daughter had gotten herself into with the mysterious Mudslinger. Not having her recently deceased husband to turn to in her time of need, the disconcerted immigrant spent the better part of a week at St. Finbar's Church, invoking unending litanies to the Holy Trinity and every other saint she could recall. She paid particular homage to St. Jude, the saint of hopeless causes, and her name saint and patron of miracles, St. Anthony.

The ultimate solution was, however, less than spiritual. A visit to Antoinette's younger sister, Ida, and Ida's husband, Dominick, who was a drummer in Las Vegas, was hastily arranged for Connie. Aunt and uncle were very sympathetic, and suggested that their niece remain with them not only till the baby was born, but at least until it was more than six months old in case any busybodies back in Brooklyn were counting.

Mother and daughter were still dickering over a suitable story for her projected return when Connie boarded a United DC-7 at Idlewild.

Ida and Dominick tried their best to cheer Connie up, but to no avail. When they wanted to introduce her to young people they knew, she refused. The same went for sight-seeing, gambling, or nightclub shows. Her occasional concession was to have dinner with them at the Flamingo Hotel, where Dominick played in the lounge.

Connie's first three months in Las Vegas were filled with gloom. She was torn between the torturous separation from her ex-lover and her resentment toward him for not placing her first in his life. Her perplexed aunt and uncle stood helplessly by as their hysterical niece packed to leave on several occasions, once traveling as far as McCarran International before returning to their home. There was no way she'd capitulate and go back to Mudslinger's belittling terms. If he really loved her, he'd pursue her to the altar—nothing less.

The second half of Connie's pregnancy was marked by severe physical discomfort. Swollen ankles, lower back pains, and chronic insomnia compounded her emotional fray. The longer she agonized alone, the more she began to despise the one man she wanted more than anything else in the world.

Ida swore it would be a boy by the way Connie was carrying, all in the front like she'd swallowed a basketball. Uncle Dom laid seven-to-five odds on them needing pink bows for the crib.

Around that same time, Antoinette indicated in her weekly calls from Brooklyn that she'd been exhibiting more of the weakness and listlessness that had begun shortly before Connie had left. She dismissed her symptoms as being attributable to aggravation because of her daughter's predicament, and to a lingering cold. When her daughter offered to return, Antoinette stopped complaining; said she was feeling better.

At the beginning of her ninth month, Connie received a call from her uncle Al, saying that her mother had entered Victory Memorial Hospital for some routine tests, that at worst she might have contracted a mild case of walking pneumonia, and that she had begged him to tell her daughter not to even consider a flight back until after the baby was born. Uncle Al and Aunt Millie would see to Antoinette's every need.

Two weeks later Antoinette Partinico was dead, victim of a rare form of leukemia that had ravaged her body virtually overnight.

Connie was inconsolable. Over strenuous objections by family on both coasts, and her obstetrician, she made a reservation to accompany Dominick and Ida back to New York on the following day's noon flight.

None of them made it.

On the way to the airport, Connie suddenly broke her water and went into heavy labor. At 3:51 P.M. Michael Antonio Partinico arrived, angrily screaming and kicking at his troublesome new world.

It wasn't until almost a month after the funeral that Connie arrived home. On the second day, her cousin, Al, Jr., drove her to visit her mother's grave at Calvary Cemetery. Through a sedative-induced stupor, she reacted as if she were two distinct people. While her conscious mind couldn't associate her flesh-and-blood parent with the freshly turned earth she saw, her body was racked by convulsive bawling.

Back alone in her mother's house, Connie became prisoner to haunting memories. She prayed that Mudslinger would somehow learn what had happened, and surprise her by suddenly appearing at her door. She envisioned him standing there, a little-boy look on his tough mug and his fat fist clutching a bunch of roses.

For the next three months she wallowed in guilt, daydreams, and self-pity, barely caring for her infant son. A flaming bottom from too many unchanged diapers added to the baby's piercingly vocal nature. All Connie's shopping was done by phone. She lived on bologna sandwiches and pizza.

Finally, some fifteen pounds lighter than her normal weight of 110 and disgusted with the endless howling of her raw-skinned child, Connie decided to change her life.

Despite her anorexic look, she was still an eye-catching sight the day she marched down the block to the local real estate office. She had already come to the conclusion that if she liquidated her only major asset, her home, and added the resulting cash to whatever small sum Antoinette had left in the bank, she would be able to support Michael, whom she had begun calling Mickey because he was every bit as cute as Disney's famous mouse, until he was old enough for her to go to work. If she could sell the house, she and her child would be just fine.

The broker listened to her story, and with the utmost compassion pledged every effort to secure her a buyer.

Within days an angel of mercy materialized for Connie in the form of Louis J. Salso. His ringing of the front doorbell woke her from a midmorning siesta she'd coordinated with one of her baby's infrequent naps. Upon seeing Real Estate Broker emblazoned on the business card he presented, she quickly invited him in.

Over coffee, "Call me Louis" explained that he had been contacted about her house by the firm she had listed with. Since he, coincidentally, had an out-of-towner eager to relocate into the neighborhood immediately, he had come to personally conduct the inspection and negotiations.

In keeping with his overly padded frame, Louis devoured an entire chocolate layer cake while discussing a proposal with her.

Connie found the cost of the cake well worth it. By the time Louis had left, she not only held a cash deposit on a sales price twenty percent above her earlier expectations, but the phone number of a cousin of his, with whom he'd arranged to rent her a place to live. The hundred-and-twenty-five-dollar-a-month figure he quoted her for the two-bedroom apartment was extremely fair and, out of what he claimed was human kindness, he wanted no commission for that added service. One month's rent plus one month security would do the trick. He even had a moving man who would work for half the price of anyone else.

The last thing Louis J. Salso told her before he left was that the closing and other details regarding the sale of the house would be handled by her original broker. "Professional courtesy," he said.

Though her new apartment was in Flatbush, some distance away from where she'd spent her entire life, once she got there Connie was happy to be away from the old neighborhood. Here, at least, she wouldn't be burdened with constant reminders of her mother's passing. The fruit store wouldn't have to be the store where Antoinette squeezed tomatoes till the owner screamed, and the church wouldn't be the one where she finally lay.

The new landlady, Lena Zafferamo, made it easy for Connie to feel at home immediately. A stereotype of a kindly Neapolitan grandmother, she instantly fell in love with little Mickey, and placed him and his husbandless mom under her broad wing.

Connie was relatively content, spending most of her free time with Lena and her husband, Joe. She helped the old lady around the house and learned new ways to prepare the tomatoes, eggplants, and zucchinis that Lena's retired bricklayer husband grew in their backyard.

It wasn't long before dinners with the elderly couple had become a daily routine. Over their vehement protests, Connie contributed money toward the weekly food bill. Either they accept her share, she'd argued, or upstairs she and her baby would go.

Eventually, Lena questioned Connie about a growing uneasiness she sensed in her. Though Connie denied the restlessness that had indeed been getting her down, she fooled no one.

The next weekend Lena announced that through a friend of a friend she had been able to arrange a part-time job for Connie at a new women's fashion boutique a few blocks away; the shop owner, she said, had been impressed by the fact that Connie had worked at Bergdorf's. And the job was a breeze. Connie's only duties in the shop would be to assist in the purchase of inventory during buying seasons, and to handle customers two nights a week and on Saturdays. At a flat two hundred fifty dollars per week, the salary was much too good to refuse, and it would give her a much-needed diversion.

Lena also insisted on baby-sitting for free. She said that since she had secured Connie's new position, and since Mickey seemed to be quiet and content only in her fleshy arms, it would be both ungrateful and cruel to deny her and the child the pleasure they found in each other.

A thankful Connie had little choice but to agree.

Since she was more occupied, time passed a bit easier for Connie. But a certain emptiness remained, usually becoming more exaggerated a week or so before her menstrual cycle began, and a week or so following its end. At those times, severe sensual aching attacked her entire body, and she took to masturbating in the shower or in bed late at night, when a mischievous Mickey had called it a day. Then the visions of Mudslinger would come to her easily and vividly. Then she would touch the secret places he'd touched, quicker and deeper, till she whimpered with relief. The self-gratification helped her sleep better, but also begot more frustration and accompanying feelings of guilt.

A couple of times, determined to have a man, Connie had gone out to the hotter bars in Brooklyn, like the Airport, Flamingo, or Silhouette, with a couple of the girls from work. Each time she had no trouble attracting sex-hungry males, but chickened out at the end. One time, slightly drunk, she got as far as her pickup's front door before she reneged. Drunk himself, and pissed off, he promptly chased her from his car, leaving her miles from home at 3:30 A.M. Fortunately, she was able to flag down a cab on its way to a nearby depot.

And prearranged dates were no better. Every one of the so-called gentlemen she was introduced to became a mauling machine by the wee hours. Confused and disgusted, Connie went on fewer and fewer dates and took more and more late-evening showers.

Albert Messina was leaning on his cab, waiting for a fare, one Saturday when Connie emerged from Dubrow's Cafeteria after her lunch break. Most of the time she went home for meals so she could spend a little extra time with her son, who everybody now called "Mickey Boy." On that day, however, "Papa Joe" had taken the feisty four-year-old to the Avalon Theater for a cartoon matinee.

At first Connie didn't recognize the moustachioed hackie who called her by name. It was only after a second searching look that she was able to place the large hazel eyes and broad toothy smile: New Utrecht High, class of '52. Although many of their classes had overlapped through their concurrent four years at New Utrecht, including home-

194

room for the final two, the reticent classmates had never become more to each other than perfunctory "hi's" while passing in the halls.

After twice refusing his request to meet her that evening for a bite to eat and a movie, Connie finally agreed.

Albert showed up that evening in a turquoise '56 Chevy that was in showroom condition. Their date consisted of a hamburger dinner at Mitchell's Drive-in and a visit to the Loew's to see Natalie Wood and George Chakiris in *West Side Story*. Albert was definitely no Mudslinger, but he was attentive and fun to be with. At the end of the evening, he said good night with a peck on her cheek and a request to see her again the following weekend.

Albert Messina's one date quickly multiplied. He took Connie out every subsequent Saturday night for an inexpensive meal at either Nathan's Famous, Mitchell's, or downstairs at 21 Mott Street in Chinatown. On special occasions they ate at the Carolina Italian Restaurant in Coney Island. A smitten Albert also visited Connie's home at least one other evening a week, usually carrying a bagful of square-shaped White Castle burgers and greasy french fries.

Although financial problems had forced Albert to bypass college and seek employment after graduating from high school, he was basically a cerebral type, and when he wasn't entertaining little Mickey Boy, who took to him instantly, he spent his evenings at Connie's expounding his views on everything from the newly constructed Berlin Wall to the next Patterson-Johansson heavyweight title bout. An avid reader, he gave her a rundown of each new book he'd borrowed from the library, and encouraged her to do the same. His favorite that year was Joseph Heller's *Catch-22*, hers was *The Carpetbaggers* by Harold Robbins.

More important, Connie was grateful for the intellectual atmosphere Albert had brought to her home, for little Mickey Boy's sake. If he saw her read, he might imitate, and not necessarily be limited to a blue-collar future. She began to think in terms of college for him—a doctor, lawyer, engineer. It would be up to her, and the example she set.

Though in all her private moments Mudslinger's image pervaded her thoughts, Connie tried to judge Albert on his own. She found him an attractive, seemingly healthy and pleasant male, and initiated some heavy petting after their fourth date.

The unexpected problem Connie encountered, however, was that her new boyfriend was the consummate gentleman, and took her gasping protestations to be genuine. To Albert Messina, when a girl said no, she meant no. That naïveté on his part drove Connie mad. She'd been lonely for too long to be continually frustrated, but on the other hand was reluctant to be too sexually aggressive. In addition to being embarrassed about being blunt, she feared that if she let him know how lusty her desires really were, she would somehow be diminished in his eyes and would lose him. No, Albert was no Mudslinger, who'd read her desires like a map, who'd taken her body and made her feel feminine and alive—who'd used and discarded her.

One tactic Connie did try in her plight to have sex with Albert was to stop protesting when their petting got heated up, in the hope that he'd go further. Unfortunately, he was too conditioned and always stopped anyway. *The man has to be inhuman*, crossed her mind on more than one occasion.

Stimulated by their lengthy sessions of hot foreplay, each time Albert left, Connie would go directly to the tub and relieve herself with deftly placed fingers and an active imagination.

Only after Connie had accepted his proposal of marriage did Albert allow himself the pleasure of intercourse with her. He acted both surprised and flattered that she gave herself to him so easily.

Connie was disappointed that her first sexual experience with Albert lacked the sparks she remembered. While he was a kind, selfless lover, not one moment with him came close to the emotional highs she'd felt some five years before with Mudslinger—but it would have to do.

"Connie, Connie, are you all right?" Albert asked, his brows knitting together with concern. The bride- and groom-to-be stood together on the steps of New York's City Hall, where their best man, Albert's brother Larry, waited patiently to snap their picture.

Though she felt distant and disembodied, Connie smiled warmly at the man she was about to marry.

"Looks like the excitement's getting to you," he said.

"I'm fine, Albert . . . just daydreaming."

Albert kissed her on the forehead. "I sure hope you're dreaming about us," he teased.

Connie wasn't.

Part
III

42

September 27: Sheepshead Bay, Brooklyn

Teeth tugging at Laurel's swollen nipple made her groan.

Excited by the sound of her surrender, Mickey sucked harder at the enlarged bud, then drew his tongue from the underside of her breasts down to her navel, leaving a damp trail. When he kissed the inside of her thigh, she clutched greedily at his hair and arched her pelvis toward his face.

"Please, Mickey . . . do it to me . . . please, now."

Mickey Boy stared at the glistening pink flesh that invited yet repulsed him. Curiosity tempted him to flick out the tip of his tongue and taste the quivering flower. Would it be salty? Nauseating? Pleasant?

He knew it was super-sensitive, probably more so than any single spot on his body. He had seen Laurel's molten reactions to even his gentlest touch when he probed between the folds or brushed the tiny button at its top, and wondered how she'd respond to a kiss there. Only years of brainwashing by his Mafia idols kept him from following through. *Disgusting!* they'd said. *Anyone who does that is less than a man.*

When Laurel thrust her vagina up at him again and tried to force his head forward, Mickey Boy pulled back.

"Mickey!" Laurel shrieked. "I want it so bad. Please, honey, kiss it now . . . just this once and I'll never ask you again." Her eyes rolled back and her breathing came in heavy gasps, in between which she bit down on her lower lip.

Roughly, Mickey Boy pushed her hand away and moved from between her legs. The sight and sound of her sweaty body writhing with lust and her voice, sex-husky and begging to be gratified orally, irked him.

Books my ass! he thought angrily. *All half-a-fag writers telling idiots like her what to do.* He could satisfy her as well as any goddamned muffdiver if she'd just put all that degenerate shit she'd studied out of her head.

Deciding to teach Laurel a sex lesson of his own, Mickey Boy shifted his body up toward a missionary position, then hooked his muscular arms behind her knees and pushed them back onto her shoulders.

"Mickey, no, not like that," Laurel moaned. She tried to move, but he had her too well trapped; her feet kicked at the air around his ears.

Determined to prove his point, Mickey Boy entered Laurel in that position and began to plunge in and out of her body with punishing force.

"Don't, Mickey. Let me go put the thing in . . . oh, nooo . . . stop. Mickey, please stop," Laurel whimpered through his pounding. "You're hurting me."

In addition to not having her diaphragm in place, Laurel had made Mickey Boy aware on other occasions of her distaste for that particular sexual position. In his heat, however, what she felt meant nothing. Despite her protestations, he continued to pump away.

Suddenly Laurel's pleas turned to anger. "Mickey, you bastard. Stop!" she screamed. "You're not even wearing . . ." Her sentence dropped off just as he began gushing semen into her. "Oh, Mickey, no . . ."

When, after finally allowing Laurel's legs to fall, he bent to kiss her, she bit him hard on the lip and began to pummel him with her fists.

The pain that shot from Mickey Boy's lip through his face infuriated him. He tried to restrain Laurel's flailing arms and caught a knee in the stomach. With an open hand he slapped her face, which sparked her to struggle even more, which in turn excited him and made him hard all over again.

Mickey Boy released Laurel's hands, ducked his head down to avoid her blows, then deftly flipped her naked body over so she lay on her stomach. Spreading her legs with his knees, he pressed one hand down between her shoulder blades and with the other lifted her from under her waist.

Now Laurel's face was buried in the bedding and her bottom hung in the air, legs open and vagina helplessly exposed. Mickey Boy rubbed his erection against her till he felt the wet folds open for him, then pushed into her again.

"You fuck!" Laurel yelled. "Stop! Take it out!"

Laurel's 110 pounds were no match for Mickey Boy's 185. He easily kept her pinned to the mattress, her head shoved flush against the top of the bed. Each time he drove forward, he saw her neck bend and her face forced into the pillow. That helplessness excited him beyond anything he'd experienced before.

Ignoring Laurel's screams, he inflicted sharp, humiliating slaps on her buttocks while he rode her from behind as if she were a rodeo mare. And, while she couldn't kick like a bronco, she retaliated in animal-like fashion by digging her sharp fingernails into his thighs and clawing as best she could. Each time she did, however, Mickey Boy slammed harder into her vagina. When he got through, she'd know what good sex really was, know what it was to be fucked better than any of those half-a-humps she'd gone with before could ever do.

To Mickey Boy's satisfaction, Laurel suddenly began to respond to his savaging. Cries turned to moans. Struggling became a syncopated back-and-forth movement that kept time with his. When she folded her hands under her to play with her own breasts, it freed him to place his hands on her ass and move with more mobility. His hips ground wide circles for her to follow. Sweat poured from both their bodies. And just as he discharged inside her again, Laurel began to convulse in a simultaneous climax.

"Oh, my God, it's so good," she moaned between spasms. "Don't stop now . . . I'm coming . . . harder, please."

Mickey Boy meant not to disappoint her. Even though his penis felt as though it had been skinned, and the eruption from its end felt as if it were turning him inside out, he continued to plow as fast and deep as he could until her body finally collapsed on the mattress. Panting with exhaustion, he fell on top of her.

For a long while their still-damp bodies lay intertwined, her head resting on his shoulder, his fingers exploring the ridges of her spine. Mickey Boy, physically drained but comfortably mellow, bent occasionally to plant a kiss on the top of her head. Laurel, in turn, kissed the lip and cheek she'd bitten and slapped before.

"Isn't it better when you're nice, like this?" Laurel asked. She appeared as relaxed as he felt. "I don't like when you're rough with me, like before. It felt as if I was with another person in bed, a total stranger."

"Didn't your parents ever tell you not to talk to strangers, let alone go to bed with them?"

"I'm serious," Laurel replied. "I've known since I was a kid that you've got a bad temper, but it's scary and depressing to think that you would direct it at me like you just did."

Mickey pushed her hair back and kissed her forehead. "Baby, I love you, and never, ever want to do anything to hurt you," he said. "I just got ticked off. An' the real—not the phony I put on for other people, but the real Mickey Boy—is not just one person. I hurt, I get happy, I get mad. It's the same like you're not just one way."

"Come on, I'm not a Jekyll and Hyde like you."

"Oh, no? I never thought you had so much tiger in you, even after all the time we spent together. Whattaya call that?"

Laurel pouted, then snuggled closer to him. "That's because I didn't like what you did to me."

"You sure as hell fooled me," Mickey Boy said with a laugh. "I coulda swore you sounded like you were having a helluva good time."

"Good time? I hated what you did."

"If all that carrying on about you coming was hate, boy, I'd really like to see how you get when you're doing something you love." Heat from Laurel's flushed face burned against his shoulder.

"Well, that was later on," she replied defensively. "Besides, that's no excuse for you being so insensitive . . . and especially for not using protection. After what happened to me before, you know how I worry. How could you do that to me?"

Though in the heat of sexual passion Mickey Boy had derived a satisfaction that bordered on being high, from proving himself a good lover, from feeling her body convulse with orgasm under his against her will, he now felt guilty. Laurel was right. He was sorry he'd brutalized someone so precious to him. It was just that her goddamned past always seemed to vomit itself up in his face, and he hated it.

"Don't worry, just this one time won't make you get caught," Mickey Boy said. "And I ain't insensitive. It's just that you ticked me off."

"Me?" Laurel yelled. "What could I have possibly done to make you act like Jack the Ripper? Was it my breath, maybe? Or did my twenty-four-hour deodorant run out in twenty-three?"

Choosing to ignore her sarcasm, Mickey Boy said, "You an' me were brought up very different, an' it's hard to get around that sometimes. I grew up in the streets, where one of the lowest things a guy could be was a muffdiver."

Laurel began to giggle.

"If you're gonna laugh, I ain't gonna tell you nothing!" he snapped.

"I'm sorry. It's just that you're so serious about something so unimportant."

"It may be unimportant to you, but the way I was raised it's like a test of my manhood."

"Raised by who? I'm sure your mother never told you such things."

"Of course, not my mother, especially," Mickey Boy replied. "I'm talking about the older guys I grew up around, the guys who taught me everything I know."

Laurel sat up and looked at Mickey Boy with astonishment. "I don't believe you," she said. "These guys think it's all right to commit any crime under the sun, then go and take something that's intimate, private, and normal—"

"That's not normal."

"It most certainly is, but that's besides the point. What's important is that it concerns no one but the two people involved—"

"Or three?"

"Or twenty, what difference does it make? The fact is that your friends somehow take what's private and turn it into a question of manhood or underworld status. Don't you see how ridiculous that is?"

Mickey Boy remained silent.

"And my wanting to do what's natural with the man I love made you angry?" Shaking her head, Laurel added, "I certainly am happy I wasn't raised like that, and truthfully, feel sorry for you for suffering from the complexes that these illiterate thugs gave you. The whole bunch of you need good psychiatrists."

While he acknowledged in his mind that everything Laurel said made sense, especially since that particular aspect of behavior was no longer taken so seriously by other mobsters, Mickey Boy was still influenced by the old values he'd been taught, and was disappointed that she didn't understand how he felt.

"Irregardless of what you say," he began. "An' I'm not saying you're wrong—"

"*Irregardless* is not a word."

"What?"

"*Irregardless* is not a word. The word is *regardless*."

"This is serious, an' you're playing fuckin' word games with me?"

"I guess I'm trying to show you that it's not serious."

"To you maybe. To me it is."

"Okay, I apologize," Laurel replied. "Go on."

What Mickey Boy went on to explain was that the taboo on cunnilingus had been pounded into his head since before he'd been old enough to understand what it was. Not one, but every one of the men who'd shaped his life had considered it a degenerate act. How did she expect him to feel then, when, keeping his upbringing in mind, he'd seen the girl he loved begging to be satisfied that way?

Laurel bent over and pecked him on the lips. "Like I said before, I feel sorry for you."

"Wanna know what really got me mad?" Mickey said with a chuckle. "I mean really the most? An' I would never tell anybody else this."

"I can't possibly imagine."

"It was that I was tempted. I never even thought about it before, but today I was really tempted. That's what got me more pissed off than anything. I was mad at myself." He returned her kiss. "Believe me, if I ever change my mind an' decide to try it, you'll be the first to know."

"Mickey, you're not Samson, and I'm not Delilah trying to take your manhood away. Oral sex is just a normal thing that lovers do. But if you feel it goes against your grain, that's fine with me. You have my word, I'll never mention it again. Just remember, I love you, much more than those friends of yours who lied to you. I think they do it themselves. In fact, I know of one for sure."

Anger began to rise in Mickey Boy again. Would he never be free of worrying that she might have slept with someone he knew? Was it Little Vinnie? Was that why she'd gotten so shook up the night of the feast?

"I told you before," he barked. "I don't wanna hear about who you fucked around with before me! Goddammit, I—"

"Today is certainly your day to act like an idiot," Laurel said, laughing. "I'm not talking about me, you lunkhead. I've just got the inside scoop on one of your macho friends who loves to go down on his girl, especially in a tubful of water."

"I don't wanna know," Mickey Boy said, but, while smiling, immediately added, "All right, tell me."

"Georgie, little Chrissy's boyfriend."

"Oh, him," Mickey Boy groaned, disappointed. "He's only a kid," he said. "Different generation. By the way, what do you do, give her a blow by blow of what we do in bed?" He shook his head. "You girls are amazing."

"I'm afraid what we do in bed wouldn't interest too many people," Laurel teased. "And I would be ashamed to tell anyone how you abuse me, you brute."

Serious again, she claimed surprise that he didn't know her better than that. She would never discuss personal matters with anyone, she said. On the other hand, Chrissy was a different story. She was young and having big problems with Georgie of late. And, because she had no one else to confide in, told Laurel everything, even things Laurel had no business knowing.

"I feel so sorry for her," Laurel said. "Do you think maybe you could talk to Georgie if I explain everything to you?"

"No," Mickey Boy said flatly.

"What do you mean no?"

"What part don't you understand, the *n* or the *o*?"

"I don't understand why you won't even hear what I have to say."

Mickey Boy claimed that though he liked both Chrissy and Georgie, he still wasn't interested in hearing what their problem was. He just didn't want to get involved. Period.

"Between the two of them, they're nothing but trouble," he said. "They're like an accident looking for a place to happen."

"That's not fair."

"It doesn't have to be fair, it's true. First of all, Georgie could get killed like that," Mickey Boy said with a snap of his fingers. "Read the papers; you'll see his people are dropping like flies every day. If I was Chrissy, I wouldn't walk on the same side of the street as him, let alone ride in his car or hump him in a tub of water."

Speaking of Chrissy reminded Mickey Boy that he had to pay her a visit to find out if she knew anything about Laurel and Little Vinnie being acquainted—or worse. He made a mental note to take care of it the next day.

Mickey Boy continued. "And if her old man finds out what she's doing with him, *marrone a mi*, there'll be hell to pay."

Mickey Boy knew how Joe Augusta had earned his way to the top. As a young hoodlum, Joe'd done "work"—assigned murders for his Family bosses. Though no one besides Joe and those higher-ups who had handed down the elimination orders was sure of how many he'd "clipped," whether it had been one or one hundred, word passed around the street was that he'd taken grim pleasure in strangling his victims while they faced him, so that he would be the last thing they saw as they expired.

As years went by, Joe'd traded in garrotes for guns, and had soon developed a reputation as an expert marksman, used by Don Vincenze to carry out the most difficult assassinations. Unlike most mobsters, who couldn't hit anything beyond arm's length, and relied on personal relationships with their victims to get within that range, Joe Augusta was said to have practiced shooting at the heads of running chickens until he'd become deadly within seventy-five feet.

"The best thing Chrissy could do for herself is leave him—but don't you tell her that," Mickey Boy ordered. "I don't even want to get involved that way. In fact, I wish you would stop bothering with her altogether."

"How can I abandon the poor kid? I'm the only one she has to talk to. She can't go to her mother or father and tell them her problems," Laurel argued. "The kid's really in love with Georgie, and now he's started taking drugs—cocaine and pills—and she's sick over it. Maybe just a little talk from you. He respects you, and—"

"I said *no!*"

"I thought you had a heart, Mr. Messina."

"I do. But only for people I love . . . like you." Mickey Boy smiled, then added, ". . . Sometimes."

"Oh, you showed me before just how much you love me," Laurel said, teasing him back.

"Come on, let me make it up to you. Let's take a shower together before Richie picks me up."

"Mickey!" Laurel screamed. "I take days off from work to stay with you, and you're always running somewhere with Richie. You two should get married."

Mickey Boy sat up. He took Laurel in his arms and tried to kiss her, but she turned her lips away.

"You could come with me if you want," he said. The reason he hadn't offered to take her along before, he added, was that he knew she didn't like to sit in the car while he went on appointments. What's more, she hated to accompany him when he made his parole visits to Spositoro, one of which was scheduled that afternoon.

"Now that the feast is over, we'll have plenty of time together, I promise," he said. "Today I just figured that by the time I got back you'd be all dressed an' beautiful, an' we could go to Freddie's for dinner. Then maybe we could catch the floor show at the Rainbow Grill. Choice is yours. You know you're welcome to come."

"No thanks. If I have to stay by myself, I'd rather do it here than in your car, and . . . no, Mickey, stop . . . I don't want to . . ." Laurel groaned as his lips pulled and sucked at her breast. Two of his fingers probed between her parted legs.

"Come on, let's take a shower," Mickey urged between nibbles. "I want to talk to you about something too."

Eyes closed, Laurel rotated her hips against his hand. "About what?" she asked in a barely audible voice, then gasped.

"Come on." Holding Laurel under her arms, Mickey pulled her to her feet, then lifted her and carried her to the bathroom.

Warm spray ran over their bodies while they kissed and hugged and kissed again. When they tired of sucking on each other's tongues and fondling each other's soapy bodies, Laurel slid down the length of Mickey's frame until she was on her knees. She ran her lips and tongue across, underneath, and over every inch of flesh from his navel to his thighs, then guided his penis in and out of her mouth.

Afraid his legs would collapse at any moment, Mickey pressed his back against the slippery tile wall, half sliding down on it as he fought for balance.

After only a short while Laurel grabbed onto his arms and hoisted herself to her feet.

"Do you think less of me now because I loved you like that?" she whispered throatily, licking his ear between words. "There's no part of you that I don't love." She clung to Mickey. "Does it offend you that I had you in my mouth? Would it bother you to kiss me now?"

From the minute Mickey Boy'd taken her to bed the first time, Laurel's sexuality had challenged his lifelong values. He'd struggled with them and suffered each time he looked away from things she did. But pleasure had outweighed suffering, and now there was no room in Mickey's mind or heart for anything but the physical pleasure only Laurel could give. He kissed her long and deep—giving himself a "blow job by proxy," as the old men said—proving to himself as much as her how much she meant to him.

"I love you too much," he panted when he came up for air. "An' I wanna be with you forever." Mickey kissed Laurel's eyes and nose. "I want my baby growing inside you. Honey, let's get married . . . soon . . . now."

Laurel hugged him, and with her face buried in his chest began to cry. "Oh, Mickey," she sobbed. "I love you more than life, and I really want to, honey, but I'm so afraid. I don't think I'm cut out to be a gangster's wife. I'd always be frightened to death that you'd go to jail, or even worse . . ."

Mickey Boy knew what she meant, knew that she couldn't even bring herself to mention what really scared her—the possibility of his being killed. But "killed" had no place there, with the water beating down on their heads and clouds of steam all around them. Only love did. Love and sex. Feeling and passion. And he bent and kissed her neck.

"Even now, if the doorbell rings, I jump," Laurel went on. "I don't know if I could be the kind of wife you need. We really need time to think, honey. But I do love you. . . ."

Mickey trailed his lips down from her neck to her wet breasts. "Marry me," he said.

Laurel's heavy breathing became more labored in the steamy stall. Mickey could feel her on fire.

"Mickey, please," Laurel gasped. "This isn't fair. We have to think rationally."

Mickey dragged his chin down over the soft skin of Laurel's underbelly and rested it on her mound of silky reddish-brown hair. Nothing mattered—not anyone Laurel had ever had sex with or anything he'd been taught—except that he was able to hold her.

"Marry me," he yelled, hearing his words echo off the blue ceramic tiles.

"Honey, let's think . . . aahh!" Laurel wailed as Mickey's tongue burrowed into her body. Her knees buckling, she clutched first at the slippery wall for support, then grabbed his hair with both hands.

Mickey wrapped his arms around Laurel's legs to keep her standing. "Marry me," he insisted, and took her clitoris between his lips.

"Oh, my God," Laurel cried out. "Oooh . . . Mickey, yes, right where you are, yes, yes . . . no, don't stop . . . oh, yes, yes, I'll marry you . . . oh, I love you so."

"*. . . I've got lots of plans for tomorrow, and all my tomorrows depend on you,*" Mickey sang as he walked out of his apartment building. When he saw Richie already there waiting, he trotted to the red Nissan and, still singing, threw himself into the passenger seat.

"Cruising Harlem again, pal?" Richie joked while staring at Mickey's face. "Or did you try to shave with a food processor? You know, if you wanna change your looks, it really pays to invest in a plastic surgeon."

Mickey checked his slightly swollen lip and blotchy cheek in the visor mirror. Not bad at all, he thought. It'd be clear in a couple of hours. He flipped the visor back in place, then dropped back in his seat.

"No," he said. "What happened was that I just ran into a Neapolitan girl with a Sicilian temper who decided to marry me. This was her way of saying I do."

"No shit? Congratulations, pal," Richie yelled. He shook Mickey's hand. "When's the big day gonna be? If I know you, it'll probably be yesterday."

"I wanna do it either on Christmas Eve or Christmas Day if I could."

"You ain't countin' on a lot of people showing up on those days, I hope?"

"Nah, the less the better. I just want a small thing, just family an' a few very close friends."

"And don't forget Santa and his elves." Richie shook his head. "Those really ain't good days."

"Don't worry, I got everything under control. You an' me should be made by then—that'll be out of the way—an' it'll give me plenty of time to get permission from my P.O. to go away on a honeymoon. I'll tell Spositoro today when I see him. Besides, look at all the money I'll save." Mickey rambled on, his manner light and joking. "I only gotta buy one present to cover two occasions every year. How's that for a score?" He slapped Richie playfully on the shoulder. "It's your turn next, pal. I'm telling you now, a happily married man like me can't hang out with a single whoremaster like you."

"Right after the Pope," Richie said. "That's a promise. The day after he ties the knot I'll be at the altar, even if I gotta marry a Delancey Street hooker with short shorts an' high-heeled boots. In the meantime, Buster's all the boss I could handle."

"What boss? Are you nuts? This is me, Mickey Boy."

"Yeah, yeah, I know the whole story. But just wait till she starts makin' you punch a clock," he said with a laugh. "No, I ain't ready for that shit."

They continued to tease and joke with each other, interrupting occasionally with discussions of current business problems and mounting casualties in the Rossellini–Vallo war, until they pulled in front of the

Arch Diner. Since there were no available spaces in the front lot, Richie parked on the sidewalk near the corner.

Inside, George, the diner's host, greeted Mickey Boy and Richie with a concerned look. He was puzzlingly serious as he led them to the far-most table in the closed section of the dining room.

"Holy shit!" Mickey Boy exclaimed, suddenly understanding George's strange looks. "What the fuck happened to you?" he asked the lanky man sitting at a table. "Try to stop a train with your face?"

Irwin "Ex-lax" looked up through tiny slits in swollen purple flesh. He managed a grotesque smile, lifting only the side of his lips that wasn't stitched up and encrusted with dried blood. "I never cried once," he said proudly, words from his nearly motionless mouth slurring together. He reminded Mickey Boy of a bad ventriloquist.

"I never thought I could take a beating. In fact, I never even had a fight in my life, not even in school. Now I won't be afraid anymore," he said, forcing a chuckle. Then suddenly he grimaced and clutched his midsection with the arm that wasn't in a sling. "Three fractured ribs . . . they only hurt me when I laugh."

All Mickey Boy's happiness over Laurel's acceptance of his proposal turned to gloom. Tightening in the pit of his stomach made him feel like he had to move his bowels. Because he admired the druggist's courage, however, he tried to laugh along with him and keep his spirits buoyed. Unconsciously, he brought one finger to his own bruised lip, rubbing it as if he could feel Irwin's pain there. He himself had never caught a beating like that and, though he tried, couldn't imagine the pain and humiliation involved. What was worse, the battered, gentle man sitting before him was supposed to be under his protection.

"Irwin," Mickey Boy said softly. "Tell me what happened, buddy."

"One of the men on the list I gave you, Anthony Erice, came down for his money," Irwin managed to say with obvious pain. "When I told him what you had said, he went away. A few days later he came back with another man who said he was Anthony's boss. I told him the same thing, but he kept pressing me to tell him who was involved; said that it didn't mean anything to him, that as far as he was concerned it was a fairy tale, something I made up, unless he knew who my partners were. So I told him."

Irwin slipped a straw past his disfigured lips and noisily sucked at his vanilla malted before speaking again.

"He said he knew Richie, but not you, Bruno. He kept asking what you looked like, and I tried to describe you. All of a sudden he smiled and said, 'Oh, I think I know who you're talking about. No problem.' Then he left too. That's why I didn't bother calling Richie on the beeper or saying anything when he picked up the envelope each week. He'll tell you, I was so busy, I didn't even come out to the front. Besides, I figured they'd get in touch with you on their own."

"Skip all that, Irwin," Mickey Boy said, agitated and impatient to avenge the wrong he felt was done to him as well as to the pharmacist. "Just tell me how you got hurt."

"Two nights ago I closed up like I usually do," Irwin went on. "I locked the gates, then went to get my car in the parking lot in back of the medical building two doors away. When I reached my car, another car's doors opened and three men got out . . . Anthony, his boss, and another man. The boss said, 'I've got a message for your partners,' and all three of them started to hit me."

Mickey Boy winced as Irwin told the story. What kind of animals were these, not to respect other street guys? Saying they knew who was involved was probably bullshit; they were probably outlaws, cowboys. No one who was connected to any Family would ever act that way. Avoiding incidents like this one was exactly the reason for putting the "organized" in crime in the first place. Well, he'd make sure, he vowed inwardly, that whoever it was would be taught a lesson in respect that they'd never forget.

Irwin continued. "The funny thing was that when I was down and they were kicking me, they kept yelling something about someone named Mickey Boy. Who's that?"

"Did they mention what the boss's name was?" Mickey Boy asked, not really needing an answer anymore. Blood pounded in his temples, his stomach gnarled and twisted even more, and his fists balled like hammers.

"Yes," Irwin replied. "He said his name was Vinnie—Little Vinnie."

Little Vinnie's gotta die, Mickey Boy thought while Richie drove him downtown to the parole office on Clinton Street. Three strikes was enough for anybody, and this was the dirty puke's third—and last. The auto accident on the parkway was the first, having something secret to do with Laurel was number two, and now a slap in the face by hurting someone under his wing—strike three!

Mickey Boy looked at Richie, whose college-boy features appeared drawn and worried. Could he trust Richie with something as important as killing a boss's son? Did he want to? He decided that it wasn't fair to involve his partner in something so dangerous, and that realistically, most of his vendetta against Don Vincenze's son had nothing to do with Richie. No, he'd have to take care of Little Vinnie by himself, and soon.

The first order of business was to make sure the entire incident with Ex-lax stayed under wraps—no beefs, no complaints. As long as no one knew what had happened, he wouldn't become suspect when Little Vinnie disappeared. Or, at worst, he'd be one minor suspect among the list of enemies he was sure the don's son had acquired with his less-than-charming ways.

Richie turned to stare back at Mickey Boy. His expression was sad and pained. "Please, don't do it, pal," he begged.

Mickey Boy patted him on the shoulder. "Just drive."

Richie stayed around the corner in his car while Mickey Boy entered the dismal building at 75 Clinton Street to make his scheduled parole report.

When Mickey Boy stepped into the doorway of the small fourth-floor office, Anthony Spositoro was seated at his desk, studying a group of photographs that were fanned out across the top. Another parole officer, a tall, well-built man, with sandy blond hair, was seated alongside the room's entrance.

"Well, well, speak of the devil," Spositoro said. "Come in, my boy. We were just talking about you."

Mickey Boy sensed something was very wrong. The hairs along the back of his neck stood at attention. He wanted to turn and run, but knew better, so he stepped inside with a false bravado. "Hey, hiya doing, Mr. S.?" he said. "Bag any bad guys lately?"

"I'm really glad to see you in such good spirits, Michael. This way it won't be as bad when I tell you that you're violated. Assume the position."

Shock hammered Mickey Boy like a giant mallet. Zombielike, he bent over Spositoro's desk, arms wide over the top and legs spread, while the other man stepped behind him and patted him down. The sensation of the officer's rough hands on his arms, chest, and legs, the thumbs running along the inside of his waistband, brought six years of bitter feelings flooding back. He coughed, then gagged as his stomach pushed its acid up to his throat.

Thoughts of Richie waiting downstairs and Laurel at the apartment, ready to go out for the evening, raced through his mind. Mostly Laurel.

Spositoro tightened his lips into a sarcastic "tsk-tsk" expression, then shook his head and said, "Too bad. Looks like you fucked up again, my friend."

"Don't call me your friend," Mickey Boy snapped. "I'm fussy about who I associate with."

When Mickey Boy's hands were cuffed behind his back, Spositoro waved a picture of him and Richie when they'd gone to see Buster at the fish-market dice game.

"Apparently you've overestimated your ability to choose your friends wisely," the parole officer retorted angrily. "And it's your poor choice that's sending you back to jail."

"Do I get a phone call?" Mickey Boy growled.

"You'll be able to make all the calls you want from MCC. Now, come on, 'wiseguy,' let's go."

43

September 28: Long Island Sound

A sullen frown wrinkled Tom Thumb's hawkish face, his one long connected brow dipping down at its center. *After all I did for that kid*, he thought unhappily. *How could he do this to me?*

He looked through the cabin's porthole at the gently rolling blue-green sea and the last vestige of Suffolk shore as it disappeared below the horizon. A few seconds later all that was visible to the despondent mafioso was water and sky.

Tom heard the heavy footsteps of one of his soldiers, 240-pound "Spike" Bagheria, descending from the upper deck of his sixty-five-foot Trumpy. Sharply honed senses permitted the Family leader to distinguish between the footsteps of each of his three companions.

Spike knocked on the door, but entered only after his boss had shouted permission. The towering button-man was another of the ex-pugs that Tom Thumb had made a point of inducting into his rank and file.

"You told me to let you know when we couldn't see no more land."

"Yeah, okay," Tom Thumb replied. "Now, in a half hour start puttin' out the lunch. Our friend deserves a decent last meal," he added somberly. "Who's pilotin'?"

"He is."

"Good. How's he actin'?"

"Like he ain't got a care in the world."

"Well, I guess pretty soon he won't. If he asks for me, just tell him I'm takin' a nap till lunch."

Tom began to cough and choke, his massive body heaving with the seizure. Agitation always made him suffer doubly, a cross he felt he was doomed to bear as his penance in life.

The trouble was that he loved Rock Santoro like a son, and his heart ached at the younger man's betrayal. Rock was the only person he had ever allowed to become intimately close with him, and the knowledge that his confidence had been misplaced stung him more than his underboss's actual deed.

While Tom had no firsthand knowledge of the conversation that had taken place between Rock and Don Peppino in Rock's mother's house, he had irrefutable evidence that such a meeting had taken place. That was enough. He had to assume he'd been betrayed.

Officially, Tom Thumb's Family was supposed to be at peace with the world and, except for the problem with Jimmy Del, nothing had arisen since his covert entry into the Rossellini–Vallo dispute to indicate anything else. But Jimmy Del was a problem that would soon have to be dealt with. The idiot had been too goddamn cheap to spend an extra bullet on Tony Giarre's douchebag girlfriend, and now she was singing her guts to the law about how Jimmy Del had murdered her boyfriend. Pretty soon Jimmy himself would have to turn up dead to cover his Family's involvement in the ongoing Rossellini–Vallo war. Thank God the other guy was safe—the slut, Marsha, kept claiming Jimmy Del's girlfriend had fired the gun.

Rock was a worse problem. The mere fact that the second highest officer of Tom Thumb's crew had participated in a clandestine conference with the boss and underboss of another Family did not bode well. Normally, once someone like Jimmy Del was gone, Tom could deny having knowledge of what went on. Who knows, it could have been a private beef over some broad? Having no proof, the worst that Dons Vincenze and Peppino would do would be to pass a couple of double-edged remarks, and maybe watch his activities a bit closer. But with Rock Santoro as a potential Judas . . . ?

Tom's father, who was one of the few senior members of their particular clan to die of natural causes, had taught his son three essential lessons of life: kill hard and fast without hesitation, never trust anyone where your life is concerned, and, when you want something done right, do it yourself.

That day the dispirited crime boss intended to practice all three: Rock Santoro would die to pay for his transgression and to set an example for other Family members who might have similar intentions. And, because he loved Rock too much to let anyone else touch him, Tom Thumb would commit the murder himself. *Poor, stupid bastard*, went through his mind over and over.

When Spike informed him that the table was set, Tom Thumb crossed himself and ritually apologized to God for what he was about to do. After tucking a .45 Colt automatic under his shirt-jacket, he ascended the steps to the upper deck.

Rock Santoro stood in the cockpit, ably navigating the aging yacht. Boats were one of his special loves, and over the last few summers he always made sure he accompanied Tom on the biweekly cruises he took to relax. Whenever Rock stood at the vessel's helm he felt as though he owned the entire world. The ex–ghetto prizefighter often thought that if he hadn't been swept into a life of crime at an early age, he might have chosen one at sea. Merchant marines, maybe.

Rock scanned the ocean in front of him. It was an especially good day for boating, he thought, since most of the sailboats that crowded the water all summer had already been placed in drydock. A blazing sun had raised the temperature to an unseasonably high eighty-five degrees, and the breeze off the water was just strong enough not to be a nuisance. *Too perfect*, he thought with a shake of his head.

As soon as the boat's fourth occupant, Ray Menfi, shouted a lunch call to him, Rock double-checked his depth finder to make sure he'd passed the hundred-fathom mark, then scanned his radar screen. Once satisfied the Trumpy was alone in the area and in a good position, he turned into the waves, reduced speed to ten knots, and switched on the automatic pilot.

When Rock reached the salon deck at the ship's stern, Tom Thumb was already seated at a sturdy card table that had been set up under a white canvas canopy. Spike and Ray sat on their leader's left and right, leaving the only open chair with its back to the transom. Rock went to the chair, looked down at the water behind him, then dropped into the seat.

It took nearly forty minutes for the four mobsters to fill themselves from a plentiful selection of fresh cold cuts, cheeses, and cold, marinated vegetable salad. They washed it all down with goblets of chilled Corvo white. As usual, there was very little conversation when anyone dined with Tom Thumb. The loudest sounds were the fat man's gluttonous slurps, punctuated by wheezing, coughing, and gasps for air. For the first time, Tom's noisy eating and open-mouthed chewing turned Rock's stomach.

After devouring the meal's last remnants, Tom Thumb signaled with a grunt and accompanying wave of his hand that he wanted his espresso served; he'd stalled as long as he could. Ray Menfi poured the coffee while Spike left to get a bottle of anisette from the galley.

Only a couple of minutes more, my son, Tom Thumb thought sadly as he jammed a forkful of cheesecake into his mouth. It was all he could do to keep tears from welling up in his slitty eyes.

The twisted nylon lifeline was a blur to Tom as it looped over his head and wedged itself tightly under his fleshy chin. One of his hands clutched at the rope, while the other reached down for the loaded pistol in his belt, but there was no way to remove it because Ray Menfi had grabbed his hand and was pressing it into his stomach. Tom tried to scream, but nothing could pass in or out through his collapsing windpipe. Spittle poured down over his cheeks; water filled his eyes.

The force of Spike Bagheria pulling back on the boating cord unbalanced a struggling Tom Thumb, whose legs upended the table as he and his chair fell backward. Dishes and flatware clattered and skidded over the polished teak deck. Ray Menfi still clung to Tom's rapidly expiring body, preventing any chance of the .45 being used.

In less than a minute, strategically placed knots along the rope squeezed the consciousness from the obese gangster. He involuntarily released his last hefty bowel movement into his white cotton pants, and died.

Neither the strangler nor his assistant released their holds on the corpse until Rock Santoro ordered, "Leave him alone; he's gone."

Rock stood expressionless, staring down at his fallen mentor. *Sorry, Pops*, he thought. *But ya shoulda listened when I told ya to keep us outta the war.*

The furor surrounding the Jimmy Del incident had proven the lunacy of having involved their crew in something that was none of their business. How long would it have been until Dons Vincenze and Peppino decided to eliminate both Tom Thumb and his underboss? No, he'd done the right thing, Rock assured himself. He'd saved his life— a life he would have lost for a misdeed he'd never supported.

Without wasting any time, Ray Menfi fetched a group of items he'd hidden below deck the previous day. "You want me to spread the plastic first?" he asked.

Rock Santoro's gaze remained fixed on the familiar dark, beady eyes that now bulged from his former boss's swollen purple face. He stared into Tom's mouth, hanging wide open as it had when he'd gasped for breath through his frequent coughing attacks.

With a chest-heaving sigh, Rock replied, "No, don't bother; we don't have to worry about the deck. Just use the wire." Then he turned and walked away.

Ray and Spike spread a six-foot length of chicken wire on the gleaming wooden floor and rolled Tom's body onto it faceup. After tearing open the dead man's clothes, Spike sliced him from his neck to his pubics. Blood rushed up from the incision and poured down either side of the body. When he dug the knife into Tom Thumb's stomach to make sure any air that might leave the corpse buoyant would escape, the resulting stench caused his partner to gag. Ray Menfi vomited over the brass rail while Spike continued his sanguinary work.

* * *

Rock Santoro waited at the bow, glancing intermittently at his watch, until a thirty-two-foot ChrisCraft appeared. Only after he waved did it approach. Had Rock not been there to signal, it would have continued on its way without stopping.

By the time the ChrisCraft pulled alongside the Trumpy, Spike was splashed all over with blood from breaking Tom's rib cage with a hard ax so he could repeat his air-letting work on the fat man's lungs. The area around him was so bloody that a recovered but still green-faced Ray Menfi slipped and fell twice while helping him fold the fence material over the gory heap.

The two men secured their package with iron chains they'd run through forty-five-pound weight-lifting plates, and nine heavy-duty locks—two where the chicken wire was open on top, two at the bottom, four along the lengthwise flap they'd created when they'd folded it over, and one on the chain. Once Tom Thumb sank to the ocean floor, the only way he'd surface, even when decomposed, would be in one-inch chunks.

Spike and Ray completed their task by dragging the wire-wrapped corpse across the planking to the gangway gate and shoving it through. Assisted by more than a hundred pounds of iron, Tom Thumb immediately disappeared below the water's green surface.

Ray Menfi hurried down to the engine room while the others waited on deck. He went to the spot where he had concealed a ten-gauge pump shotgun loaded with double-O buckshot shells. After removing the hatch cover that protected the ship's bilges, he fired through the fiberglass hull. Seawater quickly began to flood the boat by way of the gaping holes. The gunman repeated his action in four more spots, then ran back upstairs.

Rock and Spike had already boarded the other launch when Ray reached the deck. He trotted to the fast-sinking stern and stepped up onto the ChrisCraft to join them.

The boatload of mobsters circled the area until the Trumpy's bow pointed straight up and, with a great hiss of departing air, plummeted down to join its owner at the bottom of the ocean.

When the ChrisCraft headed back to shore, it carried four made members and the boss of the new Rock Santoro crime Family.

44

October 10: Downtown Manhattan

It had taken almost twenty-four hours from the time Spositoro had shut the door on his freedom until the time Mickey Boy was finally ushered onto the eleventh floor of the detention center. Wearing an oversize cotton jump suit of bright orange, and carrying a bedroll, he entered the south wing, where six dormitories warehoused over a hundred parole violators and prisoners brought back on writs to New York courts from other facilities.

On Eleven South he found old home week. People he hadn't seen in years, either from making the jail circuit or from before he'd gone away, were there.

Friends of his arranged for him to be assigned to H dorm, where most of the knock-around guys on the unit slept. The only exceptions were those members of the warring Rossellini and Vallo factions; the former clustering in J dorm and the latter in M. Rossellinis and Vallos associated with everyone on the floor except one another.

By the time a dinner of slimy microwaved ham hocks were served, those same friends had already furnished Mickey Boy with toiletries, cigarettes, snack food, and quarters for phone calls. He was most appreciative, however, of the spaghetti marinara one of their guys had sneaked up from the kitchen. It would take more than one day for him to be ready to eat nuked ham hocks.

Because of bureaucratic red tape, it wasn't until nearly a week later that Laurel was approved to visit, and then only because Richie had provided a counterfeit driver's license, identifying her as Ellen Messina, Alley's wife. Nonrelatives' clearance took the institution weeks to process, and Mickey Boy had no intention of being separated from his love for that long.

The day after the approval, Mickey Boy paced in front of the visiting room door as he waited for Laurel to come up. When the correctional officer shouted his name, he stepped into a ten-foot-long vestibule between the unit and visiting room to be pat-searched, have his hand stamped with invisible ink that showed up under purple light, and signed in so he could enter the small, airless room where inmates' friends and families waited.

As soon as Laurel spotted him, she ran to his arms and began to cry. "Oh, Mickey, Mickey," she said between sobs. "I was so afraid this would happen. I knew it."

It was the first time since his ordeal had begun that Mickey felt miserable. For himself he'd felt only anger, but seeing the effect his incarceration was having on Laurel made him ache inside. So this was what it was like to leave someone you loved.

With the thought running through his mind that he'd been lucky to have no one during the six years he'd spent in jail, Mickey Boy led Laurel toward a small wooden chair in a corner of the room. He dragged over another chair and sat down facing her, his knees surrounding both of hers.

"All right, baby . . . everything's gonna be okay," he said, taking her hands in his. "It's just that piece of shit, Spositoro, trying to break my balls, that's all. I'll be home with you before you know it."

While he made every effort to convince Laurel that his problem was minor, and that it would be resolved quickly in his favor, he had difficulty believing it himself. He'd seen too many guys violated on the flimsiest excuses, seen "preponderance of evidence" send friends back to prison on charges that they'd been found innocent of in court, seen the omnipotence of a system that was much like quicksand—the key was to stay out, not hope to fight your way out once you fell in.

No, as much as Mickey Boy would look and act confident for Laurel's sake, inside he knew better. In fact, just that day he'd blown up at Richie when Richie had given him a cryptically coded message over the phone, to the effect that Buster had said he should be patient and that everything would be all right. Sure, everything would be all right for Buster; he was on the outside.

"That's easy enough for the doctor to say," Mickey Boy had roared back in the same type of code. "He's not the sick one. If the kid has to be in the hospital for a long time, the fat doctor'll just say, 'Well, I thought he was all right.' If he remembers correctly, I warned him about the kid going to places where he could get sick, but the goddamn blimp didn't listen."

Richie's response annoyed Mickey Boy even more: a snappy "I don't write the messages, pal. I only deliver them."

"So, it's just like I told you on the phone," Mickey Boy said, still trying to reassure Laurel. "The lawyer says your future husband should win the hearing with no sweat and be home in your hot little arms before you know it." Convincing Laurel would have been a hell of a lot easier, he thought, if he'd even had a lawyer.

Laurel stared pleadingly into Mickey Boy's eyes, her hands clutching his. "Mickey darling, I love you and I really want to be your wife more than anything in this world," she said. "But I'm not sure I can."

When Mickey Boy tried to argue, she stopped him. "Please, this time let me finish," she said. "I tried to explain to you that day in the shower that this kind of life is not for me. I've been a wreck ever since you got violated. All I do is cry and eat. I must have gained ten pounds in a week."

"Looks good on—"

Ignoring him, Laurel continued. "Please, darling, if you love me, please, promise me you'll get away from these people and this way of life. I have relatives in Florida. We could go there and make a new start."

Why did she have to keep fighting a battle she couldn't win? Mickey Boy wondered. When would she realize that he was what he was, that there was nothing else he knew how to do? The only other thing he'd ever wanted to be was a lawyer, and Nicolo Fonte had kicked that out of him long ago. It was just too late.

What would he do in Florida, he wanted to ask her, be like Fat Louie, who went down there only to wind up digging palm trees in the middle of the night and selling them from a roadside stand in the day, just to put food on his table? Was that what he was destined to become, a palm-tree thief? No, there was no way he would give up all he'd worked and suffered for now—especially when he was so close to being made.

But if Mickey Boy lacked confidence about winning the parole violation hearing, he didn't when it came to knowing he'd be able to overcome Laurel's objections if he were freed. If he wasn't, he'd probably lose her anyway. Mickey Boy had seen too much of that too—seen too many guys suffer because their girls and wives had been too hot to trot to wait for them to come home—and would gird himself for it. Meanwhile, if there was a shot to hold on to her, he could only do it with time. Time was what he needed. Stall, stall, stall.

"Listen, hon, right now everything we talk about is just wasted breath until I get out," he said, meaning every word. Though he'd misled her, it was important to Mickey Boy that he not hold on to Laurel with an out-and-out lie.

"Let me think while I'm here about what options I got open to me, an' we'll go through them together when I come home, just you an' me. With all the pressure I got on my head now, all I'm sure of is that I love you an' wanna marry you." When he bent close to hug and kiss her, he whispered, "How about in here? Wanna get married here?"

"Are you kidding?!" Laurel snapped. "In jail? Never! Besides," she added in a bitter tone, "I'm Ellen Messina, your brother's wife. Remember?"

"Only joking," Mickey Boy lied. "But how about as soon as I get out—the same day? You could go for the license first. Make Richie sign my name."

Laurel dabbed at the moisture that remained around her eyes. "Oh,

Mickey, you're impossible," she said. "You really have no idea of how hard this is on me. You take it for granted that I'm as tough as you are, and can just let things roll off my back. Well, I'm not that kind of person. I need peace and order in my life."

"I could use a little piece too," he whispered, and winked.

"I'll say it again: you're impossible!" This time Laurel laughed. "Let's make a deal." She offered Mickey Boy her hand. "We won't discuss any plans for getting married until you come out and first decide what you want to do with your life. Okay?"

"Sounds good to me."

"Just keep in mind," Laurel added, "that there is a decision to be made—a choice."

"That means no more nagging while I'm in here?"

"None."

Mickey Boy grabbed her hand and brought it to his lips. "Deal," he muttered while kissing her fingers. Then, straightening up in his chair, he tugged at his jump suit and said, "Now that we can't talk about us, how do you like my snazzy outfit? Is this Bozo modern or what?"

"I'm surprised you haven't had your tailor make you a suit that color yet," Laurel replied. "They'd love it on Mulberry Street."

"When I get out."

"Matching shoes too, of course."

"Of course," Mickey Boy said. "Would I have it any other way?" He drew her hand toward him and placed it between his legs. "I got nothing on underneath. Wanna see?"

"Mickey, there are people around!"

"Sorry, they can't have any."

Laurel left her hand there for a moment, then squeezed Mickey Boy's testicles hard enough to force him back in his chair.

A tall, thin inmate sitting with a woman and small child waved and smiled at Mickey Boy and Laurel.

"He looks like a nice man," Laurel said, her hand empty of Mickey Boy's aching crotch. "What did he do?"

"Is it safe to move closer?"

"Only if you don't get piggy."

Mickey Boy leaned forward, his face near hers. "Nothing," he whispered. "They locked him up fifteen months ago for refusing to testify at a grand jury hearing, but now he's doing a bug-out routine. This way if the doctors say he's nuts, they can't ask him no more questions, an' they'll let him go. Meanwhile, he keeps us in stitches all day."

"He looks normal."

"He is, but the doctors are beginning to believe he's not. It all started when he made them think he ate a mouse."

"A what?"

"A mouse," Mickey Boy replied. "You know, the little gray things, with—"

"I know what a mouse is," Laurel interrupted. "But he didn't . . . ?"

"No, he didn't eat a real one. He made this little fake mouse out of a half a canned pear that he dried an' covered with cigarette ashes. Then he made these little legs out of matchsticks, an' a little tail. He put the phony mouse on one piece of bread an' held another piece in his other hand. Then he sent somebody to get the hack on the four o'clock shift, a country boy named Jefferson who sees his IQ on the weather report every day—in the winter. Just when the idiot's coming, somebody else yelled 'What are ya doing with that mouse?' When the hack looks, the guy you see covers it up fast with the other piece of bread an' starts to munch on it."

Laurel covered her mouth to stifle a laugh, then said, "You know, you and your friends are nuts. You're not really like anyone else I know. That's why I feel like such an outsider sometimes, and—"

"Hey!" Mickey Boy cut her off. "Remember, you made a deal."

"Okay, a deal's a deal." Laurel glanced again at the man who'd eaten the fake mouse, then asked, "Do you think this plan will work?"

"Who knows?" Mickey Boy answered with a shrug. "You know, there's a bookmaker friend of mine who's got a sign over the phone where he takes his action. It says: If you try, you may not succeed . . . but if you don't try, you *definitely* won't succeed."

When the guard announced that the hour-long visit was over, Mickey Boy checked Laurel's watch to see if it wasn't only half that. Though it certainly felt that way to him, it wasn't.

"Boy, time flies when you're having fun," he said, trying to hide the sudden sadness that filled him. Once more he reassured her that his lawyer promised to get a hearing within a month and emerge victorious. He still didn't mention that since Richie hadn't offered any explanation for his and Buster's shared optimism, and since he still wasn't sure if there even was a lawyer on his case, he himself remained skeptical. Instead, Mickey Boy sang a few inspirational Sinatra lines about "high hopes" to Laurel, and gave her a list of emergency phone numbers in case she had any problems.

Laurel hugged and kissed Mickey Boy, clinging to his body until the guard told them once more that their time was up. And when she finally left, it was the same way she had come in—crying.

"Excuse me, Laurie?"

A chill ran down Laurel's spine as she turned toward the familiar voice. Her eyes darted all around, looking for more goons, but he was alone, standing there with both hands behind his back, a forlorn expression on his face.

Laurel wasn't alone though. Not this time. Crowds of people passing MCC's Park Row entrance were there if she needed them. This time she'd scream loud enough to be heard all the way to Brooklyn. In spite of the protection all around, however, her knees still felt weak.

"If you know what's good for you, you'll leave me alone," Laurel threatened, acting more brave than she felt.

"Please, Laurie," Little Vinnie said defensively. "I just came to apologize to you for what happened that day in the store."

Laurel's head told her he had to be following her. But why? What did he want from her? To maul her again? Rape her? Everything inside told her to start running, but her legs felt heavy and incapable of movement. "How did you know I'd be here?" she asked, in a near-shriek.

"Chrissy told me you'd be visiting here, and I took it on myself to come."

Little Vinnie waved at the passing crowd. "I figured you'd feel safe if I stopped you here with all these people around." He tried to laugh, but came across only as clumsy and bumbling. "I didn't want to scare the life out of you, but it looks like I couldn't help it. You look like you're gonna pass out on me. An' if you do, Chrissy'll be madder'n hell. She'll never believe I didn't make it happen, or make you cry, like I see you been doin'."

With a smile Little Vinnie offered her a gold-foil box that he had been holding behind his back. "A little peace offering," he said. "Godiva. I hope they wash away some of your tears; maybe make your day a little sweeter."

Laurel looked directly into Little Vinnie's eyes. They looked sincere enough, but she knew what a monster he could be. She could still feel his hand roughly pawing her breast, feel his erection jammed against her belly. Had he really found her through Chrissy, or . . . ?

As if Little Vinnie could read her thoughts, he reached into his jacket pocket and pulled out a quarter. "Here," he said. "If you don't believe me, call Chrissy. She's home."

"No. There's no need to call her," Laurel replied, and started to walk away. Her steps were hard and measured, each one a threat to her balance.

"Listen, I only want to apologize," Little Vinnie said while hurrying alongside her.

Laurel kept moving as she spoke. "Your apology is accepted. Now please, go away!"

Little Vinnie hooked a hand inside Laurel's elbow, stopping her.

The feel of his touch made her shudder. As she looked down at his hand, a scream was already forming in her throat.

With a look of sudden self-consciousness, Little Vinnie let go of

Laurel and quickly stuffed his hand into his pocket. Shrugging, he said, "Gee, I'm sorry. I didn't mean to . . . well, it's just that I made a special trip down here 'cause I wanted to apologize, an' figured if we could sit an' talk a few minutes over a cup of coffee, I could explain everything."

Laurel stood silently, staring at Little Vinnie's form; his eyes were downcast like a little boy's. She was sure it was very difficult for him to apologize, and probably a new experience.

"I guess you don't want the chocolates," Little Vinnie said, and shrugged again. "Anyway, I'm sorry." He turned, tossed the expensive candy into a trash can, and, with his shoulders hunched and both hands jammed into his pants pockets, walked toward the curb.

The offer of an explanation for the ordeal she'd suffered in the lingerie shop interested Laurel. Sure, there was no excuse he could give for what he'd done, but why were he and Mickey Boy such bitter enemies? Could she help to end their feud? In addition, she found she actually felt sorry for Little Vinnie; he'd tried so hard to make amends.

"Vinnie, wait," Laurel called out. "Wait, I'll go with you."

45

October 30: Todt Hill, Staten Island

Little Vinnie got a hard-on every time he thought about Laurel. And for the last three weeks Laurel was all he thought about. Even now, just waking, she was the first thing on his mind.

He glanced at the digital clock on his nightstand. 1:37 P.M. His bastard of an old man had to be gone for the day by now. If not, he'd have to fake sleeping till that time.

Little Vinnie got up and went to the window, looking out for Buster's car, which had been parked in a driveway two hours before when he'd awakened to take a piss. The driveway was clear. Good. Let Buster keep the old fuck with him all day; maybe he'd even crash him into a truck or bus. That thought brought a smile to Little Vinnie's face.

Safe in the knowledge that he was alone in the house, the don's son opened the top drawer of his dresser, pulled the envelope of photos from beneath his underwear again, then lay back down on the bed. He withdrew the stack of 35mm prints and stared at the first one. Innocuous as it was, he studied it for a while, taking in every bit of Laurel, from her hair blowing in the wind to her shapely legs sticking out from the bottom of her blue minidress as she crossed Park Row.

He paid particular attention to the expression on her face. Not happy, but not fearful either. Maybe a little disturbed, but that could have been caused by a number of things. That was okay.

Little Vinnie moved the first snapshot to the rear, meticulously keeping them in the order he'd arranged them, and studied number two. Not great, but not bad. Laurel'd looked a little surprised when he'd taken her by the elbow halfway across the street, but his smile made up for it. *Who knows what I mighta said?*

Without taking his eyes from the pile, he flipped that picture to the rear. Only a few steps farther and Laurel'd already relaxed and had stayed close to him as cars had zipped by. They really did make a nice-looking couple, Little Vinnie thought. He reached down and adjusted the undershorts that was strangling his erection.

Photo number four, another masterstroke, guiding her into a classy restaurant-bar instead of a coffee shop. He looked at his hand at the small of her back, just a hairbreadth above her ass, as she walked through the door ahead of him. Boy, had he ever fought temptation that day. Going through the restaurant door, he'd remembered the handful of ass he'd grabbed a few weeks before in the lingerie store. Tight. Firm. Twitching under his touch. Goddamn if he hadn't struggled like a bastard to keep from grabbing it again that day.

Maybe more gentle, though, he thought. Little Vinnie laughed out loud. *What a great picture that would have made!*

Wine instead of coffee. That was what he had ordered and, like the lamb she was, that was what she'd drunk, Little Vinnie mused while eyeing a photograph that showed the bottle of Bouchard that had been on their table.

The fact that Laurel had been agitated by her visit with Mickey Boy had been a big help—in all areas. She'd probably welcomed the chance to unwind with a couple of drinks, but had been too embarrassed to suggest it herself; probably would have loved a toke of grass or a 'lude too. But he'd been on his best behavior, just like he'd promised Chrissy he would, and, as a result, hadn't suggested that.

What he had done that evening was play the misunderstood and injured friend. While plying Laurel with more white wine, he'd told her that Mickey Boy erringly blamed him for his being arrested and going to jail. The more she'd drunk the more she'd listened, and the more she'd listened the more receptive and sympathetic she'd become. Yes, Mickey Boy did make snap judgments, Laurel had agreed, and oh, yes, he could be extremely narrow-minded and stubborn at times. Wistfully, she'd added that no one knew better than she what his bad side was.

Photo six: his hand on hers, and him telling her some bullshit or other. By that time Laurel had loosened up. Sitting next to him on the padded bench seat, she'd stopped backing away when he gave her a harmless pat or friendly squeeze. Her eyes looked directly at his, and their knees touched. The same hanging side of the red tablecloth he'd cursed for covering most of her bare legs had also saved her from seeing the obvious bulge in his pants.

Now, lying in bed, Little Vinnie remembered having wanted to drop a hand to the exposed flesh between the tablecloth and the hemline of Laurel's dress, then slowly run it up along the inside of her thigh. Would she have stopped him immediately? When he reached her panties? Or would she have let him slip a finger underneath the panties to play with her cunt? He'd looked at her half-drooping eyelids and caught sight of her tongue licking her lips clean of wine. She'd been hot. Boy, had Laurel been hot. Little Vinnie was even more positive now than he'd been then.

Yes, Mickey Boy's girl sure as shit had wanted him, but as steamed up as he'd been himself, he'd controlled it. He couldn't have taken the chance of having misread her or moving too soon. Chrissy again.

Before removing that photo, Little Vinnie freed his erection and squeezed its tip hard to relieve the throbbing.

The don's son recalled that by the time he and Laurel had left the restaurant-bar, it was already dark outside. Laurel had become totally at ease and had leaned into him while he'd led her by the arm.

Shifting to make himself more comfortable, Little Vinnie stared at the photo of Laurel smiling up at him as they'd made their way to his car. The wine, two and a half bottles between them, had gotten to him too, and he'd wound up appearing a bit dopey in the picture.

But that was good. He looked just like any guy having a good time with the girl he was taking home to fuck; Mickey Boy's girl home to fuck. Goddammit if Mickey Boy wouldn't bust a gut when he'd see these photos in whatever prison he'd be doing his violation time in.

Was it that thought or just the heat that thinking about Laurel filled him with that made the throbbing in his dick so intense? Little Vinnie wondered. Probably both. The idea of screwing Mickey Boy was always exciting, and visions of making love to Laurel had driven him to fuck the Korean hooker at the massage parlor until his asshole hurt. He squeezed harder to keep from coming.

The picture of Laurel sliding into the front seat of his Eldorado was a gem. A clear view right up to her crotch. Boy, would he give anything to watch Mickey Boy's face when he saw that one.

Eyes closed and hand wrapped around his swollen penis, Little Vinnie remembered Laurel in the front seat of his car, her skirt still hiked up. He could still smell the musky odor of perfume and alcohol, hear his blood as it had pounded in his head that night, see her braless tits as they were outlined by the silky blue dress.

When he'd parked near her car, he'd turned to her to apologize again. Laurel hadn't flinched when his eyes had boldly roved up and down her body. Looking back through sultry, narrowed slits, she'd sat silently, the tip of her tongue enticingly snaking out again, this time to moisten dry, smoldering lips. If not for Chrissy, or if he'd have drunk a little more, he would have taken her right there on the front seat. But Chrissy had been involved. She'd set up the meeting for him to make amends for the incident at the lingerie shop, and if anything happened, even with Laurel's consent, there would have been hell to pay.

Little Vinnie began to stroke himself, remembering how he'd brought his hand up to cradle Laurel's chin while he'd thanked her for listening, how he'd rested his other hand on her thigh as he'd bent to kiss her good-bye, how he'd moved his lips from her cheek to brush her mouth—how she hadn't moved or objected, but had just sat there with her eyes closed. At that moment he wouldn't have had to squeeze her tits through a sweater or press his hard-on against her fully dressed body. At that moment he could have taken down her top and sucked on her nipples till she removed her own panties and begged him to put his dick in her. Then he could have made her use her tongue the way he'd known she'd been dying to all night; let her roll it around the tip of his—

"Ooh, ooh," Little Vinnie groaned as semen began to shoot up from his penis. Still stroking, he rolled over to let it spurt itself out into the bedding. His breathing was as heavy as if he'd been engaged in a strenuous sexual bout with a live female, and what little air he took came in short gasps. He felt flushed with heat and drained of strength at the same time. "Laurel, oh Laurel baby," he moaned over and over.

Wet with perspiration and sticky with semen, Little Vinnie stayed that way, without moving, while his rapid heartbeat leveled off and his breathing became even; the stack of photos remained clutched tightly in his left hand; a satisfied grin stretched his features. One day soon those loads he'd been dropping in bed, bath, and whorehouses would go where they were meant to, between Laurel's wide-spread legs. All he needed to accomplish that was to have her meet him once on her own, without Chrissy being in the middle. In that situation, even if somebody held her down while he fucked her, what could anybody say? Nothing. She'd have come to him of her own free will and it would be her word against his. Who'd believe her?

With his face still buried in the pillow, the thought crossed Little Vinnie's mind that the following day was Halloween, and that if he wanted to snatch Laurel and fuck her brains out, she couldn't even accuse him. Who would she say did it, Batman? Imagine sending her to visit Mickey Boy in Otisville or Lewisburg with his baby in her belly? Fantastic!

Little Vinnie sighed. No, things were going too good to pull a stunt like that. Pretty soon Laurel would be giving him that pussy instead of him having to take it. The girl was just too hot to play the virgin for four years.

If things worked out right, Little Vinnie thought, he might even wind up with everything: Chrissy as his wife and Laurel sucking his prick a couple of nights a week.

There was no way Little Vinnie would leave those two potential situations to chance; he'd been out working on both of them. Making the most of his good behavior that night with Laurel, he'd described it to Chrissy and had her call Laurel to verify it. Since then Chrissy had softened noticeably toward him. As for Laurel, once he'd won her confidence, he'd made sure to bump into her on two different occasions at the Kings Plaza shopping mall. Both times Laurel had hesitantly refused to meet him again, but both times they'd been photographed together. Three different times, three different outfits she'd worn, three different dates together for Mickey Boy to see.

No way an incarcerated Mickey Boy would ever believe Laurel's smiling conversations in the photos had been promises to Little Vinnie not to mention their meeting to her boyfriend or try to mediate the misunderstanding between him and Mickey Boy until Mickey Boy was released from jail.

Gradually though, Laurel would give in. Guaranteed by the holidays. Thanksgiving wasn't too bad, but a lonely Christmas? Lonely New Year's? No way. Not for hot, sexy Laurel. Till that time he'd continue to play the gentleman, scoring point after point with her until she weakened—just once.

Then Mr. Mickey Boy'll wish he was never born, Little Vinnie thought on his way to the shower to relieve yet another painful erection.

46

November 9: Gravesend, Brooklyn

Red, gravy-covered mounds of hot and sweet pork sausages, large, crumbly meatballs, and pig's-skin brascioles with boiled eggs stuffed inside still partially filled the four oval platters on Don Peppino's dinner table when his eighteen guests finished their Sunday meal. The two large pans of baked rigatoni were, however, scraped clean.

As she had nearly every Sunday for the past fifty-two years, thirty of those in their present home, the don's wife, Sofia, rose to clean up after the meal she'd begun cooking at seven A.M. for everyone to eat at two.

Now the other females at the table including the children rushed to help Sofia condense the leftovers that the adults would divide later for their own homes, remove all the dinnerware to the dishwasher in the kitchen, and brush clean the white lace tablecloth before resetting it for dessert.

The male family members either left the table to stretch their legs in the parlor or remained and chatted among themselves, leaving the don to entertain the only guest who was not a member of his immediate family, Don Vincenze Calabra. Early that morning Don Vincenze had surprised his old friend and fellow mafioso by phoning to accept an open and long-standing dinner invitation.

"Peppino, my brother," Don Vincenze said in their Sicilian dialect. "I haven't had a meal this good since my Anna died." He placed both hands over his distended stomach. "You know, I miss the dinners we used to have at my house, like this."

"You know you're always welcome here; it's like your home. But what about your daughters? Don't tell me they are too modern to make a Sunday gravy?"

No, Margie and Linda were fine cooks, Don Vincenze said, though they just missed having that little bit extra that made the old-timers like Sofia and his late wife Anna great. But of late he'd taken less and less to traveling out to Huntington, where Margie and her Jewish-accountant husband lived, or Massapequa to have dinner with Linda, Gus the plumber, and their four kids. Though both daughters treated him royally, he said, he never felt as comfortable in their homes as he had in his own. There, he hadn't thought twice about wearing comfortable slippers all day, or frying up a last-minute batch of zeppoles, or sneaking off after dinner to nap for an hour or two.

"Don't get me wrong," he said with a chuckle and a dramatic flourish of his hand. "I'm still king . . . but more like a visiting king."

"Of course, my friend. I understand you very well," Don Peppino said. "You and me, we're cut from the same piece of material. Unfortunately, today there are not many others that are, even in the old country." He shook his head sadly. "We are truly the last of our kind."

Peppino was right, they were the end of a species, Don Vincenze thought. He, Peppino, and their contemporaries had been bred in poverty, and today, for the Italian majority, the poverty was gone. With it had gone the toughness that had made La Cosa Nostra thrive.

When he looked back, Don Vincenze could remember not only the good, solid wiseguys he'd grown up with, but a host of Italian prizefighters too: Marciano, Graziano, LaMotta. Theirs had been just another way to struggle out of the ghettos.

But today there were no more white fighters. The hunger was gone. What young boy, growing up in a middle-class home, with plenty of food in his belly and a television in his room, would have the heart to stick out his face and say, "Here, see if you could mess this up"? None. Italian prizefighters were as outdated as knickers and cold-water flats.

And by the same token, how many young, so-called "tough guys" could stand tall after hearing prison gates clang shut behind them? How many could say, "Where you're sending me is like a resort compared to where I grew up"? Not many.

Yes, Peppino's sad observation about their being the last of their kind was right, Don Vincenze thought, but not entirely. "Mostly," he replied. "But there is at least one more generation we can count on. Don't forget, we still have my prince."

"Ah, yes. How could I forget your prince? Forgive this sign of old age, my friend. Yes, let us hope he is not our last prince," Don Peppino said. He pushed himself from his red velour throne at the head of the table. "Come, Vincenze, let us have our coffee in the den."

Don Peppino stooped to plant a gentle kiss on the head of his six-year-old great-grandson. "A doctor, this one," he said with no attempt to hide his disappointment. "Not too many years ago he would have been a prince too. Good blood, bad times." Shaking his head, he shuffled off to the room where he spent most of his days.

Don Peppino's den was a room overstuffed with the artifacts he treasured. Aside from a new black leather recliner chair, everything in view was related to or reminiscent of the land of his birth. Commissioned landscapes of the Castellammarese region of Sicily where he'd spent his youth, handcarved busts of Caesar and Garibaldi, and Italian reading matter that ran the gamut from Machiavelli to Montale shut out modern America and created for Don Peppino his desired illusion of an unchanging world. Even the walls were covered with old-fashioned red-on-red flocked paper instead of more modern denlike paneling, and light fixtures resembled turn-of-the-century gaslights. Decades of stale cigar odor that lingered in the airless room added to its mausoleum effect.

While Don Vincenze made himself comfortable on the sofa, Don Peppino went to a stereo that had been customized to resemble an old gramophone, placed a recording of Verdi's *I vespri siciliani* on its turntable, then walked to the room's lone window.

"Let me make sure we can talk without those *dizgraziata* sonoma-bitches listening," he said while pulling the room's heavy brocade drapes tightly shut. Now their conversation, absorbed by the fabric, would be out of reach of a possible FBI surveillance team using shotgun microphones, which pick up reverberations of voice on glass from up to hundreds of feet away.

Next, Don Peppino opened a leather attaché case that sat on his desk. He pulled an antenna up, turned a dial, then silently read the meter on his one necessary concession to modern living, an electronic bug detector.

Once the old mafioso was satisfied that the room was free of listening devices, he poured two glasses of Strega, handed one to Don Vincenze, and settled back into his La-Z-Boy.

Don Vincenze looked around the room as he sipped the fiery cordial. Instead of finding the peacefulness and comfort his host did in the Mediterranean surroundings, he became melancholy.

"You know, Peppino, in the last few years I got a strong desire to go back to the old country," Don Vincenze said, still using their native tongue. "Maybe tour the mainland and then walk barefoot along the beautiful shore of the Golfo di Catania, like I did when I was a boy. Mother of God, I ain't seen nothing like it in over fifty years, but you know what, my friend, I picture it more clear every day."

An instant vision of the water's different shades of blue, the whitest sand, and the brightest sun he'd ever seen came rushing to him more vividly than ever. Don Vincenze could actually smell the salty sea and feel the hot sand between his toes. No artist could ever capture the true essence of his homeland as it lived in his heart.

"Even though we were poor," he continued, "we were rich in life." Don Vincenze chuckled remorsefully, then added, "You know, I never felt poor till I came to this country, an' then, for a while, I even resented the years I grew up in Sicilia."

But all that had changed with age. Lately Don Vincenze would find himself digging deeper and deeper into his past, trying to remember.

". . . An' this room, my brother, makes things especially real for me," he said. "Sitting here now, I feel like if I walk outside that door I'm gonna see *a buon oumo* my father sewing up the big fishing nets he used to work with." He sipped his drink and closed his misty eyes once more.

Sad. So sad, Don Vincenze thought. He reminisced to Don Peppino about when his wife, Anna, had been alive. What a good woman; a saint. Anna had always longed to go back home for visits, and when she finally had gotten to make trips to their hometown in Sicily, he'd never accompanied her. Always too busy. Instead, he'd sent her sister Josephine along, with all their combined kids, for a month or so every few years. By that time, footing the bills for everyone had become easier than spending time with them.

"Even *a buon oumo* Joe Carlo used to beg me to go stay at his villa in Sorrento an' I never went," Don Vincenze lamented. "Poor bastard, what they did to him." Remembering his friend, he cursed the government, cursed the parole officer who had refused to let Joe visit Italy. Unfortunately, by the time the parole period was nearly up, Joe had developed lung cancer and died.

"Whatta shame," Don Vincenze said, "how short our lives really are. Nobody realizes how much you an' me suffered, how much we sacrificed out of our short lives for our obligation to La Cosa Nostra."

"That's why, my friend, there's no one who can wear our shoes," Don Peppino replied, his speech flowery with Sicilian dialect. "Of course, we have hundreds of our people who think they are the same as us . . . but they're not."

Forty years ago, the withered old don claimed, most of the current mob members would never have been accepted. He drew a comparison to the only thing he loved about American culture: baseball. "In the old days, when there were only eight teams in each league, only the best made it," he said. "If they went back to the old way, half the ball players today would be sweeping streets or waiting on tables—just like the *imbecilli* we've let in."

Don Vincenze was about to argue that, to the contrary, forty years earlier they could have easily doubled their numbers, that the reserve pool to choose from was overflowing with good men, when he and Don Peppino were interrupted by one of Don Peppino's young granddaughters bringing them a tray that held a large *maganette* of espresso, demitasse cups, a bottle of anisette, and an assortment of the miniature pastries Don Vincenze had brought to the dinner. The two men fawned over the girl a bit, Don Vincenze giving her a twenty-dollar bill, then Don Peppino sent her on her way with a kiss on the head and a pat on her bottom.

It wasn't until the two mafiosi had finished one cup of the bitter coffee that Don Peppino spoke again. "I hope we can realize our dream before long," he said while pouring them both second servings. "I would hate to have to pass on from this miserable world without seeing our task completed."

"Sooner than you think," Don Vincenze assured his host, who seemed to be sensing the end of his time more and more each day. Don Vincenze continued, saying that their operation might have been nearly over had Tom Thumb not meddled in things that didn't concern him. Now, without the fat man around to upset the balance between the Rossellinis and Vallos, events would follow, according to schedule, the course the two old dons had planned.

"By this time next year things should be the way they should've been for the last twenty-five years." Don Vincenze paused, and with a confident but sad smile, added, "Only two Families—yours an' mine."

It was not a sense of pleasure Don Vincenze took in the consolidation of New York's Mafia Families under himself and the older Don Peppino. The thought of additional power didn't excite him. He had enough now, with the minor bosses kowtowing to his wishes. All added troops meant to him at that point was extra headaches. But it had to be done, and Vincenze Calabra had never avoided his duty, not for the United States of America when it was at war, and never for La Cosa Nostra.

Don Vincenze loved La Cosa Nostra. To him it represented the ethnic fortitude that had helped Sicilians survive a host of invading rulers, the spirit that had driven them to grow from impoverished immigrants in a wealthy land to rich men, the honor that had provided the only justice for Italians in a court system dominated by Irishmen—an honor that had allowed men like him to truly become "men of respect."

And he believed in the system of five separate and distinct New York City Families as set up in 1931 by Lucky Luciano, after he had eliminated the old order of "Moustache Petes" by having dozens of them murdered during the forty-eight hours they called "The Night of the Vespers."

But Vincenze Calabra had had a vision. Not an instant apparition, like in the Bible, but a slow, creeping, ever-expanding picture that came together like a jigsaw puzzle. He saw the end. Long before he'd been made a boss, he'd seen the first pieces of their apocalypse falling into place: internal moral decay due to greed, enforcement of harsh new laws sending their people away to prison for lifetimes, loss of the resource pool to choose new members from. Most of all, the loss of the pool. No new prizefighters.

Recently, things had deteriorated to the point where Don Vincenze had felt put upon to take the situation in hand. At nearly seventy years of age he could have looked the other way for his remaining years and let those who were left fend for themselves. Or he could fight to preserve a way of life that had nurtured Sicilians for centuries, the way ancient works of literature and art were preserved for the world to learn from and understand. Don Vincenze was a fighter.

After much thought, he decided that the only hope La Cosa Nostra had to survive a bit more—for he knew it could not last forever—was to pare down, tighten up, send a small, unified force of their descendants into the future. That would be his legacy. And when that was accomplished, he could die for all he cared. He would be a happy man.

To implement his self-imposed mandate, however, Don Vincenze needed help. He needed to eliminate the ego-driven leaders of the other Families, especially the powerful Don Peppino. He'd accomplished that first by enlisting Don Peppino as an ally. The oldest of all five bosses had been willing to do anything to "keep these young punks in their place."

The second thing he'd done was set up the meeting in May, which had pitted one imbecile against another. Let's get together at the feast, they'd said, believing the issues he'd raised that night in the funeral chapel would be foremost on their minds, not realizing he'd given them a much greater problem, one that would make them forget all else.

Now, only a few short months from the two dons reaching their mutually shared but differently motivated goals, Don Peppino capped both their tiny demitasse cups with anisette, then lifted his in the air. "I think the coming end of our struggle deserves a little toast. *A salute e cent'anni*," he proclaimed, the wish translating as "a hundred years."

Raising his cup, Don Vincenze replied, "*Salute*," then brought the coffee to his mouth and sipped. "Yes, my friend, it won't be long now," he said, setting the cup aside. "To be honest with you, I didn't think this maneuver would take so long, but, besides that idiot Tom Thumb slowing things down, it turned out that Petey Ross was a much stronger fighter than either one of us expected."

"Yes," Don Peppino agreed. "In spite of his being *eccitabile* . . . hotheaded, he turned out to be a better man than I ever thought he would be. Unfortunately, he is in the wrong place at the wrong time, and must be swept aside. Too bad he came up with the wrong Family. He could have gone far with me."

"A lot of things in life are too bad. I happen to like him an' Sonny too," Don Vincenze added. "Both of them could've done all right with me very easy, but they would never give up control of their Family to move up in mine. The way it stands now, all they are are thorns in our sides."

If the incompetent Vallo brothers couldn't finish their job soon, he and Peppino would have to step in to push things along, he said. Not a difficult task now that he had an ambitious underling of Petey Ross's, Ralphie "The Eye" Burgio, keeping him up-to-date on every move Petey made. There wasn't anything about the inner workings of the Rossellini war machine that Ralphie The Eye didn't know or wouldn't reveal to Don Vincenze for a chance to be a future officer in the larger Calabra clan once Petey Ross's Family had been dissolved.

"And what about our friend, *'Don Alphonso'*?" Don Peppino asked, derisively referring to Junior Vallo as one of their special status.

Once Petey Ross was finished, then Junior would be no problem, Don Vincenze said. The man had never been leadership quality anyway, and he had a lesson coming for the error he'd made by using a bomb to do away with his old boss, John-John.

After Junior Vallo was out of the picture, and Don Peppino's *paisano* from the other side, Jack The Wop, took over, that Family would be agreeably split up and assimilated by those of the two old dons. Payment to Jack The Wop for his cooperation: a *caporegime* spot with Don Peppino's Family.

At the same time, for his part in merging Tom Thumb's family into the two major ones, Rock Santoro would become Don Peppino's *consigliere*.

Don Vincenze had gladly offered to let Don Peppino acquire both temporary bosses into his crew. As for himself, he despised turncoats, and preferred to take lower-level button-men whose loyalty he would have a better chance of relying on.

"Once that's all out of the way, and we really got ourselves tightened up, then maybe we could work to save La Cosa Nostra for another generation," Don Vincenze suggested hopefully, then laughed. "Maybe by that time I'll have a grandson to carry on for another one on top of that."

Don Vincenze looked at his watch. Joe Augusta would be arriving in a few minutes to pick him up.

"Joseph's always on time, you know," he told Don Peppino. "I guess that's from keeping a tight schedule for all the bodies he's gotta bury."

"We buried a few in our time too, eh, Vincenze?" Don Peppino asked. "And not on schedules either." He laughed at his own joke.

Don Vincenze only smiled.

Don Peppino reached for the bottle of Strega. "Come, my friend, one last drink before you go," he said. "Then I'll walk you to the garage."

With small glasses of imported liqueur and soft kisses on both cheeks, the two men who'd begun their lives in Sicily at the outset of the twentieth century toasted the eventual success of their scheme to shape organized crime in New York for the twenty-first.

Don Vincenze waved farewell to Don Peppino as Joe Augusta backed his black Cadillac out of Peppino's garage. He smiled, wondering how long it would take after Peppino died for him to complete the consolidation of the five New York City Mafia Families under one banner—his own. And, of course, his prince's. He hoped he'd be able to outlast the older Don Peppino, to wait until the crusty, *bitticuse* man who was the only challenge to his power expired naturally. Peppino deserved that—if he didn't take too long.

"How'd everything go?" Joe Augusta inquired once they'd pulled away from the Palermo home.

"What was that?" the don responded blankly, still lost in thought.

"Oh, yes, Peppino," he said after his underboss had repeated the question. "Everything went very good. We took care of the few differences we had with his people even before we ate. I let them have the guy with the frozen pizzas. They been in that business a long time an' could probably do better with him than us anyway. But we got the union in his factory."

"I'll give that to Tommy Stitch-Head in the Bronx," Joe Augusta said. He then asked, "What about my cousin with the school buses?"

"Peppino's sending a message to his guy in Jersey City that he's gotta drop out of the bidding in the district your cousin's in. Tell your cousin he's got a free ride—on us," Don Vincenze said with a dismissing wave of his hand.

"Thank you. I'm sure Cousin Anthony will do the right thing anyway. He's a good man."

"The only other thing is the construction for that office complex on the West Side," Don Vincenze continued. "We're gonna split it forty-forty, with twenty points for Rock's crew. Nothing for Petey Ross or Junior Vallo."

To Don Vincenze, Joe Augusta appeared satisfied by the outcome of the minor disputes that had accumulated between their Family and Don Peppino's. His college-educated underboss had continually argued that the future of their secret society rested on their ability to involve themselves more in legitimate business without the costly wars like the one the Rossellini and Vallo factions were engaged in.

Didn't Joe think he knew all that? What did he think, that his boss was still some peasant fisherman from Sicily who couldn't see past the bow of his boat? For all Joe Augusta's education, Don Vincenze often thought, he wasn't smart. Not street smart anyway. He'd lost that gift somewhere between the covers of one of his business management books. What the hell could a book tell him about surviving intra-Family conflicts like the one between Charlie Lucky and Vito Genovese, when your own brother could be the enemy?

More and more Joe reminded him of Frank Costello. And how did Frank wind up after Lucky died and Vito Genovese was left as a rival? When one of Vito's bullets grazed his head instead of air-conditioning it, as had been intended, Frank yelled "I quit" and stayed home to watch over his "businesses." Guys like Frank Costello and Joe Augusta had lost sight of the fact that businesses were meant as camouflage to protect their way of life, not as a substitute for it. Vincenze Calabra would be damned if he would have surrendered as easily as Frank had. Vito would have had to either make sure his murder attempt worked the first time, or wind up in a body bag himself.

Now what irritated Don Vincenze most was that even after he'd explained to Joe Augusta why he'd instigated the bloody struggle between the other Families, Joe had still argued against it.

Of course, the don hadn't elaborated on his personal reason for the manipulation of the other Families: to preserve enough of their decaying institution for his bloodline to rule into the next century—Joe wasn't part of that. Calabras, and Ragusos on Don Vincenze's maternal side, had been "men of respect" for at least a hundred recorded years in

Sicily and the United States, and, if he could help, it would continue for a hundred more.

What Don Vincenze had pointed out to his underboss was the necessity for ridding all the Families of the scum they'd accumulated over the years by greedy bosses, which he and Peppino were not among, "selling" memberships rather than bestowing them on men who'd earned them through deeds. He'd explained that his intention was to condense the fittest that would remain after the purge into a tightly knit organization, like they'd had in the old days. Joe had understood that the resource pool of Italian ghettos, from which they had been able to draw on for strong-hearted, obedient youths, had virtually dried up. Even a college boy had to see there were no more Italian fighters.

Yet, in the face of those truths, and to the irritation of Don Vincenze, Joe Augusta continued to object at every possible opportunity.

Even now Joe turned to him, while driving, and, in his college-boy way, asked, "What about Petey and Junior? When are you going to stop them?"

All his impatient or snappy replies hadn't deterred Joe one bit, Don Vincenze thought. *When's he gonna smarten up and learn not to push me?* he wondered. *You'd think after all these years . . .*

In a tone he'd usually reserved for those low enough to be casually dismissed, Don Vincenze answered, "We're gonna stop them when we accomplish what we started—an' not a minute before."

For a while afterward silence weighed heavily in the car, Don Vincenze bristling as he lit, then puffed on a fresh cigar.

"You know, Joseph," he finally said, deciding to try a different approach, "knowing the way you feel about how we should operate, I would think you'd be the first to understand how important it is that we get down to two Families. Those others have been like cowboys for years, nothing but fight, fight, fight since the fifties. This is the only way we can get a hundred percent control over them without going to war ourselves."

"I know all that," Joe replied. "It's just that it's beginning to look like the cure is worse than the disease. All this publicity is terrible for business—all of our businesses."

Don Vincenze smiled. "For you, Joseph, I'm gonna bring this thing to a quick end."

Despite being disappointed by Joe Augusta having lost the ferocity he was known for in his earlier days, Don Vincenze still remembered all the good the man had done, and cared for him as he would a loyal nephew.

Soon he would be ready to place Buster in his rightful place as underboss and move Joe into the less active position of *consigliere*, a position much better suited to his bright mind and complacent ways.

All he needed, the aging don mused, was a little more time. Just time.

Time, however, was not to be wasted, and, keeping that in mind, Don Vincenze told his underboss, "Oh, by the way, I want you to stop by Buster after you drop me off at Pauline's." His last reference was to the woman he'd kept company with for years. Once his wife, Anna, had died, he'd continued to take Pauline out at least two nights a week, as he had during his marriage, and now also made it a point to spend Sunday evenings at her home. It was a routine that both relaxed him and filled some of the emptiness in his life, though he considered himself not to be a lonely man, but a man alone.

"Buster'll be at his club till about seven or eight," the don continued. "Call the Focacceria next door an' leave a message for him to make sure he waits for you."

Though Joe Augusta's face remained passive, Don Vincenze was aware of the distaste Joe felt toward going to the Little Italy location. On several occasions his underboss had made known his preference that appointments take place at restaurants, offices, or his funeral home, not in the social clubs that were often targeted by various law enforcement agencies for surveillance.

"What do I tell him?" Joe asked.

"Tell him that I want him to send somebody on the q.t. to cop a sneak on that Irish kid, whatever the hell his name is, that had the beef with my son. Let Buster make sure that Vinnie an' his friends stay far away from where the kid hangs out, an' that they always have somebody good around them for an alibi."

That he found the order repugnant was written all over Joe Augusta's face. "Listen, Vince," he said. "You know I'll do whatever you say, but it's my responsibility to tell you when I think we might be making a mistake . . . and I think this is a major one. First of all, this Irish piece of shit doesn't mean a thing in the war—"

"You know it has nothing to do with the war," Don Vincenze interrupted. "It's just a good time to get rid of the pest and have the world think somebody else did it."

"Even so, I don't like to see our men get anywhere near that whole mess. What if something goes wrong? Look how Tom Thumb got exposed by his guy getting pinched for that hit in Tarrytown."

"I'm not Tom Thumb. And I know you're no Judas turncoat like Rock Santoro."

"Of course not. I'm only thinking of what's good for you and our Family."

"I know you are, and I appreciate your honesty, but that's the way I want it. Besides, it's only one less *babania* dealer around," Don Vincenze said. "The mayor might even give us a medal. Then we'd be heroes to your precious public, right?"

"What do I tell them about that other kid, Georgie, that stays with the Irishman?" Joe asked, his features sagging in surrender. "He's a good boy."

Don Vincenze gave the question virtually no thought, immediately answering, "If they could leave him out, okay. If not . . . let them do what they gotta do anyway. You know the old saying, 'Tell me who you stay with, an' I'll tell you what you are.' The kid's probably a dope pusher too, an' ain't worth a pile of shit himself. Either way's okay with me. An' tell Buster to make sure he sends a couple of proposed guys to do it. Let them get a little work under their belts; it's about time we made these guys really earn their places in our thing."

Joe sighed. "You're the boss."

"Always remember that an' you'll be okay," Don Vincenze replied. "Oh, an' Joseph, we only got a few weeks to Thanksgiving, so please, make sure they get this Irish problem taken care of soon, before the holiday. This way we could all enjoy our turkey."

Wanting no mistake about the pressure he meant to exert or the threat implied for failure, Don Vincenze reached over and gripped Joe Augusta by the arm. He stared sternly at his underboss, and asked, "Understood?"

"Understood."

47

November 15: Downtown Manhattan

At 2:30 P.M. Mickey Boy was elevatored down to the third floor of the federal detention center. He was led into a small, bare, windowless room, where two parole commissioners from the Northeast Regional Office sat at the long side of a wooden conference table. The younger of the two was small, dark, and weasel-faced, and wore round tortoiseshell-framed glasses. Weasel-Face tinkered with a portable tape recorder that had been placed on the table between him and his partner, who was also thin, but wore no glasses and had gray hair instead of black. Otherwise, they looked like relatives. The older, gray-haired commissioner busied himself reading something in a folder, which Mickey Boy assumed was his parole file.

Anthony Spositoro was also present, and sat at the same side of the table as the commissioners. Alongside him, the blond agent who had slapped the handcuffs on Mickey Boy almost two months earlier thumbed through a black notebook.

That was what he'd become again, Mickey Boy thought: folders, notebooks, files—not a human, just a number.

The only friendly face at the table was that of Ira J. Golden, the Park Avenue attorney Buster had insisted Mickey Boy hire. Golden, who sat directly across from the commissioners, asked for and was granted a few minutes to confer with his client outside the room.

Once they were in the hallway, the cherub-faced lawyer said, "Your friend Richie brought me what he was supposed to yesterday."

Mickey Boy stared at Golden without speaking. *Sonofabitches always think about money first*, he thought. *Here I am, fighting for my life, and he tells me he's happy I sent him cash. They should call him Golden Ira instead of Ira Golden.*

"Buster was in my office at nine-thirty this morning," Golden continued. "Quite unusual for him to roll out of bed that early. You must be very special to him."

The lawyer paused, waiting for a response, got only a stony look, then went on. "Anyway, true to his word, he came up with what to me looks like a winner . . . and at the last minute. Unfortunately, as you heard for yourself from the commissioner, we're running late and he didn't give me enough time to fully explain to you what our game plan is. I don't want to piss them off by us talking out here too long, so all I'll tell you now is that you're not going to testify in your own behalf, as I had suggested you might at our last meeting."

You mean our only meeting, went through Mickey Boy's mind. Golden had visited him once in all the weeks he was in MCC, and then only to introduce himself, make arrangements for his fee to be paid, and deliver a message from Buster for him to sit tight.

None of the questions Mickey Boy'd asked had been answered. Golden had claimed he possessed no information other than what the government had supplied, and had repeated Buster's message.

For the ten thousand dollars he'd been forced to pay, Mickey Boy felt he was worth more attention than what he'd received so far. He wished Buster had minded his own goddamned business and let him choose his own lawyer.

"Just relax and trust me," Golden now assured him. He placed a fatherly arm over Mickey Boy's shoulders and led him back into the hearing room.

Trust, my ass! Mickey Boy thought as he dropped into a green plastic chair.

As Mickey Boy's case agent, Anthony Spositoro directed the government's argument in support of Mickey Boy's being violated on parole and sent back to prison for the remainder of time owed. He made good use of his evening law school studies as he methodically presented and documented with both photographs and statements from confidential informants his contention that Michael Messina, a.k.a. "Mickey Boy," was closely associated with elements of the city's organized crime community.

Spositoro's first witness was his parole team partner, Dennis Van Brun, who testified from where he sat about his own surveillance of the accused violator.

Mickey Boy squirmed when the officer stated for the record that he had followed him on several occasions, and submitted log entries to support the fact that he never observed him do what he himself considered to be a full day's work.

After providing the commissioners with a list of all the times he had called Mickey Boy's apartment after ten A.M. on supposed workdays and had hung up when the parolee answered, Van Brun completed his testimony with an account of the day he'd assisted Spositoro in remanding him.

The two commissioners appeared slightly annoyed when Ira Golden announced that he had some questions for Van Brun. They looked at their watches to let him know they were impatient to conclude the proceedings. Golden spoke from where he sat, and in gentle tones.

GOLDEN: Officer Van Brun, on the thirty or so occasions that you called Mr. Messina, did you ever talk to him?

VAN BRUN: No.

GOLDEN: You mean you never asked him why he was home, or when he was going to work? Nothing?

VAN BRUN: No sir, nothing.

GOLDEN: And so you really don't know if Mr. Messina was home doing paperwork for his accounts, or taking orders on the phone, or entertaining a company client, do you?

VAN BRUN: No, I don't.

GOLDEN: And the same goes for the days you followed Mr. Messina. You have no idea if he conducted business at some of the stops on this paper you submitted, or if he used the phones there to call accounts of his. Is that correct?

VAN BRUN: (hesitantly) That is correct.

GOLDEN: One last question, Officer Van Brun. Did you ever observe Mr. Messina, on those days that you followed him around, consorting with any known felons?

VAN BRUN: No, I did not, but he was with one Richard DeLuca quite often, who—

240

GOLDEN: Excuse me for interrupting you, Officer Van Brun,
but does Mr. DeLuca have a police record? To your
knowledge, has he ever been arrested for anything?

VAN BRUN: Well, no, not to my knowledge, but—

GOLDEN: Thank you, Officer, that will be all.

With a snide smile Spositoro told the commissioners that Richie
DeLuca was believed by local authorities to be a bookmaker. Ira Golden
pointed out, in a brief and sarcastic reply, that unsupported labels were
supposed to have gone out with Joseph McCarthy.

Mickey Boy took little heart from his attorney's cutting remarks and
the apparent upper hand he'd won in the confrontation. Small victories
were worthless. As far as he was concerned, Spositoro and the weasel-
faced commissioners received their paychecks from the same source,
and would work in collusion against him.

The next witness for the government was FBI Special Agent Arnold
Selkower, who was brought in by Spositoro from a nearby room where
he had been sequestered. He was seated at the near end of the table.

Selkower's testimony began with his assignment to watch the Lower
Manhattan Fishing Association and his initial curiosity when Mickey
Boy had left his girlfriend alone in a parked car for an inordinate amount
of time while he entered the Focacceria Villarosa, next door to the club.
Reading from his diary, he continued relating events in a monotonous
official manner until he came to his confrontation with two giants in
the restaurant's backyard. His humorous exaggeration of their size and
his reaction to finding them there brought chuckles from everyone
except Mickey Boy, who found the agent's confidence intimidating.

Mickey Boy also noted that the two parole commissioners did nothing
to hide their irritation at Golden's insistence on questioning Selkower.

In his mind, Mickey Boy added more time to what he'd calculated
his sentence would be. Now it was up to two years out of the four
remaining on paper for his parole.

GOLDEN: On the first occasion when you noticed Mr. Messina,
did you talk to him at all?

SELKOWER: No, sir. I was in a truck.

GOLDEN: So you don't know that he wasn't in the restaurant
all that time, do you?

SELKOWER: No, sir.

GOLDEN: Now, Agent Selkower, on the second occasion, when
you followed Mr. Messina into the restaurant, did
you ask anyone for him? A waiter? Owner? Anyone?

SELKOWER: No, I didn't.

GOLDEN: Thank you, Agent Selkower. Oh, and one other thing:
            Do you know if there are any other means of entrance
            or egress from the restaurant? Other than the front
            or back doors, that is?
SELKOWER: *(puzzled)* Not that I know of . . . unless they've got a
            trapdoor that leads to the sewer system.
GOLDEN: Who knows? Stranger things have happened in this
            wonderful city of ours. Thank you, Agent Selkower,
            that will be all.

Mickey Boy was just as annoyed at Golden's useless questioning of
Agent Selkower as the commissioners appeared to be. He viewed the
cross-examination as nothing more than an attempt by Golden to justify
his weighty fee of ten thousand dollars for what would amount to a
couple of hours' work.

Spositoro himself made the final presentation on the government's
behalf. He produced his own logbook for the day he'd followed Mickey
Boy to the frankfurter warehouse building near the Seaport, photographs of Mickey Boy, Richie, and at least a dozen known mob figures
going in and out of the building at various times, and a written assessment by a city detective as to the use he believed the old structure
was being put to: an illegal gambling casino controlled by mob boss
Vincenze "Mr. Vincent" Calabra and his lieutenant, the aforementioned
Buster Alcamo.

Anthony Spositoro's delivery ended with a remark directed at Mickey
Boy's attorney, Ira Golden. "And before you ask, Counselor," he said,
"no, I did not stop him, question him, or go in to shoot craps with
him."

The parole commissioners cast knowing glances at one another. Their
conclusion appeared to be foregone: Michael "Mickey Boy" Messina
was guilty of violating conditions of his parole—conditions he'd signed
under threat of not being released—and would be sent back to jail. The
only question was, for how long?

Mickey Boy was now positive he'd draw the full four years he owed.
Disgusted, he closed his eyes. Would Laurel wait for him all that time?
he wondered. Could she wait? Had the sexual weapon she'd developed
after Alley's leaving been turned on her? Was sex now an addiction?
He shook his head, trying to clear it of Laurel. How the hell could he
think of her now, when his freedom was at stake? The thought that
maybe he was the one who was hooked crossed his mind.

Cherub-cheeked Ira J. Golden cleared his throat, then rose from his
chair. He buttoned his gray suitjacket over his sizable girth, and slowly

began to walk toward where parole officers Spositoro and Van Brun sat.

"A couple of questions for Mr. Spositoro," Golden bellowed suddenly. "Who I'm glad doesn't shoot craps."

Thank God they can't give me any more than four years, Mickey Boy thought when he looked at his judges' faces. He wished Golden would just be quiet and play for some leniency.

Spositoro smirked, first at the commissioners in a what-is-this-guy-kidding? way, then at Golden. "I thought I had covered everything you might want, or not want, to hear."

Golden seemed to grow taller than his five feet eleven inches. His back straightened and his pudgy smile became artificially wide. He snapped open his jacket button.

GOLDEN: It just goes to show that you think a lot of things that aren't always so.

SPOSITORO: What do you mean by that?

GOLDEN: Just what it sounds like. You have some preconceived notions about certain things, including my client, Michael Messina, which don't always prove to be correct. Isn't that so, Officer Spositoro?

SPOSITORO: I assure you, Counselor, any notions I have about Michael are quite correct.

GOLDEN: You're very sure of yourself. *(pause)* Do you hate Michael Messina?

SPOSITORO: Hate him? No. I dislike the things he does and the people he associates with, but I don't hate him.

GOLDEN: You mean the things you *think* he does, and the people you *assume* he associates with. Are you jealous of him?

SPOSITORO: Are you crazy? Why would I be jealous of an ex-con?

GOLDEN: Do you have any girlfriends?

SPOSITORO: That's none of your goddamn business!

Seeing Golden's performance thrilled Mickey Boy. He loved the sight of his parole officer becoming unnerved, and, if he was going to lose the parole violation hearing anyway, was all for going down swinging.

COMMISSIONER #1: Gentlemen, please. Mr. Golden, I don't think your line of questioning has a place at these proceedings, or, for that matter, is doing your client any good.

GOLDEN: Excuse me if it appears that way, but I'm trying to find out why a case agent never confronts a parolee about possible violations. Why he seems set on seeing only the bad side! *(turning to Spositoro)* Did you ask him why he was in that particular building that day?

SPOSITORO: No, I didn't. What was he going to tell me, that he sells them dice made of mozzarella cheese?

GOLDEN: There we go again, another supposition. You'd be angry if Michael Messina were found innocent today, wouldn't you?

SPOSITORO: You bet your life I would, because I know that he's violated the conditions of his parole. *(grinning)* But why discuss the impossible?

GOLDEN: *(turning his back to Spositoro)* We'll see about that. I'd like to call my first witness on behalf of Michael Messina: his employer, Mr. Guido Vizzini, the president of Viva L'Italia, Incorporated.

COMMISSIONER #2: *(impatiently)* Just how many witnesses have you, Mr. Golden?

GOLDEN: Just two.

COMMISSIONER #2: Very well, let's proceed.

Guido Vizzini was a small, unimpressive, grandfatherly type of man whose timid demeanor hid the fact that he was a millionaire many times over. Next to the imposing figure of Ira J. Golden, the balding and stooped wholesaler looked defeated. When he sat at the end of the table, Vizzini disappeared almost to the shoulders of his ill-fitted brown suit.

Golden led his witness through a brief résumé of his Italian provisions business and personal background, then focused his questions on the man's relationship with the defendant.

Vizzini explained that Mickey Boy, and he called him that, had been recommended to him by a restaurateur friend of his who'd asked him to give the young ex-convict an opportunity to earn a decent living. He portrayed Mickey Boy as a personable, hardworking asset to his firm, who was extremely well liked by their clientele and who operated under no restrictions as far as either his time or movement was concerned.

"As long as he produces like he does, he's his own boss."

Mickey Boy laughed inside at the knowledge that Vizzini had been a second cousin of his deceased boss, Sam LaMonica. He and Vizzini had become acquainted when Sam had sent him and a dozen of his friends to help the purveyor break a strike at one of his other businesses. On their boss's command, the youngsters had used Louisville Sluggers on the strikers' heads, legs, and collarbones. Now Vizzini owed him.

GOLDEN: And the account of yours on Mulberry Street in Manhattan, the Focacceria Villarosa, how did you get it?

VIZZINI: Mickey Boy brought it in a little while after he started with me.

GOLDEN: Is the Villarosa a good account?

VIZZINI: A hell of an account! They use just about everything from us, and also let me supply their paper goods from another company I own. Mickey Boy even got my brother, Sal, all their produce business . . . he's in Hunt's Point Market, you know.

GOLDEN: That's very nice, Mr. Vizzini. I have only one more question for you. Do you think that Michael might be spending too much time at the Villarosa? I mean, if he were to stay an hour or two at a time, he could be visiting other accounts instead?

VIZZINI: Like I told you before, as long as he produces like he does, he can sleep with them for all I care.

GOLDEN: Thank you, Mr. Vizzini. You've been extremely helpful.

SPOSITORO: *(forcing a smile)* No questions.

Mickey Boy had to admit to himself that he liked Golden's style. *If only I had something for him to work with*, he thought. *What a waste of good talent.*

When Golden ushered in his next witness, Mickey Boy did a double take.

In walked a luscious-looking brunette who made even the commissioners sit upright in their seats. The girl appeared to Mickey Boy to be no older than twenty or twenty-one at most. The simple black square-necked dress she wore in no way hid her large breasts, invitingly wide hips, or healthy, well-formed legs. Shiny black curls cascaded down over her shoulders.

When she waved to him and blew a kiss, Mickey Boy nearly fell off his seat. Suddenly he was conscious of the cheap orange jump suit he wore, and straightened the collar as though that would enhance its appearance.

What a knockout, he thought as the girl settled into the seat at the table's end. To him, she epitomized the lusty Italian country girls of the movies: Sylvana Mangano, Sophia Loren, Gina Lollobrigida. He could visualize her working a farm all day, then, still sweaty and dirt-splotched, fuck her husband half to death on the living room floor. *Wow!*

Since Golden elected to remain standing while he questioned the girl, the only thing that stood between her and Mickey Boy were a scant few feet of tabletop. When he stared at her, Mickey Boy felt his body come alive.

The room had suddenly become charged with electricity, everyone in it seeming more alert as Golden began to address the girl.

GOLDEN: May we have your name, Miss . . . ?
ROSALIE: Rosalie DeStefano.
GOLDEN: And your age?
ROSALIE: Nineteen.
GOLDEN: Rosalie, do you work or attend school? Or both? Or neither?

Ira Golden smiled at Rosalie when he asked the last question, as did the two commissioners. Only Spositoro kept a sour face.

ROSALIE: I work—for my parents.
GOLDEN: Where is that, Rosalie, and in what capacity do you work?
ROSALIE: At the Focacceria Villarosa on Mulberry Street. I'm the Rosa in Villarosa. *(She giggled.)*

The two parole commissioners grinned even wider, as did Ira Golden when he saw them.

Golden winked at Mickey Boy, who wondered, *How the hell did I ever miss her there?*

GOLDEN: Again, dear, what is your job at the Villarosa? Your duties?
ROSALIE: I take care of my father's bookkeeping, I do most of the ordering for him, and I even sign his checks. I'm the secretary-treasurer of his corporation.
GOLDEN: That's very good, Rosalie. I'm sure your parents are as proud of your work as you obviously are. For the moment, though, I'd like to concentrate on your duties in ordering, as you mentioned. What exactly do you order?

ROSALIE: Oh, just about everything that we need in the store, except the meat. My father likes to go to Fretta Brothers every morning and buy the meat himself. This way he gets to see the men there and talk to them for a while. They're friends since he came to this country.

GOLDEN: So then, let me see if I understand you correctly. Outside of the meat, as you explained, you would be responsible for ordering, say, the plum tomatoes, or the mozzarella cheese, or the olive oil, and so on and so forth. Correct?

ROSALIE: That's right . . . even down to the toothpicks and the toilet paper.

Everyone laughed except Spositoro.

GOLDEN: When you say you order these items, do you order by phone or do you deal with salesmen in person?

ROSALIE: Both. In the morning there's always a list of what we have in stock, and I figure out by whether it's a weekday or the weekend's coming up, what we need. Then either I call in the order, or if the salesman comes by I give it to him—like our bread man, he stops by every day.

GOLDEN: Does Michael Messina ever come around? You know Michael, sitting over there in the lovely orange designer jump suit?

ROSALIE: Mickey comes around a lot.

Rosalie smiled warmly at Mickey Boy, who was thoroughly confused. He knew he'd never seen her before, realized Buster must have sent her, but couldn't figure out of what benefit her testimony would be. Maybe she was a hooker, there as a bribe for the two parole commissioners? That would certainly have a better shot than his defense so far.

GOLDEN: Since when has Michael, or Mickey, as you call him, been coming into your parents' and your restaurant?

ROSALIE: Since sometime last spring, when he wanted to sell us stuff from Viva L'Italia.

GOLDEN: And what happened?

ROSALIE: My father sent him up to my office on the second floor. I knew his products were no different from what we were using, but his prices were good, and I thought he was really cute (giggle), so I gave him an order.

247

GOLDEN: I guess being cute helped. I don't think I could have done quite as well.

ROSALIE: *(innocently)* Why? You're cute too.

GOLDEN: *(smiling at commissioners)* Thank you, Rosalie. Now, about that office you mentioned . . . on the second floor. How would someone, for example Mr. Spositoro over there, go about getting upstairs if he wanted to speak to you?

ROSALIE: I have one entrance upstairs, but two downstairs. He could either ring the front doorbell—that's the wooden door on the left side of the restaurant—or they could buzz open the door inside the restaurant, back where the rest rooms are, and he would go from the hall to the front, where the same stairs are that he'd take if he used the outside door.

GOLDEN: *(looking directly at Spositoro)* So if someone wanted to come up, they would not have to leave the building. Correct?

ROSALIE: Yes.

GOLDEN: Now, Rosalie, if you remember, how did Michael, er, Mickey, come up to see you when he did? By which door downstairs?

ROSALIE: Oh, always by the inside door.

GOLDEN: How can you be so sure?

ROSALIE: Well, if he used the outside door, he would have had to buzz me. Besides, we're afraid of getting robbed . . . I'm alone with the safe upstairs, so I really don't let anyone in from the front. They have to come through the inside so that my father knows who's with me.

GOLDEN: So Mickey used to walk into the restaurant, ask for you, and get buzzed through the inside door. That means if someone followed him in after a little while, and didn't bother asking for him, they'd have no idea where he went. Correct?

ROSALIE: That's right.

Everyone in the room became animated: Van Brun whispered something into Spositoro's ear, the two commissioners huddled together, and Golden turned to Mickey Boy and made a victory sign with his fingers.

Mickey Boy was too stunned to do anything. His mind seemed unable to focus. Elation followed, then quickly subsided when he realized Golden still couldn't overcome his presence at the downtown crap game.

GOLDEN: Now, Rosalie, I realize that the next few questions are very personal, and embarrassing to answer. If it weren't so important, believe me, I'd never ask them of you.

ROSALIE: I know, but remember what you promised.

GOLDEN: Yes, Rosalie. I promised that whatever you testified to here would remain confidential, and that I would never let your parents know. I'm sure these gentlemen here will tell you the same.

Both commissioners nodded their heads accordingly, while Spositoro sat expressionless.

When Rosalie glanced questioningly at the parole officer, Ira J. Golden said, "Even though Mr. Spositoro has not indicated for the record that he will keep everything you say confidential, I will be glad to vouch for his honor."

SPOSITORO: As long as she tells the truth.

Everyone, including Spositoro's fellow parole officer, Dennis Van Brun, just glared at him.

GOLDEN: Now, Rosalie, when Mickey used to come and see you, in the beginning he used to leave quickly, but then as time went on, he began to stay longer. Is that correct?

ROSALIE: Yes.

GOLDEN: Why was that?

ROSALIE: We became friends.

GOLDEN: Just friends, Rosalie?

ROSALIE: *(blushing)* Very good friends.

GOLDEN: When you were upstairs at the restaurant, how friendly did you become? Did you talk, play checkers, hold hands? How good?

ROSALIE: We . . . er . . . well, we started to make out a lot. You know what I mean by that?

GOLDEN: I may look old to you, Rosalie, but I'm not exactly ancient.

Everyone laughed again. Spositoro visibly burned.

GOLDEN: I hate to seem like a dirty old man now, but when you made out, did you do it for a little while, or hours, or what?

ROSALIE: *(giggling)* Well, we used to do it for longer and longer times. A couple of times I had to let Mickey go out the front door so my father wouldn't know how long he was up there with me.

GOLDEN: So what you're telling me is that as time went on, it wouldn't have been unusual for Mickey to spend an hour or two with you?

ROSALIE: Or more. One of the times I let him out the front, he was with me for over three hours. After that, though, I got scared that my parents would catch us. Then I really would have died.

GOLDEN: So what did you do? Did you give him up?

ROSALIE: Oh, no, I love him.

Jesus, this broad's terrific, Mickey Boy thought. *I wouldn't mind making this fantasy of hers real one day—as long as Laurel don't find out.*

Ira J. Golden walked to the table where the two commissioners sat, shuffled through the photographs that lay in front of them, and brought one over to Rosalie.

GOLDEN: Now, Rosalie, I want you to study this picture carefully, and tell me if it looks familiar to you.

ROSALIE: *(imploringly)* Remember, you promised.

GOLDEN: I remember. Your parents will never find out anything from us. Now, please answer my question, Rosalie. Do you recognize this photo?

ROSALIE: Yes. I . . . uh . . . I have an apartment in that building.

GOLDEN: You mean with your parents?

ROSALIE: No, by myself. It's a small apartment on the top floor.

GOLDEN: Now, Rosalie, look at the other photo. Do you recognize the two men going in?

ROSALIE: Yes, that's Mickey and his friend Richie when they came there the first time.

GOLDEN: Do you see the date on the back of the picture? Is that the date they visited you?

ROSALIE: Yes.

GOLDEN: Now, Rosalie, remember, I don't want to embarrass you, but I must ask you how or why you recall that particular date?

ROSALIE: *(looking down)* Because that's the first time Mickey and I went all the way. You know, we . . .

GOLDEN: Yes, I understand, and without going into explicit detail, just tell us how Mickey and Richie happened to come there that day, and what happened.

ROSALIE: I told Mickey that I got the apartment and that I wanted to cook dinner for him. He told me that he had this really nice friend, so I brought my girlfriend, Cathy, and we made it a double date.

GOLDEN: Were there other "dates" when this photograph might have been taken?

ROSALIE: No. That was the only time Richie was up. He and Cathy never really got started, then she went back with her old boyfriend—she's getting married next year.

GOLDEN: *(smiling)* My congratulations to Cathy. Now, please go on, what happened next, that evening . . . the evening of the photo?

ROSALIE: After we cleaned up the table, we wanted to make out a little bit, so we left Richie and Cathy in the kitchen, and we went into the bedroom. Well, one thing led to another, and, well, I guess knowing my parents weren't there, well, we both gave in, and by the time I knew it, we fell asleep in each other's arms and didn't wake up until it was dark.

Rosalie shot a loving look at Mickey Boy, who smiled back warmly. He wanted to rush up and swing her fleshy body around in his arms for bringing victory within his reach, a victory so close he could taste it.

Spositoro's face flushed bright red. His cheek muscles rippled from tightly gritted teeth, and his fists clenched the table's edge so hard that his knuckles turned bloodless white.

The mutual glances that now passed between the commissioners had changed from one of impatience to convict Mickey Boy Messina to one of resignation to their loss.

Ira J. Golden cast Mickey Boy a cautious smile, then turned his attention back to the witness.

GOLDEN: Only two more questions, Rosalie, and then I'm finished. First of all, do you remember what time Mickey left that evening?

ROSALIE: When we woke up, the eleven o'clock news was on, and by the time we left to get Richie's car from the parking lot, Johnny Carson already had started.

Perfect! Mickey Boy thought. The times indicated in Rosalie's answer coincided perfectly with the receipt Spositoro held from the Pearl Street garage where Richie had parked the evening he and Mickey Boy had gone for dinner with Don Vincenze and Buster at the seafood restaurant.

GOLDEN: Finally, Rosalie, do you know who rents the floors below you in the building?

ROSALIE: The floor below me is empty and the floor below that is some kind of club. A lot of the men that go there are members of the club that's next door to our restaurant. In fact, that's how I knew about the apartment, from Cathy's cousin Bobby, who's a member of both clubs.

GOLDEN: Do you know what the men do at the club downstairs?

ROSALIE: That's none of my business.

GOLDEN: But you know?

ROSALIE: I said, that's none of my business.

Great move by Golden, Mickey Boy thought, not to have Rosalie say she didn't know what was going on two floors below her apartment, by men she was familiar with from her parents' restaurant. Had she done that, she would have appeared to be an idiot, or, worse, a liar.

Ira J. Golden shrugged helplessly at Rosalie's stubborn refusal to answer his question, then continued.

GOLDEN: Okay, Rosalie, let me ask you this: did Mickey stop in the club that night, that first night you two, uh, spent together?

ROSALIE: No. He was with me from the time he got there until he drove home.

GOLDEN: (smiling) Thank you, Rosalie, you've been very helpful. And again, I apologize for having to pry into your personal life.

SPOSITORO: One question, Miss DeStefano. Do you know that Michael Messina has a steady live-in girlfriend, and that she sits around in his car while he "makes out" with you?

Every face in the bare room glared "cheap shot" at the parole officer.

ROSALIE: (indignantly) Yes. I know all about Laurel. Mickey explained everything to me. He was going steady with her before he met me and doesn't want to hurt her . . . but eventually I know he'll be all mine.

Anthony Spositoro waved a dismissing hand and slumped down in his chair. He'd been taken, and there was nothing in the world he could do about it. Putting pressure on Rosalie at that point would only evoke sympathy for her.

Though she'd been informally dismissed, Rosalie continued to sit there, her dark eyes defying Spositoro to attack her story.

Looking down at his folded hands, the parole officer said, "No further questions."

The older of the commissioners immediately announced, "We find no evidence that Michael Messina violated the conditions of his parole, and order him released forthwith." The weasel-faced commissioner added, "Of course, it will take from ten days to two weeks until our determination is ratified by the national office. Mr. Messina will remain in custody at this facility until that time."

Rosalie leaned over and took the gray-haired commissioner's hand in hers. "May I please kiss Mickey good-bye?" she asked sweetly. "Just once?"

The commissioner seemed mesmerized by the milky breasts in front of him, staring down at the bit of cleavage the table had pushed into view.

"Well, er, I don't see anything wrong in it," he said, not moving his eyes from Rosalie's swelling chest. "But only for a moment."

"Thank you," Rosalie said, already on her way around the corner of the table to where Mickey Boy now stood, having risen from his seat. As soon as she reached him she flung herself into his arms as though they were long-lost lovers.

Mickey Boy felt the full length of Rosalie's robust body press against his with no reserve. When she kissed him, she parted her lips slightly, allowing him to taste the cool wetness of her mouth, the fruity leftover of some gum.

Embarrassed at first by his erection pushing against Rosalie's stomach, Mickey Boy relaxed as he received only unashamed pressure from her in return.

"Thanks," Mickey Boy whispered into Rosalie's ear, his lips brushing her lobe. His nostrils greedily sucked in her musky scent, so faint it said, Just for you.

"Anytime . . . and anything," Rosalie replied as intimately as he had, her breath making love to his ear. "You know where I am."

Though Mickey Boy's surroundings remained gray, and would for the next couple of weeks until his actual release, inside he was bursting with bright scarlets and golds. He felt truly alive for the first time in the nearly two months since he'd been locked up, and floated all the way back up on the elevator to the eleventh floor.

Only two more weeks and he'd be free again, to feel again, to get his life in gear—hopefully in time for Thanksgiving.

Mickey Boy owed Buster a debt, and Rosalie too. Though Buster would collect a lifetime of loyal service from him, he'd make it a point to buy him some gift, a watch or other personal item to show his respect and gratitude immediately. As far as Rosalie went, she would have to be repaid long-distance—a piece of jewelry, candy, flowers, delivered by some messenger service—she was just too hot to get involved with in person.

Foremost in Mickey Boy's mind was Laurel. Now he'd push her to marry him as soon as he was released. An inner urgency made the Christmas wedding he'd originally planned seem too far away. Maybe he could push it up to Thanksgiving? New Year's would be his outside bargaining limit if Laurel resisted—like all girls, Mickey Boy expected her to see the lengthy preparations for her wedding as a joy equal to the affair itself. Worse to worst, he'd fly his and her families to Vegas for a quickie ceremony and celebration, then let her plan a huge party for later on.

Mickey Boy would begin his campaign to convince Laurel to marry him immediately in little more than an hour, when she would be up to visit.

Uplifting Sinatra lyrics found their way into Mickey Boy's head for the first time since having been locked up. The way things had turned around made him sure that all his tomorrows certainly would belong to Laurel.

Whatta day, Mickey Boy mused. *Whatta goddamn wonderful day!*

Laurel shifted impatiently from one leg to the other as she stood on line in front of the Park Row entrance to the Metropolitan Correctional Center. Tasting the dryness in her mouth again, she pulled another piece of Dentyne from her pocketbook, transferred the tasteless lump she'd been chewing to the wrapper, and popped the fresh piece onto her tongue, the cinnamon immediately inflicting a refreshing burn. Only one piece of unchewed gum remained from the two packages she'd started out with only an hour before.

Laurel had arrived early, hoping to be included in the first group of visitors brought upstairs at five-thirty. Then, at last, she would be able to find out how the parole board had ruled in Mickey Boy's case. A half dozen calls to Ira J. Golden's office had gotten her nowhere. All she'd been told each time was that "Mr. Golden hasn't called in yet."

Laurel checked her watch. 4:42. Less than an hour to go until she would finally get to trade news with her fiancé. Why did his goddamn future have to be so important to hers?

When Laurel looked up from checking the time again, she spotted Mickey Boy's attorney rushing out of the building. Not caring whether or not she forfeited the place on line she'd held for an hour, she immediately ran to him.

"Mr. Golden," Laurel called. "Remember me? I'm Mickey Messina's fiancée, Laurel Bianco. I was at your office with Richie when Mickey first got violated."

Laurel's eyes automatically went to the pretty young brunette accompanying Golden, a girl she assumed was his secretary. She smiled at the brunette, but received only a discomfortingly icy stare in return.

"Of course I remember you," Golden replied. "I never forget a pretty girl . . . or a happy one. And today, my dear, you are both. We just won the hearing, and Mickey will be home with you within two weeks."

Laurel jumped up and hugged Ira J. Golden around the neck. "Oh, thank you, thank you," she said. "But why two weeks?"

After a brief explanation of the red tape involved in getting someone out of jail as opposed to the few seconds it takes to lock them up, Golden hastily departed without so much as an introduction to the brunette at his side.

I'll bet he's going to bed with her, Laurel speculated to herself. *I really wouldn't blame him, with that set of boobs—God, I wish I had a pair like that.*

While Laurel was still watching the attorney and the girl hurry away, a bitter voice assaulted her from behind.

"The competition's not bad, is it?"

Laurel spun around to face a sneering Anthony Spositoro. Anger burned openly in his eyes. His blotchy red skin looked almost magenta.

"Both you girls must be happy as kids at Christmas."

"Excuse me?" Laurel responded coldly.

"You and Michael's other girlfriend, Rosalie." He pointed at Ira J. Golden and the brunette, who were already crossing the street. "Over there with his shyster lawyer. You must both be thrilled that he won his hearing, although she might be a bit happier since she's the one who actually saved him. I'm sure she feels her efforts will move her into the number-one slot."

The implication of Spositoro's statement hit Laurel like a moving train; the urge to vomit swelled inside her.

"Just what are you talking about?" she snapped, not sure whom to be angry at.

"Don't tell me you and Rosalie never met?" Spositoro asked with a smirk. "Miss Goodbody just got through confessing that she's been humping your boyfriend all over the place. Why, you two are practically sisters-in-law."

"You're crazy!" Laurel shrieked.

"Me? No, you maybe. It seems that when I followed Michael to a building by the fish market, it was her apartment he went to, and they spent the entire night doing great but dirty things to each other."

Mickey Boy had told Laurel that the incident Spositoro was using for his parole violation had taken place on the night he had stood her up for her parents' anniversary outing on Broadway.

Laurel remembered the fight, one of countless arguments over his thoughtless treatment of her, they'd had afterward. His excuse had been that he'd gotten stuck with very important people. She'd ranted that he was full of shit. He'd stuck to his guns. But the fact that that particular story had never really satisfied Laurel made her especially vulnerable to Spositoro's jibes.

Oh, no, please God, don't let it be true, Laurel prayed. *Especially not today.*

"Listen," the parole officer said, obviously reading her face. "You look like a nice girl. Do yourself a favor and find yourself a decent guy who deserves you."

Before Laurel could find the clarity of thought to answer, Anthony Spositoro turned his back and walked away.

When an excited Mickey Boy entered the small visiting room, he found Laurel already seated. One of her shapely legs crossed over the other, its foot tensely bouncing up and down; her lips pursed tightly, as if in preparation for a fight.

"Hi, babe," Mickey Boy called jovially, acting as though he hadn't noticed her foul mood. He figured his news would cheer her up, and if not, she'd eventually tell him what was on her mind, with or without his asking. When he bent to kiss her she turned her face, coldly offering him her cheek.

"Guess who's got some good news?" Mickey Boy asked, ignoring her action.

"I know all about it . . . who's Rosalie?"

"What?"

"No, not *what*—who? Actually, I shouldn't ask who, because I already know who she is; I just saw Miss Bigtits. What I want to know is what the hell has been going on between you and her? Or should I just use my imagination?"

Mickey Boy burst out laughing. Laurel's jealousy both amused and flattered him. Wrapping his arms around her, he tried to give her a proper kiss, which she resisted. Other couples turned to watch them.

"Don't think you'll get out of this by joking," Laurel warned. "There's nothing funny about your goddamned whoring around!"

Embarrassed by the attention Laurel was drawing, Mickey Boy snapped, "Stop being a jerk!" He proceeded to give her a detailed account of the hearing, including his shock at having a total stranger testify about a string of sexual encounters he'd supposedly participated in. The only part he omitted was Rosalie's scorching farewell kiss.

When Mickey Boy finished, Laurel still claimed a bit of skepticism. A little more arguing on his part and she agreed to give him the benefit of the doubt. However, even if he hadn't bedded Rosalie, she said, she was still fed up.

"Mickey, I told you before, and I'm telling you now, hopefully for the last time, I'm not cut out for this type of life. I can't take the insecurities, the competition for your time, or the subterfuges that are part of it."

"Listen, I know you're a schoolteacher. You don't have to use no twenty-five-dollar words on me," Mickey Boy said, backing away from Laurel.

Goddamn if she couldn't find a way to take the joy out of what was supposed to be a glorious moment, Mickey Boy thought. Every fucking thing had to turn into a discussion about her hating his way of life. That day, however, he absolutely refused to participate in any of her games.

"Besides," he continued. "We made a deal not to talk about this until after I get out, which won't be long at all. Now, what are you gonna do? You gonna keep your promise an' not ruin our visit, or what?" Mickey Boy leaned forward and took both Laurel's hands in his. "C'mon, babydoll, give me a break—not today."

As usual, Laurel capitulated. "Okay, you win . . . for now. But as soon as you get out of here, we have to sit down and talk. I have to tell—"

"You don't have to tell me nothing," Mickey Boy interrupted. "There's nothing you *have* to do except kiss me."

With that, Mickey Boy kissed Laurel full on the mouth, ending their conversation.

48

November 22: Bay Ridge, Brooklyn

Georgie The Hammer's black 'Vette was already parked across the street and waiting when Chrissy Augusta slipped out the door of Fontbonne Hall High School. She'd cut out on her last three classes to spend an extended day with Georgie, whom she had been having severe problems with of late.

When her boyfriend had first begun using cocaine, Chrissy had been disturbed, but had accepted it as a by-product of the enormous pressure he was under, what with being close to the Rossellini–Vallo war and constantly worrying about her father finding out about their affair. She'd overlooked it, however, only in the belief that things would improve as the mob conflict petered out and she and Georgie drew closer to announcing their planned engagement.

But over the last few months Georgie's occasional snort of coke had evolved into a more frequent and varied use of drugs, leaving him stoned more often than not. When in that condition, he was demanding and insatiable in bed, not sensitive and caring like before; sex was becoming a chore for Chrissy instead of an expression of her love.

Worse yet, out of bed Georgie was just as bad, either ignoring Chrissy when he was around his new druggie friends or berating her for her refusal to experiment with the different substances he always seemed to have in his possession.

No problem was too large for Chrissy to handle, however, as long as she believed the one necessary element in her and Georgie's relationship was still there—that he loved her. Now she wasn't sure that was the case any longer, and she'd made up her mind to find out. If Georgie would agree to try turning over a new leaf, it would prove to the seventeen-year-old how much she meant to him; if he refused, then she'd know the worst, for sure. She'd either change Georgie or leave him.

If the worst did happen, Chrissy had thought while working out her "Plan Georgie," she might accept Little Vinnie's offer of an evening out on the town. In spite of all his bad points, the don's son was crazy about her, did have a great future ahead of him, and, most important, seemed to be making a sincere effort to change some of his nastier ways. Just the way he'd treated Laurel, with the utmost respect, when he'd met her to apologize for the lingerie shop fiasco was some indication of the man he could be.

One thing was for certain: If she ever married Little Vinnie, no matter what his bad points, he would always treat her royally. The don's son would definitely follow the typical wiseguy pattern of providing a good home for his wife and kids—best furnishings, best clothes, best schools. If he would have any fault as a husband, it would never be drugs, but probably the same one her father and everyone else in that life had: keeping one or more mistresses after their married lives had become settled and routine. All the other mob wives lived with it, content in the fact that no matter where their husbands strayed, they'd always return, and often glad that constantly having to satisfy the male libido wasn't their burden to bear. And, though Chrissy was positive that she could keep a husband sexually interested more than her mother had with her father, if it went the other way, she'd live with that too.

Yes, if the afternoon didn't turn out well with Georgie, she definitely would give Little Vinnie a chance—maybe invite him to her house for Thanksgiving, which was only three days away.

Disappointment enveloped Chrissy immediately when she opened the Corvette's door and saw a strange couple squeezed into the rear seat.

Shit! she thought. If she had any hope for success with Georgie that day, it depended on them being alone, on her being able to use every tool in her possession, from sex to tears, to change him—it was his, and their, last chance.

The female stranger in Georgie's Corvette was an overly made up blonde whose purple spandex pants and low-cut white blouse did little to conceal her voluptuous figure. She sat atop a bearded youth who was stretched sideways across the narrow back section.

Georgie sat in the driver's seat with a paper cup in his hand. "Hi, babe. I want you to meet two friends of mine, Barry and Ramona," he said sweetly. Turning toward Barry and Ramona, he added, "This is Chrissy. I told you all about her."

Then, with a display of consideration Georgie hadn't shown in months, he offered Chrissy the drink he'd been holding. "Here, love, this is for you," he said. "We all had sodas while we waited, an' I made sure I saved you some."

"I'm not really thirsty," Chrissy replied, trying not to show her annoyance. To her, finding unexpected guests was also a nuisance because they'd keep her from changing to the clothes she carried in her large duffel-type schoolbag. Like most of the teens in her school, she found it embarrassing to be with people who were dressed normally while she remained in Catholic school uniform.

"Come on, babe. I can't drive with a cupful of soda in my hand," Georgie said. He smiled charmingly. "C'mon, look how I worried about you. Wanna make me feel bad?"

Georgie's changed attitude encouraged Chrissy. Thinking that her task might possibly be easier than expected, she downed the soft drink just not to spoil his mood.

"Barry an' Ramona wanna spend a little time together at the Emerald East, so I'm gonna drop them off." Georgie winked, and squeezed Chrissy's bare thigh underneath the plaid school skirt she wore. "Then you an' me could be alone."

Though Chrissy resented the intrusion upon time she'd so carefully arranged to spend with Georgie, she was somewhat placated by the thought that she'd be rid of Barry and Ramona soon enough. The adult "hot-bed" motel, which she considered sleazeball, with its porno films and vibrating beds, was no more than a half hour away.

Resigned to what appeared to be a minor inconvenience, Chrissy settled into her seat and looked out the window through most of the parkway ride, glancing back occasionally to catch glimpses of the couple in the back sucking on each other's tongues and feeling each other up.

About halfway to the Queens motel, Chrissy began to feel strange. At first she attributed the queasiness in the pit of her stomach and the little pubic vibrations she felt to a touch of horniness from watching

Barry and Ramona make out. The couple of symptoms, however, rapidly expanded to include light-headedness and warm flushes. It couldn't be her period, she reasoned, because she'd finished that only a week before.

"Georgie," Chrissy whined. "I don't feel good. I feel very funny."

The three others in the car only laughed, and assured Chrissy that she'd be just fine once they reached the motel.

But the light-headed feeling worsened, and by the time the Corvette pulled into the Emerald East's parking lot, Chrissy was well on her way to being stoned. When she finally realized that the soda Georgie had given her had been drugged, her brain was too fuzzy and her speech too slurred to mount a credible protest.

A wonderful sense of floating accompanied Chrissy through the hall and into a room of the motel. Soft greens, blues, and violets seemed to jump up and caress her. Nausea had long passed, leaving behind euphoria and heightened senses in its place. Even when Georgie sat her on the edge of the bed, it was as if he'd put her on a cloud. And when he switched on a pornographic video, she was mesmerized by the naked, writhing bodies on the screen.

Hands grabbed at Chrissy, wonderful, gentle hands caressing every part of the body. Tiny electric pulses trilled down her neck to her pelvis and into her vagina. She felt those same hands remove her shoes, and she wiggled her toes—great to be free. So nice to have someone take off that ugly blue and gray plaid school skirt, open her starched white blouse to give her air, free her tender breasts from the confinement of her bra. Every scraping of fabric against her flesh felt sensually delightful, especially the lace panties rolling down her thighs.

Feeling weirdly suspended from her body, Chrissy continued to stare at the movie until Georgie blocked her view. She tried to push him to the side, but he wouldn't move. Instead, Georgie held something to her nose and ordered her to sniff hard, which she tried to do—anything to get him away so she could watch those people fucking. One looked like Daddy. Was it Mommy or his girlfriend Rita with her mouth on his dick? She heard everyone around her laughing, and this time joined in. Everything was funny. Daddy was funny. He looked so silly with long hair and a moustache.

Chrissy felt herself being lowered onto her back. She closed her eyes to better enjoy the tingling sensation she felt every time Georgie touched her electrically charged skin. In her stupor it seemed like he was everywhere at once, kissing, nibbling, sucking, and massaging her earlobes, her neck, her belly, her thighs. Simultaneous sparks shot from both breasts, where tongues circled and flicked her swollen nipples, and from between her legs, where it felt like he was rubbing a hairy brush against her vagina while he licked it. Surrendering her inhibitions to total sensual abandonment, she lifted her legs and clamped her thighs over his head, squeezing so he'd never stop. It was sooo good, sooo good.

Despite the tremors pulsating from her crotch every time Georgie teased her clitoris with his tongue and hairy face, Chrissy still felt the weight of him sitting on her chest, crushing both breasts till they felt ready to explode. The interweaving pleasures were almost unbearable, sweeping her along toward the threshold of sexual peak. Sighs and groans filled her ears. She wiggled and squirmed, making her body available for more and more pleasure. Her mouth gaped open, and when she bent forward to fill it with Georgie's penis, she found nothing. Opening her eyes, she saw Ramona's face staring down between those beautiful big tits. Ramona moved forward to tickle her chin with hair, to wet her chin. Chrissy let her tongue taste the wetness, then probe, dreamlike, past Ramona's soft clump of hair and into her body.

Suddenly, waves of fireworks burst from the junction of Chrissy's thighs to the darkness of her brain, igniting it with flashes of light: red, yellow, green. She was floating and burning, and expanding inside her body till she felt her skin would pop. Wave after wave of rapture rushed through her, and the faster they came, the faster and deeper she moved her tongue into the damp, salty cavity before her. Delicious, Ramona.

Chrissy was still riding the crest of the flow, floating, only aware of her feelings, when the weight shifted off her chest. She felt Georgie spread her legs and fill her vagina with a sharp thrust.

"Harder. Harder," Chrissy heard herself demanding. She clawed and sucked at his flesh, then pulled at his buttocks to force him deeper into her. "Don't stop. Fuck me harder!" her voice echoed in her ears. "Love me, Georgie. Oh, please don't stop!"

Funny thing, though, when Chrissy turned her head to the side and opened her eyes, she saw Georgie there, too, humping Ramona doggie-style. How cute.

"Barry!" the faraway voice that sounded to Chrissy like her own said when she looked up at the bearded male who was pushing his dick into her so fantastically. "Barry, Barry, Barry," came out mixed with laughs and giggles. Then, when the waves began to carry her away again, she closed her eyes, locked her ankles behind his back, and screamed, "More, Georgie! Oh, God, more!"

Darkness had already fallen when Georgie dropped Barry and Ramona off at a bar in Coney Island and headed back toward his own neighborhood. Chrissy sat on the passenger side, glaring out the window while hot tears streamed down over her cheeks.

"Whatsa matter, Miss Prissy," Georgie taunted. "Didn't ya have a good time? You sure looked like a girl who was enjoyin' herself. Even the three of us together couldn't give you enough. Boy, I never seen anybody beg for more like that in my life."

Chrissy refused to answer. She hated Georgie more than she'd ever imagined herself capable of. How could he turn her into something so cheap and dirty? Chrissy had vomited on the side of the parkway when the Quaalude Georgie had mixed into the soda he'd given her had worn off and she'd realized how badly she'd been debased. If she'd had a pistol, she would have shot him dead—then put the gun to her own head.

Every part of Chrissy's private body ached. Her breasts throbbed with pain and her vagina felt like it had been peeled raw; even her rectum hurt. What was worse was that her head was still not totally clear, and the thoughts she tried desperately to sort out seemed to evade any kind of order or control. What would she do now? Who could she talk to? There was no way she could confide in her parents or schoolmates. Her poor mother would die. School would be a horror.

After deliberating over every person she knew, the thought of each one's reaction more painful than the other, Chrissy decided there was only one person she could possibly tell: Laurel. Should she go to her first? Could she stop at home and clean herself up and then go? Would her family see her degradation on her face?

Question after question swirled around in Chrissy's mind. She cried silently, still unable to believe that someone she had once loved so much had subjected her to be treated like a common whore, not only by himself, but by two total strangers.

Georgie pulled in front of a bar on Avenue X, where Chrissy knew Skinny Malone hung out.

"I'm goin' in for a minute to get a little blow," Georgie said. "If you're smart, you'll take a few sniffs an' loosen up," he added with a sneer. "Then maybe you'll stop actin' like somebody copped your fuckin' cherry."

When Georgie left the car, Chrissy broke down and cried hysterically. She pulled her hair and banged her forehead against the glass while screaming "No! No!" It couldn't have happened. Not to her. Not to Joe Augusta's daughter. "No!" she shrieked again. "No! No!"

But it did happen. The pain in Chrissy's body couldn't be lying; the stickiness of dried semen between her legs told the truth. She was a whore, a pig, a slut, a cunt—every filthy word she'd ever heard.

As her crying turned to sobs, it seemed to Chrissy that everyone on the sidewalk was staring her way—watching, knowing, intruding on her private sorrow. Spotting a lightweight blue cap that Skinny had left in the car, she placed it on her head so it slanted down over her eyes, then leaned back against the car seat to cry alone.

Chrissy's indecisiveness persisted. She wanted to leave the car before

Georgie returned, to run away, but still felt weak-kneed, and was both ashamed and afraid to face the people in the street. Could she get to Laurel before Georgie caught up with her? What if he did catch her trying to run away? Would he beat her? Kill her? What difference did it make now? Maybe he'd come out and want to fuck her again? Or make Skinny fuck her too? Which way to run?

When Chrissy moved toward the door, she felt wet stuff oozing out of her vagina and fell back against the seat, weeping even harder.

I'll see you dead yet for what you did to me, Chrissy vowed silently at Georgie The Hammer Randazzo. *I'll see you dead!*

"Simpleminded bitch," Georgie muttered to himself as he entered the dimly lit cocktail lounge. What difference did having a little fling make when half the world was out to kill you and the other half was too worried about its own ass to help save yours? Fuck Chrissy if she couldn't take a joke. Yeah, fuck her is exactly what they'd done, him, Barry, and Ramona, he thought, laughing to himself; little bitch was too spoiled anyhow.

He spotted Skinny sitting in his regular spot at the far end of the bar, as usual entertaining all those around by trading witty barbs with Margo, the bleached-blond barmaid who stood nearly six feet tall.

"Boy, would I like to get into your pants," Skinny called to Margo loud enough for every one of the dozen or so customers to hear. He downed his drink bottom-up.

"No thanks," the brassy-looking Margo shouted back, one hand on her hip, the other resting on a beer tap. "I've got one asshole in there already."

Wiping his nose with his sleeve, Georgie made his way toward the rear of the bar, where Skinny roared with laughter.

"Isn't she a scream?" Skinny asked when he spotted Georgie.

Asshole is right, Georgie thought, not answering. He grabbed Skinny by the arm and dragged him toward the men's room. "I need some blow, Skin," he said. "Just this one time an' I won't bother you for nothing for a while."

"Goddamn, Georgie, if I ever thought in a million years that you'd use this shit, I never woulda got you involved. You were only supposed to get customers. How could you—"

"Fuck the lectures! Are you gonna help me out or what?" Georgie hated to beg for anything, and would have liked to kick Skinny in the balls for making him do it. But scoring something to feel good was more important at that moment, something to take away the pressure from his fuckin' rotten life and that fuckin' rotten war he was stuck in the middle of. He could always get even with Skinny later on.

Skinny pushed back the new leather cap he'd bought for the coming winter months, stared at Georgie for a moment or two, then threw his hands up in disgust. "I don't know, man," he said. "I mean, you really need help. It's like tuberculosis: if you catch it in time, you could cure it, but—"

"Enough of the medical shit!" Georgie snarled. "If I wanted my balls broke, I coulda got it from Little Miss Prissy." He wiped his runny nose again. "Well, whattaya gonna do?"

"You know I can't refuse you nothin', pal," Skinny said, his mouth turned downward at the sides. He pulled a small packet from inside his sock and handed it to Georgie. "What does Chrissy say about you fuckin' around with this shit? She's gotta know by now."

Between snorts of cocaine, which lifted him immediately, Georgie replied, "The little stuck-up bitch is snivelin' in the car." He rubbed some coke on his gums, enjoying both the numbing sensation of the drug and seeing the shocked look on Skinny's face—Irish bastard always did have a hard-on for Chrissy. Now he'd know for sure who she belonged to, Georgie thought, and added, "Her majesty's sore 'cause I slipped her a leg-spreader an' got her into a scene with Barry an' Ramona at the Emerald East. That was her Thanksgiving present."

"No, Georgie, you didn't?!"

A gray Buick Regal carrying three young men swung onto Avenue X, then slowly drove past the bar where Georgie The Hammer and Skinny Malone were meeting.

"Boy, did we get lucky," Little Vinnie shouted from the front seat of the Buick when he spotted Georgie's black Corvette parked outside the cocktail lounge's front door. He focused on the passenger side and the figure sitting there, a familiar newsboy cap pulled down over its face.

"Look, the Irishman's sittin' in the car. That means Georgie's gotta be inside the joint." Unable to keep from smiling, Little Vinnie added, "Like Buster said, if Georgie gets in the way, clip him too—this is perfect!"

And it was perfect, the perfect opportunity to prove himself, to kill someone and make his bones—despite his father and Buster. They must've thought they were cute, the two old cocksuckers, leaving him out of this contract. But he was cuter. Once he'd found out what was going down, he'd used his position as the don's son to not only pressure the proposed hit men to let him become part of the operation, but to take charge of it as well. No one would stop him from becoming a boss—no one!

Little Vinnie looked at Mickey Boy's partner, Richie DeLuca, sitting in the Buick's backseat. Too bad he couldn't kill Richie too, Little Vinnie complained to himself. That would be a fitting message to send that

Mickey Boy bastard, almost as good as the one he'd send later, when he fucked Laurel silly.

After weeks of effort Little Vinnie had finally convinced Laurel to agree to meet him for a drink. In fact, their meeting was scheduled for later on that same evening, after he'd gotten rid of the Irishman and would need a good hot fuck to bring him down. Sure, he'd had to work like crazy to persuade Laurel, claiming that the two of them had to work out a plan for straightening out the problem between him and Mickey Boy before Mickey Boy was released from jail, but that was part of the game—her game of holding back to ease her conscience before finally letting him lead her into bed. He'd patiently played his part, and now she was taking the big step. Maybe when Mickey Boy heard that his girl had had her cunt reamed by him, Little Vinnie Calabra, the don's son thought, he'd hang-up, saving him the trouble of having to kill him when he got out. Maybe he'd be twice blessed.

Little Vinnie checked his watch. Plenty of time to hit Skinny and still get to fuck Laurel. What a night!

"Why don't we try to catch Skinny when he's alone," Richie suggested. "I mean, Georgie could walk out any minute."

"Tough shit!" Little Vinnie growled back. His words were meant as much for Richie, who he knew hated the idea of him being along, as they were for Georgie. "It'll teach him not to hang out with fuckin' potato eaters."

While inspecting the chamber of his .357 Magnum, Little Vinnie issued orders to the driver of the Buick, Butch Scicli, a fat, lackluster third cousin of Buster's.

"Drop us off three or four cars behind him, then go one block up and make a U-turn," Little Vinnie said.

As soon as the shooting started, Butch was to drive back, making sure the power door locks were open for Little Vinnie and Richie to re-enter the car, and all the windows were down in case all hell broke loose and they had to dive in to get away. Once they were back safely inside, Butch's job was to take off as quickly as possible, drop the two gunmen off close to where their own cars were parked, then dump the stolen Buick.

After Butch had repeated his instructions satisfactorily, Little Vinnie turned to Richie. "You go up on the driver's side," he ordered. "I'll come up on the Irishman's side an' do the blasting. You just make sure you don't come up past the backseat so we don't hit each other."

It gave Little Vinnie a thrill to add, "An' if Georgie comes out, make sure you get him too—unless you wanna be on his side?"

To Richie DeLuca, attempting a murder on the busy Brooklyn street was insane. Of course he was no expert, never having killed anyone before, but neither was the scumbag running the show. For his money, if he was forced to commit the act in order to secure his future as a wiseguy, he still would prefer it to be done in private. And what if an innocent bystander, by some poor stroke of luck, got hurt? Who would be the fall guy then? Certainly not the don's flesh and blood.

However, despite feeling strongly that they should wait for a more opportune time to kill Skinny Malone, Richie didn't argue. Much as he hated Little Vinnie, he realized the prick would probably be his boss one day, and could literally make him suffer to death. Besides, this was not the time for him to look bad in anyone's eyes. He was too close to being straightened out to have Little Vinnie bad-mouth him. That button was worth everything to him—not only worth killing for, but worth taking a chance on an idiotic way of doing it.

When Butch dropped them off, Richie waited for Little Vinnie to cut between cars to the sidewalk, then walked parallel to him on the gutter side as they moved briskly toward their intended victim. Richie's hand became so soaked clutching the .32 automatic in his pocket that when he drew the gun to his side he prayed it wouldn't slip away and fall to the ground.

Please God, please let everything go all right, Richie begged silently as he approached his assigned spot on the driver's side of the Corvette. He slowed by the rear fender, then stepped forward so he could see the figure in the darkened front seat: blue poorboy cap, black curly hair, bare legs jutting out from beneath a blue and gray plaid Catholic school skirt.

"No, no, don't shoot!" Richie screamed to Little Vinnie, who was already raising his gun to fire. "Vinnie, don't shoot!"

Seventeen-year-old Chrissy Augusta felt nothing after the impact of the first bullet that passed through the back of her skull, ripped out her left eye, and splattered her brains over the dashboard; two more shells tore open her head, face, and body.

Dragging Georgie by the sleeve, Skinny was near the front of the bar on his way to comfort Chrissy, when he heard three shots explode outside. Georgie pulled away from his grasp and rushed to the window ahead of him and, by the time Skinny got there to catch a glimpse of what was going on, Georgie was screaming and halfway through the door.

Two more shots instantly rang out and Georgie burst back into the tiny vestibule, hit the wall, and slid down, blood pouring from his abdomen onto the floor.

A millisecond later another bullet shattered the window above Skinny's head, shards of glass showering him as he dove for the ground.

Skinny began to crawl toward his unconscious partner to see if he had a pistol on him to fire back with, then suddenly realized what had happened to Chrissy. After glancing one last time at Georgie, who sprawled awkwardly in a crimson puddle, Skinny, lying where he was with broken glass over and about him, buried his face in his hands and cried.

When off-duty patrolman Peter Tsakalis reached the corner of Avenue X and McDonald, it sounded like he was back in Da Nang. Three shots, then two, then one. Glass shattering. Hysterical screams. All echoed in through the open window of the officer's Mercury Bobcat as he swung it onto Avenue X and sped toward the commotion.

Officer Tsakalis pulled to a screeching stop in the middle of the street near where two men were running. Gun drawn, he jumped from his car and shouted for them to halt.

Instead of stopping, however, both men darted back to the sidewalk, then split up to run in different directions, the black-haired young man taking off to Tsakalis's left, the blond man with a gun in his hand bolting to his right.

The patrolman made for the sidewalk, then turned right to chase after the blond man. He prepared to fire, but as his finger began to squeeze off a shot, a group of women exited a restaurant, blocking his view. Right shoulder lowered like in his Boys High School football days, Tsakalis banged through them, knocking one to the ground. Curses followed him as he continued his chase.

A couple of seconds later the suspected gunman cut between two parked cars and raced toward a gray Buick sedan that had stopped to pick him up. Patrolman Tsakalis made the identical move, then, once he had a clear view, crouched and fired repeatedly at the automobile door his target was about to reach.

Only Richie DeLuca's gun got through the Buick's window before three bullets smashed him against the door and knocked him off his feet. Burning pain tore through his entire body, yet he stretched to grab for the Buick's tire, getting his hand caught underneath as it squealed away toward Ocean Parkway. Defeated, he dropped his head to the pavement, listening to the thunder of feet running his way and watching his blood slowly spread outward into an ever-darkening pool till he could hear and see no more.

49

November 23: Todt Hill, Staten Island

When the doorbell rang at 7:03 A.M., Don Vincenze was already awake and expecting his visitor.

Buster's phone call at a quarter past six had been unusual due to the hour, expectedly urgent for the same reason, and routinely brief because not a minute went by that some law enforcement agency wasn't tapping in on the don's line. All Buster had said was "I'm on my way over . . . we got big problems."

Now, alone at the kitchen table, his worn maroon robe hanging loosely over rumpled blue pajamas, and his second cup of coffee in hand, Don Vincenze checked a security monitor on a wall shelf in front of him. Using a remote control device, he alternated the images transmitted by four roof-mounted cameras so that the screen displayed the entire front area of his home, from driveway to driveway and from the sidewalk to the bare building line. The first thing the don had done upon acquiring the spacious Cape Cod, even before moving in, was to have the front denuded of the hedges and trees behind which would-be assassins could hide.

Once satisfied it was indeed Buster at the door, Don Vincenze pressed a button on the wall to let him in.

Buster rushed through the living room, carelessly tossing his topcoat over the back of an armchair, as he'd done thousands of times when Anna Calabra had been around to hang it away, and entered the kitchen.

"You won't believe what troubles we got," Buster complained while pouring himself a cup of the hot brew. "August's oldest daughter got whacked out by mistake last night."

It took a while until the meaning of Buster's words sunk into Don Vincenze's head. He'd heard them, but no, maybe he hadn't. The look on Buster's face, however, finally hit home, and Don Vincenze felt as though his insides had collapsed. He slumped back in his seat, his hand knocking over the coffee cup as he moved.

"Oh, no, not Christina," Don Vincenze moaned. "Not that poor, sweet little girl." Neither he nor Buster bothered to stem the brown pool of coffee spreading across the table.

In an instant Don Vincenze's sadness turned to rage. Slamming a fist on the table's edge, he shouted, "Who did it?! I'll kill the bastard with my own hands!" When he received no answer, he demanded, "Well, who did it? I wanna know!"

Buster's eyes remained downcast, staring into his cup. "We did," he said. "Your son Vinnie pulled the trigger."

"Vinnie?! What the hell are you talking about?!" the don screamed. "Are you nuts?!"

"I did just what August told me to do. I gave out the sneak hit on the Irishman that had the beef with your kid to a couple of our proposed guys: Mickey Boy's partner, Richie DeLuca, an' my cousin's nephew, Butch—boy, do I wish Mickey Boy was outta jail. I know he wouldn't've fucked up like this."

"Forget about who would've or could've, just tell me what the hell happened," Don Vincenze snapped.

Buster splashed his coffee into the sink, then nervously poured a fresh steaming cup and, as if he meant to punish his tongue for the words it was forced to convey, took a large gulp, his face immediately turning a bright red.

After sucking in cool air, Buster said, "It seems that Vinnie heard our conversation when we met with August down the basement here a few months ago. . . ."

That news stunned the don even more than hearing of his godchild's violent death. "The whole conversation?" he asked.

"I don't know if he heard everything," Buster said with a shrug, his face sagging in a frown. "But he heard exactly what he wasn't supposed to hear."

Don Vincenze squeezed his eyes shut. He could have kicked himself for being so careless. *Now what do I do?* he wondered. *Who is there to help me but me? Where do I go from here?*

According to Buster, Little Vinnie had somehow found out about the contract on Skinny Malone and, prompted by what he'd overheard at the basement meeting, had put it into his head that he wanted to do it, that it was the perfect opportunity to prove himself. Going behind Buster's back, he'd forced the two assigned hit men to let him go along and take charge.

"When they got there, though, something went wrong," Buster said. "They found the Irishman . . . or who they thought was the Irishman, sittin' in the other kid, Georgie's, car. They saw the hat that the Irishman wears an' all. There was no way they coulda knew it was August's kid wearing the hat. No way!"

"What the hell was she doing in that bum's car in the first place?! Didn't my *goombah* bring her up better than that?"

"Who knows?" Buster replied. "You know how these fuckin' kids are today. Who knows what they got in their heads? I'm sure if she was seein' this asshole, August didn't know nothin' about it. You know how he was with that kid . . . she was his eyes . . . he lived for her."

"Poor Joseph. How my heart breaks for him."

"An' you have no idea how sick Vinnie is," Buster added. "He probably never told you, but everybody else knows that he was crazy for Christina. All she woulda hadda do was say the word an' he woulda jumped through a hoop of fire. He—"

"Don't tell me nothing about that goddamned idiot!" the don yelled. "I shoulda flushed the load that made him down the goddamned toilet!"

Buster remained silent until the don calmed himself, then continued. "That asshole Georgie came out of the bar while Vinnie was blowin' Christina away—who he thought was the Irishman—an' caught a couple of bullets himself; he's in critical. The cocksucker shoulda died instead of her."

Despite a deep, painful sorrow for the teenager whom he'd baptized, then loved like a daughter as she'd grown from infancy, Don Vincenze's first obligation was to his Family, and concern about repercussions from Little Vinnie's error rushed to the forefront of his mind.

"Does anybody know we're involved?"

A sigh escaped from Buster's lips. "Does anybody not know we're involved? That's the question," he said. "Some off-duty cop was drivin' by at the time an' wound up shootin' Richie. He's also in critical condition, and under heavy police guard; it's all over the radio an' probably TV too. They say the doctors don't know if he'll pull through, but if he does, the D.A.'s gonna charge him with Murder One."

"Mother of God, what the hell did we do to deserve this?" Don Vincenze wailed. It seemed to him that every time Buster opened his mouth, their problem worsened, the possibilities of disastrous consequences becoming endless.

When his left eye began to twitch, the don thought, *I'm getting too old for this bullshit*, then asked, "What about Butch an' that idiot son of mine?"

"They got away. I sent the two of them to my uncle's farm in the Catskills. When I left to come here, they left for upstate." Buster checked his watch. "They should be there by ten. I'll call just to make sure they got there okay."

"I wish you woulda let me know right away. Maybe I coulda did something."

"What could anybody do once it happened? Besides, those jerkoffs didn't come tell me what happened till five o'clock in the morning. They drove around all night, scared to death 'cause they fucked up."

"Bastiano, Bastiano, were we idiots like this when we were young?"

"Vincenze, you know we were never young," Buster replied. "We grew up like old men. But at least we were men. Except for one or two we got, like Mickey Boy, they're all assholes today. Sometimes I

270

think we'd be better off if we closed the books for good an' let La Cosa Nostra die. At least it would be an honorable death."

The weight of his sixty-seven years bore down heavily on Don Vincenze's shoulders. It was as if each of the five decades he'd devoted to their cause had drained double that in his and his subculture's lifeblood, leaving nothing for him now but two tired shells. Every day he could sense the end approaching, a final rest coming for him. But the subculture that his bloodline had been a part of for generations? Never. In spite of the realization that its days were numbered, that the resource pool was rapidly drying up—no more Italian prizefighters— Don Vincenze could no more helplessly witness the end of La Cosa Nostra than allow himself to expire without a fight. And he told Buster so.

Though both Don Vincenze and his way of life were near the point of no return—his, he was sure, no more than a few short years away— for his way of life there was still a glimmer of hope, an artificial heart that might postpone its demise. And only he had the foresight and expertise to get the operation done.

So far, he'd nurtured his survival plan for La Cosa Nostra along perfectly, keeping a glove on, as the Sicilian proverb went, in order not to expose his hand. But to continue doing that, he had to overcome the horrible incident of the previous night without allowing it to peel the glove away prematurely.

When the time was right, he explained to Buster, it wouldn't matter what was revealed of his intentions, for it would be too late for anyone to forestall the operation's success. Only three to four more months, that was all that was needed. Three to four months at most.

"What we have to do is think this thing out," Don Vincenze said, "and fix it just enough to give us that time."

Buster seemed to notice the spilled coffee for the first time. He lumbered to the sink and began rinsing a sponge while asking Don Vincenze, "Where do you wanna start?"

Like an athlete who gets a second wind, Don Vincenze shed the aches and weariness of old age and instantly became the general under siege. He shoved sympathy and self-pity from his consciousness and began tackling his Family's problems in the order of their importance.

"First, what about Joseph?" he asked.

Sopping up the coffee on the table, Buster shrugged. "I don't know," he said. "I just found out a couple of hours ago myself, an' figured the worst thing for me to do was go near him right now, bein' as I sent the kids to make the hit."

Don Vincenze's mind flashed back to when he'd ordered the Irish kid disposed of, remembering Joe's reluctance to see the order carried through. If the underboss/funeral director would blame anyone, it would be him, Don Vincenze, as boss. But Joe was a good soldier, and would carry on—he hoped.

"He can't blame you," Don Vincenze told Buster. "He's just gotta understand."

"Who could explain how a guy thinks when something like this happens?" Buster said. "Imagine how the poor bastard's gonna feel when he realizes he was the one who gave me the word, that he ordered his own kid whacked."

"Well, make sure you get reports of everything he says or does. Keep somebody close to him all the time. I think Joseph will be all right, but who knows? God forbid, he could turn out to be another Sally Burns," Don Vincenze reminded Buster.

Of course, Joe Augusta was nothing like the Little Italy mobster who'd sworn revenge over the casket of his murdered son, a son who'd used the protection of his mafioso father to step on a few too many toes. But who could say what a father's grief could do to him? Sally Burns had died for his vocalization of his grief; it would be a shame if the same fate had to befall Joe.

"No problem," Buster answered the don's order to have Joe Augusta's every move monitored and reported to him. "We'll have guys around him all through the wake."

"Good. I was almost ready to put you in your rightful place as my underboss anyway, as soon as you completed that task of ours. What I'll do now is make you acting underboss right away—that will let you do what you gotta do—an' make Joseph my *consigliere*. That is, if he holds together."

Don Vincenze's next priority was Petey Ross. The young mob boss would be furious when he found out that proposed members of the Calabra Family had tried to "cop a sneak" on one of his guys. Of course, Don Vincenze would swear he knew nothing about it, and, of course, Petey would know better. But could he prove it? No. Not for the time being anyway. Richie DeLuca was being held incommunicado by the police, and the other two imbeciles were tucked away in the mountains. No one could make a liar out of him without access to Richie, Butch, or Little Vinnie. Thank God for little favors.

"We just gotta insist that we don't know who else besides Richie is involved, or why," Don Vincenze said. "If Petey should find out that the other two ain't around, we could always say we're looking for Butch too, to find out what's going on."

"What about Vinnie?"

"Petey'll never press the issue with my son." Don Vincenze smashed his fist on the table. "Oh, how I hate to call that goddamn fool my son!"

The don pushed himself out of his seat and paced the kitchen. Worse to worst, he told Buster, if they were really pressed against the wall they'd have to sacrifice Richie and Butch—and, if need be, an innocent third party.

"Sorry about Butch," Don Vincenze said.

Buster shrugged. "Those things happen," he said. "Besides, who the fuck ever seen him unless he wanted something? I didn't even know he was alive till he got pinched for the first time an' my cousin called me for help."

"Much as I'd like to kill him myself," Don Vincenze continued, "my son Vinnie will live."

There was no way Petey Ross would challenge that decision, even if he were strong enough. Saving face would definitely be more on his mind than exacting revenge for two broken-down dope pushers who happened to fall under his protection by way of Crazy Angelo. Numbers would satisfy everyone—three shooters; three bodies. Richie DeLuca and Butch Scicli deserved to die anyway for screwing up. As for the third sacrifice, there were certainly enough young imbeciles around who, under the circumstances, were worth more dead than alive.

"A few bodies might satisfy Joseph too," the don said. Then, finding a morbid touch of humor in his predicament, joked, "We'll kill two— or three—birds with one stone."

"What about Little Vinnie?" Buster asked. "You wanna talk to him? Tell him what to do?"

"Talk to him? Only if I could choke him over the phone," the don replied. "No. Keep that poor excuse for a son away from me." After a pause, he added, "Just tell him to thank God every night that I don't want to disrespect the memory of his poor mother. Otherwise, I'd peel the skin off his moron body myself."

The issue of Little Vinnie closed, Don Vincenze turned once again to Family matters. Until they could determine if they would have any problems with Petey Ross or Joe Augusta, he ordered Buster to have his men keep extremely low profiles. They were to stay out of sight, but be available to Buster at all times. That also went for Mickey Boy, who would be released from jail shortly. Buster was to send him a message while he was still in MCC.

Now that his major problems were thought out and put into some kind of working plan, Don Vincenze's mind wandered to his late god-child, Christina. His heart hurt and his eyes welled with tears. It was with a cracking voice that he asked about funeral arrangements for her.

"I don't know if they'll lay her out today or tomorrow, because of the autopsy," Buster said. "An' with Thanksgiving this week . . ." He shook his head from side to side, and moaned, "Oh, shit, what a mess."

"Anything I forgot, before I go up an' change?" Don Vincenze asked, weariness making him feel older than the ancient Don Peppino.

"Not that I could think of."

"Good. We gotta get over to Peppino an' fill him in now, in case Petey Ross goes crying to him today. Can't leave him in the dark, not knowing what to say."

Don Vincenze started up the stairs, still thinking about the cross he had to bear. Halfway up, he turned and called, "Oh, an' Bastiano, don't forget to send flowers for Christina—send a lot; make a good show."

50

November 23: Flatbush, Brooklyn

Like a drunk who finds her way home by instinct, Laurel staggered into the duplex apartment she'd shared with her parents until moving in with Mickey Boy some four months before, and, ignoring the otherworldly ringing of the phone, made her way up the stairs to her old bedroom.

She paused for a moment by her vanity mirror, staring blankly at the clownish image that stared back—streaks of mascara running over her cheeks; swollen, smudge-encircled eyes; smeared copper lipstick—then threw herself onto the spread; Squirrel Nutkin fell to the rug.

Laurel grabbed the lavender bunny that had been her favorite since childhood and, clutching it to her breast, began to bawl hysterically. Each time her crying reduced itself to spasmodic sobs, images of Chrissy would invade her thoughts and she'd break down again.

The phone continued to ring.

Laurel's day had taken off on a sour note from the moment she'd opened her eyes and seen that she'd overslept by nearly half an hour. Washing up, slapping on some makeup, and getting dressed had been frenzied acts that had left her with a pulsating headache, a yearning for caffeine, and missing the early morning news program she usually watched. Had she risen on time, she would have caught Deborah Norville's story accompanied by Chrissy's face on the screen, and would never have set foot out of the apartment.

As it turned out, it wasn't until she stopped at the candy store near her school for a container of coffee that she learned of the previous evening's tragedy. Stacked high in front of the counter were Four-Star Final editions of the *Daily News*, their headline:

TEEN GIRL KILLED IN MOB HIT!

Directly below the bold-typed announcement was a large snapshot of the grisly scene of the crime plus two inset photos: a Catholic school picture of Chrissy and one of a blood-covered Richie DeLuca on a stretcher.

At first Laurel had blinked her eyes twice, in the belief that they were playing a nasty trick on her. When her mind finally accepted the fact that the photo was really Chrissy's, she let out a piercing "Noooo" that stopped all other sound and movement in the store.

For the second time that morning she'd felt her insides rising up into her throat, and ran from the store just in time to vomit all over the sidewalk. Passersby eyed her strangely and altered their paths to avoid her.

Distraught and weakened, Laurel had managed to drive away from the area, stopping twice more to puke out the door. She had needed to lie down, but couldn't bring herself to go back to the apartment she shared with Mickey Boy. The only place for her was home—her home, the home that had seen her through mumps, Alley, and high school.

The phone continued to ring intermittently throughout the morning, its noise the background music in someone else's dream.

Lying there, eyes open, in a trancelike state, Laurel's mind viewed a kaleidoscope of surrealistic human images. First Chrissy: chasing a Frisbee in Central Park—modeling a flesh-colored string bikini—dropping ice cream on herself and laughing. Always laughing.

Then came Richie, beginning as a black dot in a corner of her mental screen, then gradually becoming larger until he loomed grotesquely over the entire background, a pistol dripping blood from its barrel stuck out of his fist.

"No, no!" Laurel protested when Richie's features were replaced by those of Mickey Boy, who now hovered over a gore-splattered Chrissy.

More tears. Worse visions. More tears again.

It was early afternoon when an emotionally and physically drained Laurel was finally abandoned by haunting images and attacked by reality. Conversations with Chrissy rolled over in her head, conversations in which the perky teenager had spoken of mobsters as if they were deities—the only ones to marry. No one else for her, she'd gushed.

What do you think of your wonderful gangsters now? Laurel's mind questioned Chrissy, and a tear rolled down her face. *Real exciting guys, huh?*

Thoughts of Mickey Boy were next to descend upon Laurel. Only the negatives seemed important to her now. Had there been any good times? She couldn't remember. But the fear was there. And the anxieties. And the anger over being treated like a second-class citizen compared to his Mafia friends. Scars were left from every one of those feelings as reminders.

Laurel thought of how much she'd given because she'd loved Mickey Boy; how in spite of the abuse she'd suffered at Little Vinnie's hands she'd put herself in the middle of his and Mickey Boy's conflict, even having agreed to meet Little Vinnie the night before just to act as peacemaker. Was she out of her mind? Did it matter anymore which of them was wrong or right? Was one any worse than the other? Thank God Little Vinnie hadn't shown up, she thought, saved her from yet another mistake.

Forcing herself up from the bed, Laurel weakly managed to strip naked and start for the shower. She stopped at the bathroom door's full-length mirror and stared at her own nude form, envisioning bloody bullet holes across her breasts, stomach, and lower belly—especially her belly.

No . . . oh, no. I must do something, she thought. *I must . . . for both of us*.

Suddenly she screamed, "I must, goddammit! I must!"

Disregarding the shower, Laurel ran to her closet, yanked out two pieces of matched burgundy luggage, and frantically began to stuff them with clothing; whatever was at Mickey Boy's apartment could stay where it was. Fuck everything!

Through a heavy stream of tears Laurel repeated, "I must . . . I must . . . I must," while she packed.

When done, and still crying, she grabbed a black dress that had remained on a hanger and tugged it over her bare flesh. Black shoes, no stockings. Dark sunglasses. Ready to go.

Downstairs in the kitchen, Laurel wrote a note for her parents— Mom, Dad, all's fine; had to get away for a while; blah, blah, blah— then reached for the phone to reserve a seat on the next available flight to Florida.

As Laurel was about to lift the receiver, it began to ring again. She hesitated for a moment, then picked it up, but remained silent through two or three hellos.

"My God, Laurel, where the fuck've you been?" Mickey Boy shouted through the jail's pay phone.

Even though Laurel hadn't answered, Mickey Boy continued to rant. "I've been worried sick. I called the school, and they said you never came in. I called our apartment . . ."

For a while there was silence, then Mickey Boy asked, "You know about Chrissy?"

Tears ran down Laurel's cheeks onto her neck.

"Laurel? Honey, are you okay?"

"Mickey," Laurel managed between sobs. "I'm leaving."

"Leaving what? Where? What the hell are you talking about?" Mickey Boy yelled, his voice filled with alarm. "Laurel?"

Laurel took a deep breath, trying hard to pull herself together. As soon as she felt calm enough to answer, she said, "Mickey, I've had enough. I'm leaving for my aunt's home in Florida."

"Florida? No, Laurel, just wait till—"

"If you want to come and make a life with me there when you get out of jail, fine," she continued on her own track. "You can get the address from my mother. If not, then good-bye."

"Laurel!"

"You can either drop off my things here, or throw them out; I don't care."

Speaking over Mickey Boy's objections, Laurel added, "And, Mickey, I mean it; don't come to see me unless you've made your mind up to stay. Please. Otherwise you'll be wasting your time . . . and mine. Please, don't do that to either one of us."

"Laurel honey, I know you're upset, but—"

"Upset?!" she screamed. "Upset?!" Laurel began to cry again. "Your fucking gangster friends murdered that poor, sweet innocent child in cold blood. Mickey, she didn't even begin to live and they killed her," she wailed. "Your partner did it—your goddamned, fucking partner!"

After pausing for control, Laurel added, "And if you weren't in jail, it might have been you who shot her."

When Mickey Boy tried to defend himself, Laurel cut him off, shrieking, "I hate your life; I hate your friends; I even hate your goddamn Sinatra! I can't handle it anymore. Make your choice, Mickey: them or me."

"Lau—"

Laurel slammed the receiver back in its cradle. *The hell with a reservation*, she thought, and left for Kennedy Airport.

51

November 26: Bensonhurst, Brooklyn

The air pervading the crowd of mourners in front of the Shore Haven Funeral Home was exceptionally somber, in direct proportion to the tragic circumstances that had brought its members there. The fact that it was the morning after Thanksgiving made their mood even more glum.

Despite that same morning being cold, dreary, and cloud-blanketed, most of those gathered wore dark glasses; too many eyes inflamed from three days of constant weeping. Behind the tinted lenses, each participant found him or herself alone with private, bittersweet memories of Christina Marie Augusta. Valiums and Libriums were passed around as if they were breath mints.

Equally morose journalists mingled with the outer perimeter of grievers, forming a border between them and the clusters of law-enforcement personnel that had been monitoring the appearances of reputed mafiosi throughout the wake. News photographers and TV cameramen stationed themselves on nearby rooftops, car tops, and in one case a treetop, in an attempt to record the finale to a murder that had outraged the general public, spurring new calls by politicians for greater pressure on the mob and a reinstatement of the death penalty.

Inside the funeral parlor, the closest friends and relatives of the deceased teenager's family were crammed into a chapel overflowing with lavish floral arrangements. Sobbing and moaning, they listened while a priest intoned a final prayer before moving the closed coffin to St. Bernadette's Church for a Requiem Mass.

Slumped in the front row of seated mourners, a haggard Theresa Augusta, her once-ebony chignon now streaked with gray, cried steadily. On Mrs. Augusta's left sat her eight-year-old daughter, Elizabeth. The only remaining child of Theresa and Joe Augusta, Elizabeth clung to the black crepe of her mother's dress, afraid to relinquish her grip on that small bit of security.

Joe Augusta sat erect and rigid, as he had for the past three days and nights, hidden from the world behind a pair of extremely dark sunglasses.

After having identified the body of his murdered daughter, the grief-stricken mafioso, who had been a link in the chain of command that had ordered the hit, had locked himself in the basement of his home and had cried until his body was drained of tears. Through those hours of convulsive sobbing, he'd intermittently vented his anger by way of tantrums that left the room totally destroyed.

Awakening in the rubbled basement the next morning, Joe had ordered his brother-in-law, Nunzio, to handle all the arrangements for the coming days, donned his black glasses, and cloaked himself in monastic silence. The only time he'd spoken since then was when he'd been alone at home with his wife and daughter. Even Nunzio hadn't heard Joe Augusta's voice since he'd been given instructions on the morning after the murder.

To the visitors that had filed past the white pearlized casket and paid their respects to the dead girl's family, Joe Augusta was handling the shock of the appalling tragedy by lapsing into a walking coma. Don

Vincenze's soldiers who had been assigned to keep a close watch on their underboss reported that it was impossible to determine how far off the deep end Joe had gone, if at all, since he remained absolutely motionless and acknowledged no one. He just sat.

Joe Augusta, however, a man weaned and nurtured in Brooklyn's toughest ghetto streets, was aware of everything. To him, his catatonic pose was a protective measure for the offense he would eventually mount. He'd learned enough from his lifetime of underworld experience to know that if he gave any indication of his intent, he wouldn't live long enough to see his yet undetermined retribution through. He, too, remembered Sally Burns being murdered for his vow of vengeance.

Another thing Joe recognized was that once he opened his mouth to speak, especially to anyone even remotely connected with his daughter's death, he wouldn't be able to control the venom in his heart from spewing forth; he didn't know what he would have done to Don Vincenze if he had shown up.

Yes, total silence was the only strategy Joe could think of to keep everyone at bay until he could fulfill his pledge to Chrissy and destroy everyone involved in her death—including himself. No excuses, no mercy for a man who'd helped kill his own child, the light of his life.

Eight pallbearers, all Augusta relatives, carried the coffin down to a virginal white hearse parked at the head of seventeen black vehicles, including five overstuffed flower cars. There was one official auto for every year Chrissy had spent on earth and one for her eternal life in heaven.

Behind the retinue of funeral cars, forty-six privately owned automobiles fell into a line that snaked around the corner and crossed onto two more blocks. Once the procession had actually begun to move, press and police vehicles added to its morbid spectacle as it crept along 13th Avenue toward St. Bernadette's Church, where Chrissy had attended elementary school, and where her funeral services would be held.

The church was SRO by the time a priest stepped to the pulpit to eulogize and pray for the lifeless body of Chrissy Augusta. The white casket, a gilt-framed photograph of the deceased teenager atop it, lay in back of the priest.

Behind the immediate family sat the entire senior class of Fontbonne Hall High School, a picture of virtuous youth in their blue and gray parochial school uniforms. Their reddened eyes and tear-streaked faces were a chilling reminder of the heinousness of the crime.

"Who can comprehend the will of Our Lord Jesus Christ in calling Christina Marie Augusta to His side so soon?" the priest began. The mention of the dead girl's name brought a fresh wave of wails and moans from the misery-filled audience.

Joe Augusta's body didn't budge an iota, but his brain was bursting with movement. Though his eyes remained riveted to the pearly white box and the picture above it, what he saw were visions of himself and his beloved little girl when she was eight years old—rocking her in his arms, kissing her bare feet, wiping away her tears. To her crushed father, Chrissy would always be eight.

Joe smiled inside as his mind spoke to Chrissy. *Don't worry, baby, you're going to be fine. You wait with the angels until Daddy makes everybody pay for hurting you.*

"We are upset that this pure and innocent child won't be able to enjoy the world that God gave us," the priest incanted. "But we can take comfort in the fact that He will care for her now."

God?! You stay the hell away from us! Stay away from me and my baby! Joe screamed silently. His exterior remained passive. *Where the hell were You when we needed You? Huh? Now You're too damn late. I'll take care of my baby now. Leave us the hell alone!*

". . . Till the day that we join our Child of Light, Christina Marie Augusta, in God's Kingdom. Amen."

A solitary tear broke through and ran down Joe Augusta's face as the service ended.

Don't cry, baby. Daddy will come to you before you know it. Then we'll stay together for ever and ever. No one will ever be able to separate us again. Just give Daddy some time to teach the bad men that they can't hurt his baby and get away with it, and then I'll come to you. I promise, Chrissy . . . I swear it!

Joe Augusta clenched his hands so tightly that his knuckles turned white. To help restrain the other tears threatening to escape, he shifted his thoughts to his own post-funeral arrangements—and his mind smiled.

A steady drizzle added to the eeriness of the blocks-long funeral procession that crawled, headlamps on, through each of the Brooklyn streets that had been meaningful to a once-vital Chrissy Augusta, toward the cemetery where her now-lifeless body would be forever interred. Those who had loved Chrissy were reminded of various experiences they'd shared with her as they followed her coffin past her home, past Fontbonne Hall High School, past Dyker Beach Park, where she'd played as a child, and past the Pizza Plate, which was the center of her teenage social activities—and in front of which she'd first met Georgie The Hammer Randazzo. Each location seen brought renewed bursts of tears from members of the caravan.

Joe Augusta's brother-in-law, Nunzio, snatched the cigarette he had placed in Joe's hand when he noticed it burning down near the bereaved father's fingers.

While Nunzio tried to comfort his sister, Theresa Augusta, with religious clichés about her daughter's future glory in heaven, Joe was transported back in time to happier days. Images of Peter Rabbit, Winnie-the-Pooh, and Paddington Bear entertained him—and his little girl, whom he pictured on his lap. Joe's lips moved faintly while his brain sang to Chrissy lyrics that over the years had bound their hearts as surely as their shared blood: *You're the end of the rainbow, my pot o' gold. You're Daddy's Little Girl to have and hold . . .*

Don Vincenze's image appeared, to spoil Joe's vision. *Get away, Vince, you old bastard, I'll see you later! A precious gem is what you are. You're mommy's bright and shining star.*

The drizzle had become a light but steady rain by the time the hearse reached St. Charles Cemetery. Joe's wife and daughter hanging on either side of him forced his shoes deep into the soft, muddy earth, soaking his feet as well as the rain did his head as they walked toward the newly dug grave.

Nunzio tried to help support Theresa Augusta from her other side, while unsuccessfully wielding an umbrella over her and Joe.

When everyone finally stood graveside, Theresa's wails of anguish pierced the hum of those who stood sobbing their last good-byes to Chrissy in the rain.

You're the spirit of Christmas, my star on the tree . . . You're the Easter Bunny to mommy and me.

The cries that accompanied the mourners as they each sloshed by the open pit to toss a flower onto the coffin caused even the normally stolid cemetery workers to weep.

You're sugar, you're spice . . . Good-bye, Vince. Good-bye, Buster. Ha-Ha! Hello, my baby Chrissy . . . You're ev'rything nice . . . Good-bye, Richie . . . And you're Daddy's Little Girl.

The last one to pull out of the burial grounds, with the father, mother, and sister of the dead girl, was a limousine driver who had worked for the Shore Haven Funeral Home for years. He made his way to Woodhaven Boulevard, then turned right toward the Belt Parkway that would take them to Gargiulo's Restaurant in Coney Island, where close to two hundred people would be attending the traditional post-funeral luncheon.

Gargiulo's had been Chrissy's favorite.

"Scotty, do me a favor," Joe Augusta suddenly asked a couple of blocks before reaching the highway. "Stop by that newsstand and get me a pack of Benson and Hedges."

The chauffeur, looking happily surprised to hear his boss speak again, pulled over and left the car to purchase the cigarettes.

A few seconds later Joe Augusta shifted the hearse into gear and drove away—minus his chauffeur, who was left standing under the newsstand's awning.

When Lizzie questioned her father about leaving the chauffeur behind—Theresa was too out of it to notice or care—Joe replied, "Shhh. Everything's gonna be okay, baby. Just lay back and try to sleep."

Driving the same route the chauffeur would have taken, Joe Augusta continued past the scheduled Coney Island exit, on to the Verrazano Bridge, through Staten Island, and over the Goethals Bridge into New Jersey. He stopped on Bayway Avenue in Elizabeth, where he opened the garage door of a green frame house.

Five minutes after that, Joe Augusta, his wife, and their eight-year-old daughter, Lizzie, sat in the front seat of another hearse, headed south on the New Jersey Turnpike to a property he owned outside of Washington, D.C. In the back of the vehicle was a casket exactly like the one in the ground at St. Charles Cemetery, except that this one had the actual physical remains of Christina Marie Augusta.

You're sugar, you're spice, you're ev'rything nice . . . And you're Daddy's Little Girl!

52

December 10: East Side, Manhattan

Though weatherman Storm Field had called for a low of thirty-five degrees, it felt much colder to Mickey Boy, standing alongside his mother, Connie, while she admired the Christmas display in Saks's front window—certainly too chilly to have spent the entire afternoon strolling along Fifth Avenue. If not for a desire to please his mother, he'd have been long gone, long before the stops at Gucci, Godiva, and F.A.O. Schwarz, long before a visit to St. Patrick's Cathedral, where he'd bought his mother a hand-carved statue of St. Jude.

Mickey Boy stared at Saks's window, seeing nothing of the moving dolls and colorful background scenes, then glanced at his watch through a puff of his own breath. When he looked up at the window again, it was without having registered the time. Instead, his mind was haunted by the sounds of Frank Sinatra's voice, singing . . . *Oh, how the ghost of you clings. These foolish things remind me of you.*

"Sorry if I'm boring you," Connie said, linking her arm in his. "Let's just see the tree, then we'll go." She'd insisted they bypass Rockefeller Center all day, saving it until they could see its seventy-five-foot tree sparkle like motionless fireworks against evening's black sky.

"Take your time," Mickey Boy said. "Christmas only comes once a year."

At Rockefeller Center they chose to remain at street level rather than venture down to the ice. Connie, red-cheeked and exuberant, leaned over the rail to watch the skaters below, then craned her neck to gaze at the top of the glittery tree.

Mickey Boy just stood.

"Smile a little," Connie teased. "Halloween's for scaring people, not Christmas."

But smiling wasn't on that year's agenda for Mickey Boy. The holiday spirit of others, rather than being contagious as it had for him in the past, seemed only to accent the negative thoughts that filled his head.

The loss of Laurel was at the forefront of things troubling Mickey Boy. She'd opened up a wound when she left that still felt fresh; he missed her terribly. And though he argued to himself that their relationship, having lasted less than a year, had been too short to hurt so much, he still felt as though a part of his body were gone. How long that feeling would last was something he didn't want to consider.

Much as he tried not to, Mickey Boy also thought often about the recent death of Chrissy Augusta, and was deeply saddened by it. How could something so horrible happen in their supposedly organized world? He found the specter of chaos on so large a scale disorienting— and frightening. How could Laurel even think that he might have been involved?

Richie DeLuca was another major concern of Mickey Boy's. Through brief, whispered half-sentences, he'd heard that his partner hadn't fired even one shot when Chrissy was killed. But that was all he'd been able to gather. The subject of Chrissy's murder was strictly taboo among Calabra Family members and associates—orders from the top. According to the newspapers, however, which were Mickey Boy's only source of information about his partner, Richie's internal injuries hadn't yet been determined, though he remained in serious condition in Bellevue's prison hospital. If he recovered, the papers said, he would be transferred to the Brooklyn House of Detention, where he'd be held on first-degree murder charges for his involvement in Christina Augusta's death. What a future ahead of the poor bastard.

Thank God the one worry that wasn't immediate anymore was Little Vinnie, Mickey Boy thought repeatedly. Rumor had it that the don's son was basking in the sun of northern Sicily while visiting relatives. Fuck him. Maybe a volcano would open up over the prick and end problems for a lot of people.

Now, standing like a wooden Indian in New York's most enchanting Christmas location, Mickey Boy made a supreme effort to mask his poor mood so not to spoil his mother's happy one. He answered her barbed comment about his gloomy appearance, saying, "Sorry, I just got lost in my own thoughts," then took her gloved hand in his. "Come on," he offered, "let's get some hot chestnuts before we go up to Freddie's. Christmas ain't Christmas without 'em."

After nibbling on the chestnuts, which Mickey Boy found disgustingly dry and tasting like burnt cardboard, he suggested they take a hansom cab to Numero Uno. "Unless you're too cold?" he said.

"Are you kidding?" Connie replied. "Thanks to you, I'll be as warm as toast." She turned around in an exaggerated model's swirl to show off the full-length sheared beaver Christmas gift Mickey Boy had given her the day before. Even though he hated giving gifts ahead of time, he'd said, her enjoying it when he squired her around Manhattan would be worth losing the surprise for.

"But what about you?" Connie asked. She lifted the coat's hood over her tightly knotted hair. "Won't it be cold for you, especially your head?"

"Nah, I'm fine. Besides, you know I got nothing in there to protect anyway."

They walked the ten blocks to the Plaza Hotel, where they found a well-kept horse and carriage by the fountain in front. The driver's black cape and top hat were perfectly matched to the evening's elegant air, Connie said.

To Mickey Boy, the man looked like Dracula.

"Ooh, I'm so tired," Connie groaned, settling into the tufted red-leather upholstery. "My poor feet are killing me. I haven't walked this much since we went to the feast in September. That's what happens when you get old."

"You're not getting old!" Mickey Boy hastily objected. To him the words *old age* meant to die, and to die meant for her to leave him. Even though fifty-two certainly wasn't an age that fell into the old category by any standards, his mother's self-deprecating teasing frightened him.

"Your problem is that you stay up there in Boston with all those snobs who are dead from the neck up . . . including Alley," Mickey Boy said. "Why don't you move back to Brooklyn? I know you really ain't happy up there."

Connie laughed. She looped her arm through Mickey Boy's and snuggled close, the beaver, thankfully, warming him up a bit.

"What is happy?" Connie asked. "I'm happy when I can take care of Alley and Ellen and Kimberly, and happy when I'm here with you. My happiness is where my children are. Unfortunately, they live in two distant places."

After kissing her son on the cheek, Connie continued. "Mickey, you and I understand each other enough for me to explain to you how I really feel. In fact, in many ways you're closer to me than any person on earth. We've been through a lot together, we two."

Connie kissed him again, and smiled in a way that warmed him more than her fur had. She went on to claim that she'd love to be back in New York, especially to spend more time with him. But she had her reasons for remaining with his brother. Primarily, even though Alley had a wife, Connie believed he needed her more than Mickey Boy did.

"You've always been so manly and self-reliant," she said. "I'd only be a bother to you."

"Never! Are you kidding?!"

Manly? Self-reliant? Mickey Boy certainly hoped so. He was proud of the strong man he'd become, a man forged that way by a lifetime of hurts both big and small, by the lack of a father to run home to and look to for support. Yes, he was manly and self-reliant, and made sure everyone around him knew it. But she was his mother, he was still her boy, and she was supposed to be aware of the vulnerable side he hid from others; he was all alone—no Kimberly, no Ellen, no Laurel—and needed someone too. As a mother, she should have sensed that need even if it didn't show. And her not wanting to bother him was just a bullshit excuse not to hurt his feelings; she knew better, she had to. What did he have to do to get some maternal attention, be like his spoiled, lard-assed brother who'd even call someone from another room to switch TV channels for him?

However, more important to Mickey Boy than his own needs at that moment was his belief that it was in his mother's best interest to move back to Brooklyn. At least there she would find comfort in the familiarity of places she'd known from childhood, have distant cousins to visit from time to time, and be able to look up long-lost friends—and, of course, she'd have him, her oldest son, to look after her every desire. It was about time, he felt, that his mother was catered to instead of doing the catering.

But none of Mickey Boy's arguments budged Connie; not even his offer to pay her rent—or mortgage, if a house was what she wanted—or open a small boutique where she could outfit others in the simple yet elegant style she'd developed during her days at Bergdorf's.

"Mickey darling, I thank you for your generous offer," Connie replied. "But, thankfully, money is not one of my concerns." What was, however, was him, she claimed. With a pained expression Mickey Boy's mother told him that she was incapable of providing the support system he believed he required. What he needed was a wife—someone who could give him comfort and solace when things got tough—and children to build a loving home for. Laurel was that girl, she said; she was sure of it. Whatever his differences with Laurel were, there had to be a middle ground to solve them on. Why was he holding back when he should be chasing her to Florida? Because of his underworld ties? Were they worth losing her for?

285

"I don't want to nag, believe me, but the people you're involved with are as despicable as their way of life," Connie said. "You're still young enough to make a new, better life for yourself . . . and without giving up someone you claim you love so much." She clutched his sleeve, and, tugging it to emphasize each phrase, implored him, "Go to her, now, before it's too late. Stay in Florida with Laurel."

"Mom, don't you think I wish I could," Mickey Boy answered, throwing his head back to look at the sky. A lump in his throat seemed to tug at muscles and nerves under his ears and behind his eyes. His face throbbed in time with the clip-clopping of the white horse up front. "You an' her just don't understand what it means to me to give up something that I paid my dues on since I was a kid. All I ever wanted to be, except for when I went through that stupid lawyer stage, was a man of respect, if you know what I mean. Now I'm almost there."

"Now you're almost nowhere," Connie replied. "I think, somehow, the word *stupid* has lost its direction in your mind. It certainly doesn't belong before *lawyer*."

"Yes, it does!" Mickey Boy snapped back, then stopped himself from going on. He turned toward his mother, and added, "But that doesn't matter anymore. It's way too late to even talk about it."

"But it's not too late for you, for a good future."

"I have a future," he said with the single-mindedness that made him Mickey Boy.

Connie just shook her head.

"What could I do now, at this stage of the game, pack it in to clean pools or maybe drive a cab in Miami?"

"Your dad drove a cab and was quite a man," Connie snapped. "In many ways, much more of a man than your so-called friends."

"But living like a cabbie just ain't me. Different blood, I guess."

Sensing immediately what was behind the stricken look that overcame his mother, Mickey Boy followed with, "Is that it? Do I look like him?"

"Excuse me?" Connie said, seeming to grope for those few words. Eyes wide, she stared beyond him, and beyond the view of gracious town houses the open carriage provided.

Mickey Boy wished he could see the images he knew had replaced reality for his mother, wished he could see his father's face just once.

For most of his life Mickey Boy had found the father image he sought among mobsters, a replacement for that mysterious man he'd never known—the man his mother refused to discuss. (Was he that terrible? A drunk? A spy?)

All Connie had told Mickey Boy was that she'd had a brief marriage to someone who'd deserted her and who had later been killed in a plane crash. (Air force pilot, Mommy? No, she'd said with a laugh, a soldier.)

Mickey Boy had never quite believed that story, and as a youth had scoured their home, sneaking around to gather bits and pieces—a gift card from flowers buried in her lingerie drawer and signed M (Michael Sr.? Manny? Moe?); a diamond cross wrapped in tissue and pinned inside a dress she never wore (Was he a priest?); two ticket stubs to *My Fair Lady* in the zipper compartment of her handbag (an actor, maybe?)—as he searched for clues to his own identity by way of a stranger's.

As a youth, Mickey Boy had never mentioned his discoveries, only slightly afraid of revealing he'd been snooping but terrified that he wouldn't find anything more—maybe a photograph—that everything else would be destroyed or better hidden by his mother. What he had done was try to question her beyond the parameters she'd set, but those early, childishly direct attempts drew only chilly silence from Connie.

Later, when Mickey Boy was old enough to be certain there were too many loose ends to her version of his conception, he chose to be more considerate of her feelings than he believed she was of his, and not agitate her.

But that didn't mean surrender. Without relatives to question—he knew he had a few second and third cousins on his mother's side, but had never even met them—Mickey Boy had turned to his first mob mentor, Sam LaMonica, for help.

After first trying to discourage him, Sam had finally helped. The now-deceased mobster had even hired a private detective—who Mickey Boy had had to pay for, of course—who, for all his expensive efforts, came up with zilch. Nothing but dead ends. Even hospital records showed only a blank space after the word *father*.

For all Mickey Boy's consideration of his mother's feelings, however, the issue of who his father was had always gnawed at him, enough to make him realize that he and she would ultimately have to settle it at some future date. And that December evening, with Mickey Boy cold and alert in an open hansom cab, was it.

"Tell me, am I a lot like my father?"

"Mickey, I'd rather not—"

"Mom, for Christ's sake!" Mickey Boy bellowed. "First you tell me what a man I am, then you wanna treat me like a goddamned kid!" He looked to see if the driver had turned to watch them, which, discretion being a cornerstone of the trade, he hadn't, then, noticing that they were only a block from Numero Uno, ordered the man to tour the area before dropping them off.

Turning back to his mother, Mickey Boy said, "I never really bothered you too much about him 'cause I knew you didn't like to talk about it. I figure the bastard hurt you a—"

"Don't you dare call your father any names!" Connie shouted, her vehemence startling Mickey Boy. "He was a fine man . . . and I loved him very much."

"Then tell me about him. I deserve to know who gave me this goddamn miserable life!"

"Mickey . . ."

"Please."

"I don't think—"

"Don't think, just talk," Mickey Boy said, then, in a soft, almost pleading voice, added, "Mom, please, I need to know."

Though his mother still hesitated, reluctant to talk, Mickey Boy knew she would. Some magic threshold had been crossed that had softened her resolve. What it was, he had no idea. All he did know was that he was too thrilled to question it, too afraid to break her spell to speak.

A wistful shine filled Connie's eyes, and, with a defeated yet relieved smile, she began, saying, "I might be old now, but I was once young. I was young, and impulsive, and in love . . . and I became pregnant without being married. You, my dear lovely boy, are the result of that love affair."

How to control the slightest expression of his shock? How to hear that his proper, sainted mother was fucking around before she was married? Legs spread wide in the backseat of some jalopy or on a beach or in a cheap motel's bed. Naked. Some faceless guy sticking it to her. My God!

Mickey Boy fought to keep his eyebrows from rising or his mouth from dropping open. Only his hand, squeezing the edge of the leather seat, would have given any hint to dispute his outward calm. Couldn't stop her; she had to go on.

"Unfortunately, he was . . . married, that is," Connie said. "It was one of those arranged, loveless marriages that were common centuries before, but he still insisted he couldn't get out of it."

"But if he loved you . . . I don't understand?"

Connie laughed. Sharp. Bitter? Eyebrows raised challengingly, she said, "You should . . . more than anyone. Your father was what you would call a man of respect, and claimed that his obligation to his code was bigger than both of us. He let those contemptible men you idolize so much keep us apart. Now you know why I hate them so. And to make matters worse, I see the same thing happening with you. Aren't you doing the same thing to Laurel?"

Mickey Boy hadn't heard a syllable past the word *respect*. In his wildest dreams, he would never have seen his father as a mafioso.

288

With his mother? Envisioning her with such a man was like seeing Mike Tyson fucking Princess Di—no way!

"Where is he now?" Mickey Boy asked, struggling not to appear as anxious as he felt.

"I asked you a question first, about you and Laurel. Didn't you push her on the side for your street life?" Connie asked angrily.

Why did women always have to mix apples and oranges? Mickey Boy wondered. In the case at hand, he concluded, he'd probably just pressed her too much and she was backing up. Consideration to hell, he had to have an answer, had to know where his father was. Just that one vital answer and he'd leave her alone. Just that one—for now.

"Laurel's and your situation brings all the years of pain I felt back to haunt me," Connie continued. "That's why, in spite of your suffering—and believe me, my heart breaks for you—I have to admire Laurel for being strong and sticking to her guns. Maybe one of you stupid, egotistical males can be bent straight by a woman's love."

Like a determined halfback, Mickey Boy looked for daylight to rush his own ball through, and, finding none, pulled away to look for another opportunity. He remained silent.

"You didn't answer me," his mother said. "Aren't you doing the same thing with Laurel as your father did with me?"

Too many things were swirling in Mickey Boy's mind to try to find differences or similarities between his and his father's situations. Who cared? What was important was for him to be vague enough to avoid admitting that he and his father were wrong, yet still satisfy his mother so she'd drop the subject of Laurel and give him the answer he'd waited a lifetime for.

"In a way, I guess you are right," Mickey Boy said. "But there's still a lot I gotta think out, especially about Laurel," he said. "I need time." *Show's over.* "Now it's your turn . . . where is he?"

Connie looked Mickey Boy directly in the eye, and, with a certainty that made his heart sink, said, "He's dead . . . he died many many years ago."

When Mickey Boy and Connie entered Numero Uno one hour beyond their reservation time, Freddie Falcone had already surrendered their table to another couple. Promising it would be only a few minutes till another table was prepared, Freddie led them to the bar for a drink. Red garlands and twinkling white lights were tastefully strung about the area, making it even more cozy than usual. Live poinsettias dotted the room.

While Connie went to the ladies' room to freshen up, Mickey Boy and Freddie discussed the turmoil that filled their world. The continuing

Rossellini–Vallo war had taken second place to the mystery surrounding Joe Augusta's disappearance. Various rumors had it that the Calabra Family underboss had gone to pieces, was in a hospital, was dead. All hush-hush, although neither Mickey Boy nor Freddie could figure out why.

What Petey Ross's response would be to Chrissy Augusta being murdered during an attempt on one of his men's lives ran a dull third. Petey would holler and rant, but in the end, they knew, would do nothing—nobody fucked with Don Vincenze.

Though he participated in the gossip, in truth, none of it interested Mickey Boy a bit. He was too lost in his own problems to give a damn who did what.

As soon as Connie returned, the headwaiter signaled that a table was ready, and led them to their seats.

During the meal, neither Mickey Boy nor his mother discussed any of the things that troubled them. Instead, they limited their conversation to mundane chitchat: what Connie should wear when they attended *The Nutcracker* at Lincoln Center the following night; which Hollywood star was reported to be the latest AIDS victim; do lobster tails really come from lobsters, or are they crayfish?

By the time they were ready for dessert, the dinner rush had passed and Freddie was able to take a break. He carried to their table a small silver tray with fresh raspberries and zabaglione, two hot lemon soufflés, and two cheesecake tarts.

"Get fat," Freddie said, pulling up a chair. "On the house."

Mickey Boy immediately dug into the soufflé—nerves always made him crave sweets. As he took the first mouthful, he felt doubly relieved to have a third party sit down, especially the ebullient restaurateur, who could always be counted on to lift the spirits.

"Everything was sinfully good," Connie said.

"Aw, shucks, ma'am," Freddie said while tilting his head to the side and batting his eyelashes at her. "You must tell that to all the top restaurant owners in New York who happen to have the finest Piedmontese chefs working for them." He turned to Mickey Boy. "I got a great story I gotta tell you about a couple of crooks we both know. That is, if your mom don't mind?"

Connie smiled. "Mr. Falcone, I am well over twenty-one and can decide for myself what I will or will not hear; I don't need my son to approve. Usually, as long as it's not an X-rated story, I'd say go ahead . . . but to be honest with you, tonight I'm not particularly interested in hearing about the type of person I understand your story is about."

Freddie looked puzzlingly at Mickey Boy, who just shrugged. What could he say? Women were women.

Thankfully, nothing could put a damper on Freddie. To accommodate Connie, he told a couple of humorous stories, which didn't involve knock-around guys and which also, Mickey Boy felt, fell far short of his usual mark of excellence.

Though constantly interrupted by his staff about restaurant business, Freddie managed to sit with his two guests throughout their dessert. He winked at Mickey Boy—who had devoured all the desserts on the tray—to show him he understood there was a problem, and continued in his efforts to make them smile.

When there was nothing else to eat, joke about, or discuss without treading on exposed nerves, Mickey Boy signaled for the check, then paid, leaving a fifty-dollar tip. Freddie accompanied him and Connie to the front door.

As it had throughout dinner, the evening's earlier conversation about his inception churned through Mickey Boy's mind while he and his mother, backs to the door, said their farewells. There was so much more to ask, he was thinking when the door opened behind them and a male voice called, "There's a table for me, or I need a reservation?"

"Don Vincenze, of course," Freddie gushed, hurrying around Mickey Boy. "You know for you there's always a table, even if I gotta throw somebody out."

If there was ever a wrong time for his boss to show up, Mickey Boy thought, that was it. And to call him don like Freddie had, while Connie was on an antigangster kick. Shit!

Mickey Boy himself greeted Don Vincenze with reserve, trying to downplay his importance, then said, "This is my mother, Connie. Mom, Mr. Vincent and er, uh . . . ?"

"Pauline," Don Vincenze replied, referring to the fortyish redhead who stood at his side, no differently than if he'd been asked the color of the car he'd driven up in.

"Mickey Boy never told me he had such a pretty mother," the don said.

"Thank you," Connie answered politely but with a distinct coolness. "You made an excellent choice . . . the food here is delicious."

"That's why I come here . . . I always go for the best." Don Vincenze kissed Mickey Boy good-bye and extended a hand to Connie.

"Nice to meet you both," Connie said as she and Mickey Boy moved to leave.

Don Vincenze stepped back to hold the door open. He patted Mickey Boy on the cheek with his free hand, then turned to Connie and said, "Believe me, the pleasure's all mine."

53

1979: Brooklyn

It was the day after *The Deer Hunter* had won the Academy Award for best motion picture that Connie Messina had the most distasteful, yet necessary, appointment of her life. From where she sat, in the front window of Fourth Avenue's Fisherman's Corner Restaurant, she could see anyone who approached. As she waited, sipping occasionally on a Campari and soda, she reflected on how her life had gone in a complete circle. . . .

When Connie Partinico married Albert Messina, she was determined to be a good wife and to forever banish the ghost of the lost love that haunted her. Though she felt no grand passion with her new husband, she was confident that in time, through mutual respect and shared experiences, a deeper, more substantial love would evolve. Besides, Mickey Boy needed a father, and Albert was perfect in that department.

At first the new couple lived in Connie's old apartment in the Zafferamos' house. Albert drove a day-shift taxi for a fleet located a short way from their home; he was at the table for dinner by five P.M. each day.

In order to supplement Albert's less than spectacular income as a cabbie, Connie continued in her position as buyer-salesgirl at the fashionable boutique she'd been working in. While he'd protested against the idea of his wife being employed, Albert eventually accepted the fact that the few hours she devoted to the store nearly doubled their gross income, and that they could never hope to better themselves without it.

Albert's big break came quickly and unexpectedly, in the form of an owner-driver he hardly knew offering to turn over his taxi medallion for a minimal down payment and the balance to be paid over five years. The seller explained that he was embarking on a new career, wanted to give another driver an opportunity to be his own boss, and had chosen Albert because of his reputation as a dependable, honest, hard worker.

But Albert was skeptical, afraid there was a gimmick, some hidden trick that would make him a loser. There was no free lunch in America, he said. Why would a virtual stranger pick him to bestow such good fortune on? With only a limited number of medallions issued by the city, they were in great demand and steadily increasing in value. If there wasn't a catch, the owner would never be offering it for sale at such incredible terms. Besides, at Bob-Net he could make a living with no risk.

Connie would hear none of that. If she'd learned any positive lesson from the flamboyant Mudslinger, it was "nothing ventured, nothing gained." She'd seen her small inheritance dwindle over the last few years, and was willing to back up their opportunity with whatever was left.

After ten days of frustrating debates—Connie was almost ready to drive the cab herself—she won her point. Con-Al Operating Company was formed and the Messinas were in business.

Once the threshold of ownership was crossed, Albert's entrepreneurial spirit and determination to provide a decent life for his family took over. He worked their new cab over seventy hours a week. The money was good, enabling them to live comfortably and still add sizable chunks to the balance Connie still had in the bank.

It was time for them to have their own child, Connie felt, and if that were to happen, they'd need more room for the baby to grow in. Again, Albert was afraid. Wait a year or two, save more cash before she'd have to quit her job. Security, security, security.

The only point Albert won, to Connie's delight, was that before they had any child together, he would formally adopt Mickey Boy, who they'd decided to tell that his natural father had died while he, Mickey Boy, was still in the womb. Hiring a lawyer to arrange for the child to carry the Messina name was the fastest move Albert had made since having asked Connie for their first date. His sensitivity to how her son might feel after the new baby was born earned him a special place in her heart.

Three months into her pregnancy, Connie pushed her husband to reach for another slice of the American Dream: a house of their own.

Once again "Call me Louis" appeared out of nowhere to provide a tremendous deal. This time it was a one-family brownstone on Carroll Street that Louis claimed he had scooped up at a price so far below the market that it was near impossible to say no.

Both she and Albert were exhilarated by how lucky they were as a pair, though the South Brooklyn neighborhood was not exactly where Connie wanted to move. To her, the overwhelmingly working-class Italian population would not give Mickey Boy the kind of example and support to go on to college. With its closely surrounding areas of blacks and Hispanics, it represented little more than a ghetto to her. Also, too many memories of Mudslinger there.

Connie argued against buying the house, wanting, instead, to search for one in a higher-income, more ethnically mixed location, but lost. It was the one time Albert was adamant. If their children were college material, he said, they would seek their own level and wind up there; young people from much worse neighborhoods had attained greatness. Also, he insisted, in a complete turnaround from his earlier positions, the price was just too good to pass by.

Right after the Fourth of July, with Connie's belly at a sizable swell, she, Albert, and Mickey Boy moved into their new home on Carroll Street near Third Avenue.

On August 20, 1963, near the end of Nat King Cole's "Lazy, Hazy, Crazy Days of Summer," a seven-pound ten-ounce Albert Messina, Jr., was delivered to Connie at Lutheran Hospital. The infant went home five days later to meet his big brother, Mickey Boy, and take up residence in a nursery already stocked by Albert, Sr., with blocks and books.

Despite Connie's misgivings about their new neighborhood, life was fine for the Messina family. Albert provided well enough for his wife and children, all of whom he adored. What little time he had to spend with them was spent well, too—reading the kids stories, Saturday night movies with Connie, trips to the Prospect Park Zoo.

Connie, who had quit her job during her sixth month of pregnancy, with a surprise going-away gift of two thousand dollars, spent most of her time at home, cooking and cleaning for her husband and children— and daydreaming.

Mickey Boy loved little Alley and was a perfect angel at home, but was already in the process of providing his teachers at school with ulcers. In a district filled with troublemakers, he was being called a monster.

Alley played with his blocks and laughed a lot.

But Connie's comfortable if lackluster existence was shattered one July morning in 1969. Half done mopping the kitchen floor, she had stopped to watch TV coverage of Neil Armstrong's first step onto the surface of the moon, when the doorbell rang. Annoyed at the interruption, Connie swung the door open to face a policeman—big, Irish face as long as a stepladder.

Sorry, the officer announced, but her husband was dead; looked like a heart attack behind the wheel of his cab.

Connie collapsed.

Unable to accept the fact that once again death had shaken her world, she sat in a zombielike trance in Chapel A of the Shore Haven Funeral Home, where her former landlady, Lena Zafferamo, had made the arrangements.

Throughout the three days and nights of the wake for Albert Messina, faceless mourners stopped at the first row of seats to offer Connie their condolences. From there, most went to see Lena's nephew, Sal, who stood by the door collecting donations to help the young widow pay for the funeral.

After all expenses had been taken care of, Connie was left with an incredible ten thousand dollars.

She'd had no idea Albert was so popular.

Now, after ten long years of raising her son alone, of fending for herself, Connie Messina sat and waited for a rendezvous with Mud-slinger. She needed him to help save her son.

Connie recognized him when he was only halfway out the rear door of a white Lincoln Town Car. The intervening twenty-three years had thinned his hair and padded his middle, but, to her, his face looked exactly the same; a bit older, but unmistakable.

Two rugged-looking young men escorted him into the restaurant, then waited by the bar while he slowly limped to where Connie was seated.

"Hello, Connie."

"Hello, Vince."

"It's been a long time," Vincenze Calabra said sadly. He sat down across from her. "How've you been?"

Words welled up in Connie, years of bitter sentences that had tucked themselves away in every cell of her body, but she held them back, saying only, "As well as can be expected under the circumstances."

Thank God her speech was coherent, she thought. Dry as her mouth was, she'd been doubtful, had pictured herself mumbling like a fool. The bastard hadn't even kissed her on the cheek.

A waitress approached with another Campari and soda for Connie— she'd much rather have had the Harvey's on the rocks he'd introduced her to, back when, but wouldn't give him that satisfaction—and a small bottle of white wine for him.

Connie looked over toward the bar at the goons, who obviously took care of everything for Vincenze, from ordering drinks to things she didn't even want to imagine.

"I see I don't have to ask you the same question," she said, unable to keep the acidity from her tone. "It seems you got what you always wanted above all else: to be king."

"Don't get smart with me," the aging mafioso snapped. "You know very well what I wanted. One thing out of my whole goddamn life woulda made me happy. One thing!" He banged the table with his fist, then pointed at Connie. "To have you an' my son."

Still glaring, Vincenze took a swallow of wine. He looked toward the bar, where his two men, the bartender, and the waitress all made a point of turning their heads to face the opposite direction; the few customers eating at that off hour looked down at their plates or across at their companions.

After what seemed to Connie like an interminable and tension-filled pause, Vincenze continued. "What I got on the outside was my destiny . . . and my burden," he said, his voice even once again. "You could never understand the obligation of leadership. Sure, I got power, but it's a double-edged sword. I also got responsibility for people whose lives depend on the justice an' guidance I give them. I ain't king yet, but I will be soon. An' when I am, it'll only be until the time a capable prince comes along to give me a rest."

The accumulated misery of years Connie'd spent alone all focused on the person sitting across from her. She wanted to strike out at her ex-lover, to hurt him in any way possible.

"You mean your bastard prince, don't you?" she asked, spitting the words at him as if they were poisoned darts.

Vincenze turned frighteningly red. He jabbed a finger at Connie's face. "Don't you ever call him that! Not ever again! My son's got as good blood as anybody, an' don't you forget it!"

"All of a sudden he's your son?" Connie lashed out, her fury too strong to be intimidated. "Where were you when he had his runny noses or measles or nightmares? Why weren't you with your precious son then?"

When he began to speak, Connie raised a palm toward him and added, "No, don't tell me, I know already . . . you had your obligations."

"Connie, how the hell could you say that? You walked out on me, remember? You told me to stay away." Continuing, Vincenze said, "If I didn't love an' respect you so much, I woulda made sure I was there all those times. An' if you wanna know the truth, there wouldn't've been a goddamn thing you could've done about it!"

If only he'd have been that forceful, that determined, in her and their child's behalf, Connie thought. *Damned idiot!* she cursed inwardly, then wondered, *Or liar?*

Vincenze's tone changed to one of sadness and regret. "Connie, Connie . . . if you only knew what you did to me, how it killed me to stay away."

When the nearly sixty-year-old father of Connie's son looked at her, his eyes full of the same sadness, the same anguish she remembered from their last time together, it pained her more than she thought possible, more than she cared to admit. Had he really been tormented all these years? Really lived as wretched a life as she? No, she argued to herself. It didn't matter. Even if he wasn't lying, everything was his doing, and she hoped he'd suffered.

"Anybody could do what's easy for them," Vincenze went on. "A true man is the one who hates what he has to do but does it anyway."

Connie studied the melting ice in her glass. Anything not to be taken in by that sad-sack look on Vincenze's face while he reminisced.

"For years I had to watch everything you an' my son did from far away," he said. "I was tempted to come to you so many times, but I knew how strong you felt about marriage, an' I wanted to give you every chance to get it . . . because I truly did love you. I'm only sorry that it took you so long to get what you wanted, an' then you hadda lose it almost before it started. Believe me, my heart broke for you when your husband died."

Startled, Connie looked up. She stared incredulously into Vincenze Calabra's eyes. "You knew everything?" she asked.

Vincenze smiled and patted her hand across the table. "More than you could imagine," he replied softly.

Events that Connie had previously dismissed as good fortune, from the unusually profitable sales and purchases of her houses, to her high-paying job in the clothing store, to Albert's surprisingly advantageous cab deal, suddenly made sense. Mudslinger had never left her. He'd always been there, hovering invisibly over her and her son, Mickey Boy, protecting and manipulating them.

The impact of Vincenze's revelation left Connie confused, unsure whether she was offended or flattered by his lengthy interference in her existence. How far had he gone? What was he actually responsible for? How could she possibly uncover twenty-three years of her life bit by bit to see where he had touched it?

"Did you arrange my marriage too?" she asked, while thinking, *He couldn't have . . . Oh, Lord, not that!*

"How could you ask me such a thing?" Vincenze replied in a teasing way. "You know you were, an' still are, as a matter of fact, an attractive an' wonderful woman. Any guy would be nuts not to want you. After all, look how I fell for you."

Answer my goddamn question! Connie thought, afraid to press the issue in words, afraid of what she might hear. She braced herself as Vincenze's lighthearted expression passed, a glint of sadness showing in his eyes.

"You know, I even kept that ugly maroon bathrobe you gave me for my birthday," he said. "I still wear it."

Connie stared at him for a minute or two. Vincent Calabra confounded her as much that day as he had twenty-three years earlier. She felt as though her heart were being sucked into a whirlpool. If she didn't fight him, she'd drown for sure.

"If you care for me and our son, as you claim, and you knew everything that was going on, how could you have let him ruin his life? Why didn't you try to stop him? How did you twist him so he could inherit your throne one day? Look what you've done."

"I never interfered with how the boy was raised," Vincenze retorted. "That was a responsibility that sat with you alone; you refused to share it."

Over the years he'd respected her wishes and had never contacted Mickey Boy, Vincenze claimed. And there was nothing he'd ever done to encourage the boy to follow in his footsteps. How, he asked, if he'd observed his son only from afar, could he have been expected to discourage his entry into a mob life-style? What would she have expected him to do? Send somebody to beat him up? What?

"Whether you like it or not, our son will seek his own destiny, just like I did. He's got the blood of our fathers, an' there's nothing that you or me . . . or anybody else in this world could do about it."

What had she expected? Connie wondered. But she already knew. She'd wanted him there, with her and their son, no matter what the price; she'd wanted him to be as tough as he'd be with his brother mafiosi, to come chasing and force her back, to remove the burden of decision from her shoulders.

But what she had wanted wasn't important. What did matter was what he had wanted. That's what had counted. And now, regardless of what Vincenze Calabra claimed, as far as she was concerned, he'd shown how he felt: He just hadn't loved her enough.

"An' as for me wanting him to inherit some kind of throne I'm supposed to have," Vincenze continued, "don't accuse me if you don't know what you're talking about. First of all, men in our life earn their positions . . . we don't hand them down like old silverware." He looked straight at Connie, his eyes pained but unyielding, and added, "An' secondly, if I had that kind of ego, I got another son to do it with."

"But I thought . . . ?"

"A couple of years after you left . . . it just happened," Vincenze said, quickly dismissing it with a wave of his hand. "But, Connie, we're here to help our son now. Unfortunately, he got himself in a terrible spot, where they wanna give him fifty, sixty years in jail, an' they don't wanna know nothing. If it was the state, we could make a deal where he'd be out before he had a chance to take his shoes off, but the feds are tough."

"You know all about that too, I see."

Vincenze smiled. "I told you before, I know everything." He reached over and took her hand firmly in his. "I realize how hard it must've been for you to come to me after all these years, but you did it for our son. It makes me positive that I was always right about you. You're a good woman, Connie . . . but very, very stubborn."

For the moment, Vincenze Calabra ceased to be the enemy of twenty-three years. To Connie, it was as if they had traveled back to when he'd been her Mudslinger—warm, caring, able to reach inside her at will.

"You're pretty stubborn yourself, Vince," Connie said. "But please, let's talk about Mickey Boy. What can you do for him?"

Still gripping her hand, Vincenze answered, "Connie, I gotta be honest with you . . . I don't know. I went to the best lawyers around. Jimmy LaRossa an' Henry Rothblatt both told me there's not much they could do. Roy Cohn says he tried, but can't even make a deal for cash. The prosecutors are looking for a minimum of fifty years . . . you know, they're trying to make a reputation for themselves an' don't care who they destroy getting it."

Connie's spirits drooped. Vincenze had been her only hope to save Mickey Boy from spending most of his adult years in prison, and once again he was letting her down when it counted.

When he saw her expression, Vincenze squeezed her hand. "Don't give up just yet," he said. "I still got one more shot to help him. We can't hope for him to walk away one hundred percent clean, but I might be able to swing a smaller sentence. I ain't sure I could do it, but I promise you I'll try my damnedest."

"No guarantees?"

"No guarantees. What I will promise you, though, is that I'll make the lawyers stall it in the courts for a couple of years. He'll have eighteen months to two years to play an' I'll have plenty of time to try an' make my deal. If it works, he'll do a few years an' come home. He's young an' strong, God bless him, an' could handle it."

Any straw at that point was enough for Connie to cling to. She felt tired and scared and would pray that this man, who had handed her the most bitter disappointment of her life, would now come through for Mickey Boy.

With a strained chuckle Connie said, "I don't know, Vince. I don't know if I can handle it."

"You do pretty good at handling hard knocks," Vincenze said. "Let's just hope I could pull it off. Other than that, there's not too much we could discuss about Mickey Boy for now. How about you, Connie? How're you doing personally?"

"How can I be, Vince? I'm a lonely forty-four-year-old widow—" Connie stopped in mid-sentence, angry with herself for revealing too much, for letting him see past the wall. In as neutral a tone as she could manage, she corrected herself, saying, "I'm a widow, with a son going to jail, for God only knows how long. Not an enviable position to be in. But I'm lucky in that I—"

"Did you love him?" Vincenze interrupted.

"Who?"

299

"Messina."

Vincenze's question caught Connie off guard; it stunned her. Heat rushed through her skin and her pulse quickened. The only protest she could think of was to pull her hand away from his, which she immediately did.

"He . . . Albert . . . was a good man," Connie said. "Kind, considerate, and—"

"But did you love him?"

Connie averted her eyes from Vincenze's glare. Focusing on the restaurant's flatware, she answered, "Of course . . . yes, I loved him." That sonofabitch across the table knew her too goddamn well, much too goddamn well.

"What about you?" she retorted as snappily as possible. "How's your wife . . . and the kids?"

Acting as though he hadn't noted the spiteful tone of her voice, Vincenze answered seriously, "My wife's getting old, like me, and she's pretty sick. My two daughters gave me lovely grandchildren." Then, after a pause, he added, "I also got my son, Vinnie."

Either he was the best actor in the world, Connie thought, or he was the loneliest man she'd ever seen.

"Do you also wanna know if I have girlfriends?" he suddenly snapped. "Yes! For years! But I never forgot you, goddammit! Oh, Connie, Connie," Vincenze said, shaking his head. "What happened to us? We coulda been so good together."

Pull yourself together, Connie told herself, then responded sharply, "You let your mob get in the way."

As much as she knew Vincenze to be intolerant of any type of disrespect from others, to her chagrin he continued to ignore her baiting.

"Connie, we still got some good years left, you an' me," he said. "Why don't we put the past where it belongs . . . in the past. Have dinner with me one night." He reached for her hand again. "C'mon."

For an instant Connie let him hold her, torn between the pleasure of his touch and the agony of his memory, then began to cry.

"Please, Vince," she sobbed while standing up. "It's too late for us . . . much too late. Just help my son . . . our son. That's all I ask."

Almost in one motion Connie bent, kissed Vincenze Calabra on the cheek, and ran, weeping, from the restaurant.

Part
IV

54

December 24: Midwood, Brooklyn

Lightly falling snow turned the amber, pink, and white glows radiating from yet-to-be-closed stores into dots and splashes, adding a fairy-tale aura to that Christmas Eve. But not for Mickey Boy. Marching briskly along Kings Highway, his coat collar up and his shoulders hunched, he watched like a voyeur the apple-cheeked smiles passersby exchanged.

"Some fuckin' Christmas," he grumbled more than once as others' cheerful spirits only sank him deeper into melancholia.

When Mickey Boy stepped into a card store crowded with last-minute shoppers, the blond cashier greeted him with a broad smile and a "Merry Christmas."

"Yeah, same to you," he muttered inaudibly, moving away from her and into a narrow aisle. He squeezed through other customers' bulky outerwear and the garments' damp, musty smells to a rack marked GENERAL XMAS.

The second card Mickey Boy plucked suited his purpose, and he began to fight his way back through the crush, pausing only once, briefly, at the section labeled SWEETHEART XMAS.

He frowned, and moved on.

Once inside his automobile, Mickey Boy turned the heater on full blast, sealed the red envelope on the card he'd just bought, and pulled out of the parking spot onto a snow-bumpy road. He drove as he had for weeks, in abject silence. Not even Sinatra was permitted to invade his morose solitude—the singer's torch songs too painful to hear, the uplifting ones too infuriating.

He rode through Brooklyn's heavily decorated streets, under ropes of twinkling garland and between store windows alive with Santas and elves, feeling like a visitor to a foreign land. The only difference was that instead of the physical surroundings being strange, Mickey Boy's alienation was internal. Like the cheerier Sinatra songs, nothing about the holiday had anything to do with him.

As he crossed McDonald Avenue into Bensonhurst, Mickey Boy took stock of the seven months he'd been home from jail: he was well on his way to being made—that was a plus; his relationship with his brother, Alley, was still cold, but civilized; and he'd loved and lost Laurel.

Laurel—always fuckin' Laurel! Almost as often as he prayed for her return, he cursed the day he'd met her, hating himself for what he considered his one weakness—caring for her.

"Stubborn bitch!" he yelled; this was the Christmas they should have been married.

When he reached the block he was looking for, Mickey Boy slowed down, checking house addresses, which he was able to see only when the necklaces of Christmas lights around their windows and doorways flashed on.

The house that went with the address on a slip of paper he held was an all-brick one-family; Season's Greetings on the window, welcome wreath on the door.

Mickey Boy pulled into the open space by a fire hydrant directly in front of the house. He snatched a cylindrical package wrapped in poinsettia-print paper from the backseat, made sure he had the card he'd just purchased, and, leaving his car running, went up the five steps to the front door and rang the bell.

Real fir smell rushed to Mickey Boy's nostrils as soon as the door swung open. Between him and the large living room scattered with holiday celebrants, a seven-foot tree, and an operating electric train set stood a red-haired woman: plain, but attractive, around forty, pleasant smile.

"Hello," the woman said. "Can I help you?"

Mickey Boy stood there for a moment, looking over the woman's shoulder into the room, watching people enjoy. But not for him. Not this year. Maybe never.

He was tempted to turn and go away.

"Can I help you?" the woman repeated.

"Oh, yeah, yes, uh, excuse me, but does Phil Ragusa live here?"

"Yes."

Holding out the red envelope and Christmas-wrapped package, Mickey Boy said, "I got something to deliver to him."

"All right. Come in."

"Sorry"—pointing—"but I'm by the hydrant. Could he come out for a minute?"

"I'll get him," the woman said, smiling, then closed the door.

Looking down at the icy steps, Mickey Boy pictured himself falling. He could see himself spread-eagle in the snow, a circle of people from the house staring down at him and laughing. No way, José. Slowly, he stepped down to street level.

While he waited, Mickey Boy paced around in a circle, inspecting his footprints in the soft white plush as he came up behind himself. It was the same pattern he'd made since first having been allowed to play in the snow as a child.

The wreathed wooden door opened again, releasing a flood of yellow into the night. A short, stocky man with a walrus moustache stood framed in the breach.

"Yeah? You wanna see me?"

Gruff, not nice—yet even he had a Christmas.

Mickey Boy stood in place. He turned the card over and studied it as though he were trying to make out some writing on the envelope.

"If you're Phil Ragusa, I got a card here, from . . ."

Phil Ragusa shut the door and, with his hand outstretched to receive the envelope, started down the stairs.

When only the smoke from their breaths separated the two men, Mickey Boy swung a gift-wrapped iron pipe from about knee level into a high arc and, while yelling "Merry Christmas from Buster," smashed it down on Phil's head. Vibrations from the blow shot up through Mickey Boy's shoulder; Phil Ragusa fell backward onto the steps, blood streaming from his forehead into the pure white snow.

Phil was the enemy. He was all the haunting demons rolled into one. He was Laurel. He was Little Vinnie. He was Mickey Boy's own self.

For a few seconds Mickey Boy remained there, shaking, wanting to strike out again to release more of the poison that permeated his system. Then he caught himself, harnessing in the anger that might have made him beat Phil Ragusa into a lifeless mass.

Mickey Boy flipped the unsigned card that bore the message "Thinking of you at Christmas" onto Phil's chest, then hurried back to his car.

Laurel accompanied Mickey Boy all the way to Buster's house in Howard Beach. He fantasized that she was there beside him while he pointed out the magnificent electrical displays that turned ordinary private homes along their route into glittering Christmas castles.

Daydreams soured quickly, though, and depression recaptured

Mickey Boy. Spending Christmases, New Years, and birthdays without Laurel pained him as much inside as Phil Ragusa's head did at that moment. But who, except people who didn't love easily, could understand that?

Buster's wife, Claire, answered the door. An overweight woman who Mickey Boy decided must have been a beauty in her day, she ushered him into a foyer, then the kitchen.

In his arms Mickey Boy carried a five-foot-tall gift basket of nuts, fruits, and jellies he'd had made up earlier that day. Through ceiling-high arches he could see a meal was about to commence in the mirrored dining room.

Three other women, one familiar, busied themselves in preparation for the feast, while their mates—must be the husbands—lounged around the living room, talking to Buster. Two small children sat on a breakfast-nook bench in the kitchen watching TV.

Another nice family. None for him.

When Buster saw Mickey Boy, he left his guests and led him down to his wood-paneled basement. Buster poured a couple of Chivas Regals over rocks while Mickey Boy threw the few quarters from his pocket into a new Joker Poker machine.

No pair—lose. No pair—lose.

"*Buon Natale*," they each toasted with their drinks, then made themselves comfortable on opposite ends of a leather sofa.

"There's two people upstairs who I could swear I seen before," Mickey Boy said. "The lady with the white hair an' blue outfit, an' the guy in the black velour shirt you were talking to."

"That's my sister an' her husband," Buster answered, then quickly asked, "Well, what's new?"

Mickey Boy taxed his memory to place the two familiar faces. When he couldn't, he put them out of his mind. The brief high he'd felt when he'd hit Phil Ragusa had worn off long ago, leaving behind nothing. He wasn't sorry about what he'd done; he was too numb for that. He wasn't happy about it either, but knew Buster would be.

Hoping the older mafioso's coming good spirits would rub off, Mickey Boy played to them, saying, "Do I have a Christmas present for you."

"I seen it upstairs," Buster said. "Beautiful, thanks."

"Nope. That's only the small part."

Buster perked up. "Oh, yeah? Well, what's the rest?"

"Guess."

"C'mon, Mick, don't play no fuckin' games," Buster said, mocking impatience but obviously enjoying himself. "Either you got a new Caddy in my driveway, or the present's in your pocket. So if the front of the house is clear, all I gotta do is shake ya upside down."

Teasing was no fun either. Take the glory.

"Neither one," Mickey Boy said. "Remember that guy, the dress contractor you told me to talk to? Well, I gave him the message."

"Today?"

"Tonight."

"Tonight? You *sfatcheem*. Tell me all about it."

Even glory was dull.

"Nothing to tell," Mickey Boy said. "I did what I hadda do and got the hell out." He did, however, tell Buster about the Christmas card he'd left.

"You hit him good?"

Tempted to reply, *No, I did a shitty job. I punk-smacked him and he hit me back*, Mickey Boy just nodded. "Any better," he finally said, "an' he wouldn't be able to pay."

Ignoring Mickey Boy's lack of enthusiasm, Buster praised his efficiency, shaking his hand and patting him on the shoulder more than once.

"But why tonight of all nights?" Buster asked. "Not that he won't remember the lesson better. There won't be a Christmas Eve that he don't think of me . . . or be afraid to go answer the door." He laughed. "I love the bit about the card."

Mickey Boy had originally intended to fulfill Buster's command after New Year's. The previous day, however, he had been having lunch at the Tiffany Diner when two friends of his who were underlings of another wiseguy, Mario Piazza, came in and joined him. After a bit of swapping war stories it came out that the two men had a contract to take care of for their boss, Mario. Did Mickey Boy know a Phil Ragusa? they asked. He was a ladies' dress manufacturer who owed Mario ten thousand dollars and had been jerking him around. That was Ragusa's game, they said: borrowing from mob guys then pitting them against each other to collect dribs and drabs. His nickname: Philly-Pay-Nobody.

When he'd first heard the story, Mickey Boy had been pissed—at Buster, Mario, and all the other shylocks and bookmakers who had Phil Ragusa on their lists. To begin with, why had Buster saved this problem for him? If the dress manufacturer was as bad a payer as they claimed, Buster had to have been behind the eight ball with him for some time. Couldn't he collect his own goddamn money? Or have sent some punk to do it months before? Did it have to wait until the insult was at a point where a borrower had to be badly hurt?

And what about the other guys Phil owed money to? If anybody deserved a beating, it was them. Greed. Overextensions of credit. Nothing new. If they would only use their heads, he'd thought, and observe strict territories, it would force potential customers to borrow and gamble near their homes or jobs. All it would take is cutting down their ranks, which were too swollen with worthless members anyway, then keeping close contact within those territories to check borrowers' debts and payment histories. A little forward thinking and things like this wouldn't happen. No one would ever have to be hurt over money. Disgraceful and, in view of the changing attitudes of the public and law enforcement, just plain dumb.

That Phil Ragusa deserved to have his head broken, there was no doubt, Mickey Boy had thought. Philly-Pay-Nobody was no Ex-lax who wanted to pay but was too jammed up to do it all at once. He was a scumbag who stole wiseguys' money and thumbed his nose at them, who dishonored what Mickey Boy felt they stood for by forcing them into dangerous and belittling situations.

Partially because he wanted to humiliate Phil Ragusa as much as Buster wanted him hurt, and partially because he wanted to get there before Mario Piazza's men, he'd made up his mind at the table to take care of the contract on Christmas Eve. Without Laurel, there was going to be no Christmas for him anyway. Fuck Christmas!

Once he'd set his mind on making an example of Philly-Pay-Nobody, Mickey Boy goaded Mario Piazza's men into a five-hundred-dollar wager against who would fulfill their assignment first. Sure win. Like most everyone else, Mario's underlings would be busy with loved ones on Christmas Eve. Mickey Boy'd be kicking ass.

Claiming that he'd done what he'd done on the holiday only to win a bet, Mickey Boy related to Buster the story of his encounter with Mario Piazza's men.

"That's great!" Buster shouted. "I love it! Can't wait to grab Mario an' ask him how he's doin' with Philly-Pay-Nobody, an' how come he got such slow-movin' guys around him. He'll shit, that fuckin' asshole."

Buster shook Mickey Boy's hand again, praised him some more, then said, "An' Mick, you don't even hafta give me half of the five hundred." He laughingly added, "That's my Christmas present to you."

The little girl who had been watching television in the kitchen when Mickey Boy'd first arrived bounded down the stairs.

"Grandpa, it's time to eat," she said, tugging on Buster's arm. "Everybody's waiting for you, and I'm starving."

"Okay, baby, but first I want you to meet my friend, Mickey Boy. Mick, this is my favorite granddaughter, Daphne. But you could call her Daffy, like the duck."

"Oh, Grandpa," the child said with a huff, her hands on her hips. "I'm your only granddaughter, and I'm not a skinny black duck who talks funny."

"Don't feel bad," Mickey Boy said. How he'd love to have a child like this—to tease, to hug, to baby, and to love. "When I was little, everybody started calling me Mickey, like the skinny black mouse who squeaks funny. My real name is Michael, but guess what? Now I like Mickey better."

Mickey Boy pulled a roll of bills out of his pocket, peeled off two twenties, and offered them to Daphne. "Here's a little Christmas present for you and the little boy upstairs."

"That's my brother, Courtney."

"Oh . . . Courtney," Mickey Boy repeated, glancing over at Buster, who shrugged helplessly.

"Maybe if you ask Mickey Boy nice, he'll stay an' eat with us," Buster said.

"Could you?" Daphne asked, taking the money.

"Sorry, maybe some other time. Tonight I got some more stops to make."

Stops? Booze and bed. If he got lucky, maybe he'd find some equally lonely bimbo hanging around to share both with him. Fuck Christmas!

The child kissed Mickey Boy and her grandfather, then ran up the stairs, yelling, "Courtney! Courtney! We got money from Grandpa's friend."

Once he was sure Daphne was out of earshot, Mickey Boy turned to Buster, and, with eyebrows raised, asked, "Courtney?"

Buster threw his arms up in the air. "Whattaya want from me?" he said. "My kid went an' married a bitch who wants her kids to sound like they're part of the social register. When I heard that they named my first grandkid Daphne, *meenkya*, I thought that was bad. But then to go an' stick a moniker like Courtney on a boy?" He made the sign of the cross in front of his chest. "My God!"

Using his fat forefinger to accent each name, Buster added, "Courtney—Stanford—Alcamo. They tell me the Stanford is for me 'cause Stanford an' Sebastiano both start with S. I'm supposed to be honored. What happens every time they call him a sonomabitch? Is that for me too?"

Well, that was one generation that wouldn't be in the streets, Mickey Boy thought while laughing at Buster's chagrin. Imagine threatening someone with having Courtney sent to get them.

"We should introduce your daughter-in-law to my brother, Alley. Two wannabe blue bloods."

"Ah, Mickey Boy," Buster said, sighing. "The world is changin' around us. Things just ain't the same no more."

"Change don't always have to be bad."

"It is for guys like us. So far I got over half a century in this life, an' all I see lately is things gettin' worse. We're breakin' down from the inside—guys roll over so fast it makes your head spin—and we're gettin' hammered from the outside at the same time: twenties, fifties, hundred-year sentences."

Buster shook his head sadly. "I wouldn't say this to no one who wasn't really close to me, but I believe we're like the cowboys in the Old West. One day they was there shootin' up Dodge City, an' the next thing you knew they was gone, all skyscrapers an' cars around."

Mickey Boy didn't believe that for a minute. Maybe the old guys like Buster would be a thing of the past, but not him. He was no dinosaur who couldn't adjust to a changing world and became extinct because of it. Though he wasn't sure how, in his heart he knew he'd find a way to conquer any conditions the world would impose and carry on a tradition that had been born centuries before in Sicily. No way he would drop the ball that generations before had handed down, a ball that he was now aware had been given directly to him by a father he'd never known.

". . . Pretty soon all anybody'll remember about us is gonna be what they see in bullshit pictures like *The Godfather*," Buster went on. "All phony stuff, like callin' a boss Don Corleone. Could you ever imagine if I ever called Don Vitone 'Don Genovese'? Or if I called the old man Don Calabra instead of Don Vincenze? *Meenkya!* They woulda hit me with a two-by-four—an' that's if I was lucky! No, I don't envy you, kid. You really picked a shitty time to be born . . . for a wiseguy anyway."

Although Buster's apparent lack of faith in their future was disconcerting, Mickey Boy tried to put on a positive face.

"Don't worry, we ain't finished yet; not by a long shot," he said. "Maybe we'll have to operate a little different, but we'll survive. The problem with the cowboys was that they weren't Italian," he said with a snicker. "If they were, they'd still be shooting up Dodge City . . . or own it."

"I hope so, kid . . . for your sake."

But Buster wasn't finished talking. He ignored another dinner call from Daphne to review the state of the Rossellini–Vallo war, and how it affected their Family. As Mickey Boy had expected, Buster said that, yes, Petey Ross was angry and insulted that an attack had been made on Georgie The Hammer by Calabra gunmen, but he was much too weak to do anything but sulk.

However, when Mickey Boy tried to pursue the topic and get some information about the events surrounding Chrissy's murder, Buster backed up.

"There are so many things I wanna tell you, but I can't. So many," Buster said. Orders were orders, even for him, and the subject had been ordered off limits. What he did reveal, though, was a worry about what Joe Augusta was up to. That was their real problem, he said.

"We got no idea where he is," Buster continued.

"Don't he go visit Chrissy's grave?"

"That's the sick part: He ain't even been there once. We know; we got it staked out twenty-four hours a day." Buster shook his head. "An' the way he loved that kid . . ."

Hadn't anyone run across Joe? Mickey Boy asked. Or his wife?

"No. We heard a rumor that he went to Washington, but we're still checking it out," Buster replied. "Joe took it pretty bad about the accident with his kid, an' we're afraid that he'll either hurt himself or try to do something stupid . . . especially if he *is* in D.C."

Incredulously, Mickey Boy asked if anyone really believed Joe Augusta would turn to the authorities.

"Who knows? One thing's for sure, though, if his mind popped, an' he decides to go in the witness protection program, we'll all be ruined. We'll have more guys in jail than they got in Ucciardone Prison in the *maxi-processo* . . . you know, that big case in Sicily, where they got a couple of hundred of our friends locked up."

To Mickey Boy, it was beyond the realm of possibilities that Joe Augusta would ever be a rat, no matter what the hidden circumstances. Joe was, however, the guy who could shoot heads off chickens. If they thought that he had snapped and might possibly direct his vengeance against them, wouldn't it make more sense that he'd strike a physical blow, an armed attack?

"No chance," Buster replied. "We got the old man guarded better than Fort Knox. There's never less than three good fellas with him all the time. Poor guy can't take a shit by himself."

So Don Vincenze was the target of Joe Augusta's anger, Mickey Boy thought. Why? Surely Joe didn't believe the old man had anything to do with it. If Don Vincenze had, Joe, as underboss, would had to have known in advance.

Unless Little Vinnie had been mixed up in the incident some way? After all, the prick's money was at the heart of the beef with Georgie, who, according to the newspapers, had recovered from his gunshot wounds but was being held in protective custody, against his will, as a material witness in Chrissy's murder. Was that why they thought Joe'd be pissed at Don Vincenze? For something his scumbag son had engineered? Was that why Little Vinnie was still away in Sicily?

And, if that was the case, why was Richie involved? Poor Richie, though more badly hurt than Georgie, was also recovering but still locked up on first-degree murder charges. Too bad he, Mickey Boy, being on parole, couldn't visit Richie and get some firsthand information. Mickey Boy knew his partner would never have gone along on the attempted hit for Little Vinnie. Buster would have had to have sent him. But then, why wasn't Buster worried about his own safety? Nothing made any sense.

"Yeah, it's a shame about Joe," Buster said. "He was a good man."

Wrapping a thick arm around Mickey Boy's shoulders, he led him toward the stairs. As they reached the bottom step, he stopped and turned Mickey Boy to face him. "You know, you might not realize it till later on in your life, but I'm the best friend you ever had. I done more for you than anybody else on this earth would."

Yeah, right, Mickey Boy thought.

"Be careful," Buster continued, "and make me proud."

In spite of the pessimistic, sometimes maudlin tone of Buster's conversations (which was the last thing Mickey Boy needed in the mood he was already in) and Buster's comment about being his best friend (which seemed like a snow job), he was glad he'd spent the time with him. In that period of less than two hours, he'd felt more of a sense of belonging than he had at any time in his life, with anyone.

Upstairs, Mickey Boy wished everyone a happy holiday. His inability to place the faces of Buster's familiar relatives still bothered him.

"I can't get over how I can't make out where I know your sister an' her husband from," he said, standing at the front door. "But I'm sure I do know them. What's their last name?"

Buster hesitated for a moment, then, with the slightest trace of a smile, answered, "Zafferamo."

"My God!" Mickey Boy exclaimed. "That's where I know them from. When I was a kid our landlady who practically raised me was a Zafferamo. I probably seen your sister an' her husband a thousand times. Boy, ain't it a small world?"

Buster smiled broadly. "You know how we guineas are," he said. "You could never tell who we're related to."

55

January 10: Pennsauken, New Jersey

It was in the earliest blue-gray stage of dawn that Don Vincenze drove along the well-plowed Jersey Turnpike. At the Exit 4 toll plaza he turned in the computerized rate card with his money, then proceeded west on Route 73. The outlines of restaurants, motels, and gas stations on both sides of the road were slowly becoming visible against the waking sky. Snow was piled everywhere.

Driving alone was a strange sensation for the don—free yet vulnerable. For years now he'd been used to having underlings take him from place to place, but had always managed occasional privacy, at least when he'd taken Pauline out or dated some overawed employee of one of the businesses under his control. Since Joe Augusta had disappeared, however, some six weeks before, he hadn't spent a waking minute without Buster and one or more of his captains around.

But there were some places even Buster wasn't welcome. Don Vincenze had waited until his acting underboss's snores reminded him of the Luftwaffe buzzing overhead during World War II, then had sneaked out of Harrah's and sped from Atlantic City. With any luck he'd be back before Buster or the other two late sleepers in the adjoining room awoke.

A chill ran down Don Vincenze's spine when a black funeral car pulled to a stop alongside him at a traffic light. No way he could see through its darkened side window.

Without losing sight of the car in his peripheral vision, the don checked the area in front for the best route of escape. Could he back up? Was someone blocking him from behind? Couldn't chance looking in the mirror. Impossible to turn right—shit! Quickly, he shifted his left foot to hold the brake and moved his right foot to the gas pedal, ready to roll. His eye never left the other vehicle's window, waiting for the slightest sign that the glass had begun to drop, waiting to see Joe Augusta's tragedy-maddened face staring at him over the barrel of a gun.

Suddenly, the hearse jolted forward and drove on, leaving Don Vincenze sitting alone at the green light, motionless, waiting for the palpitations in his chest to subside; his testicles were still shriveled up into his body as they hadn't been since the old days—when he'd been subject to higher-ups calling him out from home during the night's darkest hours, each of which might have been his last.

After a couple of minutes, when his hand steadied, the don continued on his way, cursing Joe Augusta for making him have to go through all this in the first place. After thirty years in the streets, he'd have thought his ex-underboss would have understood that when you live in a world as violent as theirs, accidents sometimes happen—that no one is immune to the gun backfiring in his hand. Instead of blaming him—though no one had heard from Joe, it was Don Vincenze's and Buster's consensus that he would fault the don for having issued the order that had ultimately resulted in Chrissy's death—Joe should have come closer to the nest, let all his friends share his grief. After all, that's what Families were for.

Don Vincenze stepped down heavily on the gas pedal. The faster he reached his destination, the faster he could get the hell back to his men.

At the cloverleaf interconnecting with Route 70, he turned around and headed back on 73 until the snow-topped letters of the Red Coach Diner came into view. Without signaling, he made a jarring turn into the diner's parking lot, then hurried out of his car toward the door.

As soon as he entered, Don Vincenze spotted the man he'd come to meet sitting in the last booth on the right. Neither of them offered the slightest signal of recognition as the old mafioso, carefully checking his surroundings, shuffled his way to the back.

"Good morning, Vince," FBI Supervisor Paul Trantino said. He pointed to a cup of steaming coffee. "I ordered it for you when I saw you fly in. And a belated Happy New Year."

"Thanks," Don Vincenze replied; a shot of cognac was more what he needed, but coffee would do. "A Happy New Year to you an' your family too."

Don Vincenze hung his gray cashmere coat and matching fedora on the brass spokes that grew out of the booth's divider, then waited for the burly agent to shift to the opposite side of the table.

He learns well, the don thought while sliding onto the leather bench facing Paul—and the doorway.

After scanning the premises again, then glancing out the window to check the parking lot, Don Vincenze asked, "How's your father? You sent him my regards?"

Vincenze Calabra and Paul Trantino's father, Frank, had been neighbors, inseparable friends, and burglary partners until induction into the army broke them up in 1941. Vincenze wound up getting his leg shattered in Italy, while Frank was losing an arm in the Pacific Theater.

But the two men's lives, which had converged so closely together for so many years, splintered and cast off in opposite directions after the war. Whereas after having been discharged Vincenze went back to Brooklyn to continue his life of crime, Frank took advantage of the GI Bill and entered Columbia University. Eight years later, while an already made Vincenze was planning his ascent in the industry Meyer Lansky liked to describe as "bigger than U.S. Steel," Frank was admitted to the New York State bar and began a career as an assistant district attorney for the farmland of Suffolk County.

Though more than a hundred miles and conflicting professions had kept the two men physically apart, they'd continued to keep track of each other's lives through little notes scribbled on greeting cards for every occasion from Christmas to Halloween—until one of them had needed a sizable personal favor.

Now, Paul, with his father's dark Sicilian coloring and the impish Irish features of his late mother, had become the older generation's occasional greeting device.

"Pop's fine," Paul Trantino said. "I sent him your regards after we met last time, and he said to send you his love. But naturally, since you and I don't see each other too often . . ." The FBI man shrugged.

"Of course," Don Vincenze replied, thinking, *The less often, the better.* He then said, "Anyway, tell him that I was asking for him again, an' that one of these days I'm gonna take him up on that fishing trip he promised me."

"Absolutely. I speak to him once a week, and, in fact, I'll be flying down to Tampa to see him in three weeks, two days, and twelve hours. But who's counting?"

"I don't blame you," Don Vincenze said, chuckling along with the government agent who might have been one of his own men under slightly altered circumstances. ". . . Especially with this goddamn weather." Then: "Speaking of weather, how'd you find the roads coming down from New York?"

"They were okay; it's me that's out of service. You know, this is a hell of a hike to take at this time of night under any conditions. Janice thought I was nuts when I set my alarm for two-thirty. But I knew that for you to want to meet, it had to be important."

"Well, you understand how tough it is for me to get away without either your people or mine watching me. My trip to Atlantic City was the only time there'd be enough confusion to sneak away."

Don Vincenze checked his watch. "As a matter of fact, if we could take care of business quickly," he said, "I could probably be back at Harrah's before my friends wake up an' start panicking."

"I can understand how they feel," Paul said with a laugh. "I wouldn't want to be the poor schnook who let his boss get kidnapped or killed. That could mean suddenly looking like a slab of Swiss cheese."

Smiling, Don Vincenze shook his head slowly. "Now, now, Paolo, you guys must be getting your ideas from television again."

"Yeah, like the seven o'clock news. Your friends are dropping like flies. A nasty little dispute they've got going for themselves."

"There are a few minor problems in every business," Don Vincenze said. He checked his watch again; no time to bullshit around. "The key is to keep them from getting out of hand. That's why I called you. I'm gonna give you an opportunity to end that problem you been seeing on TV, an' make you score some more brownie points in Washington besides."

"Why is it, Vince, that every time you've offered me help during these last eight years or so—since I helped you with that Messina kid's case—I wind up feeling like I'm walking into a revolving door in front of you and coming out in back?"

Because that's the way it's supposed to be, Don Vincenze wanted to say.

"Not that I don't appreciate the effect your offerings have had on my career," Paul said. "But somehow, when the smoke clears, I'm never as big a winner as you."

"Paolo, Paolo. I'm just an old man trying to repay a debt to my boyhood friend's son. What you imagine my benefit is is, well, let's say just the product of a mind that's been brainwashed by the government."

Paul Trantino laughed out loud. "Thank God you and Pop didn't stay partners. I don't know how either side would cope."

"What a shame your father went wrong when he did," Don Vincenze teased. "Him an' me together were a helluva team."

Frank Trantino had been a good hoodlum, and somehow, Don Vincenze thought, his son Paul would've been one, too, if he'd grown up in the right neighborhood. But there wasn't enough time to theorize or reminisce. Too many pressing problems; too little time to spend getting them solved.

"Let me tell you what I came to say so we could both go about our business," the don continued. "In a couple of weeks you'll probably get a call telling you a time an' place. Now, if I was a betting man, I'd lay odds that if your guys happened to lay a couple of bugs in that place before the time that's mentioned, you might hear a certain Mr. Rossellini an' his friends planning a couple of murders."

Paul Trantino whistled. "Boy, there's a big fish on my plate this time."

"And if you raided the place after you got some good tapes, you might get lucky an' find a whole shitload of guns there."

"What happened, is Ross too hot to handle, or are you just a closet Vallo fan?"

"I'm sure your father taught you the old saying about looking a gift horse in the mouth."

"Absolutely . . . along with a couple of others about things that are too good to be true."

"Well, this is good *and* true, as I'm sure you already know. I think I did more than the right thing about returning the favor you did for me when I called on you."

"No question," the FBI man agreed. "I'm just trying to figure out how dumping Petey Ross and his boys benefits you."

"You know, people who worry too much about what's in the other guy's pockets sometimes find theirs have been picked," the don said, then sternly added, "Worry about your own pockets . . . not mine."

Under normal circumstances, that would be one hundred percent correct, Paul said. The problem was that with an operation of that magnitude, the Bureau had to be backed up when the onslaught of Rossellini attorneys came. There wouldn't be any part of the investi-

316

gation that wouldn't be torn apart and scrutinized under a microscope once indictments were handed down.

"We've got to be prepared for the possibility of their coming up with the source that we used to initiate the taps and warrants," Paul said. "And even if they don't, which is probably the case, we'll surely have to justify everything in camera before the trial judge. I can't very well use your name."

Don Vincenze smiled the kind of smile usually reserved for cute children. "Don't worry, Paolo. Would I give you a car with the ignition missing?" he asked, pleased at how easy manipulating the FBI man was; Paul Trantino couldn't have asked more perfect questions or given better responses if the don had written them for him in advance.

Don Vincenze printed on a paper napkin and shoved it across the table at Paul. "When you go to get your court orders, just use this name."

Paul took the napkin, knitted his eyebrows questioningly as he read it, then asked, "Ralphie Burgio? The Eye? He's one of Ross's top lieutenants." He shook his head slowly from side to side. "You guys are amazing; turn on each other in a heartbeat." Still shaking his head, he added, "It's a wonder any of you are able to sleep after all the treachery."

Don Vincenze ignored Paul's remarks. What the hell did a suburban-raised asshole like him know about what it took to survive? Nothing. He'd never had to go for "coffee and a coat," like his father, Frank, and a young Vincenze Calabra had been forced to every winter, the don thought, remembering how he and Frank Trantino had waited until the weather had turned harsh each year before making a special trip to Bickford's Cafeteria as though it were Howard Clothes, and, after paying for the cheapest item on the menu, coffee, had walked out wearing winter coats that had been hung on a rack by unsuspecting but wealthier patrons. What did anyone know?

"What do we do if Ralphie The Eye is at the meeting?" Paul Trantino asked. "Pinch him?"

"Mr. Burgio will be conveniently absent from the meeting. He's as anxious to see everyone who will be at that place removed from the scene as you are."

"Do we look forward to having a Burgio Family among us instead of a Rossellini Family?"

"Please, Paolo, don't trouble yourself about what may or may not be. Just feel confident that the angel that watches over you will take care of everything."

"Okay, you win . . . Uncle Angel," Paul said, throwing open his palms in surrender. "And anytime we at the Bureau can do anything—

even cleaning house occasionally for you—don't hesitate to ask. You were right before, you have more than repaid the favor."

All that passed before during their conversation was only convenience to Don Vincenze; he could have easily taken care of Petey Ross in three or four different ways. Turning him over to the FBI had been the cleanest, and had given him a bit of leverage to get his real goal, the necessary, accomplished.

"There is one small thing I would appreciate. A very close friend of mine is missing, and I'd like to locate him."

"Please," Paul said, smiling. "If a friend of yours is missing, chances are he's wearing cement Jockey shorts."

"Would I ask you to find him if that was the case?" the don snapped. It annoyed him that he'd lost patience, possibly enough to expose his hand. He continued in a much more moderate tone. "My friend had a terrible tragedy in his home, and disappeared with his wife and kid. It's almost two months now. His name is Joseph Augusta."

Don Vincenze searched Paul's face for the slightest hint that Joe had already gone over to the feds, but saw only sadness.

"Oh, the funeral director," Paul said. "What a shame about his kid. That was a really messy thing for any parent to have to deal with, even if they are executives of yours. Being a father, I can sympathize with him." He shook his head. "No, we haven't heard anything about him, but I'll see if I can find out if he's okay. Do you think he might have left the country?"

"I don't know. Whatever you could do will be appreciated." Taking advantage of the fact that Paul Trantino was no match for him, Don Vincenze allowed his anxiety curtain to drop, pressing, "And please, it's been a long time and I'm worried about him. The faster I know something, the better I'll feel."

Paul nodded seriously. "I understand."

Don Vincenze smiled inside. He looked at his former crime partner's son and compared Paul's life against Mickey Boy's. Though being an FBI agent was about the lowest profession he could think of, and he would have been sick if Mickey Boy, God forbid, had become one, the don was sure that Paul had never suffered in his life as Mickey Boy had.

For the first time Don Vincenze questioned whether or not he'd done the right thing by forcing that two-bit *avvocato*, Nicolo Fonte, to chase Mickey Boy, to get all those thoughts of being a nobody like Fonte out of his head.

He'd purposely had Mickey Boy moved to South Brooklyn, by way of "Call me Louis" and a house that he'd bought and had Louis sell to Connie and Al Messina at a loss, to keep the boy where he could watch, guide, and protect him—form him into the type of man who could inherit and handle all that he himself had put his life on the line for. Then came Fonte, with his bleeding-heart shit to soften Mickey Boy's head.

Did I really fuck up an' hurt this kid more than I helped him? the don wondered, remembering having scared Fonte all the way back to Italy and thereby dashing any hopes Mickey Boy might have had of becoming an attorney. *Or am I just getting old now, and soft in the head?*

Don Vincenze shook off his thoughts to return to FBI Agent Paul Trantino. Satisfied their business was done, he excused himself to Paul, saying he had to get back to Harrah's.

As Don Vincenze slipped into his coat, Paul, who had remained seated, asked, "By the way, whatever happened to that Messina kid? I got someone to push up his parole hearing date like you asked, but I never checked to see how he made out."

"He beat the violation, an' he's home again. His only problem is that that ballbreaking P.O. he's got is gonna stay on his back till the last day."

"Sorry, can't help with that one without exposing something. If I don't mention you, which obviously I can't, the parole officer will think we made a deal with the kid."

"No, forget about it. We can't have that happen."

"Just tell him to take it easy," Paul said. "He should listen to you. After all, if not for you getting involved back when he had the hijacking case, he'd have gotten hit with so much time he'd have looked like George Burns by the time he saw the streets."

"Thanks to you, he won't. Even the year an' a half you stalled his case helped, and was appreciated."

"Messina must be very special for you to do what you did. Usually the only time we've ever been able to work with guys in your position was when they wanted to deal for either themselves or their sons. This case is highly unusual. I just hope the kid is worth it . . . and stays out of trouble."

Adjusting his fedora so the brim snapped down over his eyes, Don Vincenze replied, "He'll be just fine. He's a good boy, with good blood in him . . . like you."

Before walking away, the don added, "And please, Paolo, don't forget Joe Augusta. It's important."

56

February 13: Canarsie, Brooklyn

Le Parc was packed elbow to elbow on the eve before St. Valentine's Day. The mostly single crowd at the popular Canarsie disco was ostensibly celebrating its status by way of an "I'm Glad I'm Single" party. Mickey knew, however, that in spite of their cheery smiles, erotic dance floor gyrations, and flip conversations, each male and female present was hopeful that the evening would spawn a new and lasting relationship—all, that is, except him. In the midst of that sybaritic atmosphere of sex-dim lighting, sex talk, and thumping sexy music, Mickey Boy stood alone—well on his way to becoming drunk—thinking that the party's theme was a bad joke aimed specifically at him.

Since Laurel had left, more and more of his evenings were spent downing enough Johnnie Walker Red to obliterate her memory. Holidays being especially depressing, Valentine's Eve would require an extra dose.

Mickey Boy had hoped to see Laurel in January, when he'd flown down to Miami to pick up a package of forged identification from one of his former cellmates, but had never gotten the chance. Instead of having a couple of days to spend waiting for the bundle of driver's licenses, social security cards, and voter registration cards to be cut, sorted, and packed as usual, his friend had met him in the airport's lounge with everything done and wrapped. Mickey Boy had come back to New York, and his profit from selling the thousands of pieces to the city's top stolen credit card ring, without ever leaving the terminal.

Hopefully, when he returned to Miami in a couple of days to pick up samples of phony toll tickets, he'd have a little more time to spend and a lot more chance of running into Laurel.

Here's to hopes, Mickey thought, and gulped his drink bottoms-up. Maybe he would be better off with her in Florida, no matter what he had to do. At least there would be no more pain. Or would there?

The last drop of scotch had just about cleared his throat when he felt someone grab his arm. Through the rhythmic blasting of some rock tune, a vaguely familiar voice asked, "Mickey Boy, is that you?"

Though he recognized the earthy-looking brunette immediately, Mickey pretended not to, leaving his face as blank as he felt inside.

The girl smiled conspiratorially, her eyes hooded and sexy from drink. "Remember . . . Rosalie?" she asked.

A black knit halter criss-crossed her breasts, making them look even larger than he remembered and leaving her shoulders strikingly bare.

"From the Villarosa."

Well schooled, Mickey Boy thought. Most bimbos would have blurted out a whole speech about the violation hearing by then.

"Oh, yeah, Rosalie, how are you?" he said. "What're you doing here?"

"What is anybody doing here?" Rosalie lifted both hands and with curved fingers issued the universal sign for quotation marks. "Having a, quote, good time. I see I don't have to ask you the same question," she said, eyeing his empty glass.

Each time Rosalie completed a sentence, her mouth remained slightly parted with the tip of her tongue resting seductively on her lower lip.

"What are you drinking?" Mickey asked, hoping she would say "nothing" and wander off.

"Seven and Seven."

When a pert teenager who didn't look old enough to drink abandoned the barstool next to Mickey, Rosalie pounced on it. Rosalie's miniskirt—black, leather, wider than it was long—shrunk to a narrow band that hardly covered her crotch. Her legs, thankfully covered in sheer black nylon, crossed. Looking toward where the teen had been swallowed by the crowd, she said, "Cute, huh?"

"Yeah, I guess so," he replied blandly while handing Rosalie her drink. "You know, I never got to see you in person to thank you for what you did, but I don't want you to think I don't appreciate it."

"How could I ever?" Rosalie gushed. "You must have sent me half of the Botanic Gardens, and the candy was simply sinful . . . although I should be mad at you," she said, affecting an exaggerated pout and tickling his chest with her fingernail. "I'll bet I put on five pounds stuffing my face with it."

Mickey Boy let his eyes soak in her lush body for a brief moment, then looked away. "It doesn't look like it did you any harm," he said, then swallowed another drink. While signaling the bartender for more, he mechanically added, "You must've put it on in all the right places."

"Why, thank you," Rosalie sang. She rested a hand on his sleeve. "Are you always such a ball of fire, or is it me?"

Liquor-loose, Mickey began to laugh. "No, this is as good as it gets. You should see me when I'm in a pissy mood." He leaned against her—soft, compliant, so good—and drank another scotch.

"It's a girl, isn't it?"

"How'd ya guess? Is it written on my forehead?"

"All in the eyes." Rosalie's words slurred slightly and her eyelids dropped a bit more—bedroom eyes. The touchy-feely type, she ran her hand along his arm. "Don't tell me she found another guy; I won't believe it."

"Nah, she just don't like gangsters," Mickey Boy said. *Some joke*. He casually dropped his hand into Rosalie's lap, let his fingers burrow in and rest between her crossed thighs; her nylons felt coarse and scratchy.

"You know, there is an antidote," Rosalie purred. "There are plenty of girls who'd love the chance to cure a real gangster instead of the wannabes that hang around a place like this. If you'd only give one of them a chance, you might surprise yourself and find that you didn't lose much at all." Her tongue snaked out a bit farther; moved side to side to moisten her lips; glistened in the dim lights.

Mickey Boy thought about the day of his parole violation hearing, how Rosalie's body had felt pressed boldly against his own, and he began to get hard. Remembering her fiery kiss that day, he impulsively bent and kissed her full on the mouth, which opened for him as it had the first time.

Barely able to walk, let alone manage a car, Mickey Boy allowed Rosalie to drive him home in her TransAm. He leaned on her as the two of them stumbled to the elevator of his building, then once inside, draped all over her—arms looped around her shoulders, tongue down her throat, eyes closed. Hair spray and perfume fragrances filled his head like helium. Loose fur from her coat tickled his nose.

Before the door to his apartment had even slammed shut, Mickey Boy had Rosalie's halter up around her throat, mashing her tits with one hand, while he clung to her with his other for support. He bent to lick her nipple, but felt dizzy and straightened up immediately.

"Whoa, slow down," Rosalie said, laughing and pushing away from him. Her milk-white breasts hung free beneath her black knit top and between the open front sections of her silver fox. She smiled while removing her coat. "Give me a minute to wash up, lover. Gotta smell nice and clean for you down there." Breasts dangling, she wobbled off in search of the bathroom.

"Through there," Mickey Boy mumbled on his way to the bed. He shucked his jacket and shirt, dropped them to the floor as he went. Once bedside, he propped up his pillows, then threw himself against them like a sultan awaiting his harem.

By the time Rosalie entered the room, however, Mickey Boy saw her naked form through narrow, lash-webbed slits. His eyes shut all the way while she kissed his face, chest, and tip of his dick. And amid the echo of a voice that sounded amazingly like his own crying out "Laurel," consciousness slipped away.

* * *

Torrid Florida sunshine broiled Mickey's left arm while he rested it on the open window of his Lincoln. Mouth parched and head pounding with disgust, he drove slowly, looking from string bikini to string bikini for a hint of the familiar. But flesh and fabric had become as uniform as the bleached sand or the tropical-blue sky and water as they melded together on the horizon. It seemed like forever that he'd been scouring Miami's beaches and hotels, poking his nose under stupidly bright umbrellas and inside worn register books, searching for Laurel—all to no avail.

Farther along at the end of the beach he spotted an X-rated bar nestled among a group of palm trees. A one-story flamingo-pink box of a building, it was topped by a towering neon sign that flashed LIVE SHOW! GIRLS! GIRLS! GIRLS!

Deciding he needed to refuel himself, he parked in front of the bar's white colonial doors and went in.

Blinded by the sudden darkness, Mickey had to wait near the door until he could distinguish his surroundings. A thick cloud of smoke burned his eyes and the loud reverberations of drums assaulted his ears. He stepped to the bar and ordered a Johnnie Walker from a bare-bosomed brunette who bore a striking resemblance to the girl who had saved him from being sent back to jail.

To his left, a large crowd of men cheered and clapped in tune to the throbbing beat of a conga. They stood in a circle around a beam of dusty-blue light that shone down from the ceiling. Drink in hand, he nudged his way to the back for a peek at what was going on.

When Mickey squeezed through to the outer layer of chanters, he saw their attention was focused on a round stage that seemed to have been sunken to basement level. In the center, perched atop a small platform that revolved in slow gear, were three nude figures—two men on their knees with a lone female sandwiched on all fours between them. From where he stood, Mickey caught a side-rear view of the action. He could see the woman's blue legs splayed wide and the sweaty blue male behind her driving into her stretched rectum. Every time the man in back plunged into her buttocks, he forced her head forward onto his partner's penis. Her breasts swayed beneath her with every jolt.

Little by little the angle changed so that Mickey caught a full side view of the glistening blue trio. Their movements kept time with the pounding of the drum. Another push from behind sent the second stud's organ deep into the whore's mouth.

The stage turned some more.

The crowd chanted louder.

Both naked men smiled and laughed with each push and shove. They stroked the whore's head, her back, her ass. Beads of blue sweat danced on their bodies like stars sparkling on the sea.

The stage kept turning.

A wanton smile stretched across the girl's face as she sucked—that face!

Mickey pulled the man in front of him away by the hair and started for the stage. Blood banged loudly in his ears, obliterating the angry curses of viewers he battered aside.

The two males kept forcing themselves deep into the female's mouth and ass. She slid back and forth as if on a greased pole, faster and faster as the drumbeat intensified. Another nude man lay down beside her and began sucking on her hanging breasts.

Mickey punched a man who wouldn't move.

The girl moved faster and faster.

Hands from behind grabbed Mickey's arms, legs, chest, holding him back.

The nympho-female rocked back and forth at a frantic pace . . . back . . . front . . . back . . . huge erection in her mouth . . . Little Vinnie pushing into her rectum . . . Little Vinnie in front.

"Laurel! Laurel!" Mickey screamed.

"Laurel! Laurel!"

Mickey bolted upright in the bed. Drenched with icy perspiration and heart palpitating wildly, his lips still mimed her name. It took a while for him to recognize where he was.

"Laurel," Mickey whispered. Far from his dreams fading with time, it seemed to him that they had only intensified. Badly hung over, he slid off the bed and immediately stumbled to his knees.

"What the fuck?!" he yelled, kicking at the bunched-up pants that had tripped him. Being nude from the ankles up confused him until he remembered Rosalie bringing him home.

"Aw, shit," Mickey Boy muttered, picturing his car still parked on a Canarsie street. He leaned back against the bed and pulled off the garment he was tangled in. "Now I'll have to call a fuckin' car service."

Cursing, Mickey Boy stomped off toward the bathroom for some Alka-Seltzers, only to be stopped by his mirror. Scrawled across from one side to the other, large, frantic letters in bloodred lipstick: "FUCK LAUREL!"

"I guess she wasn't too happy when she left," he said to himself, wondering what he could have possibly done to her. "Fuckin' broads."

Whatever it was, he'd just send some more candy and hope it soothed her.

He started for the bathroom again, flicked on the television as he passed.

". . . New York mob boss, Pietro 'Petey Ross' Rossellini. 'This,' said a government spokesman, 'may mark the end of one of the city's most brutal Mafia Families.' "

Each step jarring his brain, Mickey Boy ran back to the TV. He reached it just as a photo of Petey Ross was being replaced on the screen by the face of the news commentator. The man shuffled some papers, saying, "We'll have an update on that story on *The Five O'Clock Report.*"

Mickey Boy jumped from channel to channel, but got nothing more about whatever had happened to Petey Ross, just soap operas and commercials. "Fuck it," he murmured. He'd find out either on the car radio or when he got to the club.

What a day to feel like shit, he thought, punching off the TV. He'd been told to show up at Don Vincenze's club on Bath Avenue for the first time. Two other proposed guys he knew had been ordered to gather there at the same time. Was it really to be just an introductory get-together, as Buster had said, or was it to be a surprise induction ceremony? In either event, it was a good sign, too good to be messed up by worrying about what he'd done to Rosalie or pining over his loss of Laurel.

Almost there, Mickey Boy thought, then toasted himself with a double Alka-Seltzer cocktail and jumped in the shower.

57

February 14: Ridgewood, Queens

Junior Vallo approached the small pizzeria-restaurant cautiously. Even though the Mafia chieftain knew his bitter and costly struggle with the Rossellini faction was virtually over, he took no chances. With a flick of his wrist he ordered his driver to pass the eatery by the first time around, while he examined parked cars, doorways, and faces that lined the old tenement block. Since Junior was uncomfortable with anyone sitting behind him, the third member of his group, another bodyguard, had to scan the area from the rear driver-side seat.

They turned left by the plant nursery on Metropolitan Avenue, made a quick U-turn, then swung back onto Fresh Pond Road for another look. Once satisfied nothing appeared out of the ordinary, Junior gave his driver permission to stop and ordered his other man to scout the premises. Hopefully, his younger brother, Sally, would have arrived at the Floridia Pizzeria and Restaurant before and would have already checked the rest rooms, back entrance, and all other spots where danger could be lurking. If not, the button-man Junior had sent ahead would take care of things.

Only when the scout waved an all-clear signal from the front doorway of the food shop did the driver shut the ignition and escort Junior Vallo inside.

Salvatore "Sally The Soldier" Vallo was already seated at a square table set in the farmost corner of the Floridia's small, dingy, wood-paneled dining room. Yellowed travel posters of Venice, their edges torn and curling inward, clung to the wall by peeling Scotch tape and brown kitchen thumbtacks. A smoke- and dust-encrusted wagon-wheel chandelier barely illuminated the ten-table area.

Junior seated himself at Sally's left, leaving both of them with their backs to the corner walls.

One of the bodyguards who had arrived with Junior posted himself inside the kitchen next to a single stainless-steel door that led to where the brothers sat; the other button-man stood outside the dining room, in the counter area.

The Vallo soldier who had accompanied Sally The Soldier earlier played waiter and took his bosses' orders: one sealed bottle of Bardolino and two unopened Pellegrino waters. He then disappeared.

Sally The Soldier dropped a *Daily News* on the red and white checked tablecloth. He smiled confidently. "I think we should be celebratin' with something stronger than a Bolla an' soda."

"We got plenty of time for that bullshit later," Junior said. He'd seen too many seeming victories turn to defeat at the last moment to be cocky. His favorite proverb: It ain't over till it's over.

"Let me see what the paper says," Junior continued, pulling the *News* in front of him; its headline:

FEDS BUST MOB WAR PARTY
Foil St. Valentine's Massacre II

"Catchy headline," Junior said. "The only thing those jerkoffs woulda massacred, though, woulda been themselves."

He read on:

Feb 14–AP/UPI–FBI officials yesterday announced the arrest of nine alleged members of the old Favara, new Rossellini, crime Family while they were planning the murders of numerous members of the rival Vallo clan. . . .

The biggest fish caught in the early evening raid was the man who is reported to be in charge of that mob while Benedetto

"Benny Brown" Favara sits in jail: forty-seven-year-old Pietro "Petey Ross" Rossellini of Great Kills Road in Staten Island. . . .

Also arrested was Rossellini's reputed underboss, Antonio "Sonny" Fortunato, sixty-eight, of Shore Road in Brooklyn. . . .

"Don't those fuckups know Sonny's *consigliere*, that Benny Brown's kid is underboss?" Sally interrupted. "They pinched the kid too, five million, which means no bail, but they don't even know what he is." Ignoring his brother, Junior continued reading:

. . . Rossellini and Fortunato were each held by Judge Mark Constantino in lieu of ten million dollars bail, on a variety of RICO charges, including murder, attempted murder, and possession of illegal weapons. Each count carries a maximum prison sentence of twenty years. The remaining seven mobsters were held on bail ranging from one to five million dollars. A hearing date has been set for March 6th. . . .

As a government spokesman said early this morning, "This culminated a long-time investigation, and should just about finish that particular Mafia Family. One down, four to go!"

Junior folded the paper. "I'll bet those other two old bastards, Vince an' Peppino, are jumpin' for joy. They got lucky this time . . . though I should say we all got lucky."

But luck had never been Junior's strong suit, and such a large dose of it all at once made him uneasy. He'd have much rather dealt in tangibles and events easily explained, like if the Rossellini top echelon had been murdered.

As a matter of fact, even when things seemed to be going his way, Junior Vallo had always tried to function from a pessimistic position instead of a cocky, lax-defense spot. He attributed the fact that he was still alive to that attitude.

"We should send the feds a singin' thank-you telegram," Sally The Soldier said while pouring the red wine and sodas for them.

Disregarding his brother's lightheartedness, Junior asked, "What time did Blackie say Peppino'd be here?"

"In about fifteen minutes from now. We're a little early, an' he might be havin' a hard time losin' the law."

Sally touched his glass in toast to Junior's, which remained on the table, then downed his wine in one gulp. "Peppino's gonna be pissed when he sees we got three guys here," he said, smacking his lips.

"Fuck him!" Junior barked. "Whatta we look like, shit? I mean, if you wanna get down to it, I'm as good as either him or Vincenze; we're all bosses. If those two greaseballs think I'm gonna jump every time they walk into a room, they got another think comin'."

"Yeah," Sally agreed. "They mighta opened the door, but we're the guys who did all the work. It's our guys that got whacked out, not theirs. The only thing they might be right about is not makin' everybody know we're meeting, what with John-John gettin' bombed, an' all."

"That's all bullshit! Nobody gives a flyin' fuck about John-John anymore; he's yesterday's news."

Junior slammed a palm on the table. "I want those two fuckin' greasers to treat me with the respect I deserve. After all, what're they gonna do, go tell the commission we fucked up the hit they ordered on John-John 'cause we blasted him with plastic instead of shooting him? That would be a cute one."

Junior was the first to notice two poncho-clad figures enter the room. He nudged Sally, who looked up from pouring more wine to catch sight of them.

Despite the brothers' instinctual sense of mortal danger, the scene moved so quickly that their minds never unjumbled enough to register even one coherent thought.

Knocking over their table, Junior charged for the kitchen door while Sally dropped to the floor behind the upended table and lay flat, as though he were trying to squeeze through to the basement.

Pandemonium began instantly. Fire and smoke spat from two 9mm Uzi machine guns that screamed at an ear-shattering pitch. Bullets tore up the furniture and shredded Venice. Paneling flew off the walls in big chunks.

Junior Vallo nearly reached the kitchen before 140-grain metal jackets began to rip through his body. The barrage made him seem to dance along the final couple of feet of wall to the stainless-steel door—which had been bolted from the kitchen side. Blood pouring from dozens of holes, Junior succumbed while staring in disbelief through the small shattered window into the abandoned room where his bodyguard was supposed to be.

Meanwhile, Sally The Soldier was being torn apart along with carpet and shabby furnishings. Blood gushed through his sharkskin suit like small geysers. The top of his skull was totally removed. A survivor of numerous vicious attacks along the Mekong Delta, Sally expired on the floor of the Floridia Pizzeria and Restaurant long before his assailants stopped firing.

The two assassins, dressed in Mexican ponchos and long-haired wigs, dropped their weapons to the floor, then calmly walked from the deserted establishment to a waiting car.

Within minutes, the men, who up until they'd begun firing had been

Vallo gunmen, would report to their new boss, Giacomo Jack The Wop LoPresti, who would in turn call his friend and *paisano*, Don Peppino Palermo, and inform him that his order to eliminate the Vallo brothers had been carried through.

58

February 14: Bath Beach, Brooklyn

Since there was no back entrance connected to an adjacent yard like at Buster's, Mickey Boy had to take different precautions before entering the Bath Avenue club that Don Vincenze ran his empire from.

First he parked his Lincoln near a cab stand on Bay Parkway, then took the lead taxi on line for the remaining few blocks. As the cab approached the corner where the club sat, Mickey Boy jammed an Irish walking hat down over his head, stuck on a pair of sunglasses, and lifted the wide collar of his leather jacket around his ears.

When he finally darted out of the cab and into the Sons of Siracusa social club, Mickey Boy Messina surrendered nothing of his identity to the FBI agents parked by the gas station across the street.

Coming out, though, might be a different matter. What if lawmen stopped him when he left? he'd asked Buster when given the appointment. What if they checked his ID?

Not to worry, Buster had said. All would be taken care of. Buster had better have another Rosalie up his sleeve, Mickey Boy thought as he slammed the Siracusa's door behind him.

"What a bitch," Mickey Boy complained to Freddie Falcone, who sipped caffè espresso in the club's front room while reading a folded newspaper. "If you ain't on parole, it's no big thing; you just smile for the camera an' give 'em the finger." He shucked his disguise and tossed the items, except for the glasses, on a wooden chair. "But especially with the P.O. I got, one picture coming in here sends me directly to jail—do not pass Go, do not collect two hundred dollars."

Freddie looked up over half-glasses he'd pushed almost to the tip of his nose. "Fear not, my son. If they look for anybody, after takin' your picture, it'll be Basil Rathbone." He then tossed the paper to Mickey Boy's side of the table. "Did you see what happened to Petey Ross an' his crew?"

"Just heard it on the radio," Mickey Boy replied. He stared at the photo that lay on the table. In it, Petey Ross appeared about twenty years younger and twenty pounds lighter than he did at the time of his arrest. Wondering what he himself would look like in twenty years, Mickey Boy began to read the article's text.

"The feds knew where the meeting was, when it was gonna happen, an' who was gonna be there," Freddie said while Mickey Boy continued to read. "They had the joint bugged from top to bottom. I'll tell you, you can't take a shit today without a dozen cocksuckers crawlin' over each other to rat you out."

Having spent substantial time in prison, Mickey Boy had seen first-hand the damage caused by informers; he'd seen the wrecked lives of those betrayed by former partners, friends, and even blood relatives— and he hated those informers no less than Freddie or anyone else in the streets.

But Mickey Boy had witnessed the other side of the coin too. For years he'd seen mob bosses protect stool pigeons as long as there was money to be earned with them, bosses who felt that as long as they themselves were too big to be told on, it was okay for them to look the other way when a big earner went bad. Those were the ones that Mickey Boy blamed for the deterioration of honor within their ranks. As a result, he had less sympathy for a Petey Ross than for those low-level victims who'd go to jail without ever having had an opportunity to change things. Of course, Mickey Boy kept those opinions to himself.

"You know, things are gonna get so bad with these rats," Freddie went on, "that one day, when you'll walk by guys hangin' out by a club, one'll turn to the others an' say, 'Shhhh, don't talk in front of Mickey Boy. I hear he's a stand-up guy.' "

"Didn't that happen yesterday?" Mickey Boy joked without looking up. When he'd finished reading, he shoved the paper back toward Freddie. "That crew's finished," he said. "Maybe now they'll break the rest of those guys up an' add 'em to the other four crews. Probably the best thing all around."

Why leave four? Freddie asked. Three Families would be better. Or better still, two. That idea had been kicked around for at least twenty-five years that he could remember, he said, but had never amounted to anything—too much ego spread around.

"How do you get a guy who's boss of a crew," Freddie asked, "to be less in another? He'd rather be number one over ten guys than number two or three over a hundred. Ego."

"That don't make sense."

"You don't talk sense where egos are involved," Freddie said. He went on to ask why men, sometimes sixty to eighty years old, don't run away when they've been indicted. Why don't they go on the lam to South America?

"So guys after them'll still get bail."

"Bullshit! These guys never worried about nobody but themselves.

What it is is that they'd rather do the rest of their life in the can, where guys follow 'em around and kiss their ass, than live free in South America, where nobody knows 'em. Ego."

However, if there was ever a time that a paring down of the five Families and tightening of their ranks was necessary, Freddie claimed, they were smack in the middle of it.

Mickey Boy was surprised both by Freddie's candor on that delicate mob matter and the fact that Freddie shared his own vision.

Though he disagreed with Freddie's assessment of why mob leaders never jumped bail and ran to South America, choosing to believe they were instead motivated by a sense of honor and responsibility toward others, he did believe that maintaining five Mafia Families in New York was an antiquated idea, that three would serve everyone concerned better. He'd felt that way for quite a while, but prided himself on being smart enough to keep it to himself.

What Mickey Boy did wonder was why, if two nobodies could see things so clearly, all the bigshots couldn't put their heads together and make it work. So what if a few had to make some concessions, swallow a little pride? Wasn't it better to be an Indian in a strong tribe than a chief in one that was doomed?

Freddie continued. "The way it's going, it really don't pay to be in this thing no more, especially if you're gonna hang out an' be up front all the time. No, today you gotta stay in the background to survive."

That was why he was happy to go to work in his restaurant each day, Freddie said. Less exposure; less trouble. In fact, if he hadn't been ordered to appear for dinner at the don's club that evening, he would never have come within ten blocks of the place.

"What bugs me is that once we get straightened out, they expect us to come to one of these joints an' eat with them once a week." Freddie laughed. "I think we might be better off staying nobodies."

"Oh, shit, I forgot," Mickey Boy said, reaching a hand forward to shake Freddie's. "Congratulations! I heard you were proposed too."

"Only 'cause they run out of warm bodies."

"Yeah, sure. I heard all about you, from the old days. What I don't understand is what took 'em so long."

"Always in the wrong place at the right time or the right place at the wrong time," Freddie said. "Story of my life." On the serious side, he added, after a little prodding from Mickey Boy, he'd been too young to be inducted into the Family before the books were closed in 1954, and by the time they were opened again—some twenty-five years later—he was under the oppressive thumb of his wiseguy boss, Vito The Bug.

"Between us, The Bug knew he wasn't going nowhere, an' he hated to lose the earn he had with me."

"Couldn't you go upstairs with it?"

Freddie laughed. "One thing you gotta learn in this life, my son, is that bosses stick together over captains, captains stick together over regular good fellas, and everybody sticks together over nobodies. For me to go complain, they'd only put me down as a crybaby, an' it would be dead-end-street time—Freddie who?"

Besides, Freddie said, when he'd previously been kept from mob entry he'd been busy building his restaurant and hadn't much cared what they'd done.

But years of Vito The Bug's hand always being out were enough, and this time when Vito stalled at having him made, Freddie had friends from another Family send Don Vincenze a message that if he wasn't interested in bringing the restaurateur into his clan, then they were.

"That's the rule, you know. If another crew wants to make you, either your guy has to do it himself or give you up."

"Great move," Mickey Boy said. For years he'd been enjoying Freddie's humor too much to see the real substance below the surface. Now he looked at him in a new light, admiring his political savvy and patient planning. He told Freddie, "This is not for publication, but believe me, one day The Bug'll be answering to you."

"From your mouth to God's ears."

"It'll happen. The old man likes guys who are legitimate earners but tough guys too." Mickey Boy thought of Joe Augusta, how far he'd gone with Don Vincenze, but since the name was officially taboo, he said nothing.

"If you know so much about what the old man likes, how come you don't do it?" a smirking Freddie asked.

"What?"

"Business. You just told me he likes guys who earn legit."

"I don't know. I meant to, but . . ."

"Think about it. To collect some shy money or get a new sports customer you'll run twenty-five hours a day, but to put a few hours into building a legit business, even if it's just to keep that fuckin' P.O. off your back, you won't do it. You'd rather dodge bullets with the prick than give him a real business to keep him off your back."

"It ain't that," Mickey Boy said. He'd intended going into business for himself one day, he told Freddie, but just hadn't gotten around to it yet. Besides, what did he know? Was he a bagel baker, or a hair stylist, or did he have any trade at all he could cash in on?

"Save the bullshit for your girl or your P.O.," Freddie replied, striking an exposed nerve at the mention of Laurel. "Does R. H. Macy sell shoes? Or squeeze grapefruit juice in the basement? Or demonstrate ski equipment? No. He uses his head an' hires help who know what they're doing. You're a bright guy who's selling yourself short. If you used half the brain power you use for scheming, you'd have everything it takes to move up the ladder—not that you won't go anyway, but just faster, higher, an' maybe safer.'"

Somehow, Freddie's breaking his balls about business didn't bring out the same resentment in Mickey Boy as when Laurel had. He saw clearly that the arguments were the same, and wondered why he felt the way he did. Maybe it was because he knew Freddie wasn't trying to change him. Or was he?

When Mickey Boy didn't answer, Freddie said, "Don't worry, I ain't gonna nag you, just give you something to think about. You're a kid who's got a helluva future if you could just show the old man you're stable, an' got your feet on the ground—it's called maturity."

Depression shrouded Mickey Boy. Laurel again. Had he blown it with her for nothing? Could he have tried to meet her halfway by really trying to open some kind of business? Would that have been enough?

In fact, when Mickey Boy had left prison, it had been with the intention of finding some business to build a solid foundation upon. Once outside, however, he'd wavered, unsure of himself and afraid of blowing his money because he wasn't equipped to handle a business properly.

Laurel might have helped if she hadn't been so pushy, Mickey Boy thought. Would she have ever been satisfied with him dividing his life, as Freddie'd suggested? Or would she have only tried to manipulate him away from what he'd wanted all his life? Or was that just another excuse? Can't lie to yourself. Was he the clown in Sinatra's "Send in the Clowns"? Was it really all his fault?

"Listen, it's nothing to get fucked up over; it was just a suggestion," Freddie said. "I didn't wanna see you lookin' like a kid who just found out he was adopted by Norman Bates."

"Naah, I'm fine."

"Come on. You looked like shit when you walked in, an' you look worse now. What is it?"

"I said I'm okay," Mickey Boy snapped, not intending to.

Freddie's silent stare made Mickey Boy uncomfortable. He tried looking away, then returned to see Freddie's gaze hadn't budged an iota.

"Okay," Mickey Boy said. "Just stop fuckin' staring like that." Freddie had done that to him when he was only a kid hanging around the bar. It had bugged the shit out of him then, and had since lost none of its effect.

"Then tell Uncle Fred what's on your mind . . . besides your girl."

"What—do I have a fuckin' sign on my face?" Mickey Boy barked. "You're the second one in twenty-four hours that said that. I'd better start wearing a fuckin' mask."

"Or start looking for another girl. I don't know what your problem is with her, but trust me, there's a zillion broads out there just waiting to welcome a guy like you with open arms . . . an' legs."

"Yeah, I know all about it. That's the trouble, they're all broads."

It occurred to Mickey Boy, at that moment, that if Freddie were to ask, But, what is Laurel? Isn't she a broad? he wouldn't have been able to answer. What did make her different? he wondered. She was hotter than most of the girls he called whore, prettier than some, not as nice as others. Didn't anything in life make sense?

"Don't worry," Mickey Boy finally said. "It's just something I gotta get over by myself."

Freddie grinned. "Leave it to Dr. Fred to cure you. Prescription number one is for you to come hang out by my joint for a while. I got more girls than I know what to do with—nice girls," he said, sarcastically drawing out the last two words. "Number two, I got a story that'll make you bust a gut."

"I'm a piss-poor audience lately. Why don't you save it for when I could really appreciate it."

Freddie put on a mocking frown. "Okay, reject my story if you want, but remember this, Messina, you fuck: There'll be a day when you'll beg for one of my much-in-demand stories, an' you know what I'll say?" He stuck his tongue between his lips and blew out a loud raspberry.

"Ain't it a shame for you to waste a good story on me when I'm in this kind of mood? I mean, Fred, your stories are too precious to waste on a mope."

"Mope, shmope. The way the Jews got chicken soup for a cold, Freddie's got stories to make the sick at heart well. Whattaya say, wanna hear?"

Mickey Boy smiled. To him, Freddie was indeed the best doctor, and friend, a guy could have when he was feeling down in the dumps.

"Okay, before I get pinched for mopery in the first degree, let's have your story. But if I don't laugh, don't get insulted."

"Hundred bucks says you do."

"You're on," Mickey Boy replied, sure, and now determined, that he would win.

Beaming, Freddie began. "A while back, this guy from downtown is up to his eyeballs in shylocks—he lays out more juice every week than Tropicana squeezes in a whole year. Anyway, the guy's all jammed up an' wants to go on the lam. The only problem is that he knows wherever he runs the shys are gonna find him. So what does he do?"

Mickey Boy shrugged.

"He comes up with a brilliant scheme: He's gonna make believe he croaked himself, so when he takes off nobody'll look for him. Make sense?"

Without waiting for an answer, Freddie continued. "The next day he puts his name in the obituary column of the *Post*, an' arranges to get himself laid out at Baciagalupe's Funeral Parlor . . ."

59

February 14: Sheepshead Bay, Brooklyn

The desk officer of the Sixty-second Precinct woke Susan Fernley at 8:05 A.M. He informed the groggy barmaid that a white Riviera registered in her name was blocking a driveway across the street from Lafayette High School, and that she should make arrangements to retrieve it. Since her car had not been reported stolen, he said, getting it back would be an easy task; no red tape; just go and pick it up.

But no task was an easy one with less than two hours' sleep, and Susan fumbled blindly for the pad she kept on her nightstand. She wrote down the address she was given without looking at the paper. With any luck it would be legible when she was able to open her eyes.

After two attempts to speak, the first of which came out as a squeak and the second as a raspy groan, she finally managed to tell the policeman that she'd be down as soon as she got dressed and had had a shot of caffeine. He laughed and told her to have more than one, and to send a tow truck instead.

"Lady, your car's got at least two front flats and a busted windshield. Who knows if it's even got an engine in it. With the thieves we got in this neighborhood, you're lucky they left anything at all."

Susan cursed her irresponsible boyfriend, who had borrowed her car, and who she was sure was sound asleep under some slut's blankets in the precinct where it was found.

"Some Valentine's Day present," she muttered while crawling out of bed. "That sonofabitch!"

It took two cups of black Taster's Choice for Susan to muster enough energy to grope in her bag for the business card of a new collision shop that had opened in the area, and another cup to help her dial. She had met one of the partners in the corner luncheonette just a few days before, and when he'd given her the card, she'd wondered what excuse she might use to call without appearing too easy. He was cute, and this was her chance.

This whole bullshit might just be fate, Susan thought, running a hand through her heavily lacquered red hair to try to stop the pain that each low ring on the other end of the phone brought to her head. *Fuck the car. He paid for it anyway.*

A half hour later, with one more cup of coffee and a hot-needle shower behind her, Susan began dressing.

Maybe I'll get lucky and find a new valentine today, she thought with amusement. *It'd serve the bastard right.*

By ten o'clock Susan Fernley stepped outside her front door on spike heels. The tightest-fitting Calvins she owned covered the lower half of her Playmate-of-the-Month figure, and a powder-blue silk blouse colored her enviable breasts. A lynx jacket hung casually off her shoulders. Obsession encircled her like a ten-foot aura.

Outside the collision shop, Susan's Riviera hung nose-up from a company tow truck in the middle of the street. To her delight, not one, but four attractive males were at work around the shop.

Eeny, meenie, minie, mo, she thought greedily. *Susan, you jerk. Why didn't you come here sooner?*

Joe, the owner who had given her the business card, greeted her inside the office. Smiling, and holding on to her arm, he explained that he wouldn't have time to assess the damage on the auto until later that day. With no hesitation, Susan jotted down her address and number and pressed it into his hand.

Joe accompanied Susan to the Riviera to remove three triple-X-rated video cassettes from its trunk. She had meant to return them to the rental club earlier and had forgotten. Now, especially if Joe decided to visit, they might be handy to have around the house.

Susan slid the round GM key into the lock, but couldn't turn it because of the cold. Offering to help, Joe placed his hand over hers and squeezed.

Squeeze me, squeeze me.

When the white trunk-lid snapped up, Susan not only found her pornographic tapes and spare tire, but the bullet-ridden body of her boyfriend, Ralphie The Eye Burgio—Don Vincenze's only link to the arrest of Petey Ross.

60

February 14: Bath Beach, Brooklyn

". . . Meanwhile," Freddie continued, "after all the shys went through all kinds of things, like how much they're sorry, an' how they would've helped him out of trouble if he came to them instead of killing himself, this guy's feeling pretty good. He's figuring, 'Rio, here I come!' when in walks the last guy he owes money to.

"Well, this *animale* starts carrying on how he always hated the guy in the coffin, how he never made a quarter with him, an' how, just for satisfaction, he's gonna stab the guy in the heart."

As usual, Freddie had difficulty containing his own laughter, punctuating his story with snorts and chortles, as he went on. ". . . The shylock's got the knife up in the air, ready to make this guy a shish ke-bob, when from the coffin, the supposed-to-be stiff puts his finger on his lips an' whispers, 'Shhh . . . *you* I'll pay!' "

Every profession from astronaut to zookeeper has its own inside jokes, jokes that are rarely found humorous by outsiders. Bookmakers and shylocks are no different. Bookmakers joke about a customer who, when surprised by two masked stick-up men, hands his bookie the money he owes for the week, saying, "You're paid." Shylocks repeat the one about the guy in the coffin. And though Mickey Boy had heard the story many times, Freddie's style of telling it still made him laugh.

"I'll tell you," Mickey Boy said. "With your talent for telling stories, you should be on the stage instead of in a restaurant or hangin' around a joint like this."

Freddie smiled warmly on his appreciative audience of one. He recalled the early days of his life in the Navy Yard area of lower Brooklyn, claiming that for many years he'd harbored a secret desire to be a comedian.

"I used to look at the guys who were top bananas in those days, like Phil Harris, or Red Skelton, or Durante, an' I used to say, 'Freddie, you sonofabitch, you could do anything they do, an' do it funnier.' I was some funny kid. But you know how it is." He shrugged.

"I grew up downtown, around the corner from Toddo Del's club, an' before you know it I'm hanging around there, an' doing some scores with the guys around my age, an' partying an' stuff. Toddo was my hero . . . him an' guys who I heard of all the time but never met. Guys like Vito, Tommy Ryan, Johnny Bathbeach. There were loads of them in those days, an' I wanted to be just like 'em. After all, these guys were living the high life while in my parents' house we were eatin' potatoes on a Monday night. That's no bullshit either. Every Monday was potato night: boiled potatoes mashed with gravy over them. That's it, potatoes!"

Mickey Boy sat quietly. He enjoyed hearing Freddie reveal his serious side. Even more, he liked the stories and anecdotes about the old-time wiseguys, men who for some reason he'd always felt a strange kinship with. Not the blind idol worship that most of his friends had, but an affection and understanding that struck him as weird. In fact, had their glory days not overlapped with his birth, he'd have sworn he'd been reincarnated from some top name or other. Maybe Lucky Luciano? Or Joe Adonis?

Freddie continued. "But I still wanted to make people laugh, an' thought about trying to get hooked up where I could do a few gigs, either in the Borscht Belt . . . you know, in the Catskills?"

Mickey Boy nodded.

"Or in Brooklyn; we had tons of clubs then. There was the Elegante, where Don Rickles worked as a maître d', an' the Town and Country on Flatbush Avenue, an' *tutta marrone* . . . clubs up the kazoo. Anyhow, I wanted to see how I could do in front of a real audience."

But to the mafiosi that Freddie had given his allegiance, entertainers were either homosexuals or some other form of degenerate. Even though the mafiosi had the power and connections to get him started as a comedian, he'd been ashamed to ask, afraid he'd be chased off the block. Street rules back then were too, too strict, he said. Bosses and underlings carrying out their edicts controlled every aspect of the lives of those who gravitated to them.

"My biggest fear," Freddie said, chuckling, "was that one of the dunskies—that's what we used to call wiseguys in those days—would want me to marry one of his dog-faced daughters. I'da had no choice if I wanted to stay around . . . and breathing."

"Thank God some things change."

"Maybe too many," Freddie said. "You know how today you hear stories about this good fella who uses coke or that one who's a fag—but he makes a lot of money so he's okay? Well, it wasn't like that back then. If you used any kind of drug, an' you were made?" He drew a thumb across his throat. "No second chances, even if you had the Bank of America under your belt."

Given the good and bad sides, Mickey Boy still longed for those more honorable times, sometimes wishing he could step into a time machine.

Freddie said, "In those days, do you know there was even no such thing as a connected guy with a moustache?"

"I know, a cuntlapper."

"Yes an' no. After the new guys, like Lucky an' Costello, took over from the 'moustachios'—or the 'Moustache Petes' as they called 'em— they passed the word that any guy with a moustache was either a stool pigeon or a muffdiver, but the real reason was mostly because it reminded them of the old-timers they hated."

Freddie raised a palm defensively. "Not that they didn't hate guys who *mangiare* the broccoli. Today going down on a broad is no felony, but in them days if they found out you did it, zingo, you were out— not a man, not to be trusted. Just like any girl who gave head was a *putana*, a slut. Let their wives ever try it an' they'd knock her head half off. 'Only whores do that,' they used to say. Then they'd go run after some barroom bimbo to suck them silly."

"Yeah, I know," Mickey Boy said, sadly remembering his last day with Laurel. He stopped, feeling as though he'd been punched in the chest, then went on. "I heard the same things when I was growing up. But then every other week I'd find out that some guy who called everybody else a cuntlapper was going down on some neighborhood rag who went around afterward talking about it. Me personally? I could never bring myself to do it, but I know what goes on."

"Sure, sure, you never did it," Freddie teased. "Spoken like a true wiseguy; you even said it with a straight face. Now I *know* you got a good future."

A mob future was all he had left, Mickey Boy thought. It had damn well better be a good one.

In the past, Freddie went on to say, a conversation like theirs, joking about taboo sex, would never have taken place. Certain subjects were just too sensitive.

"An' God forbid you got mad an' called a guy a lapper. You either had to be ready to bang him out, or get killed yourself. Believe me, they were dead serious about it. The big difference, though, was as tough as they were, they were still honorable men—not like today."

Freddie smiled the forlorn smile of those who had never dared to fulfill their dreams, and returned to his original subject—himself. "So in that atmosphere I just kept what I wanted to do to myself, an' was satisfied to be the life of the party. To me, it was like I had the best of everything: money from the scores I was doing, respect of the wiseguys I wanted to impress, an' all the girls in the neighborhood to get laid with 'cause I was fun to be around."

But the bug had never left him, he said, and even till that day, when having a few drinks in Catch a Rising Star or The Comic Strip, he'd get the urge to jump up on the stage. Especially with the newfound status he was about to receive, however, he resisted—image, and all that bullshit.

"You heard the old saying, 'Tough guys don't dance'? Well, wiseguys ain't supposed to be funny."

When Mickey Boy looked at Freddie, thought about his entertaining mannerisms when telling stories or jokes, he could see that he had the talent to be a top comedian. He felt himself lucky to be doing what he knew best, what he was cut out for, and, though Freddie was good, extremely good, at what he did, both in his restaurant and in mob-related activities—like a check-cashing deal he'd set up between Antigua and the Dominican Republic—he sympathized with him for having missed his real calling.

"Don't worry, pal," Mickey Boy said. "When I become king I'm gonna wave my magic wand an' change all that. It'll be a law in the streets that everybody's gotta be like Freddie Falcone an' laugh at the world . . . God knows, we cry enough."

"I'll settle for *consigliere*," Freddie said, laughing.

It wasn't long afterward that Don Vincenze and Buster entered the club. Two Calabra Family button-men followed close behind.

So the old man was still under pressure from Joe Augusta, Mickey Boy thought. He viewed the fact that neither of the don's bodyguards came in ahead of him as a security lapse, but would not bring it up to Buster. It wasn't his place. One day, he vowed, there would be nothing he would be excluded from saying because of rank.

A few steps into the club Buster turned and brusquely ordered the two button-men to posts by the door, one inside and the other out. "Turn on the TV!" he barked as he continued after Don Vincenze, who just waved solemnly to the men already in the room on his way toward the back.

"Some mood they're in," Mickey Boy said in a low voice.

"They're always like that when they're hungry," Freddie joked. "They musta smelled the food. Especially Buster. You ever eat with that guy? They shoulda named him Hoover instead of Buster—he sucks up everything in sight like a vacuum cleaner."

Mickey Boy's stifled laugh was like a cue to go onstage. "No, I swear it," Freddie said. "When that guy gets up from a table in my joint, it looks like locusts got there. I could seat another party without my busboys touching a thing. There ain't a crumb on the table or a stain in his plate."

"No, sonofabitch. Stop!" Mickey Boy whispered through a hand covering his mouth. He forced a couple of coughs. "Don't make me laugh. Not now!"

"Okay, truce. No laughing," Freddie said. He bent close to Mickey Boy. "But he does suck up a fuckin' table."

Suddenly a bulletin interrupted the soap opera that Buster had settled for after having an underling nearly strip the channel selector as he ordered him from station to station.

The room was silent except for the announcer's voice: "We interrupt this program for a special news story from Queens. We've got Milton Lewis standing by. Come in, Milton."

On the screen a large crowd stood behind police barricades that had been erected in a semi-circle around an old storefront building.

The camera panned in on Milton Lewis: "I'm standing here in front of the Floridia Pizzeria and Restaurant on Fresh Pond Road in Queens, where just a short time ago the reputed leader of one of New York's warring crime families, Alphonse 'Junior' Vallo, and his younger brother, Salvatore 'Sally The Soldier' Vallo, were machine-gunned down on this Valentine's Day, just as a group of their forerunners were in Chicago, almost sixty years ago.

"This latest round of bloody deaths threatens to escalate the months-long conflict that has claimed umpteen lives in both the Vallo and Rossellini camps. C'mon, boys, shake hands and make up . . . it can't be that bad."

Milton Lewis pressed a listening device to his ear to hear the announcer ask if the authorities could place the blame squarely on Petey Ross or if there were any other suspicions. When Lewis answered, it was with clouds of breath in front of him and teenagers mugging and waving at the TV audience from behind.

"As you well know, since last night the alleged executive board of the Rossellini Corporation is sitting on ice in their pretty orange jump suits, on the ninth floor of the Metropolitan Correctional Center, down on Park Row. So no matter what anyone might think, I guess they won't be charged with this one."

To the next question, about body count and other details of the actual crime, Lewis pointed at uniformed policemen scurrying in and out of the restaurant and detectives with badges hung off their coats milling around the front, and replied, "Now, I haven't been inside yet, but some of the cops who have told me that it looks like the final scene from the movie *Scarface* in there . . . that's the Pacino version. They also say that there's a group of young gang leaders who've vowed to fight to the death . . . and, as a matter of fact, to prove the boys mean business, in another seemingly related incident, the murdered body of one Ralphie 'The Eye' Burgio, who was a captain on the 'other' side . . . that's the guys in j-a-i-l . . . was found in the trunk of his girl-friend's car in the Sheepshead Bay section of Brooklyn this morning."

A patrolman manning the barricade in back of the reporter realized he was on camera and stiffened his expression to a grim pose.

"This is getting so confusing," Lewis said. "All I can say, folks, is if you happen to see any mobsters you might know coming your way, do yourself a favor and cross to the other side of the street. And if they live next door to you, for goodness' sake, *move!* . . . or at least stay home. This is Milton Lewis for Channel Seven *Eyewitness News*."

"Shut it!" Buster yelled.

"Whattaya make of it?" Mickey Boy whispered to Freddie.

"Sounds like a helluva epidemic of lead poisoning to me. That's all."

The club's custodian, old and craggy, cleared a large, round poker table in the back corner of the room, near the coffee bar. When Don Vincenze took a seat there, the eagle-topped copper espresso machine stared out over his shoulder and the door faced him.

First the don had a cup of coffee, then, with Buster in attendance, began interviewing each of his newly proposed Mafia members. To the table, each future button-man brought his wiseguy sponsor, most of whom congregated in the larger back room until they were sent for.

Mickey Boy remained in the front, and was third. He found the charged-up demeanor that had entered with the old man and Buster had disappeared as swiftly as Milton Lewis had faded from the screen.

"Well, Mickey my boy," Don Vincenze began after they had hugged and kissed in greeting. "I been hearing a lot of good things about you, and a few that ain't so good."

The last part of the don's opening statement disturbed Mickey Boy. He girded himself for a dressing-down over some deal he might have hidden that had been discovered by the Family brass.

Don Vincenze leaned close, intimate, speaking so softly that Mickey Boy felt as though he were about to be hypnotized.

"I especially like the faith you showed in Bastiano here, when he told you to show up today," the don said. "You didn't bitch and moan about your parole problems, even though we know you got a big one. Bastiano told you that he'd make sure you got out of here okay, and he will, of course, just like he straightened out your last beef with the P.O. But it was the way you respected his word that proved to me that you're the kind of man I want around. Then again, I been watching you for a long time, and you always looked like . . . well, sorta special to me."

The unexpected accolades from Don Vincenze made Mickey Boy's heart jump. What surprised him most was that the old man had been aware of him in more than a superficial way for some time.

". . . What I heard that disturbs me," Don Vincenze continued, "is that you're having some kinda domestic problems that are making you drink a little too much. What seems to be the trouble?"

Mickey Boy's head spun a bit more with each of Don Vincenze's statements. *How the fuck does he keep track of everybody's love life?* he wondered.

His first instinct was to deny that Laurel's departure bothered him that much, but he was sure the old man would see through any lie. Mickey Boy felt naked and transparent before the don. He looked to Buster for support, but found nothing more than an amused twinkle in the underboss's eyes.

"My girl can't get used to this life of mine," Mickey Boy finally blurted out.

"You mean our life," Don Vincenze corrected him. "Is she Italian?"

"Yeah, but a different kind. Her father's a shoe salesman an' her mother's a square too. She just can't accept that I'm not a regular working stiff, an' wants me to give up our life . . . which I wouldn't even think about doing."

"Do you still see her?"

"No. She's in Florida."

"Did you go after her?"

"No."

"Why not?"

"It wouldn't do any good."

"How do you know unless you try?"

"I can't beg. That's what chasing her would be," Mickey Boy replied, hoping the don wouldn't pry any further. The last thing he wanted to disclose was the role Chrissy Augusta's death had played in his estrangement, but felt there was nothing he could withhold from this man if grilled.

"Believe it or not, I understand and sympathize with you," Don Vincenze said. "When I was about your age, give or take a couple of years, I lost the only girl I ever loved too—same thing: because she couldn't understand our life."

The old mafioso smiled. "I see you looking at me strange and I know what you're thinking," he said. "Yes, I loved my wife until she died last year, but in a different way. She was a very good woman. But you gotta understand that in my day marriages were arranged for us."

Unwilling to become involved in a discussion of love and its accompanying pain, Mickey Boy let his mind wander, allowed it to focus and dwell on the element least associated with his own life: arranged marriages. A thing of the past that he couldn't imagine himself putting up with. It had affected his mother's life—she'd told him so just a few weeks before—and had even screwed up the life of a man as powerful of spirit and personality as the don. *It must've been a hell of a thing*, he thought, never associating the two stories.

". . . Anyway, I loved that other girl so much that it broke my heart when she left. I didn't know how to handle it at all. You know, women are strange creatures; they're so goddamn confusing."

Mickey Boy nodded, the don's words striking him as probably the truest ever spoken.

The don continued. "I took it pretty bad at first . . . Bastiano knows . . . he went through it with me, an' to tell you the truth, I never got over her."

Don Vincenze paused, looking as though the past were rematerializing before him, then went on. "But that didn't stop me from carrying out my obligations to my—I mean our—Family."

Mickey Boy felt drawn to the old, sad-faced leader as he had never been to Buster or Sam LaMonica before him. "I won't lie an' tell you that it don't hurt . . . a lot," he offered. "Like you said, it's the only girl I ever cared for. But the same way you did, I'll get over it."

Though the don smiled again, this time sadness remained in his eyes. "I'm sure you will."

Don Vincenze reached over and put his hand over Mickey Boy's. "You know, you an' me got a lot more in common than you could ever imagine." The old mob boss paused, letting his words sink in, while he looked first to Buster, who sat stony-faced, then to Mickey Boy, who was too awestruck to move a muscle.

The don continued. "Yes, you see, the name Messina is a big city where my father used to take me now an' then when I was a kid. It's north of Catania, where I grew up, along the gulf. Golfo di Catania— boy, was it beautiful there," he said with a shake of his head.

Mickey Boy could feel the eyes of everyone in the room, but didn't dare turn around to look. Though no one knew what was being said, the intimacy the don showed by leaning forward and holding on to the younger man's hand was unusual and attention-grabbing, and made Mickey Boy uncomfortable.

"My family name, though, Calabra, means that my ancestors probably came to Sicilia a few generations before from the southern part of the boot, an' before that from Calabria, further north. Even though we're Sicilian for as long as we could remember, somewhere along the line we got some Calabrese grandfather hidden away in my family." The don rapped his skull with his knuckles. "That's why I'm so goddamn thickheaded."

"But I'm not really a Messina. That's my adopted name, from my stepfather."

"I know all about it. You forget we check out your heritage a long way back. You were born a Partinico, which is also a good Sicilian name."

When Mickey Boy started to interrupt, Don Vincenze raised a silencing palm. "And I know that Partinico's your mother's maiden name, and all about your father . . . probably more than you do. Maybe one day down the line we'll talk about it."

That Don Vincenze knew his father sent Mickey Boy soaring. For the first time he had someone who had nothing to hide to question about his parentage. One way or another, he would get the don to point him in the right direction, to link him with his past. Even if it meant just standing over a small patch of earth where dusty bones lay, and reading an unfamiliar name etched in stone, at least he'd know to whom he belonged, and therefore who he himself was.

"But for now," the don went on, "all I'm trying to tell you is that you got good blood, and that you would make any father proud—if he was around. Now, keep up the good work, an' you'll be wearing the same shoes as us within a couple of weeks. I got big plans for you—very big plans."

344

When Mickey Boy brushed his cheek against Don Vincenze's to end their meeting, he had the urge to lift the don in a bear hug and plant sloppy wet kisses all over his face. The don had given him much more than a future that day, he'd promised him a past—and Mickey Boy felt more love for him than he'd ever felt for anyone besides his mother or possibly Laurel.

Before Mickey Boy left the table, Don Vincenze grabbed him by the sleeve. "Oh, an' Mickey Boy," he said. "Try an' cut down on the booze."

It was issued as an order and received the same way.

A half hour later the club's combination caretaker-cook announced that dinner was ready. Most of the room's occupants rushed to the larger rear area to take their places at two long banquet tables that were piled high with sausages in gravy, stuffed eggplant, and baked ziti.

Four men remained to finish a game of pinochle in the corner by the front window, which had been painted black for privacy.

The bodyguard that had stayed inside—fat, curly black chest hair running rampant over the top of his open shirt, a shiny twenty-dollar gold piece hanging from his neck by a thick rope chain—filled a plate from the back room, then stopped by the TV, which had been put back on in preparation for the news, on his way back to his post by the door.

Don Vincenze sat at his table, reviewing a tally sheet that had been given him by one of his top numbers bankers.

The only other person in that oblong room was Mickey Boy, who, too excited to eat, busily played a video game, trying to keep one step ahead of multicolored blobs that were attempting to devour his single yellow blob. He grinned inwardly as he played, still basking in the old man's aura—and promises.

At the sound of the door opening, Mickey Boy cast a lazy glance over his shoulder. A thick, bearded man in a tan raincoat paused in the doorway, scanning the interior. The gold badge that hung from his collar caught Mickey Boy's eye first, as it must have everyone else's, because silence instantly smothered the room.

Panicked by the thought of an arrest, Mickey Boy's eyes darted wildly from the dark glasses to the arm that hung straight down and slightly to the back of the man's thigh; a long metal barrel ran down past the bottom of his coat.

But this was no arrest; despite the changes, the face was familiar.

Oh, shit! Mickey Boy thought, judging the distance to the door too far while he pushed himself off the machine and spun around at the same time.

Though his actions were furious, and the passing seconds measurable in fractions, Mickey Boy's perception took on that of an eternity of slow motion:

After three giant steps he launched himself headfirst into the air at the same moment a simply disguised Joe Augusta raised his revolver to fire.

In one motion Don Vincenze's fat bodyguard, who stood eating in front of the television, tossed his food in the air and threw himself down to hide beside the TV stand.

Screaming "Noooo," Mickey Boy belly-landed on the don's table, collapsing it toward the surprised old man and sending coffee cups and ashtrays scattering.

Gunshots rang out.

Loud blasts.

One, two, three.

Searing pain ripped through Mickey Boy's shoulder, then leg, just as his outstretched hand reached the don's face, his momentum smashing them both to the wall.

Four.

Mickey Boy's head seemed to explode at the scalp. The floor rushed at him.

Then darkness.

By the time Buster rushed out from the rear, ahead of those cowering underneath the banquet tables or pushing each other into the bathroom, what he found was his boss's lame leg sticking out from beneath the overturned table and Mickey Boy Messina lying motionless, his blood spreading a carmine gloss over the dirty beige floor tiles.

61

February 15: Acireale, Sicily

"Piacere, Signore Vincenze . . . glad to meet you," the white-haired proprietor of the café said. *"Come sta . . .* how are you?" He wiped his palm on his wear-shiny black trousers before extending it in greeting.

Little Vinnie shook hands, wondering how the old man had known who he was. The young bodyguard assigned to the don's son seemed to read his puzzled expression, and smiled. Sicily was like that.

And when Little Vinnie and his bodyguard were seated outside against the building's cool lime-washed wall, two more grandfatherly types, brown as chestnuts and with peaceful smiles grown out of uncomplicated living, came forward to shake hands and pass along their hopes that all was well.

The don's son stood to clasp each man's hand in both of his and regally offer slight nods to accept their goodwill. *"Grazie,"* he repeated to each of them. *"Molto grazie."*

For nearly three months, since his bastard of a father had shuttled him off to the land of their ancestors, there wasn't a place that Little Vinnie stopped—a café, a gas station, a church—where people hadn't been previously informed that he was the visiting son of the great American don, Vincenze Calabra, and the houseguest of their own *padrone*, Don Genco Salso. Everyone from Don Genco's personal winemaker to the town's chief of police placed themselves personally at his disposal.

So far, no one seemed to have any idea why he was there, and hopefully no one would find out. If Don Genco knew, he said nothing, and, from the first moment they'd met, had treated Little Vinnie like the son he'd never had. The gnomish Mafia boss of Acireale and the surrounding province lavished unending attention on his American counterpart's son, flashing porcelain and gold-capped teeth at little actions the boy's father would have ignored, and praising him constantly for his manliness and good carriage.

Just past dawn each morning, Don Genco would cover his shiny pate with a worn gray flannel cap, grab a black walking stick with a hand-carved head of a dog at its top, and drag Little Vinnie for *una passeggiata* . . . a walk . . . around his wooded estate before breakfast. Two peasant bodyguards carrying *luparas*, the traditional Mafia shotguns, followed enough paces behind to be out of earshot but close enough to kill.

Don Genco was also the last person Little Vinnie saw each night, over a cup of steaming chamomile tea and anisette-flavored *biscòtti*.

"Due espresso, per favore," Little Vinnie now ordered from beneath the shade of a Cinzano umbrella. His eyes roamed from the fountain-centered piazza on his left, along the sleepy cobblestoned street before him and to the dusty road that led colorfully painted donkey carts up into the hills. Almost eleven thousand feet up, Mount Etna towered in the distance against a cloudless pale-blue sky.

The strangely intimate ways and slower pace of Sicily might take a while to get used to, but were definitely worth the effort, he thought. It was too beautiful.

I could stay like this forever, Little Vinnie mused as he had more and more often of late.

A pretty, dark-haired young girl sneaked him a demure smile as she walked by with a woman who appeared to be her mother. The girl reminded him of Chrissy. Poor Chrissy. Why did she have to choose that piece of shit Georgie The Hammer over him? If she'd only accepted the affection he'd tried so many times to give, she'd be alive now—walking, breathing, laughing.

But then he'd still be stuck back in Brooklyn, trying to please his father and never succeeding—his rotten whoremaster of a father.

The morning that he'd eavesdropped on Don Vincenze's meeting with Buster and Joe Augusta haunted Little Vinnie's memory. As it turned out, he had been haunted from the time he'd been born, but hadn't realized it until that sweltering July day.

". . . About my son." Don Vincenze's voice had carried up from the basement. "This is what we must do . . ."

Little Vinnie remembered with bitterness how ecstatic he had been to hear the brilliant future the don had charted, until, "My son . . . my son, Mickey Boy."

Once more those words echoing through his brain ignited a spark of silent rage.

"*Tu sei malato?* Are you ill?" Little Vinnie's bodyguard asked.

Little Vinnie glared at the burly young peasant who would undoubtedly sacrifice his own life to protect him, but saw only the face that had ruined his life—the face of that whore's son—the face of his brother—Mickey Boy's face. He twisted a worn linen table napkin tightly in both hands.

"Signore Vincenze?"

"*Sta bene* . . . I'm fine," Little Vinnie answered, snapping back to reality. He looked up at the worried face of the café owner. "*Ho sete* . . . I'm thirsty," he said hoarsely to the old man. "*Vorrei un po' di acqua minerale, per favore* . . . I'd like a little mineral water, please."

Within seconds a bottle of Fiucci and a clean glass stood before him. He guzzled straight from the bottle.

At that moment Little Vinnie privately answered a question that had been nagging him for weeks, possibly the most important question of his life. No, he wouldn't go back to America. Sicily was where he would stay. Away from his loveless father. Away from his bastard half brother. Away from his failure and shame.

Yes, he, Vincenze Calabra, Jr., who had missed being born on that sunny Mediterranean island by less than one generation, would remain with the shriveled old mafioso who affectionately called him *figlioli* . . . dear son, a term his own father had never used.

There was no doubt in Little Vinnie's mind that Don Genco Salso would more than welcome the opportunity to become his surrogate father, eventually sponsor him for Mafia membership, and designate him heir to his throne.

Vincent Calabra, Jr., of Brooklyn, New York, would eventually become Don Vincenze di Acireale, and if he played his cards right, Don Vincenze di Catania too, giving him absolute power over the entire province. Only then would he return to the United States, with enough strength to take his rightful place there—and destroy Mickey Boy Messina.

In the meantime it wouldn't hurt to punish Mickey Boy a bit, make him eat his gut as he himself had for more than half a year. Tonight he'd call Muffin-Face and get him to pull the pictures of Laurel from the dresser drawer, where they'd been lying when he'd been forced to leave the country, and make sure they got to Mickey Boy. Perfect.

Little Vinnie smiled from ear to ear. He'd inform Don Genco of his plans for resettlement immediately.

Turning to his confused bodyguard, he ordered, *"Mi conduca a casa, subito!* Take me home at once!"

62

February 16: East Side, Manhattan

Connie sat alongside the bulky hospital bed. The bed's side rail was pushed down to permit her easy access to Mickey Boy's clammy right hand, which she held in hers. With an alcohol-soaked cloth she swabbed the exposed portion of his forehead.

If appearances were the yardstick of condition, then Mickey Boy was critical—one leg, mummified in plaster of paris, hung in the air off traction equipment; his left arm and shoulder were wrapped in tape, with the arm secured against his body by a blue cloth sling; a band of gauze and adhesive stretched from a beanie-size sprout of black hair at the top of his head to about an inch and a half above his eyebrows.

The only damage of any consequence, however, was to Mickey Boy's leg, which had been shattered, then reconstructed during hours of surgery. His shoulder had been dislocated above where a bullet had passed cleanly through fatty tissue, and his head had required nothing more than a bunch of stitches to close a wound that had opened upon impact with the wall's ledge.

"Vincent?" Mickey Boy moaned when he opened his eyes. "Is the old man all right?" He'd asked the same question each and every time he'd wandered out of his Demerol sleep. In the drowsier stages his only words had been for Laurel.

"He's fine," Connie answered once more. "And you will be too.

Just try to rest." She bent and kissed her son's alcohol-dried skin.

"What about Joe?"

Connie had no idea to whom her son referred, nor did she care. "He's fine too," she replied.

To Connie, the past forty-eight hours seemed as if they had lasted for weeks; that first phone call eons away.

And if she lived to be a hundred, she would never forget the initial terror she'd felt when the familiar voice had informed her, *"Connie, Mickey Boy was shot; he's in Bellevue."*

Silence on the receiving end must have startled the caller. He asked in a panicked voice, "Connie, you okay?"

Connie's heartbeats threatened to suffocate her. More than thirty years of visions flashed before her in rapid succession: Mickey Boy being baptized, marching off to kindergarten, receiving confirmation— leaving for jail. Her head spun around inside and her eyes began to well with moisture.

"Connie?"

"I'm okay," Connie gasped. "How is Mickey Boy doing? Is he going to . . . ?" The words needed to complete that dreadful question refused to pass her lips.

The baritone voice of Mickey Boy's natural father cracked, then became husky. "He'll be okay, Connie . . . he'll be okay. They're almost finished operating right now."

"I'm coming right away!" she screamed. "I have to go to my baby!"

"Connie, listen, honey, there's nothing you could do for him right now. He's in Bellevue; they helicoptered him over there because they got the best doctors for microsurgery in the city."

Connie began to sob.

Alley's wife, Ellen, who had been in her daughter's bedroom when she heard Connie's cry, came running down the stairs with the child in her arms.

"Mother, what is it?"

"It's my Mickey Boy," Connie wailed. "It's my baby."

"Mother, please, is he all right?"

Connie quickly regained her composure. Ignoring Ellen, she asked into the phone, "Why does he need microsurgery?"

"It's his leg, Connie, an' he ain't gonna die from that," Vincenze Calabra said. "Just try not to go nuts. You can't be no help to him if you're falling apart yourself, can you?"

Slightly reassured, Connie thought about how Vincenze had always had the right words for her—except that once, the once that had counted.

"No, I guess you're right," she said. "But I'm still coming down to the city. Nothing's going to stop me from being with my baby."

"But it's late. Why don't you just wait till the morning?"

"No, I'm coming now."

"I figured you'd say that," Vincenze replied. "Just relax an' get dressed slow. There's a brown limo on its way to you now. Figure it'll be by your door in an hour or so. Remember," he cautioned her, "if it ain't a brown stretch with a skinny white-haired guy named Charlie, you don't go no place with nobody. Is that clear?"

"Yes," Connie answered meekly, glad to have someone take charge.

"Good. Now, get yourself together an' make yourself real pretty so that you don't scare your son . . ." Vincenze hesitated for a second, then corrected himself. ". . . our son, when he wakes up. The kid's been through enough," he teased.

An affectionate grin crossed Connie's lips. She said, "All right," then wiped her soggy eyes with the palm of her hand.

"And, Vince . . . thanks."

"Don't thank me, Connie. Mickey Boy got shot saving my life," he said, and hung up.

Connie stood with the phone in her hand long after the line had been disconnected.

Though the Fleetwood limousine arrived nearly a half hour earlier than expected, Connie was ready to go, pacing furiously in the front vestibule of Alley's home.

The man, Charlie, whom Vincenze had told her about over the phone, rode in the back with her. His was a new face, warm smile and watery blue eyes, that must have slipped into her ex-lover's circle after 1956, at which time Connie had known most of his friends.

Charlie's best point as far as Connie was concerned was that when she responded to his first attempts at friendliness with abrupt replies, he took the hint and remained silent for the balance of their journey.

When Connie reached the floor where Mickey Boy's room was, she found Vincenze Calabra seated on a wooden bench. Alongside him sat Buster, who she'd known when she'd dated Vince. Another man, a giant who she didn't know but who she could visualize eating raw meat and nails for breakfast, leaned against the wall—massive arms folded; jaw set; eyes alert.

Vincenze struggled to his feet as Connie approached.

Up close, the sight of him made Connie gasp. Outside of a swollen eye filled with blood, all his face color looked drained. His one good eye appeared glassy with pain and his features were downturned and especially jowly. Normally a neat dresser, Vincenze's brown suit was rumpled and splattered with dark stains; red spots soiled his open-collared white shirt. He looked at least ten years older than he had when she'd bumped into him at Numero Uno just two months before.

He stepped toward her.

"Connie, I been here all the—"

"Bastard," she hissed while rushing past him into the room.

Despite knowing her son had been badly hurt, actually seeing him swathed in bandages sapped the strength from Connie's legs. Just as they began to buckle and the room began to spin, strong hands caught her by the arms. Cradled across her back and under her knees, she was lifted and carried to the bench in the hall. Someone slapped a cold wet washcloth on her head, startling her back to full consciousness.

Once revived, Connie began a tirade against Vincenze. She reached deep inside herself to spit up weapons that would wound: he'd ruined her life, sold her out, never loved anyone but himself; he'd destroyed Mickey Boy, manipulated him into the life of crime which had landed him in jail, and now he'd nearly had him killed. When would he be satisfied, when she and her son were both dead? Why didn't he go away and leave them alone? Why didn't he just die?

Doing nothing more than waving everyone else in the corridor away, Vincenze silently endured Connie's outburst until she exhausted herself and collapsed into tears.

The arms of consolation Vincenze Calabra wrapped around Connie were like a time machine, hurling her back to another time when she'd cried in his arms. He was her Mudslinger once again—only this time he wouldn't let her down; this time he'd see their problem through.

Connie refused to let Vincenze release her until her sobs had reduced themselves to spasmodic whimpers.

A short time later, after the night-duty doctor had assured Connie that her son was out of any danger and would remain too sedated to recognize her until the following day, she allowed Vincenze to take her for something to eat. The last meal she'd consumed had been a brunch of cottage cheese and canned grapefruit sections, more than half a day earlier.

Over poached eggs and coffee Vincenze explained that the shooting was the irrational act of a man who'd gone to pieces over a personal tragedy; he'd lost a teenage daughter to an accident by one of the club members.

Why had the despondent father chosen him to try to kill?

"Well, I guess 'cause I'm the boss. When anything goes wrong, he's the guy who always gets the blame."

"It still doesn't make any sense. If you didn't have anything to do with it . . . ?"

"How could you figure out why a guy who went nuts does anything?" he asked. "You'd have to be cuckoo yourself to understand."

"What if he comes back again?"

"Don't worry yourself over that."

Vincenze wiped a chunk of English muffin through Connie's plate to mop up some leftover yolk.

"Now that I know what's on his mind, I'll take care of it. Like I said, there was no reason for him to take a crack at us."

"You."

Suddenly all his talk about how scared he'd been when he'd discovered Mickey Boy had been hurt, how he'd insisted on riding with him in the ambulance and helicopter, and how he'd refused to leave him at the hospital meant nothing. With one razor-precise word, Connie had slashed a bottom line to the entire incident.

Vincenze Calabra winced in obvious pain, as he had all evening; his bloodshot eye was blackened underneath and swollen practically shut.

Without bending his head he stared down at his plate for a time, then, raising his one good eye to stare at Connie, whispered, "Yes, me."

Now, even as she ministered to her son, waiting for him to regain consciousness after almost two days, battles that had raged within Connie during that time continued: Connie versus Mudslinger and Connie versus Connie.

During her more comforting moments, such as watching the lights of the nearby Water Club—where she'd agreed to have dinner with Vincenze the night before—sparkle like sequins on the East River's cloak of tiny waves, or just having him there to ease her burden, Connie wondered how different life might have been had she gone along with his offer in 1956 to be his mistress.

Of course, he would have bought the house he'd promised in the suburbs, and would have spent no less time there than most husbands who regularly commute to full-time jobs. Life would have been pleasantly punctuated by filet mignons at restaurants like the Water Club or champagne at nightclubs in Atlantic City hotels.

And maybe Mickey Boy, growing up away from the city, with its street toughs and mob idolizers, would have followed a more acceptable path, possibly gone to college; he certainly had the ability.

She could have made domestic life so attractive for her son and Mudslinger that Vince might have eventually left his wife for her, given her what she'd wanted all along.

But each time Connie forced herself back, she made herself examine the more probable side of the coin. Aside from the few sessions of satisfying sex that would have replaced her continued bathtub sessions with cheap novels, most of her time would have been spent alone. Some of Vincenze's weekdays would have been spent in the city on mob business; Saturday nights, Sundays, and holidays with his wife and other kids.

Connie would have had to settle for the traditional "girlfriend" Friday nights out, maybe two other evenings relaxing with him at home and an occasional sneakaway vacation to Miami or Las Vegas. She would have never been able to accompany him to a wedding, christening, or funeral.

And Mickey Boy? The odds were greater that he would have turned out worse under the direct influence of his mobster father, though Connie tried not to imagine what worse could be. God knows, working against Vincenze's charm, power, and money, she might have had no balancing effect on Mickey Boy at all.

Worse than that, there would have been no Alley, no architect son to show it wasn't all her fault. Instead, she might have given birth to a slew of little gangsters that she would have to visit in prison or mourn for at wakes.

No, she decided, she'd made the right decision in 1956.

Or had she?

Sensing a presence in the room, Connie turned to see Vincenze standing in the doorway. On his neck was the white brace he'd been fitted for the previous day to correct an injury he'd sustained during the shooting; dark glasses covered his damaged eye.

As usual, Buster and the giant, who'd been introduced to her as Eddie DaDa, stood behind their boss.

When Connie turned around, Don Vincenze had been standing silently for some time, watching her while she bent over their son, mopping his brow and dry lips with a wet cloth. Hers was the loving attention he remembered and had longed for most of his adult life.

At that moment the old mafioso felt the full weight of personal burden his underworld obligations had placed on him. The same emptiness overcame him that he had agonized over during the months after Connie had left, more than thirty years before.

Only he knew how he'd suffered. He and Buster, of course. Buster, who had nursed him through drunken binges that had gone on for days at a time; Buster, who'd handled all the details of his covert participation in Connie's and Mickey Boy's lives throughout the years that followed the split; Buster, who had temporarily sacrificed his position as captain and rightful underboss in order to nurture and "propose" Mickey Boy, who under mob rules could not be directly under anyone higher than a common soldier until he was formally inducted into their "thing."

No, Connie would never know or appreciate how much he and his loyal friend Buster had gone through in her and Mickey Boy's behalf.

If only, Don Vincenze thought, he'd been able to handle his personal affairs with the clarity and foresight that he did his Family's. Maybe then he would have pursued and recaptured her, spent a lifetime together with her and their son.

But, then again, maybe he would have frightened her away, lost her and their son for all time? Who knew? Fuckin' broads.

When Mickey Boy stirred, Connie held a fluted paper cup of water to his lips. He sipped with his eyes closed, then fell off to sleep again. Connie turned back to the don and shrugged.

Don Vincenze crooked a finger at Connie, motioning her outside the room.

"How's he doing?" he asked.

Connie absentmindedly brushed back wisps of mostly black hair that dangled near her eye.

"Better," she said. "Once he gets through the hangover he's amazingly alert. I think it's the pain. He refuses to let them give him shots on time; pushes them off until it's too much for him to bear. Says he doesn't want to become a junkie."

She shook her head in noncomprehension. "Ridiculous, but you know how stubborn he can be."

"Takes after his mother."

That brought a tired smile to Connie's face. Weariness seemed to bring out the best in her, added a vulnerability Don Vincenze could remember from her youth. God, he still loved her.

"I ordered us some scungilli and calamari from Vincent's Clam Bar," he said. "Charlie went an' get it."

"Thank you, but you don't have to fuss. A hamburger—"

"And fried shrimps."

Connie touched his arm. "You're still crazy, but thanks."

"And mussels," he said, covering her hand with his. Since his head was immobile in the brace and his eyes were shaded in black, he gestured toward Mickey Boy's room with his shoulder, which sent a fiery sting up to his brain.

"Maybe he'll be able to taste some?" he asked.

"Oh, I don't know. The doctors . . . ?"

"The hell with them. Whatta they know about what heals a Sicilian? Besides, if they okayed him for visitors today, he should be okay for scungilli."

What Don Vincenze didn't mention was that for the nearly fifteen thousand dollars he'd spread around to the staff as "tips" and "gifts" to have him and his men take up residence there and be treated as though they were invisible, he could have brought in a chorus of naked dancing girls and never have raised so much as an eyebrow.

". . . And, I bought enough for everybody up here," he added with a wink.

"Never lost your charm, I see," Connie smilingly said, her hand still wedged between his palm and forearm. "Or your instinct for bribery."

Buster and Eddie DaDa both laughed, filling Don Vincenze with a sense of déjà vu—a young man in the mid-1950s, relaxing and joking with his favorite girl and his friends.

"C'mon," Don Vincenze said, taking Connie by the hand. "Let's sit in the lounge for a while, till Charlie brings the food. Mickey Boy won't be up yet, anyway."

When Connie hesitated, the don added, "Don't worry, I'll leave Bastiano in the room in case Mickey Boy wakes all the way up. He'll call us."

Walking down the hallway toward the lounge, Connie said, "Vince, I appreciate your being here every waking minute, but it really isn't necessary. You must have business to take care of. . . ."

Because of the neck brace, Don Vincenze had to stop fully to turn and face Connie. He lifted her hand to his lips and briefly kissed it.

Smiling, he said, "This is my business."

. . . You put your lips close to mine and I kissed them, and you didn't mind it at all . . .

Little by little the music slowed, and with it the dancing couple began to fade, him in a tuxedo, her in a sunny yellow gown.

Frank Sinatra's words slurred deeper and deeper in resonance: *When I'm awake such a break never happens . . .*

Yellow paling to near white; the voice, lower and lower: *. . . How long can a guy go on dreaming?*

Mickey Boy opened his eyes. He'd been awake for some time, but then again he hadn't, off instead in a netherworld of fanciful thoughts, daydreams that transported him away from physical pain and painful realities.

As usual, Pagliacci winked from the ceiling, surface imperfections that Mickey Boy had discovered resembled a clown's face. Though he had never seen the opera, he knew the jester's name from the late Sam LaMonica and felt it sounded better for his ceiling companion than Bozo or Clarabelle.

"Mickey honey?" He heard his mother's voice. She dabbed his forehead with a wet cloth. "You have some visitors."

When he let his head roll to the right, Mickey Boy saw Don Vincenze standing behind his mother, one hand on her shoulder, a neck brace pushing the fat on his face up to make him look like an old Shar Pei with sunglasses.

The don stepped by Connie and bent over the bed to kiss Mickey

Boy. Since he couldn't bend his head, however, and Mickey Boy could barely lift his, the greeting landed up near Mickey Boy's eye.

"What shape we're in," Don Vincenze said, laughing. "Two broken-down valises."

The don and Connie stepped back to let Buster, Eddie DaDa, and Charlie Bones take turns kissing Mickey Boy, then returned to the side of the bed.

"Your eyes okay?" Mickey Boy asked Don Vincenze.

"Walked into a doorknob, that's all."

As the last of the cobwebs cleared, Mickey Boy was struck by the incongruity of seeing his mother and the don together.

"I guess you remembered my best girl?" he said. "Ain't she beautiful?"

Taking Connie's hand in his, Don Vincenze replied, "How could I ever forget her?" He then added, "And, yes, she is very beautiful."

Mickey Boy smiled. The completeness of having the most important man in his future standing alongside the most important woman in his life felt good. Low-key, comforting good. Satisfying good. Bittersweet good, when he thought of the piece still missing from the picture—Laurel.

Closing his eyes, Mickey Boy forced his head back onto the pillow as if it could disappear into the fluffiness. He concentrated on the throbbing behind his eye sockets, taking pleasure and pitying himself at the same time.

"You okay?" the don asked. "If not, I could see you a little later on."

"No, don't go," Mickey Boy said; he couldn't insult the old man. "I was just resting my eyes."

No sooner had the words left Mickey Boy's mouth than everyone moved about, shutting the lights, curtains, and the door so that the room was almost dark enough to develop film in.

"No, it wasn't the light," Mickey Boy said, enjoying the sight of everyone scrambling to flick on the lamps and reopen the drapes and door. Feeling important rivaled feeling just plain good any day.

"Now, if you're feeling up to it, an' if your lovely mom don't mind, I'd just like a few minutes to talk to you alone. Not that we ain't gonna miss her," Don Vincenze told Mickey Boy while looking at Connie. "But she won't be far away; we ain't gonna let her disappear that easy."

Still staring at Connie, the don asked, "You don't mind, dear, do you?"

Connie withdrew her hand from his as if it had been seared. For a time she didn't answer, but just looked over at her son.

Finally, she said huffily, "I want to call Boston anyway. My other son is in Europe on business and is waiting to hear from his wife about

Mickey Boy's condition. I'll call her from the visitors' lounge." She touched her fingertips to Mickey Boy's cheek. "I'll be there when you're finished."

As soon as Connie had left, with Eddie DaDa and Charlie Bones following, Don Vincenze pulled a chair to Mickey Boy's bedside. Buster was the only one to remain in the room with them; he shoved a chair over by the door and sat down.

"I didn't wanna ask in front of your mom, but how are you really feeling today?" the don asked.

"Like the Twin Towers fell on me."

Don Vincenze laughed, then replied, "Good. For a while there I was worried you were in bad shape. You know it takes more than falling buildings—or bullets—to stop guys like us."

To Mickey Boy there was no greater compliment than to be lumped together in the same category as the don, by the don, and he told him so.

Don Vincenze brushed away Mickey Boy's sentimentality with a wave of his hand. "Hungry?" he asked. "We saved you some scungilli an' calamari from lunch. Buster could throw it in the microwave the nurses use."

Sending food down to his stomach to stop the burning was tempting. Couldn't waste the moment, though, and eat when the old man obviously wanted to talk.

"Maybe later," Mickey Boy said.

Before he went on, however, Don Vincenze gave Mickey Boy a couple of large white pills to swallow. He said he'd been told of Mickey Boy's fear of drug addiction and felt exactly the same way. The pills he'd given him were non-narcotic pain relievers he'd had a doctor friend of his provide.

Cautioning him not to let the nurses find them, the don slipped a vial of the pills into Mickey Boy's sling, then said, "What I really want to tell you is that I won't ever forget what you did. You know, all of us are sworn to throw ourselves in front of a bullet for the guy above us, but between you an' me, there ain't too many of our own kind who would really do it. I woulda done it when I was young, an' it looks like you're cut from the same piece of cloth."

Don Vincenze's fingers dug into Mickey Boy's arm. "You, like me, got the blood of our fathers—the heart that made us survive in Sicily for centuries an' kept us on top here in America," he said. "That's a blessing, Mick, but today also, the way the world is, it could be a curse."

If, as Don Vincenze said, his balls and spirit had been inherited, then it had to come through his father, Mickey Boy thought. On the Partinico side there were no wiseguys, just bricklayers and long-shoremen.

Mickey Boy hung on each syllable the don uttered, searching for some message about his heritage that might be cloaked in the obliquely worded manner so common to the underworld.

But nothing. Just straightforward lamenting about the rapid decline of their way of life. Omitting the modern Mafia's own contributions—allowing themselves to be motivated by greed instead of honor, swelling their ranks with unproven or worthless members (in many cases their own sons and nephews), refusing to keep pace with the changing morals and technology of the last decades, settling problems among themselves with violence (which resulted in incidents like the one that had landed Mickey Boy in the hospital)—Don Vincenze complained about a government that was persecuting them with the support of a public that had permitted itself to be brainwashed.

Once he realized no new information would be forthcoming about his father, Mickey Boy listened half attentively while the don droned on about the government's attempts to drive mob guys out of the gambling business so that the states themselves could monopolize it; about the average sucker's acceptance of that Communist-style takeover because he realized that in today's America he was going nowhere fast and resented anyone who had more than he did; about how their people were being driven from the streets, where they had exercised some kind of civilized control, leaving those territories open to Jamaicans and Latins, who massacred whole families—". . . Women, children, everybody."

On and off Mickey Boy drifted into his own thoughts of Laurel, then back out to pick up sections of the don's speech, which reminded him of a more detailed version of the one Buster had made on Christmas Eve.

Yes, he realized what all the problems were without all the lectures; he'd spent his entire adult life in the streets and had seen the changes firsthand. But why the hell bother him now, of all times? What could he do about it anyway?

Suddenly it occurred to Mickey Boy that all the discouraging talk about what their life had become might be a prelude, a roundabout way of preparing him for the fact that he was out. Was that their way of rewarding him for nearly getting killed, early retirement?

"Now, why am I telling you all this?"

Dry as it had felt before, now Mickey Boy's mouth felt cement-coated. Defeat insulted his nostrils along with the smell of his own bad breath.

He didn't answer.

"Because there's a lot of things to be fixed an' I'm depending on you to help fix 'em."

Sure, from a pool-cleaning job in Miami. At least there he'd have Laurel. Probably a big pot belly and whiskey habit too.

"I see that going legit is the way of the future, an' that you're the guy to make that future happen. You're the spark of life that's gonna make my vision come true."

Now Mickey Boy was sure he was being put out to pasture. He girded himself for the decision, scrambling inside his brain for the protest he would mount: He'd been loyal, he'd absorbed the hard knocks; if they had problems, he'd earned the right to help solve them from the inside, not out.

Leaning closer, Don Vincenze said, "Next week we're gonna make the guys we promised. Naturally, you won't be able to be there. . . ."

Shit, here it comes. The pain in Mickey Boy's leg that had been masked by medication jackhammered up to his hip.

"So what we're gonna do is straighten you out right up here, in this room."

Every muscle in Mickey Boy's body collapsed. If any pain had been surging back into his leg, it was now ebbing away and too minimal to notice.

"Right after that I'm making you a skipper."

Mickey Boy nearly jumped off the bed; Don Vincenze had to press him back against his pillow.

Buster hurried over, and seeing he wasn't needed, wandered back to guard the door.

"Don't be too excited just yet. You got an awful lot to learn, an' not that much time to learn it in. I told you, it might wind up being a curse."

Curse or not, as far as Mickey Boy was concerned it was all his, had been destined for him. Fuck being an *avvocato* in some poor Italian ghetto or a pool cleaner in Miami.

What Mickey Boy needed at that moment were tranquilizers instead of the pain-killers that filled his system. His heart raced and his head swam.

Fighting with his own mind, he shoved thoughts of Laurel into the background and paid close attention to each word the don said.

There were men across the entire country, Don Vincenze went on, that he wanted Mickey Boy to meet. Some were "men of respect" like themselves, others businessmen with whom the Calabra Family had sizable investments. Mickey Boy's duties would be to make use of these people, and gradually switch their Family's enterprises over from gambling, loansharking, and other illegal businesses to legitimate ones.

"The key is that to keep all that legit stuff, we gotta keep our crew strong in the streets—leave the dirty stuff to the other *borgatas*, but still strike the fear of God in them so they don't think we became hooples an' get any ideas about moving in on us."

So far, everything the don had said made sense to Mickey Boy. And at least the mob stuff looked easy. As far as the business end went, he was sure the don had someone else capable of handling that better than he could.

"The trouble is," Don Vincenze continued, "business guys make lousy street bosses. They ain't got the strength to keep the hoodlums underneath 'em in line. Before you know it, their own men wind up eating them up."

Don Vincenze removed his dark glasses and pressed close enough for Mickey Boy to smell his Macanudo breath. His devil's-red eye shone above his squashed smile as he said, "You could be both."

"Me? No, I ain't got—"

"Yes, definitely you. The hoodlums we gotta keep to make sure our businesses stay on top will listen to you 'cause they know where you been, that you earned your position the hard way."

"But I don't know that much about business. I ain't been to college, I—"

"Fuck college," Don Vincenze said, squeezing Mickey Boy's arm hard enough to hurt. "You been through our college, which is more important. There is no substitute for the learning you experienced through living our life and suffering its worst. Thousands go to college, but very few ever learn what you did, and what you will."

Though excited by the idea of moving into the top echelon of the Calabra Family, and thereby the top echelon in the country, Mickey Boy felt it a matter of duty to remind the don that as much life experience as he, Mickey Boy, had had, there would still be decisions to be made that would require more formal learning than he'd had. There had to be someone better qualified to lead their Family in a business capacity.

"Don't sell yourself short," Don Vincenze replied. "Remember how I said you got the blood of our fathers? The heart? Well, the way you made the decision to throw yourself in front of a bullet, not to save me but to save our way of life, that's the way you'll make the tough decisions in business. Trust me, when the time comes, you'll do the right thing."

"You got more faith in me than I got in myself."

"That alone should teach you something."

"But how would I learn all—"

"Don't worry about that now. When the time comes, you'll hire pros; there's plenty of them around to be bought. But you'll be around to take care of their problems. Nobody will dare rob any of our accounts or try to bury us with bad paper, or pull any of the other shit that so-called legitimate businessmen pull. One way or another, you'll make sure we survive."

For the first time in as long as he could remember, Mickey Boy felt frightened. Yes, he'd seen the handwriting on the wall just as the don had. Little by little to be sure, but he'd absorbed the changing future through his conversations with Buster, Freddie Falcone—and, yes, even Laurel. He just wasn't convinced he possessed the capabilities to lead that kind of major change in their Family's direction.

And what if their next boss didn't share his and Don Vincenze's vision? A new boss with his own ideas might easily decide to sweep house, eliminating anyone closely associated with Don Vincenze's policies. Would he have to spearhead a bloodbath within their Family just to survive?

Above all the contradictions was a thunderous roaring in Mickey Boy's chest that he hoped the don couldn't hear.

"Do all this for me—for us; all of us," Don Vincenze went on. Then, as if he had read Mickey Boy's troubled mind, he said, "Make my vision come true, and when I die, Buster will move to become boss and you will be his underboss. When he dies, you'll take over, number one. You'll be Don Migito."

First Don Vincenze bent and solemnly kissed Mickey Boy on the lips, then Buster followed.

Tears filled Mickey Boy's eyes. After nearly twenty years of being driven by a force too deeply internal for him to comprehend, he now stood at the threshold of accomplishments far greater than he'd ever realistically imagined.

"I don't know what to say," he murmured.

"There's nothing to say. Just get better an' get ready to take on a whole lot of new obligations."

"I'll never let you down."

"I know that better than you. If I didn't, I would never put you where I'm putting you. Don't worry, you'll be just fine," he said, chuckling. "Especially now that I know what a nice mother you came from, I'm sure of it. Your father was a lucky man," Don Vincenze added. His lips pursed reflectively.

Buster looked away.

"I never knew my old man; he died when I was a baby," Mickey Boy replied. "I don't know how lucky or unlucky he was, but me an' my mom ain't been too lucky in that department—my stepfather croaked, too, when I was thirteen."

"I know all about it," Don Vincenze said. "But your luck is changing. You got two fathers now—me an' Bastiano."

"That's better than anyone could ask for, an' I really am grateful, but there's something I gotta—"

"*Aspetto.*" The don silenced Mickey Boy with a raised palm. "I know what you want, and you have my sacred word that when the time is right, I will tell you what you want to know . . . about your father."

"But, when is—"

"No more," Don Vincenze said, cutting Mickey Boy off again. "I will not forget my promise, and you will not mention it again. Just trust me, it will be soon."

"You don't know how good that makes me feel."

Don Vincenze stared at Mickey Boy for a moment silently with the most somber look on his face that Mickey Boy had seen all night.

Was he going to break down and tell him something about his father? Mickey Boy wondered, afraid to ask.

When Don Vincenze finally did speak, however, the subject was changed. "The only bad news I got for you tonight is that the doctors say you're gonna probably wind up a little lame—like me."

Deflated, but still aware of his blessings, Mickey Boy said, "Any way I could be like you is okay with me. Even if it means limping around a little."

When the don kissed him again, Mickey Boy felt a bit of moisture rub off the old man's cheek onto his.

"Just one thing," Mickey Boy asked, remembering the only sore spot in his life besides Laurel. "What about your son, Little Vinnie? Ain't he—"

Don Vincenze raised a hand to stop Mickey Boy's question. "I might be a father, but I'm a boss first. My first obligation is to my men, men whose lives an' families' lives depend on me. Little Vinnie's my son, but he ain't got what it takes to be a boss. You do. Because of who his father is, Little Vinnie will be made to protect him for once I'm gone, but he will eventually answer to you—and you will treat him as though he was your own brother. Do I have your word?"

Mickey Boy winced inside, hesitated, then reluctantly agreed.

"I know my son has done you a major injustice in your life," Don Vincenze said, shocking Mickey Boy again. "But I want you to know that by the time I found out about it, it was too late to change things. In spite of that, you must swear to what I asked."

If the don knew that Little Vinnie had set him up to go to jail, Mickey Boy wondered, had he really learned too late? Or had he just covered up like most other wiseguys would have, to save his own son, his own flesh and blood, at the expense of a stranger? Did he also know that Little Vinnie had tried to kill him?

To the last question Mickey Boy answered himself no. That was an issue he'd have to straighten out with Little Vinnie himself.

As for the questions surrounding his having been set up to go to prison, that was past, a dead issue. There was no point in letting his anger get the best of him now. He couldn't retrieve those lost years no matter what he did. Deciding that forward was the only way to go, he thrashed the questions from his mind and replied, "I swear."

The balance of their time was spent on small talk, plans, and a fleeting discussion of Joe Augusta—the poor man was sick in the head,

Don Vincenze said, but was no responsibility of Mickey Boy's; Joe would be taken care of soon.

By dinner time Connie had looked in twice and both times had been asked by Don Vincenze for some more time alone with Mickey Boy. Each time had obviously burned her up.

The nurse had also been sent away with a plate of gray meat, mashed potatoes, and canned beets—and Mickey Boy's shot of Demerol.

Though the pills Don Vincenze had brought were less effective than the injection for pain, they did the job well enough to at least allow Mickey Boy to remain awake and coherent; everything that was happening was too good to be missed. If only Laurel were there to share his joy . . . but then, his joy would probably only piss her off.

In the early evening, with Connie back in the room, they heard a commotion in the hall. Buster left to see what the disturbance was all about while Don Vincenze and Connie remained seated by Mickey Boy's side.

Not a minute later Buster returned to announce that Mickey Boy's parole officer was outside and wanted to come in, but that Eddie DaDa and Charlie Bones wouldn't admit him without approval.

"Sorry, honey, but just go out for a few minutes more," Don Vincenze said.

This time Connie didn't seem to mind leaving. She went out quickly and without protest.

Mickey Boy was surprised by the don's presumption of familiarity with his mother, but quickly forgot it to worry about Spositoro.

After cursing himself inwardly for not having bribed the hospital staff to keep Mickey Boy off limits to visitors, or at very least to announce anyone who showed up from downstairs, Don Vincenze told Buster to have Eddie and Charlie let Spositoro enter. Talking slightly above a whisper, he said, "Just make sure you tell him first that the kid's in bad shape an' that he can't stay long. Talk nice to him."

The don turned to Mickey Boy. "You just make like you're real groggy an' don't understand him."

Using a dimmer switch, Don Vincenze lowered the light to a coziness more suited to a cocktail lounge than a hospital room, then shuffled over to the window, where he stood looking out, his back to the room. He edged close to the right-hand panel of the open drapery, hoping he'd go unnoticed by the parole officer.

"Well, Michael," Spositoro declared upon entering. "You really got yourself into a hell of a mess this time."

Reflected in the glass, Don Vincenze could see Spositoro standing in the cone of yellow light that spilled in through the doorway.

Cocksucker couldn't wait, the don thought.

As the parole officer slithered into the darkness, Buster took his place between the doorjambs, his wide, folded arms and barrel chest nearly eclipsing the hallway's beam.

"You must be a bigger shot than I thought, rating goons around you," Spositoro said.

Don Vincenze could feel the parole officer's eyes manhandling his back.

Mickey Boy groaned, then made a feeble attempt to speak. "Uncles," he mumbled.

"You might as well tell me that you're Santa Claus and these are your elves."

"Mother's side."

Though Mickey Boy's voice sounded faint, it also sounded ridiculously phony to Don Vincenze. He snapped the stem of a yellow carnation that jutted asymmetrically from a get-well arrangement on the sill.

"At this point, who they are is unimportant," Spositoro replied. "The reason I stopped by is to let you know that I'm going to do you a big favor and not drop a paper on you while you're here—even though there's a lovely prison ward right in this building. You've suffered enough for the moment, but when you leave here, it will be with United States marshals, my friend."

"Didn't do nothing," Mickey Boy groaned. "Just got hurt."

"You did more than enough just being in that club where you were shot. None of your lying guinea girlfriends are going to be able to get you off the hook this time."

That getting old was a bitch went through Don Vincenze's mind. Twenty years ago the first thing he would have done after the shooting was transfer the victim to another spot before calling an ambulance; took the heat off the joint. But when he'd seen Mickey Boy—his son—lying unconscious in a mess of blood, he'd panicked, not outwardly, but inside. He'd just been too goddamn scared to move him, too afraid he'd die. As a result, even though he'd spread around enough money in the precinct to have the incident written up as a robbery attempt by an unknown gunman, which would quickly be filed as "unsolved" and forgotten, the report had named Mickey Boy as the victim and had left him vulnerable to a parole problem.

Spositoro continued to berate Mickey Boy, saying, "You'll just have to kiss your mafioso friends good-bye for the next few years."

As a young man Don Vincenze would not have been able to control himself with someone like Spositoro, and he didn't expect Mickey Boy to do so for long either. In fact, he sensed the crack in Mickey Boy's demeanor a millisecond before it came.

In a clear, lucid voice Mickey Boy said, "Listen, I'm hurtin' too much now to give a fuck what you do."

"You will when you have to finish up those three to four years you owe."

"No years," Mickey Boy replied. "Consorting's a technical violation an' only carries nine months. Check the Rastelli and Cataldo cases. I could read too, you know."

"Oh, yeah? Well, read this, you smartass punk: By the time I get through playing with you the way you played with me, you'll do it all—every single day."

"Excuse me," Don Vincenze interrupted politely while turning. He began to limp toward Spositoro.

"Wow, we are in the big time," Spositoro exclaimed.

"Could I talk to you outside for a minute?"

"There's really nothing I have to say to you except that your presence makes it a lot easier to keep Mafioso Junior here behind bars, where he belongs."

Buster didn't wait for a signal from Don Vincenze to summon their other two men. He and Eddie DaDa positioned themselves on either side of Spositoro, leaving Charlie Bones to guard the door.

"Your goons don't frighten me," Spositoro said. "I am the government of the United States."

Despite the parole officer's brashness, Don Vincenze could sense a weakness in him, almost as though it had a smell to it, his bravado the odor of cheap perfume to cover up the stink of fear.

Standing directly in front of him, the don studied Spositoro's face for an instant, caught the telltale roadmap of alcoholism around his nose, then, without saying a word, spat straight in his face.

Spositoro's first reaction was just to jerk his head back as if he'd been punched; his eyes widened in disbelief. An instant later his right hand shot underneath his jacket toward his waistband.

Buster and Eddie DaDa moved faster, however, grabbing both his arms and violently twisting them up behind him.

"Are you crazy?!" he screamed, his face twisted in agony. "I'm a federal officer!"

The only response he received was more pressure on his twisted limbs.

"Aargh!"

Don Vincenze registered, with pleasure, the shock on Spositoro's face, the incomprehension of anyone having the audacity to insult him that way.

But the don understood the power of intimidation by quiet insult; no yelling; no screaming. Breaking the parole officer's arms would never have the same effect as spitting in his face. Let his coward's heart deal with what a man confident enough to let him walk away after the insult could have done to him if he'd wanted.

Wielding humiliation as a weapon, Don Vincenze spoke in a quiet, measured tone. "Listen, you piece of shit, I don't care if you're Jesus Christ. You can't come in here an' insult men who could chew you up an' spit you out. That kid in the bed is more of a man than you could be if you lived twice. Now, you do what the fuck you gotta do for your job, but you treat him with respect. Understand?"

When Spositoro refused to answer, Buster and Eddie yanked on his arms once again, nearly ripping them from their sockets.

"Y-yes," Spositoro begrudgingly moaned.

"If I find out you didn't, that you said one disrespectful thing to this kid, you got my word that I personally will chop your ugly head off. An' when I say chop your head off, mister, I don't mean give you a beating. I mean chop your head off."

Don Vincenze removed and slowly emptied the parole officer's gun. After pocketing the bullets, he replaced the gun in his holster.

"I know you," the don said, staring into Spositoro's eyes. "I know what makes you tick." He paused, holding the parole officer's gaze. "I know what you really are."

Spositoro's eyes dropped toward the floor.

"Now my friends are gonna let you go. If you insist on creating a disturbance, they'll kill you right here."

When Spositoro looked up in surprise, Don Vincenze said, "I know, they always told you that the one thing we never do is kill an officer of the law. Don't believe it."

Getting the expression of fear he wanted in return, the don added, "If, by some chance, you think I'm kidding, just try me."

Spositoro looked first at Buster then at Eddie DaDa, who were themselves looking to Don Vincenze for an order to either let their victim go or snuff the life out of him.

"All right, all right," Spositoro groaned. "Just let go of me."

The two powerfully built men maintained their holds until receiving a nod of consent from their boss.

Once released, Spositoro's arms dangled helplessly at his sides. Grimacing, he attempted to wipe the thick spittle from his face by lowering his head toward his hands, which only reached up to chest height.

"Now, go quietly. My friends'll show you the way out."

As Spositoro approached the door, however, Don Vincenze called, "Oh, one more thing. I know I'm gonna hate myself in the morning for allowing you to live. So if you think you might want to start a vendetta against me, please, don't even hesitate. I'd like a chance to correct my error."

After the trio had left the room, Don Vincenze turned to Mickey

Boy, whose mouth hung open and whose eyes looked like doughnuts, and said, "I don't think he'll bother you no more."

A half hour later the current that had crackled through the air during and immediately following the don's confrontation with Spositoro had all but dissipated.

Only Buster remained in the room with Mickey Boy, Don Vincenze and Connie having gone off to unwind in the lounge, with the don's two bodyguards following.

Tension had ebbed from Mickey Boy's body, too, leaving behind a throbbing that he was sure the pills the don had given him were too weak to cure. Surrendering to the pain, he'd asked the nurse to prepare a shot of Demerol.

He wanted to sleep too; painless sleep; forgetful sleep, sleep without worry about his being capable of handling the transition to legitimate business for the Calabra Family. Sleep without Laurel.

Suddenly a flash of yellow bursting into the room startled him. Before he could mount a verbal response, the swirl of color had hesitated a fraction of a second, then charged his way, finally engulfing him in arms, hair, and heady perfume.

"Oh my God, Mickey, I was so scared," Laurel cried. "Thank God you're alive."

Laurel's warm tears swept down over Mickey Boy's cheek, and when he threw his one good arm around her and hugged her tight, she shuddered.

Greedily clinging to Laurel, Mickey felt the sorrow and self-pity of the past months drain from his body as surely as if it were gangrenous blood being drawn through an open wound. He rubbed his eye against her hair to wipe away his own tear.

Buster picked up the white wool cape that Laurel had dropped when she'd charged into the room. He carefully draped it over the back of the chair, then gave Mickey an awkward wave and stepped outside the door.

Holding Mickey's face in both her hands, Laurel kissed his lips, eyes, and bandaged head. The past few months had been terribly painful for her too, she exclaimed between smooches. She'd missed him so; cried every day; been tempted so often to return.

Mickey stared at Laurel, trying to etch every visible micron of her flesh into his brain. His eyes remained moist and the upper portion of his head felt ready to explode. All the upbeat music in his life—Sinatra's ballads of requited love—that had left with Laurel on that plane to Florida came rushing back in one joyous symphony.

"I think I should get shot more often," he said. "As a matter of fact, if I knew it woulda brought you back so fast I woulda got it done sooner. How'd you find out?"

Her eyes glistening like watery sapphires, Laurel lovingly wiped her tears from his face.

"Your mother called my mother this morning and told her what had happened," she said. "Then my mother called me. Since Pan Am and I were going to be in the neighborhood anyway, I thought I'd stop by and say hello."

"I'll tell you," Mickey responded dreamily to Laurel's joking. "You got a hell of a way with hellos—it's your good-byes I can't stand."

"Mickey darling, I never want to say good-bye to you again. If you only knew how miserable I've been since I left. There was just no other way."

The nurse appeared with his injection, but Mickey Boy waved her away, choosing instead two more of Don Vincenze's pain-killers from his sling.

When Laurel stepped from the bed to pour him water from a pitcher on the nightstand, Mickey soaked in each of her movements, scanning her from her white Reeboks to her baggy painter-style jeans to the full sunshine-yellow overblouse.

Laurel handed him the water, then returned to the nightstand to pour some for herself.

Still staring, Mickey thought, *She either gained a lot of weight, or . . .*

Only the traction equipment kept Mickey from bolting upright in the bed. Fiery pain raced from his injured shoulder down his arm and back up to his neck.

"What the fuck is wrong with you?!" he roared. "Why didn't you tell me you were pregnant?!"

Strings of questions erupted in Mickey's mind. Could she have been married in Florida? Was she pregnant from a new lover? No. No. He absolutely knew he was the father of the embryo growing in Laurel's womb. He had to be.

"Don't you yell at me!" Laurel shrieked, then began to cry again.

While sobbing, Laurel vented her misery through bitter accusations: "If you weren't so goddamned devoted to your goddamned friends, and really cared for me, you would have been the first to know . . . you never once came looking for me . . . you just didn't care."

At that moment Mickey couldn't imagine anyone caring more than he did. He was thrilled by the realization that he'd soon be a father. Soon he'd have a miniature version of himself on which to heap all the wholeness he'd always missed. A child that he'd carve the time out to roll on the carpet with and take to the zoo; that he'd care for and about.

And then there'd be more, maybe one or two right away. Given his way, he'd fill her with babies, keep her so busy she wouldn't have time to worry or complain about what he was up to.

Amid his jubilation, Mickey felt a warm flush of tenderness for Laurel—the mother of his child.

"Laurel, please, baby, come here."

After the briefest bit of wavering, Laurel threw herself on him.

"Oh, Mickey, I thought you loved me." Her crying intensified as she repeated, "I thought you loved me . . . I thought you loved me."

"But I do, baby," Mickey answered through his own tears. "I love you more than anything else in this world. Always remember that, baby. You're the only one I ever loved."

Mickey stroked Laurel's hair while she clung tightly to him.

"It's just that I couldn't chase you, baby," he said. "You didn't leave me no room to try, an' I'm not the kind of guy who could crawl; it just ain't in me."

If she thought he didn't know how she felt, Mickey said, well, she had no idea how much it killed him every day that she was gone. He'd wanted to go after her on numerous occasions, but gave up each time before leaving because he didn't know how to convince her to return, didn't know what to say.

During that time, he added, he became more and more miserable and, as a result, took his frustration out on everyone around him.

"Boy," he added in a lighter tone, "there's a lot of abused guys up here who'd love to give you a black eye."

"Let them try it," Laurel replied, sniffling.

"That's my girl . . . tough to the end. Only this ain't the end, sweetheart, nobody'll be able to separate me from you—except maybe with a crowbar. You're gonna be so tired of me, you're gonna beg me to leave you alone."

"Oh, Mickey my love," Laurel whispered, snuggling closer. "I've waited so long to hear that. You'll see, you won't even miss that rotten gangster life of yours."

No, this can't be; not again, ran through Mickey Boy's head. How could he and Laurel have run in opposite directions for three months and wound up in the exact same place?

Disengaging his arm from around Laurel's shoulders, Mickey Boy pushed her back to face him.

"Honey, please," he said. "We seen this movie before an' neither one of us like the way it ended. I never said nothing about changing my way of life. All we were talking about was you an' me getting married an' spending the rest of our lives together."

"But I just thought . . . I mean, after your getting shot . . . when I heard, I just ran, but on the plane I began to think . . . hope . . . that . . . and with the baby coming."

Laurel stared at Mickey Boy as if he were growing horns.

"Especially with the baby," she said. "How in the world can you not put that nonsense behind you?"

Mickey Boy felt as though Laurel had just kicked him in the balls. The same way happiness had come charging into his life with that sudden flash of yellow was how he saw it evaporating before his eyes.

"Laurel, this life is anything but nonsense," Mickey Boy replied, thinking of the future Don Vincenze had just laid in his lap. "We suffer an' put up with this unbelievable shit for the respect that most people never even dream of getting. That's not only for me, but for everybody I love . . . most of all you an' that little peanut you got growing in your belly."

"I told you before, I can't live in that kind of environment. That's not the type of life I want for me or my husband—and certainly not for my child."

"What type of life? You don't even know what the hell you're talking about. Everything's changing. Everything's gonna be just the way you want."

Speaking rapidly to keep Laurel from interrupting, Mickey Boy went on to draw his and Don Vincenze's vision of the future for Laurel. He emphasized the transition from illegitimate enterprises to legal ones, but omitted any mention of the street muscle they'd have to maintain to ensure that their businesses thrived.

But someone had to spearhead those changes, he said. Who better than him? He'd seen the darker side, having both been in jail and been shot, and had returned with a clearer insight as to what their tomorrows should be. And he had Don Vincenze's blessing. He'd been anointed.

Yes, she'd been right all along; legitimate was the way. He just needed time.

"How long?"

"Honey, I love you too much to lie to you. It's gonna take years—one, ten, I don't know. But at least we'll be moving in the right direction."

"You've got the we all wrong. You, me, and our baby are the we, not your murdering gangster friends. We can change our lives for the better immediately. We don't have to wait for them to catch up."

"You just don't understand," Mickey Boy said, collapsing inside. "You don't know what it means to belong, to have a family that's big enough so that when something happens to one, the family still stays whole.

"Me an' my mother were always limping; there was always a leg missing from our family. First my father died, then Alley's old man. Sometimes I think she never married again 'cause she was afraid, scared that once she started walking straight again she'd lose the next guy, an' not being used to it anymore, she'd flop straight on her face."

"But they're not your family," Laurel implored. "We are." She patted her stomach. "This child of ours and me—if you'll let us."

"But they're my family too—and their wives; and their kids. Different from you and our baby, but all family in a way. You'll see, when we get married, there'll be a thousand people come."

"Sure, five hundred trying to kill you and five hundred trying to stop them. Lovely."

Laurel got off the bed.

"No, sorry, not for me," she said. "If you insist that being with murderers, and God knows whatever else, is more important than being with me and your child, then you'll just have to live in their world—alone."

All the painful emotional turmoil Mickey Boy had experienced for the first time when Laurel had walked out on him rushed back in one stunning blow.

"What do you think," he screamed. "You think my fuckin' life's a big party that you're just gonna decide to send me to stag?" Smashing a fist on the bed, he yelled, "Goddammit, Laurel, you're so goddamn smart with everything else, except when it comes to me! Then you get stupid!"

"Maybe I am stupid!" Laurel shouted right back. "If I had any brains, I would never have come back! It's just that with you I don't think, I just feel . . . and hope . . . and dream."

"Laurel, dreams are great, but this is reality, and we're real people. This ain't some TV character that you're just gonna rewrite the script and change. I'm Mickey Boy, remember me? I'm the same guy that seen you grow up, that fell in love with you, that ate and slept with you. I'm the same guy that you claim you loved all your life—no different."

At that moment, in Mickey Boy's head, Frank Sinatra's voice begged, *. . . But, if you stay, I'll make you a day like no day has been, or will be again . . .*

If Laurel could only hear those words, if he could only make her feel them the way he did.

Instead, Mickey Boy's emotions cried out softly, "Laurel, please, I beg you. Please don't do this to us."

"Don't you dare try to put the blame on me for this," Laurel replied after a tearful silence. "I had no idea when I met you, or fell in love with you, how horrible the life you're a part of is."

"Laurel, please, just try to understand. . . ."

. . . But if you stay, I'll make you a day like no day has been, or will be again . . .

"Why don't you understand that I can't live every day not knowing if you're going to jail, or being murdered somewhere, or murdering

372

someone else. I can't raise my baby knowing that one of your filthy enemies might kill him or her—the way they did to that poor, sweet innocent child, Chrissy."

Sensing the futility of his situation, Mickey Boy shut his eyes; his fists balled and his head pounded.

. . . We'll sail the sun, we'll ride on the rain, we'll talk to the trees, 'n worship the wind . . .

"No, I can't, I can't, I can't!" Laurel screamed. "And I won't!"

. . . Then if you go, I'll understand. Leave me just enough love to fill up my hand . . .

After regaining her composure, Laurel continued. "If you don't love us enough to tear yourself away from these monsters, then forget we're alive."

Tears welled behind Mickey Boy's closed lids. He escaped deeper within his own mind, cushioning himself from a reality he couldn't control.

. . . If you go away, as I know you must, there'll be nothing left in the world to trust. Just an empty room, full of empty space, like the empty look I see on your face . . .

Mickey Boy opened his eyes in time to see Laurel rushing toward the door.

"Go and marry your fuckin' Rosalie!" she yelled on her way out.

Please, don't go away.

The door slammed.

Suddenly aware of a pulsating ache throughout his body, Mickey Boy rang for the nurse, and his Demerol.

At the sound of the door to Mickey Boy's room slamming, Connie and Don Vincenze rushed from the lounge to find themselves directly in Laurel's path as she ran down the corridor.

Connie grabbed Laurel by both arms. "Laurel . . . Laurel, what's wrong?"

Streaming eyes shut tight, Laurel wordlessly shook her head from side to side. The white cape she carried hung down onto the floor.

Connie motioned with her head for Don Vincenze to attend to Mickey Boy, then put an arm around Laurel's shoulders and led her into the lounge. She seated the sobbing girl on a plastic sofa, then brought her a bottle of Pellegrino water from a small refrigerator the don had had installed.

Once Laurel's crying had subsided, Connie said, "You'd be surprised how talking to a third party can clear up a dispute between lovers. I don't mean to pry, but I do want to help." She patted around Laurel's eyes with a tissue.

"Is it about the baby? Is that why you two fought?"

Laurel looked up.

"You may not be showing a lot, but it is pretty obvious," Connie said with a warm smile. "Especially to a grandmother who's been pregnant twice herself and senses her second grandchild on the way."

"None of us could ever fool you."

Laurel's attempt to laugh and control her sobbing at the same time came out like hiccups and sniffles.

"That's a little bit of it," Laurel went on. "But the baby only added another dimension to the problems we already had."

"Sorry, I'm at a loss there, not knowing what went on between you two," Connie replied.

At first, when Connie had questioned Mickey Boy about her not having heard from Laurel for a few days, he'd said Laurel had gone off to visit relatives in Florida and that she'd be back once he was released from MCC.

Later, when Connie'd become suspicious about Laurel not having returned, Mickey Boy'd admitted to their having quarreled, but refused to discuss it further.

Dead issue.

"You can't learn very much from someone who avoids discussion," she went on. "What I did learn, however, is that he missed you terribly. That's why I didn't tell him that I phoned your parents. He'd been calling your name in his sleep, and I didn't want him disappointed if you decided not to come. Anyway, I thought the surprise of it, if you did show up, might do wonders for him."

Judging that Laurel was composed enough to speak, Connie questioned her again. "Well, have you decided to confide in me how you feel, or are you still afraid of me, as you told my son?"

"Ooh, that rat." Laurel groaned. "I wasn't afraid. I just told him that . . . I don't know . . . that you were always so . . . well, regal . . . and that I was embarrassed over the situation between him and Alley . . . and me." She added, "But that was all before you and I spoke."

"Well, I hope you are aware that the facade I present for the public only disguises the insecurities of a kindly old grandmother."

"Some old grandmother. I hope I look half as good as you when I'm a grandmother . . . if I ever get to be one."

Suddenly Laurel's inner turmoil ballooned to the surface. "Oh, Connie, Connie, I'm so sick. I'm in a position where no matter what I do, it's wrong; just like *Catch-22*. I love your son so much, Connie, that sometimes I can't believe it myself. The time I've been away from him has been sheer torture. I think about him all the time and cry constantly. Sometimes I feel like I'm going crazy."

"That, my dear girl, doesn't sound like anything more serious than a young girl in love. However, that does not explain why you two can't settle your differences instead of staying apart."

Laurel bowed her head. "Connie, leaving your son was the most difficult decision I ever made in my life, and today I had to make it for the second time—for me and my baby. It's very difficult for someone who's not in my situation to understand."

"Try me. You know, I was young once too."

"But this is different," Laurel insisted.

"I repeat: Try me."

"Okay, but I warn you, it's going to be impossible for you to understand. Just remember that my decision is well thought out, and is crucial to my life."

"It sounds ominous," Connie teased.

Laurel answered seriously. "Oh, it is, Connie, much more than you imagine." She sipped her mineral water, then continued. "I love your son more than anything in this world, but I can't exist as part of the kind of life he insists on living. That's what our differences are about."

Connie thought back to the frigid night she and Mickey Boy had discussed Laurel as they rode around Manhattan in the hansom cab, remembering how she, not aware of why Laurel had left, had urged him to give up his mob-connected life to follow her to Florida. Now she understood why he had refused to talk about it after that. Mickey Boy had known where she stood and had simply avoided her nagging.

"Connie, I don't want to offend you, but I just don't think I can make it as a gangster's wife."

"You don't offend me. If anything, I support you one hundred percent in trying to get my son out of that life."

"But he's not going. Not for me . . . not for our baby . . . not for anyone."

Her situation in the open, Laurel then related the entire story, from the effect that Mickey Boy's continuing trouble with his parole officer had had on her to the death of Chrissy Augusta.

Connie sat rigid and expressionless throughout the telling.

"So you see, I had to make a choice. Once he showed me that his street life was more important than I was, I was devastated and decided that rather than take second place, I'd leave him and make a life for myself."

Laurel shrugged helplessly. "The only problem is that I can't forget him, and I suffer because of it."

Looking defeated, Laurel added, "I warned you it would be hard to understand why someone would have to take a stand with someone they love, and stick by it—in spite of the chance of their baby having no father."

Though Connie was aware of Laurel, it was in a detached, dreamlike way.

Inside her head, however, her world was active and alive as Connie's mind labored to sort out reels of images—Vince; Mickey Boy; 1956; Laurel; back to Vince again—that melded together into one sad collage.

Alongside the chaos a level of order existed too, with Connie wondering how different things might have been for Mickey Boy, and through him Laurel, if, back in 1956, she had given herself to a doctor, lawyer, or even a longshoreman like her father, instead of a married gangster.

While she heaped blame on herself for the inevitability of her son's life, voices called to Connie from a long, spiraling tunnel. Faces; male faces: Mickey Boy . . . Vince. Females: Connie . . . Laurel . . . Laurel. Laurel's voice began to overpower the others . . . Laurel.

"Connie! Connie, are you all right?" Laurel cried. "Connie, please, say something."

The first thing Connie recognized was the pregnant girl's petrified gaze. Inside, she could see Laurel eating alone, raising a child alone, spending time alone in a tub to relieve her sexual frustration.

"Oh, Laurel, Laurel, we must talk."

Noticing other visitors staring at her, Connie rose and literally dragged Laurel from the room. She pulled her to a bench against the opposite wall of the corridor.

Nothing mattered to Connie now except the younger vision of herself incarnate.

"Laurel, how long have we known each other?"

Laurel looked at her questioningly. "I, uh, guess about ten or twelve years, maybe thirteen. Connie, are you feeling okay?"

"Laurel honey, I'm fine," Connie said. "Right now I'm a little shocked, disturbed, and certainly concerned—for you, and that lovely grandchild of mine that you're carrying. But that does not mean I'm anything other than of perfectly sound mind and body."

With her wits about her once more, Connie was determined to have her say, to have a chance to make things right.

"Now, listen to me, and listen to me carefully," she said. "We've known each other for many years, and for most of those years I've treated you like a daughter instead of like one of my sons' girlfriends. From those years you know that I can be tough when I have to be and can be a very bitter enemy."

"I—I don't understand. Why are you talking about enemies?"

"Because, my dear, I've got to have your sworn promise that what we discuss here will never—and I do mean never—pass your lips. If you betray me, you will become the most mortal enemy I've ever known."

"I would never—"

"Swear to me, Laurel. Swear on your unborn child and my grand-child—my blood."

"But—"

"Swear!"

Appearing frightened, Laurel replied hesitantly, "All right, Connie. If that's what you want, I swear—on my baby's life, and mine. I swear never to repeat a word you say."

The words of Laurel's oath, which Connie would have normally found repugnant, satisfied her. She began to speak evenly and unemotionally.

"Laurel, before I mentioned that I was young once, in a joke, but believe it or not, it's true."

Smiling, Connie continued in a more wistful tone. "Oh, yes, I was young. In fact, at the time the story I'm about to tell you took place, I was a bit younger than you are now.

"One hot, humid day, which I can remember like it was yesterday, I was standing on a corner, waiting to cross the street, when a car raced around the block and splashed mud all over me . . ."

For the first time in her life, Connie told the complete story of how she'd met and fallen in love with Mickey Boy's father. She spared no detail, save his identity, telling Laurel of the flowers from Mudslinger, of where they'd gone together, of what they'd eaten—of their first time in bed.

Throughout Connie's recounting, Laurel sat mesmerized, her mouth agape.

It was nearly an hour before Connie reached her final scene in the motel room, when she'd told Mudslinger she was pregnant, over thirty years before.

"I was furious, hurt, indignant, every word you can think of. The nerve of him, placing me behind those goons he hung around with, and an old greaseball uncle. If I'd had a pistol that night, I think I would have shot him—and myself afterward. Oh, boy, was I mad." Connie giggled, mostly from relief.

Being able to tell someone what she had kept bottled up for so long made Connie feel as though a heavy burden had been lifted from her.

"There was only one minor problem: I loved him. Oh, Laurel, I loved him so much that the pain of being away from him was unbearable. I cried and cried, and packed and unpacked. I was like an insane person.

"My aunt and uncle, God bless them, used to run away from me. In the morning they'd sort of glance out from the corners of their eyes to try to forecast my mood for that day. But I was oblivious to them. Sweet people that they were, they might as well have been cedar chests for all the attention they got from me. I never was able to return their love because Mickey Boy's father had stolen all I had."

Connie wiped a tear from her eye and sipped from Laurel's bottle of mineral water, which by that time had become warm and somewhat flat.

"One thing I was, though—I was stubborn," Connie went on. "Oh, yes, Connie Partinico wasn't going to bend for anyone. I'd show Mr. Mudslinger that he couldn't place me anywhere but first in his life. And I did."

Connie's next words seemed to come simultaneously with her mind's discovering their meaning for the first time.

"I know I made him suffer," she said, "because I'm sure now that he sincerely loved me."

Using her forefinger for emphasis, Connie added, "But, Laurel honey, no one—not one single, solitary person in the world—suffered as much as I did because of that stubbornness. I've spent more than half my life in misery, loving a man I wouldn't allow myself to have."

Eyes misted over and lips parted, Laurel had the entranced look of a child listening to a favorite fairy tale.

"But didn't you love your second, no, then he was your first husband—Alley's father?"

"Albert was the kindest, gentlest, most understanding man I have ever met," Connie replied. "He was an absolutely wonderful husband and father, especially to my Mickey Boy, and I loved him dearly."

Sighing deeply, she added, "But, Laurel, that love was never whole. There was always that one spot in my heart that constantly cried for my one grand passion: my Mickey Boy's father."

Connie bent over and kissed Laurel on the cheek.

"Laurel honey, when you told me what had happened between you and my son, it was as if I had been reincarnated in you. And what that insight offered me was a chance to change something that I've regretted all these years, a chance to see you have a happier life than I did."

"Oh, Connie, I'm so confused," Laurel said. "I just don't think I can live your son's kind of life."

"But you knew Mickey Boy. You weren't a stranger who just met him and started dating. You knew what his life was about for years."

"Yes, I knew, but I didn't want to see. I tried so hard to wear blinders, not to imagine what more there was than a simple after-hours club or a few football bets . . . until Chrissy. Then the truth smacked me in the face; I couldn't look away anymore."

Laurel looked down at her lap. "When I made up my mind to stick by my decision, I did it with the hope that Mickey loved me enough to give it all up and follow me. I can make him happy, they can't."

"Did he follow?"

378

"No, but now I've got his baby—our baby."

Though surprised by the sudden change of outlook that seemed to gush up from a broken drum within herself, a drum she'd reinforced through the years with bitter layers of resentment, that surprise took a backseat to Connie's determination to compensate for what she now viewed as her ruined adulthood by convincing Laurel to change her mind.

Never having known Laurel to be a fighter, Connie was also surprised to find the young girl every bit as unyielding as she herself had been at her age.

Laurel claimed that although she'd come rushing back to Mickey Boy's side the moment she'd heard he'd been hurt, now she felt like a mother who panics when her child is in danger, then, once he's safe, smacks him for having created the situation in the first place. Mickey Boy had certainly created this situation, and now she felt angry and used.

When Connie pointed out that that anger was temporary, and that she should consider the larger picture, including what was right for her coming child, Laurel responded, "Maybe there is no right or wrong. I have friends whose parents are divorced, who say that they'd have put up with anything to have had their parents together while they were growing up, and another friend whose parents lived under the same roof but fought constantly, who says she wishes they'd have divorced years ago so she wouldn't have had to grow up with that hatred surrounding her."

In that there was no right or wrong, in her heart Connie believed Laurel was a hundred percent correct. What was worse was that she felt Laurel would be a loser to some extent no matter which decision she made.

Despite a determination to see Laurel return to Mickey Boy, Connie felt impelled to be honest with Laurel and spelled out her misgivings. What was important, however, she said, was that Laurel choose the lesser of the impending evils, which in this case, she believed wholeheartedly, was to spend her life with the man she loved, and who loved her, regardless of the sacrifices involved.

"Yes, I do love him, but I don't know how long that love would survive if I had to be worn down each day by fear of his going to jail or being, God forbid, killed."

Sure, she'd been miserable every day she'd been away from Mickey Boy, Laurel said, but as much as her heart hurt, her mind knew that all hurts heal in time. Maybe if she gave herself that time, she could learn to love someone else—someone who wouldn't bring those same types of encumbrances to a marriage.

"I just don't know."

"I don't want you to do anything you really don't want to," Connie said. "But take it from me, you don't learn to love people. You can respect them and feel affection for them, like I did for Albert. But love? That feeling that words don't adequately define? It's either there or it's not."

"I wish I could be as sure as you are."

"To do that, my dear girl, you will have to have lived through whatever decision you make, just as I have—and suffered through it."

Much as she argued, Connie could feel certain defeat slowly surrounding her.

In a last-ditch attempt to sway Laurel, she said, "You know, if anyone would have told me before tonight that I would be here arguing in any man's behalf, even my son's, in a situation like this, I would have had them committed. Up until recently, though, I never understood men like Mickey Boy's father—or my Mickey Boy himself—and I probably still don't, at least not one hundred percent."

The difference was that now she could look on them and their "Family obligations" without the bitterness she had before, Connie said. And, in this particular case, she claimed, she could view things much more objectively than when she herself had been involved, and like Laurel in her present predicament, had been able to think only with her heart instead of her head.

"Laurel, believe me, I don't mean to romanticize them or the violent life they lead, but they are special men in a way. They love as fiercely and passionately as they fight, and to be the object of that love is something you shouldn't be so quick to just throw out the window."

"It's not me who's throwing our relationship out the window," Laurel insisted. "It's him. He's got so much more to him, so much more capability than he even realizes. If only he would try to break away, to change the destructive elements in his life, I'd do anything to help him—work three jobs with babies hanging off my neck, anything."

"Well, if there is a chance, no matter how remote, to change my Mickey Boy, it certainly can't be done long distance."

"If I truly thought being here with him would help, I would stay. But frankly, I'm not sure anything I do can change a thing."

Laurel's head and shoulders drooped, her look tired and worn-down.

"I want so badly to make the right decision."

"Laurel, I can't tell you to commit yourself and your child to the kind of life-style my son is offering you. That has to come from your own sense of what you want, and can live with. What I can tell you is that I've experienced one side of the coin, and, as a result, have spent a miserable life. My conscience wouldn't be too clear if I didn't try to save you from the mistake I made, and the hell I've been through because of it."

Tears began to trickle down Laurel's cheeks as she gathered up her cape.

"I'll call and let you know what I decide."

Seeing Laurel cry, coupled with the taste of defeat, brought a gush of tears from Connie too.

"One more thing you must promise me, Laurel," she said, sobbing. "No matter what your decision is as far as my Mickey Boy is concerned, you won't hide my grandchild from me. Even if I have to travel to wherever you are, and go along with whatever story you decide to tell the child. Just don't shut me out."

Laurel stood, then bent to kiss Connie on the forehead. "I swear by God," she said barely above a whisper. "There's only one question, though, that I have to ask: Where is Mickey Boy's father today?"

Connie looked up at her and, forcing a smile, said, "In the room with his son."

Shaking her head, Laurel almost whispered, "You have to tell him."

"I can't. It's too embarrassing; I just wouldn't know how."

"You'll have to find a way."

Weariness overcame Connie. "I guess you're right, but it's not my decision alone," she said. "I'll speak to his father about it. Just remember, you swore."

Laurel kissed Connie again, smiled back at her weakly, then walked off toward the elevator.

63

February 17: LaGuardia Airport

Buster's car had barely pulled up to the meter when Don Vincenze was out the door and hurrying across the roadway toward the Delta terminal.

Eddie DaDa and Charlie Bones kept pace on either side of the don as he rushed ahead, his hobbled leg making him feel as though he were skipping. Each jolt of his good heel on the cement made his neck burn with pain beneath the brace. Luckily, foot and vehicle traffic were light at that midnight hour, allowing him to move along unimpeded.

Fast as Don Vincenze was able to go, however, by the time he reached the terminal's glass door Buster was already holding it open with one foot pressed on the sensitized floor mat.

The electronic monitor overhead showed the Miami flight delayed from 12:45 to 1:15.

Great.

They stopped a porter for directions to Gate E, then, with the clatter of their soles echoing in the corridor, the don's group charged toward the flight's waiting area.

Don Vincenze saw her immediately, sitting alone at the end of a row of attached plastic chairs. She had the forlorn look of a soldier on the way home from a lost war. A suitcase stood on the seat next to her.

As he reached her, Don Vincenze asked, "Laurel?" And when she looked up, her face lifeless, he said, "My name is Vince. I'm a friend of Mickey Boy's and Connie's."

"I know who you are." Still no expression.

Laurel crossed her arms around her middle as if protecting herself from an expected assault.

When Connie had called, crying that Laurel had phoned her to say she was leaving for Florida that night, thereby abandoning Mickey Boy again, Don Vincenze and his men had just sat down at his kitchen table to catch up on that day's missed dinner. Leaving the sausage and eggs Charlie'd prepared, they'd immediately run from the house.

Though he certainly had his own misgivings about the girl, the fact was that Mickey Boy wanted her, and the don was determined to do something for his son, give him some fatherly gift to make up for all the times he'd let him down.

Now that he was at his destination, however, standing in front of this sorrowful-looking girl who was carrying his grandchild, what could he do? Threaten her with the scope of his might? Offer her money? Beat her?

Though Don Vincenze Calabra could direct mob matters and solve the problems of those within his sphere of influence almost instinctively and with a decisiveness envied by even other bosses, he'd never been good at handling female situations. Not thirty years before with Connie. Not that night.

"I'd like to talk to you," Don Vincenze said, having no idea how to approach the subject he was there to discuss.

All he'd told Connie, jumping into action without thinking, was that he was on his way. As soon as the phone had hit its cradle he'd grabbed the packed envelope he'd been saving, stuffed it into his jacket pocket, and run out.

"But I feel ridiculous sitting here at this time of night with dark glasses; I look like an old junkie."

382

Laurel forced a smile.

Playing for sympathy, the don adjusted his medical collar. "Believe me, this thing is a pain someplace besides my neck."

"Pain goes with your territory, doesn't it?" Laurel said dryly. "Ask Mickey—or Chrissy Augusta's parents."

Thinking, *bitch*, but showing nothing of that feeling in his outward appearance, Don Vincenze said, "Why don't we see if there's a coffee shop open? We could grab a bite an' sit in a booth an' talk."

The don waved his men away, but they moved only a few feet back; the area was too open to protect him from a distance.

"I'm sorry," Laurel said. "But I'd rather stay here. I don't want to miss my flight."

Reflexively, Don Vincenze checked his watch; time was running out. He sat in the seat on the other side of her suitcase and waved his men back again when he noticed her looking from one to the other.

"I guess they're worried what you'll do to me," he said, trying to lighten the strained air.

Laurel smiled another weak smile.

Looking at her over the top of the luggage, Don Vincenze said, "You know, on my way here I was thinking that everybody's got a price."

When Laurel began to protest, the don stopped her, saying, "No, no, don't take it wrong, I'm just talking in general. But there's always a price to make somebody change their position in any dealing—not necessarily money, but a price. Sometimes it could be a guy who stops beating up his wife that makes her give up a divorce. Or a lazy partner who agrees to do more work to keep the other guy from quitting. See?"

"But we're not dealing for anything, and I haven't been beaten up."

"Maybe we are, who knows? And maybe you were but don't even know it."

Dissatisfied with the conversation's lack of progress, Don Vincenze blurted out, "I came here to try to convince you not to go away, not to leave Mickey Boy, but I find I don't know where to start."

"There's really nothing to say," Laurel replied. "Mickey knows why I'm leaving, and he knows what he can do about it if he wants to. It has nothing to do with anyone but him and me."

"Wrong again. Don't forget, that kid you're lugging around in you is part of me too."

The don had played for some shocked reaction, something to put Laurel off balance, but received nothing. Connie had obviously filled her in earlier about his being Mickey Boy's father. Shit!

And when Laurel dryly informed him that she was sorry if he was affected but didn't feel that she was willing to sacrifice her life for others' pleasure, he knew he was off in the wrong direction anyway.

What he would have liked to do at that moment was simply throw a burlap sack over her head and carry her off.

Oddly, though, the don found Laurel's stubbornness exciting, and glanced down toward her breasts, her hips, her legs, beginning to understand the uniquely female combination that had bewitched his son so.

"Let's go back a minute to what I said about dealing," Don Vincenze said. "No, let's go back even further an' start fresh. Do you love him?"

"Yes—but I can survive without him."

"Good, that's tough. I like that." And he did.

Nothing the don's investigators had told him had indicated the qualities he was uncovering about Laurel firsthand. Between her 139 IQ and the strength of character he saw, she'd be a hell of a wife for Mickey Boy. A hell of a wife—if she could only keep herself from being a cunt.

Laurel would be smart enough to bring out the side of Mickey Boy he'd kept hidden, the intelligence and inherited management ability he'd played down while making his mark as a tough guy, the parts that would give him the balance to build on and control the legitimate assets the Calabra Family already had while still keeping their army in line.

Besides, she was probably a hellfire in the sack and would definitely produce prize grandchildren, maybe a fine boy to carry on the tradition of La Cosa Nostra for yet another generation.

Yes, the don thought, Laurel Bianco would marry his son no matter what he had to do to convince her, no matter what promises he had to make.

Laurel went on. "And he can live without me if he gives himself a chance."

"Maybe he doesn't want to. But we're getting off the road. Please, just answer what I asked," Don Vincenze said firmly.

Maybe a strong approach was what this bitch needed.

"So far you said you love him. To me that means you would really want to be with him if you could. Is that right?"

"But I can't. There are some things that—"

"Do all teachers talk so goddamn much? Maybe if they listened more, kids would do better in school."

"My students do fine, thank you."

Though Don Vincenze felt like slapping Laurel across the mouth, he controlled himself, snapping, "How fine are they gonna do, thank you, when you desert them?"

"There are other—"

"Please, I appreciate how smart-mouthed you are, an' understand how hurt an' angry you are, but we're wasting time with nonsense. I ain't here to do a pissing contest with you."

Upon seeing his aggressiveness back Laurel up, the don continued. "Bottom line is that if you could only stay with Mickey Boy under certain conditions, I'm the guy who could make 'em happen," he said.

"I could also guarantee that the kid inside you, an' any other kids you have, will always have everything you want for them—best private schools, colleges, security for the rest of their lives an' their kids' lives."

"Money isn't everything."

"No? What are you gonna give a kid without it? Shit, that's what! An' what makes you think I'm just gonna sit by an' let my grandchild live like that? You think I'm just gonna leave him with you while you whore around in Florida?"

"Whaa—?"

"I know more about you than you think, miss, about you an' his brother, Alley, for starters."

Don Vincenze pulled the envelope from his inside pocket and laid it on top of her suitcase. Why he'd brought it along had not been clear to him until that moment. To him it was just another example of the instinct that had always seemed to flow from an unconscious well at crucial moments, and that had boosted him along the way to the top all his life.

It suddenly occurred to the don that if he'd conducted his personal affairs as if they were mob business, using the same toughness that had served him in the streets instead of worrying how to protect and shield from hurt the ones he loved, he might have been better off.

As Laurel pulled the photos from the envelope and glared at them, Don Vincenze studied her, watched her face for the slightest sign of guilt.

When he'd caught that pockmarked bastard pocketing the package of photos and negatives, he'd pressed him for the story, and, like the weasel that any friend of his son's had to be, the kid had ratted Little Vinnie out, said it was part of a plot to get back at Mickey Boy for some insult.

No, the don assured himself, nine out of ten nothing had happened between Little Vinnie and Laurel. Little Vinnie had probably just conned her into meeting him so he could get pictures that appeared incriminating. That slimy half-a-hump he was ashamed to call a son.

"How dare you spy on me!" Laurel snapped.

Don Vincenze found the vein bulging on her neck incredibly sexy. Everything about her was innocent shock. Now he would have bet his life that her indignation was real.

"I didn't," he said. "But somebody thought it was important enough to do it."

"Was it Mickey?"

"If it was, he woulda spit in your face an' never looked at you again."

"But I never did anything with Vinnie."

"You'd never know it from those pictures."

Don Vincenze had studied the photos over and over, absorbed every bit of Laurel's body language. In his mind, if she hadn't gotten laid that night, it was only because his idiot son had been too inept and stupid to capitalize on her weaknesses, on her hot nature. Now, if it had been him at that age . . .

"Listen," the don said. "My son loves you, an' what's more important, I like you—I think you'd be good for him."

"And the hell with me?"

Where were the goddamned tears? Don Vincenze wondered. He'd certainly worked for them.

"No, wrong," he said. "You get everything—for you, your kids, even your parents. There's nothing you want that I can't make sure you get. All we gotta do, you an' me, is find your price an' make a deal."

"I want Mickey out of the rackets," Laurel said, her eyes challenging him.

"That's the easiest of all," Don Vincenze said. "If you're patient. In another couple of years our way of life will be gone; we're finished. But we have people and assets that have to make the change to legitimate business. That takes time."

"I know, your son gave me the same story."

Laurel seemed taken aback for a moment by her offhand mention of Mickey Boy as the don's son, then asked, "How could you not tell him he's your son?"

Don Vincenze cursed Laurel in his mind for having struck him in a spot that hurt him more and more the older he got. He loved Mickey Boy in his own way, and blamed himself for being so clumsy and inept in the handling of his personal life that the boy had stayed apart from him all these years. But he was supposed to strike the blows that counted, not Laurel.

"That's none of your business," the don said, then softened and added, "But, I will tell him—soon."

"What's soon?"

"When I decide the time is right," the don replied. "But, please, we're getting off the track again."

Don Vincenze moved Laurel's suitcase to the floor and took her hand in his, patting it in a soothing, grandfatherly manner.

"Look at me," he said. "I'm an old man an' haven't got the time to make things right. I need Mickey Boy to help me get it done. I need my son."

Laurel eyed him suspiciously. She fingered the photographs.

"And you never showed these to Mickey?"

"You could answer that for yourself."

"Yet you kept the pictures."

Laurel stared directly into the don's eyes much as he had done to others all his life to discern the truth. Unlike any of those times, however, when he'd been in the superior position, and had felt free to break eye contact when his purpose had been served, Don Vincenze had to fight the desire to break away from Laurel's soul-stripping stare.

"Was it an ax to hold over my head in case I ever went back with him?" Laurel asked. "What could you possibly want from me?"

One finger rested on Laurel's pursed lips as she tossed the questions over in her mind. Suddenly her eyes brightened to a wicked gleam and her finger wagged at the don.

"Unless it was to use me to control him. That's it, isn't it?"

Don Vincenze only smiled.

"You're a terrible old man," Laurel said, returning his smile.

At that moment Don Vincenze felt a kindredness with Laurel, a sympatico with a darker side of her nature he was positive existed, and which would complement his son even more nicely than he'd previously thought.

"Not always terrible," he replied. "But always smart."

"Slick is more like it. Have you ever been in jail?"

"Not more than overnight. Why?"

"Too bad Mickey doesn't have that much guile in him. It might have kept him out too."

"He's got it—after all, he is my son. Just give him time to learn how to use it."

A loudspeaker announced the commencement of boarding for the Miami flight.

"My plane is here," Laurel said. "My uncle will be waiting to meet me. I'll think about—"

"Please," Don Vincenze said. "Give me a little more time." He smiled. "Just a little. Let's go bargain a little over a cup of coffee."

Paziènza repeated in the don's head, and he reminded himself of the old Sicilian proverb: *Con la santa pazienza l'elefante si inculo la pulce* . . . With enough patience, the elephant fucked the flea.

"If we can't make a deal, you have my word I'll take you over to the private terminal here an' charter a plane just for you; you'll be in Miami in no time. C'mon."

Laurel looked undecidedly toward the gate again, then turned back to him and shrugged.

With a wave of his hand Don Vincenze signaled for Eddie DaDa to take Laurel's luggage, then, still holding her hand in one of his, helped her up. He hooked his arm in hers and led her away quickly, before she could have a change of heart.

"You know," the don said, "if I was a little younger, I think I'd marry you myself."

64

March 25: Bensonhurst, Brooklyn

". . . Lord, hear our prayers for Michael Antonio and Laurel Elise," Father Anthony intoned.

The gray-haired priest's words echoed off the beige plaster walls of St. Finbar's Roman Catholic Church and settled on an unusually tense wedding group.

Mickey Boy leaned on one crutch and glanced back over his shoulder to make sure everything was in order.

All ten tuxedo-clad men were in place, either standing guard by an exit or sitting in a pew. Each kept his hand close to a hidden .357 Magnum and each remained fully alert.

Good.

Mickey Boy had no doubt that the six men posted out front of the church and the four more diverting traffic at either corner with heavy-construction equipment were on their toes as well. The disappearance of the two bodyguards who, having been fooled into thinking Joe Augusta was a detective, had let him handcuff them and thus take his shots at the don would keep everyone wired up.

Mickey Boy looked over at Don Vincenze and gave an almost imperceptible nod.

Though the don had removed his neck brace for the wedding, he was unable to take a precautionary look around without turning his entire body and alarming the women even more than they already were. Mickey Boy had literally become the eyes in back of his head.

". . . With faith in You and in each other they pledge their love today," Father Anthony went on. "May their lives always bear witness to the reality of that love."

At that same moment an equally large crew was going through a mock wedding at Laurel's first choice of church, Mary Queen of Heaven, in Flatbush.

That location had been discussed on phones the don was sure were tapped and printed on announcements that were distributed to all the members, associates, and friends of their Family. No precautions were too light to keep a determined lunatic like Joe Augusta, who was said to have accumulated "a graveyard behind him," from marring the wedding. If they could fool the law into following the other affair, they could fool Joe too.

Mickey Boy prayed there would be no problem at the other site either.

". . . Bind Michael Antonio and Laurel Elise in the loving union of marriage and make their love fruitful so that they may be living witness to Your divine love in the world. We ask this through our Lord Jesus Christ, Your Son, who lives and reigns with You and the Holy Spirit, one God, for ever and ever."

The priest then led the couple through the standard wedding vows.

Don Vincenze, as best man, stepped forward to present Mickey Boy with a black velvet ring box.

Connie, who Laurel had chosen as her maid of honor, stood in place.

The only other guests—Alley and his wife, Laurel's parents with nearly a dozen of their relatives, Buster, and Freddie Falcone—filled the second-row pew.

Saying, "With this ring, I thee wed," Mickey Boy slipped a diamond wedding band on Laurel's finger.

". . . Michael Antonio and Laurel Elise, you are now united in marriage before God's altar. You may kiss each other."

Mickey Boy shifted his weight onto one crutch, threw his good arm around Laurel's shoulders, and kissed her. Laurel's body was stiff and her lips dry. A patch of deep-set creases was left in the front of Mickey Boy's tuxedo where her damp hands had clutched it.

Father Anthony said a final nuptial blessing, ending with "May they live to see their children's children. And, after a happy old age, grant them fullness of life with the saints in the Kingdom of Heaven. We ask this through Christ our Lord."

Connie, slinky in a gold beaded sheath, and Laurel, in white organdy that camouflaged her swollen abdomen, then kissed each other.

Don Vincenze did the same with Mickey Boy—who still had no idea that his best man was in fact his natural father.

After kissing Laurel, Don Vincenze said to Mickey Boy, "What a bargain you got today." He patted Laurel's stomach. "One wife an' one almost kid for one 'I do.' Not a bad deal at all."

Laurel blushed livid pink and glared at Don Vincenze, who smiled back at her. To Mickey Boy, it was as if she and the don had a private battle going, to the exclusion of everyone else.

Though Mickey Boy smiled, shook hands, and kissed Laurel's parched lips again, he felt oddly detached—as though he had somehow transcended his body to get a Peeping Tom's view of the group's jittery movements.

Laurel hugged Mickey Boy once more, then turned to chat with her mother and aunts.

It had been six weeks since she had met at the airport with Don Vincenze—Connie'd slipped and told Mickey Boy that, and had made him promise silence—but so far Laurel had not said a word about it.

What had the old man promised that he himself couldn't to keep her? Mickey Boy wondered.

Since that time, Don Vincenze had put a substantial down payment on a twelve-room house in Staten Island for Mickey Boy and Laurel, and had bought them a new silver-gray Mercedes.

The don said it was out of gratitude for Mickey Boy's having saved his life, but was it? Or was it part of a deal with Laurel? Was money what she'd been about all along? He didn't believe that—or, more precisely, didn't want to believe that.

Whatever Laurel's motivation was, however, each day she kept the meeting a secret was another brick added to an invisible barrier Mickey Boy felt she was erecting between them.

Services over, the bodyguards from the pews and rear doors formed a cordon around the wedding party as it moved toward the front of the church.

Don Vincenze and Connie walked just ahead of Mickey Boy and Laurel, talking with Father Anthony as if they were the bride and groom.

Though he felt he owed the don everything, Mickey Boy smarted at Don Vincenze's continual running of what he considered his own personal show.

Sure, Don Vincenze had provided his future and had become the key to his past, in fact recently having promised to sit down with Mickey Boy after his honeymoon and tell him anything he wanted to know. The don had even given him Laurel.

But all the gifts were becoming overbearing. Being manipulated with good, as opposed to being manipulated as he had by Little Vinnie—into prison—still made Mickey Boy uncomfortable.

Little Vinnie was the biggest deficit that came along with the new close relationship with Don Vincenze. Mickey Boy still felt he owed the worthless little shit for the six years that had been taken from his life and for the car crash with Laurel beside him.

Those were things that were not supposed to go unanswered, according to underworld law, but Mickey Boy had made a vow to Don Vincenze and intended to honor it to the letter.

What about Little Vinnie though? Would he honor a truce too, or continue trying to kill him? Don or no don, Mickey Boy wouldn't let himself and Laurel become ducks in an arcade for anyone.

If he could only find some way of communicating with Little Vinnie in Sicily, Mickey Boy thought, even by phone, maybe the two of them could come to some acceptable understanding—at least for whatever years the don had left.

Chiana, chiana, met en ghoule.

That lately he'd been thinking too much went through Mickey Boy's mind. He'd been looking too many gift horses in the mouth, especially as far as Laurel was concerned.

Now was a time to celebrate, and luxuriate in his newfound status as both a captain in the Calabra Family and a husband to the girl he loved.

"Wait a minute," Mickey Boy said, stopping everyone at the door. He stepped out from the protective ring of bodyguards and pointed at two of the men who stood at the door.

"You an' you, go outside an' make sure everything's okay before we go out," he ordered, then turned to Laurel and winked. "Just to make sure the limo starts, honey."

To the other guests, who were laughing at his good-humored approach to their stressful situation, Mickey Boy said, "If you're gonna throw any rice, throw it in here. I don't want things flying in our faces once we get outside."

Don Vincenze stood by quietly, a satisfied smile on his face.

To Mickey Boy, the old man had slipped by not having the front of the church checked, but that was okay. At his age he should have nothing more to do than enjoy his family and play golf, or whatever else it was that pleased him.

If the day ever came when he replaced Don Vincenze as boss, Mickey Boy told himself, he'd definitely retire his men at sixty or sixty-five, take them off the front lines where they were exposed to either jail or being murdered, let them live out their last years in peace—maybe just let them advise younger guys who could benefit from their storehouses of experience and knowledge.

Yes, acting like a boss felt good, Mickey Boy thought. He looked at Don Vincenze and smiled back at him. Maybe it was time for the old man to retire.

When the bodyguard returned with an all-clear, Mickey Boy stepped back into place beside Laurel and, amid a hailstorm of dry white rice, prepared to walk out into the brilliant March sunshine to fulfill the balance of his destiny.

65

March 25: Bensonhurst, Brooklyn

White sheets and pillowcases flapped gently on a rooftop clothesline as the sun dried them.

At a corner of the roof a lone man leaned against the waist-high protective wall, staring down four stories and across the top of the traffic being detoured a block away. He looked beyond the men in hard hats who were guiding a bus off the avenue of its regular route into a narrower side street, and settled on a group of six in tuxedos who stood outside the entrance of a church.

When the church's door opened, the man on the roof raised a Weatherbee .270 and brought the doorway within the crosshairs of its scope.

A seventh formally dressed male came out of the house of worship, spoke briefly to the others, then ducked back inside.

The man on the roof smiled, but held the rifle in place.

Soon.

Through his mind jingled, *You're sugar, you're spice, you're ev'rything nice . . . And you're Dad-dy's Lit-tle Girl!*

66

March 28: Bensonhurst, Brooklyn

"It's cheaper to eat twenty-dollar bills than to go to his fuckin' joint for dinner," Freddie Falcone whispered, his face still as a ventriloquist's, his eyes staring straight ahead.

The object of Freddie's remark was the owner of one of New York's finest French restaurants—and a made man in the Calabra Family. The restaurateur nodded and hand-shook his way toward the staircase leading out of the Shore Haven Funeral Home's lower lounge.

Under normal circumstances, Mickey Boy would have broken up over Freddie's comment. Now he barely paid attention, waiting instead for Buster to usher over another member of their Family for him to meet.

It had been that way for Mickey Boy for two days, since the police had released what was left of Don Vincenze's corpse following their autopsy.

For two days Mickey Boy had held court in the funeral parlor's basement, being introduced to formally inducted members of the Calabra Family who had come to pay their last respects to their don and to meet their new boss. There were men from all walks of life and from various parts of the country. Different men, yet—in that they'd all sworn a secret oath of allegiance to La Cosa Nostra—the same. The group included restaurant owners (like the jet-setter Mickey Boy'd just met), a union president, a garment center manufacturer, a furniture company owner who Mickey Boy had seen promoting his stores on television, even a doctor. (What could he have possibly done to earn his way in, Mickey Boy had wondered when introduced. Refused some enemy of the Family their digitalis?) Other men came from places Mickey Boy would never have believed a wiseguy could exist. There was one from Texas, complete with western-style boots, hat, and string tie and a button-man from New Orleans, who muttered Italian words with a southern drawl.

And there were the others—hard-nosed warriors with shiny black suits and white-on-white shirts who'd earned their memberships in the streets. Bookmakers. Shylocks. Thieves. If he didn't know each of them personally, Mickey Boy was at least familiar with most by reputation.

Much as he'd known before, Mickey Boy was staggered by the scope of his Family's power and influence—and numbed by his own.

"I gotta go get a drink or something," Mickey Boy said to Freddie.

"I'll get you something. Whattaya want? Soda? Coffee?"

"Please, I'll go myself," Mickey Boy replied. "I need air more than anything else."

With Freddie Falcone, the new acting *consigliere* of their Family, beside him, Mickey Boy started for the stairway.

Wiseguys and associates alike, who were packed into the small lounge area like a rush-hour subway car, pushed back into the crowd to clear a path for their boss, who limped along with a cane for support. Only a thick cloud of tobacco smoke remained in his way.

"Everything okay?" Buster asked. He stood alongside the bottom step, immediately next to a brown leather chair where Don Peppino sat.

"Just taking a break," Mickey Boy replied.

"Want me to come along?"

"No, that's okay. Freddie's with me."

Mickey Boy nodded to Don Peppino, who just smiled. God, how he hated that fuckin' sneaky smile. Though Don Peppino had been supportive these last couple of days, Mickey Boy harbored an instinctive

393

mistrust of the man, and a resentment that he, frail and withered as last year's Easter plants, still lived while his father—and it sounded so natural to him—was dead.

"You sure?" Buster asked. "There's nothing I gotta do here. I could come with youse if you want."

"No, I'm okay," Mickey Boy said, feeling smothered.

For two days it had been like that, since Buster had abdicated the throne Don Vincenze had left to him in favor of Mickey Boy becoming their Family's leader.

"I just ain't cut out to be boss," Buster had said. "I ain't smart enough."

Mickey Boy had argued till he'd had no breath left. The old man had wanted Buster to take his place, he'd said over and over. He, Mickey Boy, was only supposed to be underboss. The old man had told him so in the hospital.

But Buster would have none of it. If he became boss, there'd be those within the Family who would resent him, he'd argued, smarter, richer captains who would feel they were better suited for the job. And they would be right. His only claim to fame was that he'd spent his entire life backing up someone else. Loyally, to be sure, but still only a muscle man for Don Vincenze.

On the other hand, Buster had gone on, Mickey Boy would be accepted by all. Only a son of the respected don could keep a bloody war of jealousy from erupting within their *borgata*.

"An' who'd be a better underboss for you than me?" Buster had asked. "I know how to play backup better than anybody, even you. It's the only thing I'm really great at."

"But nobody knows he was my old man," Mickey Boy had countered.

Buster had shaken his head, then ended their argument, saying, "Except Don Peppino."

And, in spite of Don Vincenze's last wishes, that's how it had gone. Don Peppino had agreed to support Mickey Boy as temporary heir apparent to the top spot of the Calabra Family, with Buster as acting underboss, and, at Mickey Boy's insistence, Freddie Falcone as acting *consigliere* (at least he wouldn't have to worry about treachery from his two top aides, Mickey Boy had thought).

Now, all that was left was for the Family captains to get together and formally recognize Mickey Boy as permanent boss, which would automatically confirm the other two.

When they reached the top of the staircase, Mickey Boy paused. He looked out over the main room—gold-flocked foil, red floral carpets, huge crystal chandeliers—where those mourners who couldn't take constantly sitting in the chapel with the don's embalmed body, and

those who were not welcome downstairs—women, children, and legitimate relatives of the Calabras—spent their time.

Upon Mickey Boy's orders, the Shore Haven had been closed to any
other funerals while Don Vincenze's body was to be laid out.

Immediately outside the chapel where the don's body lay, Laurel
and Connie, both dressed in black, sat on a tufted gold sofa.

For nearly seventy-two hours, Mickey Boy had not spoken to either
one. Not since the moment after the don's brains had exploded over
Laurel's snow-white wedding gown, when Connie had cried, "Help
him, Mickey Boy! Help him, please! He's your father."

Mickey Boy burned, even as he remembered that moment.

When the don's head had burst as they hit the church's front steps,
Mickey Boy had moved like a soldier in action, dropping his crutch to
the ground and flinging his body over Laurel's.

He could hear his own shouts as he'd directed bodyguards to shove
everyone inside the church and not to return any gunfire until they
saw who was firing.

But no more shots had come.

Just screams, whimpers, and moans.

Connie, covered with blood, had clung to the don's form as he lay
underneath the holy water font, where he'd been abandoned after the
men had dragged him in. They'd left him there under Mickey Boy's
brutally shouted orders to attend to the living.

It was then that his consciousness had been penetrated by "Help
him, Mickey Boy! Help him, please! He's your father."

His father. The man he'd been searching for all his life. Bloody. What
was left of the old man's head, swollen twice its size, was cradled in
Connie's arms. His father. Gone before he could even know him.

Now Mickey Boy looked away from his mother and Laurel, whom
he'd found out had known too. How the fuck could the only two
women he'd ever cared about have done that to him? Especially his
mother, after all the times he'd begged for some particle of truth, for
some clue to the man who had given him life. If the situation were
reversed, he could never have withheld the truth from them. Bitches.
They were all the same.

The only one Mickey Boy didn't blame was Don Vincenze. He had
already paid whatever price could be exacted; he was beyond pun-
ishment.

Mickey Boy had also forgiven Buster, who'd explained that if he
were in Don Vincenze's place, he would have told Mickey Boy long
ago that the old man was his father, but he hadn't been in his place.
Rational or not, it had been the don's decision, and there was no way
he, Buster, could have gone against it without having forfeited his life.

To Mickey Boy that made sense.

But Connie and Laurel were another story. They had no excuse. And Mickey Boy cursed them under his breath again for cheating him.

"Let's go in the chapel for a minute," Mickey Boy said.

Freddie just shrugged.

Taking hold of Freddie's sleeve, Mickey Boy said, "I know, it's a lot of times. It's just something I gotta do."

"You lead, I'll follow," Freddie replied.

Still refusing to acknowledge his mother or Laurel, Mickey Boy hobbled to the chapel's entrance.

He stepped first inside the doorway, then to the side, standing for a moment where the *a boost*—the register book that lists donations to the deceased's family—would normally be, a custom Mickey Boy had ordered dispensed with. If anyone wanted to give the don's relatives a gift, he'd said, they should bring Joe Augusta to him, preferably— but not necessarily—in one piece.

Given the opportunity, Mickey Boy would have banned flowers too, but there were just too many people who had known and either loved or respected Don Vincenze Calabra. Floral arrangements had started pouring in to the Shore Haven even before the don's body had arrived. So many had been delivered, in fact, that besides the abundance of flowers that seemed to suck the air out of the somber funeral room, two empty chapels had been filled with whatever arrangements couldn't reasonably be squeezed in.

After a deep breath, Mickey Boy, with Freddie again beside him, made his way along the perimeter of the room, past the wire stands filled with mass cards, to the front of the don's silver and gold casket.

Staring at the highly polished metals, Mickey Boy wondered how he could feel such loss over something, a father, he'd never had. The fact that the coffin was closed seemed to emphasize the finality of that loss. Not even a picture of Don Vincenze was on display to remember him by or cry over. The don had hated photos, and would have wanted it that way.

Mickey Boy genuflected slightly, as much as the rigid cast on his leg would allow, and crossed himself—a motion he made more out of habit than belief. He stood in front of the coffin as if praying or silently speaking to the dead, but thought nothing. He felt too empty for thoughts.

No tears came either, but Mickey Boy had cried plenty. Alone, like he always had. On the toilet bowl, with his naked ass exposed to the world. Now, especially with men surrounding him wherever he went, that was the only time he could break down and be human.

As usual, the don's two daughters, Margie and Linda, refused to acknowledge Mickey Boy. Overweight, auburn-haired, and shrouded in black, Margie once again looked down at her lap, while Linda, not much leaner, but with hair as black as her dress, buried her tear-swollen face in her handkerchief.

Though it felt strange to think of these two women, who without their makeup resembled men in drag, as his sisters, Mickey Boy reminded himself that they were, and not one cell less than Alley was his brother. And their two jerkoff husbands—the accountant and the plumber, obviously anxious to make his acquaintance but just as clearly too afraid of their wives to speak—were every bit as much his in-laws as Ellen; the half dozen overfed brats were his nieces and nephews.

It pained Mickey Boy not to be able to sit with these people and commiserate with them, to put his arm around them and share their grief. After all, they were his family. The only living relation he was aware of on Connie's side was her cousin Al Partinico, who, because Al's company had relocated him to Atlanta nearly thirty years earlier, he'd never met. True, Al Messina had come from a large family, many of whom Alley still kept in touch with. But then, Mickey Boy felt, they were Alley's relatives, not his.

Afraid of how the don's daughters might react if he approached them, but sure that, in time, they would have to come to him, Mickey Boy limped back around the room to leave.

As he approached the open doors of the chapel, Mickey Boy heard a commotion outside in the lobby. Not a trouble-type commotion, but a buzz in the crowd, something going on.

Hurrying, Mickey Boy left the chapel to come face-to-face—across a space of thirty feet—with his brother, Little Vinnie Calabra.

Flanked by two greaseballs—they had to be: heavy wool cuffs breaking on the fronts of their shoes, coats thrown over their shoulders like capes, cigarettes held European-style; phony smiles that never reached their dark eyes—Little Vinnie stood at the center of a group of relatives who, by the look of their adoration, either had no idea or hadn't gotten used to the fact that Mickey Boy was the don's son too.

Mickey Boy followed Little Vinnie's eyes as they shifted away from his gaze to pick out the form of his ex-gofer, Muffin-Face, standing alone near a pastoral painting.

Though Muffin-Face had obviously known he wasn't welcome to the new Calabra Family hierarchy that congregated one floor below, he'd still shown up to pay his respects and had remained upstairs with the women and legitimate relatives.

Mickey Boy liked that. It showed a certain strength of character in the young man, some potential. On the other hand, he thought, the other bum who'd stayed with Little Vinnie hadn't had the decency or balls to show his face. Worthless dogmeat.

Muffin-Face nervously looked back and forth between the two silent half brothers, then stepped over to take a place alongside Mickey Boy.

Little Vinnie's eyes narrowed.

"Go downstairs an' tell Buster I said to come up, right away," Freddie Falcone whispered to Muffin-Face from his position a half step behind Mickey Boy. As soon as the younger man had left to carry out his command, Freddie stepped into the spot he'd vacated next to Mickey Boy.

"I think we should talk," Mickey Boy said, breaking the tense silence. When he saw Little Vinnie look to his two bodyguards, he added, "Alone."

Little Vinnie pursed his lips and nodded slowly, as if thinking, then said, "Yeah, okay," surprising Mickey Boy, who'd thought he'd get some snotty reply. Maybe it would be easier than he'd expected to deal with Little Vinnie, now that his—their—father was gone.

Buster interrupted the invisible beam between the brothers by thundering up from the basement.

"Everything's okay," Mickey Boy told Buster, who'd brought a herd of Calabra Family wiseguys with him. "Me an' Vinnie's gonna go talk." He looked over his shoulder at two carved wooden doors that led to an unoccupied chapel. "Over in there," he said, pointing toward the chapel with his head.

As Little Vinnie took his first step forward, his two bodyguards followed.

Buster and his group stepped forward to challenge them.

All the other guests shuffled backward, away from the two sides.

"Nice to see ya, pal," Little Vinnie said to Buster with a sarcastic smirk, then, without turning toward his men, ordered them in Italian to stay where they were. He stretched one arm out, palm up, and told Mickey Boy, "I'm all yours."

On his way toward the chapel, Mickey Boy tried to sort out some conversation, some way to begin to reach Little Vinnie. It occurred to him that he could have easily avoided the problem by ordering the little shit disposed of, killed. While the realization of that power over life and death gave him a sudden exhilarating rush, it was tempered by the new responsibilities carried with it, responsibilities that weighed heavy in his heart. Besides, Little Vinnie was his brother.

"Want me to pat him down?" Buster asked as they walked.

"No. Just the two zips, when we're outta sight."

Once inside the chapel with Little Vinnie, Mickey Boy told Buster to make sure no one disturbed them. His first thought, as the doors closed, was, *Here goes nothing*.

Mickey Boy limped a few feet into the room. Despite the ache in his good leg, he resisted the temptation to sit on one of the sixty or so folding chairs set up in the center of the floor or one of the sofas along the wall. Standing, even with the help of a cane, would still project more power than sitting down.

"You look good," Mickey Boy said, settling against the wooden register stand. He surveyed Little Vinnie: navy pin-striped suit too full at the chest and shoulders to be anything but European; dark blue print tie, not the mourning a respectful son should have worn, but dark at least; diamond rings on both pinkies, the orange-gold settings a give-away for the eighteen karat used overseas. "You lost weight."

"Cut the crap. What's on your mind?" Little Vinnie's stance hardened, both feet apart, his gray topcoat folded inside out over his hands.

For the first time Mickey Boy was aware of the chapel's low temperature as his face flushed against the cool air. His nostrils opened to the lingering scent of yesterday's flowers. Mouth pasty, he reached into his pocket for one of the mints he'd sent Freddie for earlier, but found he'd already munched them all.

"You know what really kicks my ass," Mickey Boy began, tossing out every bit of preplanned speech that had gone through his head, "is that you had what I wanted most, you little hump—a father—our father—and you wouldn't even share him. Even when you set me up to go to the can, if I only knew you were my brother, you wouldn'ta hadda do that. I woulda went for you gladly, just to save your ass."

"Big fuckin' hero," Little Vinnie replied. "Always ready to look good an' make me look like shit."

"How could you do that to me, knowin' we had the same blood, the same father?"

"I didn't know then, 'cause if I did, I woulda—"

"Killed me . . . ?"

"Fuck you!"

"Like you tried to do?"

Taking into account every miserable thing Little Vinnie'd done, from setting him up to go to prison to engineering an attempt on his and Laurel's life to his goddamned belligerent attitude at that moment, Mickey Boy still couldn't bring himself to hate Little Vinnie.

In his heart Mickey Boy knew he could no more direct that vile emotion at Little Vinnie Calabra than he could at his other brother, Alley Messina. He could become angry with them, as he had often enough with Alley, but never hate.

What surprised Mickey Boy, however, was not being able to muster the desire to rub Little Vinnie's nose in the dirt, make him bow to an intended victim's newfound power.

What Mickey Boy found he did want to do to Little Vinnie was teach him, direct him in life as an older brother should when their father dies. Their father.

Then, after all his efforts, if Little Vinnie didn't respond, fuck him.

Little Vinnie tossed his coat over one of the folding chairs and walked toward the front of the unused chapel.

Mickey Boy followed, limping slowly about five feet behind.

"So now you're a big goddamned boss," Little Vinnie shouted, his arms spread wide as if to encompass the room, the world, or whatever. "What're you gonna do now, get one of your assholes to take me out in a boat an' shoot me, like in *The Godfather?*"

Feeling the question unworthy of a response, Mickey Boy remained silent.

When he reached the empty bier which stood directly in front of a twelve-foot statue of the Virgin Mary, Little Vinnie suddenly spun around and walked back to Mickey Boy.

"Well, is that what you're gonna do?!" Little Vinnie yelled. "Maybe tell that punk Richie, who ain't got a man's set of balls, to do it?"

"What'd you say?"

"You heard me. Your fuckin' partner's a punk. Almost made me get killed. Fucked up the whole hit on the Irishman that night."

Mickey Boy's head spun. Buster had mentioned something just that day about Richie and Little Vinnie being involved in the botch job that had killed Christina Augusta, but had quickly dropped the subject, saying he'd fill Mickey Boy in after the don had been laid to rest. With enough on his mind to occupy him for two lifetimes, Mickey Boy had brushed the matter off as low priority for that moment, and had thought nothing more about it until Little Vinnie had brought it up.

"Yeah, how?" Mickey Boy asked. "How'd Richie fuck anything up?"

For the next few minutes, as Little Vinnie coldly admitted his error in shooting Chrissy instead of Skinny Malone, Mickey Boy felt as though his heart had fallen into his bowels. One stupid but understandable misjudgment—that is, if Little Vinnie was telling the truth about Skinny's hat being on Chrissy that night—had caused Mickey Boy to be shot and their father to lose his life. Poor Richie. Poor fuckin' Chrissy.

"An' when that jerkoff Georgie come out of the joint with a fuckin' gun, Richie just froze. If I don't shoot first, I'd be fuckin' dead right now."

"An' the old man knew about the hit on the Irishman?" Mickey Boy asked, confused at why his father would even bother with such a smalltime murder.

"Knew about it? The cocksucker ordered it."

"Watch your fuckin' mouth! Ain't you got a goddamn bit of respect?"

"For who? For him? He ordered the fuckin' hit himself. If not for him, none of us would've been there."

"You're full of shit!"

"Am I?" Little Vinnie asked, sneering. "Whattaya think he was, a fuckin' saint? This guy left more guys dead than you could count. That whole war between Petey Ross and Junior Vallo was all his doing. I heard the whole thing from his own mouth."

"That's crazy," Mickey Boy said, in a low monotone, talking more to himself than Little Vinnie. "It don't make sense."

Obviously gleeful, Little Vinnie went on to explain how he'd overheard a meeting between his father, Buster, and Joe Augusta one morning when he'd come home after a night of partying. He seemed to take joy in naming murder after murder that their father had engineered, beginning with John-John and Sammy The Blond.

Little Vinnie's attitude changed to one of bitterness as he told of hearing that Mickey Boy was also the don's son; how he'd made up his mind then to do away with Mickey Boy once and for all. "What'd you think," he continued, "that I was just gonna let you come into the picture an' take everything away, after I spent my whole life kissin' ass an' only getting shit for it? I'm the one who should be boss—an' I don't give a flying fuck who, or how many, I gotta waste getting there." With the cockiness of a bantam rooster, he added, "Sure, Chrissy was a mistake, but at least now everybody knows I got the balls to kill."

Numbed, yet with his head pounding, Mickey Boy said, "You know, you're wrong. This ain't like *The Godfather*, this is real life. If the day ever comes that you gotta go, an' it might be sooner than you think, you could bet those fuckin' balls you think you got that the only one who's gonna do it is me."

Stepping close enough so that his sour breath would hit Little Vinnie directly in the face, he added, "After all, you piece of shit, you're my brother."

"You ain't my fuckin' brother!" Little Vinnie snapped back. "You're the bastard son of some two-bit whore my old man happened to be fucking!"

Mickey Boy's body rocketed into the air. With his left hand grabbing Little Vinnie's throat, he slammed him against the wall, Little Vinnie's head echoing loudly in the room.

Since he had dropped his cane, Mickey Boy used his hold on Little Vinnie for balance while he slapped his face over and over with his free hand.

"What the fuck?!" Buster shouted, as he burst into the room.

"Get out!" Mickey Boy yelled, tightening his grip on Little Vinnie's throat and slapping him again.

When Buster hesitated, Mickey Boy screamed, "I said, get out!"

Just as the double doors shut, however, Mickey Boy, who had had to turn slightly toward Buster to shout his command, felt a knee slam up into his balls. The pain loosened his hold and buckled his legs under him.

Clawing at Little Vinnie's body for balance, Mickey Boy's hand caught his suit pocket, destroying the navy worsted with a loud ripping sound as he fell to the ground.

Now he could have used Buster's help, but was too proud, and in too much agony, to call for it.

"Motherfucker!" Little Vinnie shouted, and kicked out at Mickey Boy.

Because he'd had enough sense to roll away from Little Vinnie when he fell, Mickey Boy caught the kick at the small of his back instead of the ribs, chest, or face. What pain it caused, however, shot up his spine, adding to the ache in his testicles that kept him cramped in a fetal position.

When Mickey Boy rolled away a second time, Little Vinnie's kick just glancing off his back, his face scraped the rough carpet, then hit the tip of his fallen cane. He grabbed the cane with one hand just as another kick connected, sending him rolling into the empty chairs.

The next sound Mickey Boy heard was the swoosh of the cane swung just inches above the floor, as he instinctively put to use the lesson he'd been taught as a kid, when he and his Sackett Street Boys had gone into the Red Hook projects to rumble with the all-black gang called the Chaplains.

"Niggers' heads are just too fuckin' hard," he'd been told by an older gang member. "So hit 'em on the shins with everything you got. Once they go down, then just fuck 'em up as much as you could."

"Crack!" followed the swoosh, as the cane hit bone.

Little Vinnie tumbled down on top of Mickey Boy, pushing him farther into the mess of fallen chairs. "You bastard!" got lost in the jumble of the chairs' metal banging against each other.

Mickey Boy threw a punch, which landed on flesh. He threw another one that connected on bone, and hurt his hand. When he tried to rise, however, the rigid cast on his leg stopped him. He felt arms grab him as he rolled over Little Vinnie and hit the floor with his head. He and Little Vinnie rolled back the other way, toward the bier. He was pinned and couldn't throw a decent punch or swing the cane, which he hung on to for dear life. With his free hand he grabbed a handful of hair, making Little Vinnie scream. An inside punch to the stomach caused him to release the hair. Rolling back again, he could smell Little Vinnie's flowery cologne mingled with sweat.

Yelling "Whore's son!," Little Vinnie butted him with his head. The pain started just above Mickey Boy's eye and shot up through his skull.

In the midst of his fighting, Mickey Boy caught sight of the bottom of the doors swinging open again.

"Get out!" he screamed, and bit Little Vinnie's face. The taste was salty sweat or blood, he couldn't tell which.

Little Vinnie yelped, and released his bear hug, allowing Mickey Boy to rise to one knee with the aid of the cane.

Mickey Boy was just about to push himself up to his feet, when he spotted Little Vinnie pull something from under his pants leg. Making it out to be a blade, he smashed the cane on Little Vinnie's fingers. Blood oozed from a cut on Little Vinnie's leg as the knife fell.

Little Vinnie reached for the Sicilian-style dagger again, and again Mickey Boy laced into him with the cane, an old black cane that Don Vincenze had kept around for those damp-weather days that sometimes nearly crippled him with pain. With each swing Mickey Boy felt as if their father had reached out from the dead to teach his brat of a son a lesson.

He hit Little Vinnie again.

And again.

And again.

Finally, Mickey Boy was able to use the cane to help himself rise from the bloodied carpet. Every part of his body ached, his leg so much that he wondered if it had burst, or something, beneath the metal-reinforced cast.

Without even glancing at Little Vinnie, whom he was sure was unconscious, Mickey Boy stumbled toward a chair and fell onto it. He sat there for a time, head in his hands, feeling Little Vinnie's words cut pieces out of his heart and brain as surely as if it were the dagger at work. Sure, killing had always been a daily presence in their life, a necessary force to prevent chaos. But leaving so many good men's families fatherless for no sensible reason . . . ? His father?

Yes. He knew it; could tell from Little Vinnie's voice.

So sick. So sad. Where was the honor that had motivated him all these years to want to be a wiseguy? Mickey Boy wondered. Where were the so-called men of respect now? Having jumped from low man on the totem pole to boss in such a short time, Mickey Boy had never had the secrets of each succeeding level unfolded to him. He'd believed what he was told because he'd wanted to believe; listened carefully and learned. But what had he believed? he now asked himself. What had he suffered, fought, and nearly died for? Myths, that's what. God-damn, bullshit myths that wiseguys peddled about themselves. The honor they always boasted about was just a smokescreen for treachery and deceit; the murders they justified, just for ego.

And worse, the most despicable of the lot were his own blood: a father he didn't know but had idolized just the same, and a brother as much a lowlife as anyone he'd ever met. God, how his heart broke for poor Chrissy, a victim of his own blood, his own genes. Would he himself turn out as bad as time went on? Would he have to in order to keep other sharks like his father and Little Vinnie from swallowing him up? Would the genetic disease affect his son, too, if, in fact, he had a son?

"Fuck Nicolo Fonte," Mickey Boy muttered, about the man who'd chased him out, the man who'd been his best chance to avoid this life he'd ultimately chosen, then added, ". . . and fuck me," for not having listened to Laurel and fled to Florida with her.

Suddenly the life and position that Mickey Boy had dreamed about and strived for seemed to smother him. He felt trapped, but was beyond the point of politely walking away because of the blood oath he'd taken.

Wishing there were a way to leave, alive and unharmed, before his miserable genetic inheritance destroyed him inside, he made his way to the chapel's door. For a moment, he leaned his forehead against it, sniffing in the smell of his own blood and hearing his heartbeat; taking deep breaths to prepare himself.

Then Mickey stepped outside.

When he saw the color drain from Buster's face, Mickey managed a smile. Buster would have so much to answer for in the next few days, but for now nothing would be said.

"Go get that piece of shit in there, an' make sure you get him on a plane back to Sicily." Mickey motioned toward the two bodyguards who had escorted Little Vinnie, and who were now surrounded by Calabra Family members. "Them, too. Make somebody tell them in Italian to let Vinnie know if he comes back he dies."

Buster held on to Mickey's arm while repeating the orders to his men. "Let me help you," he said. Freddie stepped over to take Mickey from the other side.

"No, I'm okay," Mickey replied, shaking them off. He looked past the crowd to where his mother and Laurel stood, appearing terrified but, after two days of his stubborn refusal to speak to them, afraid to approach.

But the poison was out. The blame. The bitterness. The feeling sorry for himself. Violence had a sad way of relieving all those tensions. It always had. And now, knowing how right Laurel and his mother had been all along, he saw them as his only salvation.

Mickey looked down at his clothes, bloody and torn; the tip of one shoe, somehow having come away from its sole, flapped open. Then he looked up at Laurel and his mother, lifted his one free arm to welcome them, and smiled.

Crying, both women, the only two ever able to claim Mickey's love, ran to him.

After Laurel and Connie had hugged and kissed him profusely, Mickey looked out, teary-eyed, at the faces in the crowd. Faces that belonged to him, as an obligation and a burden. Now he thought only of the burden, imposed on him by a murderous father who never gave him as much consideration as these strangers expected. But the obligations he'd imposed would, unfortunately, stand.

To Laurel and Connie, Mickey said, "I wanna go home." Before leaving, he looked down at Laurel's belly, swollen with his blood. And an even greater obligation. And a greater love.

With thoughts of his, Laurel's, and their baby's future in the forefront of his mind, Mickey suddenly hoped, for the first time, that the child would be a girl—because he wanted something better.